Queen of Air and Darkness

Also by Cassandra Clare

THE MORTAL INSTRUMENTS

City of Bones

City of Ashes

City of Glass

City of Fallen Angels

City of Lost Souls

City of Heavenly Fire

THE INFERNAL DEVICES

Clockwork Angel

Clockwork Prince

Clockwork Princess

THE DARK ARTIFICES

Lady Midnight

Lord of Shadows

Queen of Air and Darkness

THE ELDEST CURSES

With Wesley Chu

The Red Scrolls of Magic

The Shadowhunter's Codex

With Joshua Lewis

The Bane Chronicles

With Sarah Rees Brennan
and Maureen Johnson

Tales from the Shadowhunter Academy

With Sarah Rees Brennan, Maureen Johnson,
and Robin Wasserman

Ghosts of the Shadow Market

With Sarah Rees Brennan, Maureen Johnson,
Kelly Link, and Robin Wasserman

Queen of Air and Darkness

CASSANDRA CLARE

THE DARK ARTIFICES

BOOK THREE

Margaret K. McElderry Books
NEW YORK LONDON TORONTO SYDNEY NEW DELHI

MARGARET K. McELDERRY BOOKS
An imprint of Simon & Schuster Children's Publishing Division
1230 Avenue of the Americas, New York, New York 10020
This book is a work of fiction. Any references to historical events, real people, or real places are used fictitiously. Other names, characters, places, and events are products of the author's imagination, and any resemblance to actual events or places or persons, living or dead, is entirely coincidental.

For information about special discounts for bulk purchases, please contact Simon & Schuster Special Sales at 1-866-506-1949 or business@simonandschuster.com.
The Simon & Schuster Speakers Bureau can bring authors to your live event.
For more information or to book an event, contact the Simon & Schuster Speakers Bureau at 1-866-248-3049 or visit our website at www.simonspeakers.com.
Also available in a Margaret K. McElderry Books hardcover edition
Cover design by Russell Gordon
Interior design by Mike Rosamilia
The text for this book was set in Dolly.
Manufactured in the United States of America
First Margaret K. McElderry Books paperback edition October 2019
2 4 6 8 10 9 7 5 3 1
The Library of Congress has cataloged the hardcover edition as follows:
Names: Clare, Cassandra, author.
Title: Queen of air and darkness / Cassandra Clare.
Description: First edition. | New York : Margaret K. McElderry Books, 2018. |
Series: The dark artifices ; book three | Summary: While the Clave teeters on the brink of civil war, Julian and Emma take desperate measures to put their forbidden love aside and focus on saving the world of Shadowhunters before the parabatai curse destroys everyone.
Identifiers: LCCN 2018032682 (print) | LCCN 2018038515 (eBook) |
ISBN 9781442468436 (hardback) | ISBN 9781442468443 (paperback) | ISBN 9781442468450 (eBook) |
Subjects: | CYAC: Supernatural—Fiction. | Magic—Fiction. |
Demonology—Fiction. | Blessing and cursing—Fiction.
Classification: LCC PZ7.C5265 (eBook) | LCC PZ7.C5265 Qu 2018 (print) |
DDC [Fic]—dc23
LC record available at https://lccn.loc.gov/2018032682

For Sarah.
She knows what she did.

Lo! Death has reared himself a throne
In a strange city lying alone
Far down within the dim West,
Where the good and the bad and the worst and the best
Have gone to their eternal rest.
There shrines and palaces and towers
(Time-eaten towers that tremble not!)
Resemble nothing that is ours.
Around, by lifting winds forgot,
Resignedly beneath the sky
The melancholy waters lie.

No rays from the holy heaven come down
On the long night-time of that town;
But light from out the lurid sea
Streams up the turrets silently—
Gleams up the pinnacles far and free—
Up domes—up spires—up kingly halls—
Up fanes—up Babylon-like walls—
Up shadowy long-forgotten bowers
Of sculptured ivy and stone flowers—
Up many and many a marvellous shrine
Whose wreathed friezes intertwine
The viol, the violet, and the vine.
Resignedly beneath the sky
The melancholy waters lie.
So blend the turrets and shadows there
That all seem pendulous in air,
While from a proud tower in the town
Death looks gigantically down.

There open fanes and gaping graves
Yawn level with the luminous waves;
But not the riches there that lie
In each idol's diamond eye—
Not the gaily-jewelled dead
Tempt the waters from their bed;
For no ripples curl, alas!
Along that wilderness of glass—
No swellings tell that winds may be
Upon some far-off happier sea—
No heavings hint that winds have been
On seas less hideously serene.

But lo, a stir is in the air!
The wave—there is a movement there!
As if the towers had thrust aside,
In slightly sinking, the dull tide—
As if their tops had feebly given
A void within the filmy Heaven.
The waves have now a redder glow—
The hours are breathing faint and low—
And when, amid no earthly moans,
Down, down that town shall settle hence,
Hell, rising from a thousand thrones,
Shall do it reverence.

—Edgar Allan Poe, "City in the Sea"

PART ONE

Feel No Sorrow

In the Land of Faerie,
as mortals feel no sorrow, neither can they feel joy.
—Faerie proverb

1
Death Looks Down

There was blood on the Council dais, blood on the steps, blood on the walls and the floor and the shattered remnants of the Mortal Sword. Later Emma would remember it as a sort of red mist. A piece of broken poetry kept going through her mind, something about not being able to imagine people had so much blood in them.

They said that shock cushioned great blows, but Emma didn't feel cushioned. She could see and hear everything: the Council Hall full of guards. The screaming. She tried to fight her way through to Julian. Guards surged up in front of her in a wave. She could hear more shouting. *"Emma Carstairs shattered the Mortal Sword! She destroyed a Mortal Instrument! Arrest her!"*

She didn't care what they did to her; she had to get to Julian. He was still on the ground with Livvy in his arms, resisting all efforts by the guards to lift her dead body away from him.

"Let me through," she said. "I'm his *parabatai*, let me through."

"Give me the sword." It was the Consul's voice. "Give me Cortana, Emma, and you can help Julian."

She gasped, and tasted blood in her mouth. Alec was up on the dais now, kneeling by his father's body. The floor of the Hall was a mass of rushing figures; among them Emma glimpsed Mark, carrying an unconscious Ty out of the Hall, shouldering other Nephilim aside as he went. He looked grimmer than she'd ever seen him. Kit was with him; where was Dru? There—she was alone on the ground; no, Diana was with her, holding her and weeping, and there was Helen, fighting to get to the dais.

Emma took a step back and almost stumbled. The wood floor was slippery with blood. Consul Jia Penhallow was still in front of her, her thin hand held out for Cortana. *Cortana.* The sword was a part of Emma's family, had been a part of her memory for as long as she could recall. She could still remember Julian laying it in her arms after her parents had died, how she'd held the sword to her as if it were a child, heedless of the deep cut the blade left on her arm.

Jia was asking her to hand over a piece of herself.

But Julian was there, alone, bowed in grief, soaked in blood. And he was more of herself than Cortana was. Emma surrendered the sword; feeling it yanked from her grip, her whole body tensed. She almost thought she could hear Cortana scream at being parted from her.

"Go," Jia said; Emma could hear other voices, including Horace Dearborn's, raised, demanding she be stopped, that the destruction of the Mortal Sword and the disappearance of Annabel Blackthorn be answered for. Jia was snapping at the guards, telling them to escort everyone from the Hall: now was a time of grief, not a time for revenge—Annabel would be found—*go with dignity, Horace, or you'll be escorted out, now is not the time*—Aline helping Dru and Diana to their feet, helping them walk from the room . . .

Emma fell to her knees by Julian. The metallic smell of blood was everywhere. Livvy was a crumpled shape in his arms, her skin the color of skimmed milk. He had stopped calling for her to come back and was rocking her as if she were a child, his chin against the top of her head.

"Jules," Emma whispered, but the word sat bitterly on her

tongue: that was her childhood name for him, and he was an adult now, a grieving parent. Livvy had not just been his sister. For years he had raised her as a daughter. "Julian." She touched his cold cheek, then Livvy's colder one. "Julian, love, please, let me help you. . . ."

He raised his head slowly. He looked as if someone had flung a pail full of blood at him. It masked his chest, his throat, spattered his chin and cheeks. "Emma." His voice was barely a whisper. "Emma, I drew so many *iratzes*—"

But Livvy had already been dead when she hit the wood of the dais. Before Julian even lifted her into his arms. No rune, no *iratze*, would have helped.

"Jules!" Helen had finally forced her way past the guards; she flung herself down beside Emma and Julian, heedless of the blood. Emma watched numbly as Helen carefully removed the broken shard of the Mortal Sword from Livvy's body and set it on the ground. It stained her hands with blood. Her lips white with grief, she put her arms around Julian and Livvy both, whispering soothing words.

The room was emptying around them. Magnus had come in, walking very slowly and looking pale. A long row of Silent Brothers followed him. He ascended the dais and Alec rose to his feet, flinging himself into Magnus's arms. They held each other wordlessly as four of the Brothers knelt and lifted Robert Lightwood's body. His hands had been folded over his chest, his eyes carefully closed. Soft murmurs of "*ave atque vale*, Robert Lightwood," echoed behind him as the Brothers carried his body from the room.

The Consul moved toward them. There were guards with her. The Silent Brothers hovered behind them, like ghosts, a blur of parchment.

"You have to let go of her, Jules," Helen said in her gentlest voice. "She has to be taken to the Silent City."

Julian looked at Emma. His eyes were stark as winter skies, but she could read them. "Let him do it," Emma said. "He wants the last person to carry Livvy to be him."

Helen stroked her brother's hair and kissed his forehead before rising. She said, "Jia, please."

The Consul nodded. Julian got slowly to his feet, Livvy cradled against him. He began to move toward the stairs that led down from the dais, Helen at his side and the Silent Brothers following, but as Emma rose too, Jia put a hand out to hold her back.

"Only family, Emma," she said.

I am family. Let me go with them. Let me go with Livvy, Emma screamed silently, but she kept her mouth firmly closed: She couldn't add her own sadness to the existing horror. And the rules of the Silent City were unchangeable. *The Law is hard, but it is the Law.*

The small procession was moving toward the doors. The Cohort had gone, but there were still some guards and other Shadowhunters in the room: a low chorus of "hail and farewell, Livia Blackthorn," followed them.

The Consul turned, Cortana flashing in her hand, and went down the steps and over to Aline, who had been watching as Livvy was carried away. Emma began to shiver all over, a shiver that started deep down in her bones. She had never felt so alone—Julian was going away from her, and the other Blackthorns seemed a million miles away like distant stars, and she wanted her parents with a painful intensity that was almost humiliating, and she wanted Jem and she wanted Cortana back in her arms and she wanted to forget Livvy bleeding and dying and crumpled like a broken doll as the window of the Council Hall exploded and the broken crown took Annabel—had anyone else seen it but her?

"Emma." Arms went around her, familiar, gentle arms, raising her to her feet. It was Cristina, who must have waited through all the chaos for her, who had stayed stubbornly in the Hall as the guards shouted for everyone to leave, stayed to remain by Emma's side. "Emma, come with me, don't stay here. I'll take care of you. I know where we can go. Emma. *Corazoncita.* Come with me."

Emma let Cristina help her to her feet. Magnus and Alec were coming over to them, Alec's face tight, his eyes reddened. Emma stood with her hand clasped in Cristina's and looked out over the Hall, which seemed to her an entirely different place than it had when they had arrived hours ago. Maybe because the sun had been up then, she thought, dimly hearing Magnus and Alec talking to Cristina about taking Emma to the house that had been set aside for the Blackthorns. Maybe because the room had darkened, and shadows were thick as paint in the corners.

Or maybe because everything had changed, now. Maybe because nothing at all would ever be the same again.

"Dru?" Helen knocked gently on the closed door of the room. "Dru, can I talk to you?"

At least, she was fairly sure it was Dru's room. The canal house next to the Consul's residence on Princewater Street had been prepared for the Blackthorns before the meeting, since everyone had assumed they would spend several nights in Idris. Helen and Aline had been shown it earlier by Diana, and Helen had appreciated the light touch of Diana's loving hands everywhere: There were flowers in the kitchen, and rooms had names taped to the doors—the one with two narrow beds was for the twins, the one for Tavvy full of books and toys Diana had brought from her own home over the weapons shop.

Helen had stopped in front of a small room with flowered wallpaper. "For Dru, maybe?" she'd said. "It's pretty."

Diana had looked dubious. "Oh, Dru isn't like that," she'd said. "Maybe if the wallpaper had bats on it, or skeletons."

Helen had winced.

Aline had taken her hand. "Don't worry," she'd whispered.

"You'll get to know them all again." She'd kissed Helen's cheek. "It'll be easy-peasy."

And maybe it would have been, Helen thought, staring at the door with the note that said *Drusilla* on it. Maybe if everything had gone well. Grief's sharp agony flared up in her chest—she felt as she imagined a fish caught on a hook might feel, twisting and turning to get away from the spike of pain driven into its flesh.

She remembered this pain from the death of her father, when only the thought that she had to take care of her family, had to look after the children, had gotten her through. She was trying to do the same now, but it was clear the children—if they could even really be called that; only Tavvy was truly a child, and he was at the Inquisitor's house, having thankfully missed the horror in the Council Hall—felt awkward around her. As if she were a stranger.

Which only made the pain pierce deeper in her chest. She wished Aline was with her, but Aline had gone to be with her parents for a few hours.

"Dru," Helen said again, knocking with more force. "*Please* let me in."

The door flew open and Helen jerked her hand back before she accidentally punched Dru in the shoulder. Her sister stood in front of her, glaring in her ill-fitting black meeting clothes, too tight in the waist and chest. Her eyes were so red-rimmed it looked as if she had smeared scarlet eye shadow across her lids.

"I know you might want to be alone," said Helen. "But I need to know that you're—"

"All right?" Dru said, a little sharply. The implication was clear: *How could I possibly be all right?*

"Surviving."

Dru glanced away for a moment; her lips, pressed tightly together, trembled. Helen ached to grab her little sister and hug her, to cuddle Dru the way she had years ago when Dru was a stubborn toddler. "I want to know how Ty is."

"He's asleep," said Helen. "The Silent Brothers gave him a sedative potion, and Mark's sitting with him. Do you want to sit with him too?"

"I . . ." Dru hesitated, while Helen wished she could think of something comforting to say about Ty. She was terrified of what would happen when he woke up. He'd fainted in the Council Hall, and Mark had carried him to the Brothers, who were already in the Gard. They'd examined him in eerie silence and stated that physically he was healthy, but they would give him herbs that would keep him sleeping. That sometimes the mind knew when it needed to shut down to prepare itself to heal. Though Helen didn't know how a night of sleep, or even a year of it, would prepare Ty for losing his twin.

"I want Jules," Dru said finally. "Is he here?"

"No," Helen said. "He's still with Livvy. In the Silent City." She wanted to say he'd be back any moment—Aline had said the ceremony of laying someone out in the City as a preparation for cremation was a short one—but she didn't want to say anything to Dru that would turn out not to be true.

"What about Emma?" Dru's voice was polite but clear: *I want the people I know, not you.*

"I'll go look for her," Helen said.

She had barely turned away from Dru's door when it shut behind her with a small but determined click. She blinked away tears—and saw Mark, standing in the hallway a few feet from her. He had come close so soundlessly that she hadn't heard him approach. He held a crumpled piece of paper in his hand that looked like a fire-message.

"Helen," he said. His voice was rough. After all his years in the Hunt, would he grieve as faeries grieved? He looked rumpled, weary: There were very human lines under his eyes, at the sides of his mouth. "Ty is not alone—Diana and Kit are with him, and he sleeps on, besides. I needed to speak with you."

"I have to get Emma," Helen said. "Dru wants her."

"Her room is just there; we can certainly get her before we leave," Mark said, indicating the farther end of the corridor. The house was paneled in honey-colored wood, the witchlight lamps lighting it to warmth; on another day, it would have been a pretty place.

"Leave?" Helen said, puzzled.

"I have had a message from Magnus and Alec, at the Inquisitor's house. I must go and fetch Tavvy and tell him our sister is dead." Mark reached out a hand for her, his face twisting with pain. "Please, Helen. Come with me."

When Diana was young, she had visited a museum in London where the star attraction was a Sleeping Beauty made of wax. Her skin was like pale tallow, and her chest rose and fell as she "breathed" with the help of a small motor implanted in her body.

Something about Ty's stillness and pallor reminded her now of the wax girl. He lay partly covered with the blankets on his bed, his only movement his breath. His hands were loose and open at his sides; Diana longed for nothing more than to see his fingers moving, playing with one of Julian's creations or the cord of his headphones.

"Is he going to be all right?" Kit spoke in a half whisper. The room was papered in cheerful yellow, both twin beds covered in rag bedspreads. Kit could have sat on the empty bed that was meant to be Livvy's, but he hadn't. He was crouched in a corner of the room, his back against the wall, his legs drawn up. He was staring at Ty.

Diana put her hand to Ty's forehead; it was cool. She felt numb throughout her body. "He's fine, Kit," she said. She tugged the blanket up over Ty; he stirred and murmured, shrugging it off. The windows were open—they'd thought the air might be better for Ty—but Diana crossed the room to close them now. Her mother had always been obsessed with the idea that the worst thing that could happen to someone was catching a chill, and apparently you never forgot what your parents told you.

Beyond the window she could see the city, outlined in the early dusk, and the rising moon. She thought of a figure on horseback, riding across that vast sky. She wondered if Gwyn knew of this afternoon's events, or if she would have to send him a message. And what would he do or say when he received it? He had come to her once before when Livvy, Ty, and Kit were in danger, but he had been called upon by Mark then. She still wasn't sure if he'd done it because he was genuinely fond of the children, or if he had simply been discharging a debt.

She paused, hand on the window curtain. In truth, she knew little about Gwyn. As the leader of the Wild Hunt he was almost more mythic than human. She wondered how emotions must be felt by those so powerful and old they had become part of myths and stories. How could he really care about any mortal's little life given the scope of what he had experienced?

And yet he had held her and comforted her in her old bedroom, when she had told him what she had only ever told Catarina and her parents before, and her parents were dead. He had been kind—hadn't he?

Stop it. She turned back to the room; now wasn't the time to think about Gwyn, even if some part of her hoped he would come and comfort her again. Not when Ty might wake up any moment into a world of new and terrible pain. Not when Kit was crouched against the wall as if he had fetched up on some lonely beach after a disaster at sea.

She was about to put her hand on Kit's shoulder when he looked up at her. There were no marks of tears on his face. He had been dry-eyed after his father's death too, she recalled, when he had opened the door of the Institute for the first time and realized he was a Shadowhunter.

"Ty likes familiar things," said Kit. "He won't know where he is when he wakes up. We should make sure his bag is here, and whatever stuff he brought from London."

"It's over there." Diana pointed to where Ty's duffel had been placed under the bed that should have been Livvy's. Without looking at her, Kit got to his feet and went over to it. He unzipped it and took out a book—a thick book, with old-fashioned page binding. Silently, he placed it on the bed just next to Ty's open left hand, and Diana caught a glimpse of the title embossed in gold across the cover and realized that even her numb heart could twinge with pain.

The Return of Sherlock Holmes.

The moon had begun to rise, and the demon towers of Alicante glowed in their light.

It had been many years since Mark had been in Alicante. The Wild Hunt had flown over it, and he remembered seeing the land of Idris spread out below him as the others in the Hunt whooped and howled, amused at flying over Nephilim land. But Mark's heart had always beaten faster at the sight of the Shadowhunter homeland; the bright silver quarter of Lake Lyn, the green of Brocelind Forest, the stone manor houses of the countryside, and the glimmer of Alicante on its hill. And Kieran beside him, thoughtful, watching Mark as Mark watched Idris.

My place, my people. My home, he'd thought. But it seemed different from ground level: more prosaic, filled with the smell of canal water in summer, streets illuminated by harsh witchlight. It wasn't far to the Inquisitor's house, but they were walking slowly. It was several minutes before Helen spoke for the first time:

"You saw our aunt in Faerie," she said. "Nene. Only Nene, right?"

"She was in the Seelie Court." Mark nodded, glad to have the silence broken. "How many sisters did our mother have?"

"Six or seven, I think," said Helen. "Nene is the only one who is kind."

"I thought you didn't know where Nene was?"

"She never spoke of her location to me, but she has communicated with me on more than one occasion since I was sent to Wrangel Island," said Helen. "I think she felt sympathy in her heart for me."

"She helped hide us, and heal Kieran," said Mark. "She spoke to me of our faerie names." He looked around; they had reached the Inquisitor's house, the biggest on this stretch of pavement, with balconies out over the canal. "I never thought I would come back here. Not to Alicante. Not as a Shadowhunter."

Helen squeezed his shoulder and they walked up to the door together; she knocked, and a harried-looking Simon Lewis opened the door. It had been years since Mark had seen him, and he looked older now: His shoulders were broader, his brown hair longer, and there was stubble along his jaw.

He gave Helen a lopsided smile. "The last time you and I were here I was drunk and yelling up at Isabelle's window." He turned to Mark. "And the last time I saw you, I was stuck in a cage in Faerie."

Mark remembered: Simon looking up at him through the bars of the fey-wrought cage, Mark saying to him: *I am no faerie. I am Mark Blackthorn of the Los Angeles Institute. It doesn't matter what they say or what they do to me. I still remember who I am.*

"Yes," Mark said. "You told me of my brothers and sisters, of Helen's marriage. I was grateful." He swept a small bow, out of habit, and saw Helen look surprised.

"I wish I could have told you more," Simon said, in a more serious voice. "And I'm so sorry. About Livvy. We're grieving here, too."

Simon swung the door open wider. Mark saw a grand entryway inside, with a large chandelier hanging from the ceiling; off to the left was a family room, where Rafe, Max, and Tavvy sat in front of an empty fireplace, playing with a small stack of toys. Isabelle and Alec sat on the couch: She had her arms around his neck and was sobbing quietly against his chest. Low, hopeless sobs that struck an echo deep inside his own heart, a matching chord of loss.

"Please tell Isabelle and Alec we are sorry for the loss of their father," said Helen. "We did not mean to intrude. We are here for Octavian."

At that moment, Magnus appeared from the entryway. He nodded at them and went over to the children, lifting Tavvy up in his arms. Though Tavvy was getting awfully big to be carried, Mark thought, but in many ways Tavvy was young for his age, as if early grief had kept him more childlike. As Magnus approached them, Helen began to lift her hands, but Tavvy held out his arms to Mark.

In some surprise, Mark took the burden of his little brother in his arms. Tavvy squirmed around, tired but alert. "What's happened?" he said. "Everyone's crying."

Magnus ran a hand through his hair. He looked extremely weary. "We haven't told him anything," he said. "We thought it was for you to do."

Mark took a few steps back from the door, Helen following after him so that they stood in the lighted square of illumination from the entryway. He set Tavvy down on the pavement. This was the way the Fair Folk broke bad news, face-to-face.

"Livvy is gone, child," he said.

Tavvy looked confused. "Gone where?"

"She has passed into the Shadow Lands," said Mark. He was struggling for the words; death in Faerie was such a different thing than it was to humans.

Tavvy's blue-green Blackthorn eyes were wide. "Then we can

rescue her," he said. "We can go after her, right? Like we got you back from Faerie. Like you went after Kieran."

Helen made a small noise. "Oh, Octavian," she said.

"She is *dead*," Mark said helplessly, and saw Tavvy wince away from the words. "Mortal lives are short and—and fragile in the face of eternity."

Tavvy's eyes filled with tears.

"*Mark*," Helen said, and knelt down on the ground, reaching her hands out to Tavvy. "She died so bravely," she said. "She was defending Julian and Emma. Our sister—she was courageous."

The tears began to spill down Tavvy's face. "Where's Julian?" he said. "Where did he go?"

Helen dropped her hands. "He's with Livvy in the Silent City—he'll be back soon—let us take you back home to the canal house—"

"Home?" Tavvy said scornfully. "Nothing here is *home*."

Mark was aware of Simon having come to stand beside him. "God, poor kid," he said. "Look, Mark—"

"Octavian." It was Magnus's voice. He was standing in the doorway still, looking down at the small tearstained boy in front of him. There was exhaustion in his eyes, but also an immense compassion: the kind of compassion that came with great old age.

He seemed as if he would have said more, but Rafe and Max had joined him. Silently they filed down the steps and went over to Tavvy; Rafe was nearly as tall as he was, though he was only five. He reached to hug Tavvy, and Max did too—and to Mark's surprise, Tavvy seemed to relax slightly, allowing the embraces, nodding when Max said something to him in a quiet voice.

Helen got to her feet, and Mark wondered if his face wore the same expression hers did, of pain and shame. Shame that they could not do more to comfort a younger brother who barely knew them.

"It's all right," Simon said. "Look, you tried."

"We did not succeed," said Mark.

"You can't fix grief," said Simon. "A rabbi told me that when my father died. The only thing that fixes grief is time, and the love of the people who care about you, and Tavvy has that." He squeezed Mark's shoulder briefly. "Take care of yourself," he said. "*Shelo ted'u od tza'ar*, Mark Blackthorn."

"What does that mean?" said Mark.

"It's a blessing," said Simon. "Something else the rabbi taught me. 'Let it be that you should know no further sorrow.'"

Mark inclined his head in gratitude; faeries knew the value of blessings freely given. But his chest felt heavy nonetheless. He could not imagine the sorrows of his family would be ending soon.

2
Melancholy Waters

Cristina stood despairingly in the extremely clean kitchen of the Princewater Street canal house and wished there was something she could tidy up.

She'd washed dishes that didn't need washing. She'd mopped the floor and set and reset the table. She'd arranged flowers in a vase and then thrown them out, and then retrieved them from the trash and arranged them again. She wanted to make the kitchen nice, the house pretty, but was anyone really going to care if the kitchen was nice and the house was pretty?

She knew they wouldn't. But she had to do something. She wanted to be with Emma and comfort Emma, but Emma was with Drusilla, who had cried herself to sleep holding Emma's hands. She wanted to be with Mark, and comfort Mark, but he'd left with Helen, and she could hardly be anything but glad that at last he was getting to spend time with the sister he'd missed for so long.

The front door rattled open, startling Cristina into knocking a dish from the table. It fell to the floor and shattered. She was about to pick it up when she saw Julian come in, closing the door behind him—Locking runes were more common than keys in Idris, but he didn't reach for his stele, just looked sightlessly from the entryway to the stairs.

Cristina stood frozen. Julian looked like the ghost from a Shakespeare play. He clearly hadn't changed since the Council Hall; his shirt and jacket were stiff with dried blood.

She never quite knew how to talk to Julian anyway; she knew more about him than was comfortable, thanks to Emma. She knew he was desperately in love with her friend; it was obvious in the way he looked at Emma, spoke to her, in gestures as tiny as handing her a dish across a table. She didn't know how everyone else didn't see it too. She'd known other *parabatai* and they didn't look at each other like that.

Having such personal information about someone was awkward at the best of times. This wasn't the best of times. Julian's expression was blank; he moved into the hall, and as he walked, his sister's dried blood flaked off his jacket and drifted to the floor.

If she just stood still, Cristina thought, he might not see her, and he might go upstairs and they'd both be spared an awkward moment. But even as she thought it, the bleakness in his face tugged at her heart. She was in the doorway before she realized she'd moved.

"Julian," she said quietly.

He didn't seem startled. He turned to face her as slowly as an automaton winding down. "How are they?"

How did you answer that? "They're well taken care of," she said finally. "Helen has been here, and Diana, and Mark."

"Ty . . ."

"Is still asleep." She tugged nervously at her skirt. She'd changed all her clothes since the Council Hall, just to feel clean.

For the first time, he met her eyes. His were shot through with red, though she didn't remember having seen him cry. Or maybe he had cried when he was holding Livvy—she didn't want to remember that. "Emma," he said. "Is she all right? You'd know. She would—tell you."

"She's with Drusilla. But I'm sure she'd like to see you."

"But is she all right?"

"No," Cristina said. "How could she be all right?"

He glanced toward the steps, as if he couldn't imagine the effort it would take to climb them. "Robert was going to help us," he said. "Emma and me. You know about us, I know that you do, that you know how we feel."

Cristina hesitated, stunned. She'd never thought Julian would mention any of this to her. "Maybe the next Inquisitor—"

"I passed through the Gard on my way back," Julian said. "They're already meeting. Most of the Cohort and half the Council. Talking about who's going to be the next Inquisitor. I doubt it's going to be someone who will help us. Not after today. I should care," he said. "But right now I don't."

A door opened at the top of the steps, and light spilled onto the dark landing. "Julian?" Emma called. "Julian, is that you?"

He straightened a little, unconsciously, at the sound of her voice. "I'll be right there." He didn't look at Cristina as he went up the stairs, but he nodded to her, a quick gesture of acknowledgment.

She heard his footsteps die away, his voice mingling with Emma's. She glanced back at the kitchen. The broken dish lay in the corner. She could sweep it up. It would be the more practical thing to do, and Cristina had always thought of herself as practical.

A moment later she had thrown her gear jacket on over her clothes. Tucking several seraph blades into her weapons belt, she slipped quietly out the door and into the streets of Alicante.

Emma listened to the familiar sound of Julian coming up the stairs. The tread of his feet was like music she had always known, so familiar it had almost stopped being music.

Emma resisted calling out again—she was in Dru's room, and Dru had just fallen asleep, worn-out, still in the clothes she'd worn to the Council meeting. Emma heard Julian's step in the hall, and then the sound of a door opening and closing.

Careful not to wake Dru, she slipped out of the room. She knew where Julian was without having to wonder: Down the hall a few doors was Ty's borrowed bedroom.

Inside, the room was softly lit. Diana sat in an armchair by the head of Ty's bed, her face tight with grief and weariness. Kit was asleep, propped against the wall, his hands in his lap.

Julian stood by Ty's bed, looking down, his hands at his sides. Ty slept without restlessness, a drugged sleep, hair dark against the white pillows. Still, even in sleep he kept himself to the left side of the bed, as if leaving the space beside him open for Livvy.

". . . his cheeks are flushed," Julian was saying. "Like he has a fever."

"He doesn't," Diana said firmly. "He needs this, Jules. Sleep heals."

Emma saw the open doubt on Julian's face. She knew what he was thinking: *Sleep didn't heal me when my mother died, or my father, and it won't heal this, either. It will always be a wound.*

Diana glanced over at Emma. "Dru?" she said.

Julian looked up at that, and his eyes met Emma's. She felt the pain in his gaze like a blow to her chest. It was suddenly hard to breathe. "Asleep," she said, almost in a whisper. "It took a little while, but she finally crashed."

"I was in the Silent City," he said. "We brought Livvy down there. I helped them lay her body out."

Diana reached up to put her hand on his arm. "Jules," she said quietly. "You need to go and get yourself cleaned up, and get some rest."

"I should stay here," Julian said in a low voice. "If Ty wakes up and I'm not here—"

"He won't," Diana said. "The Silent Brothers are precise with their doses."

"If he wakes up and you're standing here covered in Livvy's

blood, Julian, it won't help anything," Emma said. Diana looked at her, clearly surprised by the harshness of her words, but Julian blinked as if coming out of a dream.

Emma held out her hand to him. "Come on," she said.

The sky was a mixture of dark blue and black, where storm clouds had gathered over the mountains in the distance. Fortunately, the way up to the Gard was lit by witchlight torches. Cristina slipped along beside the path, keeping to the shadows. The air held the ozone tang of an oncoming storm, making her think of the bitter-penny tang of blood.

As she reached the front doors of the Gard, they opened and a group of Silent Brothers emerged. Their ivory robes seemed to glimmer with what looked like raindrops.

Cristina pressed herself back against the wall. She wasn't doing anything wrong—any Shadowhunter could come to the Gard when they liked—but she instinctively didn't want to be seen. As the Brothers passed close by her, she saw that it wasn't rain after all sparkling on their robes but a fine dusting of glass.

They must have been in the Council Hall. She remembered the window smashing inward as Annabel had disappeared. It had been a blur of noise, splintering light: Cristina had been focused on the Blackthorns. On Emma, the look of devastation on her face. On Mark, his body hunched inward as if he were absorbing the force of a physical blow.

The inside of the Gard was quiet. Head down, she walked rapidly down the corridors, following the sound of voices toward the Hall. She veered aside to take the stairs up to the second-floor seats, which jutted out over the rest of the room like the balcony in a theater. There was a crowd of Nephilim milling around on the dais below. Someone (the Silent Brothers?) had cleared away the broken glass and blood. The window was back to normal.

Clear up the evidence all you want, Cristina thought as she knelt down to peer over the railing of the balcony. *It still happened.*

She could see Horace Dearborn, seated on a high stool. He was a big, bony man, not muscular though his arms and neck were ropy with tendons. His daughter, Zara Dearborn—her hair in a neat braid around her head, her gear immaculate—stood behind him. She didn't resemble her father much, except perhaps in the tight anger of their expressions and in their passion for the Cohort, a faction within the Clave who believed in the primacy of Shadowhunters over Downworlders, even when it came to breaking the Law.

Crowded around them were other Shadowhunters, young and old. Cristina recognized quite a few Centurions—Manuel Casales Villalobos, Jessica Beausejours, and Samantha Larkspear among them—as well as many other Nephilim who had been carrying Cohort signs at the meeting. There were quite a few, though, who as far as she knew were not members of the Cohort. Like Lazlo Balogh, the craggy head of the Budapest Institute, who had been one of the main architects of the Cold Peace and its punitive measures against Downworlders. Josiane Pontmercy she knew from the Marseilles Institute. Delaney Scarsbury taught at the Academy. A few others she recognized as friends of her mother's—Trini Castel from the Barcelona Conclave, and Luana Carvalho, who ran the Institute in São Paulo, had both known her when she was a small girl.

They were all Council members. Cristina said a silent prayer of thanks that her mother wasn't here, that she'd been too busy dealing with an outbreak of Halphas demons in the Alameda Central to attend, trusting Diego to represent her interests.

"There is no time to lose," Horace said. He exuded a sense of humorless intensity, just like his daughter. "We are without an Inquisitor, now, at a critical time, when we are under threat from outside and inside the Clave." He glanced around the room. "We hope that after today's events, those of you who have doubted our cause will come to be believers."

Cristina felt cold inside. This was more than just a Cohort meeting. This was the Cohort recruiting. Inside the empty Council Hall, where Livvy had died. She felt sick.

"What do you think you've learned, exactly, Horace?" said a woman with an Australian accent. "Be clear with us, so we're all understanding the same thing."

He smirked a little. "Andrea Sedgewick," he said. "You were in favor of the Cold Peace, if I recall correctly."

She looked pinched. "I don't think much of Downworlders. But what happened here today . . ."

"We were attacked," said Dearborn. "Betrayed, attacked, inside and out. I'm sure you all saw what I saw—the sigil of the Unseelie Court?"

Cristina remembered. As Annabel had disappeared, borne away through the shattered window of the Hall as if by unseen hands, a single image had flashed on the air: a broken crown.

The crowd murmured their assent. Fear hung in the air like a miasma. Dearborn clearly relished it, almost licking his lips as he gazed around the room. "The Unseelie King, striking at the heart of our homeland. He sneers at the Cold Peace. He knows we are weak. He laughs at our inability to pass stricter Laws, to do anything that would really control the fey—"

"No one can control the fey," said Scarsbury.

"That's exactly the attitude that's weakened the Clave all these years," snapped Zara. Her father smiled at her indulgently.

"My daughter is right," he said. "The fey have their weaknesses, like all Downworlders. They were not created by God or by our Angel. They have flaws, and we have never exploited them, yet they exploit our mercy and laugh at us behind their hands."

"What are you suggesting?" said Trini. "A wall around Faerie?"

There was a bit of derisive laughter. Faerie existed everywhere and nowhere: It was another plane of existence. No one could wall it off.

Horace narrowed his eyes. "You laugh," he said, "but iron doors at all the entrances and exits of Faerie would do a great deal to prevent their incursions into our world."

"Is that the goal?" Manuel spoke lazily, as if he didn't have much invested in the answer. "Close off Faerie?"

"There is not only one goal, as you well know, boy," said Dearborn. Suddenly he smiled, as if something had just occurred to him. "You know of the blight, Manuel. Perhaps you should share your knowledge, since the Consul has not. Perhaps these good people should be aware of what happens when the doors between Faerie and the world are flung wide."

Holding her necklace, Cristina seethed silently as Manuel described the patches of dead blighted earth in Brocelind Forest: the way they resisted Shadowhunter magic, the fact that the same blight seemed to exist in the Unseelie Lands of Faerie. How did he know that? Cristina agonized silently. It had been what Kieran was going to tell the Council, but he hadn't had the chance. How did Manuel know?

She was only grateful that Diego had done what she had asked him to do, and taken Kieran to the Scholomance. It was clear there would have been no safety for a full-blood faerie here.

"The Unseelie King is creating a poison and beginning to spread it to our world—one that will make Shadowhunters powerless against him. We must move now to show our strength," said Zara, cutting Manuel off before he was finished.

"As you moved against Malcolm?" said Lazlo. There were titters, and Zara flushed—she had proudly claimed to have slain Malcolm Fade, a powerful warlock, though it had later turned out she had lied. Cristina and the others had hoped the fact would discredit

Zara—but now, after what had happened with Annabel, Zara's lie had become little more than a joke.

Dearborn rose to his feet. "That's not the issue now, Balogh. The Blackthorns have faerie blood in their family. They brought a creature—a necromantic half-dead thing that slew our Inquisitor and filled the Hall with blood and terror—into Alicante."

"Their sister was killed too," said Luana. "We saw their grief. They did not plan what happened."

Cristina could see the calculations going on inside Dearborn's head—he would have dearly liked to blame the Blackthorns and see them all tossed into the Silent City prisons, but the spectacle of Julian holding Livvy's body as she died was too raw and visceral for even the Cohort to ignore. "They are victims too," he said, "of the Fair Folk prince they trusted, and possibly their own faerie kin. Perhaps they can be brought around to see a reasonable point of view. After all, they are Shadowhunters, and that is what the Cohort is about—protecting Shadowhunters. Protecting our own." He laid a hand on Zara's shoulder. "When the Mortal Sword is restored, I am sure Zara will be happy to lay any doubts you have about her accomplishments to rest."

Zara flushed and nodded. Cristina thought she looked guilty as sin, but the rest of the crowd had been distracted by the mention of the Sword.

"The Mortal Sword restored?" said Trini. She was a deep believer in the Angel and his power, as Cristina's family was too. She looked anxious now, her thin hands working in her lap. "Our irreplaceable link to the Angel Raziel—you believe it will be returned to us?"

"It will be restored," Dearborn said smoothly. "Jia will be meeting with the Iron Sisters tomorrow. As it was forged, so can it be reforged."

"But it was forged in Heaven," protested Trini. "Not the Adamant Citadel."

"And Heaven let it break," said Dearborn, and Cristina suppressed a gasp. How could he claim such a brazen thing? Yet the others clearly trusted him. "Nothing can shatter the Mortal Sword save Raziel's will. He looked upon us and he saw we were unworthy. He saw that we had turned away from his message, from our service to angels, and were serving Downworlders instead. He broke the sword to warn us." His eyes glittered with a fanatic light. "If we prove ourselves worthy again, Raziel will allow the Sword to be reforged. I have no doubts."

How dare he speak for Raziel? How dare he speak as if he were God? Cristina shook with fury, but the others seemed to be looking at him as if he offered them a light in darkness. As if he were their only hope.

"And how do we prove ourselves worthy?" said Balogh in a more somber voice.

"We must remember that Shadowhunters were chosen," said Horace. "We must remember that we have a mandate. We stand first in the face of evil, and therefore we *come first*. Let Downworlders look to their own. If we work together with strong leadership—"

"But we don't have strong leadership," said Jessica Beausejours, one of Zara's Centurion friends. "We have Jia Penhallow, and she is tainted by her daughter's association with faeries and half-bloods."

There was a gasp and a titter. All eyes turned toward Horace, but he only shook his head. "I will not utter a word against our Consul," he said primly.

More murmurs. Clearly Horace's pretense of loyalty had won him some support. Cristina tried not to grind her teeth.

"Her loyalty to her family is understandable, even if it may have blinded her," said Horace. "What matters now is the Laws the Clave passes. We must enforce strict regulations on Downworlders, the strictest of all on the Fair Folk—though there is nothing fair about them."

"That won't stop the Unseelie King," said Jessica, though Cristina got the feeling she didn't so much doubt Horace as desire to prompt him to go further.

"The issue is preventing faeries and other Downworlders from joining the King's cause," said Horace. "That is why they need to be observed and, if necessary, incarcerated before they have a chance to betray us."

"Incarcerated?" Trini echoed. "But how—?"

"Oh, there are several ways," said Horace. "Wrangel Island, for instance, could hold a host of Downworlders. The important thing is that we begin with control. Enforcement of the Accords. Registration of each Downworlder, their name and location. We would start with the faeries, of course."

There was a buzz of approval.

"We will, of course, need a strong Inquisitor to pass and enforce those laws," said Horace.

"Then let it be you!" cried Trini. "We have lost a Mortal Sword and an Inquisitor tonight; let us at least replace one. We have a quorum—enough Shadowhunters are here to put Horace forward for the Inquisitor's position. We can hold the vote tomorrow morning. Who is with me?"

A chant of "Dearborn! Dearborn!" filled the room. Cristina hung on to the railing of the balcony, her ears ringing. This couldn't happen. It couldn't. Trini wasn't like that. Her mother's friends weren't like that. This couldn't be the real face of the Council.

She scrambled to her feet, unable to stand another second of it, and bolted from the gallery.

Emma's room was small and painted an incongruously bright shade of yellow. A white-painted four-poster bed dominated the space. Emma tugged Julian toward it, sitting him down gently, and went to bolt the door.

"Why are you locking it?" Julian raised his head. It was the first thing he'd said since they'd left Ty's room.

"You need some privacy, Julian." She turned toward him; God, the way he looked broke her heart. Blood freckled his skin, darkened his stiff clothes, had dried in patches on his boots.

Livvy's blood. Emma wished she'd been closer to Livvy in those last moments, paid more attention to her, rather than worrying about the Cohort, about Manuel and Zara and Jessica, about Robert Lightwood and exile, about her own broken, messed-up heart. She wished she had held Livvy one more time, marveling at how tall and grown-up she was, how she had changed from the chubby toddler Emma recalled in her own earliest memories.

"Don't," Julian said roughly.

Emma came closer to him; she couldn't stop herself. He had to look up to meet her eyes. "Don't do what?"

"Blame yourself," he said. "I can feel you thinking about how you should have done something different. I can't let those kind of thoughts in, or I'll go to pieces."

He was sitting on the very edge of the bed, as if he couldn't bear the thought of lying down. Very gently, Emma touched his face, sliding the palm of her hand across his jaw. He shuddered and caught her wrist, hard.

"Emma," he said, and for one of the first times in her life, she couldn't read his voice—it was low and dark, rough without being angry, wanting something, but she didn't know what.

"What can I do," she breathed. "What can I do, I'm your *parabatai*, Julian, I need to help you."

He was still holding her wrist; his pupils were wide disks, turning the blue-green of his irises into halos. "I make plans one step at a time," he said. "When everything seems overwhelming, I ask myself what problem needs to be solved first. When that's solved, the next one. But I can't even begin here."

"Julian," she said. "I am your warrior partner. Listen to me now. This is the first step. Get up."

He narrowed his eyes at her for a moment, then obliged by rising to his feet. They were standing close together; she could feel the solidity and warmth of him. She pushed his jacket off his shoulders, then reached up and gripped the front of his shirt. It had a texture like oilcloth now, tacky with blood. She pulled at it and it tore open, leaving it hanging from his arms.

Julian's eyes widened but he made no move to stop her. She ripped away the shirt and tossed it to the ground. She bent down and yanked off his bloodied boots. When she rose up, he was looking at her with eyebrows raised.

"You're really going to rip my pants off?" he said.

"They have her blood on them," she said, almost choking on the words. She touched his chest, felt him draw in a breath. She imagined she could feel the jagged edges of his heart beneath the muscle. There was blood on his skin, too: Patches of it had dried on his neck, his shoulder. The places he had held Livvy close against him. "You need to shower," she said. "I'll wait for you."

He touched her jaw, lightly, with the tips of his fingers. "Emma," he said. "We both need to be clean."

He turned and went into the bathroom, leaving the door wide open. After a moment, she followed.

He had left the rest of his clothes in a pile on the floor. He was standing in the shower in just his underwear, letting the water run down over his face, his hair.

Swallowing hard, Emma stripped down to her panties and camisole and stepped in after him. The water was scalding hot, filling the small stone space with steam. He stood unmoving under the spray, letting it streak his skin with pale scarlet.

Emma reached around him and turned the temperature down. He watched her, wordless, as she took up a bar of soap and lathered it between her hands. When she put her soapy hands on his body he inhaled sharply as if it hurt, but he didn't move even an inch.

She scrubbed at his skin, almost digging her fingers in as she scraped at the blood. The water ran pinkish red into the drain. The soap had a strong smell of lemon. His body was hard under her touch, scarred and muscled, not a young boy's body at all. Not anymore. When had he changed? She couldn't remember the day, the hour, the moment.

He bent his head and she worked the lather into his hair, stroking her fingers through the curls. When she was done, she tilted back his head, let the water run over both of them until it ran clear. She was soaked to the skin, her camisole sticking to her. She reached around Julian to turn the water off and felt him turn his head into her neck, his lips against her cheek.

She froze. The shower had stopped running, but steam rose up around them. Julian's chest was rising and falling fast, as if he were close to collapsing after a race. Dry sobs, she realized. He didn't cry—she couldn't remember the last time she'd seen him cry. He needed the release of tears, she thought, but he'd forgotten the mechanisms of weeping after so many years of holding back.

She put her arms around him. "It's all right," she said. His skin was hot against hers. She swallowed the salt of her own tears. "Julian—"

He drew back as she raised her head, and their lips brushed—and it was instant, desperate, more like a tumble over a cliff's edge than anything else. Their mouths collided, teeth and tongues and heat, jolts shuddering through Emma at the contact.

"Emma." He sounded stunned, his hands knotting in the soaked material of her camisole. "Can I—?"

She nodded, feeling the muscles in his arms tighten as he swung her up into his arms. She shut her eyes, clutching at him, his shoulders, his hair, her hands slippery with water as he carried her into her bedroom, tumbling her onto the bed. A second later he was above her, braced on his elbows, his mouth devouring hers feverishly. Every movement was fierce, frantic, and Emma knew: These were the tears he couldn't cry, the words of grief he couldn't speak. This was the relief he could only allow himself like this, in the annihilation of shared desire.

Frantic gestures rid them of their wet garments. She and Julian were skin to skin now: She was holding him against her body, her heart. His hand slid down, shaking fingers dancing across her hipbone. "Let me—"

She knew what he wanted to say: *Let me please you, let me make you feel good first*. But that wasn't what she wanted, not now. "Come closer," she whispered. "Closer—"

Her hands curved over the wings of his shoulder blades. He kissed her throat, her collarbones. She felt him flinch, hard, and whispered, "What—?"

He had already drawn away from her. Sitting up, he reached for his clothes, pulling them on with shaking hands. "We can't," he said, his voice muffled. "Emma, we can't."

"All right—but, Julian—" She struggled into a sitting position, pulling the blanket up over herself. "You don't have to go—"

He leaned over the edge of the bed to grab his torn and bloodied shirt. He looked at her with a sort of wildness. "I do," he said. "I really do."

"Julian, don't—"

But he was already up, retrieving the rest of his clothes, yanking them on while she stared. He was gone without putting his boots on, almost slamming the door behind him. Emma stared into the darkness, as stunned and disoriented as if she had fallen from a great height.

* * *

Ty woke up suddenly, like someone exploding through the surface of water, gasping for air. The noise snapped Kit out of his doze—he'd been fitfully sleeping, dreaming about his father, walking around the Shadow Market with a massive wound across his stomach that seeped blood.

"This is how it is, Kit," he'd been saying. *"This is life with the Nephilim."*

Still half-asleep, Kit pushed himself up the wall with one hand. Ty was a motionless shadow on the bed. Diana was no longer there—she was probably catching a few moments of sleep in her own room. He was alone with Ty.

It came to him how completely unprepared he was for all of this. For Livvy's death, yes, though he'd seen his own father die, and he knew there were still aspects of that loss he hadn't faced. Never having coped with that loss, how could he cope with this one? And given that he'd never known how to help anyone else, how to offer normal kinds of comfort, how could he help Ty?

He wanted to shout for Julian, but something told him not to—that the shouting might alarm Ty. As Kit's eyes adjusted, he could see the other boy more clearly: Ty looked . . . "disconnected" might be the best word for it, as if he hadn't quite alighted back on earth. His soft black hair seemed crumpled, like dark linen, and there were shadows under his eyes.

"Jules?" he said, his voice low.

Kit pushed himself fully upright, his heart beating unevenly. "It's me," he said. "Kit."

He had braced himself for Ty's disappointment, but Ty only looked at him with wide gray eyes. "My bag," Ty said. "Where is it? Is it over there?"

Kit was too stunned to speak. Did Ty remember what had happened? Would it be worse if he did or didn't?

"My duffel bag," Ty said. There was definite strain in his voice now. "Over there—I need it."

The duffel bag was under the second bed. As Kit went to retrieve it, he glanced out at the view—the crystal spires of the demon towers reaching toward the sky, the water glimmering like ice in the canals, the walls of the city and the fields beyond. He had never been in a place so beautiful or so unreal-looking.

He carried the bag over to Ty, who was sitting with his legs dangling over the side of the bed. Ty took the duffel and started to rummage through it.

"Do you want me to get Julian?" Kit said.

"Not right now," Ty said.

Kit had no idea what to do. He'd never in his entire life had so little idea what to do, in fact. Not when he'd found a golem examining the ice cream in his fridge at four a.m. when he was ten. Not when a mermaid had camped out for weeks on his sofa when he was twelve and spent every day eating goldfish crackers.

Not even when he'd been attacked by Mantid demons. There had been an instinct then, a Shadowhunter sense that had kicked in and propelled his body into action.

Nothing was propelling him now. He was overwhelmed by the desire to drop down to his knees and grab Ty's hands, and hold him the way he had on the rooftop in London when Livvy had been hurt. At the same time, he was just as overwhelmed by the voice in his head that told him that would be a terrible idea, that he had no clue what Ty needed right now.

Ty was still rustling around in his bag. He must not remember, Kit thought with rising panic. He must have blanked out the events in the Council Hall. Kit hadn't been there when Robert and Livvy died, but he'd heard enough from Diana to know what Ty must have witnessed. People forgot horrible things sometimes, he knew, their brains simply refusing to process or store what they'd seen.

"I'll get Helen," he said finally. "She can tell you—what happened—"

"I know what happened," Ty said. He had located his phone, in the bottom of the bag. The tension left his body; his relief was clear. Kit was baffled. There was no signal anywhere in Idris; the phone would be useless. "I'm going to go back to sleep now," Ty said. "There are still drugs in my system. I can feel them." He didn't sound pleased.

"Should I stay?" Kit said. Ty had tossed the duffel bag onto the floor and lain back on the pillows. He was gripping the phone in his right hand, so tightly that his knuckles were white, but otherwise he showed no recognizable signs of distress.

He looked up at Kit. His gray eyes were silver in the moonlight, flat as two quarters. Kit couldn't imagine what he was thinking. "Yes, I'd rather you did," he said. "And go to sleep if you want. I'll be fine."

He closed his eyes. After a long moment, Kit sat down on the bed opposite Ty's, the one that was supposed to be Livvy's. He thought of the last time he'd seen her alone, helping her with her necklace before the big Council meeting, the way she'd smiled, the color and life in her face. It seemed absolutely impossible that she was gone. Maybe Ty wasn't the one acting oddly at all—maybe the rest of them, in accepting the fact of her death, were the ones who didn't understand.

It felt like a hundred miles between Emma's room and his, Julian thought. Like a thousand. He made his way through the halls of the canal house as if he were in a dream.

His shoulder burned and ached.

Emma was the only person he had ever desired, and the force of that desire sometimes stunned him. Never more than tonight. He had lost himself in her, in them, for some totality of time; he had felt only his body and the part of his heart that loved and was uninjured. Emma was all the good in him, he thought, all that burned bright.

But then the pain had come, and the sense of something wrong, and he had *known*. As he hurried toward his room, fear tapped against the outside of his consciousness, howling to be let in and acknowledged, like skeleton hands scratching at a window. It was the fear of his own despair. He knew that he was cushioned by shock now, that he had only touched the tip of the iceberg of grief and howling loss. It would come, the darkness and the horror: He had lived through it before, with the loss of his father.

And this—Livvy—would be worse. He couldn't control his grief. He couldn't control his feelings for Emma. His whole life had been built around exerting control over himself, over the mask he showed the world, and now it was cracking.

"Jules?"

He had reached his bedroom, but he wasn't home free. Mark was waiting for him, leaning against the door. He looked bone tired, hair and clothes rumpled. Not that Julian had any ground to stand on, since his own clothes were torn and bloody, his feet bare.

Julian stopped dead. "Is everything all right?"

They were going to be asking each other that constantly for quite some time, he guessed. And it never would really be okay, but they would reassure each other anyway about the small things, the measure of tiny victories: yes, Dru slept a little; yes, Ty is eating a bit; yes, we're all still breathing. Julian listened mechanically as Mark explained to him that he and Helen had picked up Tavvy, and Tavvy knew about Livia now, and it wasn't good but it was all right and Tavvy was sleeping.

"I didn't want to bother you in the middle of the night," Mark said, "but Helen insisted. She said otherwise the first thing that would happen when you woke up was that you'd freak out about Tavvy."

"Sure," said Julian, amazed he sounded so coherent. "Thanks for letting me know."

Mark gave him a long look. "You were very young when we lost Eleanor, your mother," he said. "She told me once there is a clock in the hearts of parents. Most of the time it is silent, but you can hear it ticking when your child is not with you and you do not know where they are, or when they are awake in the night and wanting you. It will tick until you are with them again."

"Tavvy isn't my child," said Julian. "I'm not a parent."

Mark touched his brother's cheek. It was almost more a faerie touch than a human one, though Mark's hand felt warm and calloused and real. Actually, it didn't feel like a touch at all, Julian thought. It felt like a blessing. "You know you are," Mark said. "I must ask your forgiveness, Julian. I told Helen of your sacrifice."

"My—sacrifice?" Julian's mind was a blank.

"The years you ran the Institute in secret," said Mark. "How you have taken care of the children. The way they look to you, and how you have loved them. I know it was a secret, but I thought she should know it."

"That's fine," Julian said. It didn't matter. Nothing did. "Was she angry?"

Mark looked surprised. "She said she felt such pride in you that it broke her heart."

It was like a tiny point of light, breaking through the darkness. "She—did?"

Mark seemed about to reply when a second hot dart of pain went through Julian's shoulder. He knew exactly the location of that twinge. His heartbeat sped up; he said something to Mark about seeing him later, or at least he thought he did, before going into his bedroom and bolting the door. He was in the bathroom in seconds, turning up the witchlight's brilliance as he gazed into the mirror.

He drew aside the collar of his shirt to get a better look—and stared.

There was his *parabatai* rune. It was stark against his skin—but no longer black. Within the thickly drawn lines he saw what looked like red and glowing flecks, as if the rune had begun to burn from the inside out.

He grabbed the rim of the sink as a wave of dizziness passed over him. He'd been forcing himself not to think about what Robert's death meant, about their broken plans for exile. About the curse that would come on any *parabatai* who fell in love. A curse of power and destruction. He had been thinking only of how much he desperately needed Emma, and not at all of the reasons that he couldn't have her, which remained unchanged.

They had forgotten, reaching for each other in the abyss of grief, as they had always reached for each other all their lives. But it couldn't happen, Julian told himself, biting down hard on his lip, tasting his own blood. There could be no more destruction.

It had begun to rain outside. He could hear the soft patter on the roof of the house. He bent down and tore a strip of material from the shirt he'd worn at the Council meeting. It was stiff and dark with his sister's dried blood.

He tied it around his right wrist. It would stay there until he had vengeance. Until there was justice for Livvy. Until all this bloody mess was cleared up. Until everyone he loved was safe.

He went back out into the bedroom and began to hunt for clean clothes and shoes. He knew exactly where he needed to go.

Julian ran through the empty streets of Idris. Warm summer rain plastered his hair to his forehead and soaked his shirt and jacket.

His heart was pounding: He missed Emma already, regretted leaving her. And yet he couldn't stop running, as if he could outrun the pain of Livvy's death. It was almost a surprise that he could grieve his sister and love Emma at the same time and feel both, neither diminishing the other: Livvy had loved Emma too.

He could imagine how thrilled Livvy would have been to know

he and Emma were together; if it were possible for them to get married, Livvy would have been wild with delight at the idea of helping plan a wedding. The thought was like a stabbing blow to the midsection, the twist of a blade in his guts.

Rain was splashing down into the canals, turning the world to mist and water. The Inquisitor's house loomed up out of the fog like a shadow, and Julian ran up the front steps with such force that he nearly crashed into the front door. He knocked and Magnus opened it, looking pinched and unusually pale. He wore a black T-shirt and jeans with a blue silk robe thrown over them. His hands were bare of their usual rings.

When he saw Julian, he sagged a little against the doorframe. He didn't move or speak, just stared, as if he were looking not at Julian but at something or someone else.

"Magnus," Julian said, a little alarmed. He recalled that Magnus wasn't well. He'd nearly forgotten it. Magnus had always seemed the same: eternal, immutable, invulnerable. "I—"

"I'm here on my own account," Magnus said, in a low and distant voice. *"I need your help. There is absolutely no one else that I can ask."*

"That's not what I . . ." Julian pushed sopping-wet hair out of his eyes, his voice trailing off in realization. "You're remembering someone."

Magnus seemed to shake himself a little, like a dog emerging from the sea. "Another night, a different boy with blue eyes. Wet weather in London, but when was it anything else?"

Julian didn't press it. "Well, you're right. I do need your help. And there isn't anyone else I can ask."

Magnus sighed. "Come in, then. But be quiet. Everyone's asleep, and that's an achievement, considering."

Of course, Julian thought, following Magnus into a central drawing room. This was also a house of grief.

The interior of the house was grand in its scope, with high ceilings and furniture that looked heavy and expensive. Robert seemed to have added little in terms of personality and decoration. There were no family pictures, and little art on the wall besides generic landscapes.

"I haven't seen Alec cry in a long time," Magnus said, sinking onto the sofa and staring into the middle distance. Julian stood where he was, dripping onto the carpet. "Or Isabelle. I understand what it's like to have a father who's a bastard. He's still your bastard. And he did love them, and tried to make amends. Which is more than you can say for mine." He flicked a glance at Julian. "I hope you don't mind if I don't use a drying spell on you. I'm trying to conserve energy. There's a blanket on that chair."

Julian ignored the blanket and the chair. "I shouldn't be here," he said.

Magnus's gaze dropped to the bloody cloth tied around Julian's wrist. His expression softened. "It's all right," he said. "For the first time in a long time, I'm feeling despair. It makes me lash out. My Alec lost his father, and the Clave has lost a decent Inquisitor. But you, you lost your hope of salvation. Don't think I don't understand that."

"My rune started to burn," Julian said. "Tonight. As if it had been drawn on my skin with fire."

Magnus hunched forward and rubbed wearily at his face. Lines of pain and tiredness were etched beside his mouth. His eyes looked sunken. "I wish I knew more about it," he said. "What destruction this will bring to you, to Emma. To others." He paused. "I should be kinder to you. You've lost a child."

"I thought it would wipe everything else out," Julian said, his voice scraped raw. "I thought there wouldn't be anything else in my heart but agony, but there's room in there for me to be terrified for Ty, and panicked about Dru, and there's room for more hate than I ever thought anyone could feel." The pain in his *parabatai* rune flared, and he felt his legs give out.

He staggered and went down on his knees in front of Magnus. Magnus didn't seem surprised that he was kneeling. He only looked down at Julian with a quiet, rarefied patience, like a priest hearing a confession.

"What hurts more," Magnus asked, "the love or the hate?"

"I don't know," Julian said. He dug wet fingers into the carpet on either side of his knees. He felt as if he were having a hard time catching his breath. "I still love Emma more than I ever thought was possible. I love her more every day, and more every time I try to stop. I love her like I'm being ripped in half. And I want to cut the throats of everyone in the Cohort."

"There's an unconventional love speech," Magnus said, leaning forward. "What about Annabel?"

"I hate her, too," said Julian, without emotion. "There's plenty of room for me to hate them all."

Magnus's cat eyes glittered. "Don't think I don't know what you feel," he said. "And there is something I could do. It would be a stopgap. A harsh one. And I wouldn't do it lightly."

"Please." Kneeling on the ground in front of the warlock, Julian looked up; he had never begged for anything in his life, but he didn't care if he was begging now. "I know you're sick, I know I shouldn't even ask, but I have nothing else I can do and nowhere else I can go."

Magnus sighed. "There would be consequences. Have you ever heard the expression '*the sleep of reason brings forth monsters*'?"

"Yes," Julian said. "But I'm going to be a monster either way."

Magnus stood up. For a moment he seemed to tower over Julian, a figure as tall and dark as the grim reaper in a child's nightmare.

"Please," Julian said again. "I don't have anything left to lose."

"Yes, you do," said Magnus. He raised his left hand and looked at it quizzically. Cobalt sparks had begun to burn at the tips of each of his fingers. "Oh yes, you do."

The room lit with blue fire, and Julian closed his eyes.

3
Eternal Rest

The funeral was set for noon, but Emma had been tossing and turning since three or four in the morning. Her eyes felt dry and itchy and her hands shook as she brushed her hair and wound it carefully into a knot on the back of her head.

After Julian had left, she'd run to the window, wrapped in a sheet, and stared out in mingled shock and disbelief. She'd seen him come out of the house and run into the drizzling rain, not even bothering to slow down to zip his jacket.

After that, there hadn't seemed like much she could do. It wasn't like Julian was in danger in the streets of Alicante. Still, she'd waited until she heard his step on the stairs, returning, and heard his bedroom door open and close.

She'd gotten up then and gone to check on Ty, who was still asleep, Kit beside him. She'd realized Livvy's duffel bag was still in the room and taken it, afraid that it would hurt Ty to see it when he woke up. In her room, she'd sat on the bed and unzipped it briefly. There hadn't been much to Livvy's scant belongings—some shirts and skirts, a book, carefully packed toothbrush and soap. One of the shirts had dirt on it, and Emma thought maybe she should wash Livvy's clothes, maybe that would be helpful, and then she'd realized exactly why it wouldn't be helpful and didn't matter and she'd curled up over the bag, sobbing as if her heart would crack in half.

In the end, she'd fallen into a fitful sleep full of dreams of fire and blood. She'd been woken up by the sound of Cristina knocking on her door with a mug of tea and the unpleasant news that Horace had been elected the new Inquisitor in an emergency vote that morning. She'd already told the rest of the family, who were awake and readying themselves for the funeral.

The tea had about three thousand tablespoons of sugar in it, which was both sweet and sweet of Cristina, but it didn't take the edge off the bitterness of the Inquisitor news.

Emma was looking out the window when Cristina came in again, this time carrying a pile of clothes. She was dressed all in white, the color of Shadowhunter mourning and funerals. White gear jacket, white shirt, white flowers in her loose dark hair.

Cristina frowned. "Come away from there."

"Why?" Emma glanced through the window; the house had a commanding view out over the lower part of the city. The walls were visible, and green fields beyond.

She could see a line of very distant figures in white, filing through the gates of the city. In the center of the green fields, two massive stacks of kindling rose like pyramids.

"They already built the pyres," Emma said, and a wave of dizziness came over her. She felt Cristina's warm hand close over hers, and a moment later they were both sitting on the edge of the bed and Cristina was telling her to breathe.

"I'm sorry," Emma said. "I'm sorry. I didn't mean to go to pieces."

Some of Emma's hair had come down out of its knot. Cristina's hands were skillful as she reached up to tuck the strands back in place. "When my uncle died," she said, "he was buried in Idris, and I could not come to the funeral, because my mother thought Idris was still dangerous. When she came home, I went to hug her and her clothes smelled like smoke. I thought: that is all there is left of my uncle now, this smoke on my mother's jacket."

"I need to be strong," Emma said. "I have to be there for the Blackthorns. Julian is—" *Broken, smashed up, in pieces. Missing. No, not missing. Just not with me.*

"You can grieve Livvy too," said Cristina. "She was a sister to you. Family is more than blood."

"But—"

"Grief does not make us weak," Cristina said firmly. "It makes us human. How could you comfort Dru, or Ty, or Jules, if you didn't know what they missed about her? Sympathy is common. Knowing the exact shape of the hole someone's loss leaves in your heart is rare."

"I don't think any of us can understand the shape of what Ty lost," said Emma. Her fear for Ty was intense, like a constant bitter taste in the back of her throat, mixing with her grief for Livvy until she thought she might choke.

Cristina gave Emma a last pat on the hand. "You'd better get dressed," she said. "I'll be down in the kitchen."

Emma dressed in a half-dazed state. When she was done, she glanced at herself in the mirror. The white gear was covered with the scarlet runes of mourning, over and over, an overlapping pattern that became quickly meaningless to the eye like a word that is said repeatedly becomes meaningless to the ear. It made her hair and skin look paler, and even her eyes seemed cold. She looked like an icicle, she thought, or the blade of a knife.

If only she had Cortana with her. She could go into Brocelind and scream and scream and slash at the air until she fell exhausted to the ground, the agony of loss seeping from her every pore like blood.

Feeling incomplete without her sword, she headed downstairs.

* * *

Diana was in the kitchen when Ty came downstairs. There was no one with him, and her hand tightened on the glass she was holding so fiercely that her fingers ached.

She wasn't sure what she'd expected. She'd sat with Ty much of the night as he slept, a dead, silent, unmoving sleep. She'd tried to remember how to pray to Raziel, but it had been such a long time. She had made offerings of incense and flowers in Thailand after her sister had died, but none of it had helped or come close to healing the hole in her heart where Aria should have been.

And Livvy was Ty's twin. Neither had ever known a world without the other one in it. Livvy's last words had been *Ty, I—*. No one would ever know the rest of what she'd wanted to say. How could he cope? How could anyone?

The Consul had provided them all with mourning clothes, which had been kind. Diana wore her own white gown and a gear jacket, and Ty was in full formal mourning dress. Elegantly cut white coat, white trousers and boots, his hair very stark and black against it all. For the first time Diana realized that when Ty grew up he was going to be stunning. She'd thought about him as an adorable child for so long it had never crossed her mind that one day the more adult concept of beauty or handsomeness might be applied to him.

He frowned. He was very, very, pale, almost the color of bleached paper, but his hair was neatly brushed and he looked otherwise put together and almost ordinary. "Twenty-three minutes," he said.

"What?"

"It will take us twenty-three minutes to get down to the Fields, and the ceremonies begin in twenty-five. Where is everyone?"

Diana almost reached for her phone to text Julian before remembering phones didn't work in Idris. *Focus*, she told herself. "I'm sure they're on their way—"

"I wanted to talk to Julian." Ty didn't sound demanding; he sounded more as if he were trying to remember a significant list of things he needed, in proper order. "He went with Livvy to the Silent City. I need to know what he saw and what they did to her there."

I wouldn't have wanted to know those things about Aria, Diana thought, and immediately chided herself. She was not Ty. Ty took comfort from facts. He hated the unknown. Livvy's body had been taken away and locked behind stone doors. Of course he would want to know: Had they honored her body, had they kept her things, had they cleaned the blood from her face? Only by knowing would he be able to understand.

There was a clatter of feet on the stairs. Suddenly the kitchen was full of Blackthorns. Ty moved to stand out of the way as Dru came down, red-eyed in a gear jacket a size too small. Helen, carrying Tavvy, both of them in white; Aline and Mark, Aline with her hair up and small gold earrings in the shape of mourning runes. Diana realized with a start she had been looking for Kieran beside Mark, expecting him there now, and had forgotten he was gone.

Cristina followed and then Emma, both subdued. Diana had put out toast and butter and tea, and Helen put Tavvy down and went to get him some. No one else seemed interested in eating.

Ty glanced anxiously at the clock. A moment later Kit was downstairs, looking uncomfortable in a white gear jacket. Ty didn't say anything, or even glance over at him, but the tension in his shoulders relaxed slightly.

To Diana's surprise, the last to come down the stairs was Julian. She wanted to run over to him to see if he was all right, but it had been a long time since he'd let her do that. If he ever had. He'd always been a self-contained boy, loath to show any negative emotion in front of his family.

She saw Emma glance at him, but he didn't return her glance. He was looking around the room, sizing up everyone's moods, whatever mental calculations he was making invisible behind the shield of his blue-green eyes.

"We should go," he said. "They'll wait for us, but not long, and we should be there for Robert's ceremony."

There was something different about his voice; Diana couldn't place it, exactly. The flatness of grief, most likely.

Everyone turned toward him. He was the center, Diana thought, the fulcrum on which the family turned: Emma and Cristina stood back, not being Blackthorns, and Helen looked relieved when Julian spoke, as if she'd been dreading trying to corral the group.

Tavvy went over to Julian and took his hand. They went out the door in a silent procession, a river of white flowing down the stone steps of the house.

Diana couldn't help thinking of her sister and how she had been burned in Thailand and her ashes sent back to Idris for burial in the Silent City. But Diana hadn't been there for the funeral. At the time, she'd thought she'd never return to Idris again.

As they passed along the street toward Silversteel Bridge, someone threw open a window overhead. A long white banner marked with a mourning rune tumbled out; Ty raised his head, and Diana realized that the bridge and then the street, all the way to the city gates, were festooned with white banners. They strode between them, even Tavvy looking up and around in wonder.

Perhaps they flew mostly for Robert, the Inquisitor, but they were also for Livvy. At least the Blackthorns would always have this, she thought, this remembrance of the honor that had been shown to their sister.

She hoped the election of Horace as Inquisitor wouldn't taint the day even more. Through all her life she had been aware of the uneasy truce not just between Shadowhunters and Downworlders but between those among the Nephilim who thought Downworlders should be embraced by the Clave—and those who did not. Many had celebrated when Downworlders had finally joined the Council after the Dark War. But she had heard the whispers of those who had not—those like Lazlo Balogh and Horace Dearborn. The Cold Peace had given them the liberty to express the hate in their hearts, confident that all right-thinking Nephilim agreed with them.

She had always believed they were wrong, but the election of Horace filled her with fear that there were more Nephilim than she had ever dreamed who were irretrievably soaked in hatred.

As they stepped onto the bridge, something brushed against Diana's shoulder. She reached up to flick it away and realized it was a white flower—one of the kind that grew only in Idris. She looked up; clouds were scudding across the sky, pushed by a brisk wind, but she saw the outline of a man on horseback vanish behind one of them.

Gwyn. The thought of him lit a spark of warmth in her heart. She closed her hand carefully around the petals.

The Imperishable Fields.

That was what they were called, though most people called them simply the Fields. They stretched across the flat plains outside Alicante, from the city walls that had been built after the Dark War to the trees of Brocelind Forest.

The breeze was soft and unique to Idris; in some ways Emma preferred the wind off the ocean in Los Angeles, with its sideways bite of salt. This wind felt too gentle for the day of Livvy's funeral. It lifted her hair and blew her white dress around her knees; it made the white banners that were raised on either side of each pyre drift like ribbons across the sky.

The ground sloped down from the city toward the woods, and as they neared the funeral pyres Cristina took Emma's hand. Emma squeezed back gratefully as they came close enough to the crowd for Emma to see people staring and hear the mutters rise around them. There was sympathy for the Blackthorns, certainly, but also glares for her and Julian; Julian had brought Annabel into Idris, and Emma was the girl who had broken the Mortal Sword.

"A blade as powerful as Cortana has no business in the hands of a child," said a woman with blond hair as Emma passed by.

"The whole thing smacks of dark magic," said someone else.

Emma decided to try not to listen. She stared straight ahead: She could see Jia standing between the pyres, all in white. Memories of the Dark War flooded over her. So many people in white; so very many burning pyres.

Beside Jia stood a woman with long red hair who Emma recognized as Clary's mother, Jocelyn. Beside her was Maryse Lightwood, her black hair loose down her back. It was liberally threaded with gray. She seemed to be speaking intently to Jia, though they were too far away for Emma to hear what they were saying.

Both pyres were finished, though the bodies had not been brought from the Silent City yet. Quite a few Shadowhunters had gathered—no one was required to attend funerals, but Robert had been popular, and his and Livvy's deaths shocking in their horror.

Robert's family stood close to the pyre on the right—the ceremonial robes of the Inquisitor had been draped across the top. They would burn with him. Surrounding the kindling were Alec and Magnus, Simon and Isabelle, all in ritual mourning clothes, even little Max and Rafe. Isabelle looked up at Emma as she approached and waved a greeting; her eyes were swollen from crying.

Simon, beside her, looked tense as a drawn bowstring. He was glancing around, his gaze darting among the people in the crowd. Emma couldn't help but wonder if he was looking for the same people she was—the people who by all rights ought to be here when Robert Lightwood was laid to rest.

Where were Jace and Clary?

* * *

The Shadowhunters had rarely seemed as alien to Kit as they did now. They were everywhere, dressed in their white, a color he associated with weddings and Easter. The banners, the runes, the glittering demon towers in the distance—all of it combined to make him feel as if he were on another planet.

Not to mention that the Shadowhunters didn't cry. Kit had been to funerals before, and seen them on TV. People held handkerchiefs and sobbed into them. But not here; here they were silent, pulled taut, and the sound of birds was louder than the sound of talking or crying.

Not that Kit was crying himself, and not that he had cried when his father died. He knew it wasn't healthy, but his father had always made it sound like to break down in grief meant you would be broken forever. Kit owed too much to the Blackthorns, especially Ty, to let himself shatter over Livvy. She wouldn't have wanted that. She would have wanted him to be there for Ty.

One after another the Nephilim came up to the Blackthorns and offered their condolences. Julian had placed himself at the head of his family like a shield and was coolly fending off all cordial attempts to talk to his brothers and sisters, who stood in a group behind him. Julian seemed colder and more removed than usual, but that wasn't surprising. Grief hit everyone in different ways.

It did mean he'd let go of Tavvy's hand, though, so Tavvy had gone over to stand next to Dru, pressing himself into her side. It also left Ty on his own, and Kit made his way over to the other boy, feeling resplendently silly in white leather pants and jacket. He knew it was a formal mourning outfit, but it made him feel like he was cosplaying someone in an eighties music video.

"Funerals are always so sad," said a woman who had introduced herself as Irina Cartwright, staring at Julian with a deep pitying stare. When he didn't respond, she shifted her gaze to Kit. "Don't you think?"

"I wouldn't know," said Kit. "My father was eaten by demons."

Irina Cartwright looked discomfited and hurried away after a few more trite phrases. Julian raised an eyebrow at Kit before greeting the next mourner.

"Do you still have . . . the phone?" Kit asked Ty, and felt immediately like an idiot. Who went up to someone at their twin sister's funeral and asked them if they had their phone? Especially when there was no signal anywhere in Idris? "I mean. Not that you can call. Anyone."

"There's one phone in Idris that works. It's in the Consul's office," said Ty. He didn't look like he was cosplaying an eighties music-video star; he looked icy and striking and—

The word "beautiful" blinked on and off in Kit's head like a flickering neon sign. He ignored it.

Elegant. Ty looked elegant. People with dark hair probably just looked naturally better in white.

"It's not the phone signal I need," said Ty. "It's the photos on the phone."

"Photos of Livvy?" Kit asked, confused.

Ty stared at him. Kit remembered the days in London, in which they'd been working together, solving—well, solving mysteries. Like Watson and Holmes. He hadn't ever felt like he didn't understand Ty. But he felt it now.

"No," Ty said.

He glanced around. Kit wondered if the growing number of people was bothering Ty. He hated crowds. Magnus and Alec were standing with their kids near the Consul; they were with a beautiful black-haired girl with eyebrows just like Alec's and a boy—well, he was probably in his twenties—with untidy brown hair. The boy gave Kit a considering look that seemed to say *you look familiar*. Several people had done the same. Kit guessed it was because he looked like Jace, if Jace had suffered a sudden and unexpected height, muscle, and overall hotness reduction.

"I need to talk to you, later," Ty said, his voice low, and Kit wasn't sure whether to be worried or grateful. As far as he knew, Ty hadn't really talked to anyone since Livvy died.

"You don't—want to talk to your brother? To Julian?"

"No. I need to talk to you." Ty hesitated, as if he was about to say something else.

There was a low, mournful sound as if of a horn blowing, and people turned to stare back at the city. Kit followed their gazes and saw that a procession was leaving the gates. Dozens of Silent Brothers in their parchment uniforms, walking in two lines on either side of two biers. The biers were carried at shoulder height by Council guards.

They were too distant for Kit to see which bier was Livvy's: He could see only a body lying on each platform, wrapped in white. And then they came closer, and he saw that one body was much smaller than the other, and he turned to Ty without being able to stop himself.

"I'm sorry," he said. "I'm so sorry."

Ty was looking toward the city. One of his hands was opening and closing, his long fingers curling under, but other than that he showed no signs of any emotion. "There really isn't any reason for you to be sorry," he said. "So please don't be."

Kit stood without speaking. There was a cold tension inside him, a fear he couldn't shake—that he had lost not just Livvy but Ty as well.

"They haven't come back yet," Isabelle said. She was composed, immaculate in gear, a white silk band holding back her hair. She was holding Simon's hand, her knuckles as white as the flower in her lapel.

Emma had always thought of grief as a claw. The claw of a

massive monster you couldn't see, that reached down out of the sky and seized hold of you, punching out your breath, leaving only a pain you couldn't wriggle away from or avoid. You just had to endure it for as long as the claw had you in its grasp.

She could see the pain of it in Isabelle's eyes, behind her calm exterior, and part of her wanted to reach out and hug the other girl. She wished Clary were here—Clary and Isabelle were like sisters, and Clary could comfort Izzy in the way only a best friend could.

"I thought you knew," Simon said, his eyebrows wrinkled as he looked at Emma. She thought of Clary saying that she couldn't tell Simon about her visions of death, that he'd fall apart. "I thought they told you where they were going."

No one seemed to be paying much attention to them—Jia was still deep in conversation with Jocelyn and Maryse, and the other Shadowhunters present had descended on Julian and the others to offer condolences. "They did. They went to Faerie. I know."

Simon and Isabelle moved instinctively closer to her. She hoped they didn't look too much as if they were huddling, sharing secrets, since that was exactly what was happening.

"It's just that I thought they'd be back by now," Emma said.

"They're meant to get back tomorrow." Isabelle made a cooing noise, and bent down to scoop up Max. She held him in her arms, nuzzling her chin into his hair. "I know—it's awful. If there had only been a way to get them a message . . ."

"We couldn't exactly ask the Clave to delay the funeral," said Simon. Shadowhunter bodies weren't embalmed; they were burned as soon as possible, before they began to decay.

"Jace is going to be wrecked," said Izzy. She glanced back over her shoulder to where her brother was holding Rafe by the hand, looking up at Magnus as they talked. "Especially not to have been here for Alec."

"Grief lasts a long time," said Emma, her throat tight. "Lots of people are there for you in the beginning, when it first happens. If Jace is there for Alec later, after all the noise of the funeral and all the platitudes from total strangers go away, that'll be better anyway."

Izzy's eyes softened. "Thanks. And try not to worry about Clary and Jace. We knew we wouldn't be able to be in touch with them while they were gone. Simon—he's Clary's *parabatai.* He would feel it if anything had happened to her. And Alec would as well, about Jace."

Emma couldn't argue the strength of the *parabatai* bond. She glanced down, wondering—

"They've come." It was Magnus, reaching to take Max from Isabelle. He gave Emma an odd sideways look that she couldn't read. "The Brothers."

Emma glanced over. It was true: They had glided almost soundlessly into the crowd, parting it like the Red Sea. Shadowhunters fell back as the biers carrying Livvy and Robert passed among them, and stopped between the pyres.

Livvy lay pale and bloodless, her body swathed in a white silk dress, white silk binding her eyes. Her gold necklace glittered at her throat. Her long brown hair was scattered with white flowers.

Livvy dancing on her bed, wearing a pale green chiffon dress she'd bought at Hidden Treasures. Emma, Emma, look at my new dress! Emma struggled against the memory, against the cold truth: This was the last dress she would see Livvy wear. This was the last time she would see her familiar brown hair, the curve of her cheek, her stubborn chin. *Livvy, my Livvy, my wise little owl, my sweet little sister.*

She wanted to scream, but Shadowhunters didn't cry out at death. They spoke the old words instead, handed down through the ages.

"Ave atque vale." The murmur went through the crowd. *"Ave atque vale, Robert Lightwood. Ave atque vale, Livia Blackthorn."*

Isabelle and Alec turned to face their father's bier. Julian and the other Blackthorns were still pinned in by well-wishers. For a moment, Emma was alone with Simon.

"I talked to Clary before she left," she said, the words feeling like a hot pressure in the back of her throat. "She was worried something bad was going to happen."

Simon looked puzzled. "What kind of bad thing?"

Emma shook her head. "Just—if she doesn't come back when she's supposed to—"

Simon looked at her with troubled eyes, but before he could say anything, Jia stepped forward and began to speak.

"Shadowhunters die young," said someone in the crowd. Julian didn't recognize the man: He was probably in his early forties, with thick black eyebrows. He wore a patch on his gear with the symbol of the Scholomance on it, but little else differentiated him from the dozens of other people who had come up to Julian to tell him they were sorry his sister was dead.

"But fifteen—" The man shook his head. Gladstone, Julian recalled. His last name was Gladstone. "Robert lived a full life. He was a distant cousin of mine, you know. But what happened to your sister should never have happened. She was only a child."

Mark made a strangled noise behind Julian. Julian said something polite to send Gladstone on his way. Everything felt distant, muffled, as if he or the world had been wrapped in cotton padding.

"I didn't like him," said Dru, after Gladstone had gone. The skin under her eyes was shiny and tight where tears had left traces that couldn't be washed away.

It was as if there were two Julians. One was Julian Before, the Julian who would have reached over to comfort Dru, ruffle her hair. Julian Now didn't. He remained motionless as the crowd started to surge apart to make way for the funeral procession, and saw Helen lift Tavvy up into her arms.

"He's seven," he said to her. "He's too old to be carried everywhere."

She gave him a half-surprised, half-reproachful look but said nothing. The Silent Brothers were walking between them with their biers, and the Blackthorn family stilled as the air filled with the chant of the Nephilim.

"Ave atque vale, Livia Blackthorn. Hail and farewell."

Dru jammed the heels of her hands into her eyes. Aline put an arm around her. Julian looked for Ty. He couldn't stop himself.

Mark had gone over to Ty and was talking to him; Kit stood beside him, hands shoved in his pockets, shoulders hunched, altogether wretched. Ty himself was staring at Livvy's bier, a spot of red burning on each of his cheeks. On the way down from the city, he had peppered Julian with questions: *Who touched her in the Silent City? Did they wash the blood off her? Did they brush her hair? Did they take her necklace? Did they let you have her clothes? Who picked the dress for her to be buried in? Did they close her eyes before they tied the silk over them?* until Julian had been exhausted and near snapping.

Ladders had been placed beside the pyres, each one a massive stack of logs and kindling. A Silent Brother took Livvy's body and began to climb the ladder. When he reached the top, he laid her body down; at the second pyre, a Silent Brother was doing the same with Robert Lightwood's corpse.

Diana had also gone to stand beside Ty. There was a white flower tucked into her collar, pale against her dark skin. She said something quietly to him, and Ty looked up at her.

Julian ached inside, a physical ache, as if he'd been punched in the stomach and was just now getting his breath back. He could feel the bloody cloth tied around his wrist, like a circle of fire.

Emma. He looked for her in the crowd, saw her standing beside Simon. Cristina had come to stand with them. The ladders had been drawn away, and the Silent Brothers stepped forward with their lit torches. Their fire was bright enough to illuminate even the daylight scene. Emma's hair sparked and caught its brilliance as the Silent Brothers took their places around the pyres.

"These flames, this burning," said Mark, who had appeared at Julian's side. "In the Wild Hunt we practiced sky burial."

Julian glanced at him. Mark was flushed, his pale curls disordered. His mourning runes had been applied with care and precision, though, which meant he hadn't done them himself. They were beautiful and delicately done—Cristina's work.

"We would leave bodies at the tops of glaciers or high trees, for the birds to pick clean," Mark said.

"How about you not suggest that to anyone else at this funeral," said Julian.

Mark winced. "I'm sorry, I don't always know the right thing to say."

"When in doubt, don't say anything," Julian said. "Literally, it's better if you don't talk at all."

Mark gave him the same look Helen had before—half hurt and half surprise—but before he could say anything, Jia Penhallow, in ceremonial robes of dazzling snow white, began to speak.

"Fellow Shadowhunters," she said, her rich voice carrying across the Imperishable Fields. "A great tragedy has come to us. One of our most faithful servants of the Clave, Robert Lightwood, was slain in the Council Hall, where our Law has always prevailed."

"Good job not mentioning he was a traitor," muttered someone in the crowd.

It was Zara. A hissing spurt of giggles erupted around her, like a teapot exploding. Her friends, Manuel Villalobos, Samantha Larkspear, and Jessica Beausejours, stood around her in a tight circle.

"I can't believe they're *here*." It was Emma. Somehow she had come up beside Julian. He didn't remember it happening, but reality seemed to be flickering in and out like a camera shutter opening and closing. She looked slightly taken aback when Julian didn't reply, but she stalked off into the crowd, stiff-arming Gladstone out of the way.

"Also one of our youngest and most promising Shadowhunters was murdered, her blood spilled in front of us all," said Jia as Emma reached Zara and her friends. Zara jumped back slightly, then tried to hide her loss of poise with a glare.

Emma wouldn't care one way or another, Julian thought, about Zara's poise. She was gesturing at Zara, and then at the Blackthorns and Ty, as Jia's voice rang out over the meadow:

"We *will not* let these deaths go unpunished. We *will not* forget who was responsible. We are warriors, and we will fight, and fight back."

Zara and her friends were looking mulish—all but Manuel, who was smiling a sideways smile that under other circumstances would have given Julian the creeps. Emma turned and walked away from them. Her expression was grim.

Still, Zara had stopped talking, which was something.

"They are gone," said Jia. "The Nephilim have lost two great souls. Let Raziel bless them. Let Jonathan Shadowhunter honor them. Let David the Silent remember them. And let us commend their bodies to the necropolis, where they will serve forever."

The Consul's voice had softened. Everyone was looking toward her, even the children like Tavvy, Rafe, and Max, so everyone saw her expression change and darken. She spoke the next words as if they tasted bitter in her mouth.

"And now, our new Inquisitor wants to say a few words."

Horace Dearborn stepped forward; Julian hadn't noticed him until that moment. He wore a white mourning robe and a suitably grave expression, though there seemed to be a sneer behind it, like a shadow behind glass.

Zara was grinning openly, and more of her friends from the Scholomance had gathered near her. She gave her father a little wave, still grinning, and Manuel's smirk spread until it covered most of his face.

Julian saw the nausea in Isabelle's and Simon's expressions, the horror on Emma's face, the anger on Magnus's and Alec's.

He strained to feel what they felt, but he couldn't. He felt nothing at all.

Horace Dearborn took a long moment to survey the crowd. Kit had gleaned enough from the others to know that Zara's father was an even worse bigot than she was and that he'd been named the new Inquisitor by a majority of the Council, all of whom seemed more scared of the Unseelie Court and the threat of Downworlders than they were of investing a clearly evil man with power.

Not that Kit found any of this surprising. Just depressing.

Ty, beside him, didn't seem to be looking at Horace at all. He was staring up at Livvy, or the little of her they could see—she was a scrap of white at the top of a tall pile of kindling wood. As he looked at his sister, he drew his right index finger across the back of his left hand, over and over; otherwise he was motionless.

"Today," Horace said finally, "as the Consul says, may indeed be a day for grief."

"Nice of him to acknowledge," murmured Diana.

"*However!*" Horace's voice rose, and he stabbed a finger out into the crowd, as if accusing them all of a terrible crime. "These deaths did not come from nowhere. There is no question who was responsible for these murders—though foolish Shadowhunters may have allowed them to occur, the hand of the Unseelie King and all faeries, and all Downworlders by connection, were behind this act!"

Why would that be? Kit thought. Horace reminded him of politicians shouting on TV, red-faced men who always seemed angry and always wanted you to know there was something you needed to be afraid of.

The idea that if the Unseelie King was responsible for Livvy's and Robert's deaths, all Downworlders were guilty, made no sense to Kit, but if he was hoping for a protest from the crowd, he was disappointed. The gathering was strangely quiet, but Kit didn't get the sense that they were against Horace. Rather they seemed as if they felt it would be impolite to cheer. Magnus looked on with no expression at all, as if it had been wiped from his face with an eraser.

"Death serves as a reminder," said Horace, and Kit glanced over at Julian, whose dark brown hair was blowing in the rising wind. Kit doubted this was a reminder Julian had needed. "A reminder that we have only one life and we must live it as warriors. A reminder that we have only one chance to make the correct choices. A reminder that the time is coming soon when all Shadowhunters will have to decide where they stand. Do they stand with traitors and Downworlder-lovers? Do they stand with those who would destroy our way of life and our very culture? Do they—young man, what are you doing? Get down from there!"

"Oh, by the Angel," Diana whispered.

Ty was climbing up the side of his sister's pyre. It didn't look easy—the wood had been piled up for maximum-efficiency burning, not for clambering, but he was finding handholds and footholds anyway. He was already high enough off the ground that Kit felt a bolt of fear go through him at the thought of what would happen if one of the logs of wood came free and he fell.

Kit started after him without thinking, only to feel a hand close on his collar. He was jerked back by Diana. "No," she said. "Not you." Her face was set in grim lines.

Not you. Kit saw what she meant in a moment: Julian Blackthorn was already running, shoving past the Inquisitor—who squawked indignantly—and leaping for the pyre. He began to climb after his brother.

"Julian!" Emma called, but she doubted he could hear her. Everyone was shouting now—the Council guards, the mourners, the Consul and Inquisitor. Zara and her friends were hooting with laughter, pointing at Ty. He had nearly reached the top of the pyre and didn't seem to hear anyone or anything around him: He was climbing with a dogged intensity. Julian, below him, climbing more carefully, couldn't match his speed.

Only the Blackthorns were utterly silent. Emma tried to push forward, but Cristina held on to her wrist, shaking her head. "Don't—it's not safe, better not to distract Julian—"

Ty had reached the platform atop the pyre. He sat down there, perched beside his sister's body.

Helen gave a little whimper in her throat. "*Ty.*"

There was no protection from the wind at the top of the pyre. Ty's hair whipped around his face as he bent over Livvy. It looked as if he were touching her folded hands. Emma felt a wave of empathic sorrow like a punch to the gut, followed by another wave of anxiety.

Julian reached the platform beside Ty and Livvy. He knelt beside his brother. They looked like two pale chess pieces, only the color of their hair—Ty's a little darker—differentiating them in color.

Emma felt her heartbeat in her throat. It was one of the hardest things she'd ever done, not to run to the pyre and climb it. Everything else but Julian and Ty seemed distant and far off, even when she heard Zara and her friends giggle that the Silent Brothers should light the pyre, should burn Ty and Julian along with Livvy if they wanted to be with her so badly.

She felt Cristina stiffen beside her. Mark was walking across the grass, toward the two pyres. Zara and her friends were muttering about him now, about his pointed ears, his faerie blood. Mark walked with his head down, determined, and Emma couldn't stand it anymore: She broke away from Cristina and ran across the grass. If Mark was going to go after Julian and Ty, then she was too.

She caught a glimpse of Jia, beside Maryse and Jocelyn, all of them motionless, a horrified tableau. Shadowhunters didn't do this sort of thing. They didn't make a spectacle of their grief. They didn't scream or rage or collapse or break down or climb to the tops of pyres.

Julian had bent and taken his brother's face in his hands. It made for a peculiarly tender portrait, despite their location. Emma could imagine how difficult this was for him: He hated showing emotion in front of anyone he couldn't trust, but he didn't seem to be thinking about that; he was murmuring to Ty, their foreheads almost touching.

"The ladders," Emma said to Mark, and he nodded without asking anything further. They pushed past a knot of onlookers and grabbed one of the heavy ladders the Silent Brothers had carried to the Field, propping it against the side of Livvy's pyre.

"Julian," Emma called, and she saw him glance down at her as she and Mark held the ladder steady. Somewhere Horace was shouting at them to leave it alone and for the Council guards to come and drag the boys down. But nobody moved.

Julian touched Ty once on the cheek and Ty hesitated, his arms coming up to hug himself briefly. He dropped them and followed Julian as they climbed down the ladder, Julian first. When he hit the ground he didn't move, just looked up, poised to catch his brother if he fell.

Ty reached the ground and walked away from the pyre without

stopping to catch his breath, heading across the grass toward Kit and Diana.

Someone was shouting at them to move the ladder: Mark hoisted it and carried it over to the Silent Brothers, while Emma took hold of Julian's wrists and drew him gently away from the site of the pyres.

He looked stunned, as if he'd been hit with enough force to make him dizzy. She stopped some distance from any other people and took both his hands in hers.

No one would think anything odd of it; that was a normal sort of affection between *parabatai*. Still, she shivered, at the combination of touching him and the horror of the situation and the blank look on his face.

"Julian," she said, and he winced.

"My hands," he said, sounding surprised. "I didn't feel it."

She glanced down and sucked in her breath. His palms were a crazy quilt of bloody splinters from the kindling wood. Some were small dark lines against his skin, but others were bigger, snapped-off toothpicks of wood that had gone in at an angle, oozing blood.

"You need an *iratze*," she said, letting go of one of his wrists and reaching to her belt for a stele. "Let me—"

"No." He drew his other wrist free of her hold. His expression was colder than glacial ice. "I don't think that would be a very good idea."

He walked away as Emma struggled to breathe. Ty and Mark had returned to where the Blackthorns were standing: Ty was near Kit, as he almost always was, like a magnet clicking into place.

She saw Mark reach out to take Cristina's hand and hold it and thought: *I should be holding Julian's hands, I should be there for him, reminding him there are still things in the world worth living for.*

But Julian's hands were bloody and wounded and he didn't want her to touch them. As his soul was torn and bloody and maybe he didn't want anyone near that, either, but she was different, she was his *parabatai*, wasn't she?

It is time. The silent voice of one of the Brothers rippled across the Fields: They all heard it—except Magnus and Max, who looked around in confusion. Emma barely had time to brace herself before the Silent Brothers touched their torches to the kindling wood at the foot of each pyre. Fire blasted upward, rippling in shades of gold and red, and for a moment it was almost beautiful.

Then the roar of the flames hit her, like the sound of a crashing wave, and the heat rolled across the grass, and Livvy's body vanished behind a sheet of smoke.

Kit could barely hear the soft chant of the Nephilim over the greedy crackle of the flames: "*Vale, vale, vale. Farewell, farewell, farewell.*"

The smoke was thick. His eyes stung and burned, and he couldn't stop thinking of the fact that his own father had had no funeral, that there had been little of him left to bury, his flesh turned to ash by Mantid venom, his remains disposed of by the Silent Brothers.

Kit couldn't bear to look at the Blackthorns, so he stared at the Lightwoods. He had overheard all their names by now: he knew Alec's sister was Isabelle, the girl with the black hair who stood with her arms around Alec and her mother, Maryse. Rafe and Max held each other's hands; Simon and Magnus stood close to the others, like small moons of comfort orbiting a planet of grief. He remembered someone saying that funerals were for the living, not the dead, so that they could say good-bye. He wondered about the burning: Was it so that the Nephilim could bid good-bye in fire that reminded them of angels?

He saw a man come toward the Lightwoods and blinked his watering eyes. He was a young man, handsome, with curling brown hair and a square jaw. He wasn't wearing white, like the others, but plain black gear. As he passed Maryse he stopped and laid a hand on her shoulder.

She didn't turn or seem to notice. Neither did anyone else. Magnus glanced over quickly, frowning, but looked away again; Kit realized with a coldness in his chest that he was the only one who actually could see the young man—and that the smoke seemed to flow through the stranger, as if he were made of air.

A ghost, he thought. *Like Jessamine.* He looked around wildly: Surely there would be more ghosts here, in the Imperishable Fields, their dead feet leaving no traces on the grass?

But he saw only the Blackthorns, clinging together, Emma and Cristina side by side, and Julian with Tavvy, as the smoke rose up and around them. Half-reluctantly he glanced back: The young man with the dark hair had moved to kneel beside Robert Lightwood's pyre. He was closer to the flames than any human could have gotten, and they seemed to eddy within the outline of his body, lighting eyes with fiery tears.

Parabatai, Kit thought suddenly. In the slump of the young man's shoulders, in his outstretched hands, in the longing stamped on his face, he saw Emma and Julian, he saw Alec as he spoke about Jace; he knew he was looking at the ghost of Robert Lightwood's *parabatai.* He didn't know how he knew it, but he did.

A cruel sort of bond, he thought, that made one person out of two people, and left such devastation when half was gone.

He glanced away from the ghost, realizing that smoke and fire had made a wall now, and the pyres were no longer visible. Livvy had disappeared behind the boiling darkness. The last thing he saw before tears blinded him was Ty beside him, lifting his face and closing his eyes, a dark silhouette outlined by the brilliance of the fire as if he was haloed in gold.

4

Nothing That Is Ours

The pyres were still burning as the procession turned and headed back toward the city. It was customary for the smoke to rise all night, and for families to gather in Angel Square to mourn among others.

Not that Emma thought it was likely the Blackthorns would do that. They would remain in their house, sequestered with each other: They had been too much apart all their lives to want comfort from other Shadowhunters who they barely knew.

She had trailed away from the rest of the group, too raw to want to try to talk to Julian again in front of his family.

"Emma," said a voice beside her. She turned and saw Jem Carstairs.

Jem. She was too surprised to speak. Jem had been a Silent Brother once, and though he was a Carstairs, he was a very distant relative, due to being more than a century old. He looked only about twenty-five, though, and was dressed in jeans and scuffed shoes. He wore a white sweater, which she guessed was his concession to Shadowhunter funeral whites. Jem was no longer a Shadowhunter, though he had been one for many years.

"Jem," she whispered, not wanting to disturb anyone else in the procession. "Thanks for coming."

"I wished you to know how sorry I am," he said. He looked pale and drawn. "I know you loved Livia like a sister."

"I had to watch her die," said Emma. "Have you ever watched someone you loved die?"

"Yes," said Jem.

This was the thing about nearly immortal people, Emma thought. It was rare that you had a life experience that they hadn't.

"Can we talk?" she said abruptly. "Just us?"

"Yes. I wished to speak alone with you myself." He indicated a low rise some distance away, partially hidden by a stand of trees. After whispering to Cristina that she was going to talk to Jem—"*The* Jem? The really old one? Who's married to a warlock? *Really*?"—she followed Jem to where he was sitting on the grass, among a tumble of old stones.

They sat for a moment in silence, both of them looking out over the Imperishable Fields. "When you were a Silent Brother," Emma said abruptly, "did you burn people?"

Jem looked over at her. His eyes were very dark. "I helped light the pyres," he said. "A clever man I knew once said that we cannot understand life, and therefore we cannot hope to understand death. I have lost many I loved to death, and it does not get easier, nor does watching the pyres burn."

"*We are dust and shadows*," Emma said. "I guess we're all ashes, too."

"It was meant to make us all equal," said Jem. "We are all burned. Our ashes all go to build the City of Bones."

"Except for criminals," said Emma.

Jem's brow furrowed. "Livia was hardly that," he said. "Nor you, unless you are thinking of committing a crime?"

I already have. I'm criminally in love with my parabatai. The desire to say the words, to confess to someone—to Jem, specifically—was like a pressure behind Emma's eyes. She said hastily, "Did your *parabatai* ever pull away from you? When you, you know, wanted to talk?"

"People do strange things when they're grieving," said Jem gently. "I was watching from a distance, earlier. I saw Julian climb to the top of the pyre for his brother. I know how much he has always loved those children. Nothing he says or does now, in these first and worst days, is who he is. Besides," he added, with a slight smile, "being *parabatai* is complicated. I hit my *parabatai* in the face once."

"You did *what*?"

"As I said." Jem seemed to enjoy her astonishment. "I struck my *parabatai*—I loved him more than anyone else in the world I've ever loved save Tessa, and I struck him in the face because my heart was breaking. I can hardly judge anyone else."

"Tessa!" Emma exclaimed. "Where is she?"

Jem's hand made a fist in the grass. "You know of the warlock illness?"

Emma recalled hearing of Magnus's weakness, the swiftness with which his magic was depleted. That it wasn't just him, it was other warlocks too.

"Is Tessa sick?" she said.

"No," Jem said. "She was ill, but recovered."

"Then the warlocks can get better?"

"Tessa is the only one who has conquered the sickness. She believes she is protected by her Shadowhunter blood. But more and more warlocks are falling ill now—and those who are older, who have used more magic and more powerful magic, are sickening first."

"Like Magnus," Emma whispered. "How much does Tessa know about it? What have they figured out?"

"Tessa thinks it might be connected to the spells Malcolm Fade used to raise Annabel," said Jem. "He used the ley lines to power his necromantic magic—if they're poisoned with that darkness, it might be communicating that poison to any warlock who uses them."

"Can't warlocks just not use them?"

"There are only a few sources of power," said Jem. "Ley lines are the easiest. Many of the warlocks *have* stopped using them, but it means they're exhausting their powers very quickly, which is also unhealthy." He gave her an unconvincing smile. "Tessa will solve it," he said. "She found Kit—she'll discover the answer to this as well."

Jem bent his head. He kept his hair short, and Emma could see the marks of his Silent Brother scars, where runes of silence had once been placed, along his cheek.

"I wanted to talk to you about Kit, actually," he said. "It's partly why I came."

"Really? Because of Kit? He's all right, as far as I know. Sad, like the rest of us."

"Kit is more than just a Herondale," he said. "The Herondales are important to me, but so are the Carstairs and Blackthorns. But Tessa and I knew Kit was in danger from the first time we found out what his heritage was. We rushed to find him, but Johnny Rook had hidden him well."

"His heritage? Johnny Rook was a con man and Kit says his mother was a showgirl in Vegas."

"Johnny *was* a con man, but he also had some Shadowhunter blood in his family—from a long time back, probably hundreds of years. That's not what's significant about Kit, though. What's significant is what he inherited from his mother." He hesitated. "Kit's mother's family has been hunted by faeries for many generations. The Unseelie King has been bent on their destruction, and Kit is the last of their line."

Emma fell sideways onto the grass. "Not more faeries," she groaned.

Jem smiled, but his eyes were troubled. "Kit's mother was murdered by a Rider," he said. "Fal. I believe you knew him."

"I believe I killed him," said Emma. She pushed herself back up to sit beside Jem. "And now I'm glad. He murdered Kit's mom? That's awful."

"I cannot tell you as much as I wish I could," said Jem. "Not quite yet. But I can tell you there is faerie blood in Kit's family. Kit's mother was hunted, and so was her father, on through the generations. Kit is alive because his mother went to great lengths to conceal the fact that he was born. She covered every link between them, and when she died, the King thought the line died with her."

"And that's changed?" said Emma.

"We fear it might have," said Jem. "Tessa and I left Kit with you at the Institute because the warlock sickness was already beginning. We did not know then whether it was something that could spread to humans. We also needed to be in the Spiral Labyrinth and they would not let us bring Kit. We always intended to return for him—we had no idea the Riders would be dispatched to find you. We cannot know whether or not they recognized him. He looks a great deal like his mother."

"I don't think so," said Emma. Kit looked just like Jace, in her opinion.

"So are you going to take Kit with you now?" said Emma. "We don't want to lose him, but if you have to—"

"The warlock sickness has only worsened. Tessa and I are working day and night in the Spiral Labyrinth to find a cure. And there is something else." He hesitated. "Tessa is pregnant."

"Oh! *Congratulations!*" It was the first good news Emma had gotten in what felt like forever.

Jem smiled the sort of smile that made it look as if a light had turned on inside him. He had been alone so long, Emma knew, imagining that he would never have a family. To have a wife now and a baby on the way—the very ordinary sort of miracles that made up an ordinary life—must be extraordinary for him.

"It is wonderful," he said. He laid a hand on hers. "I trust you,

Emma. I wish only to ask you to look out for Kit, and if you see something suspicious—if you see any signs of a search—please tell me. I will come at once."

"Should I send a fire-message?" Emma said, her happiness over the baby fading.

"Sometimes it is not possible to send a fire-message. There are easier ways." He pressed something into her hand. A simple silver ring with a clear stone set into it. "It's glass," he said. "Smash the ring and Tessa will know; she has the matching one."

Emma slid the ring onto her finger. She thought of Kit, standing faithfully beside Ty at the funeral. She thought of his pale curls and blue eyes and gamine face; should she have guessed he had faerie blood somewhere? No. He didn't look like Mark. He looked like a Herondale. Like that was all he was. "You can trust me," she said. "I'll look out for Kit. Is there anything I can do about the ley lines?"

"It would be useful to have a Shadowhunter in Los Angeles checking out the locus point of Malcolm's magic," said Jem. "When you get home, contact Catarina Loss. She may want your help."

"I will," Emma said. "It's good for me to have a purpose, I think. Livvy's dead—Jace and Clary are on a mission and can't be reached—and Horace Dearborn is the Inquisitor. It's like there's no hope for anything now."

"There is *always* hope," said Jem. "When I was very young, it was still permitted to take spoils—the property of Downworlders could be confiscated by any Shadowhunter. I knew a man who kept the heads of slaughtered faeries in the Institute he ran."

Emma made a nauseated noise.

"There has ever been this strain of poison running through the dark heart of the Clave. But there are many more who know Downworlders are our brothers. We are all children under the Angel." He sighed. "And though I cannot remain with you, simply smash this ring and I will come, no matter how distant I may be." He put an arm around her and hugged her close for a moment. "Take care, *mèi mei.*"

"What does that mean?" Emma asked. But he was already gone, vanishing into the trees as swiftly as he'd come.

Kit stood and watched the smoke rising in the distance through the window of the room he shared with Ty.

At least, he assumed he shared the room with Ty. His bag was here, tossed into a corner, and nobody had ever bothered to tell him whether he was supposed to be in a different room. He'd gotten dressed in the bathroom that morning and emerged to find Ty pulling his T-shirt on over his head. His Marks seemed unusually black, probably because his skin was so pale. He looked so delicate—Kit had to glance away from the shape of his shoulder blades, the fragility of his spine. How could he look like that and be strong enough to fight demons?

Now Ty was downstairs, with the rest of his family. People tended to cook when someone died and Shadowhunters were no exception. Someone was probably making a casserole. A demon casserole. Kit leaned his head against the cold glass of the window.

There was a time he could have run, Kit thought. He could have run and left the Shadowhunters behind, lost himself in the underground world of Shadow Markets. Been like his father, not part of any world, existing between them.

In the reflection of the window glass, Kit saw the bedroom door open and Ty come in. He was still wearing his mourning clothes, though he'd taken off the jacket and was just in a long-sleeved T-shirt. And Kit knew it was too late to run, that he cared about these people now, and specifically Ty.

"I'm glad you're here." Ty sat down on the bed and started unlacing his boots. "I wanted to talk to you."

The door was still slightly open and Kit could hear voices

coming from the kitchen downstairs. Helen's, Dru's, Emma's, Julian's. Diana had gone back to her own house. Apparently she lived in a weapons store or something like that. She'd gone back to get some kind of tool she thought could fish the splinters out of Julian's bleeding hands.

Ty's hands were fine, but he'd been wearing gloves. Kit had seen Julian's when he'd gone to rinse them at the sink, and they'd looked like shrapnel had blown into his palms. Emma had stood nearby looking worried, but Julian had said he didn't want an *iratze*, that it would just heal the skin closed over the bits of wood. His voice had sounded so flat, Kit had barely recognized it.

"I know how this is going to sound," Kit said, turning so his back was against the cold glass. Ty was hunched over, and Kit caught the gleam of gold at his neck. "But you're not acting the way I expected."

Ty kicked his boots off. "Because I climbed up the pyre?"

"No, that was kind of actually the most expected thing you did," said Kit. "I just . . ."

"I did it to get this," Ty said, and put his hand to his throat. Kit recognized the gold chain and the slim disk of metal attached to it: Livvy's locket, the one he'd helped her with in London. It had a circlet of the family thorns on the front, and she had told him Julian had added an etching to the back: a pair of crossed sabers, Livvy's weapon.

Kit vividly remembered untangling her hair from the thin chain, and the smell of her perfume. His stomach lurched with sadness.

"Livvy's necklace," he said. "I mean, I guess that makes sense. I just thought you would . . ."

"Cry?" Ty didn't look angry, but the intensity in his gray eyes had deepened. He was still holding the pendant. "Everybody is supposed to be sad. But that's because they accept that Livvy is dead. But I don't. I don't accept it."

"What?"

"I'm going to get her back," said Ty.

Kit sat down heavily on the windowsill. "How are you going to do that?"

Ty let go of the necklace and took his phone out of his pocket. "These were on Julian's phone," he said. "He took them when he was in the library with Annabel. They're photos of the pages of the Black Volume of the Dead."

"When did you get these?" Kit knew texting didn't work in Idris. "Does Julian know you have them?"

"I set up his phone so it would back up to mine. I guess he didn't realize. Then when I saw these in London, I—" Ty gave Kit a worried frown. "You won't tell him, will you?"

"Of course not."

"Will you come and sit down next to me so you can see them?"

Kit wanted to say no; he couldn't say it. He wanted this not to be happening, but it was. When he sat down next to Ty on the bed, the mattress sagged, and he knocked against Ty's elbow accidentally. Ty's skin felt hot against his even through his T-shirt, as if the other boy had a fever.

It never crossed his mind that Ty was lying or wrong, and he didn't seem to be either. After fifteen years with Johnny Rook, Kit was pretty familiar with what bad spell books were like, and this one looked decidedly evil. Spells in cramped handwriting littered the pages, along with creepy sketches of corpses crawling out of the grave, screaming faces, and charred skeletons.

Ty wasn't looking at the photos like they were creepy, though; he was looking at them like they were the Holy Grail. "This is the most powerful spell book for bringing back the dead that's ever existed," he said. "That's why it didn't matter if they burned Livvy's body. With spells like these, she can be brought back whole no matter what happened to her, no matter how long—" He broke off with a shuddering breath. "But I don't want to wait. I want to start as soon as we get back to Los Angeles."

"Didn't Malcolm kill a lot of people to bring Annabel back?" said Kit.

"Correlation, not causation, Watson," said Ty. "The simplest way to do necromancy is with death energy. Life for death, basically. But there are other sources of energy. I would never kill anyone." He made a face that was probably supposed to be scornful but was actually just cute.

"I don't think Livvy would want you to do necromancy," Kit said.

Ty put his phone away. "I don't think Livvy would want to be dead."

Kit felt the words like a punch to the chest, but before he could reply, there was a commotion downstairs. He and Ty ran to the top of the stairwell, Ty in his stocking feet, and looked down into the kitchen.

Zara Dearborn's Spanish friend Manuel was there, wearing the uniform of a Gard officer and a smirk. Kit leaned forward more to see who he was talking to. He caught sight of Julian leaning against the kitchen table, his face expressionless. The others were ranged around the kitchen—Emma looked furious, and Cristina had her hand on the other girl's arm as if to hold her back.

"Really?" Helen said furiously. "You couldn't wait until the day after our sister's funeral to drag Emma and Jules to the Gard?"

Manuel shrugged, clearly indifferent. "It has to be now," he said. "The Consul insists."

"What's going on?" Aline said. "You're talking about my mother, Manuel. She wouldn't just demand to see them without a good reason."

"It's about the Mortal Sword," Manuel said. "Is that a good enough reason for all of you?"

Ty tugged on Kit's arm, pulling him away from the stairs. They moved down the upstairs hallway, the voices in the kitchen receding but still urgent.

"Do you think they'll go?" Kit said.

"Emma and Jules? They have to. The Consul's asking," said Ty. "But it's her, not the Inquisitor, so it'll be all right." He leaned in toward Kit, whose back was against the wall; he smelled like a campfire. "I can do this without you. Bring back Livvy, I mean," he said. "But I don't want to. Sherlock doesn't do things without Watson."

"Did you tell anyone else?"

"No." Ty had pulled the sleeves of his shirt down over his hands and was worrying at the fabric with his fingers. "I know it has to be a secret. People wouldn't like it, but when Livvy comes back, they'll be happy and they won't care."

"Better to ask forgiveness than permission," Kit said, feeling dazed.

"Yes." Ty wasn't looking directly at Kit—he never did—but his eyes lit up hopefully; in the dim light of the hallway, the gray in them was so pale it looked like tears. Kit thought of Ty sleeping, how he'd slept the whole day of Livvy's death and into the night, and the way Kit had watched him sleep in terror of what would happen when he awoke.

Everyone had been terrified. Ty would fall apart, they'd thought. Kit remembered Julian standing over Ty as he slept, one hand stroking his brother's hair, and he'd been praying—Kit didn't even know Shadowhunters prayed, but Julian definitely had been. Ty would crumble in a world without his sister, they'd all thought; he'd fall away to ashes just like Livvy's body.

And now he was asking Kit for this, saying he didn't want to do it without him, and what if Kit said no and Ty crumbled from the pressure of trying to do it alone? What if Kit took away his last hope and he fell apart because of it?

"You need me?" Kit asked slowly.

"Yes."

"Then," Kit said, knowing already that he was making a huge mistake, "I'll help you."

It was cold in the Scholomance, even during the summer. The school had been carved into a mountainside, with long windows running all along the cliff face. They provided light, as did the witchlight chandeliers in nearly every room, but no warmth. The chill of the lake below, deep and black in the moonlight, seemed to have seeped into the stone of the walls and floor and to radiate outward, which was why, even in early September, Diego Rocio Rosales was wearing a thick sweater and coat over his jeans.

Dusty witchlight sconces cast his shadow long and thin in front of him as he hurried down the hallway toward the library. In his opinion, the Scholomance was direly in need of an update. The one time his brother Jaime had ever visited the school, he'd said it looked as if it had been decorated by Dracula. This was unfortunately true. Everywhere there were iron chandeliers (which made Kieran sneeze), bronze dragon-shaped sconces holding ancient witchlight stones, and cavernous stone fireplaces with huge carved angels standing forbiddingly on either side. Communal meals were taken at a long table that could have accommodated the population of Belgium, though at the moment there were less than twenty people in residence at the school. Most of the teachers and students were either at home or in Idris.

Which made it much easier for Diego to hide a faerie prince on the premises. He'd been nervous about the idea of concealing Kieran at the Scholomance—he wasn't a good liar at the best of times, and the effort of maintaining a "relationship" with Zara had worn him down already. But Cristina had asked him to hide Kieran, and he would have done anything for Cristina.

He'd reached the end of the corridor, where the door to the library was. Long ago the word "*Biblioteca*" had adorned the door in gold lettering. Now only the outlines of the letters remained, and the hinges squeaked like distressed mice when Diego shoved the door open.

The first time he'd been shown the library, he'd thought it was a prank. A massive room, it was on the top floor of the Scholomance, where the roof was made of thick glass and light filtered down through it. During the time that the school had been deserted, massive trees had taken root in the dirt beneath the floor: Kieran had commented that they seemed to have the strength of faerie oaks. No one had had the time or money to remove them. They remained, surrounded by the dust of broken stone; their roots had cracked the floor and snaked among the chairs and shelves. Branches spread out wide above, forming a canopy over the bookshelves, dusting the seats and floors with fallen leaves.

Sometimes Diego wondered if Kieran liked it in here because it reminded him of a forest. He certainly spent most of his time in a window seat, somewhat grimly reading everything in the section on faeries. He had made a pile of books he considered accurate. The pile was small.

He glanced over as Diego came in. His hair was blue-black, the color of the lake outside the window. He had put two books into his accurate pile and was reading a third: *Mating Habits of the Unseelie*.

"I do not know anyone in Faerie who has married a goat," he said irritably. "In either the Seelie *or* the Unseelie Court."

"Don't take it personally," Diego said. He pulled a chair over and sat down facing Kieran. He could see them both reflected in the window. Kieran's bony wrists stuck out below the sleeves of his borrowed uniform. Diego's clothes had all been too big for him, so Rayan Maduabuchi had offered to lend Kieran some—he didn't seem bothered that Diego was hiding a faerie in his room, but nothing much ruffled the surface of Rayan's calm. Divya, on the other hand, Diego's other best friend at the school, leaped nervously into the air every time anyone mentioned they were going to the library, despite Kieran's uncanny ability to hide himself.

Divya and Rayan were the only people Diego had told about Kieran, mostly because they were the only people currently at the Scholomance that he trusted. There was only one professor in residence—Professor Gladstone, who was currently in Idris for the Inquisitor's funeral. Besides, while there'd been a time that Diego would have trusted a professor without a second thought, that time was past.

"Have you heard anything from Idris?" said Kieran, looking down at his book.

"You mean Mark," said Diego, "and I haven't heard anything from him. I am not his favorite person."

Kieran glanced up. "Are you anyone's?" Somehow he managed to ask it as if it weren't an insulting question, but something he merely wished to know.

Diego, who sometimes wondered the same thing himself, didn't answer.

"I thought you might have heard from Cristina." Kieran closed the book, marking his place with his finger. "About whether she is all right, and Mark—I thought the funerals were today."

"They were," Diego said. He also thought he might have heard from Cristina; he knew she'd been fond of Livia Blackthorn. "But funerals for us are very busy times. There is a great deal of ceremony, and a lot of people who visit and express condolences. She might not have much time."

Kieran looked pained. "That seems as if it would be annoying. In Faerie we know to leave those who are grieving to themselves."

"It's annoying, but also not," Diego said. He thought of the death of his grandfather, how the house had been full of *velas*, candles that burned with a beautiful light. How visitors had come and brought gifts of food, and they had eaten and drunk together and remembered his *abuelo*. Everywhere there had been marigolds and the cinnamon smell of *atole* and the sound of laughter.

It seemed cold to him, and lonely, to grieve by yourself. But faeries were different.

Kieran's eyes sharpened, as if he had seen something revealing in Diego's expression. "Is there a plan for me?" he asked. "Where am I to be sent, when my time hiding here is over?"

"I had thought you might want to return to Los Angeles," said Diego, surprised.

Kieran shook his head. Locks of his hair had turned white; his hair color seemed to change with his mood. "No. I will not go back to where Mark is."

Diego was silent—he hadn't really had a plan. Cristina had asked him to hide Kieran but had never said for how long. He had wanted to do this for her because he knew he owed her; he had thought of Zara—had remembered the hurt on Cristina's face when she'd first met Zara.

It had been his fault. He hadn't told her about Zara because he'd been desperately hoping something would happen that would get him out of the engagement before it was necessary. It was the Dearborns who had insisted on the marriage contract. They had threatened to expose the Rocio Rosales family's secrets if Diego didn't do something to prove to them that he was truthful when he said he didn't know where his brother was and didn't know where the artifact was that Jaime had taken.

There had never been a question of him loving Zara, nor of her loving him. She seemed to feel it was a feather in her cap to be engaged to the son of an important family, but there was no passion in her except passion for the horrible causes her father espoused.

Kieran's eyes widened. "What's that?"

That was a bright light, like a will-o'-the-wisp, over Diego's shoulder. A fire-message. He caught it out of the air and the paper unrolled in his hand: He recognized the handwriting immediately. "Cristina," he said. "It's a message from Cristina."

Kieran sat up so fast the book tumbled out of his lap to the floor. "Cristina? What does she say? Is she all right?"

Odd, Diego thought; he would have imagined Kieran would have asked if *Mark* was all right. But the thought flew from his mind almost immediately, scrawled over by the words he was reading.

Feeling as if he had been kicked in the gut, Diego handed the message over to Kieran and watched the other boy turn ashen as he read that Horace Dearborn had been made the new Inquisitor.

"This is a slap in the Blackthorns' face," said Kieran, his hand shaking. "They will be heartbroken, as will Cristina. And he is a dangerous man. A deadly man." He looked up at Diego, his eyes night black and storm gray. "What can we do?"

"It is clear I know nothing of people," Diego said, thinking of Zara, of Jaime, of all the lies he had told and how none of them had accomplished what he had wanted, but had only made everything worse. "No one should ask me how to solve anything."

As Kieran looked at him, astonished, he dropped his face into his hands.

"I know these words must seem empty at this point," said Jia, "but I'm so sorry about Livia."

"You're right," Julian said. "They do."

It was as if grief had plunged Julian into a bath of ice, Emma thought. Everything about him was cold—his eyes, his expression, the tone of his voice. She tried to remember the boy who'd clung to her with such passion the night before, but it felt a million miles away.

It was late afternoon, and the demon towers were strung across the skyline of Alicante like a row of jagged diamonds. Emma looked around, remembering the last time she'd been in this room—she'd been twelve, and she'd been so impressed at how plush it was, with thick rugs underfoot and a desk of gleaming mahogany. She, Julian, and Diana were all seated in wingback armchairs before Jia's desk. Diana looked furious. Julian just looked blank.

"These kids are tired and grief-stricken," Diana said. "I respect your judgment, Jia, but does this have to be now?"

"It does," she said, "because Horace Dearborn wants to interrogate Helen and Mark, and any other Downworlders or part Downworlders in Alicante. Magnus and Alec are already packing their things to Portal out tonight. Evelyn Highsmith returned to the London Institute, so they can go home to New York." Jia pressed her fingers against her forehead. "I would have thought you would have wanted Helen and Mark to leave as well."

"He wants to *what?*" Emma sat up straight, indignant. "You can't let him."

"I don't have a choice. He was elected by a majority vote." Jia frowned. "Interrogating people is what the Inquisitor does—the decision is at his discretion."

"Horace Dearborn has no discretion," said Diana.

"Which is why I'm giving you advance notice," said Jia. "I suggest that Helen and Mark—and Aline, since she won't leave Helen—be Portaled to Los Angeles tonight."

There was a moment of silence. "You're offering to send Helen to Los Angeles?" said Julian finally. "Not Wrangel Island?"

"I'm suggesting Helen and Aline temporarily run the Los Angeles Institute," said Jia, and Emma actually felt her mouth fall open. "As the Consul, that is within *my* power, and I believe I can make it happen now, while Dearborn is distracted."

"So you're saying we should *all* Portal back?" Emma said. "And Helen and Aline can come with us? That's great, that's—"

"She doesn't mean all of us," said Julian. His hands were both bandaged. He'd gotten most of the splinters out himself, with the tip of a sharp knife, and there was blood on the bandages. He didn't seem to have felt it—Emma had felt the pain herself, watching his skin split under the blade, but he had never wavered. "She means Diana, you, and I are going to stay here, in Idris."

"You've always been clever, Julian," said Jia, although not as if she admired the quality all that much.

"If Helen and Mark aren't here, he'll interrogate us," said Julian. "Isn't that true?"

"No," Diana said sharply. "They're *children.*"

"Yes," said Jia. "And one of them broke the Mortal Sword. The Inquisitor, like everyone else, is desperate to know how. Cortana is a legendary sword, but still just a sword. It should not have been able to shatter Maellartach."

"He can ask me, but I don't *know* why it was broken," Emma said. "I swung at Annabel because she was trying to kill me. It was self-defense—"

"People are terrified. And fear isn't logical," said Jia. "Thank the Angel that the Cup and Mirror are unaffected." She sighed. "This was the worst possible time for the Mortal Sword to be broken, at a time of serious instability and on the eve of a possible war with faeries. And after the Unseelie King snatched Annabel from the Council Hall—don't you understand how aware the Clave is that you brought her here?"

"That was just me." Julian was white around the mouth. "Emma didn't have anything to do with it."

Emma felt a faint spark of relief light among her fear. *He still has my back.*

Jia looked down at her hands. "If I were to send all of you back home right now, there would be a riot. If Dearborn is allowed to question you, then public attention will swing away from you. The

Cohort suspects your loyalty, mostly because of Helen and Mark."

Julian gave a harsh laugh. "They suspect us because of our brother and sister? More than because I brought that thing—because I brought Annabel into the city? And promised everything would be all right? But it's Mark and Helen's blood that matters?"

"Blood always matters, to the wrong sort of people," said Jia, and there was a rare bitterness in her voice. She passed a hand over her face. "I'm not asking you to be on his side. God, I'm not asking that. Just get him to understand that you're victims of Annabel. Those not in the Cohort are very sympathetic to you right now because of Livia—he won't want to go too much against public opinion."

"So this is like a pointless little dance we're doing?" Emma said. "We let the Inquisitor question us, mostly for show, and then we can go home?"

Jia smiled grimly. "Now you understand politics."

"You're not worried about making Aline and Helen the heads of the Los Angeles Institute? Given the Cohort's concerns about Helen?" said Diana.

"It'll just be Aline." Julian gazed unwaveringly at Jia. "The Consul's daughter. Helen won't be running anything."

"That's right," said Jia, "and no, I don't like it either. But this may be a chance to get them back permanently from Wrangel Island. That's why I'm asking for your help—all three of you."

"Am I going to be interrogated as well?" There was a sharp tension in Diana's voice.

"No," Jia said. "But I'd like your help. As you helped me before with those files."

"Files?" echoed Emma. "How are files important right now?"

But Diana looked as if she understood some secret language Jia was speaking. "I'll stay, certainly," she said. "As long as the understanding is clear that I'm helping *you* and that my interests are in no way aligned with the Inquisitor's."

"I understand," said Jia. *Nor are mine* hung unspoken in the air.

"But the kids," said Emma. "They can't go back to Los Angeles without us." She turned to look at Julian, waiting for him to say that he wouldn't be separated from his younger siblings. That they needed him, that they should stay in Idris.

"Helen can take care of them," he said, without glancing at her. "She wants to. It'll be all right. She's their sister."

"Then it's decided," said Jia, rising from behind her desk. "You might as well get them packed—we'll open the Portal for them tonight."

Julian rose as well, pushing back the hair that had fallen into his eyes with one of his bandaged hands. *What the hell is wrong with you?* Emma thought. There was something going on with Julian beyond what could be explained by grief. She didn't just know it, she *felt* it, down in the deep place where the *parabatai* bond tugged at her heart.

And later tonight, when the others were gone, she would find out what it was.

5

Wilderness of Glass

When Emma came into Cristina's room, she found her friend already packing. Cristina packed like she did everything else, with neatness and precision. She carefully rolled all her clothes so they wouldn't get wrinkled, sealed anything damp into plastic, and put her shoes into soft bags so they didn't mark up any fabric.

"You realize that when I pack, I just throw everything into a suitcase, and then sit on it while Julian tries to zip it, right?" said Emma.

Cristina looked up and smiled. "The thought gives me hives."

Emma leaned against the wall. She felt bone tired and strangely lonely, as if Cristina and the Blackthorns had already departed. "Please tell me you'll be at the L.A. Institute when I get back," she said.

Cristina stopped packing. She glanced down at the suitcase the Penhallows had provided, open on the bed, worrying her lower lip between her teeth. "Do you know how long it will be?"

"A few days."

"Do you think the family will want me to stay?" Cristina turned wide, dark eyes on Emma. "I could just go home. My study year isn't over, but they would understand. I feel as if I'm intruding. . . ."

Emma pushed herself off the wall, shaking her head vigorously. "No, no—you're not, Tina, you're not." Quickly, she described her conversation with Jem and the issue of the ley line contamination. "Jem thought I was going back to Los Angeles," she said. "He asked me to contact Catarina and help her find out more about the ley lines, but it'll have to be you. Helen and Aline will be so overwhelmed with the kids, and with their grief, and everyone—I know you can do it, Cristina. I trust you."

Cristina gave her a slightly watery smile. "I trust you, too."

Emma sat down on the bed. It creaked a protest, and she kicked it, bruising her heel but relieving her feelings somewhat. "I don't mean that Helen and Aline won't be any help. It's just that everyone's destroyed with grief. They're going to need someone who isn't destroyed to turn to—they'll need *you*." She took a deep breath. "Mark will need you."

Cristina's eyes widened, and Emma suddenly remembered Mark's face an hour ago in the kitchen, when she and Julian had broken the news that the family would be returning to Los Angeles tonight without the two of them.

His expression had stiffened. He had shaken his head and said, "Ill news. I cannot—" Breaking off, he'd sat down at the table, his hands shaking slightly. Helen, already sitting at the table, had gone white but said nothing, while Aline had put her hand on her wife's shoulder.

Dru had silently walked out of the room. After a moment, Mark had risen and gone after her. Tavvy was protesting, offering a hundred different arguments for why Julian should go with them and why they didn't need to stay and the Inquisitor could come to Los Angeles instead or they could do the interrogation over Skype, which would have made Emma laugh if she hadn't felt so awful.

"We're going home?" Helen had said. Julian had bent down to talk to Tavvy in a low voice; Emma could no longer hear them. "Back to Los Angeles?"

"I'm really happy for you, and Jia says she thinks you can stay," Emma had said.

"She *hopes*," Aline said. "She hopes we can stay." She looked calm, but her grip on Helen was tight.

"But not without you," Helen said, looking troubled. "We should stay as long as you're here—"

"No." To everyone's surprise, it was Ty. "That would be dangerous for Mark, and for you. This plan makes sense."

Kit had given Ty an almost indecipherable look, half concern and half something else.

"Home," Helen said, her eyes glimmering with tears. She looked at Julian, but he was picking up a protesting Tavvy. He carried him out of the room. "I don't know if I'm crying because I'm sad or happy," she added, brushing away the tears with damp fingers.

Aline had kissed the top of her head. "Both, I imagine."

Emma had been halfway up the stairs on the way to Cristina's room when she had seen Mark, leaning against the wall on the landing and looking dejected. "Dru won't let me in to talk to her," he said. "I am worried. It is like a faerie to grieve alone, but not, I understand, like a Shadowhunter."

Emma hesitated. She was about to say that it wasn't unlike Dru to lock herself in her room alone, but Dru had looked more than a little upset when she'd left the kitchen. "Keep trying," she advised. "Sometimes you have to knock for twenty minutes or so. Or you could offer to watch a horror movie with her."

Mark looked glum. "I do not think I would enjoy a horror movie."

"You never know," Emma said.

He had turned to head back up the stairs, and hesitated. "I am worried about you and Jules as well," he said, more quietly. "I do not like the Inquisitor, or the idea of you being questioned by him. He reminds me of the King of Unseelie."

Emma was startled. "He does?"

"They give me the same feeling," Mark said. "I cannot explain it, but—"

A door opened on the landing overhead: It was Cristina's. She stepped out, glancing down. "Emma? I wondered if you were—"

She had stopped when she saw Mark, and she and Mark stared at each other in a way that made Emma feel as if she had disappeared completely.

"I didn't mean to interrupt," Cristina said, but she was still looking at Mark, and he was looking back as if their gazes were hopelessly tied together.

Mark had shaken himself, as if he were casting off cobwebs or dreams. "It is all right—I must go speak with Drusilla." He had bounded up the stairs and out of sight, disappearing around the bend in the corridor.

Cristina had snapped out of it and invited Emma in, and now it was as if the moment with Mark had never happened, though Emma was itching to ask about it. "Mark will need you," she said again, and Cristina twisted her hands in her lap.

"Mark," she said, and paused. "I don't know what Mark is thinking. If he is angry at me."

"Why would he be angry at you?"

"Because of Kieran," she said. "They did not end things well, and now Kieran is at the Scholomance, and far away, which was my doing."

"You didn't break him up with Kieran," Emma protested. "If anything, you helped keep them together longer. Remember—hot faerie threesome."

Cristina dropped her face into her hands. "Mrfuffhfhsh," she said.

"What?"

"I said," Cristina repeated, lifting her face, "that Kieran sent me a note."

"He *did*? How? When?"

"This morning. In an acorn." Cristina passed a small piece of paper to Emma. "It isn't very illuminating."

> *Lady of Roses,*
> *Though the Scholomance is cold, and Diego is boring, I am still grateful that you found enough value in my life to save it. You are as kind as you are beautiful. My thoughts are with you.*
> *Kieran*

"Why did he send you this?" Emma handed the note back to Cristina, shaking her head. "It's weird. He's so weird!"

"I think he just wanted to thank me for the escape plan," Cristina protested. "That's all."

"Faeries don't like thanking people," said Emma. "This is a *romantic* note."

Cristina blushed. "It's just the way faeries talk. It doesn't mean anything."

"When it comes to faeries," Emma said darkly, "*everything* means something."

Dru ignored the pounding on the door. It wasn't hard—since Livvy died she'd felt like she was underwater and everything was happening at a distant remove, far above the surface. Words seemed to be echoes, and people were blurs that came and went like flickers of sunshine or shadow.

Sometimes she would say the words to herself: *Livvy, my sister Livvy, is dead.*

But they didn't feel real either. Even watching the pyre burn had felt like an event that was happening to someone else.

She glanced out the window. The demon towers gleamed like shards of beautiful glass. Dru hated them—every time she'd ever been in Alicante, horrible things had happened. People had died. Helen had been exiled.

She sat down on the windowsill, still holding a rolled-up T-shirt in her hand. Helen. For so long they had all wanted Helen back. It had been a family goal, like wanting Mark back and wanting the Cold Peace over and wanting Jules to be happy and for that forever worried line between his eyes to go away. But now Helen *was* back. She was back, and she was apparently going to take over for Jules.

Helen will be taking care of you, he'd said. As if he could just walk away from that and Helen could pick it up, as if they weren't a family but were a carelessly dropped penny. Or a gerbil. *You're treating me like a gerbil*, she thought, and wondered what would happen if she said that to Jules. But she couldn't. Since Livvy had died the worried line had gone from between his eyebrows, replaced by a blank look that was a thousand times worse.

Getting Mark back had been one thing. Mark had been happy to be with them, even when he'd been strange and said odd faerie things, and he'd told Drusilla that she was beautiful, and he'd tried to cook even though he couldn't. But Helen was thin and beautiful and remote; Dru remembered when Helen had gone off to Europe for her study year with a dismissive wave and an eagerness to be gone that had felt like a slap. She'd returned with Aline, sparklingly happy, but Dru had never forgotten how glad she'd been to be leaving them.

She isn't going to want to watch horror movies with me and eat caramel corn, Dru thought. *She probably doesn't eat anything except flower petals. She isn't going to understand a thing about me and she isn't going to try.*

Unwrapping the T-shirt she was holding, she took out the knife and the note that Jaime Rocio Rosales had given her in London. She'd read the note so many times that the paper had grown thin and worn. She hunched over it, curled up on the windowsill as Mark knocked on her door and called her name in vain.

The house felt echoingly empty.

The trip back and forth to the Portal room at the Gard had been chaotic, with Tavvy complaining, and Helen frantically asking Julian about the everyday running of the Institute, and the odd electricity between Cristina and Mark, and Ty doing something odder with his phone. On the walk back Diana had mercifully broken the silence between Emma and Julian by chatting about whether or not she was going to sell the weapons shop on Flintlock Street. Emma could tell Diana was making a conscious effort to avoid awkward breaks in conversation, but she appreciated it all the same.

Now Diana was gone, and Emma and Julian climbed the steps to the canal house in silence. Several guards had been posted around the place, but it still felt empty. The house had been full of people that morning; now it was only her and Julian. He threw the bolt on the front door and turned to go up the stairs without a word.

"Julian," she said. "We need—I need to talk to you."

He stopped where he was, hand on the banister. He didn't turn to look at her. "Isn't that sort of a cliché?" he said. "*We need to talk?*"

"Yeah, that's why I changed it to 'I need to talk to you,' but either way, it's a fact and you know it," Emma said. "Especially since we're going to be alone with each other for the next few days. And we have to face the Inquisitor together."

"But this isn't about the Inquisitor." He did finally turn to look at her, and his eyes burned, acid blue-green. "Is it?"

"No," Emma said. For a moment she wondered if he was actually going to refuse to have a conversation, but he shrugged finally and led the way upstairs without speaking.

In his room, she closed the door, and he laughed, a tired sort of noise. "You don't need to do that. There's no one else here."

Emma could think of a time they would have been delighted to have a house to themselves. When it was a dream they'd shared. A house to themselves, forever, a life of their own, forever. But it did seem almost blasphemous to think about that, with Livvy dead.

She had laughed, earlier, with Cristina. A flicker of joy in the dark. Now she wanted to shiver as Julian turned around, his face still blank, and looked at her.

She moved closer to him, unable to stop herself from studying his face. He had explained to her once that what fascinated him about painting and drawing was the moment when an illustration took on lifc. Thc dab of paint or flick of a pen that changed a drawing from a flat copy to a living, breathing interpretation—the Mona Lisa's smile, the look in the eyes of the *Girl with a Pearl Earring*.

That was what was gone from Julian, she thought, shivering again. The thousands of emotions that had always lived behind his expressions, the love—for her, for his siblings—behind his eyes. Even his worry seemed to have gone, and that was stranger than anything else.

He sat down on the edge of his bed. There was a spiral-bound drawing notebook there; he shoved it carelessly aside, almost under one of his pillows. Julian was usually fastidious about his art supplies; Emma pushed back the urge to rescue the sketch pad. She felt lost at sea.

So much seemed to have changed.

"What's going on with you?" she said.

"I don't know what you mean," Julian said. "I'm grieving my sister. How am I supposed to be acting?"

"Not like this," Emma said. "I'm your *parabatai*. I can tell when something's wrong. And grief isn't wrong. Grief is what I'm feeling, what I know you were feeling last night, but Julian, what I feel from you now *isn't that*. And it scares me more than anything."

Julian was silent for a long moment. "This is going to sound strange," he said finally. "But can I touch you?"

Emma stepped forward so that she was standing between his legs, within arm's reach. "Yes," she said.

He put his hands on her hips, just over the band of her jeans. He drew her closer, and she put her hands gently on the sides of his face, curling her fingertips against his cheekbones.

He closed his eyes, and she felt his lashes brush the sides of her fingers. *What is this?* she thought. *Julian, what is this?* It wasn't as if he'd never hidden anything from her before; he'd hidden a whole secret life from her for years. Sometimes he'd been like a book written in an indecipherable language. But now he was like a book that had been shut and locked with a dozen heavy clasps.

He leaned his head against her, soft wavy hair brushing her skin where her T-shirt rode up. He raised his head slightly and she felt the warmth of his breath through the fabric. She shivered as he pressed a soft kiss to the spot just above her hip bone; when he looked up at her, his eyes were fever bright.

"I think I solved our problem," he said.

She swallowed down her desire, her confusion, her tangle of unsorted feelings. "What do you mean?"

"When Robert Lightwood died," Julian said, "we lost our chance of exile. I thought maybe grief, the overwhelming pain of it, would make me stop loving you." His hands were still on Emma's hips, but she didn't feel comforted by that: His voice was terrifyingly flat. "But it didn't. You know that. Last night—"

"We stopped," Emma said, her cheeks flushing as she remembered: the shower, the tangle of sheets, the salt-and-soap taste of kisses.

"It's not the actions, it's the emotions," said Julian. "Nothing made me stop loving you. Nothing made me even slow down. So I had to fix it."

A cold knot of dread settled in Emma's stomach. "What did you do?"

"I went to Magnus," Julian said. "He agreed to do a spell. Magnus said this kind of magic, messing with people's emotions, can have dangerous repercussions, but—"

"Messing with your emotions?" Emma took a step back, and his hands fell to his sides. "*What do you mean?*"

"He took them away," said Julian. "My emotions. My feelings for you. They're gone."

"I don't understand." Emma had always wondered why people said that when it was clear they did understand, perfectly. She realized now: It was because they didn't want to understand. It was a way of saying: *No, you can't mean it. Not what you just said.*

Tell me it isn't true.

"As long as our feelings aren't mutual," he said, "it's not a problem, right? The curse can't come to pass."

"Maybe." Emma took a deep, shaking breath. "But it's not just how you feel about *me*. You're different. You didn't fight Jia about leaving the kids—"

He looked a little surprised. "I suppose I didn't," he said. He stood up, reaching out a hand for her, but she backed away. He dropped his arm. "Magnus said this stuff wasn't precise. That that was why it was a problem. Love spells, real love spells, the kind that make you fall for someone, those are black magic. They're a way of forcing emotion on people. Something like what he did to me is almost the opposite—he wasn't forcing anything on me, I asked for it, but he said emotions aren't *singular*—that's why there are no real 'cancel out love' spells. All your feelings are tied to other feelings, and they're tied to your thoughts and to who you are." Something fluttered on his wrist as he gestured: It looked like a loop of red fabric. "So he said he would do his best to affect only one part of my emotions. The *eros* part. Romantic love. But he did say it would probably affect everything else I felt too."

"And has it?" Emma said.

He frowned. And watching him frown tore at her heart: It was an *emotion*, even if it was just frustration or wonderment. "I feel as if I'm behind a pane of glass," he said. "And everyone else is on the other side. My anger is still there, I can feel that easily. I was angry at Jia. And when I climbed the pyre after Ty, it was atavistic, the need to protect him, there was no conscious thought to it." He glanced down at his bandaged hands. "I still feel grief, over Livvy, but it's *bearable*. It doesn't feel like it's ripping away my breath. And you . . ."

"And us," Emma said grimly.

"I know I loved you," he said. "But I can't *feel* it."

Loved. The past tense was like being punched; she took another step backward, toward the door. She had to get out of the room.

"*Entreat me not to leave thee*," she said, reaching for the doorknob, "but you've left me. You've left me, Julian."

"Emma, stop," he said. "Last night—when I went to Magnus—the curse was *happening*. I felt it. I *know*, I know I couldn't stand one more person dying."

"I never would have agreed to stay here with you if I'd known what you'd done," Emma said. "You could at least have told me. Honesty isn't an emotion, Julian."

At that, she thought, he did flinch—though it could have been a start of surprise. "Emma—"

"No more," she said, and fled from the room.

She wasn't waiting for Gwyn, Diana told herself. She was definitely not sitting on her bed in the early hours of the morning, wearing a nice silk top she'd found in her closet, even though she would normally have put on her pajamas hours ago, for any reason except that she was up cleaning swords.

She had three or four swords strewn across the coverlet, and she'd been polishing them in an attempt to bring back some of their original glory. They'd once been etched with twining roses, stars, flowers, and thorns, but over the years some had darkened and discolored. She felt a twinge of guilt at having neglected her father's shop, mixed with the old familiar guilt that always accompanied thoughts of her parents.

There had been a time when all she had wanted was to be Diana and own Diana's Arrow, when she had ached for Idris and the chance to be herself in the Shadowhunter home country. Now she felt a restlessness that went beyond that; the old hopes felt too confining, as if they were a dress she had outgrown. Perhaps you outgrew your dreams, too, as your world expanded.

Tap. Tap. Diana was up and off the bed the moment the window rattled. She threw up the sash and leaned out. Gwyn was hovering at eye level, his dappled horse shining in the light of the demon towers. His helmet hung by a strap from his horse's neck; there was a massive sword over his back, its hilt blackened with years of use.

"I could not come sooner," he said. "I saw the smoke in the sky today and watched from above the clouds. Can you come with me to where it is safe?"

She began to climb out the window before he was even done with his question. Sliding onto the horse's back in front of him felt familiar now, as did being circled by his enormous arms. She had always been a tall woman, and not much made her feel small and delicate, but Gwyn did. It was, if nothing else, a novel feeling.

She let her mind wander as they flew in silence past the city, over its walls and the Imperishable Fields. The pyres had burned away to ash, covering the grass in eerie circles of blanched gray. Her eyes stung, and she looked away, hurriedly, toward the forest: the green trees approaching and then stretching out below them, the rills of silver streams, and the occasional rise of a stone manor house at the fringes of the woods.

She thought of Emma and Julian, of the lonely shock on Emma's face when the Consul had told them they'd have to stay in Idris, of the worrying blankness on Julian's. She knew the emptiness shock could force on you. She could see it in Ty, as well, the deep silence and stillness brought on by a pain so great that no wailing or tears would touch it. She remembered her own loss of Aria, how she had lain on the floor of Catarina's cottage, turning and twisting her body as if she could somehow get away from the pain of missing her sister.

"We are here," Gwyn said, and they were landing in the glade she remembered. Gwyn dismounted and was reaching up to help her down.

She stroked the side of the horse's neck, and it nudged her with its soft nose. "Does your horse have a name?"

Gwyn looked puzzled. "Name?"

"I'm going to call him Orion," said Diana, settling herself on the ground. The grass under her was springy, and the air was scented with pine and flowers. She leaned back on her hands and some of the tension began to leave her body.

"I would like that. For my steed to be named by you." Gwyn seated himself opposite her, large hands at his sides, his brow creased with concern. His size and bulk somehow made him seem more helpless than he would have otherwise. "I know what happened," he said. "When death comes in great and unexpected ways, the Wild Hunt knows it. We hear the stories told by spilled blood."

Diana didn't know what to say—that death was unfair? That Livvy hadn't deserved to die that way, or any way? That the broken hearts of the Blackthorns would never be the same? It all seemed trite, a hundred times said and understood already.

Instead she said, "I think I would like it if you kissed me."

Gwyn didn't hesitate. He was beside her in a moment, graceful despite his bulk; he put his arms around her and she was surrounded by warmth and the smell of the forest and horses. She wrinkled her nose slightly and smiled, and he kissed her smiling mouth.

It was a gentle kiss, for all his size. The softness of his mouth contrasted with the scratch of his stubble and the hard musculature under her hands when she put them timidly on his shoulders and stroked.

He leaned into the touch with a low rumble of pleasure. Diana reached up to gently cup his face, marveling at the feeling of someone else's skin. It had been a long time, and she had never imagined something quite like this: Moonlight and flowers were for other people.

But apparently not. His big hands stroked her hair. She had never felt so warm or so cared for, so completely contained in someone else's affection. When they stopped kissing it was as natural as when they had started, and Gwyn pulled her closer, tucking her into his body. He chuckled.

"What?" she asked, craning her head up.

"I wondered if kissing a faerie was different than kissing a Shadowhunter," he said with a surprisingly boyish smile.

"I've never kissed one," she said. It was true; long ago, she had been too shy to kiss anyone, and too deeply sad, and later . . . "I've kissed a few mundanes. I knew them in Bangkok; a few were trans, like me. But back then I always felt too much as if I were keeping the secret of being Nephilim, and it fell like a shadow between me and other people. . . ." She sighed. "I feel like you're maybe the only person besides Catarina who really knows everything about me."

Gwyn made a low, thoughtful noise. "I like everything about you that I know."

And I like you, she wanted to say. She was shocked at how much she *did* like him, this odd faerie man with his capacity for great gentleness and equal capacity for enormous violence. She had experienced him as kind, but from Mark's stories she knew there was another side to him: the side that led the Wild Hunt on their bloody pathway between the stars.

"I'm going to tell them everything," she said. "Emma and Julian. We're all stuck here in Idris together, and I love them like they were my little brother and sister. They should know."

"Do it if it will bring you ease to do it," said Gwyn. "You owe them nothing; you have cared for them and helped them and they know you as who you are. None of us owe every piece of our soul's history to another."

"I *am* doing it for me. I'll be happier."

"Then by all means." Gwyn dropped a kiss on her head. Diana sat in the warm circle of his arms and thought of Livvy and how grief and contentment could share a place in the human heart. She wondered what losses Gwyn had sustained in his life. He must have had a mother, a father, brothers and sisters, but she couldn't imagine them and couldn't yet bring herself to ask.

Later, when she was walking to Gwyn's horse for the return journey to Alicante, she noticed that the tips of her fingers were smudged with ash, and frowned. Ash must have blown on the wind from the pyres that morning, but still. It was very odd.

She put it from her mind as Gwyn lifted her onto Orion's back and they sailed up, into the stars.

The rooms in the Scholomance were neither as pleasant as the rooms in most Institutes nor as unpleasant as the ones in the Shadowhunter Academy. They were clean and bare and had, in Diego's opinion, a monkish feel. Each room came with two beds, two heavy desks, and—thanks to the absence of closets—two massive wardrobes.

Due to low enrollment, Diego didn't usually have a roommate, but at the moment, Kieran lay in a grouchy lump on the floor, wrapped in blankets.

Folding his arms behind his head, Diego stared at the ceiling. He'd memorized the lumps and bumps in the plaster. For the first time in his life, he didn't have the concentration to read or meditate; his mind skittered like a nervous spider over thoughts of Jaime, of Cristina, of the Dearborns and the new Inquisitor.

Not to mention the unhappy faerie prince who was currently thrashing around on his floor.

"How long are you planning to keep me here?" Kieran's voice was muffled. He pulled a piece of blanket away from his face and stared at the ceiling as if he could come to understand what Diego saw in it.

"Keep you here?" Diego rolled onto his side. "You're not a prisoner. You can go whenever you like."

"I cannot," Kieran said. "I cannot return to the Wild Hunt without bringing the wrath of the King upon the Hunt. I cannot return to Faerie, for the King will find and slay me. I cannot wander the world as a wild fey, for I will be recognized, and I do not know even now if the King is seeking me."

"Why not return to the Institute in Los Angeles? Even if you're angry with Mark, Cristina would—"

"It is because of Mark and Cristina that I cannot go there." Kieran's hair was changing color in the dim light, deep blue to pale white. "And I am not angry with either of them. It is only that I do not want . . ." He sat up. "Or perhaps I want too much."

"We can figure it out when the time comes," Diego said. "What will be best for you."

Kieran looked at him, an uncanny, sharp look that made Diego push himself up on his elbow. "Isn't that what you always do?" he said. "You decide you will find a solution when the time comes, but when the worst happens, you find yourself unprepared."

Diego opened his mouth to protest when there was a sharp rap on the door. Kieran was gone in a flash, so quickly that Diego could only guess where he'd disappeared to. Diego cleared his throat and called, *"Pásale!"*

Divya slipped into the room, followed by Rayan. They were in their uniforms, Rayan wearing a thick sweater over his. Both he and Divya had found it difficult to get used to the cold air in the Scholomance.

Divya carried a witchlight, its rays illuminating her anxious expression. "Diego," she said. "Is Kieran here?"

"I think he's under the bed," said Diego.

"That's strange," said Rayan. He didn't look anxious, but Rayan rarely betrayed much emotion.

"He could be in the wardrobe," Diego said. "Why?"

"The Cohort," said Divya. "Zara and some of the others—Samantha and Manuel and Jessica—they've just Portaled in with Professor Gladstone."

Kieran rolled out from under the bed. There was a dust ball in his hair. "Do they know I'm here?" He sat up, eyes gleaming. "Give me a weapon. Any weapon."

"Hold on there." Divya raised a hand. "We were actually thinking of a more restrained approach. Like hiding you."

"I was already hiding," Kieran pointed out.

"He *was* under the bed," Diego said.

"Yes, but since Zara Dearborn is on her way to talk to Diego, this isn't the safest room," said Rayan. "And the Cohort suspects Diego's loyalty to their cause, anyway."

"They do," said Divya. "We heard them talking." She held out a hand to Kieran as if to help him up. He eyed it with surprise, then rose to his feet unassisted.

"I would not kill her if she was unarmed," said Kieran. "I would challenge her to a fair fight."

"Yeah, and then everyone would know you were here, including the Clave," said Divya. She snapped her fingers. "Come on. Let's go. Quit wasting time."

Kieran looked slightly stunned. He cut his eyes sideways toward Diego, and Diego nodded. "It'll be safer for both of us."

"As you command, then," Kieran said, and followed Rayan and Divya out of the room, the witchlight wavering over them all. They slipped into the shadows and were gone; Diego barely had time to get out of bed and shrug on a T-shirt before the door banged open.

Zara stood in the doorway with her hands on her hips, glowering. Diego wondered if he should thank her for knocking but decided that she probably didn't understand sarcasm.

"I'm just about fed up with you," she said.

Diego leaned back against the wardrobe and crossed his arms over his chest. Zara's eyes skated over his biceps. She smirked.

"I really had hope for our alliance," she said. "But you'd better straighten up and stop sympathizing with Downworlders, criminals, and ingrates."

"Ingrates?" Diego echoed. "I'm only allowed to hang out with the grateful?"

Zara blinked. "What?"

"I'm not sure that word means what you think it means," said Diego. "English is my second language, but . . ."

"The Blackthorns are ingrates," she clarified. "You need to drop them and everyone associated with them." Her eyes bored into him.

"If you mean Cristina, we are only friends—"

"I don't care. The Blackthorns are awful. Mark's a half-breed, Ty is a weird little recluse, Dru is fat and stupid, and Julian is like—like Sebastian Morgenstern."

Diego burst out laughing. "He's *what?*"

She flushed. "He raised the dead!"

"He didn't, actually," said Diego, though he knew it didn't matter. The Cohort constantly changed the rules of the game when they were trying to make a point. They didn't care too much whether their evidence was accurate, nor were they going to be interested in the difference between raising the dead and just associating with them.

"You'll be sorry when he's burning the world down," she said darkly.

"I bet I will," said Diego. "Look, do you have anything else to say? Because it's the middle of the night and I'd like to get some sleep."

"Remember why you agreed to get engaged to me in the first place," she said, with a sharp little grin. "Maybe you should have thought of what the consequences would be if I had to break it off."

She turned to go, and Diego saw her pause, as if she'd caught sight of something that surprised her. She shot a last glare at him and stalked off down the corridor.

There was no lock on the door. All Diego could do was kick it shut before flopping back down on his bed. He stared at the ceiling again, but this time it provided no distraction.

6

From a Proud Tower

Emma awoke with a pounding headache to a knocking on her bedroom door. She'd fallen asleep on the floor in all her clothes; her hair was damp, sticking to her cheeks. She felt, and suspected she looked, like a shipwreck.

"Come in," she called, and the door swung open. It was Julian.

She sat up. For a moment they simply stared at each other. Emma felt cold all over; he would notice her blotchy face, her rumpled clothes. Even if he didn't love her, he would feel—

"You'd better get dressed and cleaned up," he said. He wore jeans and a blue sweater and looked as if he'd slept fine. He looked *good*, even. Like a handsome stranger, someone she didn't know.

There was nothing harsh in his voice, just a calm pragmatism. She hadn't needed to worry he'd feel pity for her, she realized, or even guilt; he didn't *feel* anything at all.

"Dane Larkspear just came by the house with a message," he said. "The Inquisitor wants to see us right away."

The moment Cristina opened the door to the kitchen, Helen popped up from behind the counter, holding a ladle and smiling brightly. "Good morning!"

Cristina had woken early, her body scrambled by the time difference between L.A. and Idris, and sleepwalked her way to the kitchen, meaning to throw together some toast and coffee. Helen's energetic greeting made her want to lie down and nap on the table. She would never understand morning people, especially those who functioned without a caffeine injection.

"I'm making oatmeal," Helen went on.

"Oh," said Cristina. She didn't really like oatmeal.

"Aline's up in the office, trying to make sense of all the papers. It looks like the Centurions tore the place apart." Helen grimaced.

"I know." Cristina looked longingly at the coffeemaker. Would it be rude to push past Helen and grab for the coffee beans and filter?

"Don't bother," Helen said. "The Centurions left moldy coffee in the pot." She gestured toward the sink, where the coffeepot was soaking.

Cristina instantly hated the Centurions even more than she had before. "Is there anything they don't ruin?"

"They left laundry," Mark said, coming in with his hair wet. He must have just showered. Cristina felt the immediate and uncontrollable spark of nerves in her stomach, and sat down on a counter stool. She could still see the healing weal of skin around Mark's wrist, where the binding spell had cut him; she had one that matched. His eyes glowed in the morning sunlight, blue and gold as the heart of the ocean; she turned quickly away from looking at him and began studying a kitchen tile depicting Hector's body being dragged around the walls of Troy. "So much laundry. Piles and piles of laundry."

"I'll do the laundry." Helen had moved to the stove and was stirring a pot industriously. "I'm making oatmeal."

"Oh," said Mark. He met Cristina's eyes briefly. A shared moment of oatmeal dislike passed between them.

More Blackthorns started piling into the kitchen: Ty, followed by Kit and then Dru and Tavvy. There was a babble of voices, and for a moment, things felt nearly normal. Nearly. Without Emma, she knew, the Institute would never be normal for her. Emma had been the first person she'd met in Los Angeles; Emma had befriended her instantly and without hesitation. Her introduction to L.A. had been going to all of Emma's favorite places, her secret beaches and canyon trails; it had been driving in the car with her with the radio on and their hair down, hot dogs at Pink's, pie at the Apple Pan at midnight.

It was hard not to feel anchorless now, an unmoored boat on the tide. But she clung to what Emma had said to her: *They'll need you. Mark will need you.*

Ty grabbed a bag of potato chips off the counter and handed it to Kit, who gave him a thumbs-up. They had a way of communicating without words, almost like Emma and Julian did.

"You don't need those," Helen said. "I'm making oatmeal!" She pointed at the table with her spoon: She'd set it with matching bowls and even a vase with a sprig of wildflowers.

"Oh," said Kit.

"I want pancakes," announced Tavvy.

"We're not staying for breakfast," said Ty. "Kit and I are going to the beach. We'll see you later."

"But—" Helen began, but it was no use; they'd already left, Ty dragging Kit behind him with a firm grip on his wrist. Kit shrugged apologetically before disappearing through the door.

"I hate oatmeal," said Dru. She sat down at the table, frowning.

"I hate oatmeal too," said Tavvy, pushing in next to his sister. He frowned too, and for a moment the resemblance between them was almost comical.

"Well, oatmeal is what there is," Helen said. "But I can make toast, too."

"Not toast," said Tavvy. "Pancakes."

Helen shut the stove off. For a moment she stood staring down into the pot of cooling oatmeal. In a small voice, she said, "I don't know how to make pancakes."

Cristina got hurriedly off her stool. "Helen, let me help you make some eggs and toast," she said.

"Julian can make pancakes," said Tavvy.

Helen had made room for Cristina at the counter by the stove. Cristina handed over bread; as Helen loaded up the toaster, Cristina saw that her hands were shaking.

"I really don't want eggs for breakfast," said Dru. She picked one of the flowers out of the vase on the table and plucked off its head. Petals showered down onto the table.

"Come on, both of you," said Mark, going over to his younger brother and sister and ruffling their hair affectionately. "We just got back. Don't give Helen a hard time."

"Well, she doesn't *have* to make breakfast," said Dru. "We could make our own."

Helen hurried over with the plate of toast and set it on the table. Dru stared at it blankly. "Come on, Dru," she said. "Just eat the bread."

Dru stiffened all over. "Don't tell me what to eat and not eat," she said.

Helen flinched. Tavvy reached for the jam and upended it, shaking it until sticky jelly splattered all over his plate, the table, and his hands. He giggled.

"Don't—*no*!" Helen said, grabbing the jam out of his hands. "Tavvy, don't do that!"

"I don't have to listen to *you*," Tavvy said, his small face flushing. "I don't even know *you*."

He pushed his way past Dru and bolted from the kitchen. After a moment, Dru shot Helen a reproachful look and darted after him.

Helen stood where she was, holding the empty plastic jam jar, tears running down her face. Cristina's heart went out to her. All she wanted was to please her siblings, but they couldn't forgive her for not being Julian.

She moved toward Helen, but Mark was already there, putting his arms around his sister, getting jam on his shirt. "It's all right," Cristina heard him say. "When I first got back, I was always messing things up. I got everything wrong. . . ."

Feeling like an intruder, Cristina slipped out of the kitchen; some family scenes were private. She headed down the hall slowly (she was *sure* there was a second coffeemaker in the library), half her mind on what Mark had said to Helen. She wondered if he really felt that way. She remembered the first time she'd seen him, crouched against the wall of his bedroom as the wind blew the curtains around him like sails. The bond she had felt with him had been immediate—she hadn't known him before the Hunt had taken him, and had no expectations of what he was like or who he should be. It had tied them together as strongly as the binding spell, but what if everything had changed? What if what they had was broken and could never be repaired?

"Cristina!"

She spun around. Mark was behind her, flushed; he'd been running to catch up to her. He stopped when she turned and hesitated a moment, looking like someone about to take a step off a high cliff.

"I have to be with Helen now," he said. "But I need to talk to you. I've needed to talk to you since—for a long time. Meet me in the parking lot tonight, when the moon is high."

She nodded, too surprised to say anything. By the time it occurred to her that "when the moon is high" wasn't very helpful—what if it was cloudy?—he'd already vanished down the hall. With a sigh, she headed off to send Catarina Loss a fire-message.

* * *

It had been only a few days since Robert Lightwood's death, but Horace Dearborn had already completely redecorated his office.

The first thing Emma noticed was that the tapestry of the Battle of the Burren was missing. The fireplace was lit now, and over it Alec Lightwood's image had been replaced by Zara Dearborn's. It was a portrait of her in gear, her long blond-brown hair falling to her waist in two braids like a Viking's. ZARA DEARBORN, CLAVE HERO, said a gold plaque on the frame.

"Subtle," Julian muttered. He and Emma had just come into Horace's office; the Inquisitor was bent over and poking around in his desk, seemingly ignoring them. The desk at least was the same, though a large sign hung behind it that announced: PURITY IS STRENGTH. STRENGTH IS VICTORY. THEREFORE PURITY IS VICTORY.

Dearborn straightened up. "'Clave hero' might be a bit simple," he said thoughtfully, making it quite clear he'd heard Julian's comment. "I was thinking 'Modern Boadicea.' In case you don't know who she was—"

"I know who Boadicea was," said Julian, seating himself; Emma followed. The chairs were new as well, with stiff upholstery. "A warrior queen of Britain."

"Julian's uncle was a classical scholar," said Emma.

"Ah yes, so Zara told me." Horace dropped heavily into his own seat, behind the mahogany desk. He was a big man, rawboned, with a nondescript face. Only his size was unusual—his hands were enormous, and his big shoulders pulled at the material of his uniform. They must not have had time to make one up for him yet. "Now, children. I must say I'm surprised at you two. There has always been such a . . . vibrant partnership between the Blackthorn and Carstairs families and the Clave."

"The Clave has changed," said Emma.

"Not all change is for the worse," said Horace. "This has been a long time coming."

Julian swung his feet up, planting his boots on Horace's desk. Emma blinked. Julian had always been rebellious at heart, but rarely openly. He smiled like an angel and said, "Why don't you just tell us what you want?"

Horace's eyes glinted. There was anger in them, but his voice was smooth when he spoke. "You two have really fucked up," he said. "More than you know."

Emma was jolted. Shadowhunter adults, especially those in positions of authority, rarely swore in front of anyone they considered children.

"What do you mean?" she said.

He opened a desk drawer and took out a black leather notebook. "Robert Lightwood's notes," he said. "He took them after every meeting he had. He took them after the meeting he had with *you*."

Julian went white; he clearly recognized the notebook. Robert must have written in it after Emma had left his office with Manuel.

"I know what you told him about your relationship," Dearborn said with relish. "*Parabatai* in love. Disgusting. And I know what you wanted from him. Exile."

Though the color had left his face, Julian's voice was steady. "I still think you should tell us what you want from us."

"To fall in love with your *parabatai* is, shall we say, a breach of contract. The contract you've made as Nephilim, with the Clave. It desecrates our holiest of holy bonds." He set the notebook back in its drawer. "But I am not an unreasonable man. I've come up with a mutually beneficial solution to all our little problems. And a few of the big ones."

"Solutions aren't usually mutually beneficial when one party has all the power," said Julian.

Dearborn ignored him. "If you agree to be sent on a mission to the Land of Faerie, if you promise to find and to kill Annabel Blackthorn there and bring back the Black Volume of the Dead, I'll honor the terms Robert set out. Exile and secrecy. No one will ever know."

"You can't be sure she's in Faerie—" Julian began.

"You have *got* to be kidding," Emma said at the same time.

"My sources say she's in the Unseelie Court, and no, I am not 'kidding,'" said Dearborn. "I would swear it on the Mortal Sword, if Carstairs hadn't broken it."

Emma flushed. "Why do you want the Black Volume? Planning on raising some dead?"

"I have no interest in some warlock's pitiable book of necromantic amusements," said Horace, "save keeping it *out* of the hands of Annabel Blackthorn and the King of Unseelie. Do not even consider trying to fob me off with imitations or fakes. I will know, and I will punish you. I want the Black Volume in the control of Nephilim, not Downworlders."

"You must have older, more capable people who can do this?" said Julian.

"This mission must be carried out with the utmost secrecy," Dearborn snapped. "Who has a better reason to keep it a secret than you?"

"But time works differently in Faerie," said Julian. "We could wind up coming back ten years from now. That won't help you much."

"Ah." Dearborn sat back. There was a pile of cloth behind him, in one corner of the room: Emma realized with a jolt that it was the tapestry of the Battle of the Burren, thrown away like so much trash. Strange for a man who claimed to value Nephilim history. "A long time ago, three medallions were given to the Clave by the Fair Folk. They prevent time slippage in Faerie. One is missing, but you'll be given one of the remaining two. You can return it when you yourselves come back."

A medallion? Emma remembered Cristina's necklace, its power to control time in Faerie. *One of them is missing. . . .*

"And how are we supposed to get back?" Emma said. "It's not as if returning from Faerie is easy for a human."

"You will use the map we give you to locate a place called Bram's Crossroads," said Horace. "There you will find a friend ready to bring you home." He steepled his fingers together. "I will conceal the fact that you are not in Alicante. There are already guards around the Princewater house. The word will be that you are under house arrest until the matter of the Mortal Sword is cleared up. But I must insist that you find the book and return within four days. Otherwise I may assume you decided to strike out on your own, in which case I will have no choice but to reveal your secret."

"What makes you think we can do this in four days?" said Julian.

"Because you have no choice," Horace replied.

Emma exchanged a look with Julian. She suspected his feelings, such as they were, mirrored her own—suspicion and helplessness. They couldn't trust Horace Dearborn, but if they didn't agree to this plan, he would destroy their lives. Their Marks would be stripped. They would never see the other Blackthorns again.

"There's no need for you to look so untrusting," said Dearborn. "We are in this together. None of us want Annabel Blackthorn or the Unseelie King to possess such a powerful item as the Black Volume." He gave a yellowish smile. "Besides, Julian, I thought you'd be pleased. This is your chance to kill Annabel Blackthorn and take her precious book from her. I would have thought you'd want revenge."

Unable to bear the way the Inquisitor was looking at Julian, Emma stood up. "I want Cortana," she said. "It was my father's before mine, and it has belonged in my family since before Jem and Cordelia Carstairs. Give it back to me."

"No," Horace said, his thin mouth flattening. "We are still investigating how it managed to shatter the Mortal Sword. We will furnish you with weapons, food, a map, and all the gear you need, but not Cortana."

"Seraph blades don't work in Faerie," said Julian. "Neither will our runes."

Dearborn snorted. "Then you'll be given daggers and swords and crossbows. You know we have every weapon you might need." He rose to his feet. "I don't care what you use to kill Annabel Blackthorn. Just kill her. You brought that bitch to us. It's your responsibility to rid us of her."

Julian slid his boots off the desk. "When are we supposed to be leaving?"

"And how will we get there?" said Emma.

"That's for me to know," said Dearborn. "As for when you leave, it might as well be now. It's not as if you have anything you need to be doing in Alicante." He gestured toward the door, as if he couldn't wait to be rid of them. "Go home and retrieve whatever personal items you require. And don't waste time. Guards will be coming to get you shortly. Be ready."

"Fine," Emma said. She strode over to the corner and picked up the tapestry of Alec. "But I'm keeping this."

It was surprisingly heavy. Dearborn raised his eyebrows but said nothing as she staggered out of the room clutching it.

"Where are we going?" Kit said. He was holding the bag of potato chips, salt and grease on his fingers. It was a weird breakfast, but he'd had weirder in his life. Besides, the ocean breeze was lifting his hair off his forehead, the beach was deserted, and he and Ty were walking into a golden haze of sand and sunshine. Despite everything, his mood was lifting.

"Remember that cave?" Ty said. "The one we were in when we saw Zara talking to Manuel?"

"Yeah," Kit said, and almost added, *when we were with Livvy*, but he knew that was what Ty meant by "we." It was a word that for him would always include Livvy. The shadow of memory fell over

Kit's good mood: He remembered that night, Livvy laughing, Ty holding up a starfish—the salt air had tangled his usually straight hair, and his eyes had echoed the silver color of the moon. He had been smiling, his real, shining Ty-smile. Kit had felt closer to the two of them than he had ever felt to anyone else. "Wait—why are we going there?"

They had reached the part of the beach where long fingers of pocked granite reached out into the ocean. The waves rushed in from the sea, slamming against the rocks, whipping themselves up into white-silver spray.

Ty reached into the bag of chips, his arm brushing against Kit's. "Because we need help to do necromancy. We can't do it on our own."

"Please tell me we don't need help from an army of the dead. I hate armies of the dead."

"Not an army of the dead. Hypatia Vex."

Kit nearly dropped the chips. "Hypatia Vex? The warlock from London?"

"Yep," said Ty. "Keep up, Watson."

"That's not a 'keep up,'" said Kit. "How would I know you contacted her? I didn't think she liked us very much."

"Does it matter?"

"You make a good point." Kit stopped, sand kicking up around his sneakers. "Here we are."

The dark hole in the bluff opened up in front of them. Ty paused too, rooting around in the pocket of his hoodie. "I have something for you."

Kit rolled up the bag of chips and stashed it behind a rock. "You do?"

Ty produced a small white stone, about the size of a golf ball, with a rune etched into it. "Your witchlight rune-stone. Every Shadowhunter has one." He took Kit's hand unselfconsciously and pressed the stone into his palm. A hot flutter went through Kit's stomach, surprising him. He'd never felt anything like it before.

"Thanks," he said. "How do I activate it?"

"Close your fingers around it and think of light," said Ty. "Imagine a light switch flicking on; that's what Julian said to me. Come on—I'll show you."

Kit held the stone awkwardly as they headed up the path to the cave entrance. A few steps into the cave and the darkness enveloped them like velvet, muffling the sound of the waves outside. Kit could barely see Ty, the shadow of a shadow beside him.

Like flicking a switch, he thought, and closed his fingers around the rune-stone.

It gave a little kick in his palm, and light rayed out, illuminating the familiar stone corridor. It was much as it had been before, rough-walled and spidery, reminding Kit of the underground tunnels in the first *Indiana Jones* movie.

At least this time they knew where they were going. They followed the curve of the tunnel around a bend, into an enormous stone chamber. The walls were granite, though black lines scored through them showed where they had cracked long ago. The room smelled like something sweet—probably the smoke that rose from the candles placed on the wooden table in the room's center. A hooded figure in a black robe, its face lost in shadow, sat where Zara had been sitting the last time they'd been here.

"Hypatia?" said Ty, stepping forward.

The figure raised a single, silencing finger. Both Kit and Ty hesitated as two gloved hands rose to push back the enveloping hood.

Ty licked his dry lips. "You're—not Hypatia." He turned to Kit. "That's not her."

"No," Kit agreed. "Seems to be a green fellow with horns."

"I'm not Hypatia, but she did send me," said the warlock. "We have met before, the three of us. In the Shadow Market in London."

Kit remembered quickly moving green-tinted hands. *I have to say I never thought I'd have the pleasure of entertaining the Lost Herondale.*

"Shade," he said.

The warlock looked amused. "Not my real name, but it'll do."

Ty was shaking his head. "I want to deal with Hypatia," he said. "Not you."

Shade leaned back in his chair. "Most warlocks won't touch necromancy," he said quietly. "Hypatia isn't any different; in fact, she's smarter than most. She wants to run the Shadow Market herself one day, and she's not going to endanger her chances."

Ty's expression seemed to splinter, like the cracked face of a statue. "I never said anything about necromancy—"

"Your twin sister just died," said Shade. "And you reach out to a warlock with a desperate request. It doesn't take a genius to guess what you want."

Kit put his hand on Ty's shoulder. "We don't have to stay here," he said. "We can just leave—"

"No," said Shade. "Hear me out first, little Shadowhunters, if you wish for my help. I understand. Grief makes people mad. You search for a way to end it."

"Yes," said Ty. "I want to bring my sister back. I *will* bring my sister back."

Shade's dark eyes were flinty. "You want to raise the dead. Do you know how many people want to do that? It's not a good plan. I suggest you drop it. I could help you out with something else. Have you ever wanted to move objects with your mind?"

"Sure," said Kit. "That sounds great." *Anything but this.*

"I have the Black Volume of the Dead," said Ty. "Or at least, I have a copy."

He didn't seem to recognize the absolute astonishment on Shade's face, but Kit saw it. It increased both his pride in Ty and, at the same time, his apprehension.

"Well," said Shade finally. "That's better than the real thing."

Odd thing to say, Kit thought.

"So it's not the spells we need help with," said Ty. "We need your help in gathering spell components. Some are easy to get, but Shadowhunters aren't welcome at the Shadow Market, so if you could go, I could give you money, or we have a lot of valuable weapons in the Institute—"

Kit was pleased. "I thought about selling those once, myself."

Shade held up his gloved hands. "No," he said. "I'll help you, all right, but it won't be fast, and it won't be easy."

"Good," said Ty, but Kit was instantly suspicious.

"Why?" said Kit. "Why would you help us? You don't approve—"

"I don't," said Shade. "But if it isn't me, it'll be someone else, some other warlock with fewer scruples. At least I can make sure you do this as cleanly as possible. I can show you how to cast the spell properly. I can get you a catalyst—a clean energy source that won't corrupt what you do."

"But you won't go to the Shadow Market?" said Kit.

"The spell only works if the spell caster collects the components themselves," said Shade. "And you'll be the one casting this spell, even if you need me to direct you. So whatever is between you two and the people of the Shadow Market—and I saw some of it myself, so I know it's personal—clean it up." His voice was gruff. "You're clever, you can figure it out. When you've got what you need, come back to me. I'll remain here in the cave for as long as you're committed to this insane project. But send a note if you're planning on dropping by. I like my privacy."

Ty's face was alight with relief, and Kit knew what he was thinking: This was step one accomplished, one move closer to getting Livvy back. Shade looked at him and shook his head, his white hair gleaming in the candlelight. "Of course, if you reconsider, and I never hear from you again, that will be even better," he added.

"Consider this, children. Some lights were never meant to burn for long."

He closed his gloved fingers around the wick of the largest candle, extinguishing it. A plume of white smoke rose toward the ceiling. Kit glanced at Ty again, but he hadn't reacted; he might not even have heard Shade. He was smiling to himself: not the blazing smile Kit had missed on the beach, but a quiet, private smile.

If we go forward, I have to shoulder this alone, Kit thought. *Any guilt, any apprehension. It's only mine.*

He glanced away from the warlock before Shade could see the doubt in his eyes.

Some lights were never meant to burn for long.

"I can't believe the Centurions left such a *mess*," Helen said.

For years, Helen had promised Aline that she would take her on a full tour of the Institute and show her all her favorite places from her childhood.

But Helen's mind was only partly on showing Aline around.

Some of it was on the destruction wrought by the Centurions inside the Institute—towels left everywhere, stains on the tables, and old food rotting in the fridge in the kitchen. Some of it was on the message she'd paid a faerie to take to her aunt Nene in the Seelie Court. But most of it was on her family.

"Those jerks aren't what's really bothering you," said Aline. They were standing on an overlook some distance from the Institute. From here you could see the desert, carpeted with wildflowers and green scrub, and the ocean as well, blue and gleaming below. There had been ocean at Wrangel Island, cold and icy and beautiful, but in no way welcoming. This was the sea of Helen's childhood—the sea of long days spent splashing in the waves with her sisters and brothers. "You can tell me anything, Helen."

"They hate me," Helen said in a small voice.

"Who hates you?" Aline demanded. "I'll kill them."

"My brothers and sister," said Helen. "Please don't kill them, though."

Aline looked stunned. "What do you mean, they hate you?"

"Ty ignores me," said Helen. "Dru snarls at me. Tavvy despises that I'm not Julian. And Mark—well, Mark doesn't hate me, but his mind seems far away. I can't drag him into this."

Aline crossed her arms and stared thoughtfully at the ocean. This was one of the things Helen loved about her wife. If Helen said something was the case, Aline would consider it from all angles; she was never dismissive.

"I told Julian to tell all the kids I was happy on Wrangel Island," said Helen. "I didn't want them to worry. But now—I think they believe I spent all these years not caring about being separated from them. They don't know how much I missed them. They don't know how horrible I feel that Julian had to shoulder all that responsibility, for all those years. I didn't *know*."

"The thing is," said Aline, "they don't just see you as replacing Julian as the person who takes care of them. You also stepped into their lives just as Livvy left them."

"But I also loved Livvy! I also miss her—"

"I know," Aline said gently. "But they're just children. They're grief stricken and lashing out. *They* don't know this is why they feel angry. They just feel it."

"I can't do this." Helen tried to keep her voice steady, but it was nearly impossible. She hoped the strain would be covered by the sound of the waves crashing below them, but Aline knew her too well. She could sense when Helen was upset, even when she was trying hard not to show it. "It's too hard."

"Baby." Aline moved closer, wrapping her arms around Helen, brushing her lips softly with her own. "You can. You can do anything."

Helen relaxed into her wife's arms. When she'd first met Aline, she'd thought the other girl was taller than she was, but she'd realized later it was the way Aline held herself, arrow straight. The Consul, her mother, held herself the same way, and with the same pride—not that either of them was arrogant, but the word seemed a shade closer to what Helen imagined than simple confidence. She remembered the first love note Aline had ever written her. *The world is changed because you are made of ivory and gold. The curves of your lips rewrite history.* Later, she'd found out it was an Oscar Wilde quote, and had said to Aline, smiling, *You've got a lot of nerve.*

Aline had looked back at her steadily. *I know. I do.*

They both had, always, and it had stood them in good stead. But this wasn't a situation where nerve mattered so much as patience. Helen had expected her younger brothers and sister to love her; she had needed it, in a way. Now she realized she had to show them her love first.

"In a way, their anger means good things," said Aline. "It means they know you'll always love them, no matter what. Eventually they'll stop testing you."

"Is there any way to speed up 'eventually'?"

"Would thinking about it as 'someday' help?"

Helen sniffled a laugh. "No."

Aline stroked her shoulder gently. "It was worth a try."

There were a dozen or more guards posted when Emma and Julian returned to the house. It was a bright day, and sun sparkled off the swords slung over their shoulders and the water in the canal.

As they went up the stairs, Dane Larkspear was slouching against one side of the doorway, his whippety face pale under a shock of black hair. He winked at Emma as Julian, ignoring him, reached for his stele. "Nice to see you."

"Can't say the same," said Emma. "Where's your evil twin? And

I mean that literally. She's your twin, and she's evil."

"Yeah, I got that," said Dane, rolling his eyes. "Samantha's at the Scholomance. And you've got guests."

Emma tensed. "In the house? Isn't the point of guards to keep them out?"

Dane chuckled. "Please. The point of us is to keep you in."

Julian scrawled an unlocking rune on the door and gave Dane a dark look. "Fifteen against two?"

Dane's smirk got wider. "Just showing you who's in power," he said. "We control the odds. I don't feel bad about that at all."

"You wouldn't," Julian said, and stalked into the house.

"Just in case I wasn't feeling really crappy about this situation already," Emma muttered, and followed Julian. She was wary—she hadn't liked the way Dane had said the word "guests." She closed the front door slowly, hand on the hilt of the dagger in her weapons belt.

She heard Julian call her name. "In the kitchen," he said. "It's all right, Emma."

Usually she trusted Julian more than she trusted herself. But things were different now. She went carefully toward the kitchen, only dropping her hand from the dagger when she saw Isabelle seated on the kitchen table, her long legs crossed. She was wearing a short velvet coat and a long tulle skirt. The bright glint of silver jewelry shone on her wrists and ankles.

Simon was seated at one of the kitchen chairs, elbows on the table, sunglasses pushed up on his head. "Hope you don't mind," he said. "The guards let us in."

"Not at all," said Julian, leaning against one of the counters. "I'm just surprised they agreed."

"Friendly persuasion," said Isabelle, and smiled a smile that was mostly teeth. "The Cohort doesn't have all the power yet. We still know a lot of people in high places."

"Where were you?" Simon inquired. "The guards wouldn't tell us anything."

"The Inquisitor wanted to talk to us," said Emma.

Simon frowned. "Dearborn? You mean he wanted to interrogate you?"

"Not exactly." Emma took off her jacket and slung it over a chair back. "He had a favor he wanted us to do. But what are you doing here?"

Isabelle and Simon exchanged a glance. "We have some bad news," Simon said.

Emma stared harder at both of them. Izzy looked tired, Simon tense, but that wasn't surprising. She could only imagine how she looked herself.

"My brothers and sisters—" Julian began, his voice tight, and Emma glanced at him; she remembered what he'd said about climbing up the pyre after Ty; *it was atavistic, the need to protect him, there was no conscious thought to it.*

"Nothing like that," said Simon. "Jace and Clary didn't come back at the appointed time."

Speechless, Emma sank into a chair opposite Simon.

"That's interesting," Julian said. "What do you think happened?"

Simon looked at him oddly. Isabelle nudged him with her knee, and through her surprise and worry Emma heard her mutter something about how Julian's sister just died, he was probably still in shock.

"Maybe they're just late because of the time being different in Faerie," said Emma. "Or did they get one of the medallions?"

"They're not affected by the time magic in Faerie, because of their angel blood," said Isabelle. "That's why the Clave chose to send them. Their runes still work, even in the blighted lands." She frowned. "What medallions?"

"Oh." Emma exchanged a look with Julian. "The Clave has medallions that prevent time slippage in Faerie. Dearborn gave us one."

Isabelle and Simon exchanged a bewildered glance. "What? Why would they give you—?"

"The favor that Dearborn asked us to do," said Julian. "It involved traveling to Faerie."

Simon straightened up. His face had gone tight-jawed, in a way that reminded Emma that he wasn't just Isabelle Lightwood's mild-mannered fiancé. He was a hero in his own right. He'd faced down the Angel Raziel himself. Few besides Clary could say that. "He did *what*?"

"I'll explain," said Julian, and he did, with a dry economy uncolored by emotion. Nevertheless, when he was done, both Isabelle and Simon looked furious.

"How dare he," said Simon. "How can he think—"

"But he's the Inquisitor now. He'd know Clary and Jace haven't come back," interrupted Isabelle. "The Clave knows it's dangerous, especially now. Why would he send you?"

"Because Annabel escaped into Faerie, and he thinks Annabel is our problem," said Emma.

"It's ridiculous; you guys are just kids," Simon said.

Isabelle kicked him lightly. "We did a lot when we were kids."

"Because we *had* to," said Simon. "Because we had no choices." He turned back to Emma and Julian. "We can get you out of here. We can hide you."

"No," Julian said.

"He means that we don't have choices either," said Emma. "There's too much chance of the Black Volume being put to terrible use, either by Annabel or the Unseelie King. There's no telling who might get hurt, and we have the best chance of finding the book. No one else has dealt with Annabel for centuries—in a weird way, Julian knows her the best."

"And we can look for Jace and Clary. It's not like Horace is going to send anyone else to find them," said Julian.

Isabelle looked flinty. "Because he's a jerk, you mean?"

"Because he doesn't like the support they have, or the way people look up to them and Alec and you guys," said Julian. "The longer they're gone, the better for him. He wants to consolidate power—he doesn't need heroes coming back. I'm sure Jia will try to help, but he won't make it easy for her. He can always throw delays in her path."

Julian was very pale, and his eyes looked like the blue sea glass in his bracelet. Her *parabatai* might not be feeling anything himself, Emma thought, but he still understood other people's feelings, almost too well. He had made the one argument Simon and Isabelle wouldn't be able to push back against: Clary and Jace's safety.

Still, Simon tried. "We can figure out something ourselves," he said. "Some way to look for them. The offer to hide you still stands."

"They'll take it out on my family if I disappear," Julian said. "This is a new Clave."

"Or maybe just what was always hiding under the old one," said Emma. "Can you swear you won't tell anyone, not even Jia, about us going to Faerie?"

No one can know. If Jia confronts Horace, he'll tell her our secret.

Simon and Isabelle looked troubled, but they both promised. "When are they asking you to leave?" said Isabelle.

"Soon," said Julian. "We just came back here to pack our things."

Simon muttered a curse. Isabelle shook her head, then bent down and unclipped a chain from one slender ankle. She held it out to Emma. "This is blessed iron. Poisonous to faeries. Wear it and you can pack a hell of a kick."

"Thanks." Emma took the chain and wrapped it twice around her wrist, fastening it tightly.

"Do I have anything iron?" Simon looked around wildly, then

reached into his pocket and pulled out a small miniature figure of an archer. "This is my D&D character, Lord Montgomery—"

"Oh my God," said Isabelle.

"Most figurines are pewter, but this one's iron. I got it on Kickstarter." Simon held it out to Julian. "Just take it. It could be helpful."

"I don't understand about half of what you just said, but thanks," said Jules, pocketing the toy.

There was an awkward silence. It was Isabelle who broke it, her dark gaze passing from Julian to Emma, and back again. "Thank you," she said. "Both of you. This is an incredibly brave thing to do." She took a deep breath. "When you find Clary and Jace, and I know you will, tell Jace about Robert. He should know what's happened to his family."

7
STONE FLOWERS

It was a clear California night, with a warm wind blowing inland from the desert, and the moon was bright and very definitely high in the sky when Cristina slipped out the back door of the Institute and hesitated on the top step.

It had been an odd evening—Helen and Aline had made spaghetti and left the pot on the stove so anyone who liked could come along and serve themselves. Cristina had eaten with Kit and Ty, who were bright-eyed and distant, caught up in their own world; at some point Dru had come in with bowls and put them in the sink. “I had dinner with Tavvy in his room,” she’d announced, and Cristina—feeling completely at sea—had stammered something about how she was glad they’d eaten.

Mark hadn’t appeared at all.

Cristina had waited until midnight before putting on a dress and denim jacket and going to see Mark. It was strange to have her own clothes back, her room with its *árbol de vida*, her own sheets and blankets. It wasn’t quite coming home, but it was close.

She paused at the top of the stairs. In the distance, the waves swayed and crashed. She’d stood here once and watched as Kieran and Mark kissed each other, Kieran holding Mark as if he were everything in the world.

It felt like a long time ago now.

She moved down the steps, the wind catching at the hem of her pale yellow dress, making it bell out like a flower. The "parking lot" was really a large rectangle of raked sand where the Institute's car spent its time—at least the Centurions didn't seem to have set it on fire, which was something. Near the lot were statues of Greek and Roman philosophers and playwrights, glowing palely under the stars, placed there by Arthur Blackthorn. They seemed out of place in the scrubby chaparral of the Malibu hills.

"Lady of Roses," said a voice behind her.

Kieran! she thought, and turned. And of course, it wasn't Kieran—it was Mark, tousled pale blond hair and blue jeans and a flannel shirt, which he'd buttoned slightly wrong. The *Markness* of him made her flush, partly at his nearness and partly that she'd thought for a moment that he might be someone else.

It was just that Kieran was the only one who called her Lady of Roses.

"I cannot bear all this iron," Mark said, and he sounded more tired than she had ever heard anyone sound. "I cannot bear these inside spaces. And I have missed you so much. Will you come into the desert with me?"

Cristina remembered the last time they were in the desert and what he had said. He had touched her face: *Am I imagining you? I was thinking about you, and now here you are.*

Faeries couldn't lie, but Mark could, and yet it was his painful honesty that caught at Cristina's heart. "Of course I will," she said.

He smiled, and it lit up his face. He cut across the parking lot, Cristina beside him, following a nearly invisible trail between tangled scrub and fern-shrouded boulders. "I used to walk here all the time when I was younger," he said. "Before the Dark War. I used to come here to think about my problems. Brood about them, whatever you want to call it."

"What problems?" she teased. "Romantic ones?"

He laughed. "I never really dated anyone back then," he said. "Vanessa Ashdown for about a week, but just—well, she wasn't very nice. Then I had a crush on a boy who was in the Conclave, but his family moved back to Idris after the Mortal War, and now I don't remember his name."

"Oh dear," she said. "Do you look at boys in Idris now and think 'that might be him'?"

"He'd be twenty now," said Mark. "For all I know he's married and has a dozen children."

"At *twenty*?" said Cristina. "He'd have to have been having triplets every year for four years!"

"Or two sets of sextuplets," said Mark. "It could happen."

They were both laughing now, softly, in the way of people who were just glad to be with each other. *I missed you*, he had said, and for a moment Cristina let herself forget the past days and be happy to be with Mark in the beautiful night. She had always loved the stark lines of deserts: the gleaming tangles of sagebrush and thornbushes, the massive shadows of mountains in the distance, the smell of sugar pines and incense cedar, the golden sand turned silver by moonlight. As they reached the flat top of a steep-sided hill, the ground fell away below them and she could see the ocean in the distance, its wind-touched shimmer reaching to the horizon in a dream of silver and black.

"This is one of my favorite places." Mark sank down onto the sand. "The Institute and the highway are hidden and the whole world goes away. It's just you and the desert."

She sat down beside him. The sand was still warm from the sunlight it had absorbed during the day. She dug her toes in, glad she'd worn sandals. "Is this where you used to do your thinking?"

He didn't answer. He seemed to have become absorbed in looking at his own hands; they were scarred lightly all over, calloused like any Shadowhunter's, his Voyance rune stark on his right hand.

"It's all right," she said. "It's all right for you not to be able to stand the iron, or inside spaces, or closed rooms or the sight of the ocean or anything at all. Your sister just died. There is nothing you could feel that would be wrong."

His chest hitched with an uneven breath. "What if I told you—if I told you that I am grieving for my sister, but since I five years ago decided she was dead, that all my family was dead, that I have already grieved her in a way? That my grief is different than the grief of the rest of my family, and therefore I cannot talk to them about it? I lost her and then I gained her and lost her again. It is more as if the having of her was a brief dream."

"It might be that it is easier to think of it that way," she said. "When I lost Jaime—though it is not the same—but when he disappeared, and our friendship ended, I grieved for him despite my anger, and then I began to wonder sometimes if perhaps I had dreamed him. No one else spoke of him, and I thought perhaps he had never existed." She drew up her knees, locking her arms around them. "And then I came here, and no one knew him at all, and it was even more as if he had never been."

Mark was looking at her now. He was silver and white in the moonlight and so beautiful to her that her heart broke a little. "He was your best friend."

"He was going to be my *parabatai*."

"So you did not just lose him," Mark said. "You lost that Cristina. The one with a *parabatai*."

"And you have lost that Mark," she said. "The one who was Livia's brother."

His smile was wry. "You are wise, Cristina."

She tensed against the feelings that rose in her at the sight of his smile. "No. I'm very foolish."

His gaze sharpened. "And Diego. You lost him, too."

"Yes," she said. "And I had loved him—he was my first love."

"But you don't love him now?" His eyes had darkened; blue and gold to a deeper black.

"You shouldn't have to ask," she whispered.

He reached for her; her hair was down and loose, and he took a lock of it and wound it around his finger, his touch impossibly gentle. "I needed to know," he said. "I needed to know if I could kiss you and it would be all right."

She couldn't speak; she nodded, and he wound his hands into her hair, lifted a handful of strands to his face, and kissed them. "Lady of Roses," he whispered. "Your hair, like black roses. I have been wanting you."

Want me, then. Kiss me. Everything. Everything, Mark. Her thoughts dissolved as he leaned into her; when she murmured against his mouth, it was in Spanish. "*Bésame*, Mark."

They sank backward into the sand, entwined, his hands running through her hair. His mouth was warm on hers and then hot, and the gentleness was gone, replaced by a fierce intensity. It was gorgeously like falling; he drew her under him, the sand cradling her body, and her hands ran over him, touching all the places she'd ached to touch: his hair, the arch of his back, the wings of his shoulder blades.

He was already so much more *present* than he had been when he'd first come to the Institute, when he'd looked as if a high wind might blow him away. He'd gained weight, put on muscle, and she enjoyed the solidity of him, the long elegant muscles that curved along his spine, the breadth and warmth of his shoulders. She ran her hands up under his shirt where his skin was smooth and burning hot, and he gasped into her mouth.

"*Te adoro,*" he whispered, and she giggled.

"Where did you learn that?"

"I looked it up," he said, cupping the back of her neck, brushing kisses along her cheek, her jaw. "It's true. I adore you, Cristina Mendoza Rosales, daughter of mountains and roses."

"I adore you, too," she whispered. "Even though your accent is terrible, I adore you, Mark Blackthorn, son of thorns." She smoothed her hand along his face and smiled. "Though you are not so prickly."

"Would you rather I had a beard?" Mark teased, rubbing his cheek against hers, and she giggled and whispered to him that his shirt was buttoned wrong.

"I can fix that," he said, and pulled it off; she heard some of the buttons pop and hoped it hadn't been a favorite shirt. She marveled at his lovely bare skin, flecked with scars. His eyes deepened in color; they were black as the depths of the ocean now, both the blue and the gold.

"I love the way you look at me," he said.

Both of them had stopped giggling; she ran the flat of her palms down his bare chest, his stomach, to the belt of his jeans, and he half-closed his eyes. His own hands went to the buttons that ran down the front of her dress. She continued to touch him as he undid them, neck to hem, until the dress fell away and she was lying on it in only her bra and underwear.

She would have expected to feel self-conscious. She always had with Diego. But Mark was looking at her as if he were stunned, as if he had unwrapped a present and found it to be the one thing he'd always wanted.

"May I touch you?" he said, and when she said yes, he exhaled a shaky breath. He lowered himself slowly over her, kissing her mouth, and she wrapped her legs around his hips, the desert air on her bare skin like silk.

He trailed a path of kisses down her throat; he kissed her where the wind touched her skin, on her belly and breasts, the peaks of her hips. By the time he slid back up her body to her mouth she was shaking. *I want to touch him, I have to,* she thought hazily; she slipped her hand down his body and under the waistband of his jeans. He inhaled sharply, murmuring between kisses for her not to stop. His body kept time with the movement of her hand, his hips pressing harder and harder against her. Until he pulled away, sitting up, his breath coming in harsh gasps.

"We have to stop—or it'll be over *now*," he said, sounding more human and less faerie than she remembered him ever sounding before.

"You told me not to stop," she pointed out, smiling at him.

"Did I?" he said, looking surprised. "I want it to be good for you, too, Cristina," he said. "I don't know what you and Diego—"

"We didn't," she interrupted. "I'm a virgin."

"You are?" He looked absolutely shocked.

"I wasn't ready," she said. "Now, I'm ready."

"I just thought—you'd been dating a long time—"

"Not all relationships are about sex," she said, and then wondered if making that statement while lying half-naked on a hill made it slightly more unconvincing. "People should only have sex if they want to, and I do want to, with you."

"And I want to with you," he said, his eyes softening. "But do you have the rune?"

The rune.

The birth control rune. Cristina had never put it on; she'd never thought she was that close to needing it. "Oh, *no*," she said. "My stele is down in the Institute."

"Mine as well," he said. Cristina almost giggled at the disappointed look on his face, though she felt the same. "Still," he said, brightening. "There is much else I can do to make you feel good. Allow me?"

Cristina settled back into the sand, feeling as if she might die from blushing. "All right."

He came back into her arms, and they held each other and kissed through the night, and he touched her and showed her he did indeed know how to make her feel good—so good she shook in his arms and muffled her cries against his shoulder. And she did the same for him, and this time he didn't ask her to stop, but arched his back and cried out her name, whispering afterward that he adored her, that she made him feel whole.

They decided to return to the Institute when dawn began to turn the sky rose-colored, and fingers of light illuminated their hilltop mesa. They wandered back down the path holding hands, and only unlinked their fingers when they reached the back door of the Institute. It stuck when Mark pushed on it, and he took his stele out to scrawl a quick Open rune on the wood.

It popped open, and he held it for Cristina, who slipped past him into the entryway. She felt incredibly disheveled, with sand stuck to half her body, and her hair a tangled mess. Mark didn't look much better, especially considering that most of the buttons had been ripped off his shirt.

He smiled at her, a heart-meltingly sweet smile. "Tomorrow night—"

"You have your stele," Cristina said.

He blinked. "What?"

"You have your stele. You told me that you didn't, when I needed to make the birth control rune. But you just used it to open the door."

He glanced away from her, and any hope Cristina had that he'd simply forgotten or been wrong vanished. "Cristina, I—"

"I just don't know why you lied to me," she said.

She turned away from him and walked up the stairs that led to her room. Her body had been humming with happiness; now she felt dazed and sticky and in need of a shower. She heard Mark call after her, but she didn't turn around.

Diego was asleep and dreaming restlessly about pools of blue water in which a dead woman floated. So he was only a little bit upset to be woken by the impact of a flying boot.

He sat up, reaching automatically for the ax propped next to his bed. The next thing that hit him was a ball of socks, which didn't hurt but was annoying. "What?" he sputtered. "What's going on?"

"Wake *up*," said Divya. "By the Angel, you snore like an outboard motor." She gestured at him. "Put your clothes on."

"Why?" said Diego, in what he felt was a very reasonable manner.

"They took Kieran," Divya said.

"Who took Kieran?" Diego was up, grabbing a sweater and jamming his feet into socks and boots.

"The Cohort," Divya said. She looked as if she'd just woken up herself; her thick dark hair was tangled, and she wore a gear jacket unbuttoned over her uniform. "They burst into my room and grabbed him. We tried to fight them off, but there were too many."

Diego's heart raced: Kieran had been under his protection. If he was harmed, Diego would have failed, not just Cristina but himself. He grabbed for his ax.

"Diego, stop," Divya said. "You can't ax Manuel to death. He's still a *student*."

"Fine. I'll take a shorter blade." Diego shoved the ax back against the wall with a clang and reached for a dagger. "Where did they take Kieran?"

"The Place of Reflection, or at least that's what they said," said Divya. "Rayan's out looking for them. Come on."

Diego shook the last cobwebs of sleep from his head and bolted after Divya. They jogged down the corridors, calling for Rayan.

"The Place of Reflection," said Diego. "That doesn't sound so bad. Is this a room for quiet meditation, or—?"

"*No.* You don't understand. It's called the Place of Reflection because there's a reflecting pool in it, but it isn't a regular reflecting pool. Some people call it the Hollow Place."

Oh. Diego did know of the Hollow Place, a secret room where, it was said, a pool had been filled with enchanted water. To gaze into the water was to gaze into your own soul: to see all the evil you had ever done, intentionally or otherwise.

"It's awful for anyone," said Divya. "And for someone in the Wild Hunt, it could kill them."

"*What?*" They turned a corner and encountered a blaze of light. It was Rayan, standing in the middle of a long corridor, wearing a grim expression. He had a massive sword strapped to his back.

"They just went into the Hollow Place," he said. "I couldn't follow them—I don't have my stele on me. Do either of you?"

"I do," said Diego, and they jogged down a short, sloping hallway to a set of closed doors. Loud giggles spilled out from inside the room.

Diego scrawled a quick Open rune on the door. It wrenched open with a puff of rust and they charged inside.

The Hollow Place was a wide space with granite floors, clear of any furniture. The walls were rough rock, glittering with mica. In the center of the room was a tile-lined pool with water so clear and clean it reflected like a mirror. Gold metal lettering decorated the floor: *And God split open the hollow place, and water came out from it.*

"Well, thank the Angel," drawled Manuel, who was leaning against a far wall in a pose of total disinterest. "Look who's here to save us all."

Zara giggled. She was surrounded by a group of other Cohort members—among them Diego recognized several Scholomance students and their family members. Mallory Bridgestock and Milo Coldridge. Anush Joshi, Divya's cousin. Several Centurions were there too: Timothy Rockford, Samantha Larkspear, and Jessica Beausejours were standing around smirking while Anush dragged Kieran toward the pool in the center of the room. Kieran was jerking and twisting in his grip; there was blood on his face, his shirt.

"It's a fair punishment for the princeling, don't you think?" said Zara. "If you look or swim in the water of the pool, you feel the pain you've inflicted on others. So if he's innocent, it should be just fine for him."

"No one is that innocent," said Rayan. "The pool is to be used sparingly, to allow students to seek for truth within themselves. Not as a torture device."

"What an interesting thought, Rayan," said Manuel. "Thank you for sharing. But I don't see Gladstone running in here to stop us, do you? Is it possible you didn't want to get in trouble for harboring a faerie fugitive?"

"I think it's interesting you know so much about Kieran," said Divya. "Is it possible you knew he was here and didn't want to report it so you could torture and kill him yourself?"

She was right, Diego thought, but none of this was helping Kieran, who was gagging and choking on his own blood.

I swore I would protect him. Diego reached for his ax, only to realize it wasn't there. He saw Zara's eyes narrow and turned; Divya had yanked Rayan's sword from its scabbard and was pointing it at the Cohort.

"Enough," she said. "Stop it, all of you. And I'm especially ashamed of you, Anush," she added, shooting her cousin a dark look. "You know what it's like to be treated unfairly. When your mother finds out . . ."

Anush let Kieran go with a shove. He landed at the edge of the pool with a grunt of agony. *Move away from the water,* Diego thought, but Kieran was clearly wounded; he knelt in place, dazed and gasping.

"We're just having a little fun," protested Anush.

"What are you going to do, Divya, attack us?" said Samantha. "Just for having a little fun?"

"He's bleeding," said Diego. "That's more than just 'a little fun.' And what happens if you kill him? Do you really want to deal with the consequences? He's the son of the Unseelie King."

There was a rumble of discontent among the Cohort. Clearly they'd never thought about that.

"Fine, fine," said Zara. "Be killjoys. But I knew he was here, hiding out in your room," she said to Diego. "I saw a hollowed acorn on your floor. So this is your fault. If you hadn't brought him here, none of this would have happened."

"Give it a rest, Zara," said Divya, still holding the sword levelly. "Diego, go get Kieran."

Diego started across the room, just as Manuel spoke. "Why don't you look in the water yourself, Rocio Rosales?" he said. "If you think your soul is so clean. It should be painless for you."

"Cállate la pinche boca," Diego snapped, nearly at Kieran's side; the faerie prince was coughing, blood on his lips. He'd started to pull himself upright when Manuel moved with the speed of a snake: Planting a boot in Kieran's back, he kicked him into the water.

Diego lunged forward, catching at the back of Kieran's shirt, but not before Kieran had gotten a faceful of pool water. Diego yanked him out, coughing and gasping, and tried to set him on his feet; Kieran staggered and Rayan caught him.

"Just get out," Samantha said, striding toward them. "When the Inquisitor hears about this—"

"Samantha!" Jessica called in alarm, but it was too late;

Samantha had slipped on the water at the edge of the pool and tumbled in with a scream.

"By the Angel." Divya lowered her sword, staring. "Is she—"

Samantha surfaced, screaming. It was a terrible scream, as if she were dying, or watching someone she loved die. It was a scream of horror and revulsion and misery.

The Cohort members stood stunned; only a few moved toward Samantha. Hands reached into the water, grasped her arms, and drew her out.

Kieran's hands. Still coughing blood, he deposited Samantha on the side of the pool. She rolled over, retching and gagging water, as Zara shoved herself between Samantha and the faerie prince. "Get away from her," she snarled at Kieran.

He turned and limped toward Diego. Diego caught Kieran as he nearly collapsed. The Cohort was occupied with Samantha; there was no time to waste. As Diego hurried from the room, half-supporting Kieran between himself and Rayan, Divya following with her sword, he was almost sure he could hear Manuel laughing.

"Okay," Julian said. "Let's see what we've got."

They were in what Emma could only describe as a glade. Glades were the sort of thing she didn't have a lot of experience with—there weren't too many in L.A.—but this was definitely one: open and grassy, surrounded by trees, filled with sunlight and the low humming of what might have been insects or tiny pixies.

You never could tell in Faerie.

She was still dizzy from the trip through the faerie gate, buried deep in the woods of Brocelind Forest. How Horace had known about it, she couldn't guess. Perhaps it was information given to all the high officials of the Clave. He had been impatient, nearly shoving them through without ceremony, but not too impatient to give

Emma the medallion, and both of them black rucksacks packed with weapons, gear, and food.

The last thing he'd said was: "Remember, you're heading toward the Unseelie Court. Follow the map."

A map wouldn't work in Faerie, Emma had thought, but Horace had shoved her toward the gate of twisted branches, and a moment later she was thudding to her knees on green grass and the scent of Faerie air was in her nose and mouth.

She reached up a hand and touched the medallion. It didn't have an angel on it, like Cristina's; in fact, it looked as if it had once borne a Shadowhunter family crest that had since been scratched away. Otherwise it looked much like the Rosales necklace. It made a comforting weight at the base of her throat.

"The Clave packed us sandwiches," Julian said, fishing around in his rucksack. "I guess for today, because they won't keep. There's cheese, bread, dried meat, and fruit. Some bottles of water."

Emma moved closer to him to see what he was unpacking and spreading on the grass. He'd taken out two gray blankets, an assortment of weapons—they also carried weapons on their belts—and folded clothes. When Julian shook them out, they turned out to be smooth linen in earth tones, fastened with laces and loops, no zippers or buttons.

"Faerie clothes," Emma said.

"It's a good idea," said Julian. Both outfits consisted of a long overshirt, trousers that laced up the front, and vests made of tough hide. "We should change. The longer we stand around in Shadowhunter gear, the longer we're a target."

Emma took the smaller set of clothes and went behind a copse of trees to change. She wished she could have asked Julian to go with her, especially when she was hopping on one foot, pulling on her trousers with one hand while gripping her weapons belt with the other. She'd rarely felt more vulnerable to attack, but even though Julian had seen her with no clothes on at all, it felt awkward now. She wasn't sure how this new Julian, the one without feelings, would react, and wasn't sure she wanted to know.

The faerie clothes were comfortable at least, soft and loose. When she emerged from the trees, she stood blinking in the bright sunlight for a moment, looking for Julian.

She saw him as he turned; he was holding up what looked like a piece of old parchment, frowning. He had put on the faerie trousers, but he was naked from the waist up.

Her stomach tightened. Emma had seen Julian shirtless at the beach plenty of times, but somehow this was different. Maybe because now she knew what it was like to run her hands over his shoulders, pale gold in the sunlight. He was smoothly muscled all over, the ridges in his abdomen sharply defined. She had kissed her way down that skin while he ran his hands through her hair, saying *Emma, Emma*, in the gentlest voice. Now she was staring like a curious onlooker.

But she couldn't stop. There was something about it—illicit, nerve-racking—as if Julian were a dangerous stranger. Her gaze slipped over him: his hair, soft and dark and thick, curling where it touched the nape of his neck; his hips and collarbones made elegant arches under his skin; his runes described whorls and spirals across his chest and biceps. His *parabatai* rune seemed to glow under the sun. Around his wrist was the same knotted rag of red-brown cloth.

He looked up at that moment and saw her. He lowered the parchment he was holding, angling it to cover the thing on his wrist. "Come here," he called, "and look at the map," and turned away, reaching for his shirt. By the time she'd gotten near him, he'd pulled it on and the rag was covered.

He handed over the map and she forgot everything else. She

stared at it as he knelt down, unpacking the food from one of the rucksacks.

The parchment showed a sketch of Faerie—the Thorn Mountains, various lakes and streams, and the Courts of Seelie and Unseelie. It also showed a bright red dot that seemed to be trembling slightly, as if it weren't a part of the page.

"The dot is us," Julian said, putting out sandwiches. "I figured the map out—it shows where we are in relation to the Courts. No real map would work here. The landscape of Faerie always shifts, and the Unseelie Court moves around. But since this shows where we are *and* where the Unseelie Court is, as long as we keep walking toward it we should be all right."

Emma sat down on the grass across from him and picked up a sandwich. They were both cheese, lettuce, and tomato—not her favorite but she didn't care, since she was hungry enough to eat pretty much anything.

"And what about Jace and Clary? We said to Simon and Isabelle that we'd look for them."

"We only have four days," Julian said. "We have to find the Black Volume first, or Horace will destroy our lives."

And the kids' lives. And Helen's and Aline's. And even Cristina's, because she knew our secret and she didn't tell. Emma knew it was all true, and Julian was being practical. Still, she wished he seemed more regretful that they couldn't look for their friends yet.

"But we can look for them if we find the book?" said Emma.

"If we still have time left on Horace's clock," said Julian. "I don't see why not."

"Four days isn't that much time," said Emma. "Do you think this plan could work? Or is Horace just trying to get us killed?"

"Be a pretty elaborate way to kill us," said Julian. He took a bite out of his sandwich and looked meditatively into the distance. "He wants the Black Volume. You heard him. I don't think he cares how he gets it, and we'll probably have to watch our step. But as long as we have it in our hands . . ." He pointed at the map. "Look. Bram's Crossroads."

The fact that their extraction point actually existed made Emma feel slightly better.

"I wish I knew what he was going to do with the Black Volume," Emma muttered.

"Probably nothing. He wants it so the faeries can't have it. It would be a political coup for him. The Consul couldn't get it, now he does, he gets to hold it up at the next Council meeting and praise himself."

"He'll probably say Zara found it," Emma said—and then paused, staring at Julian. "You're eating lettuce," she said.

"Yes?" He was leaning over the map, his fingers keeping it flat.

"You hate lettuce." She thought of all the times he'd eaten lettuce in front of the kids to be a good example and then complained to her later that it tasted like crunchy paper. "You've *always* hated it."

"Have I?" He sounded puzzled. He rose to his feet, starting to gather up their things. "We should head out. This time we travel by daylight. Too much weird stuff abroad in Faerie at night."

It's just lettuce, Emma told herself. *Not that important.* Still, she found herself biting her lip as she bent to pick up her rucksack. Julian was strapping his crossbow to his back; his rucksack went across the other shoulder.

From the woods came a cracking noise, the kind a breaking branch might make. Emma whirled around, her hand at her hip, feeling for the hilt of a knife. "Did you hear that?"

Julian tightened the strap of his crossbow. They stood there for long moments, on their guard, but there was no second sound, and nothing appeared. Emma wished fiercely for a Vision or Hearing rune.

"It could have been nothing," Julian said, finally, and though

Emma knew he wasn't really trying to comfort her, just trying to get them on the road, it still seemed like something the Julian she knew would say.

In silence they headed away from the clearing, which moments ago had been bright with sunlight and now seemed ominous and full of shadows.

8
Long-Forgotten Bowers

Diana hurried toward the canal house on Princewater Street, the cool morning wind lifting her hair. She felt shot through with adrenaline, tense at the prospect of spilling her history to Emma and Jules. She'd kept it hugged so close to herself for so many years, telling Gwyn had been like cracking open her ribs to show her heart.

She hoped the second time would be easier. Emma and Julian loved her, she told herself. They would—

She stopped dead, the heels of her boots clacking on the cobblestones. The cheerfully painted blue canal house rose in front of her, but it was surrounded by a ring of Council guards. Not just Council guards, in fact. Quite a few of them were young Centurions. Each was armed with an oak *bo* staff.

She glanced around. A few Shadowhunters hurried by, none of them glancing at the house. She wondered how many of them knew Jules and Emma were even still in Alicante—but then, the Inquisitor had planned to make an example of their testimony. They'd have to know eventually.

At the top of the steps was Amelia Overbeck, who had been giggling with Zara at the funeral. Annoyance sped up Diana's stride, and she pushed past the first ring of guards and ascended the steps.

Amelia, who had been leaning against the door talking to a girl with long orange-red hair, turned to Diana with a brittle smirk. "Miss Wrayburn," she said. "Is there something you want?"

"I'd like to see Julian Blackthorn and Emma Carstairs," said Diana, keeping her voice as neutral as possible.

"Gosh," said Amelia, clearly enjoying herself. "I just don't think so."

"Amelia, I have every right," said Diana. "Let me by."

Amelia slewed her gaze toward the redhead. "This is Diana Wrayburn, Vanessa," she said. "She thinks she's *very* important."

"Vanessa Ashdown?" Diana looked more closely: Cameron's cousin had left for the Academy as a spindly teen, and was almost unrecognizable now. "I know your cousin Cameron."

Vanessa rolled her eyes. "He's boring. Emma's whipped puppy. And no, don't think you can get into the house by making nice with me. I don't like the Blackthorns or anyone who pals around with them."

"Great news, since you're supposed to be protecting them," said Diana. Her adrenaline was coiling into rage. "Look, I'm going to open this door. If you want to try to stop me—"

"Diana!"

Diana turned, pushing hair out of her face: Jia was standing outside the ring of guards, her hand raised as if in greeting.

"The Consul." Vanessa's eyes bugged out. "Oh sh—"

"Shut up, Vanessa," hissed Amelia. She didn't look worried or afraid of Jia, just annoyed.

Diana pushed her way down the steps and to Jia's side. Jia wore a silk blouse and trousers, her hair held back with a jeweled clip. Her mouth was an angry slash. "Don't bother," she said in a low voice, placing her hand on Diana's elbow and guiding her away from the crowd of hooting guards. "I heard them say Emma and Julian were with the Inquisitor."

"Well, why didn't they just tell me that?" Diana snapped, exasperated. She glanced back over her shoulder at Vanessa Ashdown, who was giggling. "Vanessa Ashdown. My mother used to say some people had more hair than sense."

"She does seem to aptly prove that theory," said Jia dryly. She had stopped some distance from the house, where a small stone bank inclined into the canal. It was thick with moss, bright green under the silver water that slopped up the side. "Look, Diana, I need to talk to you. Where can we not be overheard?"

Diana looked at Jia closely. Was it her imagination, or when the Consul glanced at the Centurions surrounding the small canal house, did she look—afraid?

"Don't worry," said Diana. "I know exactly what to do."

She was climbing a spiral staircase that seemed to reach toward the stars. Cristina didn't remember how she had found the staircase, nor did she recall her destination. The staircase rose from darkness and soared into the clouds; she kept the material of her long skirts clutched in her hands so she wouldn't trip over them. Her hair felt dense and heavy, and the scent of white roses thickened the air.

The stairs ended abruptly and she stepped out in wonder onto a familiar rooftop: She was perched atop the Institute in Mexico City. She could see out over the city: El Ángel, shining gold atop the Monumento a la Independencia, Chapultepec Park, the Palacio de Bellas Artes lit up and glowing, the bell-shaped towers of the Guadalupe Basilica. The mountains rising behind it all, cupping the city as if in an open palm.

A shadowy figure stood at the edge of the rooftop: slender and masculine, hands looped behind his back. She knew before he turned that it was Mark: No one else had hair like that, like gold hammered to airy silver. He wore a long belted tunic, a dagger thrust through the leather strap, and linen trousers. His feet were bare as he came toward her and took her in his arms.

His eyes were shadowed, hooded with desire, his movements as slow as if they were both underwater. He drew her toward him, running his fingers through her hair, and she realized why it had felt so heavy: It was woven through with vines on which grew full-blown red roses. They fell around Mark as he cradled her with his other arm, his free hand running from her hair to her lips to her collarbones, his fingers dipping below the neckline of her dress. His hands were warm, the night cool, and his lips on hers were even warmer. She swayed into him, her hands finding their way to the back of his neck, where the fine hairs were softest, straying down to touch his scars. . . .

He drew back. "Cristina," he murmured. "Turn around."

She turned in his arms and saw Kieran. He was in velvet where Mark was in plain linen, and there were heavy gold rings on his fingers, his eyes shimmering and black-rimmed with kohl. He was a piece torn out of the night sky: silver and black.

One of Mark's arms went around Cristina. The other reached for Kieran. And Cristina reached for him too, her hands finding the softness of his doublet, gathering him toward both her and Mark, enfolding them in the dark velvet of him. He kissed Mark, and then bent to her, Mark's arms around her as Kieran's lips found hers. . . .

"Cristina." The voice pierced through Cristina's sleep, and she sat up instantly, clutching her blankets to her chest, wide-eyed with shock. "Cristina Mendoza Rosales?"

It was a woman's voice. Breathless, Cristina looked around as her bedroom came into focus: the Institute furniture, bright sunlight through the window, a blanket loaned to her by Emma folded at the foot of the bed. There was a woman sitting on the windowsill. She had blue skin and hair the color of white paper. The pupils of her eyes were a very deep blue. "I got your fire-message," she said as Cristina stared at her, dazed. *What did I just dream?*

Not now, Cristina. Think about it later.

"Catarina Loss?" Cristina had wanted to talk to the warlock, granted, but she hadn't expected Catarina to just appear in her bedroom, and certainly not at such an awkward moment. "How did you get in here . . . ?"

"I didn't. I'm a Projection." Catarina moved her hand in front of the bright surface of the window; sunlight streamed through it as if it were stained glass.

Cristina tugged discreetly at her hair. No roses. *Ay.* "What time is it?"

"Ten," said Catarina. "I'm sorry—I really thought you'd be awake. Here." She made a gesture with her fingers, and a paper cup appeared at Cristina's bedside.

"Peet's Coffee," Catarina said. "My favorite on the West Coast."

Cristina hugged the cup to her chest. Catarina was her new favorite person.

"I really wondered if I'd hear from you." Cristina took a sip of coffee. "I know it was a weird question."

"I wasn't sure either." Catarina sighed. "In a way, this is warlock business. Shadowhunters don't use ley lines."

"But we do use warlocks. You're our allies. If you are getting sick, then we owe it to you to do something."

Catarina looked surprised, then smiled. "I wasn't—it's good to hear you say that." She glanced down. "It's been getting worse. More and more warlocks are affected."

"How is Magnus Bane?" said Cristina. She hadn't known Magnus for long, but she'd liked him a great deal.

She was startled to see tears in Catarina's eyes. "Magnus is—well, Alec takes good care of him. But no, he's not well."

Cristina set her coffee down. "Then please let us help. What would a sign of ley line contamination be? What can we look for?"

"Well, at a place where the ley lines have been compromised, there would be increased demon activity," said Catarina.

"That's something we can definitely check."

"I can look into it myself. I'll send you a marked map via fire-message." Catarina stood up, and the sunlight streamed through her transparent white hair. "But if you're going to investigate an area with increased demon activity, don't go alone. Take several others with you. You Shadowhunters can be so careless."

"We're not all Jace Herondale," said Cristina, who was usually the least careless person she knew.

"Please. I've taught at Shadowhunter Academy. I—" Catarina began to cough, her shoulders shaking. Her eyes widened.

Cristina slid out of bed, alarmed. "Are you all right—?"

But Catarina had vanished. There wasn't even a swirl of air to show where her Projection had been.

Cristina threw on her clothes: jeans, an old T-shirt of Emma's. It smelled like Emma's perfume, a mixture of lemons and rosemary. Cristina wished with all her heart that Emma was here, that they could talk about last night, that Emma could give her advice and a shoulder to cry on.

But she wasn't and she couldn't. Cristina touched her necklace, whispered a quick prayer to the Angel, and headed down the hall to Mark's room.

He'd been up as late as she was, so there was a high possibility he was still sleeping. She knocked on the door hesitantly and then harder; finally Mark threw it open, yawning and stark naked.

"Híjole!" Cristina shrieked, and pulled her T-shirt collar up over her face. "Put your pants on!"

"Sorry," he called, ducking behind the door. "At least you've already seen it all."

"Not in good lighting!" Cristina could still see Mark through the gap in the door; he was wearing boxer shorts and pulling on a shirt. His head popped through the collar, his blond hair adorably ruffled.

No, not adorable, she told herself. *Terrible. Annoying.*

Naked.

No, she wasn't going to think about that, either. *Am I awake?* she wondered. She still felt wobbly about the dream she'd had. Dreams didn't mean anything, she reminded herself. It probably had something to do with anxiety, and not Mark and Kieran at all.

Mark reappeared in the doorway. "I'm so sorry. I—we often slept naked in the Hunt, and I forgot—"

Cristina yanked her shirt back down. "Let's not discuss it."

"Did you want to talk about last night?" He looked eager. "I can explain."

"No. I don't," she said firmly. "I need your help, and I—well, I couldn't ask anyone else. Ty and the others are too young, and Aline and Helen would feel like they had to tell Jia."

Mark looked disappointed, but rallied. "This is something the Clave can't know about?"

"I don't know. I just—at this point, I wonder if we can tell them anything."

"Can you at least tell me what this is about? Demons?"

"For a change, yes," said Cristina, and explained about the ley lines, the warlock sickness, and her talk with Catarina. "All we are doing is going to see if there's anything unusual to report on. We probably won't even get out of the car."

Mark perked up. "You'll be driving? It'll just be the two of us?"

"I will," she said. "Be ready by seven tonight." She started to walk away, then paused and glanced over her shoulder. She couldn't help it. "Just do me a favor tonight. Wear some pants."

When Kit came into the kitchen, Ty wasn't there.

He almost turned around and left, but the others had already seen him. Aline, in black jeans and a tank top, was at the stove, her hair tied up on top of her head, a frown of concentration on her face. Dru, Mark, Cristina, and Tavvy were at the table; Dru was fussing over Tavvy, but Cristina and Mark both greeted Kit with a wave.

He sat down and was immediately overwhelmed by awkwardness. He'd never spent much time with any of the Blackthorns besides Ty and Livvy. Without either of them there, he felt as if he'd wandered into a party full of people he barely knew with whom he was expected to make small talk.

"Did you sleep well?" Cristina asked him. It was hard to feel awkward around Cristina—she seemed to radiate kindness. Kit managed it, though. Johnny Rook had defrauded plenty of extremely kind people in his life and Kit doubted he lacked the capacity to do the same.

He mumbled something in response and poured himself some orange juice. Had he slept well? Not really. He'd spent half the night awake worrying about going to the Shadow Market with Ty, and the other half being oddly excited about going to the Shadow Market with Ty.

"Where's Helen?" Dru said in a low voice, eyeing Aline. Kit had been wondering the same. She'd looked pretty stressed out the previous day. He wouldn't blame her if she realized what she'd taken on and ran screaming into the desert.

"The Conclave is meeting today," said Mark. "Helen's attending."

"But isn't Aline the one who's supposed to be running the Institute?" Dru looked puzzled.

"Helen thought the Conclave should get used to her," said Mark. "Be reminded she's a Shadowhunter like any other Shadowhunter. And that she's a Blackthorn, especially since they might wind up talking about things like whether Diana needs to be replaced as our tutor—"

"I don't want another tutor!" Tavvy exclaimed. "I want Diana!"

"But surely she is only going to be away a few more days?" said Cristina anxiously. "At the most?"

Mark shrugged. "All of us bouncing around here without a tutor or a schedule is the kind of thing that makes Conclaves nervous."

"But Tavvy's right," Dru said. "We're already studying with *Diana*. We don't need to start with someone else. Isn't that right, Kit?"

Kit was so startled to be addressed that his juice glass almost flew out of his hand. Before he could answer, Aline interrupted them by stalking over to the table holding a frying pan. Fantastic smells wafted from it. Kit's mouth began to water.

"What's that?" Tavvy asked, his eyes big.

"This," said Aline, "is a frittata. And you're all going to eat it." She slammed it down onto a metal trivet in the center of the table.

"Don't like frittata," said Tavvy.

"Too bad," said Aline, crossing her arms and glaring at each of them in turn. "You made Helen cry yesterday, so you're going to eat this frittata—which, by the way, is goddamn delicious—and you're going to like it. It's what's for breakfast, and since I'm *not* Helen, I don't care if you starve or eat Cheetos for every single meal. Helen and I both have a lot of work to do, the Clave isn't giving us an inch, all she wants is to be with you guys, and you are *not* going to make her cry again. Understood?"

Dru and Tavvy both nodded, wide-eyed.

"I'm very sorry, Aline," said Cristina in a small voice.

"I didn't mean you, Cristina." Aline rolled her eyes. "And where's Ty? I'm not repeating this lecture again." She glared at Kit. "You're the one glued to his side. Where is he?"

"Probably sleeping," said Kit. He guessed Ty had stayed up late, researching dark magic. Not that he'd say that out loud.

"Fine. Tell him what I said when he wakes up. And put the frying pan in the freaking sink when you're done with breakfast." Aline grabbed her jacket off the back of a chair, slid her arms into the sleeves, and stalked out of the room.

Kit braced himself for either Tavvy or Dru to start to cry. Neither of them did. “That was pretty cool,” said Dru, helping herself to some frittata, which turned out to be a mixture of eggs, sausage, cheese, and caramelized onions. “I like the way she stood up for Helen.”

“*You* yelled at Helen the other day,” Mark pointed out.

“She’s my sister,” said Dru, heaping frittata on Tavvy’s plate.

Mark made an exasperated noise. Cristina took a bite of frittata and closed her eyes in pleasure.

“I bet you used to yell at your dad,” Dru said to Kit. “I mean, every family fights sometimes.”

“We weren’t really a yelling family. Mostly my dad would either ignore me or spend his time trying to teach me to pick locks.”

Dru’s face lit up. She still looked wan and tired, and very young in her oversize T-shirt, but when she smiled, she reminded Kit of Livvy. “You can pick locks?”

“I can show you how, if you want.”

She dropped her fork and clapped her hands together. “Yes! Mark, can I go learn how to pick locks now?”

“We have Open runes, Dru,” Mark said.

“So? What if I was kidnapped by a tentacle demon and I dropped my stele and I was handcuffed to a chair? What then?”

“That won’t happen,” said Mark.

“It could happen,” said Tavvy.

“It really couldn’t. Tentacle demons can’t operate handcuffs.” Mark looked exasperated.

“*Please?*” Dru begged him with her eyes.

“I—suppose it would do no harm,” Mark said, clearly out of his depth. He glanced sideways at Cristina, as if seeking her approval, but she looked quickly away. “Just don’t commit any actual crimes with your newfound knowledge, Dru. The last thing we need is something else for the Clave to be annoyed about.”

* * *

"That water is eldritch magic," Kieran said. He was leaning heavily against Diego's side as they made their way as quickly as possible down the corridors of the Scholomance. Divya and Rayan had remained behind at the doors of the Hollow Place, to keep the Cohort from chasing after Kieran and Diego. "I heard them laugh about it, as they dragged me down the halls, blindfolded." There was a haughty bitterness in his voice, still the tones of a prince. Beneath it was a layer of rage and shame. "I did not believe they knew of what they spoke, but they did."

"I am sorry," Diego said. He put a hand on the faerie prince's shoulder, tentatively. It seemed as if he could feel Kieran's heartbeat thrumming even through bone and muscle. "I was meant to protect you. I failed."

"You did not fail," Kieran said. "If it were not for you, I would have died." He sounded uncomfortable. Faeries weren't fond of apologies or debts. "We cannot go back to your room," Kieran added as they turned another corner. "They will look for us there."

"We have to hide," said Diego. "Somewhere we can get you bandaged up. There are dozens of empty rooms—"

Kieran pulled away. He was walking like a drunk, unsteadily. "Bandages are for those who deserve to heal," he said.

Diego looked at him, worried. "Is the pain bad?"

"It is not my pain," said Kieran.

A scream echoed down the halls. A tortured female scream, abruptly cut off.

"The girl who fell in the waters," said Kieran. "I tried to reach her sooner—"

Samantha. Diego might not have liked her, but no one deserved pain that would make you scream like that.

"Maybe we should get out of the Scholomance," said Diego. The main entrance was through the side of the mountain but was always guarded. There were other ways out, though—even a glass corridor that snaked through the waters of the lake to the other side.

Kieran raised his chin. "Someone is coming."

Diego reached for Kieran with one hand and his dagger with the other, then froze as he recognized the figure in front of him. Black hair, set jaw, scowling eyebrows, eyes fixed on Kieran.

Martin Gladstone.

"You won't be leaving the Scholomance," Gladstone said. "Not any time soon."

"You don't understand," said Diego. "The others—Zara's group—they tried to kill Kieran—"

Gladstone raked contemptuous eyes over Diego and his companion. "So you really had the gall to bring him here," he said, clearly meaning Kieran. "The faerie is a member of an enemy army. A high-ranking one at that."

"He was going to testify against the Unseelie King!" said Diego. "He was going to risk himself—risk the King's anger—to help Shadowhunters!"

"He never quite got that chance, did he," sneered Gladstone. "So we don't know what he would have done."

"I would have testified," said Kieran, leaning against the wall. "I bear my father no love."

"Faeries can't lie," said Diego. "Can you not listen?"

"They can trick and deceive and manipulate. How did he get you to aid him, Diego Rocio Rosales?"

"He did not 'get' me to do anything," said Diego. "I know who I trust. And if you kill Kieran, or let those bastards hurt him, you will be breaking the Accords."

"Interesting escalation," said Gladstone. "I have no intention of killing or harming Kingson. Instead you will be sequestered in the library until the Inquisitor can arrive and deal with you both."

* * *

Emma and Julian had been walking for some hours when Emma realized that they were being followed.

It had actually been a fairly pleasant walk along a tramped path in the woods. Julian was easy enough to talk to when Emma tried not to think about the spell, or how he felt about her, or about how he felt, period. They avoided the topics of Livvy and the *parabatai* curse, and talked instead about the Clave and what its next plans might be, and how Zara might figure into them. Julian walked ahead, holding the map, consulting it when enough light rayed down through the trees to make the map readable.

"We could reach the Unseelie Court by tomorrow morning," he said, pausing in the middle of a clearing. Blue and green flowers nodded in patches on the forest floor, and the sunlight turned the leaves to green veils. "Depending on how much we're willing to travel at night—"

Emma stopped in her tracks. "We're being followed," she said.

Julian stopped as well and turned to her, folding the map into his pocket. "You're sure?"

His voice was quiet. Emma strained to hear what she'd heard before: the tiny breakage of branches behind them, the thump of a footfall. "I'm sure."

There was no doubt in Julian's eyes; Emma felt a faint gratification that even in his current enchanted state, he trusted her skills implicitly. "We can't run," he said—he was right; the trail was too rocky and the undergrowth too thick for them to be sure they'd outrun a pursuer.

"Come on." Emma grabbed Julian's hand; a moment later they were skinning up the trunk of the tallest of the oak trees surrounding the clearing. Emma found the fork of a branch and settled into it; a second later, Julian swung up onto a branch across from hers. They clung to the tree trunk and looked down.

The footfalls were getting closer. Hoofbeats, Emma realized, and then a kelpie—dark green, with a mane of shimmering seaweed—strode into the clearing, a rider on its back.

Emma sucked in her breath. The rider was a man, wearing Shadowhunter gear.

She leaned down, eager to see more. Not a man, she realized, a boy—whippet thin and narrow-faced, with a shock of black hair.

"Dane Larkspear on a kelpie," Julian muttered. "What is this?"

"If I see Zara come up riding the Loch Ness monster, we're going home," Emma hissed back.

The kelpie had stopped dead in the middle of the clearing. It was rolling its eyes—deep black with no whites. Closer up, it looked less like a horse, even though it had a mane and tail and four legs, and more like a frightening creature, something that had never been meant to be out of the water.

"Hurry up." Dane jerked on the kelpie's bridle and a memory flickered in the back of Emma's mind—something about how bridling a kelpie forced it to obey you. She wondered how Dane had managed it. "We need to find Blackthorn and Carstairs's trail before nightfall or we'll lose them."

The kelpie spoke. Emma jolted. Its voice sounded like the grinding of waves against rock. "I do not know these creatures, Master. I do not know what they look like."

"It doesn't matter! Pick up their trail!" Dane smacked the kelpie across the shoulder and sat back, glowering. "Okay, I'll describe them for you. Julian's the kind of guy who would have a girl as a *parabatai*. Get it?"

"No," said the kelpie.

"Spends all his time chasing little kids around. Has like a million children and he acts like he's their dad. It's creepy. Now, Emma, she's the kind of girl who'd be hot if she ever shut up."

"I'll kill him," Emma muttered. "I'll kill him while *talking the whole time.*"

"I don't understand human attitudes toward beauty," said the kelpie. "I like a fine sheen of seaweed on a woman."

"Shut up." Dane jerked the bridle and the kelpie exposed needlelike teeth in a hiss. "We need to find them before the sun goes down." His smile was ugly. "Once I get back with the Black Volume, Horace will give me anything I want. Maybe Julian Blackthorn's last sister to play with. Dru whatsit. Best tits in the family."

Emma was out of the tree so fast that the world was a blur of green leaves and red rage. She landed on Dane Larkspear and knocked him clear of his saddle, forcing a gasp of pain from him when they hit the ground together. She punched him hard in the stomach and he doubled up while she sprang to her feet. She grabbed for her sword; for a moment she had been worried Julian wouldn't have followed her but he was already on the ground, yanking off the kelpie's bridle.

"My lord!" The kelpie bowed its forelegs to Julian. Dane was coughing and gagging, rolling on the ground in pain. "Thank you for freeing me."

"Don't mention it." Julian tossed the bridle aside, and the kelpie dashed into the forest.

Emma was still standing over Dane with her sword pointed at his throat, where something gold flashed. Lying flat on the ground, he glared at her.

"What are you doing here, Larkspear?" she demanded. "We were sent to get the Black Volume, not you."

"Get away from me." Dane turned his head and spit blood. He wiped his mouth, leaving a red smear on his hand. "If you hurt me at all, the Dearborns will have your Marks stripped."

"So what?" Emma said. "We don't even have the Black Volume. So you just wasted your time following us, Dane. Which, by the way, you suck at. You sounded like an elephant. A sexist elephant. You're a terrible Shadowhunter."

"I know you don't have it," Dane said in disgust. "But you will. You'll find it. And when you do—"

Dane broke off.

"What?" Emma's voice dripped scorn. "Am I talking too much?"

Emma suddenly realized Dane wasn't staring at her but behind her; Julian had come up and was standing with his longsword in his hand, gazing at Dane with a frightening coldness. "You do know," he said quietly, "that if you ever touched Dru, I would kill you?"

Dane pushed himself up on his elbows. "You think you're so special," he hissed in a thin, whining voice. "You think you're so great—you think your sister's too good for me—"

"She's too *young* for you," said Emma. "She's thirteen, creep."

"You think the Inquisitor sent you on some special mission because you're so great, but he sent you because you're disposable! Because you don't matter! He wants you *gone*!"

Dane froze, as if he realized he'd said too much.

Emma turned to Julian. "Does he mean—"

"He means the Inquisitor sent him to kill us," said Julian. "He's wearing one of the medallions Horace gave us. The ones that prevent time slippage."

Dane put a hand protectively to his throat, but not before Emma saw that Julian was right.

She glared at Dane. "So Horace sent you to get the Black Volume and kill us and return with it alone?"

"And then he'd tell everyone we were murdered by the Fair Folk," said Julian. "Extra bonus for him."

A flicker of fear crossed Dane's face. "How did you guess that?"

"I'm smarter than you," said Julian. "But I wouldn't give myself big props. So is sawdust."

"There's a difference between sending someone on a dangerous mission and sending someone after them to stab them in the back," said Emma. "When the Clave finds out—"

"They won't find out!" Dane shouted. "You're never coming back from here! You think it's just me?" He staggered to his feet; Emma took a step back, unsure what to do. They could knock Dane out, but then what? Tie him up? Return him to Idris somehow? "The Cohort has a long reach and we don't need traitors like you. The fewer of you there are in the world, the better—we got a good start with Livvy, but—"

Julian's sword flashed like lightning as he drove the blade into Dane's heart.

Emma knew it was Dane's heart, because Dane's body spasmed and arched, like a fish caught with a hook through its body. He coughed out blood in a red spray, his eyes fixed on Julian with a look of incredulity.

Julian jerked his sword free. Dane slid to the ground, his mouth half-open, his expression glassy and flat.

Emma whirled on Julian. "*What did you just do?*"

Julian bent to clean the blade of his sword on a patch of grass and flowers. "Killed the person who was planning to kill us."

"You murdered him," Emma said.

"Emma, be practical. He was sent here to murder *us*. He would have done it to us if I hadn't done it to him. And he said there might be others, too, other Cohort members. If we left him alive, we could have been facing a lot more adversaries pretty soon."

Emma felt as if she couldn't catch her breath. Julian had sheathed his sword; the flowers at his feet were stained with blood. She couldn't look at Dane's body. "You don't just kill other Shadowhunters. People don't do that. People with *feelings* don't do that."

"Maybe," said Julian. "But he was a problem, and now he's not."

There was a rustle in the underbrush. A moment later the kelpie reappeared, shimmering green in the sunlight. It nosed its way over to Dane. Emma wondered for a second if it was mourning its previous master.

There was a crunching sound as it sank its needle teeth into Dane's bloodstained side. The coppery smell of blood exploded onto the air. The kelpie swallowed and looked up at Julian, its green teeth glinting red, like a disturbing vision of Christmas.

"Oh God." Emma stepped back, revolted.

"Sorry," said the kelpie. "Did you want to share? He's very tasty."

"No, thanks." Julian looked neither bothered nor amused by the grisly spectacle.

"You are very generous, Julian Blackthorn," said the kelpie. "Be sure I will repay you some day."

"We need to leave," said Emma, trying not to gag. She looked away, but not before she saw Dane's rib cage gleam white in the sun. "We need to get out of here *now*."

She whirled blindly. She kept seeing the blood on the flowers, the way Dane's eyes had rolled up in his head. The air was suddenly thick with the copper smell of blood, and Emma reached out to steady herself on the narrow trunk of a birch tree.

"Emma?" Julian said behind her, and suddenly there was the explosive thunder of hooves, and two horses, one gray and one brown, burst into the clearing. A faerie rider sat astride each: a fair-haired woman on the gray horse, and a wheat-skinned man on the brown.

"Is this Faerie Grand Central?" said Emma, leaning her forehead against the tree. "Does everyone come here?"

"Emma Carstairs?" said the fair-haired woman. Emma recognized her through blurred vision: It was Mark's aunt Nene. Beside her rode one of the Seelie Queen's courtiers, Fergus. He was scowling.

"Is that a dead *Shadowhunter*?" he demanded.

"He took me prisoner and these kind people freed me," said the kelpie.

"Go, kelpie," said Fergus. "Leave this place. The words of Seelie courtiers are not for you."

The kelpie gave a whinnying sigh and dragged Dane's body into the underbrush. Emma turned slowly, keeping her back to the tree. She was fervently glad the corpse was gone, though the ground was still wet with blood, the petals of the flowers weighed down by it.

"Emma Carstairs and Julian Blackthorn," said Nene. "Your course was bound toward the Seelie Court. Why?"

"No, we were on the way to the Unseelie Court," said Emma. "We were—"

"We know which paths in the Lands lead to what destinations," said Fergus sharply. "Do not try your human tricks."

Emma opened her mouth to protest—and saw Julian shake his head at her, a tiny fraction of a negation, but she knew immediately what it meant. They *had* been traveling the wrong way. For whatever reason, he had lied to her; every time he had consulted the map, it had brought them closer to the Seelie Court.

The taste of betrayal was bitter in her mouth, more bitter than the copper of blood.

"We have the Black Volume," Julian said to Nene, to Fergus, and Emma stared at him in total astonishment. What was he talking about? "That is why we have returned to Faerie. The Queen asked us to retrieve it for her, and we have, and we have come for what she promised."

He straightened, his head thrown back. His face was very pale, but his eyes were shining, bright green-blue, and he looked beautiful; even with blood on his face he was beautiful, and Emma wished she couldn't see it, but she could.

"We formally request audience with the Seelie Queen," he said.

9

Up Kingly Halls

Soaring through the air with Gwyn, Diana felt free, despite her nagging worry over Emma and Julian. She supposed they were safe in the house, but she didn't like not being able to see them. It made her realize how much they had become her family over the past five years, and how disconnected she felt from Alicante.

Walking through the streets, even familiar faces felt like the masks of strangers. *Did you vote to bring Horace Dearborn in as the Inquisitor? Do you blame the Blackthorns for their own sister's death? Do you believe faeries are monsters? Who are you, really?*

She held Gwyn more tightly as they landed in their now-familiar small clearing among the linden trees. The moon had thinned, and the glade was full of silence and deep shadow. Gwyn dismounted first and helped Diana down; this time he had not brought saddle-bags full of food, but a blunt sword at his waist. Diana knew he trusted her, and he had asked no questions when she'd requested that he bring her here tonight. He didn't trust other Shadowhunters, though, and she couldn't blame him for that.

A light sprang up among the shadows, and Jia stepped out from behind a tilted rock. Diana frowned as the Consul approached them. The last time Diana had been here, the earth had been green under her feet. Now Jia's shoes crunched on dried moss, brown and sere. It could simply be because fall was approaching, but the blight . . .

"Diana," Jia said. "I need your help."

Diana held up a hand. "First I need to know why I am not allowed to see Emma and Julian. Why am I being kept away from them?"

"Everyone is meant to be kept away from them," said Jia. She sat down neatly on a flat stone, her ankles crossed. She didn't have a hair out of place. "Horace says he doesn't want to compromise their testimony."

Diana made a disbelieving noise. "How is he planning to force them to give testimony? There's no Mortal Sword!"

"I understand how concerned you must be," said Jia. "But I spoke with Simon before he left for New York. He and Isabelle managed to see Emma and Julian this morning and said that they were fine and their meeting with Horace went as well as could be expected."

A mix of relief and annoyance washed over Diana. "Jia, you have to do something. Dearborn cannot keep them isolated until some imaginary future time when the Sword is repaired."

"I know," Jia said. "It's why I wanted to meet. Remember when I asked you to stand with me?"

"Yes," Diana said.

"The Cohort are aware of the blight in the forest," Jia said. "After all, Patrick took Manuel with him to see it, before we realized how dangerous they all were—even the children." She sighed and glanced at Gwyn, who was expressionless. With his years of experience in the political duelings of the Faerie Courts, Diana couldn't help but wonder what he thought of all this. "They've decided to use it as a political tool. They are going to claim it as the work of faeries specifically. They want to burn the forest to kill the blight."

"That will not kill the blight," said Gwyn. "It will only kill the forest. The blight is death and decay. You cannot destroy destruction itself any more than you can cure poison with poison."

Jia looked at Gwyn again, this time hard and directly. "*Is* it faerie magic? The blight?"

"It is not any faerie magic I have ever seen, and I have lived a long time," said Gwyn. "I am not saying that the Unseelie King has no hand in it. But this is a more demonic magic than any wielded in Faerie. It is not natural but unnatural in nature."

"So burning the forest won't accomplish anything?" said Diana.

"It will accomplish *something*," said Gwyn. "It will drive out the Downworlders who call Brocelind home—all the faeries and the werewolf packs who have lived here for generations."

"It is an excuse, I believe, to begin driving the Downworlders out of Idris," said Jia. "Dearborn intends to use the current mood of fear among the Nephilim to push for stricter anti-Downworlder laws. I knew he would, but I did not expect his attempt to empty Idris of Downworlders to come so quickly."

"Do you think the Clave would ever fall in line with him?" asked Diana.

"I fear so," Jia said with a rarely expressed bitterness. "They are focused so much on their fear and hatred that they don't even see where they are injuring themselves. They would eat a poisoned banquet if they thought Downworlders were feasting beside them."

Diana hugged her arms around herself to keep from shivering. "So what can we do?"

"Horace has called a meeting in two days. It will be his first opportunity to present his plans to the public. People respect you—the Wrayburns are a proud family and you fought bravely in the Dark War. There must be those of us who stand up to resist him. So many are afraid to speak out."

"I am not afraid," said Diana, and she saw Gwyn give her a warm look of admiration.

"The world can change so quickly," Jia said. "One day the future seems hopeful, and the next day clouds of hate and bigotry have gathered as if blown in from some as yet unimagined sea."

"They were always there, Jia," said Diana. "Even if we did not want to acknowledge them. They were always on the horizon."

Jia looked weary, and Diana wondered if she had walked all the way here, though she doubted it was physical exertion that had tired the Consul. "I do not know if we can gather enough strength to clear the skies again."

"Okay," said Kit. "First we're going to make a tension wrench out of a paper clip."

"We're going to make a what out of a what?" Dru hooked her hair behind her ears and looked at Kit with wide eyes. They were both sitting on top of one of the long tables in the library, with a padlock and a pile of paper clips in between them.

He groaned. "Don't tell me you don't know what a paper clip is."

She looked indignant. "Of course I do. Those." She jabbed a finger. "But what are we making?"

"I'll show you. Take a clip."

She picked one up.

"Bend it into an L shape," he instructed. "The straight part is the top part. Okay, good." Her face was screwed up with concentration. She was wearing a black T-shirt that said FROM BEYOND THE GRAVE on it and featured a cracked tombstone.

Kit picked up a second clip and straightened it completely. "This is your pick," he said. "What you're holding is the tension wrench."

"Okay," she said. "Now how do you pick the lock?"

He laughed. "Hold your horses. Okay, pick up the padlock—you're going to take the tension wrench and insert it into the bottom of the keyhole, which is called the shear line."

Dru did as he'd instructed. Her tongue poked out one corner of her mouth: She looked like a little girl concentrating on a book.

"Turn it in the direction that the lock would turn," he said. "Not left—there you go. Like that. Now take the pick with your other hand."

"No, wait—" She laughed. "That's confusing."

"Okay, I'll show you." He slid the second clip into the lock itself and began to rake it back and forth, trying to push the pins up. His father had taught him how to feel the pins with his lock pick—this lock had five—and he began to fiddle gently, raising one pin after another. "Turn your wrench," he said suddenly, and Dru jumped. "Turn it to the right."

She twisted, and the padlock popped open. Dru gave a muted scream. "That's so cool!"

Kit felt like smiling at her—it had never occurred to him to want a little sister, but there was something nice about having someone to teach things to.

"Does Ty know how to do this?" she asked.

"I don't think so," Kit said, relocking the padlock and handing it to her. "But he'd probably learn fast." He handed her the pick next and sat back. "Now you do it."

She groaned. "Not fair."

"You only learn by doing." It was something Kit's father had always said.

"You sound like Julian." Dru puffed out a little laugh and started in on the padlock. Her fingernails were painted with chipped black polish. Kit was impressed with the delicacy with which she handled the pick and wrench.

"I never thought anyone would say I sounded like Julian Blackthorn."

Dru looked up. "You know what I mean. Dad-ish." She twisted the tension wrench. "I'm glad you're friends with Ty," she said unexpectedly. Kit felt his heart give a sudden sharp bump in his chest. "I mean, he always had Livvy. So he didn't need any other friends. It was like a little club and no one could get in, and then you came along and you did."

She had paused, still holding the padlock. She was looking at him with eyes so much like Livvy's, that wide blue-green fringed with dark lashes.

"I'm sorry?" he said.

"Don't be. I'm too young. Ty would never have let me in, even if you hadn't showed up." She said it matter-of-factly. "I love Julian. He's like—the best father. You know he'll always put you first. But Ty was always my cool brother. He had such awesome stuff in his room, and animals liked him, and he knew everything—"

She broke off, her cheeks turning pink. Ty had come in, his damp hair in soft, humid curls, and Kit felt a slow flip inside him, like his stomach turning over. He told himself he probably felt awkward because Ty had walked in on them talking about him.

"I'm learning how to pick locks," Dru said.

"Okay." Ty spared her a cursory glance. "I need to talk to Kit now, though."

Kit slid hastily off the table, nearly knocking over the pile of paper clips. "Dru did really well," he said.

"Okay," Ty said again. "But I need to talk to you."

"So talk," said Dru. She'd put the lock-picking equipment down on the table and was glaring at Ty.

"Not with you here," he said.

It had been pretty obvious, but Dru made a hurt noise anyway and jumped off the table. She stalked out of the library, slamming the door behind her.

"That wasn't—she wasn't—" Kit started. He couldn't finish, though; he couldn't scold Ty. Not now.

Ty unzipped his hoodie and reached brusquely into an inner pocket. "We need to go to the Shadow Market tonight," he said.

Kit yanked his brain back to the present. "I'm forbidden from entering the Market. I suspect you are too."

"We can petition at the gate," said Ty. "I read about people doing that. Shadow Markets have gates, right?"

"Yeah, there are gates. They're marked off. They don't keep people out or in; they're more like meeting points. And yeah, you can petition the head of the Market, except in this case it's Barnabas and he hates me."

Ty picked up a paper clip from the table and looked at it with interest. There were bruises on his neck, Kit noticed suddenly. He didn't remember them, which struck him as strange, but then, who noticed every bruise on someone else's skin? Ty must have gotten them when they'd fought the Riders in London. "We just have to convince him it's in his interest to let us in."

"How do you plan to do that? We're not exactly master negotiators."

Ty, who had been straightening the paper clip, gave Kit one of his rare sunrise-over-the-water smiles. "You are."

"I—" Kit realized he was grinning, and broke off. He'd always had a sarcastic edge to his tongue, never been someone to take a compliment gracefully, but it was as if there was something about Ty Blackthorn that reached into him and untied all the careful knots of protection holding him together. He wondered if that was what people meant when they said they felt undone.

Ty frowned as if he hadn't noticed Kit's stupid smile. "The problem is," he said, "neither of us drive. We have no way of getting to the Market."

"But you have an iPhone," said Kit. "In fact, there's several in the Institute. I've seen them."

"Sure," said Ty, "but—"

"I'm going to introduce you to a wonderful invention called Uber," said Kit. "Your life will be changed, Ty Blackthorn."

"Ah, Watson," said Ty, shoving the clip into his pocket. "You may not yourself be luminous, but you are an extraordinary conductor of light."

Diego had been surprised that Gladstone wanted to lock them in the library. He'd never thought of it as a particularly secure room. Once they were both inside, Diego stripped of his weapons and stele, and the solid oak door had been locked behind them, Diego began to realize the advantages the library had as a prison.

The walls were thick and there were only a few sturdy windows that overlooked the deadly drop to the lake. Most of the light came in through the massive glass ceiling many feet up. The sheer walls made it impossible to climb up and break it, and nothing in the room yielded a useful weapon—they could throw books, Diego supposed, or try to flip the tables, but he didn't figure that would do much good.

He stalked over to where Kieran sat slumped at the foot of the massive tree that grew up out of the floor. If only it reached up high enough to get to the ceiling, Diego thought.

Kieran was hunched against the trunk. He had jammed the palms of his hands into his eyes, as if he could blind himself.

"Are you all right?" Diego said.

Kieran dropped his hands. "I am sorry." He looked up at Diego, who could see the marks of Kieran's palms against his cheekbones.

"It's fine. You were injured. I can look for ways out by myself," Diego said, deliberately misunderstanding him.

"No, I mean I am *sorry*," Kieran choked out. "I *cannot*."

"You cannot what?"

"Get away from it. I feel guilt like a curtain of thorns in which I am entangled. Every which way I turn I am pierced again."

The pool makes you feel every hurt you have ever caused others. "We are none of us without guilt," said Diego, and he thought of his family, of Cristina. "Every one of us has hurt another, inadvertently or not."

"You do not understand." Kieran was shaking his head. A lock of hair fell across his forehead, silver darkening to blue. "When I was in the Hunt, I was a straw floating in wind or water. All I could do was clutch at other straws. I believed I had no effect in the world. That I mattered so little I could neither help nor harm." He tensed his hands into fists. "Now I have felt the pain that was Emma's and the sorrow that was Mark's, the pain of everyone I harmed in the Hunt, even Erec's pain as he died. But how could I have been the person who caused such pain when I am someone whose actions are written in water?"

His eyes, black and silver, were haunted. Diego said, "Kieran. You have not only caused pain in this world. It is just that the pool does not show good, only hurt."

"How do you know?" Kieran cried. "We are but barely acquainted, you and I—"

"Because of Cristina," said Diego. "Cristina had faith in you. True faith, unblemished and unbroken. Why do you think I agreed to hide you here? Because she believed you were good, and I believed in her."

He stopped before he could say too much, but Kieran had already winced at the mention of Cristina. His next question puzzled Diego. "How can I face her again?" he said.

"Do you care that much what she thinks?" Diego said. It hadn't occurred to him that Kieran might. Surely he couldn't know Cristina that well.

"More than you might imagine or guess," Kieran said. "How did you ever face her again, after you engaged yourself to Zara and broke her heart?"

"Really?" Diego was stung. "We need to bring this up now?"

Kieran looked at him with wild eyes. Diego sighed. "Yes, I disappointed Cristina and I lost her regard—you must understand what that is like. To have let down someone you loved. To have disappointed yourself."

"Maybe not exactly," said Kieran, with a shadow of his old wryness. "Nobody calls me Perfect Kieran."

"I don't call *myself* Perfect Diego!" Diego protested, feeling that the conversation had degenerated. "Nobody would call themselves that!"

There was a noise at the door. Both of them turned, poised for danger, but as it swung open Diego was shocked to see Divya on the threshold.

She looked as if she'd been in a fight. Scratched and bloody, she held up the key. "I got it from Gladstone in the infirmary chaos," she said. "I doubt we have much time before he notices it's gone."

Diego stalked past her and opened the library door a crack. The corridor was empty. "What's happening? Where's Rayan?"

"Trying to see what the others know, the ones who came from Alicante and *aren't* in the Cohort. Everyone's steles have been confiscated. Zara Portaled back to Idris right after you took Kieran away. And Gladstone's in the infirmary with Samantha," said Divya. "She won't stop screaming." She bit her lip. "It's really bad."

Kieran had risen to his feet, though he was still using the tree to support himself. "You two should run," he said. "Get out of here. It's me they want, and you have put yourselves in enough danger on my account."

Divya gave him a wry look. "By the Angel, he's all self-sacrificing now he fell in that pool. Faerie, you haven't caused *me* any harm. We're fine."

"I made you worry and feel fear," said Kieran, gazing at her with a look both haunting and haunted. "You were afraid of what might happen to you and the others, retaliation for hiding me. You feared for Rayan." He glanced at Diego. "And you—"

"No." Diego held up a hand. "I don't want to hear about my feelings."

"Said every man ever," Divya quipped, but her eyes were overly bright. "Look, there's more I need to tell you. And you should both hear it. I heard Zara laughing with Gladstone in the infirmary before they brought Samantha in. The Inquisitor sent two Shadowhunters on a suicide mission to Faerie to find the Black Volume."

"Jace and Clary?" said Diego, puzzled. "That's not a suicide mission."

"Not them. Emma and Julian Blackthorn. They left yesterday."

"They would never agree to a suicide mission," said Kieran. "Julian would not leave his brothers and sisters. *Never.*"

"They don't *know* it's a suicide mission—Dearborn sent someone to follow them and kill them before they can come back."

"That's against the Law." It was all Diego could think of to say, and he immediately felt ridiculous.

"Horace Dearborn doesn't care about your Laws," said Kieran. His cheeks were flushed darkly with color. "He cares for nothing beyond furthering his own purpose. To him a Nephilim who doesn't agree with him is no better than a Downworlder. They are all vermin to be destroyed."

"Kieran's right," said Divya. "He's the Inquisitor, Diego. He's going to change all the Laws—change them so he can do whatever he wants."

"We must go," said Kieran. "There is not a moment to lose. We must tell the Blackthorns—Mark and Cristina—"

"All the exits are guarded," said Divya. "I'm not saying it's impossible, but we're going to need Rayan and Gen and the others. We can't fight the Cohort alone. Especially not without steles. We'll need to plan—"

"We do not have time to plan—" Kieran began.

Diego thought suddenly of Cristina, of the way she'd written about Kieran in her letter asking Diego to hide him. The fascination she'd had with faeries even when she was a little girl, the way she'd cried when the Cold Peace was passed, telling Diego over and over the faeries were good, their powers part of the blessed magic of the world.

"Kieran," Diego said sharply. "You are a prince of Faerie. *Be* a prince of Faerie."

Kieran gave him a wild, dark look. His breath was ragged. Divya glanced at Diego as if to say *what are you doing?* just as Kieran reached up to seize a branch of the tree.

He closed his black and silver eyes. His face was a pale mask. His jaw tightened even as the leaves on the tree began to rustle, as if in a high wind. It was as if the tree were calling out.

"What's happening?" whispered Divya.

Light crackled up and down the tree—not lightning, but pure bright sparks. It circled Kieran as if he were outlined in gold paint. His hair had turned an odd gold-green, something Diego had never seen before.

"Kieran—" Diego started.

Kieran threw his hands up. His eyes were still closed; words poured from his mouth, a language Diego had never heard. He wished Cristina were here. Cristina could translate. Kieran was shouting; Diego thought he heard the word "Windspear" repeated.

Windspear? thought Diego. *Isn't that—?*

"There are people coming!" Divya cried. She ran to the door of the library, slammed it closed, and locked it, but she was shaking her head. "There are way too many of them. Diego—"

The glass ceiling exploded. Both Diego and Divya gasped.

A white horse crashed through the ceiling. A *flying* white horse, proud and beautiful. Glass sprayed and Diego dived under a nearby table, dragging Divya with him. Kieran opened his eyes; he reached up in welcome as Windspear sliced through the air, swift as an arrow, light as thistledown.

"By the Angel," Divya whispered. "God, I used to love ponies when I was little."

Kieran vaulted himself up onto Windspear's back. His hair had gone back to its more normal blue-black, but he was still crackling with energy. His hands threw sparks as he moved. He reached out toward Diego, who scrambled out from under the table, Divya beside him, their boots crunching on shattered glass.

"Come with me," Kieran called. The room was full of wind and cold, the smell of the Carpathians and lake water. Above them, the broken window opened out onto a sky full of stars. "You will not be safe here."

But Divya shook her head. Crushing down the longing to escape that rose inside him, Diego did the same. "We will stay and fight," he called. "We are Shadowhunters. We cannot all flee and leave only the worst of us to seize power. We must resist."

Kieran hesitated, just as the library door burst open. Gladstone and a dozen Cohort members swarmed in, their eyes widening.

"Stop him!" Gladstone shouted, throwing an arm out toward Kieran. "Manuel—Anush—"

"Kieran, *go*!" Diego roared, and Kieran seized Windspear's mane; they exploded into the air before Manuel could do more than take a step forward. Diego thought he saw Kieran look back at him once before Windspear cleared the ceiling and they shimmered into a white streak across the sky.

Diego heard someone step up behind him. Across the room, Divya was looking at him. There were tears in her eyes. Behind her, her cousin Anush was cuffing her hands.

"You're going to be so sorry you did this," Manuel said, his delighted whisper rasping in Diego's ear. "So very sorry, Rocio Rosales."

And then there was only darkness.

Emma was taken up behind Nene on her gray palfrey, while Julian rode behind Fergus, so there was no chance to talk. Frustration churned in Emma as they rode along under the green trees, the golden spears of light that drove down through the gaps in the trees turning to a deeper bronze as the day wore on.

She wanted to talk to Julian, wanted to make a plan for what they were going to do when they reached the Seelie Court. What would they say to the Queen? How would they get out again? What did they want from her?

But part of her was also too angry to talk to Julian—how dare he keep a massive part of their plan from her? Let her walk blind into Faerie, believing they had one mission when apparently they had another? And a smaller, colder part of her said: *The only reason he wouldn't tell you was if he knew you'd refuse to go along with his plan.* Whatever the plan was, Emma wasn't going to like it.

And down even deeper, where she barely had the words for what she felt, she knew that if it weren't for the spell, Julian would never have done this, because she had never been one of the people Julian manipulated and lied to. She was family, inside the protected circle, and because of that she had forgiven the lies, the plans, because they hadn't been directed at her. They'd been directed at the enemies of the family. The Julian who had to lie and manipulate was a persona created by a frightened child to protect the people he loved. But what if the spell had made the persona real? What if that was who Julian was now?

They had left the forest behind and were in a place of green fields that showed no sign of habitation. Just waving green grass for miles, starred with patches of blue and purple flowers, and dim violet mountains in the distance. A hill rose up in front of them like a green tidal wave, and Emma chanced a glance at Julian as the front of the hill rose like a portcullis, revealing a massive marble entryway.

Things in Faerie rarely looked the same twice, Emma knew; the last time they'd entered the Seelie Court through a hill, they'd found themselves in a narrow corridor. Now they rode under an elegant bronze gate boasting scrollwork of prancing horses. Nene and Fergus dismounted, and it was only after Emma had slid to the marble floor that she saw that both horses' reins had been taken up by diminutive fluttering faeries with outspread wings of blue and red and gold.

The horses clopped off, led by the buzzing pixies. "I could use one of those to do my hair in the morning," said Emma to Nene, who gave her an unreadable smile. It was unnerving how much Nene looked like Mark—the same curling white-blond hair and narrow bones.

Fergus narrowed his eyes. "My son is married to a diminutive pixie," he said. "Please do not ask any intrusive questions about it."

Julian raised his eyebrows but said nothing. He and Emma fell into step beside each other as they followed Nene and Fergus from the marble-clad room into an earth-packed corridor that twisted into the hill.

"I guess everything went according to your plan, didn't it," Emma said coldly, not looking at Julian. She could feel him beside her, though, the familiar warmth and shape of him. Her *parabatai*, who she would have known deafened and blindfolded. "If you're lying about having the Black Volume, it's going to go badly for both of us."

"I'm not lying," he said. "There was a copy shop near the London Institute. You'll see."

"We weren't supposed to *leave* the Institute, Julian—"

"This was the best option," said Julian. "You may be too sentimental to see it clearly, but this gets us closest to what we want."

"How does it do that?" Emma hissed. "What's the point of coming to the Seelie Queen? We can't trust her, any more than we can trust Horace or Annabel."

Julian's eyes glittered like the precious stones set into the walls of the long tunnel. They gleamed in stripes of jasper and quartz. The ground underfoot had become polished tile, a milky green-white. "Not trusting the Queen is part of my plan."

Emma wanted to kick a wall. "You shouldn't have a plan that includes the Queen at all, don't you get it? We're all dealing with the Cold Peace because of her treachery."

"Such anti-faerie sentiments," Julian said, ducking under a gray curtain of lace. "I'm surprised at you."

Emma stalked after him. "It's nothing to do with faeries in general. But the Queen is a no-holds-barred bit—why hello, Your Majesty!"

Oh crap. It seemed that the gray curtain they'd passed through was the entrance to the Queen's Court. The Queen herself was seated in the middle of the room, on her throne, regarding Emma coldly.

The chamber looked as it had before, as if a fire had swept through the room years ago and no one had truly cleaned up the damage. The floor was blackened, cracked marble. The Queen's throne was tarnished bronze, the back of it rising high above her head in a fan-shaped scroll. The walls were gouged here and there, as if a massive beast had dug out clots of marble with its claws.

The Queen was flame and bone. Her bony clavicles rose from the bodice of her intricately figured blue-and-gold dress; her long bare arms were thin as sticks. All around her tumbled her rich, deep red hair in thick waves of blood and fire. From her narrow white face, blue eyes blazed like gas flames.

Emma cleared her throat. "The Queen is a no-holds-barred bit of sunshine," she said. "That's what I was going to say."

"You will not greet me in that informal manner, Emma Carstairs," she said. "Do you understand?"

"They were waylaid on the road and attacked," said Nene. "We sent pixie messengers ahead to tell you—"

"I heard," said the Queen. "That does not excuse rudeness."

"I think the blond one was about to call the Queen a besom," Fergus murmured to Nene, who looked as exasperated as faerie courtiers ever looked.

"So true," said Emma.

"Kneel," snapped the Queen. "Kneel, Emma Carstairs and Julian Blackthorn, and show proper respect."

Emma felt her chin go up as if it had been pulled on a string. "We are Nephilim," she said. "We do not kneel."

"Because once the Nephilim were giants on earth, with the strength of a thousand men?" The Queen's tone was gently mocking. "How the mighty have fallen."

Julian took a step toward the throne. The Queen's eyes raked him up and down, assessing, measuring. "Would you rather an empty gesture or something you truly want?" he asked.

The Queen's blue eyes flashed. "You are suggesting you have something I truly want? Think carefully. It is not easy to guess what a monarch desires."

"I have the Black Volume of the Dead," Julian said.

The Queen laughed. "I had heard you had lost that," she said. "Along with the life of your sister."

Julian whitened, but his expression didn't change. "You never specified which copy of the Black Volume you wanted." As the Queen and Emma both stared, he reached into his pack and pulled out a bound white manuscript. Holes were punched into the left side, the whole thing held together with thick plastic ties.

The Queen sat back, her flame-red hair brilliant against the dark metal of her throne. "That is not the Black Volume."

"I think you will find if you examine the pages that it is," said Julian. "A book is the words it contains, nothing more. I took photos of every page of the Black Volume with my phone and had it printed and bound at a copy shop."

The Queen tilted her head, and the thin gold circle binding her brow flashed. "I do not understand the words of your mortal spells and rituals," she said. Her voice had risen to a sharp pitch. Behind her sometimes mocking, sometimes laughing eyes, Emma thought she caught a glimpse of the true Queen, and what would happen if one crossed her, and she felt chilled. "I will not be tricked or mocked, Julian Blackthorn, and I do not trust your mischief. Nene, take the book from him and examine it!"

Nene stepped forward and held out her hand. In the shadowy corners of the room, there was movement; Emma realized the walls were lined with faerie guards in gray uniforms. No wonder they'd allowed her and Julian to enter still carrying their weapons. There must be fifty guards here, and more in the tunnels.

Let Nene have the book, Julian, she thought, and indeed, he handed it over without a murmur. He watched calmly as Nene looked it over, her eyes flicking over the pages. At last she said, "This was made by a very skilled calligrapher. The brushstrokes are exactly as I remember."

"A skilled calligrapher named OfficeMax," Julian muttered, but Emma didn't smile at him.

The Queen was silent for a long time. The tapping of her slipper-shod foot was the only sound in the room as they all waited for her to speak. At last she said, "This is not the first time you have presented me with a perplexing issue, Julian Blackthorn, and I suspect it will not be the last."

"It shouldn't be perplexing," said Julian. "It's the Black Volume. And you said if we gave you the Black Volume, you would help us."

"Not quite," said the Queen. "I recall making promises, but some may no longer be relevant."

"I am asking you to remember that you promised us aid," said Julian. "I am asking you to help us find Annabel Blackthorn here in Faerie."

"We're already here to find her," Emma said. "We don't need this—this—person's help." She glared at the Queen.

"We have a map that barely works," said Julian. "The Queen will have spies all over Faerie. It could take us weeks to find Annabel. We could wander in Faerie forever while our food runs out. The Queen could lead us right to her. Nothing happens in this realm she doesn't know about."

The Queen smirked. "And what do you want of Annabel when you find her? The second Black Volume?"

"Yes," said Julian. "You can keep this copy. I need to take the original Black Volume back with me to Idris to prove to the Clave that it's no longer in the hands of Annabel Blackthorn." He paused. "And I want revenge. Pure and simple revenge."

"There is nothing simple about vengeance, and nothing pure," said the Queen, but her eyes glittered with interest.

If the Queen knew so much, why didn't she just go kill Annabel and take the Black Volume? Emma wondered. Because of the involvement of the Unseelie Court? But she kept her mouth shut—it was clear she and Julian were in no way in agreement on the Queen.

"Before, you wished for an army," said the Queen. "Now you only want me to find Annabel for you?"

"It's a better bargain for you," said Julian, and Emma noticed that he hadn't said "yes." He wanted more than this from the Queen.

"Perhaps, but I will not be the final word on this volume's merit," said the Queen. "I must have an expert agree first. And you must remain in the Court until that is done."

"No!" Emma said. "We will not stay an unspecified amount of time in Faerie." She spun on Julian. "That's how they get you! Unspecified amounts of time!"

"I will watch over the two of you," said Nene unexpectedly. "For the sake of Mark. I will watch over you and make sure no harm comes to you."

The Queen shot Nene an unfriendly look before returning her gaze to Emma and Julian. "What do you say?"

"I'm not sure," Julian said. "We paid a high price for this book in blood and loss. To be told to wait—"

"Oh, very well," said the Queen, and in her eyes Emma saw an odd light of eagerness. Perhaps she was more desperate for the book than Emma had thought? "As a sign of my good faith, I will give you part of what I promised. I will tell you, Julian, how certain bonds might be broken. But I will not tell *her*." She gestured at Emma. "That was not part of the bargain."

Emma heard him inhale sharply. Julian's feelings for her might be deadened, she thought, but for whatever reason he still wanted this desperately. The knowledge of how their bond might be dissolved. Perhaps it was an atavistic want, as he had described his desire to protect Ty—a deep-rooted need for survival?

"Nene," said the Queen. "Please escort Emma to the room she inhabited the last time she was a guest of the Court."

Fergus groaned. It had been his bedroom Emma and Julian had slept in previously.

Nene approached the Queen, placed the copy of the Black Volume at her feet, and backed away to stand at Emma's side.

The Queen smiled with her red lips. "Julian and I will remain here, and speak in private," she said. "Guards, you may leave me. Leave us."

"I don't need to," Emma said. "I know what this is about. Breaking all *parabatai* bonds. We don't need to hear about it. It's not going to happen."

The Queen's gaze was scornful. "Little fool," she said. "You probably think you are protecting something sacred. Something good."

"I know it's something you wouldn't understand," Emma said.

"What would you say," said the Queen, "if I said to you: There is a corruption at the heart of the bond of *parabatai*. A poison. A darkness in it that mirrors its goodness. There is a reason *parabatai* cannot fall in love, and it is monstrous beyond all you could imagine." Her mouth shimmered like a poisoned apple as she smiled. "The *parabatai* rune was not given to you by the Angel but by men, and men are flawed. David the Silent and Jonathan Shadowhunter created the rune and the ceremony. Do you imagine that carries no consequences?"

It was true, and Emma knew it. The *parabatai* rune was not in the Gray Book. But neither was the Alliance rune Clary had created, and that was regarded as a universal good.

The Queen was twisting the truth to suit herself, as she always did. Her eyes, fixed on Emma's, were shards of blue ice. "I see you do not understand," she said. "But you will."

Before Emma could protest, Nene took her arm. "Come," she murmured. "While the Queen is still in a good mood."

Emma glanced at Julian. He hadn't moved from where he was, his back rigid, his gaze fixed firmly on the Queen. Emma knew she should say something. Protest, tell him not to listen to the Queen's trickster words, tell him that there was no way, no matter what was at stake, that they could justify the shattering of every *parabatai* bond in the world.

Even if it would free them. Even if it would give Julian back to her.

She couldn't force the words out. She walked out of the Queen's chamber beside Nene without another word.

10
Many a Marvellous Shrine

The sight of the Shadow Market sent a punch of familiarity through Kit's chest. It was a typical Los Angeles night—the temperature had dropped as soon as the sun set, and a cool wind blew through the empty lot where the Market was, making the dozens of faerie bells that hung from the corners of white-canopied booths chime.

Ty had been full of suppressed excitement all the way there in the back of the Uber car, which he'd dealt with by pushing up the sleeve of Kit's shirt and giving him several runes. Kit had three of them: Night Vision, Agility, and one called Talent, which Ty told him would make him more persuasive. Now they were standing at the circumference of the Market, having been dropped off in Kendall Alley. They were both dressed as mundanely as possible, in jeans, zip-front jackets, and Frye boots.

But Ty was still visibly a Shadowhunter. He held himself like one, and he walked like one and looked like one, and there were even runes visible on the delicate skin of his neck and wrists. And bruises, too—all over the sides of his hands, the kind no mundane boy would have any business getting unless he was in an illegal fight club.

It wouldn't have mattered if he could have covered them up, though. Shadowhunters seemed to bleed their angel heritage through their pores. Kit wondered if he himself did yet.

"I don't see any gates," Ty said, craning his head.

"The gates are—metaphysical. Not exactly real," Kit explained. They were walking toward the section of the Market where potions and charms were sold. A booth covered in tumbling roses in shades of red and pink and white sold love charms. One with a green-and-white awning sold luck and good fortune, and a pearly gray stand hung with curtains of lace, providing privacy, sold more dangerous items. Necromancy and death magic were both forbidden at the Market, but the rules had never been strictly enforced.

A phouka was leaning against the post of a nearby streetlamp, smoking a cigarette. Behind him, the lanes of the Market looked like small, glowing streets, enticing Kit with calls of "Come buy!" Voices clamored, jewelry clinked and rattled, spice and incense perfumed the air. Kit felt a longing mixed with anxiety—he cut a quick sideways glance toward Ty. They hadn't entered the Market yet; was Ty thinking about how much he'd hated the London Market, how it had made him sweat and panic with too much noise, too much light, too much pressure, too much everything?

He wanted to ask Ty if he was all right, but he knew the other boy wouldn't want it. Ty was staring at the Market, tense with curiosity. Kit turned to the phouka.

"Gatekeeper," he said. "We request entrance to the Shadow Market."

Ty's gaze snapped to attention. The phouka was tall, dark, and thin, with bronze and gold strands threaded through his long hair. He wore purple trousers and no shoes. The lamppost he leaned against was between two stalls, neatly blocking the way into the Market.

"Kit Rook," said the phouka. "What a compliment it is, to still be recognized by one who has left us to dwell among the angels."

"He knows you," muttered Ty.

"Everyone in the Shadow Market knows me," said Kit, hoping Ty would be impressed.

The phouka stubbed out his cigarette. It released a sickly sweet smell of charred herbs. "Password," he said.

"I'm not saying that," said Kit. "You think it's funny to try to make people say that."

"Say what? What's the password?" Ty demanded.

The phouka grinned. "Wait here, Kit Rook," he said, and melted back into the shadows of the Market.

"He's going to get Hale," said Kit, trying to hide the signs of his nerves.

"Can they see us?" Ty said. He was looking into the Shadow Market, where clusters of Downworlders, witches and other assorted members of the magical underworld, moved among the clamor. "Out here?"

It was like standing outside a lighted room in the dark, Kit thought. And though Ty might not express it that way, Kit suspected he felt the same.

"If they can, they'd never show it," he said.

Ty turned toward him suddenly. His gaze slipped over Kit's ear, his cheekbone, not quite meeting his eyes. "Watson—"

"Kit Rook and Ty Blackthorn," snapped a voice out of the shadows. It was Barnabas Hale, head of the Market. "Actually, I'm assuming you're not actually Kit Rook and Ty Blackthorn, because they'd never be stupid enough to show up here."

"That seemed like a compliment," said Ty, who looked honestly surprised.

"Sure, maybe it's not us," said Kit. "Maybe someone just got the specifications for the candygram you ordered wildly off."

Hale frowned in annoyance. He looked as he always had: short and scaly-skinned, with a snake's slit-pupiled eyes. He wore a pin-striped suit that Kit assumed must have been heavily altered to fit. Most humans weren't three feet tall and three feet wide.

The phouka had returned with Hale. Silently, he leaned against the lamppost again, his dark eyes glittering.

"Prove you're Kit Rook," said Hale. "What's the password?"

"I'm still not saying it. I'm never going to say it," said Kit.

"What is it?" Ty demanded.

"Just let us in," said Kit. "We don't want any trouble."

Hale barked a laugh. "You don't want trouble? You two? You've got to be kidding me. Do you know what kind of mayhem you caused in London? You wrecked property, attacked vendors, and you"—he pointed at Ty—"destroyed a great deal of fey stock. I hate you both. Go away."

"Hear me out," Kit said. "Remember when that faerie burned half the Market down and was welcomed back the next year because she had a bumper crop of hen's teeth? Remember the werewolf and the llama and how that turned out? And he wasn't banned, because he had a line on a supply of *yin fen*."

"What's your point?" said Hale. He sighed. "God, I wish I had a cigar. Had to quit."

"The spirit of the Market is simple," said Kit. "Everything's okay as long as you make a profit. Right?"

"Sure," said Hale. "And that's why we tolerated Johnny Rook. We tolerated you because the Shadowhunters hadn't found you yet. But now they have and it's a hop, skip, and a jump until you find out who you really are—"

"What's that supposed to mean?" said Ty. The wind had picked up and was blowing his dark hair like streamers.

"Nothing for free," Hale said, with the annoyance of a man who'd said too much, and who also wanted a cigar and couldn't have one. "Besides, your money is no good here, Rook." He waved a hand in Ty's direction. "I might be able to get something in exchange for your skinny friend in the right circles, but not enough."

"Theoretically, how much?" asked Ty with interest.

Hale looked grim. "Not as good a price as I could get for Emma Carstairs—even more for just her head."

Ty blanched. Kit felt it, Ty's recollection that the Market was, in fact, truly dangerous. That it was all truly dangerous.

Kit felt the situation was getting away from him. "No heads. Look, my father didn't trust anyone, Mr. Hale. You know that. He hid his most precious items all over Los Angeles, buried in places he thought no one would ever find them."

"I'm listening," said Hale.

Kit knew this was the risky part. "One is right here in the Shadow Market. A ruby-encrusted copy of the Red Scrolls of Magic."

The phouka whistled, long and low.

"Not only will I give it to you, I'll give it to you for free," said Kit. "All you have to do is let us back into the Shadow Market. Free trade."

Hale shook his head in regret. "Now I really wish I had a cigar, so I could celebrate," he said. "I already found that, you stupid brat. We dug up your dad's stall after the Mantids killed him." He turned away, then paused, glancing back over his shoulder. The moonlight seemed to bounce off his white, scaled skin. "You're out of your depth, kids. Get out of Downworld before someone kills you. That person could even be me."

A forked tongue shot from between his teeth and licked his lips. Kit started back, revolted, as Hale melted into the Market and was swallowed up by the crowds.

Kit couldn't look at Ty. He felt as if the air had been knocked out of him, shock and shame warring for an equal chance to turn his stomach. "I . . . ," he began.

"You should have just given the password," said the phouka.

Out of patience, Kit slowly raised his middle finger. "Here's the password."

Ty muffled a laugh and grabbed Kit's sleeve. "Come on," he said. "Let's get out of here."

"I am proud to announce," said Horace Dearborn, "that the proposed Downworld Registry is ready to become a reality."

The sound that went through the rows of Nephilim seated in the Council Hall was hard to decipher. To Diana it sounded like the roar of an animal driving another hungry beast away from its prey.

Horace stood with his hands folded behind his back, a toneless smirk on his face. At his left stood Zara, in full Centurion regalia, her hair braided in a crown around her head. At his right was Manuel, his expression carefully blank, his eyes dancing with malice. They looked like a horrible mockery of a family portrait.

"All Institutes will have a short amount of time to register their local Downworlders," said Horace. "The heads of Institutes must meet a quota of registrations, based on our knowledge of local Downworld populations, in the first weeks this Law takes effect."

Diana sat, letting the words wash over her in waves of horror. She couldn't help but look at Jia, who occupied a tall wooden seat at the edge of the dais. Her face was a strained mask. Diana couldn't help but wonder if this was more extreme even than what Jia had feared Horace might propose.

"And if Downworlders refuse?" called someone from the audience.

"Then they will have their protections under the Accords stripped from them," Zara said, and Diana went cold all over. No Accords protection meant a Shadowhunter could kill a Downworlder in the street for no reason, and there would be no consequences. "We understand this will be a great burden of work on Institutes, but it is important that everyone cooperate, for the good of all Shadowhunters."

"Each Downworlder registered will be given a number," said Horace. "If a Downworlder is stopped by a Shadowhunter for any reason, anywhere, they can be asked for this number."

The noise in the room was decidedly more worried now.

"Think of it as a sort of identification card," said Manuel. "Safety and accountability are two of our chief concerns."

"I want to hear from the Consul!" shouted Carmen Rosales Delgado, head of the Mexico City Institute, from the audience. She was Cristina's mother, and looked more than a little bit like her daughter.

Horace looked annoyed; technically, as the one proposing a new Law, he had the floor and could speak for a certain number of minutes uninterrupted. Diana felt that he had already been speaking for several years.

He gestured ungraciously toward Jia, who gripped the arms of her chair tightly. "It is my opinion that this Law is not a good idea," she said. "Downworlders will resist what they will see to be a major overreach on the part of the Nephilim. It establishes an atmosphere of mistrust."

"That's because we don't trust them," said Manuel. There was a gale of laughter from the back of the room.

Diana could stand it no longer. She rose to her feet. "I have a question for the Inquisitor!"

Horace looked at her with hooded eyes. "We will take questions and comments later, *Diana*."

Diana didn't like the emphasis he put on her name. As if he found it distasteful. Probably Zara had told her father a pack of lies about Diana; Diana had once humiliated Zara in front of her fellow Centurions. Narcissists like Zara didn't forget insults.

"Let her speak," said Jia. "Everyone on the Council has a voice."

Intensely aware of the eyes on her, Diana said, "This may seem like a small action, but it's not going to seem small to Downworlders.

It will have repercussions. Even if the Registry is temporary, there will always be reasons to continue it. It is far harder to dismantle this sort of structure than it is to build it. We could face a situation where Downworlders insist that Shadowhunters also be registered, for parity. Are you prepared to have *Nephilim* carry their papers everywhere with them?"

This had the desired effect. The Council burst into angry buzzing. "No! Never!" Dearborn snapped.

"Then this effectively creates an underclass of Downworlders," said Diana. "We will have rights that they don't. Think about that."

"And why are you so bothered by that idea, Diana Wrayburn?" said Manuel in his soft, charming voice. His eyes glittered like marbles. "Is there a Downworlder, perhaps dear to you, that you worry will be affected?"

"Many Shadowhunters have Downworlders that are dear to them," said Diana evenly. "You cannot cleanly sever us from a group of human beings who have more in common with us than mundanes do."

Diana knew the answer to that: *We're not afraid of mundanes. It's Downworlders we fear, and we seek to control what we fear.* But it was unlikely Horace had that kind of self-awareness. He glared at her with open loathing as she took her seat.

"This is clearly a complex issue," said Jia, rising to her feet. "I suggest we stay this vote for a week until the Council has had time to come to terms with *all* its ramifications."

Horace transferred his glare to her, but said nothing. The Council was now a hum of relief, and even Horace Dearborn knew better than to fly directly in the face of popular opinion during a vote. He stayed on the dais as the meeting was dismissed, his supporters flocking around him in a thick crowd.

Feeling inexpressibly weary, Diana made for one of the exits. She felt as if she had been called to witness a bloody execution only to see the victim spared for a week. Relief mixed with fear of what the future would bring.

"Diana!" said a light, accented voice behind her. Diana turned to see one of the women from the Barcelona Institute—Trini Castel—approach her. She put a birdlike hand on Diana's arm.

"I was inspired by what you said, Miss Wrayburn," she said. "You are correct that rights—anyone's rights—are not to be discarded lightly."

"Thank you," said Diana, more than a little surprised. Trini Castel gave her a quick smile and scurried away, leaving Diana with a clear view of the dais.

Zara stood at its edge, her gaze fixed on Diana. In the pale light filtering through the window, the naked hatred on her face—far more than anyone might feel over a past insult—was clear as day. Shuddering, Diana turned and hurried from the Hall.

Catarina's suspicious confluence of ley lines turned out to be in a small desert park near the Antelope Valley Freeway, famous for its massive sandstone formations. Both Helen and Aline seemed faintly surprised that Mark and Cristina were planning to go out on patrol, but they hadn't done anything to stop them, as if they reluctantly acknowledged that patrolling was a normal part of Shadowhunter life, and the sooner everyone got back to normal life, the better.

The drive from Malibu—they'd taken Diana's truck, which had been left in the parking lot of the Institute—reminded Cristina of long ambling road trips she'd taken with Emma. Windows down in the truck, music playing low on the speakers, beach turning to highway turning to desert as the sun went down in a haze of fire. Mark had his long legs up on the dashboard and would sometimes turn his head to look at her as they rolled along in silence; the weight of his gaze felt like skin against her skin. Like a touch.

The Vasquez Rocks park closed at sunset, and the dirt parking lot was empty when Cristina cruised the truck into it and turned off the engine. They collected their weapons from the bed of the truck, snapping on wrist protectors and buckling weapons belts. Cristina strapped a longsword and her trusted balisong to her belt, while Mark found a runed black whip and cracked it a few times. He wore a look of pleasure on his face as it snaked across the darkening sky.

They had runed themselves before they left. Cristina could see Mark's Night Vision rune gleaming black against his throat as they passed under the lights of the ranger station and crossed onto a dirt path that wound through scrub among rocks that twisted and folded like envelopes.

Cristina breathed deeply. Of all the things she loved about California, she loved the scent of the desert the most: clear air mixed with juniper, manzanita, and sage. The sky opened above them like a secret told, scattered with a million stars.

They passed a wooden sign for a trail just as a massive rock formation rose ahead of them, nearly blocking out the moon. "The ley line confluence," Mark said, pointing.

Cristina didn't ask him how he knew; faeries had a sense for such things. They moved closer to the rocks, which rose above them in tilted slabs, like the remains of a spaceship that had crashed into the sand. Cristina's boots crunched on the sand, the sound loud in her ears thanks to her Audio rune.

A sharp, insect-like sound buzzed behind her. She turned. Mark was frowning at the Sensor in his hand. "It's making a buzzing noise, but not one I've heard before," he said.

Cristina turned around slowly. The desert stretched around her, a carpet of black and brown and dim gold. The sky was dark velvet. "I don't see anything."

"We should wait here," said Mark. "See if it happens again."

Cristina was in no mood to hang around under the romantic moon with Mark. "I think we should keep moving."

"Cristina," Mark said. "You seem wroth with me."

Cristina rolled her eyes. "Nothing gets by you, Mark Blackthorn."

Mark lowered the Sensor. "Last night—It wasn't that I didn't want to—I *did* want to—"

Cristina blushed furiously. "It's not that, Mark," she said. "You can want to or not want to. It's your business. It was that you lied."

"Humans lie," he said, his bicolored eyes suddenly blazing. "Mortals lie to each other every day, especially in matters of love. Is it that my lie wasn't good enough? Should I be more practiced?"

"No!" She whirled on him. "I like that you don't lie, Mark. It is why I was so—Mark, can't you understand? I didn't expect you to lie to me."

"You saw me lie to Kieran," he said.

"Yes, but that was to save lives," she said. "Unless you're telling me that you not wanting to have sex with me has something to do with saving lives, which I find hard to believe—"

"I did want to!" Mark exploded. "One thing you must understand—I did want to be with you in that way, and all ways, and that is not a lie."

Cristina sank down on a low rock. Her heart was pounding. And she'd just said the word "sex," which horribly embarrassed her. "Then I don't understand why you did it," she said in a small voice. "Were you trying to spare someone? Kieran?"

"I was trying to spare you," he said, his voice dark and hard, like late-winter ice.

"Spare me what?"

"You know who you are!" he cried, startling her. She looked up at him, not understanding—it was not as if she were a stranger, to him or to anyone. What did he mean? "Kieran called you a princess of the Nephilim, and rightly," he said. The moon was out fully, and the silver-white light illuminated his hair like a halo. It illuminated his eyes, too—wide and gold and blue and full of pain. "You are one of the best examples of our people I have ever known—shining, righteous, virtuous. You are all the good things I can think of, and all the things I would like to be and know I never can. I do not want you to do anything that later you would regret. I do not want you to later realize how far down from your standards you reached, when you reached for me."

"*Mark!*" She bolted up from the rock and went over to him. She heard a thump as something hit the ground, and threw her arms around Mark, hugging him tightly.

For a moment he held himself stiff and frozen. Then he softened against her, his arms encircling her body, his lips brushing her cheek, the soft curls of her hair that had escaped from her braid.

"Cristina," he whispered.

She drew back enough to touch his face, her fingers tracing the lines of his cheekbones. His skin had that impossible faerie smoothness that came from never having needed the touch of a razor. "Mark Blackthorn," she said, and shivered deep in her bones at the look in his eyes. "I wish you could see yourself as I see you. You are so many things I never thought to want, but I do want them. I want all things with you."

His arms tightened around her; he gathered her to him as if he were gathering an armful of flowers. His lips skated along her cheek, her jawline; at last their mouths met, burning hot in the cold air, and Cristina gave a little gasp at the desire that shot through her, sharp as an arrowhead.

He tasted like honey and faerie wine. They staggered backward, fetching up against a rock pile. Mark's hands were on her gear jacket; he was undoing it, sliding his hands inside, under her shirt, as if desperate for the touch of her skin. He murmured words like "beautiful" and "perfect" and she smiled and swiped her tongue slowly across his bottom lip, making him gasp as if she had stabbed him. He groaned helplessly and pulled her tighter.

The Sensor buzzed, loud and long.

They sprang apart, gasping. Cristina zipped her jacket with shaking hands as Mark bent awkwardly to seize the Sensor. It buzzed again and they both whirled, staring.

"*No mames,*" she whispered. The buzzer made another, insistent noise, and something hit her hard from the side.

It was Mark. He'd knocked her to the ground; they both rolled sideways over the bumpy, pitted earth as something massive and shadowy rose above them. Black wings spread like ragged shadows. Cristina shoved herself up on her elbow, yanked a runed dagger from her belt, and flung it.

There was a cawing scream. Witchlight lit the sky; Mark was on his knees, a rune-stone in his hand. Above them a massive white-faced demon trailing feathers like a shadowy cloak of rags flapped its wings; the hilt of Cristina's dagger protruded from its chest. Its outline was already beginning to blur as it screeched again, clawing at the hilt with a taloned claw, before folding up like paper and vanishing.

"Harpyia demon," said Mark, leaping to his feet. He reached down to help Cristina up after him. "Probably hiding in the rocks. That's why the Sensor didn't pick it up well."

"We should go." Cristina glanced around. "Judging by the Sensor, there are more."

They began to jog toward the dirt trail, Cristina glancing back over her shoulder to see if anything was following them.

"I just want to make it clear that I did not engineer the interruption of the Harpyia demon," Mark said, "and was indeed eager to continue with our sexual congress."

Cristina sighed. "Good to know." She cut sideways through

some low sagebrush. In the far distance, she could see the metal gleam of the parked truck.

Mark's footsteps slowed. "Cristina. Look."

She glanced around. "I don't see—"

"Look down," he said, and she did.

She remembered thinking that her boots had crunched oddly on the sand. Now she realized that it was because it wasn't sand. A bleak moonscape stretched around them in a twenty-foot radius. The succulent plants and sagebrush were withered, gray-white as old bones. The sand looked as if it had been blasted with wildfire, and the skeletons of jackrabbits and snakes were scattered among the rocks.

"It is the blight," said Mark. "The same blight we saw in Faerie."

"But why would it be here?" Cristina demanded, bewildered. "What do ley lines have to do with the blight? Isn't that faerie magic?"

Mark shook his head. "I don't—"

A chorus of shrieking howls ripped through the air. Cristina spun, kicking up a cloud of dust, and saw shadows rising out of the desert all around them. Now Cristina could see them more closely: They resembled birds only in that they were winged. What looked like feathers were actually trailing black rags that swathed their gaunt white bodies. Their mouths were so stuffed with crooked, jagged teeth that it looked as if they were grotesquely smiling. Their eyes were popping yellow bulbs with black dot pupils.

"But the Sensor," she whispered. "It didn't go off. It didn't—"

"Run," Mark said, and they ran, as the Harpyia demons soared screeching and laughing into the sky. A rock thumped to the ground near Cristina, and another barely missed Mark's head.

Cristina longed to turn and plunge her balisong into the nearest demon, but it was too hard to aim while they were both running. She could hear Mark cursing as he dodged rocks the size of baseballs. One slammed painfully into Cristina's hand as they reached the truck and she jerked the door open; Mark climbed in the other side, and for a moment they sat gasping as rocks pounded down onto the truck's cab like hailstones.

"Diana is not going to be happy about her car," said Mark.

"We have bigger problems." Cristina jammed the keys into the ignition; the truck started with a jerk, rolled backward—and stopped. The sound of the rocks pounding the metal roof had ceased as well, and the silence seemed suddenly eerie. "What's going on?" she demanded, stomping down on the gas.

"Get out!" Mark shouted. "We have to get out!"

He grabbed hold of Cristina's arm, hauling her over the center console. They both tumbled out of the passenger-side door as the truck lifted into the air, Cristina landing awkwardly half on top of Mark.

She twisted around to see that Harpyia demons had seized the truck, their claws puncturing the metal sides of the bed and digging into the window frames. The vehicle sailed into the air, the Harpyia demons shrieking and giggling as they hauled it up into the sky—and dropped it.

It spun end over end and hit the ground with a massive crash of metal and glass, rolling sideways to lie upended on the sand. One of the Harpyia had ridden it down as if it were a surfboard and still crouched, snarking and cackling, on the frame of the upside-down truck.

Cristina leaped to her feet and stalked toward the truck. As she got closer, she could smell the stink of spilling gasoline. The Harpyia, too stupid to realize the danger, turned its dead-white, grinning face toward her. *"The rocks are our place,"* it hissed at her. *"Poisoned. The best place."*

"Cállate!" she snapped, unsheathed her longsword, and sliced off its head.

Ichor exploded upward in a spray even as the Harpyia's body

folded up and winked out of existence. The other demons howled and dived; Cristina saw one of them dive-bombing Mark and screamed his name; he leaped onto a rock and slashed out with his whip. Ichor opened a glowing seam across the Harpyia's chest and it thumped to the sand, chittering, but another Harpyia was already streaking across the sky. Mark's whip curled around its throat and he jerked hard, sending its head bumping like a tumbleweed among the rocks.

Something struck Cristina's back; she screamed as her feet left the ground. A Harpyia had sunk its claws into the back of her gear jacket and was lifting her into the air. She thought of stories about how eagles flew high into the sky with their prey and then released them, letting their bodies smash open on the earth below. The ground was already receding below her with terrifying speed.

With a scream of fear and anger, she slashed up and backward with her sword, slicing the Harpyia's claws off at the joint. The demon shrieked and Cristina tumbled through the air, her sword falling out of her hand, reaching out as if she could catch onto something to slow her fall—

Something seized her out of the sky.

She gasped as a hand caught her elbow, and she was yanked sideways to land awkwardly atop something warm and alive. A flying horse. She gasped and scrabbled for purchase, digging into the creature's mane as it dipped and dived.

"Cristina! Stay still!"

It was Kieran shouting. Kieran was behind her, one arm lashing around her waist to pull her against him. What felt like an electric charge shot through her. Kieran was wild-eyed, his hair deep blue-black, and she realized suddenly that the horse was Windspear, even as the stallion shot downward through the crowd of Harpyia toward Mark.

"Kieran—look out—" she cried, as the Harpyia demons turned

their attention to Windspear, their popping yellow eyes swiveling like flashlights.

Kieran flung his arm out, and Cristina felt the sharp electric charge go through her again. White fire flashed and the Harpyia demons recoiled as Windspear landed lightly in front of Mark.

"Mark! To me!" Kieran shouted. Mark looked over at him and grinned—a Hunter's grin, a battle grin, all teeth—before decapitating a last Harpyia with a jerk of his whip. Splattered with blood and ichor, Mark leaped onto the horse behind Kieran, latching his arms around Kieran's waist. Windspear sprang into the air and the Harpyia followed, their grinning mouths open to show rows of sharklike teeth.

Kieran shouted something in a Faerie language Cristina didn't know, and Windspear tilted up at an impossible angle. The horse shot upward like an arrow, just as the truck below them finally exploded, swallowing the Harpyia demons in a massive corona of flames.

Diana's going to be really angry about her truck, Cristina thought, and slumped down against Windspear's mane as the faerie horse circled below the clouds, turned, and flew toward the ocean.

Kit had never been up on the roof of the Los Angeles Institute before. He had to admit it had a better view than the London Institute, unless you were a sucker for skyscrapers. Here you could see the desert stretching out behind the house, all the way to the mountains. Their tops were touched by light reflected from the city on the other side of the range, their valleys in deep shadow. The sky was brilliant with stars.

In front of the house was the ocean, its immensity terrifying and glorious. Tonight the wind was like light fingers stroking its surface, leaving trails of silver ripples behind.

"You seem sad," said Ty. "Are you?"

They were sitting on the edge of the roof, their legs dangling into empty space. This was probably the way he was supposed to live his high school years, Kit thought, climbing up onto high places, doing dumb and dangerous things that would worry his parents. Only he had no parents to worry, and the dangerous things he was doing were truly dangerous.

He wasn't worried for himself, but he was worried for Ty. Ty, who was looking at him with concern, his gray gaze skating over Kit's face as if it were a book he was having trouble reading.

Yes, I'm sad, Kit thought. *I'm stuck and frustrated. I wanted to impress you at the Shadow Market and I got so caught up in that I forgot about everything else. About how we really shouldn't be doing this. About how I can't tell you we shouldn't be doing this.*

Ty reached out and brushed Kit's hair away from his face, an absent sort of gesture that sent a shot of something through Kit, a feeling like he'd touched a live electrical fence. He stared, and Ty said, "You ought to get your hair cut. Julian cuts Tavvy's hair."

"Julian's not here," said Kit. "And I don't know if I want him cutting my hair."

"He's not bad at it." Ty dropped his hand. "You said your dad had stuff hidden all over Los Angeles. Is there anything that could help us?"

Your dad. As if Julian was Ty's father. Then again, he was in a way. "Nothing necromantic," said Kit.

Ty looked disappointed. Still dizzy from the electric-fence shock, Kit couldn't stand it. He had to fix it, that look on Ty's face. "Look—we tried the straightforward approach. Now we have to try the con."

"I don't really get cons," said Ty. "I read a book about them, but I don't understand how people let themselves get tricked like that."

Kit's eyes dropped to the gold locket around Ty's neck. There was still blood on it. It looked like patches of rust. "It's not about making people believe what you want them to believe. It's about letting them believe what they want to believe. About giving them what they think they need."

Ty raised his eyes; though they didn't meet Kit's, Kit could read the expression in them, the dawning awareness. *Does he realize?* Kit thought, in mingled relief and apprehension.

Ty sprang to his feet. "I have to send a fire-message to Hypatia Vex," he said.

This was not at all what Kit had expected him to say. "Why? She already said no to helping us."

"She did. But Shade says she's always wanted to run the Shadow Market herself." Ty smiled sideways, and in that moment, despite their difference in coloring, he looked like Julian. "It's what she thinks she needs."

The sky was a road and the stars made pathways; the moon was a watchtower, a lighthouse that led you home.

Being on Windspear's back was both utterly strange and utterly familiar to Mark. So was having his arms around Kieran. He had flown through so many skies holding Kieran, and the feeling of Kieran's body against his, the whipcord strength of him, the faint ocean-salt scent of his skin and hair, was mapped into Mark's blood.

At the same time he could hear Cristina, hear her laughing, see her as she bent to point out landmarks flashing by beneath them. She had asked Kieran if they could fly over the Hollywood sign and he had obliged; Kieran, who made a point of being disobliging.

And Mark's heart stirred at her laugh; it stirred as he touched Kieran; he was between them again, as he had been in London, and though agitation prickled his nerves at the thought, he couldn't pretend he wasn't glad to have Kieran back again.

Kieran brought Windspear down in the lot behind the Institute.

Everything was still, broken only by the sound of chirping cicadas. It was hard to believe that ten minutes previously they had been in a fight to the death with Harpyia demons.

"Are you all right?" Cristina said with a frown, as she slid from the horse's back. "You don't look well."

With a start, Mark realized she was talking to Kieran. And that she was right. Kieran had arrived at the Vasquez Rocks almost crackling with energy. It was a kind of wild, numinous magic Mark associated with the royal family but had never seen Kieran employ before.

But the energy seemed to have left him; he leaned a hand against Windspear's side, breathing hard. There was blood on his hands, his collar and skin; his face was drained of color.

Mark stepped forward, hesitated. He remembered Kieran telling him that they were done. "I didn't know you were hurt at the rocks, Kier," he said.

"No. This happened at the Scholomance."

"Why did you leave?" Cristina asked.

"There's something I need to tell you." Kieran winced, and slapped Windspear on the flank. The horse whickered and trotted into the shadows, melting into the darkness.

"First we must get you upstairs." Cristina glanced at Mark as if she expected him to step forward to help Kieran. When he didn't, she moved to Kieran's side, curving his arm around her shoulder. "We must see how badly you are wounded."

"It is important—" Kieran began.

"So is this." Cristina moved forward with Kieran leaning on her. Mark could no longer stand it; he swung around to Kieran's other side, and together they went into the house, Kieran limping between them.

"Thank you, Mark," Kieran said in a low voice. When Mark chanced a glance sideways, he saw no anger in Kieran's eyes, but hadn't Kieran been angry the last time they had been together? Had Kieran forgotten Mark had wronged him? It was not in the nature of princes to forget wrongs or forgive them.

Cristina was saying something about water and food; Mark's mind was in a whirl, and for a moment, when they stepped into the kitchen, he blinked around in confusion. He'd thought they were going to one of their rooms. Cristina helped Mark get Kieran settled into a chair before going to the sink to get damp towels and soap.

"I must speak to you of what I have learned," Kieran was saying; he was perched on the chair, all long limbs and dark, odd clothes and burning eyes. His hair shimmered deep blue. He looked like a faerie out of place in the human world, and it stabbed Mark through with a painful sympathy mixed with a fear that he might look like that himself.

"Let me see your face." Cristina brushed Kieran with gentle fingers; he leaned into her touch, and Mark could not blame him.

"What's going on?" Light blazed up in the kitchen; it was Helen, carrying a rune-stone in one hand. "Is someone hurt?"

Mark and Cristina exchanged startled looks; Kieran looked between Mark and Helen, his lips parting in realization.

"Were you waiting up for us?" Mark demanded. "It's past midnight."

"I was . . . not." Helen looked down at her sweatpants guiltily. "I wanted a sandwich." She squinted at Kieran. "Did you trade in Diana's truck for a faerie prince?"

Kieran was still looking at her with that same realization and Mark knew what he must be seeing: someone who was so clearly Mark's sister, so clearly the Helen that Mark had spoken about with such pain for so many years in the Hunt.

He rose to his feet and crossed the room to Helen. He lifted her free hand and kissed the back of it.

"The beloved sister of my beloved Mark. It is a joy to behold you well and reunited with your family."

"I like him," Helen said to Mark.

Kieran lowered her hand. "May I share my sorrow at the passing of your sister Livia," he said. "It is a shame to see such a bright and beautiful star untimely extinguished."

"Yes." Helen's eyes glistened. "Thank you."

I don't understand. Mark felt as if he were in a dream. He had imagined Kieran meeting his family, but it had not been like this, and Kieran had never been so gracious, even in Mark's imagination.

"Perhaps we should all sit down," Helen said. "I think I'd better hear about what happened tonight on your 'normal patrol.'" She raised an eyebrow at Mark.

"I must first tell you of what befell at the Scholomance," said Kieran firmly. "It is imperative."

"What happened?" Cristina said. "I thought it would be safe for you there—"

"It was, for a short time," said Kieran. "Then the Cohort returned from Idris and discovered me. But that story must wait. I came to bring you news." He glanced around at their expectant faces. "The Inquisitor of the Clave has sent Emma and Julian on a secret mission to Faerie. They are not expected either to return or to survive."

Mark felt numb all over. "What do you mean?"

"It is a dangerous mission—and someone has been sent after them to make sure they don't complete it—" Gasping, Kieran slumped back in his chair, looking terribly pale.

Mark and Cristina both reached to steady him at the same time. They looked at each other in some surprise over Kieran's bowed head.

"Kieran, you're bleeding!" Cristina exclaimed, taking her hand away from his shoulder. It was stained red.

"It is nothing," Kieran said roughly. Not a lie, precisely—Mark was sure he believed it, but his ashen face and feverish eyes told another story.

"Kier, you're unwell," said Mark. "You must rest. You cannot do anyone any good in this condition."

"Agreed." Cristina stood up, her hand still red with Kieran's blood. "We must see to your wounds at once."

"You have changed, son of thorns," said the Queen.

She had been silent for some minutes while the room emptied of guards and observers. Even then, Julian did not entirely believe that they were alone. Who knew what sprites or cluricauns might hide among the shadows?

Julian had been pacing, impelled by a restlessness he couldn't explain. Then again, he could explain little of what he felt these days. There were impulses he followed, others he avoided, angers and dislikes and even hopes, but he could not have explained the emotion that led him to kill Dane, or what he felt afterward. It was as if the words he needed to describe what he had felt had disappeared from his mental vocabulary.

He remembered someone had once told him that the last words of Sebastian Morgenstern had been *I've never felt so light*. He felt light himself, having put down a weight of constant fear and longing he had grown so used to carrying he no longer noticed it. But still, deep down, the thought of Sebastian chilled him. Was it wrong to feel lightness?

He was conscious now of impatience, and a knowledge, though it was distant, that he was playing with fire. But the knowledge did not come accompanied either by fear or by excitement. It was distant. Clinical.

"We are alone," said the Queen. "We could amuse ourselves."

Now he did look at her. Her throne had changed, and so had she. She seemed to be draped along the cushions of a red chaise, her coppery hair tumbling around her. She was radiantly beautiful, the gaunt outlines of her face filled in with youth and health, her brown eyes glowing.

The Queen's eyes are blue. Emma's are brown.

But it didn't change what he was seeing; the Queen's eyes were the color of tiger's-eye stones and shimmered as she gazed at him. Her dress was white satin, and as she slowly drew up one leg, sliding her toe along her opposite calf, it fell open at the slit, revealing her legs up to her hips.

"That's a glamour," Julian said. "I know what's underneath."

She rested her chin on her hand. "Most people would not dare to speak that way to the Seelie Queen."

"Most people don't have something the Seelie Queen wants," said Julian. He felt nothing, looking at her: She was beautiful, but he could not have desired her less if she'd been a beautiful rock or a beautiful sunset.

She narrowed her eyes and they flickered back to blue. "You are indeed different," she said, "more like a faerie."

"I'm better," he said.

"Really?" The Queen sat up slowly, her silken dress resettling around her. "There is a saying among my people, about the mortals we bring here: *In the Land of Faerie, as mortals feel no sorrow, neither can they feel joy.*"

"And why is that?" asked Julian.

She laughed. "Have you ever wondered how we lure mortals to live amongst faeries and serve us, son of thorns? We choose those who have lost something and promise them that which humans desire most of all, a cessation to their grief and suffering. Little do they know that once they enter our Lands, they are in the cage and will never again feel happiness." She leaned forward. "You are in that cage, boy."

A shiver went up Julian's spine. It was atavistic, primal, like the impulse that had driven him to climb Livvy's pyre. "You're trying to distract me, my lady. How about giving me what you promised?"

"What do you mind about the *parabatai* bond now? It seems you no longer care for Emma. I saw it in the way she looked at you. As if she missed you though you were standing beside her."

"The bonds," Julian said through his teeth. "How can they be broken?" His head throbbed. Maybe he was dehydrated.

"Very well." The Queen leaned back, letting her long hair spill over the side of the chaise and down to the ground. "Though it may not please you."

"Tell me."

"The *parabatai* rune has a weakness that no other rune has, because it was created by Jonathan Shadowhunter, rather than the Angel Raziel," said the Queen. As she spoke she drew on the air with her fingertip, in lazy spirals. "Kept in the Silent City is the original *parabatai* rune inscribed by Jonathan Shadowhunter and David the Silent. If it is destroyed, all the *parabatai* runes in the world will be broken."

Julian could hardly breathe. His heart was hammering against his chest. All the bonds in the world. Broken. He still couldn't explain what he was feeling, but the intensity of it made him feel as if he were bursting out of his own skin. "Why would I not be pleased to hear that?" he asked. "Because it would be difficult?"

"Not difficult. Impossible. Oh, it wasn't always impossible," said the Queen, sitting up and smirking at him. "When I spoke to you about it first, it was in good faith. But things have changed."

"What do you mean?" Julian demanded. "How have things changed?"

"I mean there is only one way to destroy the rune," the Queen said. "It must be cut through and through by the Mortal Sword."

11

Some Far-Off Happier Sea

The wound was long but not deep, a slice across Kieran's right upper arm. Kieran sat with his teeth gritted atop the bed in one of the Institute's empty guest rooms, his sleeve cut away by Cristina's balisong. Mark leaned nervously against a nearby wall, watching.

Cristina had been a little surprised at how muscular Kieran's arm was; even after he'd carried her through London, she'd thought of faeries as delicate, fine-boned. And he was, but there was toughness there too. His muscles seemed more tightly wrapped against his bones than a human's, giving his body a lean, tensile strength.

She finished carefully mopping the blood away from the cut and ran her fingers lightly over the skin around it. Kieran shivered, half-closing his eyes. She felt guilty for causing him pain. "I see no sign of infection or need for the wound to be stitched," she said. "Bandaging it should do the trick."

Kieran looked at her sideways. It was hard to discern his expression in the shadows: There was only one lamp in the room, and it was heavily shaded.

"I'm sorry to have brought this trouble to you," Kieran said in a soft voice. A nighttime voice, careful of waking those who might be sleeping. "Both of you."

"You didn't bring us trouble," said Mark, his voice roughened with tiredness. "You brought us information that can help us save the lives of people we love. We're grateful."

Kieran frowned, as if he weren't too fond of the word "grateful." Before Cristina could add anything, a cry split the night—a howl of miserable terror.

Even knowing what it was, Cristina shivered. "Tavvy," she said.

"He's having a nightmare," Mark confirmed.

"Poor child," said Kieran. "The terrors of the night are grim indeed."

"He'll be all right," Mark said, though worry shadowed his expression. "He wasn't there when Livvy died, thank the Angel, but I think he heard whispers. Perhaps we shouldn't have brought him to the funeral. To see the pyres—"

"I believe such things are a comfort," Cristina said. "I believe they allow our souls to say good-bye."

The door creaked open—someone ought to see to the hinges—and Helen stuck her head in, looking distressed. "Mark, will you go to Tavvy?"

Mark hesitated. "Helen, I shouldn't—"

"Please." Helen leaned exhaustedly against the doorjamb. "He's not used to me yet and he won't stop crying."

"I'll take care of Kieran," Cristina said, with more confidence than she felt.

Mark followed Helen from the room with clear reluctance. Feeling awkward at being left alone with Kieran, Cristina took a bandage from the kit and began to wind it around his upper arm. "I always to seem to end up tending your wounds," she said half-jokingly.

But Kieran did not smile. "That must be why," he said, "whenever I suffer, I now long for the touch of your hands."

Cristina looked at him in surprise. He was clearly more delirious than she had thought. She laid a hand on his forehead: He was burning up. She wondered what a normal temperature for faeries was.

"Lie down." She tied off the bandage. "You should rest."

Her hair swung forward as she bent over him. He reached up and tucked a lock behind her ear. She went still, her heart thudding. "I thought of you at the Scholomance," he said. "I thought of you every time anyone used Diego's name, Rosales. I could not stop thinking of you."

"Did you want to?" Her voice shook. "Stop thinking of me?"

He touched her hair again, his fingers light where they brushed her cheek. The sensation made goose bumps flood across her skin. "I know that you and Mark are together. I do not know where I fit into all of that." His cheeks were fever flushed. "I know how much I have hurt you both. I feel it, down in my bones. I would never want to hurt either of you a second time. Tomorrow I will leave here, and neither of you need ever see me again."

"No!" Cristina exclaimed, with a force that surprised her. "Do not go, not alone."

"Cristina." His right hand came up to curve around her other cheek; he was cupping her face. His skin was hot; she could see the blotches of fever on his cheeks, his collarbone. "Princess. You will be better off without me."

"I am not a princess," she said; she was leaning over him, one of her hands braced against the blanket. His face was close to hers, so close she could see the dark fringe of his eyelashes. "And I do not want you to go."

He sat up, his hands still cradling her face. She gave a little gasp and felt her own temperature spike at the warmth of his hands as they moved from her face to her shoulders, to the curve of her waist, drawing her toward him. She let herself fall atop him, her body stretched along his, their hips and chests aligned. He was tense as a drawn bow, tight and arched beneath her. His hands were fever hot, carding through her soft hair.

She placed her palms against his hard chest. It rose and fell rapidly. Her mind was spinning. She wanted to press her lips against the fine skin over his cheekbone, graze his jaw with kisses. She wanted, and the wanting shocked her, the intensity of it.

She had never felt such intensity for anyone but Mark.

Mark. She drew away from Kieran, nearly tumbling to the coverlet. "Kieran, I—we shouldn't, you—you have a fever."

He rolled onto his side, eyes bright as he studied her. "I do have a fever," he said. "I am not out of my mind, though. I have been wanting to hold you for a long time."

"You haven't even known me that long," she whispered, though she knew she was lying in a very human way, hiding what she really meant behind irrelevancies. The truth was that she had wanted Kieran, too, and she suspected she had for some time. "Lie back. You need to rest. We will have plenty of time to . . . talk more if you do not leave." She sat up. "Promise me you won't leave."

Kieran's eyes were averted, his lashes like the rays of a dark star. "I should not stay. I will only bring sorrow to you and to Mark."

"*Promise* me," Cristina hissed.

"I promise I will stay," he said at last. "But I cannot promise that you will not regret that I did."

Nene showed Emma into the room she and Julian had stayed in the last time they'd been in the Seelie Court. The silvery-quartz walls pulsed with low light, and the rose hedge Emma remembered was gone. Instead the waterfall cascaded fiercely down the rock wall as if powered by a flood, pouring into an unshaded pool several feet below the floor.

"It's kind of Fergus to let us stay in his room," Emma said as Nene ushered her in.

"Fergus has no choice," said Nene serenely. "It's what the Queen desires."

Emma blinked. That seemed odd and not auspicious. Why did the Queen care where they stayed? Her gaze strayed over the rest of the room—there was a table she could put her bag down on, there was a sofa made of vines twining closely together. . . . She frowned. "Where's the bed?"

"Behind the waterfall, in Fergus's bower."

"His what?"

"His bower." Nene pointed. Sure enough, a set of stone steps wound behind the curtain of the waterfall. Apparently Fergus liked to mix it up in the design area. "What is wrong with a bower?"

"Nothing," said Emma. "I was thinking of getting one myself."

Nene gave her a suspicious look before leaving her alone. Emma heard the key turn in the lock as she shut the door and didn't even bother to try the knob. Even if she escaped from the room, she'd have no way of finding her way through the corridors. And it wasn't as if she'd go anywhere without Julian, who wanted to be here anyway.

The last thing she felt like was sleeping, but she'd learned to snatch rest at any time on missions. She changed into her nightgown and mounted the stone steps behind the waterfall. They led to a stone platform hidden behind the water.

Despite her miserable mood, Emma was struck by the beauty of it. The bed was massive, piled with cloudy white cushions and a heavy coverlet. The waterfall sheeted by past the foot of the bed in a curtain of glimmering silver; the rush and roar of water surrounded the space, reminding Emma of the crash of waves against the beach.

She sank down on the bed. "Nice room," she said, to no one in particular. "Sorry. Bower."

Time to sleep, she decided. She lay down and closed her eyes, but the first image that sprang up against her lids was the image of Julian holding Livvy's body in the Council Hall. His face against her blood-wet hair. Emma's eyelids popped open, and she turned over restlessly. It didn't help; the next time she tried, she saw Dane's open, staring eyes as the kelpie sank its teeth into his body.

Too much. Too much blood, too much horror. She wanted Julian badly; she missed him as if it had been a week since she'd seen him. In a way, it had been. Even her *parabatai* rune felt strange—she was used to the pulse of its energy, but even before they had come to Faerie, reaching for that energy had been like slamming into a blank wall.

She turned over again, wishing for Cristina, who she could talk to. Cristina, who would understand. But could she tell even Cristina about the spell that had stripped Julian of his emotions? And what about his deal with the Queen? It had been an ugly sort of brilliant, she thought, to make a copy for the Fair Folk. They were both tricky and literal enough to at least consider the copy as sufficient for their purposes. It was too bad Julian couldn't simply have given the copy to Horace, but he would have laughed in their faces: Even a Dearborn knew what printer paper looked like. He didn't want to perform the spells in the book, after all; he simply wanted back the property he believed Annabel had stolen, the Black Volume that had lived so many years on the shelves of the Cornwall Institute.

She heard the door of the room open, voices, Julian's tread on the stairs, and then he was by the bed; she hadn't realized how the light pouring through the water would turn him into an effigy of silver. Even his dark hair was silvered, as if she was seeing him the way he might look in thirty years.

She sat up. He didn't move or seem as if he was about to say anything. He stood looking at her, and when he raised his hand to push his hair back, she saw again the stained cloth tied around his wrist.

"So how'd it go?" she asked finally. "Did you find out how to break all the *parabatai* bonds in the world?"

"As it turns out, it's not possible." He leaned against a bedpost. "You must be pleased."

"Yes." She kicked a pillow down to the foot of the bed. "I mean, that's a relief, but I'm still curious why you suddenly decided to trust the Seelie Queen when she's literally never been trustworthy."

"She didn't betray us before," said Julian. "We made a deal with her, but we never brought her the Black Volume—until now."

"She did terrible things to Jace and Clary—"

"Maybe they just didn't know how to deal with her properly." His blue-green eyes glittered. "The Queen only cares about the Queen. She isn't interested in causing pain for the sake of causing it. She just wants what she wants. If you remember that, you can deal with her."

"But why did we ever have to—"

"Look, it was obvious we couldn't trust Dearborn from the beginning. This isn't just a secret mission like Clary and Jace's. He brought us to Brocelind alone. He sent us through the door to Faerie without anyone else there. Horace Dearborn is not on our side," Julian said. "He thinks we're enemies. Downworlder-lovers. Sure, he thinks we can get the Black Volume back for him—but he planned for us to die doing it. What do you think happens, Emma, when we go home if we *don't* have it? In fact, how do you think we even get back—do you really feel like we can trust some guy standing at Bram's Crossroads on Horace's orders?"

She'd been so caught up in anger at Julian she hadn't stopped to think about how they might get home from Faerie. "Dane said it wasn't just him," she said. "Do you think he meant there'll be someone waiting at Bram's Crossroads to kill us?"

"There could be someone waiting around every corner to kill us," Julian said. "Dane was an idiot—he came for us too fast, before we had the real book. But they may not all be. Our lives are in danger here every second. If we have a deal with the Queen, we're under her protection."

"We need an ally," Emma said. "And she's weird and opportunistic and terrible but better than nothing. That's what you're saying?"

"Every plan involves risk," Julian said. "*Not* going to the Queen was a risk. Strategy is choosing between the risks—there is no safe way, Emma, not for us. Not since the minute Horace called us into his office."

"And if we return with the real Black Volume, he'll just kill us and take it," said Emma. "That was his plan anyway."

"No," Julian said. "That was his plan when he thought he was controlling how we returned. If we decide how and where we return, we can walk into any Council meeting and present the Black Volume, bravely rescued from our faerie foes. Horace thought he could get rid of us easily because we were in disgrace. It'll be much harder to do if we return in triumph."

"Fine," she said. "I get what you think we're doing. I don't know if I agree about working with the Queen, but at least I understand. But you know what would have been better? If you'd included me in the part where you chose what risk we were going to take."

"I didn't see the point," he said. "You would have worried, and for what?"

Emma felt tears burn behind her eyes. "This isn't you. *You'd* never say that."

Julian's eyes flashed. "You know I've always done whatever needed to be done to keep us safe. I thought you understood that about me."

"This is different. Remember—Julian, remember what Dane said, that you were the kind of guy who would have a girl for a *parabatai*?" She knelt up on the bed, raising her chin to look him directly in the eye. "That's what I always loved about you, even before I was in love with you. You never thought for a second about it diminishing you to have a girl as your warrior partner, you never acted as if I was anything less than your complete equal. You never for a moment made me feel like I had to be weak for you to be strong."

He looked away. Emma pressed on:

"You knew we were always stronger together. You've always treated me as though my opinion matters. You've always respected my ability to make decisions for myself. But you're not acting like that now. It's not some small thing that you lied to me, Julian, it's a betrayal of everything we swore in our *parabatai* ceremony. It's one thing for you to not want to treat me like your girlfriend, but it's entirely another for you to not treat me like your *parabatai*."

Julian crawled onto the bed beside her. "This isn't what I planned," he said. "I was concerned that you'd refuse to go to the Seelie Court, and I was just trying to move fast." The shimmer of the waterfall altered, and Julian's hair was dark again, his lashes making shadows against his cheeks. "I had no idea you'd be so upset about—everything."

"Of course you had no idea." Having Julian this close made her nerves feel like they were jumping inside her skin. They were both kneeling, facing each other; he was so close she could have reached out and put her arms around him without even needing to lean forward. "You have no idea because you have no feelings. Because you turned off all your emotions, not just about me, but about everything"—*about Livvy, even about Livvy*—"and that's going to come back and bite you in the end."

"I don't," he said.

"You don't what?"

He slid his hand across the bed so that his fingertips touched hers, just barely. Emma's heart kicked into a faster beat. "I don't have no feelings at all." He sounded lost and a little baffled. "I just don't entirely understand what it is that I do feel. Except that—I need you not to be angry, Emma."

She froze. His fingers curved around to stroke the inside of her wrist. Emma felt as if every nerve ending in her body was concentrated there, where his fingers touched. He was touching her pulse. Her heart.

"I'm sorry, Emma," he said. "I'm sorry."

Her heart leaped. With a low cry, she reached out for him; on their knees, they wrapped their arms around each other. He dipped his head to kiss her, and all her breath left her body.

He tasted the way she imagined faerie fruit would taste, sweeter than any sugar on earth. She was dizzy with the memory of the first time she'd kissed him, wet from seawater, hungry and desperate. This was languorous, hot with a slow desire: He explored her mouth thoroughly with his own, stroking his fingertips over her cheekbones, cupping her jaw to tilt her head back.

He pulled her closer. *His body still works the same,* she thought. *Feelings or no feelings.*

There was a terrible satisfaction in it. He felt something for her, even if it was only a physical something.

But he had said he was sorry. Surely that meant something. Perhaps that the spell was wearing off. Maybe it wasn't permanent. Maybe—

He kissed the corner of her mouth, the pulse at her neck. His lips were soft against her throat; his hands caught the hem of her nightgown, working it up her thighs.

Let it happen, her body said. *Get whatever you can of him, because there might never be anything else.*

His hands were under her gown. He knew where she liked to be touched. Knew what would make her shiver and kiss him harder.

No one knew her like Julian did.

Her eyes fluttered open, her vision hazy with desire. She started—Julian was looking at her, his own eyes open, and the expression in them was cool and thoughtful. It was like a bucket of cold water dashed in her face; she almost gasped.

I need you not to be angry, he'd said.

His hands were still curved around the backs of her thighs, holding her against him. Against his mouth, she whispered, "You're not really sorry, are you?"

His eyes shuttered: She knew that look. He was thinking of the right thing to say. Not the true thing, but the best thing: the most clever and efficacious thing. The thing that would get him what he wanted and needed.

She had always been proud of him for his cleverness; adored and understood the necessity of it. It was David's slingshot; it was Julian's only small defense against a massive world arrayed against him and his family. It was the only way he knew of protecting what he loved.

But without love as the driving force behind everything he did, what would he be capable of? A Julian without feelings was a Julian who could and would manipulate anyone.

Even her.

He sank back on his heels, his hands falling to his sides, his expression still indecipherable. Before he could speak, the sound of someone entering the room echoed from downstairs.

They scrambled off the bed in alarm. A few seconds later they were standing, in some disarray, on the steps leading down to the main room.

Nene was there, a key in her hand, looking up at them. She wore the uniform of a Seelie Court page. When she caught sight of them, her pale eyebrows raised. "What is it humans say? Is this a bad time?"

"It's fine," said Julian. His expression had gone back to normal, as if nothing much had happened. Emma didn't know what her own face looked like, but she knew how she felt: as if a gaping hole had been punched through the center of her.

"I am glad to hear that," Nene said, stalking to the center of the room and turning to face them. "Because we must speak now. Quickly, come downstairs. The Queen has betrayed you, and there is little time to act."

Tavvy was finally asleep, clutching a book, his face still stained with recent tears. Mark was kneeling, tousling his soft hair. Helen felt her heart aching—with love for Tavvy, with worry, with missing Julian, who would have been able to calm Tavvy's fears in minutes, not the hours it was taking Helen.

As Mark drew a blanket over his smallest brother, Helen got up to open the windows and let some fresh air into the room. She hadn't heard from Julian or Emma since they'd left them behind in Alicante, though Jia swore up and down to Aline that they were all right.

And yet Helen had rarely felt so far from her family. Even on Wrangel Island, where she had felt cut off from the world, she had trusted that Julian was taking care of them—that they were as happy as they could be—and the images of them, happy, in her mind had sustained her.

The reality of them here was a shock. Without Julian, they were looking to her, and she had no idea for what. Tavvy cried when she touched him. Dru glared at her. Ty barely seemed to know she was there. And Mark . . .

"I should never have let them separate us," Helen said. "In Idris. When they wanted to keep Jules and Emma behind, I shouldn't have let them do it."

"The Clave forced it," said Mark, rising to his feet. "You didn't have a choice."

"We always have choices," said Helen.

"You can't blame yourself. It's very hard to fight Julian when he's being stubborn. He has a very strong will. And he wanted to stay."

"Do you really think so?"

"I think he didn't want to come back with us. He was acting strangely before we left Idris, don't you think?"

"It's hard to say." Helen shut the window. "Julian has always been able to make sacrifices that were difficult and hide the pain it caused him."

"Yes," Mark said, "but even when he was hiding things, he was loving, not cold. Before we left he was cold."

He spoke simply, without any doubt. He glanced at Tavvy again and rose to his feet. "I have to get back to Kieran. He is hurt, and Tavvy is settled."

Helen nodded. "I will go with you."

The corridors of the Institute were dark and quiet. Somewhere down the hall, Aline was sleeping. Helen let herself think for a moment of how much she wanted to crawl back into bed with her wife, curl up to Aline's warmth and forget everything else.

"Perhaps we could try a Familias rune," said Helen. "Something that would lead us to Julian."

Mark looked puzzled. "You know that will not work over the border with Faerie. And Julian would need to be wearing one too."

"Of course." Helen felt as she had years ago, when Eleanor Blackthorn had died, as if she had frozen inside and it was difficult to think. "I—I know that."

Mark gave her a worried look as they entered the spare bedroom where they had put Kieran. The room was dim, and Cristina was sitting in a chair beside the bed, holding Kieran's hand; Kieran was very still under the blanket, though his chest rose and fell with the swift, regular breathing normal in faeries.

Helen had known only a little about Kieran, just what Mark had told her in the few quick conversations they'd had since he'd returned from Faerie, until she'd reached Idris; she and Mark had stayed up talking in the canal house after retrieving Tavvy, and she'd heard the whole story then. She knew how complicated Mark's feelings for Kieran were, though in the moment, as Mark gazed at the other boy worriedly, she might have guessed they were simpler.

But nothing ever was simpler, was it? Helen caught Mark's quick glance at her between his lashes as he sat down beside Cristina: worry, concern—for Kieran, for Emma and Julian, for all of them. There was plenty of worry to go around.

"I know you're going to want to go after Julian," said Helen. "To Faerie. Please don't do anything foolish, Mark."

Mark's eyes burned in the darkness. Blue and gold, sea and sunlight. "I will do what I need to do to rescue Julian and Emma. I will rejoin the Hunt if I must."

"Mark!" Helen was appalled. "You would never!"

"I would do what I needed to do," he said again, and in his voice she heard not the smaller brother she had raised but the boy who had come back from the Wild Hunt an adult.

"I know you lived with the Hunt for years and know things that I don't," said Helen. "But I have been in touch with our aunt Nene, and I know things *you* don't. I know how you and Julian and the others are thought of in Faerie—not as children but as fearsome enemies. You fought the Riders of Mannan. You shamed the Unseelie King in his own Court, and Emma slew Fal, who is almost like a god to the fey folk. Though you will find some friends in Faerie, you will find many, many foes."

"That's always been true," Mark said.

"You don't understand," said Helen in a harsh whisper. "Outside of Idris, every entrance to Faerie is guarded now, and has been since the disaster in the Council Hall. The Fair Folk know that the Nephilim hold them to blame. Even if you took the moon's road, the phouka who guards it would report your entry immediately, and you would be greeted with swords on the other side."

"What do you propose, then?" Mark demanded. "Leaving our brother and Emma in Faerie to die and rot? I have been abandoned in Faerie, I know how it feels. I will never let that happen to Emma and Julian!"

"No. I propose that I go after them. I am not an enemy in Faerie. I will go straight to Nene. She will help me."

Mark sprang to his feet. "You cannot go. The children need you here. Someone needs to take care of them."

"Aline can take care of them. She's already doing a better job than I am. The children don't even like me, Mark."

"They may not like you but they love you," Mark said furiously, "and I love you, and I will not lose another sibling to Faerie!"

Helen straightened up—though she was nowhere near as tall as her brother, which unnerved her now—and glared at Mark. "Neither will I."

"I might have a solution," Cristina said. "There is an heirloom of the Rosales family. We call it the Eternidad, to mean a time that has no beginning or end, like time in Faerie. It will allow us to enter Faerie undetected."

"Will you let me take it?" said Mark.

"I do not have it quite yet—and only a Rosales may properly use it, so I will go."

"Then I will go with you," said Kieran, who had propped himself up on his elbows. His hair was mussed and there were shadows under his eyes.

"You're awake?" said Mark.

"I've been awake for a while," Kieran admitted. "But I pretended to be asleep because it was awkward."

"Hmm," said Helen. "I think this is what Aline means by radical honesty."

"Cristina cannot journey into Faerie alone," said Kieran stubbornly. "It is too dangerous."

"I agree," said Mark. He turned to Helen. "I will go with Cristina and Kieran. We work best as a team, the three of us."

Helen hesitated. How could she let them go, into such danger? And yet that was what Shadowhunters did, wasn't it? Rush into danger? She wished desperately she could talk to her own mother. Perhaps the better question was, how could she stop them, when Mark and Kieran would be better at navigating Faerie than anyone else? To send Cristina alone would be like sending her into destruction; to send them all meant she might lose Mark as well as Julian. But not to let them go meant to abandon Julian in Faerie.

"Please, Helen," Mark said. "My brother went to Faerie to save me. I must be able to do the same for him. I have been a prisoner before. Do not make me a prisoner again."

Helen felt her muscles sag. He was right. She sat down on the bed before she could start crying. "When would you be leaving?"

"As soon as Jaime gets here with the heirloom," said Cristina. "It's been nearly an hour since I summoned him with a fire-message, but I don't know how long it will take him to arrive."

"Jaime Rosales?" said Mark and Kieran at the same time.

Helen glanced between them. They both looked surprised and a little watchful, as if jealous. She dismissed the thought. She was losing her mind, probably because of the strain.

"Oh, Mark," she said. In times of strain, the cadence of her voice, like his, slipped into an ancestral faerie formality. "I cannot bear to let you go, but I suppose I must."

Mark's eyes softened. "Helen. I am sorry. I promise to come back to you safely, and to bring Julian and Emma back safely as well."

Before Helen pointed out that this wasn't a promise he could truly make, Kieran cleared his throat. The sound was very ordinary and human and nearly made Helen smile despite herself.

"I would that I had ever had a sibling who loved me as much as you love each other," he said, sounding very much like a prince of Faerie. The semblance was quickly dispelled, though, when he cleared his throat again and said, "In the meantime, Helen, I must ask you to remove yourself from my leg. You are sitting on it and it is becoming quite painful."

"Some monsters are human," said Gwyn. They were in Diana's rooms on Flintlock Street. She lay crosswise on her bed, her head in Gwyn's lap as he stroked her hair. "Horace Dearborn is one of them."

Diana brushed her hand along the wool of Gwyn's tunic. She liked seeing him like this—without his helmet or mail, just a man in a worn tunic and scuffed boots. A man with pointed ears and two-colored eyes, but Diana had stopped seeing those as odd. They were just part of Gwyn.

"I believe there are good people in the Council," Diana said. "They are frightened. Of Horace as well as his dire predictions. He has seized a great deal of power in a short time."

"He has made Idris unsafe," said Gwyn. "I wish you to leave Alicante, Diana."

She sat up in surprise. "Leave Alicante?"

"I have seen a great deal of history," said Gwyn. "Terrible laws are usually passed before they are repealed after much suffering. Small-mindedness and fear have a way of winning out. You have told me Horace and his daughter do not like you."

"No," said Diana. "Though I don't know why—"

"They fear your influence," said Gwyn. "They know others listen to you. You are very persuasive, Diana, and startlingly wise."

She made a face at him. "Flatterer."

"I am not flattering you." He stood up. "I am afraid for you. Horace Dearborn may not be a dictator yet, but he yearns to be one. His first move will to be to eliminate all who stand against him. He will move to extinguish the brightest lights first, those who illuminate the pathway for others."

Diana shivered. She could hear the hooves of his horse pacing back and forth across her roof. "You are bitter, Gwyn."

"It is possible I do not always see the best in people," he said, "as I hunt down the souls of slain warriors on the battlefield."

She raised her eyebrows. "Are you making a joke?"

"No." He looked puzzled. "I meant what I said. Diana, let me take you from here. We would be safe in Faerie. At night the stars are a thousand colors and during the day the fields are full of roses."

"I cannot, Gwyn. I cannot abandon this fight."

He sat back down on the bed, hanging his shaggy head in weariness. "Diana . . ."

It was strange after so long to feel the desire to be close to someone, physically as well as emotionally. "Did you not tell me that the first time you saw me, you cared for me because I was so brave? You would now like me to be a coward?"

He looked at her, emotion naked on his lined face. "It is different now."

"Why would it be different?"

He curved his big hands around her waist. "Because I know that I love you."

Her heart gave a strong flutter inside her chest. She had not expected such words from anyone, had considered it a price she would pay for being transgender and Nephilim. She had certainly never expected to hear it from someone like Gwyn: who knew all there was to know about her, who could not lie, a prince of wild magic.

"Gwyn," she said, and cupped his face in her hands, bending to kiss him. He leaned back, gently drawing her with him until they lay upon the bed, her heart beating fast against the roughness of his tunic. He curved over her, his bulk casting a shadow across her body, and in that shadow she closed her eyes and moved with the movements of his gentle kisses and touches as they turned sweeter and sharper, until they reached together a place where fear was gone, where there was only the gentle alliance of souls who had left loneliness behind.

Helen had gone to tell Aline what was going on; Mark couldn't guess how late it was, but he could no longer see moonlight through the window. He was sitting on the mattress next to Kieran, and Cristina had curled herself into the chair beside the bed.

He avoided meeting her eyes. He knew he had done nothing wrong by kissing her, or she by kissing him. He remembered the last time he had spoken to Kieran alone, in the London Sanctuary. How Kieran had touched the elf-bolt that hung around Mark's neck. It had become a symbol, of sorts, of the two of them. What Kieran had said next still rang in his ears: *We will be done with each other.*

He didn't know if he could explain what he felt to Kieran, or even to Cristina. He knew only that he did not feel done: not with Kieran, nor with Cristina should Kieran choose to return to him.

"Do you feel any better, Kieran?" he said softly.

"Yes—Cristina is a very good nurse."

Cristina rolled her eyes. "I put on a bandage. Don't exaggerate my talents."

Kieran gazed sadly down at his bandaged arm. "I do feel a bit odd with my sleeve missing."

Mark couldn't help smiling. "It's very stylish. Big with mundanes, the one-sleeve look."

Kieran's eyes widened. "Is it?"

Both Mark and Cristina giggled. Kieran frowned. "You should not mock me."

"Everyone gets mocked," Cristina said teasingly. "That's what friends do."

Kieran's face lit up at that, so much so that Mark felt the painful urge to hug him. Princes of Faerie didn't have friends, he guessed; he and Kieran had never really talked about it. There was a time that the two of them had been friends, but love and pain had transmuted that in a way Mark now knew wasn't inevitable. There were people who fell in love but stayed friends—Magnus and Alec, or Clary and Jace, or Helen and Aline.

Kieran's smile had vanished. He moved restlessly under the covers. "There is something I need to tell you both. To explain."

Cristina looked worried. "Not if you don't want to—"

"It is about the Scholomance," Kieran said, and they both fell silent. They listened while Kieran told them of the Hollow Place. Mark tended to lose himself in other people's stories. He had always been like that, since he was a child, and he remembered how much he had loved Kieran telling him stories when they were in the Hunt—how he had gone to sleep with Kieran's fingers in his hair and Kieran's voice in his ears, telling him tales of Bloduwedd, the princess made of flowers, and of the black cauldron that raised the dead, and of the battle between Gwyn ap Nudd and Herne the Hunter, that had shaken down the trees.

Cristina never lost herself in retellings in the same way, Mark thought; she was entirely present, her expression darkening and her eyes widening with horror as Kieran told them of the Cohort, the fight by the pool, the way Diego had saved him, and how he had escaped from the library.

"They are horrible," Cristina said, almost before Kieran had finished speaking. "Horrible. That they would go that far—!"

"We must check in on Diego and the others," said Mark, though Diego Rocio Rosales was one of his least favorite people. "See if they're all right."

"I will write to Diego," Cristina said. "Kieran, I am so sorry. I thought you would be safe at the Scholomance."

"You could not have known," said Kieran. "While I was at the Scholomance, I chided Diego for not planning for the future, but this is not a future anyone could imagine."

"Kieran's right. It's not your fault," said Mark. "The Cohort is out of control. I'd guess it was one of them who followed Emma and Julian into Faerie."

Kieran shoved his blankets off with a harsh, sudden gesture. "I owe it to Emma and Julian to go after them. I understand that now. I regretted what I had done even before the water of the pool touched me. But I was never able to testify. I was never able to earn their forgiveness or make up for what I did."

"Emma has forgiven you," Cristina said.

Kieran did not look convinced. When he spoke, it was haltingly. "I want to show you something."

When neither Mark nor Cristina moved, he turned around, kneeling on the bed, and pulled up his shirt, baring his back. Mark heard Cristina suck in her breath as Kieran's skin was revealed.

It was covered in whip marks. They looked newly healed, as if a few weeks old, no longer bleeding but still scarlet. Mark dry-swallowed. He knew every mark and scar on Kieran's skin. These were new.

"The Cohort whipped you?" he whispered.

"No," said Kieran. He let his shirt fall, though he didn't move from where he was, facing the wall behind the bed. "These marks appeared on my back when the water of the pool touched me. They are Emma's. I bear them now as a reminder of the agony she would not have been caused if not for me. When the pool water touched me, I felt her fear and pain. How can she forgive me for that?"

Cristina rose to her feet. Her brown eyes glimmered with distress; she touched her hand lightly to Kieran's back. "Kieran," she said. "As we all have an infinite capacity to make mistakes, we all have an infinite capacity for forgiveness. Emma bears these scars cheerfully because to her, they are a mark of valor. Let them be the same to you. You are a prince of Faerie. I have seen you be as brave as anyone I have known. Sometimes the bravest thing we can do is confront our own failings."

"You are a prince of Faerie." Kieran smiled a little, though it was crooked. "Someone else said that to me tonight."

"To realize that you have made mistakes and hope to correct them is all anyone can hope to do," said Mark. "Sometimes we may have the best intentions—you were trying to save my life when you went to Gwyn and Iarlath—and the results are terrible. We all had the best intentions when we went to the Council meeting, and now Livvy is dead and Alicante is in the hands of the Cohort."

Wincing, Kieran turned to face them both. "I swear to you," he said. "I will fight to my last breath to help you save the ones you love."

Cristina smiled, clearly touched. "Let's just focus on Emma and Julian right now," she said. "We will be grateful to have you with us in Faerie tomorrow."

Mark reached behind his neck and untied his elf-bolt necklace. "I want you to wear this, Kieran. You must never be defenseless again."

Kieran didn't reach for the elf-bolt. "I gave it to you because I wished you to have it."

"And now I want you to have it," said Mark. "There are many who seek to harm you, here and in Faerie. I want to be certain you will always have a weapon close to hand."

Kieran slowly reached out and caught the necklace from Mark's hand. "I will wear it then, if it pleases you."

Cristina gave Mark an unreadable look as Kieran looped the necklace over his head. There was something approving in her expression, as though she were glad of Mark's generosity.

Kieran ran his hands through his hair. It slipped through his fingers in ink-blue locks. "Exhaustion claims me," he said. "I am sorry."

In the Hunt, Mark would have wrapped his arms around Kieran and held him. They would have been cushions for each other's bodies against the hard ground. "Would you like us to make you a bed of blankets on the floor?" Mark offered.

Kieran looked up, his eyes like shining polished mirrors: one black, one silver. "I think I could sleep in the bed if you stayed with me."

Cristina turned bright red. "All right," she said. "I'll say good night then—"

"No," Kieran said quickly. "I mean both of you. I want both of you to stay with me."

Mark and Cristina exchanged a look. It was the first time, Mark thought, that he had really looked at Cristina since they'd come back from the Vasquez Rocks: He'd felt too awkward, too ashamed of his own confusion. Now he realized she looked just as flushed and puzzled as he did.

Kieran's shoulders sagged slightly. "If you do not want to, I will understand."

It was Cristina who kicked off her shoes and climbed into the bed beside Kieran. She was still wearing her jeans and tank top, one strap torn by a Harpyia demon. Mark got into the bed on the other side of Kieran, pillowing his head on his hand.

They lay there for long moments in silence. The warmth from Kieran's body was familiar—so familiar it was hard not to curl up against him. To pull the blankets up over them, to forget everything in the darkness.

But Cristina was there, and her presence seemed to change the makeup of the atoms in the air, the chemical balance between Kieran and Mark. It was no longer possible to fall into forgetting. This moment was now, and Mark was sharply aware of Kieran's nearness in a way he had not been since they first met, as if the clock had been rewound on their relationship.

And he was aware of Cristina as well, no less sharply. Awkward, shy wanting anchored him in place. He glanced over at her;

he could see the gleam of her dark hair against the pillow, one bare brown shoulder. Heat muddled Mark's head, his thoughts.

"I shall dream of the Borderlands," said Kieran. "Adaon had a cottage there, in lands neither Seelie nor Unseelie. A little stone place, with roses climbing the walls. In the Hunt, when I was hungry and cold, I would say to myself, none of this is real, and try to make the cottage real in my mind. I would pretend I was there, looking out the windows, and not where I truly was. It became more real to me than reality was."

Cristina touched his cheek lightly. "*Ya duérmete*," she murmured. "Go to sleep, you silly person."

Mark couldn't help smiling. "Has anyone else ever called you a silly person before, Prince Kieran?" he whispered as Cristina closed her eyes to sleep.

But Kieran was looking over at Cristina, his dark hair tangled, his eyes soft with weariness and something else.

"I think she is the most beautiful girl I have ever seen," he said in a ruminative voice.

"I have always thought the same," said Mark.

"You are different with each other now," Kieran said. "It is clear to see. You were together while I was away."

It was not something Mark would have ever lied about. "That is true."

Kieran reached out, touched Mark's hair. A light touch, sending a shower of sparks down through Mark's body. Kieran's mouth was a sleepy, soft curve. "I hoped you would be," he said. "The thought gave me comfort while I was in the Scholomance."

Kieran curled into the blankets and closed his eyes, but Mark remained awake for a long time, staring into the dark.

12
Beneath the Sky

Mark, Kieran, and Cristina were in the library, packing for their departure to Faerie. Everyone else was there too; at least, everyone except Dru, who had taken Tavvy down to the beach to keep him distracted. Kit doubted she'd actually want to watch them preparing to leave anyway.

Kit felt bad for her—her eyes had still been red when she'd set out with Tavvy and a duffel bag full of toys and sand buckets, though she'd kept her voice cheerful when promising Tavvy she'd help him make a sandcastle city.

But he felt worse for Ty.

It wasn't just that Mark was going back to Faerie. That was bad enough. It was why he was going. When Mark and Helen had explained that Emma and Julian were on a mission in the Undying Lands and needed assistance, Kit had tensed all over with panic. Ty didn't just love Julian, he needed him the way kids needed their parents. On top of what had happened to Livvy, how would he deal with it?

They had been in the kitchen, in the early morning, the room flooded with sun. The table still scattered with the remains of breakfast, Dru teasing Tavvy by making mini seraph blades out of pieces of toast and dunking them in jelly. Then Aline had gotten up at some unspoken signal from Helen and taken Tavvy out of the room, promising to show him her favorite illustrated book in the library.

And then Helen had explained what was going on. Mark and Cristina had interjected occasionally, but Kieran had stood quietly by the window while they talked, his dark blue hair threaded through with white.

When they were done, Drusilla was crying quietly. Ty sat in absolute silence, but Kit could see that his right hand, under the table, was moving like a pianist's, his fingers stretching and curling. He wondered if Ty had forgotten his hand toys—the Internet called them stim toys or stimming objects. He glanced around for something he could hand to Ty, as Mark leaned forward and lightly touched his younger brother's face.

"Tiberius," he said. "And Drusilla. I know this must be hard for you, but we will bring Julian back and then we will all be together again."

Dru smiled faintly at him. *Don't say that*, Kit thought. *What if you can't bring him back? What if he dies there in Faerie? Making promises you can't keep is worse than making no promises at all.*

Ty stood up and walked out of the kitchen without a word. Kit started to push his chair back, and hesitated. Maybe he shouldn't go after Ty. Maybe Ty wouldn't want him to. When he glanced up, he saw that Mark and Cristina were both looking at him—in fact, Kieran was too, with his eerie light-and-dark eyes.

"You should go after him," Mark said. "You're the one he wants."

Kit blinked and stood up. Cristina gave him an encouraging smile as he headed out of the kitchen.

Ty hadn't gone far; he was in the corridor just outside, leaning back against the wall. His eyes were closed, his lips moving silently. He had a retractable pen in his right hand and was clicking the top of it, over and over, *snap snap*.

"Are you okay?" Kit said, hovering awkwardly just outside the kitchen door.

Ty opened his eyes and looked toward Kit. "Yeah."

Kit didn't say anything. It seemed desperately unlikely to him in that moment that Ty was actually okay. It was too much. Losing Livvy, and now the fear of losing Julian and Mark—and Emma and Cristina. He felt as if he were witnessing the burning away of the Blackthorn family. As if the destruction that Malcolm had wished on them was happening now, even after Malcolm was gone, and they would all be lost, one by one.

But not Ty. Please don't do this to Ty. He's good, he deserves better.

Not that people always got what they deserved, Kit knew. It was one of the first things he'd ever learned about life.

"I am okay," Ty said, as if he could hear Kit's doubts. "I have to be okay for Livvy. And if anything happens to Mark or to Julian or Emma in Faerie, that's okay too, because we can bring them all back. We have the Black Volume. We can bring them back."

Kit stared; his mind felt full of white noise and shock. Ty didn't mean it, he told himself. He couldn't mean it. The kitchen door opened behind him and Mark came out; he said something Kit didn't hear and then he went to Ty and put his arms around him.

Ty hugged him back, his forehead against Mark's shoulder. He was still gripping the pen. Kit saw again the bruises on Ty's hands and wrists, the ones he must have gotten climbing the pyre in Idris. They stood out so starkly against Ty's pale skin that Kit imagined he could feel the pain of them himself.

And now he and Kit were sitting on one of the library tables, watching the others pack. Kit couldn't shake off his feeling of strangeness. The last time Mark and Cristina had disappeared to Faerie, there'd been no warning and no preparation. They'd disappeared overnight with Emma and Julian. This time not only did everyone know about it, they were all pitching in to help as if it were a camping trip.

Mark, Cristina, and Kieran were dressed in the least Shadowhuntery clothes they'd been able to find. Cristina wore a knee-length white dress, and Mark and Kieran had on shirts and trousers that Aline had attacked with a pair of scissors to make them look ragged and uneven. They wore soft shoes, without metal buckles, and Cristina's hair was tied back with ribbon.

Helen had packed them plastic containers of food—granola bars, apples, things that wouldn't go bad. There were blankets and bandages and even antiseptic spray, since their steles wouldn't work in Faerie. And of course there were all the weapons: Cristina's balisong, dozens of daggers and throwing knives wrapped in soft leather, a crossbow for Mark, and even a bronze shortsword for Kieran, who had buckled it on at his waist with the delighted look of someone who missed being armed.

"Maybe we shouldn't pack the food now," Helen said nervously, taking a Tupperware container she'd just packed back out of the bag. "Maybe we should wait until they're leaving."

Aline sighed. She'd been flipping back and forth all day between looking as if she was going to cry and looking as if she was going to yell at Mark, Kieran, and Cristina for making Helen cry. "Most of that food will keep. That's the point."

"We can only wait so long to depart," Mark said. "This is urgent." He flicked his eyes toward Kit and Ty; Kit turned and realized that Ty had disappeared. No one had left the library, though, so he had to be somewhere in the room.

"Jaime will come as quickly as he can," Cristina said. She was deftly knotting up a roll of throwing knives.

"If he isn't here by tonight, we may need to take the moon's road," said Kieran.

"And risk being reported to the Courts?" Helen said. "It's too dangerous. No. You can't go anywhere until Jaime Rosales shows up."

"He'll come," Cristina said, shoving the roll of knives into her pack with some force. "I trust him."

"If he doesn't, it's too risky. Especially considering where you're going."

Kit slid off the table as Kieran protested; no one was paying attention to him anyway. He walked alongside the rows of bookshelves until he saw Ty, between two stacks of books, his head bent over a piece of paper.

He stopped for a moment and just looked at him. He was aware of Kieran watching him from across the room and wondered why; they'd shared an interesting conversation once, on the roof of the London Institute, where they realized they were both outsiders where the Blackthorn family was concerned.

Kit wasn't sure that was true anymore, though. Either for him or for Kieran. And they hadn't spoken since.

He slipped between the rows of books. He couldn't help noticing they were somewhat ironically in the SEA CREATURES AND THINGS AQUATIC section.

"Ty," he said. "Ty, what's going on?"

Perhaps Ty had finally snapped; perhaps the weight of grief and loss and fear had gotten to him. There was something incredibly vulnerable about the thinness of his fingers, the flush on his cheeks when he glanced up. Maybe—

Kit realized Ty's eyes were shining, and not with tears. Ty held up the paper in his hands; it was a letter. "It's from Hypatia Vex," he said in a low voice. "She's agreed to help us with the Shadow Market."

"What's going on?" Julian jogged down the curving steps from Fergus's bower, twisting his shirt around as he went. Emma followed more cautiously, having stopped to throw on clothes and grab her pack.

Nene stood in the center of Fergus's room, wearing a long green dress and a heavy green cloak over it trimmed in green and blue feathers. She flicked the hood back with impatient fingers and faced them.

"The Queen has betrayed you," she said again. "Even now she prepares to leave for the Unseelie Court with the Black Volume."

Emma started. "The Unseelie Court? But why?"

Nene gave them a hard glance. "You understand I am betraying my Court and my lady by speaking to you like this," she said. "If I am found out, it will go worse for me than you can imagine."

"You came to us," Julian pointed out. He was himself again, calm, measured. Maybe that was what being without your emotions meant; maybe you never really lost yourself in anything. "We didn't come to you."

"I came because I owe the Blackthorns," she said. "Because of the wrong my sister Celithe did to Arthur in torturing him, in shattering his mind with magic so that he might never be cured. And because I do not want the Unseelie King to have the Black Volume of the Dead."

"But he might well already have it," Emma said. "He took Annabel—and Annabel has the book."

"We have spies in the Court, of course," said Nene. "He does have Annabel. But she will not give him the Black Volume, and because she knows his true name, he cannot make her."

"So why is she staying in the Court?" Julian demanded.

"That I cannot tell you," Nene said. "Only what the Queen is doing. She does not consider any promises she made to you binding, because the book you brought her is a copy and not the original."

"That's a ridiculous technicality," said Emma.

"Faerie turns on ridiculous technicalities," said Nene. "The Queen will do what the Queen wishes to do. That is the nature of Seelie."

"But why does she want to give the book to the King? She hates the King! She said she wanted to keep it out of his hands—" Emma started.

"She did say she wanted to keep it out of his hands," Julian said. He was pale. "But she didn't say she wouldn't give it to him anyway."

"No," said Nene. "She did not."

The Queen's words echoed in Emma's head. *The Black Volume is more than necromancy. It contains spells that will allow me to retrieve the captive from the Unseelie Court.* "She's going to trade the book for the captive in the Unseelie Court, whoever he is," said Emma. "Or she."

"He," said Nene. "It is her son who is captive."

Julian sucked in a breath. "Why didn't you tell us that before? If I'd known that—"

Nene glared at him. "Betraying my Queen is no light thing to me! If it were not for my sister's children, I would never—"

"I expected the Queen to betray us," Julian said. "But not for her to do it so soon, or like this. She must be desperate."

"Because she's trying to save her child," said Emma. "How old is he?"

"I do not know," Nene said. "Ash was always hidden from us. I would not recognize him if I saw him."

"The King can't have the book. The Queen said that he was blighting the Lands of Faerie with dark magic and filling the rivers with blood. Imagine what he'd do if he had the Black Volume."

"If we can believe the Queen," said Julian.

"It is the truth as far as I know it," said Nene. "Since the Cold Peace, the Land of Unseelie has been bleeding evil. It is said that a great weapon resides there, something that but needs the spells of the Black Volume to bring its powers to life. It is something that could wipe out all angelic magic."

"We have to get to the Unseelie Court," said Emma. "We have to stop the Queen."

Julian's eyes glittered. Emma knew what he was thinking. That in the Unseelie Court was Annabel, and with Annabel lay revenge for Livvy's death. "I agree with you," he said. "We can follow the Queen—"

"You cannot travel as fast as a procession of fey horses," she said. "Not even Nephilim can run like that. You must intercept the Queen before she reaches the tower."

"The tower?" echoed Emma.

"It is the one permanent stronghold of Unseelie, the place they retreat when under siege. Its fortifications are unmatched in Faerie; none can scale the walls or brave the thorns, and the throne room at the top of the tower is guarded by redcaps. You must join the procession so that you might reach the Queen before she is inside the tower, and it is too late."

"Join the procession? We'll be noticed!" Emma exclaimed, but Nene was already seizing up a hooded cloak that had been hung by the door and tossing it to Julian.

"Wear this," she said. "It's Fergus's. Pull up the hood. No one will be looking that closely." She drew off her own cloak and handed it to Emma. "And you will be disguised as me." She eyed Emma critically as Emma put the cloak on, fastening it at the throat. "At least the blond hair is right."

Julian had disappeared up the steps; when he returned, he was carrying his weapons belt and Emma's. Fergus's cloak—black, with raven wings shimmering like oil on the breast and hood—covered him completely. "We're not going without these."

"Keep them beneath your cloaks," Nene said. "They are clearly of Shadowhunter make." She looked them up and down. "As are you. Ah well. We will do the best we can."

"What if we need to flee from Faerie?" said Emma. "What if we get the Black Volume and need to go back to Idris?"

Nene hesitated.

"You've already betrayed faerie secrets," said Julian. "What's one more?"

Nene narrowed her eyes. "You have changed," she said. "I can only hope it is grief."

Grief. Everyone in Alicante had thought it was grief that had altered Julian's behavior, his reactions. Emma had thought it herself at first.

"Make your way to Branwen's Falls," said Nene. "Beneath the falls you will find a path back to Alicante. And if you ever speak of this secret to another soul besides each other, my curse will be on your heads."

She pushed open the door, and they crept out into the corridor.

Tavvy had never been satisfied with sandcastles. They bored him. He liked to build what he called sand cities—rows of square sand structures shaped by empty milk cartons turned upside down. They were houses, stores, and schools, complete with signs made with the torn-off fronts of matchbooks.

Dru scuffed her way up and down the beach barefoot, helping Tavvy find sticks, rocks, and seashells that would become lampposts, walls, and bus stops. Sometimes she'd find a piece of sea glass, red or green or blue, and tuck it into the pocket of her overalls.

The beach was empty except for her and Tavvy. She was watching him out of the corner of her eye as he knelt on the wet sand, shaping a massive wall to surround his city—after what had happened with Malcolm, she didn't plan to take her gaze off him again. But most of her mind was filled up with thoughts of Mark and Emma and Julian. Mark was going to Faerie, and he was going because Julian and Emma were in trouble. Mark hadn't said, but Dru was pretty sure it was bad trouble. Nothing good came from going to Faerie, and Mark and Cristina and Kieran wouldn't be running to save them if they thought they'd be all right on their own.

People are leaving me one by one, she thought. First Livvy, then Julian and Emma, now Mark. She stopped to glance out at the ocean: sparkling blue waves rolling over and under. Once she'd watched that ocean thinking that somewhere across it was Helen on her island, protecting the wards of the world. She had remembered her sister's laugh, her blond hair, and imagined her as a sort of Valkyrie, holding up a spear at the entrance to the world, not letting the demons pass her by.

These days, she could tell that every time Helen looked at her she was sad that Dru wasn't more friendly, more open to sisterly bonding. Dru knew it was true, but she couldn't change it. Didn't Helen understand that if Dru let herself love her older sister, Helen would just be another person for Dru to lose?

"Someone's coming," Tavvy said. He was looking down the beach, his blue-green eyes squinted against the sun.

Dru turned and stared. A boy was walking down the empty beach, consulting a small object in his hand as he went. A tall, rail-thin boy with a mop of black hair, brown skin that shone in the sun, and bare, runed arms.

She dropped the seashells she was holding. "Jaime!" she screamed. "Jaime!"

He glanced up and seemed to see her for the first time. A wide grin spread across his face and he started to run, loping across the sand until he reached her. He grabbed her up in a hug, whooping and spinning her around.

She still remembered the odd dream she'd had before Jaime left the London Institute, in which she'd been somewhere—it had felt like Faerie, but then how would she know what Faerie felt like? She'd dismissed it, but the faint memory came back now that he was here—along with other memories: of him sitting and watching movies with her, talking to her about her family, listening to her.

"It's good to see you again, friend," he said, setting her down on the sand and ruffling her hair. "It's very good."

He looked tired, inexpressibly tired, as if he hadn't hit the ground except for running since the last time she'd seen him. There were dark circles under his eyes. Tavvy was running over to see who he was, and Jaime was asking if she still had the knife he'd given her, and she couldn't help smiling, her first real smile since Livvy.

He came back, Dru thought. Finally, someone didn't leave—they came back instead.

They crept along the corridors with Nene, keeping to the shadows. Both Emma and Julian kept their hoods drawn up; Nene had tucked her hair under a cap and, in breeches and a loose shirt, looked like a page boy at first glance.

"What about Fergus?" Emma said.

Nene smiled grimly. "Fergus has been waylaid by a dryad of the sort he most admires. A young sapling."

"Ouch," said Julian. "Splinters."

Nene ignored him. "I've known Fergus a long time, I know all about his inclinations. He'll be busy for a good long time."

They had reached a sloping hallway familiar to Emma. She could smell night air coming from one end of the corridor, the scent of leaves and sap and fall. She wondered if it was the same season in Faerie as it was at home. It felt later, as if autumn had already touched the Lands of Faerie with an early frost.

The corridor ended abruptly, opening into a clearing full of grass and stars. Trees stood around in a tall circle, shaking down leaves of gold and russet on a crowd of faerie courtiers and their horses.

The Queen herself sat sidesaddle on a white mare at the head of the procession. A white lace veil covered her face and her shoulders, and white gloves covered her hands. Her red hair streamed down her back. Her courtiers, in gold silk and bright velvet, rode behind her: most on horses, but some on massive, pad-pawed cats and narrow-eyed wolves the size of small cars. A green-skinned dryad with a mass of leaves for hair rode tucked into the branches of a walking tree.

Emma couldn't help looking around herself in wonder. She was a Shadowhunter, used to magic; still, there was something so alien at the heart of the Courts of Faerie that it still made her marvel.

Nene led them through the shadows to where her horse and Fergus's waited, already in the procession's line, between a sprite riding a winged toadstool and two faerie girls in russet dresses with identical black hair, who sat one in front of the other on a bay mare. Emma pulled herself up into the saddle of Nene's gray palfrey.

Nene patted the horse's neck fondly. "Her name is Silvermane. Be kind to her. She knows her own way home."

Emma nodded as Julian mounted Fergus's bay stallion. "What's his name?" he asked as the horse pawed the ground and snorted.

"Widowmaker," said Nene.

Julian snorted under his hood. "Does he make widows out of the people who ride him or people he takes a dislike to?"

"Both," said Nene. She reached into her cloak and drew out two crystal vials, each looped on a golden chain. She handed one to Julian and the other to Emma. "Wear these around your throats," she said in a low voice. "And keep them close."

Emma looped the chain obediently around her throat. The vial was about the size of her thumb. Pale gold liquid was visible inside it, glimmering as the vial moved. "What are these for?"

"If you are in danger in the King's Court, break the top and drink the liquid," said Nene.

"Is it poison?" Julian sounded curious as he fastened the chain around his throat. The vial fell against his chest.

"No—it will make you invisible to Unseelie faeries, at least for a time. I don't know how long the magic lasts. I have never had cause to use it."

A squawking goblin with a piece of parchment and a massive quill pen was running along the side of the procession, marking off names. He cast a quick glance at Emma and Julian. "Lady Nene, Lord Fergus," he said. "We are about to depart."

"We?" said Julian in a bored voice. Emma blinked, astonished by how much he sounded like a faerie. "Are you accompanying us, goblin? Would you enjoy a holiday in the Court of Unseelie?"

The goblin squinted. "Are you well, Lord Fergus? You sound different."

"Perhaps because I pine for goblin heads to decorate my bower," said Julian. "Off with you." He aimed a kick at the goblin, who made a hissing sound of fright and skittered away from them, hurrying down the line.

"Be careful what masks you wear, child," Nene said, "lest you lose your true face forever."

"False or true, it is all the same," said Julian, and picked up the reins as the procession began to move forward into the night.

Before Kit could answer Ty, a commotion in the library drew them out from behind the shelves.

Dru had returned to the library and was hanging back by the door, looking shy but smiling. A good-looking dark-eyed boy who resembled a narrower version of Diego Rocio Rosales was hugging Cristina. Mark and Kieran were both looking at him with uneasy expressions. As soon as Cristina let him go, Helen strode over to shake his hand. "Welcome to the Los Angeles Institute, Jaime," she said. "Thanks so much for coming on such short notice."

"Jaime Rocio Rosales," said Ty to Kit, under his breath.

"I found him on the beach and brought him straight up," Dru said proudly.

Helen looked puzzled. "But how did you recognize him?"

Dru exchanged a look with Jaime, part panic and part resignation.

"He stayed with me for a few days when we were at the London Institute," Dru said.

Everyone looked astonished, though Kit wasn't exactly sure why. The relationships between different Shadowhunter families were endlessly confusing: some, like Emma, Jace, and Clary, were treated almost like Blackthorn family; some weren't. He had to hand it to Dru, though, for managing to conceal the fact she had someone in her room in London from everyone else. It indicated a talent for deception. Along with her lock-picking skills, she definitely had a criminal bent he admired.

"You mean he was in your room?" Mark demanded incredulously. He turned to Jaime, who had backed up against one of the long tables. "She's only thirteen!"

Jaime looked incredulous. "I thought she had to be at least sixteen—"

Helen sucked in her breath. Mark handed his pack to Kieran, who took it, looking baffled. "Stay where you are, Jaime Rosales."

"Why?" said Jaime suspiciously.

Mark advanced. "So I can rain blows down upon you."

Like an acrobat, Jaime flipped himself backward, landing squarely atop the table. He glared down at Mark. "I don't know what you think happened, but nothing did. Dru is my friend, whatever her age. That is all."

Ty turned to whisper in Kit's ear. "I don't get it—why is Mark angry?"

Kit thought about it. It was one of the great things about Ty, actually—he made you consider the threads of subconscious logic that wove beneath the surface of ordinary conversations. The suppositions and assumptions people made without ever considering why, the implications of certain words and gestures. Kit didn't think he'd take those things for granted again. "You know how knights in stories defend a lady's honor?" he whispered. "Mark thinks he has to defend Drusilla's honor."

"That table is going to break," Ty said.

He was right. The legs of the table Jaime was standing on were wobbling dangerously.

Dru leaped in between Mark and Jaime, arms spread wide. "Stop," she said fiercely. "I didn't tell Jaime how old I was because he was my friend. He listened to me and he watched horror movies with me and he acted like what I said was important and I didn't want him to treat me like a little kid."

"But you are only a child," Mark said. "He should not treat you as an adult."

"He treated me like a friend," said Dru. "I might be young, but I'm not a liar."

"She is telling you that you have to trust her, Mark," said Kieran. He rarely said much around the Blackthorns; Kit was surprised, but couldn't disagree.

Cristina stepped around Mark and moved to stand next to Dru. They couldn't have looked more different—Cristina in her white dress, Dru in overalls and a black T-shirt—but they wore identical stubborn expressions.

"Mark," said Cristina. "I understand you feel you have not been here to protect your family for so many years. But that does not mean mistrusting them now. Nor would Jaime hurt Dru."

The door of the library opened; it was Aline. No one but Kit watched as she crossed the room and whispered in Helen's ear. No one but Kit saw Helen's expression change, her lips whiten.

"Dru is like a little sister to me," said Jaime, and Dru winced almost imperceptibly.

Mark turned to Dru. "I'm sorry, sister. I should have listened to you." He looked up at Jaime, and his eyes flashed. "I believe you,

Jaime Rocio Rosales. But I can't speak for what Julian will do when he finds out."

"You guys are really incentivizing me to let you use the Eternidad to get to Faerie," said Jaime.

"Stop bickering." Helen's voice rang out. "Earlier I sent word to my aunt Nene in the Seelie Court. She just returned my message. She said that Emma and Julian were there—but they've gone. They just set forth from the Seelie Court to the Unseelie Court."

Kieran's eyes darkened. Cristina said, "Why would they do that?"

"I don't know," Helen said. "But it means that we have a specific location where we know they'll be."

Kieran touched the sword at his waist. "I know a place along the road that leads between Seelie and Unseelie where we can waylay them. But once they pass it, we may be too late. If we are going to go, we should go now."

Jaime leaped down off the table with the lightness of a cat. "I'll get the heirloom." He began to rummage through his pack. "Cristina, only you can use it, because whoever uses it must have Rosales blood."

Cristina and Jaime exchanged a significant look, indecipherable to Kit.

"You can use it to get to Faerie, and also back," said Jaime. "Your passage in and out of the Lands will be undetectable. But it cannot protect you while you are there." He handed something to Cristina; Kit could only catch a glimpse of it. It looked like smooth wood, twisted into an odd shape.

Kieran and Mark were strapping their packs on. Dru had gone over to Helen, who looked as if she'd like to put an arm around her younger sister, but Dru wasn't standing close enough for that.

Something about the sight of them made Kit put his hand on Ty's shoulder. He was aware of the warmth of the other boy's skin through his T-shirt. Ty glanced at him sideways. "You better go say good-bye, or good trip," Kit said awkwardly.

Ty hesitated a moment, and then went, Kit's hand sliding off his shoulder as if Ty had never noticed it there. Kit hung back during the good-byes, the tearful hugs, the whispered promises, the ruffling of hair. Helen held fiercely to Mark as if she never wanted to let him go, while Aline went to get Tavvy, who was playing in his room.

Jaime hung back too, though he did watch Kit out of the corner of his eye, with a curious look, as if to say, *Who is that guy?*

When Aline came back, Tavvy dutifully hugged everyone who was leaving—even Kieran, who looked startled and touched. He dropped his hand to touch Tavvy's hair lightly. "Worry not, little one."

And then it was time for Ty and Mark to say farewell, and Mark touched Ty lightly on each cheek, once—a faerie good-bye.

"Don't die," Ty said.

Mark's smile looked painful. "I won't."

Helen reached for Ty, and the small group of remaining Blackthorns gathered as Cristina held the Eternidad against her chest. It was definitely a piece of polished wood, Kit saw now, twisted somehow into the infinity symbol—no beginning and no end.

"Gather together, all of you who are going to Faerie," said Jaime. "You must be touching each other."

Mark and Kieran each put a hand on one of Cristina's shoulders. She looked quite small between them. Mark rubbed the back of her neck with his thumb: a soothing, almost absent gesture; the intimacy of it startled Kit.

Jaime seemed to notice it as well; his gaze sharpened. But all he said was, "You must tell the artifact where to take you. You don't want to let it choose."

Kieran turned to Cristina. "We go to Bram's Crossroads."

Cristina lowered her gaze, her hands brushing lightly over the artifact. "Take us to Bram's Crossroads," she said.

Faerie magic was quiet, Kit thought. There was no noise, no tumult, no flashing warlock lights. In between one breath and another, Mark, Kieran, and Cristina simply disappeared.

Another meeting, Diana thought. And an emergency one at that: She'd been woken early in the morning by a fire-message summoning her to a Council meeting at the Gard.

Gwyn had tried to coax her back into bed, but Diana was too worried. Worried for Jia. Worried for Emma and Julian. She knew Horace was making an example out of them with this house arrest, but they were just children. How long was this punishment meant to last? And how long would Julian be all right separated from his siblings?

She'd left Gwyn with a kiss and hurried to the Gard, where she'd discovered Shadowhunters from all over—not just the usual Alicante crowd—pouring into the Gard through doors guarded by Centurions. She'd barely gotten a seat toward the front, next to Kadir Safar of the New York Conclave.

When the doors had been closed, they had all been left staring at a dais that was empty except for a single chair with a tall wooden back, and a black-draped table. The drapery looked as if it were covering something—lumpy—that sent a chill up Diana's spine. She told herself it couldn't possibly be what it looked like. Perhaps it was a pile of weapons.

As the Council slowly settled into their places, a silence fell over the room. Horace Dearborn, fully decked out in his Inquisitor robes, was striding onto the dais, followed by Manuel and Zara in Centurion garb, each carrying a long spear etched with the words *primus pilus*.

"*First spears*," Kadir translated. Diana had met him before: an often silent man who had been Maryse's second-in-command for years, and still headed up the New York Conclave. He looked tired and tense, a sallowness to his dark skin that hadn't been there before. "It means they have been promoted to Centurions who personally guard the Inquisitor and Consul."

"Speaking of the Consul," Diana whispered back, "where is Jia?"

Her murmur caught, like a spark in dry tinder, and soon the whole Council was muttering. Horace held up a placating hand.

"Greetings, Nephilim," he said. "Our Consul, Jia Penhallow, sends regards. She is at the Adamant Citadel, consulting with the Iron Sisters about the Mortal Sword. It will soon be reforged, allowing trials to begin again."

The noise subsided to a mutter.

"It is an unfortunate coincidence that both meetings had to be held at the same moment," Horace continued, "but time is of the essence. It will be difficult to have this meeting without Jia, but I know of her positions and will be representing them here."

His voice echoed through the room. *He must be using an Amplification rune*, Diana thought.

"The last time we met here we discussed stricter laws that would codify accountability among Downworlders," Horace said. "Our Consul, in her kindness and generosity, wished us to put off the decision to implement these laws—but these people do not respond to kindness." His face had gone red under his thinning blond hair. "They respond to *strength*! And we must make Shadowhunters strong again!"

A murmur spread through the Hall. Diana looked around for Carmen, who had spoken so bravely at the last meeting, but could find her nowhere in the crowd. She whispered to Kadir, "What is this about? Why did he bring us here to rant at us?"

Kadir looked grim. "The question is, what's he leading up to?"

Diana studied the faces of Manuel and Zara but could read

nothing on them except smugness on Zara's. Manuel was as blank as a piece of new paper.

"With all respect for our Consul, I was willing to go along with the delay," said Horace, "but events have now transpired that make waiting impossible."

A murmur of expectation ran through the room—what was he talking about?

He turned to his daughter. "Zara, let them see the atrocity the Fair Folk have committed against us!"

With a look of grim delight, Zara crossed the dais to the table and whipped the black sheet away as if she were a magician performing in front of a crowd.

A moan of horror went through the crowd. Diana felt her own gorge rise. Beneath the sheet were the remains of Dane Larkspear, splayed out on the table like a corpse ready to be autopsied.

His head was tilted back, his mouth open in a silent scream. His rib cage had been torn to shreds, bits of white bone and yellow tendon peeking through the grotesque slashes. His skin looked withered and ashen, as if he had been dead some time.

Horace's voice rose to a shout. "You see before you a brave young man who was sent on a mission of peace to Faerie, and this is what they return to us. This savaged corpse!"

A terrible scream rent the silence. A woman with Dane Larkspear's dark hair and bony face was on her feet, howling. Elena Larkspear, Diana realized. A bulky man whose features seemed to be collapsing in on themselves with shock and horror had her in his arms; as the crowd stared openly, he dragged her screaming from the room.

Diana felt sick. She hadn't liked Dane Larkspear, but he was just a child, and his parents' grief was real. "*This* is how the family found out?"

There was bitterness in Kadir's tone. "It makes for better theater. Dearborn has always been less a politician than a performer."

Across the aisle, Lazlo Balogh shot them both a dirty look. He wasn't an official member of the Cohort, as far as Diana knew, but he was definitely a sympathizer.

"And savaged it was!" Zara cried, her eyes glittering. "Behold the bite marks—the work of kelpies! Perhaps even helped by vampires, or werewolves—"

"Stop it, Zara," Manuel muttered. No one seemed to have noticed Zara's ranting, though. There was too much chaos in the crowd. Shadowhunters were cursing and swearing in a dozen different languages. Diana felt a cold despair settle over her.

"This is not all—more Downworlder crimes have come to light in just these past days," said Horace. "A group of brave Centurions, loyal to their Shadowhunter heritage, discovered an Unseelie prince hiding at the Scholomance." He turned to Zara and Manuel. "Bring forth the traitors!"

"This is not how we do things," Diana whispered. "This is not how Shadowhunters comport themselves, nor how we hold our own accountable—"

She broke off before Kadir could reply. Zara and Manuel had disappeared into one of the corridors beside the dais; they returned with Timothy Rockford by their side. Between them marched a line of students familiar to Diana—Diego Rosales, Rayan Maduabuchi, and Divya Joshi.

Their hands were bound behind them, their mouths closed with runes of Quietude, runes that usually only Silent Brothers bore. Diana's eyes met Diego's: She saw the raw fear behind them.

"Runes of Quietude," said Kadir in disgust, as the Hall erupted into screams. "Imagine being treated like this, and silenced—unable to protest."

Diana bolted to her feet. "What are you doing, Horace? These are just children! *Shadowhunter* children! It is our job to protect them!"

Horace's amplified voice made his hiss of annoyance echo through the room. "Yes, they are our children, our hope for the future! And our sympathy toward Downworlders has made them easy prey for deceit. These misguided souls smuggled a faerie 'prince' out of the Scholomance after his vicious attack on another one of our most promising young minds."

The room fell silent. Diana exchanged a bewildered look with Kadir. What was Horace talking about?

Manuel's eyes flicked to the left. He was smirking. A second later Gladstone appeared, half-carrying a girl in a ragged dress, a Centurion cloak thrown over her shoulders.

It was Samantha Larkspear. Her black hair hung down over her face in strings and her eyes darted back and forth like trapped insects. Her hands were crooked into claws at her sides: She held one out, batting it toward the audience as if she were swatting away flies.

Diana felt as if she might throw up.

Manuel stalked toward her, his hands looped carelessly behind his back. "Samantha Larkspear," he said. A groan rippled around the crowd as people realized that this was the sister of the dead and maimed boy on the table. "Tell us of Prince Kieran!"

Samantha began to whip her head back and forth, her hair swinging. "No, no! Such terrible pain!" she moaned. "Don't make me think of Prince Kieran!"

"That poor girl," Lazlo Balogh announced loudly. "Traumatized by Downworlders."

Diana could see Diego shaking his head, Rayan trying to speak, but no sound or words coming out. Divya merely stared stonily at Manuel, hatred clear in her every flicker of expression.

"Perhaps you would like to talk to the prisoners," Manuel suggested to Samantha, his tone like an oily caress. "The ones who let Prince Kieran free?"

Samantha shied away from Diego and the others, her face contorted. "No! Keep them away from me! Don't let them look at me!"

Diana sank back in her seat. Whatever had happened to Samantha, she knew it was no fault of Kieran's or the others', but she could feel the mood of the crowd: stark horror. No one would want to hear a defense of them now.

"My God, what's he going to do?" she whispered, half to herself. "What's Horace going to do to Diego and the others?"

"Put them in jail," said Kadir bleakly. "Make an example of them. They cannot be tried now, while the Mortal Sword is broken. Horace will leave them there to inspire hatred and fear. A symbol to point to whenever his policies are questioned. *Look what happened.*"

On the dais, Samantha was sobbing. Manuel had taken her into his arms, as if to comfort her, but Diana could see the force with which he held the wailing girl. He was restraining her as the crowd roared for Horace to speak.

Horace stepped forward, his amplified voice carrying over the din as Zara looked on with proud pleasure. "We cannot allow any more young Shadowhunters to suffer and die!" he yelled, and the crowd exploded with agreement.

As if Diego and Divya and Rayan weren't young Shadowhunters. As if they weren't suffering.

"We cannot allow our world to be taken from us," Horace shouted, as Manuel's fingers bit into Samantha's shoulders. "We must be strong enough to protect our children and our homeland. The time has come to put Nephilim first!" Horace raised his triumphantly clenched fists. "Who will join me in voting for the registration of all Downworlders?"

The howl of the answering crowd was like a river roaring out of control, sweeping away all of Diana's hopes.

13
Babylon

There was only a sliver of moon, but the multicolored stars of Faerie lit the sky like bonfires, illuminating the Queen's procession as it wound through silent countryside, over green hills and wide fields.

Sometimes they passed through blood-filled rivers, the scarlet fluid splashing up to stain the horses' legs. Sometimes they passed areas of blight, ghostly moonscapes of gray and black. The Seelie faeries whispered and chittered to each other nervously every time another dead patch of land came into view, but Emma could never make out exactly what they were saying.

By the time they started to hear the noise, Emma was half-asleep on Silvermane's back. Distant music woke her, and the sound of people crying out. She blinked, half-awake, pulling her hood back into place.

They were approaching a crossroads, the first she'd seen that night. Heavy mist hung over the road, obscuring the path ahead. Clusters of tall trees grew at the X where the roads met, and empty iron cages swung from the branches. Emma shivered. The cages were big enough to hold a human being.

She glanced toward Julian. He sat alert on Widowmaker, his dark hair hidden by the hood of Fergus's cloak. She could see only a sliver of his skin, like the moon overhead. "Music," he said in a low voice, drawing his horse up beside hers. "Probably a revel coming up."

He was right. They passed the crossroads, and the thick mist parted immediately. The music grew louder, pipes and fiddles and sweet flutelike instruments Emma didn't recognize. The field north of the road was dominated by a massive pavilion draped with silk and hung with the broken-crown banner of the Unseelie King.

Wildly dancing figures surrounded the pavilion. Most seemed naked, or nearly so, dressed in diaphanous rags. It wasn't much of a dance—they appeared to be mostly writhing together, giggling and splashing in and out of a massive pool of water ringed with silvery rocks. White mist rose off the water, obscuring but not covering a number of half-naked bodies.

Emma blushed, mostly because Julian was there, and looked away. The girls—they had to be sisters—on the bay mare behind her giggled, toying with the ribbons at their throats.

"Prince Oban's revel," said one. "It could be no other."

Her sister looked wistful. "Would that we could go, but the Queen would not approve."

Emma glanced back toward the revel. She had listened to Mark speak of faerie revels before as if they were more than massive wild parties. They were a way of calling down wild magic, he'd said. They had a terrifying undercurrent, a barely leashed power. Looking out at the field, Emma couldn't help but feel as if some of the laughing faces she saw were actually screaming in agony.

"Up ahead," said Julian, snapping her out of her reverie. "It's the Unseelie Court's tower."

Emma looked, and for a moment, a dizzying memory assaulted her: the mural on Julian's bedroom wall showing a castle surrounded by thorned hedges. Ahead of them a dark gray tower rose out of the hills and shadows. Only the top of the tower was visible.

Growing up all around it, their sharp spikes visible even from this distance, was a massive wall of thorns.

"Well, that's that," Helen said in a curiously flat voice. She sat down at the head of the library table. Aline frowned and put her hand on Helen's back. "They're gone."

Dru tried to catch Jaime's eye, but he wasn't looking at her. He'd glanced curiously at Kit and Ty and was now fastening up the straps of his pack.

"You can't go," she said to him a bit desperately. "You must be so tired—"

"I'm all right." He still didn't look at her. Dru felt wretched. She hadn't meant to lie to Jaime. She'd just never mentioned her age, because she'd been afraid he'd think she was a stupid kid. And then Mark had yelled at him about it.

"No, Dru is right." Helen smiled with some effort. "Let us at least give you dinner."

Jaime hesitated. He stood twisting the ties of his pack irresolutely as Kit and Ty pushed past him, and Ty said something about going up on the roof. Kit waved and the two of them slipped out of the library. Back to their private world, Dru thought. Ty would never let her in—he'd never let anyone take Livvy's place.

Not that Dru wanted to do that. She just wanted to be friends with her brother. *Like Helen just wants to be friends with you,* said an annoying little voice in the back of her head. She ignored it.

"Aline's a really good cook," she said instead. Aline rolled her eyes, but Dru ignored her. Jaime was really skinny—skinnier than he had been when she'd seen him in London. He must be hungry. Maybe if she could get him to stay, she could explain—

There was a noise like a soft explosion. Dru gave a small shriek, and an envelope fell from the ceiling and landed on the table. A faint wisp of smoke hung in the air.

"It's addressed to you, babe," Helen said, handing the envelope to Aline. "'Aline Penhallow, Head of the Institute.'"

Frowning, Aline ripped the envelope open. Her face tightened. She read aloud:

Aline Penhallow:
Pursuant to the most recent Council meeting held in Alicante, the Registry of Downworlders is now enforced. Heads of Institutes and Conclaves, it is your responsibility to make sure that the Downworlders in your region are registered and given identification numbers. You will be receiving a stamp to use in registration, in ink that will show up only in witchlight.

Downworlders must be ready to show their marked documents at any time. Records of all registrations must be handed over to the Office of the Inquisitor. Failure to do so may result in suspension of privileges or recall to Alicante. Sed lex, dura lex. The Law is hard, but it is the Law. In these troubled times, all must be held accountable. Thank you for your understanding.

Horace Dearborn

NB: As reflects our new policy of accountability, all Institute heads should be advised that the traitors Diego Rosales, Divya Joshi, and Rayan Maduabuchi are awaiting conviction in the Gard for aiding in the escape of a wanted Downworlder. As soon as the Mortal Sword is reforged, they will stand trial.

There was a crash. Jaime had dropped his pack. Drusilla moved to pick it up, but he'd already seized it.

"That bastard Dearborn," he said through white lips. "My brother is not a traitor. He is painfully honest, good—" He looked around at the stricken faces surrounding him. "What does it matter?" he whispered. "None of you know him."

Helen began to rise to her feet. "Jaime—"

He bolted from the library. A second later, Dru tore after him.

He was fast, but he didn't know the house or the way the front door stuck. Dru caught up to him as he struggled to yank it open.

"Jaime!" she cried.

He held up a hand. "Stop. I must go, Drusilla. It's my brother, you understand?"

"I know. But please be careful." She fumbled at her belt and held something out to him. Her hand was shaking. "Take your dagger. You need it more than I do."

He stared down at the blade she held; he'd given it to her, left it in her room at the London Institute when he'd gone. A gold hunting dagger carved with roses.

Gently, he took hold of her hand, closing her fingers over the dagger. "It is yours. A gift," he said.

Her voice sounded small. "Does that mean we're still friends?"

His fleeting smile was sad. He pulled at the door handle and this time it opened; Jaime slipped through it, past her, and vanished into the shadows.

"Dru? Are you all right?"

She turned around, scrubbing furiously at her stinging eyes. She didn't want to cry in front of Helen—and it was Helen, her sister standing on the bottom step of the main staircase, looking at her with troubled eyes.

"You don't need to worry about me," she said in a shaking voice. "I know you think it's stupid, but he was my first real friend—"

"I don't think it's stupid!" Helen crossed the room to Dru in swift strides.

Dru's throat hurt almost too much for her to speak. "I feel like people keep leaving," she whispered.

This close up, Helen looked even more thin and pretty and she smelled like orange blossoms. But for the first time, she didn't seem remote, like a distant star. She seemed distressed and worried and very much present. There was even an ink stain on her sleeve.

"I know how you feel," Helen went on. "I missed you so much while I was on Wrangel Island I couldn't breathe. I kept thinking about everything I was missing, and how I'd miss you getting older, all the little things, and when I saw you in the Council Hall I kept thinking . . ."

Dru braced herself.

". . . how beautiful you'd gotten. You look so much like Mom." Helen sniffled. "I used to watch her getting ready to go out. She was so glamorous, she had such style . . . all I can ever think to wear is jeans and a shirt."

Dru stared in amazement.

"I'm going to stay," Helen said fiercely. "I'm not leaving you ever again." She reached for Dru—and Dru nodded, just the smallest nod. Helen put her arms around her and held her tightly.

Dru rested her forehead against her sister and finally allowed herself to remember Helen picking her up when she was small, swinging her around while she laughed, tying ribbons in her hair and finding her lost shoes, inevitably discarded on the beach. They fit together differently now than they had then, Dru thought, as she put her own arms around Helen. They were different heights and shapes, different people than they had been once.

But even if they fit differently now, they still fit like sisters.

It was nothing like a Portal; there was no rushing tumult, no sense of being picked up by a tornado and hurled around wildly. One moment Cristina was standing in the library at the Institute, and the next she was in a green field, with Mark and Kieran on either side of her and music ringing through the air.

Mark dropped his hand from her shoulder; so did Kieran. Cristina shoved the artifact into her pack and slung it onto her back, pulling the straps tight as the boys looked around in astonishment.

"It's a revel," said Mark in disbelief. "We've landed in the middle of a revel."

"Well, not the middle," said Kieran. He was technically correct; they were just outside a field that was full of whirling, spinning dancers. Pavilions had been set up on the green, with one, more massive than the others, hung with swags of silk.

"I thought we were going to Bram's Crossroads?" Cristina said.

"We're close to it." Kieran pointed. Across the field, Cristina could see the place where two roads met, surrounding by massive oak trees. "It is the place where the Seelie Lands and the Unseelie Lands meet."

"Who is Bram?" said Cristina.

"Bram was King before my father, long ago," said Kieran. He indicated the southern road. "Emma and Julian would be coming from there. The Seelie Lands. Any official procession would pass the crossroads."

"So we have to get to the road," said Mark. "We have to go through the revel." He turned. "Disguise yourself, Prince Kieran."

Kieran gave Mark a dark look. Cristina, not wanting to waste time, unbuckled Kieran's pack, pulled out a rolled cloak, and handed it to him.

Kieran drew the cloak on, pulling the hood up. "Am I disguised?"

Cristina could still see a glimpse of blue-black hair beneath the edge of the hood but hoped no one would be looking all that closely. If they did, they could tell easily enough that he was a prince. It was in his bearing, in the way he moved, the look on his face.

Mark must have had the same thought, for he bent down, took

a handful of mud, and rubbed it firmly into Kieran's surprised face, leaving smears of dirt on his cheek and nose.

Kieran was not pleased. He glared. "You did that because you enjoyed it."

Mark grinned like a little boy and tossed the remaining mud aside. Kieran scrubbed at his nose, still glaring. He did look less princely, though. "Stop it," said Cristina.

"Thank you," Kieran said.

With a grin, Cristina grabbed some mud and smeared a bit on Kieran's cheek. "You have to get both sides."

Mark laughed; Kieran looked indignant for several seconds before giving in and laughing as well.

"Now let's not waste any more time," Cristina said a bit regretfully. She wished the three of them could simply stay here, together, and not join the revel.

But they had no choice. They pressed forward into the revel, through the area where many of the dancers had already collapsed, exhausted. A boy with smeared metallic paint on his face and striped breeches sat gazing at his hands in a drugged haze as he moved them slowly through the air. They passed a pool of steaming water surrounded by mist; slippery bodies were visible through gaps in the smoke. Cristina felt her cheeks flame red.

They moved on, and the crowd closed around them like fast-growing vines. It was nothing like the revel Cristina had seen the last time she was in Faerie. That had been a massive dance party. This was more like a slice of a Bosch painting. A group of faerie men were fighting; their bare upper bodies, slippery with blood, shone in the starlight. A kelpie feasted hungrily on the dead body of a brownie, its open eyes staring sightlessly at the sky. Naked bodies lay entwined in the grass, their limbs moving with slow intent. Pipes and fiddles screamed, and the air smelled like wine and blood.

They passed a giant lying unconscious in the grass. All over his huge body were hundreds of pixies, darting and dancing, like a moving sea. No, Cristina realized, they weren't dancing. They were—

She glanced away. Her cheeks felt like they were on fire.

"This is my brother's doing," said Kieran, staring grimly at the largest of the pavilions, the one that bore the crest of the Unseelie Court. An ornate throne-like seat had been placed there, but it was empty. "Prince Oban. His revels are famous for their duration and their debauchery." He frowned as a group of naked acrobats hooted from a nearby tree. "He makes Magnus Bane look like a prudish nun."

Mark looked as if he'd just heard that there was an alternate sun that was nine million times hotter than Earth's sun. "You never mentioned Oban."

"He embarrasses me," said Kieran. A branch broke overhead, depositing a goblin-size horse wearing a garter belt on the ground in front of them. It wore woolen hose with runs in them and golden hoof covers.

"I can see why," said Mark as the horse wandered off, nibbling at the grass. It studiously avoided the couples embracing in the tangled undergrowth.

Dancers whirled past Cristina in a circle surrounding a ribboned tree, but none of them wore expressions of enjoyment. Their faces were blank, their eyes wide, their arms flailing. Every once in a while a drunken faerie knight would pull one of the dancers from the circle and down into the long grass. Cristina shuddered.

From the top of the tree hung a cage. Inside the cage was a hunched figure, white and slimy like a pale slug, its body covered in gray pockmarks. *It looks like an Eidolon demon in its true form*, Cristina thought. But why would a prince of Faerie have an Eidolon demon in a cage?

A horn blared. The music had become more sour, almost sinister. Cristina looked again at the dancers and realized suddenly that they were ensorcelled. She remembered the last time she'd been at a revel, and how she'd been swept away by the music; she didn't feel that way now, and silently thanked the Eternidad.

She had read about faerie revels where mortals were forced to dance until the bones in their feet splintered, but she hadn't realized it was something faeries might do to each other. The beautiful young girls and boys in the circle were being danced off their feet, their upper bodies slumping even as their legs moved tirelessly to the rhythm.

Kieran looked grim. "Oban gets pleasure from witnessing the pain of others. Those are the thorns of his roses, the poison in the bloom of his gregariousness and gifts."

Cristina moved toward the dancers, concerned. "They're all going to die—"

Kieran caught her sleeve, pulling her back toward him and Mark. "Cristina, no." He sounded sincerely alarmed for her. "Oban will let them live, once he's humiliated them enough."

"How can you be sure?" Cristina asked.

"They're gentry. Court hangers-on. Oban would be in trouble with my father if he killed them all."

"Kieran is right," said Mark, the moonlight silvering his hair. "You cannot save them, Cristina. And we cannot linger here."

Reluctantly Cristina followed as they pushed swiftly through the crowd. The air was full of sweet, harsh smoke, mixing with the mist from the occasional pool of water.

"Prince Kieran." A faerie woman with hair like a dandelion clock drifted up to them. She wore a dress of white filaments, and her eyes were green as stems. "You come to us in disguise."

Mark's hand had gone to his weapons belt, but Kieran made a quick settling gesture at him. "I can trust you to keep my secret, can I not?"

"If you tell me why an Unseelie Prince would come hidden to his own brother's revel, perhaps," said the woman, her green eyes keen.

"I seek a friend," Kieran said.

The woman's eyes darted over Cristina and then Mark. Her mouth widened into a smile. "You seem to have several."

"That's enough," said Mark. "The prince would proceed unhindered."

"Now, if it were a love potion you sought, you might come to me," said the faerie woman, ignoring Mark. "But which of these two Nephilim do you love? And which loves you?"

Kieran raised a warning hand. "Enough."

"Ah, I see, I see." Cristina wondered what it was she saw. "No love potion could assist with this." Her eyes danced. "Now, in Faerie, you could love both and have both love you. You would have no trouble. But in the world of the Angel—"

"Enough, I said!" Kieran flushed. "What would it take to end this bedevilment?"

The faerie woman laughed. "A kiss."

With a look of exasperation, Kieran bent his head and kissed the faerie woman lightly on the mouth. Cristina felt herself tense, her stomach tightening. It was an unpleasant sensation.

She realized Mark, beside her, had tensed as well, but neither of them moved as the faerie woman drew back, winked, and danced away into the crowd.

Kieran wiped the back of his hand across his lips. "They say a kiss from a prince brings good luck," he said. "Even a disgraced one, apparently."

"You didn't need to do that, Kier," said Mark. "We could have gotten rid of her."

"Not without a fuss," Kieran said. "And I suspect Oban and his men are here in the crowd somewhere."

Cristina glanced up at the pavilion. Kieran was right—it was still empty. Where was Prince Oban? Among the rutting couples in the grass? They had begun to make their way across the clearing again: Faces of every hue loomed out of the mist at her, twisted in grimaces; Cristina even imagined she saw Manuel, and remembered how Emma had been forced to see an image of her father the last time they had been in Faerie. She shuddered, and when she looked again it was not Manuel at all but a faerie with the body of a man and the face of a wise old tabby, blinking golden eyes.

"Drinks, madam and sirs? A draft to cool you after dancing?" said the tabby faerie in a soft and cooing voice. Cristina stared, remembering. Mark had bought her a drink from this cat-faced faerie at the revel she'd been to with him. He held the same gold tray with cups on it. Even his tattered Edwardian suit had not changed.

"No drinks, Tom Tildrum, King of Cats," said Kieran. His voice was sharp, but he clearly recognized the cat faerie. "We need to find a Seelie procession. There could be several coins in it for you if you lead us to the road."

Tom gave a low hiss. "You are too late. The Queen's procession passed by here an hour ago."

Mark cursed and flung his hood back. Cristina didn't even have time to be startled that usually gentle Mark was cursing; she felt as if a hole had been punched through her chest. Emma. Emma and Jules. They'd missed them. Kieran, too, looked dismayed.

"Give me a drink, then, Tom," said Mark, and seized a glass of ruby-colored liquid from the tray.

Kieran held out a staying hand. "Mark! You know better!"

"It's just fruit juice," Mark said, his eyes on Cristina's. She flushed and glanced away as he drained the glass.

A moment later he sank to the ground, his eyes rolling back in his head. "Mark!" Cristina gasped, flinging herself to the ground beside him. He was clearly unconscious, but just as clearly breathing. In fact, he was snoring a bit. "But it was just fruit juice!" she protested.

"I like to serve a variety of beverages," said Tom.

Kieran knelt down by Cristina. His hood had partly fallen back, and Cristina could see the concern on his face as he touched Mark's chest lightly. The smudges on his cheeks made his eyes stand out starkly. "Tom Tildrum," he said in a tight voice. "It's not safe here."

"Not for you, for the sons of the Unseelie King are at each other's throats like cats," said Tom Tildrum with a flash of incisors.

"Then you see why you must lead us through to the road," Kieran said.

"And if I do not?"

Kieran rose to his feet, managing to exude princely menace despite his dirty face. "Then I will yank your tail until you howl."

Tom Tildrum hissed as Kieran and Cristina bent to lift Mark and carry him between them. "Come with me, then, and be quick about it, before Prince Oban sees. He would not like me helping you, Prince Kieran. He would not like it at all."

Kit lay on the roof of the Institute, his hands behind his head. The air was blowing from the desert, warm and soft as a blanket tickling his skin. If he turned his head one way, he could see Malibu, a chain of glittering lights strung along the curve of the seashore.

This was the Los Angeles people sang about in pop songs, he thought, and put into movies; sea and sand and expensive houses, perfect weather and air that breathed as soft as powder. He had never known it before, living with his father in the shadow of smog and downtown skyscrapers.

If he turned his head the other way, he could see Ty, a black-and-white figure perched beside him at the roof's edge. The sleeves of Ty's hoodie were pulled down, and he worried their frayed edges with his fingers. His black eyelashes were so long Kit could see the breeze move them as if it were ruffling sea grass.

The feeling of his own heart turning over was now so familiar that Kit didn't question it or what it meant.

"I can't believe Hypatia agreed to our plan," Kit said. "Do you think she really means it?"

"She must mean it," said Ty, staring out over the ocean. The moon was hidden behind clouds, and the ocean seemed to be absorbing light, sucking it down into its black depth. Along the border where the sea met the shore, white foam ran like a stitched ribbon. "She wouldn't have sent us the money if she hadn't. Especially enchanted money."

Kit yawned. "True. When a warlock sends you money, you know it's serious. I guarantee you that if we don't get this done like we said we would, she's going to come after us—for the money, at least."

Ty pulled his knees up against his chest. "The issue here is that we have to get a meeting with Barnabas, but he hates us. We've already seen that. We can't get near him."

"You should maybe have thought of that before you made this deal," said Kit.

Ty looked confused for a moment, then smiled. "Details, Watson." He ran a hand through his hair. "Maybe we should disguise ourselves."

"I think we should ask Dru."

"Dru? Why Dru?" Now Ty looked baffled. "Ask her what?"

"To help us. Barnabas doesn't know her. And she does look a lot older than she is."

"No. Not Dru."

Kit remembered Dru's face in the library when she'd talked about Jaime. *He listened to me and he watched horror movies with me and he acted like what I said was important.* He remembered how happy she'd been to be taught lock picking. "Why not? We can trust her. She's lonely and bored. I think she'd like to be included."

"But we can't tell her about Shade." Ty was pale as the moon. "Or the Black Volume."

True, Kit thought to himself. *I'm definitely not telling Drusilla about a plan that I hope falls apart before it ever comes to fruition.*

He sat up. "No—no, definitely not. It would be dangerous for her to know anything about—about that. All we need to tell her is that we're trying to get back on good terms with the Shadow Market."

Ty's gaze slid away from Kit. "You really like Drusilla."

"I think she feels very alone," said Kit. "I get that."

"I don't want her to be in danger," said Ty. "She can't be in any kind of danger." He tugged at the sleeves of his hoodie. "When Livvy comes back, I'm going to tell her I want to do the *parabatai* ceremony right away."

"I thought you wanted to go to the Scholomance?" said Kit without thinking. If only Ty could see that was a possibility for him now, Kit wished—and instantly hated himself for thinking it. Of course Ty wouldn't want to consider Livvy's death to be any form of freedom.

"No," Ty said sharply. "Remember, I told you, I don't want to go there anymore. Besides, you can't have *parabatai* at the Scholomance. It's a rule. And rules are important."

Kit didn't even want to think about how many rules they were breaking right now. Ty had clearly compartmentalized what it would take to bring Livvy back, but nothing like that ever worked perfectly. He was worrying hard at the cuffs of his hoodie now, his fingers shaking a little.

Kit touched Ty's shoulder. He was sitting slightly behind him. Ty's back curved as he hunched forward, but he didn't avoid the touch.

"How many windows does the front of the Institute have?" Kit said.

"Thirty-six," said Ty. "Thirty-seven if you count the attic, but it's papered over. Why?"

"Because that's what I like about you," Kit said in a low voice, and Ty's shaking stilled slightly. "The way you notice everything. Nothing gets forgotten. Nothing"—*and no one*—"gets overlooked."

Emma had begun to nod off again as the night wore on. She woke when her horse stopped in its tracks and pushed her hood back slightly, gazing around her.

They had reached the tower. Dawn was breaking and in the first threads of light, the only permanent manifestation of the Unseelie Court looked less like Julian's mural and more like something from a nightmare. The hedge of thorns surrounding the tower was nothing like modest rosebushes. The thorns were steel-colored, each easily a foot long. Here and there they were studded with what looked like massive white flowers. The tower's walls were smooth and dark as anthracite, and windowless.

Emma's breath made tracks against the chilly air. She shivered and drew Nene's cloak closer, murmurs rising all around as the sleepy procession of Seelie faeries began to come back to wakefulness. The girls behind her were chattering about what kind of rooms and welcome they might expect from the King. Julian was motionless beside Emma, his spine straight, his hood concealing his face.

There was a loud clang, like the ringing of a bell. Emma peered ahead to see that there were gates set into the thorny hedge, tall bronze gates that had just been flung open. She could see a courtyard just past the gates, and a great black archway leading into the tower.

Unseelie knights in black cloaks guarded either side of the gates. They were stopping each member of the procession before allowing them to pass through into the courtyard, where two lines of Unseelie faeries flanked the path to the tower doors.

The multicolored stars were beginning to fade out of the air, and in their absence, the light of the rising sun cast dull gold shadows over the tower, darkly beautiful as a polished gun barrel. All around the hedge was a flat, grassy plain, punctuated here and there by stands of hawthorn trees. The line of Seelie faeries lurched forward again, and a loud grumble rose among the riot of silks and velvets, wings and hooves. The girls on the bay mare were muttering to each other: How slow they are here in the Night Court. How rude to keep us waiting.

The morning air caught the edge of Emma's hood as she turned. "What is this about?"

One of the girls shook her head. "The King is suspicious, naturally. Too long has there been enmity between the Courts. The Riders are inspecting each guest."

Emma froze. "The Riders of Mannan?"

The other girl laughed. "As if there were other Riders!"

Julian leaned toward Emma and spoke in a low voice: "There's no way we can get through those gates with the rest of the procession without the Riders recognizing us. Especially you. We need to get out of here."

The place where Cortana usually hung at Emma's back ached like a phantom limb. She had killed one of the Riders with her sword—there was no chance they wouldn't remember her. "Agreed. Any idea how to do that?"

Julian glanced up and down the restless line of Seelie folk. It stretched from the gates of the tower into the distance, as far as the eye could see. "Not currently."

A noise erupted from the line ahead. The dryad in the tree was arguing with a pair of goblins. In fact, small arguments seemed to breaking out up and down the line. Occasionally a faerie knight would ride lazily by and call for order, but no one seemed too interested in keeping things calm.

Emma gazed anxiously at the horizon; it was dawn, and soon there would be more light, which would hardly help any attempt on her and Julian's part to try to get away. They could bolt for the gates, but the guards would block them; if they ran for the thorn hedges or tried to leave the line, they'd certainly be seen.

Then accept that you'll be seen, Emma thought. She turned to Julian, drawing herself up imperiously. "Fergus, you fool!" she snapped. "The Queen explicitly demanded that you bring up the rear of this procession!"

Julian's lips shaped the word "What?" silently. He didn't move, and the girls on the bay mare giggled again.

Emma struck his shoulder lightly, her fingers sliding across his back, drawing a quick symbol they both knew. It meant: *I have a plan.* "Distracted by a dryad, were you?" she said. She dug her heels into Silvermane's side and the horse, startled, trotted sharply in place. "The Queen will have your head for this. Come along!"

Giggles spread throughout the nearby faeries. Emma turned Silvermane and began to ride toward the back of the procession. After a moment, Julian followed her. The giggles faded behind them as they trotted down the line; Emma didn't want to attract notice by going too fast.

To her relief, no one paid much attention to them. As they rode away from the tower, the Seelie procession's order began to deteriorate. Faerie folk were grouped together laughing, joking, and playing cards. None of them seemed interested in their progress toward the tower, much less anything closer at hand.

"This way," Julian murmured. He bent low over Widowmaker, and the horse bolted toward a nearby thicket of trees. Emma grabbed her own reins tightly as Silvermane leaped after the stallion. The world rushed by in a blur—she was galloping, which was like flying, the horse's feet barely seeming to touch the ground. Emma caught her breath. It was like the terror and freedom of being in the ocean, at the mercy of something far stronger than you. Her hood flew back and the wind tore at her, her blond hair whipping like a banner.

They pulled up at the far side of the thicket, out of sight of the Seelie folk. Emma looked at Julian, breathless. His cheeks were flushed to brightness by the cold air. Behind him, the horizon had turned to bright gold.

"Nice work," he said.

Emma couldn't suppress a smile as she slid from Silvermane's back. "We might not have angelic magic here, but we're still Shadowhunters."

Julian dismounted beside her. Neither needed to say they couldn't keep the horses with them; Emma struck Silvermane lightly on the flank, and the mare took off toward the lightening horizon. *She knows her own way home.*

Widowmaker vanished after her in a dark blur, and Emma and Julian turned toward the tower. The long shadows of dawn were beginning to stretch out across the grass. The tower rose before them, the high hedge circling it like a deadly necklace.

Emma eyed the grass between their trees and the hedge nervously. There was no cover, and though they were out of sight of the gates, anyone watching from the tower could see them approach.

Julian turned toward her, pushing his hood back. Emma supposed it no longer mattered; he was done pretending to be Fergus. His hair was tousled and sweat-dampened from the hood. As if he had read her mind, he said, "We can't worry about cover. We'll have to brazen it out till we get to the hedge."

He slid his hand into hers. Emma tried to stop herself from jumping. His palm was warm against her palm; he drew her toward him and they began to walk across the grass.

"Keep your head turned toward me," Julian said in a low voice. "Faeries are romantics, in their way."

Emma realized with a jolt that they were playing at being a

couple, taking an affectionate walk in the dawn light. Their shoulders brushed, and she shivered, even as the sun rose higher, warming the air.

She glanced sideways at Julian. He didn't look like someone on a romantic walk; his eyes were wary, his jaw set. He looked like a statue of himself, one carved by someone who didn't know him well, who had never seen the sparkle in his eyes he saved for his family, who had never seen the smile he had once saved for Emma alone.

They had reached the hedge. It rose above them, a tangle of closely woven vines, and Emma drew her hand out of Julian's with an indrawn breath. Up close, the hedge looked as if it were made out of shining steel, the thorns sticking out everywhere at jagged angles. Some were as long as swords. What Emma had thought were flowers were the whitening skeletons of those who had tried to climb the wall, a warning to future trespassers.

"This might be impossible," said Julian, looking up. "We could wait until nightfall—try to sneak through the gates."

"We can't wait that long—it's dawn now. We have to stop the Queen." Emma drew a dagger from her belt. It wasn't Cortana, but it was still Shadowhunter steel, long and sharp. She laid the edge against one of the thorns, cutting at an angle. She had expected resistance; there was none. The thorn sliced away easily, leaving behind a stump that dripped grayish sap.

"Ugh," she said, kicking the fallen thorn away. An odd scent, dull and green, rose from the damaged hedge. She took a deep breath, trying to push down her unease. "Okay. I'm going to cut my way through. I can even see the tower through the vines." It was true; this close up, it was clear that the hedge wasn't a solid wall, and there were gaps between the vines big enough to shove a human body through.

"Emma—" Julian made as if to reach out to her, then dropped his hand. "I don't like this. We're not the first people who've tried to get through the hedge." He indicated the skeletons above and around them with a jerk of his chin.

"But we're the first Shadowhunters," said Emma, with a bravado she didn't feel. She slashed at the hedge. Thorns pattered down around her in a light rain.

Light began to fade as she pushed on, farther into the hedge. It was as thick as the lane of a highway, and the vines seemed to weave together above her, forming a shield against the sunlight. She thought she heard Julian call out to her, but his voice was muffled. She glanced back in surprise—and stiffened in horror.

The hedge had closed up behind her like water. She was surrounded by a thick green-gray wall, studded with deadly spikes. She slashed out wildly with her dagger, but the edge of it bounced off the nearest thorn with a clang, as if it were made of steel.

A sharp pain stabbed at her chest. The vines were moving, pressing in toward Emma slowly. The sharp tip of one jabbed her above her heart; another stabbed at her wrist; she jerked her hand away, dropping the dagger; she had more in her pack, but there was no way she could reach them now. Her heart was pounding as the vines surged toward her; she could see flashes of white through the vines as they moved, others who had been trapped in the heart of the hedge wall.

The tip of a thorn slashed along her cheek and blood ran warmly down her face. Emma shrank back, and more thorns stabbed into her back and shoulders. *I'm going to die,* she thought, her thoughts blackening with terror.

But Shadowhunters weren't meant to be afraid, weren't meant to feel fear. In her mind, Emma begged the forgiveness of her parents, her *parabatai*, her friends. She had always thought she'd die in battle, not be crushed to death by a thousand blades, alone and without Cortana in her hand.

Something stabbed into her throat. She twisted, trying to pull away from the agony; she heard Julian call her name—

Something slammed into her palm. Her fingers closed reflexively around it, her body knowing the feel of the sword's hilt before her mind registered what she was holding.

It was a sword. A sword with a white blade, like a slice cut out of the moon. She recognized it immediately from illustrations in old books: It was Durendal, the sword of Roland, brother blade to Cortana.

There was no time to ask questions. Against the thorns, she swung her arm up, Durendal a silvery blur. There was a scream, as of twisting metal, as Durendal sliced through thorns and vines. Sap sprayed, stinging Emma's open cuts, but she didn't care; she cut again and again, the blade whipsawing in her hand, and the vines fell away around her. The hedge writhed as if in pain and the vines began to draw back as if afraid of Durendal. A path opened both ahead of her and behind her, like the parting of the Red Sea. Emma fled through the narrow gap between the vines, calling for Julian to follow her.

She exploded out the other side into a world of color and light and noise: green grass, blue sky, the distant sounds of the procession advancing to the tower. She fell to her knees, still clutching Durendal. Her hands were slicked with blood and sap; she was gasping, bleeding from long rents in her tunic.

A shadow darkened the sky above her. It was Julian. He fell to his knees across from her, his face bone white. He caught at her shoulders and Emma held back a wince. Having his hands on her was more than worth the pain, as was the look on his face. "Emma," he said. "That was incredible. How—?"

She held up the sword. "Durendal came to me," she said. Blood from her cuts pattered down onto the blade as it began to shimmer and fade. In a moment, she was holding only empty air, her fingers still curved around the place the golden hilt had been. "I needed Cortana, and it sent Durendal to me."

"'I am of the same steel and temper as Joyeuse and Durendal,'" Julian murmured. "Twinned blades. Interesting." He released her shoulders and tore a strip of cloth from the hem of his tunic, wadding it up to press against the cut on her cheek with a surprising gentleness.

Joy surged through her, brighter than her pain. She knew he couldn't love her, but in that moment it felt as if he did.

"Mother?" Aline said. "Mother, are you there?"

Helen squinted. She was seated on the desk in the Institute's office, Aline next to her. Jia seemed to be trying to appear as a Projection against the far wall, but at the moment she was just a rather wobbly shadow, like an image taken with a handheld camera.

"Ma!" Aline exclaimed, clearly exasperated. "Could you please appear? We really need to talk to you."

Jia sharpened at the edges. Now Helen could see her, still in her Consul robes. She looked drawn, so thin as to be worryingly emaciated.

The texture of the wall was still visible through her, but she was solid enough for Helen to read her expression: It mirrored her daughter's in annoyance. "It isn't easy to Project from the Gard," she said. "We could have spoken on the phone."

"I wanted to see you," said Aline. There was a slight tremble in her voice. "I needed to know what's going on with this Registry. Why did the Council pass this piece of trash?"

"Horace—" Jia began.

Aline's voice cracked. "Where were you, Mom? How did you let this happen?"

"I did not *let* it happen," Jia said. "Horace lied to me. A very significant meeting was set up this morning, a meeting with Sister Cleophas of the Iron Sisters about the Mortal Sword."

"Is it fixed?" said Aline, diverted momentarily.

“They have made no progress reforging it. It was created by angels, not humans, and perhaps only an angel can heal it.” Jia sighed. “Horace was meant to run a very standard meeting about border protocols while I was at the Adamant Citadel. Instead it became this fiasco.”

“I just don’t understand how he convinced people that this was a good idea,” Helen said.

Jia had begun to pace. Her shadow wobbled up and down the wall like a puppet being pulled back and forth on a stage. “Horace should never have been a politician. He should have had a career in the theater. He played upon everyone’s worst fears. He sent a spy into Faerie and when he came to harm, claimed he was an innocent, murdered child. He claimed Kieran Kingson drove Samantha Larkspear mad—”

“Mark told me she went out of her mind because she fell into the pool in the Hollow Place while the Cohort was tormenting Kieran,” said Helen indignantly. “*She* tried to murder *him*.”

Jia looked bleakly amused. “Should I ask where Kieran is now?”

“Back in Faerie,” said Aline. “Now, you should tell me where Horace is now so I can punch him harder than he’s ever been punched in his life.”

“Punching him won’t help,” said Jia. This was a conversation she and Aline had often. “I have to think about how to take constructive steps to undo the damage he’s done.”

“Why did he arrest the Scholomance kids?” Helen said. “According to Mark, Rayan and Divya and Diego were the most decent of the Centurions.”

“To make an example of them. ‘This is what happens if you help Downworlders,’” said Jia.

“We can’t actually register people,” said Aline. “It’s inhumane. That’s what I’m going to tell the Clave.”

Jia’s Projection fizzed angrily at the edges. “Don’t you dare,” she said. "Haven't you heard what I just said? Dearborn has it in for Helen because of her faerie blood. You'll wind up in jail if you do, and someone more compliant will be installed in your place. You have to at least look like you're going along with it."

"How do we do that?" Helen had always been a little afraid of her Consul mother-in-law. She always imagined that Jia couldn't possibly be pleased that Aline had chosen to marry a woman, much less a half-faerie one. Jia had never indicated by word or deed that she was disappointed in Aline's choice, but Helen felt it just the same. Still, she couldn't help but speak up now. "Downworlders are meant to come to the Sanctuary and we have to turn in the registrations to the Clave."

"I know, Helen," Jia said. "But you can't ignore the orders. Horace will be watching to make sure the L.A. Institute meets its quota. I just got you two back from exile. I'm not losing you again. You're clever. Find a creative way to undermine the registration mandate without ignoring it."

Despite everything, Helen felt a little shock of happiness. *You two*, Jia had said. As if she had missed not just Aline but Helen, too.

"There is one bright spot," Jia said. "I was with Sister Cleophas when the news came through, and she was furious. The Iron Sisters are definitely on our side. They can be formidable when they choose. I don't think Horace will enjoy having them as enemies."

"Mom," Aline said. "You and Dad have to get out of Idris. Come here for a while. It's not safe there."

Helen took Aline's hand and squeezed, because she knew what the answer would be. "I can't just leave," Jia said, sounding not like Aline's mother but like the Consul of the Clave. "I can't abandon our people. I swore an oath to protect Nephilim, and that means weathering this storm and doing everything I can to reverse what Horace has done—to get those children out of the Gard prison—" Jia looked over her shoulder. "I must go. But remember, girls—the

Council is basically good, and so are the hearts of most people."

She vanished.

"I wish I believed that," said Aline. "I wish I understood how my mother could believe that, after all this time as Consul."

She sounded angry at Jia, but Helen knew that wasn't what was going on. "Your mom is smart. She'll be safe."

"I hope so," said Aline, looking down at her hand and Helen's, intertwined on the desk. "And now we need to figure out how to register people without actually registering them. A plan that doesn't involve punching Horace. Why do I never get to do the things I want to do?"

Despite everything, Helen laughed. "Actually, I have an idea. And I think you might like it."

The clearing overlooked the road below, visible as a white ribbon through the trees. The moon overhead was caught in the branches, casting enough illumination that Cristina could see the glade clearly: Surrounded by thick hawthorn trees, the grass underfoot was springy and cool, damp with dew. She had spread out Mark's blanket roll and he lay asleep on it, curled partly on his side, his cheeks flushed.

Cristina sat beside him, her legs stretched out before her in the dew-wet grass. Kieran was nearby, leaning against the trunk of a hawthorn. In the distance, Cristina could hear the sounds of the revel, carried on the clear air.

"This," said Kieran, his gaze fixed on the road below, "was not how I was expecting the events following our arrival in Faerie to transpire."

Cristina brushed Mark's hair back from his face. His skin was fever hot; she suspected it was a side effect of whatever the cat faerie had given him to drink. "How long do you think Mark will be unconscious?"

Kieran turned to press his back against the tree. In the darkness, his face was a map of black-and-white shadow. He had fallen into silence the moment they had reached the glade and gotten Mark settled. Cristina could only imagine what he had been dwelling on. "Another hour or so, most likely."

Cristina felt as if a lead weight were pressing against her chest. "Every moment we wait brings us farther away from Emma and Julian," she said. "I do not see how we could possibly catch up with them now."

Kieran stretched his hands out in front of them. Long-fingered faerie hands, almost double-jointed. "I could summon Windspear again," he said a little haltingly. "He is swift enough to reach them."

"You do not sound as if you like that idea much," Cristina observed, but Kieran only shrugged.

He drew away from the tree and came toward Mark, bending to tuck a corner of the blanket over Mark's shoulder. Cristina watched him consideringly. Windspear was a prince's steed, she thought. Windspear would catch attention, here in Faerie. He might alert the kingdom to Kieran's presence, put him in danger. But Kieran seemed willing to summon him regardless.

"Not Windspear," she said. "Even if we had him—what would we do, try to pluck them from the procession out of the air? We would be noticed, and think of the danger—to Mark, to Jules and Emma."

Kieran smoothed the blanket over Mark's shoulder and stood up. "I do not know," he said. "I do not have answers." He pulled his cloak around him. "But you are right. We cannot wait."

Cristina glanced up at him. "We cannot leave Mark, either."

"I know. I think you should let me go alone. You remain here with Mark."

"No!" Cristina exclaimed. "No, you're not going alone. And not without the artifact. It's our only way out."

"It doesn't matter," said Kieran. He bent down to lift his bag, swinging it over his shoulder. "It doesn't matter what happens to me."

"Of course it matters!" Cristina started to her feet and winced; her legs were stinging with pins and needles. She hurried after Kieran nonetheless, limping a little.

Moving swiftly, Kieran had reached the edge of the glade when she caught up with him. She seized hold of his arm, her fingers digging into the fabric of his sleeve. "Kieran, *stop*."

He stopped, though he didn't look back at her. He was staring out at the road and the revel beyond. In a remote voice, he said, "Why do you prevent me?"

"To go alone on that road is dangerous, especially for you."

Kieran didn't seem to hear her. "When I touched the pool at the Scholomance, I felt the confusion and pain that I caused to you," he said.

Cristina waited. He said nothing else. "And?"

"And?" he echoed in disbelief. "And I cannot bear it! That I hurt you like that, hurt you and Mark like that—I cannot stand it."

"But you must," said Cristina.

Kieran's lips parted in astonishment. "What?"

"This is the nature of having a soul, Kieran, and a heart. We all stumble around in the dark and we cause each other pain and we try to make up for it the best we can. We are all confused."

"Then let me make up for it." Gently but firmly, he pried her hand from his sleeve. "Let me go after them."

He started down the hill, but Cristina followed, blocking his way. "No—you must not—"

He tried to step around her. She moved in front of him. "Let me—"

"I will not let you risk yourself!" she cried, and caught at the front of his shirt with her hands, the fabric rough under her fingers. She heard him exhale with surprise.

She had to tilt her head back to look into his eyes; they glittered, black and silver and remote as the moon. "Why not?" he demanded.

She could feel the warmth of him through the linen of his shirt. There had been a time she might have thought him fragile, unreal as moonbeams, but she knew now that he was strong. She could see herself reflected in his dark eye; his silver eye was a mirror to the stars. There was a weariness to his face that spoke of pain, but a steadfastness, too, more beautiful than symmetry of features. No wonder Mark had fallen in love with him in the Hunt. Who would not have?

"Perhaps you are not confused," she said in a whisper. "But I am. You confuse me very much."

"Cristina," he whispered. He touched her face lightly; she leaned into the warmth of his hand, and his fingers slipped across her cheek to her mouth. He outlined the shape of her lips with his fingertips, his eyes half-closed. She reached up to wrap her arms around his neck.

He pulled her against him, and their mouths came together so swiftly she could not have said who kissed who. It was all fire: the taste of him on her mouth, and his skin smooth where she touched it, sliding her fingers under the collar of his cloak. His lips were fine-grained, soft but firm; he sipped at her mouth as if drinking fine wine. Her hands found his hair and buried themselves in the soft locks.

"My lady," he whispered against her mouth, and her body thrilled to the sound of his voice. "Lady of Roses."

His hands slipped down her body, over her curves and softness, and she was lost in the heat and fire of it, in the feeling of him against her, so different from Mark but just as wonderful. He gripped her waist and pulled her tight to him and a shock went through her: He was so warm and human, and not remote at all. "Kieran," she breathed, and she heard Mark's voice in her head, saying his name: *Kier, Kieran, my dark one,* and she remembered Mark and Kieran kissing in the desert and felt a flutter of excitement deep in her bones.

"What's going on?"

It was Mark's voice—not just in her head, but cutting through the night, through the fog of desire. Cristina and Kieran jerked away from each other, almost stumbling, and Cristina stared at Mark, a silver-and-gold silhouette in the darkness, blinking at them.

"Mark," Kieran said, a catch in his voice.

Suddenly the clearing was full of light. Mark threw up an arm, flinching away from the sudden unnatural brilliance.

"Mark!" Kieran said again, and this time the catch in his voice was alarm. He moved toward Mark, drawing Cristina after him, his hand in hers. They stumbled together into the center of the clearing just as a contingent of faerie guards burst from the trees, their torches blazing like banners against the night.

They were led by Manuel Villalobos. Cristina stared in shock. He wore their same livery: a tunic with the symbol of the broken crown hovering over a throne. His sandy hair was tousled, his grin slightly manic. A medallion like the one Cristina always wore glimmered at his throat.

"Prince Kieran," he said as the guards surrounded Kieran, Mark, and Cristina. "How delighted your brother Oban will be to see you."

Kieran had his hand on the hilt of his sword. He spoke flatly. "That will be a first. He has never been delighted to see me before."

"What are you doing here, Manuel?" Cristina said.

Manuel turned to her with a sneer. "I'm here on business. Unlike you."

"You don't know why I'm here," she snapped.

"Apparently, to whore for a faerie and his half-breed lover," said Manuel. "Interesting activities for a Shadowhunter."

Mark's sword flashed out. He lunged at Manuel, who leaped back, snapping an order to the prince's guards. They swarmed forward; Cristina barely had time to get her balisong free and slash it forward, slicing a long cut across the chest of a guard with purple-and-blue-streaked hair.

Mark and Kieran were already fighting, each with a sword in hand. They were beautifully fast and deadly; several guards fell, shouting in pain, and Cristina added two more to the pile of wounded.

But there were far too many of them. Through the blaze of torches and flash of blades, Cristina could see Manuel lounging against the trunk of a tree. As she caught his eye, he grinned and made an obscene gesture at her. He clearly wasn't worried about who was going to win this.

Mark shouted. Three guards had grabbed Kieran, who was struggling as they twisted his arms behind his back. Two more were advancing on Mark, and another leaped for Cristina; she sank her balisong into his shoulder and pushed past his falling body toward Mark and Kieran.

"Bind them!" Manuel called. "Prince Oban would take them to the King for questioning! Do not harm them." He grinned. "The King wants to do that himself."

Cristina's eyes met Mark's as the two guards seized him. He shook his head at her frantically, shouting through the clamor:

"Cristina! Take the artifact! Go!"

Cristina shook her head—*I can' t leave you, I can't*—but her eyes fell on Kieran, who was looking at her with naked hope and pleading. Reading the meaning in his gaze, she leaped for her pack where it lay on the ground.

Several of Oban's guards dashed toward her, weapons outstretched, as Manuel cried out for them to stop her. She thrust her hand into the bag and seized the artifact. With all her will, she concentrated her mind on the one person she thought could help them.

Take me to him. Take me.

The glade flashed out of existence just as the guards closed in.

14

THE VIOL, THE VIOLET, AND THE VINE

The search for Dru took a little longer than Kit had expected. She wasn't in the library, or in her bedroom, or down by the beach. They found her eventually in the TV room, sorting through a pile of old videotapes with names like *Scream and Scream Again* and *Bloody Birthday*.

The look she gave them when they came in wasn't friendly. Her eyes were swollen, Kit saw, as if she'd been crying recently. He wondered if it was about Emma and Julian being in trouble in Faerie, or Jaime, or some combination of both. She'd seemed heartbroken when he'd fled.

"What?" she said. "Helen and Aline are with Tavvy, if you came to tell me to watch him."

"Actually," said Ty, sitting down on a piano bench, "we need your help with something else."

"Let me guess." Dru dropped the videotape she was holding and Kit held himself back from commenting on the fact that he didn't think anyone under eighty owned videotapes anymore. "Dishwashing? Laundry? Lying down in front of the Institute so you can use me for a step?"

Ty furrowed his eyebrows. "What—"

Kit cut in quickly. "It's nothing like that. It's a mission."

Dru hesitated. "What kind of mission?"

"A secret mission," said Ty.

She tugged on a braid. Both of her braids were short, and stuck out almost horizontally on either side of her head. "You can't just ignore me until you want me to do something," she said, though she sounded torn.

Ty started to protest. Kit interrupted, holding up a hand to quell them both. "We did want to ask you to join in before," he said. "Ty didn't want to put you in danger."

"Danger?" Dru perked up. "There's going to be danger?"

"So much danger," said Kit.

Dru narrowed her eyes. "What are we talking about here, exactly?"

"We need to get on better terms with the Shadow Market," said Ty. "Since we can't go to Faerie, we want to see if there's anything we can do to help Emma and Julian from this side. Any information we can get."

"I would like to help Emma and Jules," Dru said slowly.

"We think there are answers in the Market," said Kit. "But it's run by this really awful warlock, Barnabas Hale. He's agreed to a meeting with Vanessa Ashdown."

"Vanessa Ashdown?" Dru looked stunned. "She's in on this?"

"No, she's not," said Ty. "We lied to him about who wanted to see him so we could get the meeting."

Dru snorted. "You don't look like Vanessa. Either of you."

"That's where you come in," said Kit. "Even if we weren't pretending to be Vanessa Ashdown, he'd never stay if we showed up at the meeting place, because he hates us."

Dru smiled a little. "Don't you mean he hates *you*?" she said to Kit.

"He also hates me," Ty said proudly. "Because Livvy and I were with Kit at the Shadow Market in London."

Dru sat up. "Livvy would have done this for you, right, if she was here?"

Ty didn't say anything. He had raised his eyes to the ceiling, where the fan spun lazily, and was staring at it as if his life depended on it.

"I don't look anything like Vanessa Ashdown," Dru added hesitantly.

"He doesn't know what she looks like," said Kit. "He just knows she's got a lot of money for him."

"He probably thinks she isn't thirteen," said Dru. "He's got to imagine she's an adult, especially if she's got a lot of money. Which incidentally, why do you have a lot of money?"

"You look a lot older than you are," said Kit, ignoring her question. "And we thought . . ."

Ty got up and went into the hall. They both looked after him, Kit wondering if the mention of Livvy had sent him running. Whether any cracks were starting to appear in the wall of his belief that Livvy was coming back.

"Did I upset him?" Dru said in a small voice.

Before Kit could respond, Ty had returned. He was carrying what looked like a pile of gray cloth. "I've noticed people look at clothes a lot more than they look at other people's faces. I thought maybe you could wear one of Mom's suits." He held out a slate-colored skirt and jacket. "I think you were similar sizes."

Dru stood up and reached out for the clothes. "Okay," she said, taking them into her arms carefully. Kit wondered how much she remembered of her mother. Did she have dim recollections, like he did, of a soft kind voice, the sound of singing? "Okay, I'll do it. Where are we going?"

"Hollywood," Kit said. "Tomorrow."

Dru frowned. "Helen and Aline don't know about this. And they said they'd be in the Sanctuary all tomorrow night. Something to do with Downworlders."

"Good," Kit said. "So they won't be wondering where we are."

"Sure—but how are we getting there?"

Ty smiled and tapped his side pocket, where his phone was. "Drusilla Blackthorn, meet Uber."

For the third time, Emma and Julian paused in the shadow of a doorway to consult their map. The inside of the tower was nearly featureless—if it weren't for the map, Emma suspected, they would have been wandering lost for days.

She winced and ached every time she moved. Julian had done his best to patch her up outside the tower, using torn strips from his shirt as bandages. They were so used to functioning with healing runes and the Silent Brothers' skills, Emma thought, that they never expected to be working hurt, not for more than a brief amount of time. Pushing past the pain where the thorns had driven into her body was exhausting, and she found herself glad for the chance to rest for a moment while Julian stared at the map.

The inside of the tower resembled the inside of a seashell. The corridors twisted around and around in circles, ever narrowing as they ascended, keeping to the shadows. They had discussed whether to use Nene's potion, but Julian had said they should save it until they absolutely needed it—right now, the corridors were crowded enough with faeries both Seelie and Unseelie that no one was taking too close a look at two hurrying figures in torn cloaks.

"The corridors split here," Julian said. "One leads down, one up. The throne room isn't marked on the map—"

"But we know it's near the top of the tower," said Emma. "The Queen's probably already there. We can't let the King get his hands on the Black Volume."

"Then I guess we go that way," Julian said, indicating the ascending corridor. "Keep going up, and hope for some kind of helpful signage on the way."

"Sure. Because faeries are so big on helpful signage."

Julian almost smiled. "All right. Keep your hood down."

They headed up the steeply sloping corridor, their hoods pulled low. As they ascended, the crowds of faeries began to thin out, as if they were reaching rarefied air. The walls became lined with doors, each one more elaborately decorated than the one before, with chips of rare stones and inlaid gold. Emma could hear voices, laughter and chatter, from behind them; she guessed this was the area where the courtiers lived.

One doorway was half-obscured by a tapestry patterned in stars. Standing outside it were two guards dressed in unusual gold-and-black armor, their faces hidden by helmets. Emma felt a shiver of cold as they went by, passing into an area where the corridor narrowed, and narrowed again, as if they were truly winding closer to the heart of a seashell. The torches burned lower in their holders, and Emma squinted ahead, wishing for a Night Vision rune.

Julian clamped his hand down on her arm, drawing her into a shallow alcove. "Redcaps," he hissed.

Emma peered around the wall. Indeed, two lines of redcaps stood guarding a tall archway. Redcaps were among the most vicious of faerie warriors. They wore scarlet uniforms dyed in the blood of those they had slain. Unusually for faeries, these guards were bearded, with weathered faces. They carried pikestaffs whose metal spearheads were crusted with dried blood.

"This must be it," Julian whispered. "The throne room."

He drew the chain with the vial on it over his head, snapped off the top, and swallowed the liquid inside. Emma hurried to do the same, and stifled a gasp. It burned, as if she had swallowed liquid fire. She saw Julian make a pained face before he dropped his empty vial in his pocket.

They stared at each other. Other than the burning in her throat and stomach, Emma felt the same. She could still see her own hands and feet, clear as day, and Julian hadn't so much as started to get fuzzy around the edges. It wasn't quite what she'd imagined.

"Nene did say we'd only be invisible to Unseelie faeries," said Julian quietly after a long moment. His eyes suddenly narrowed. "Emma . . . ?"

"What?" she whispered. "What is it?"

Slowly he raised his hand and tapped his chest, where his *parabatai* rune was, beneath his clothes. Emma blinked. She could see a dark red glow emanating from the spot, as if his heart itself were glowing. The glow was moving, shifting, like a tiny sandstorm.

"Julian . . ." She glanced down. There was a glow surrounding her own rune too. It was uncanny enough to make her shiver, but she pushed the feeling away and stalked out into the corridor. A moment later Julian was at her side.

The line of redcaps was still there, in front of the dark archway. Emma began to move toward them, conscious of Julian beside her. She could see him clearly, and hear his footsteps, yet as they moved toward the throne room and slipped between the rows of redcaps, no one turned toward them. Not a single redcap appeared to hear or see them.

Emma could see the dark light as if it were strapped across Julian's chest. But why would an invisibility potion make his *parabatai* rune glow? It didn't make sense, but she didn't have time to wonder about it—they were passing the last pair of redcaps. She felt like a mouse walking blithely in front of an oblivious cat.

A moment later they were over the threshold and inside the throne room of the King.

It was not what Emma had expected. Rather than glimmering gold and rich decor, the room was bare, the floor dark gray stone. The walls were windowless, except for the north wall: A massive glass rectangle looked out onto a blowing nighttime view. The room was scattered with heaps of tumbled boulders, some as big as elephants, many smashed into smaller pieces. It looked like the ruins of a giant's playground.

There were no seats in the room except for the throne, which was itself a boulder into which a seat had been carved. Stone rose all around its back and sides, as if to shield the King, who sat motionless on the throne's seat.

In his hands was Julian's copy of the Black Volume.

As they entered, the King looked up, frowning, and for a moment of panic Emma thought that he could see them. His face was as awful as she remembered it: Divided exactly down the middle as if by a blade, it was half the face of a beautifully striking man, and half stripped skeletal bone. He wore a rich red velvet doublet, a cloak was fastened to his shoulders with rows of golden aiguillettes, and a golden crown bound his brow. A clear vial dangled on a chain around his throat, filled with some scarlet potion.

Reflexively, Emma and Julian ducked behind the nearest heap of broken stone just as four guards strode in, surrounding a woman in white with long dark hair. Behind her marched a young boy with a golden circlet around his head. Two guards accompanied him. They wore the unusual black-and-gold armor Emma had noted before, in the corridor.

She didn't have much time to think about it, though, because as the woman in white moved into the room, she turned her head, and Emma recognized her.

It was Annabel Blackthorn.

Memory surged in the back of Emma's throat, a bitter wave. Annabel on the dais in the Council Hall. Annabel, her eyes wild, driving the shards of the Mortal Sword into Livvy's chest. Annabel covered in blood, the dais swimming with it, Julian holding Livvy in his arms.

Beside Emma, Julian sucked in a harsh, choking breath. He had gone rigid. Emma grabbed his shoulder. It felt like granite: unyielding, inhuman.

His hand was at his belt, on the hilt of a shortsword. His eyes were fixed on Annabel. His whole body was tense with barely leashed energy.

He's going to kill her. Emma knew it the way she knew each of his next moves in a fight, the rhythm of his breath in battle. She tugged at him, pulling him around to face her, though it was like trying to move a boulder.

"No." She spoke in a harsh whisper. "You can't. Not now."

Julian was breathing hard, as if he'd been running. "Let me go, Emma."

"She can see us," Emma hissed. "She's not a faerie. She will see us coming, Julian."

He looked at her with wild eyes.

"She'll raise the alarm, and we'll be stopped. If you try to kill Annabel now, we'll both be caught. And we'll never get the Black Volume back."

"She needs to die for what she did." Two harsh red dots burned on his cheekbones. "Let me kill her and the King can keep the god-damn book—"

Emma caught at his cloak. "We'll both die here if you try!"

Julian was silent, his fingers closing and unclosing at his side. The red glow above his *parabatai* rune flared like fire, and black lines chased through it, as if it were glass about to shatter.

"Would you really choose revenge over Tavvy and Dru and Ty?" Emma shook him, hard, and let go. "Would you want them to know that you did?"

Julian sagged back against a rock. He shook his head slowly, as if in disbelief, but the red glow around him had dimmed. Maybe the mention of the Blackthorn kids had been a low blow, Emma thought, but she didn't care; it was worth it to keep Julian from flinging him-self headlong into suicide. Her legs were still shaking as she turned around to peer at the throne room through a gap in the rocks.

Annabel and the boy had approached the throne. Annabel looked nothing like she had before—she wore a dress of bleached linen, gathered under her bosom, falling to brush her ankles. Her hair fell down her back in a smooth river. She looked quiet and ordinary and harmless. She held the hand of the boy in the crown carefully, as if ready to shield him from harm if necessary.

They were still surrounded by Unseelie guards in gold and black. The King smiled at them with half his face, a horrible smile. "Annabel," said the King. "Ash. I have had this day some interesting tidings."

Ash. Emma stared at the boy. So this was the Seelie Queen's son. He had silver-fair hair and deep green eyes like forest leaves; he wore a high-collared velvet tunic and the golden band around his forehead was a smaller version of the King's. He was probably no more than Dru's age, thin in a way that didn't look healthy, and there was a bruise on his cheek. He carried himself with the same straight posture Kieran did. Princes probably weren't supposed to slump.

He looked familiar in a way she couldn't quite place. Was it just that he resembled his mother?

"This day I have had a visit from the Queen of the Seelie Court," said the King.

Ash lifted his head sharply. "What did my mother want?"

"As you know, she has long bargained for your return, and only today she has brought me what I asked for." The King sat forward and spoke with relish. "The Black Volume of the Dead."

"That's impossible," said Annabel, her pale cheeks flushing. "I have the Black Volume. The Queen is a liar."

The King tapped two gloved fingers against his bony cheek. "Is she," he mused. "It is something of an interesting philosophical question, isn't it? What is a book? Is it the binding, the ink, the pages, or the sum of the words contained?"

Annabel frowned. "I don't understand."

The King drew the copy of the Black Volume from where it had rested at his side. He held it up so that Annabel and Ash could see it. "This is a copy of the Black Volume of the Dead," he said. "The book that is also called the Dark Artifices, for it contains within it some of the most formidable magic ever recorded." He caressed the front page. "The Queen says it is an exact duplicate. It was made with the assistance of a wizard of great power called OfficeMax, of whom I know nothing."

"Jesus Christ," Julian muttered.

"The Queen has left it with me for the span of a single day," said the King, "that I might decide whether I wish to trade Ash for it. I have sworn to return it to her at the rising of the sun tomorrow morning."

"The Queen is deceiving you." Annabel drew Ash closer to her side. "She would trick you into trading Ash for this—this flawed copy."

"Perhaps." The King's eyes were hooded. "I have yet to make my decision. But you, Annabel, you also have your decisions to make. I have observed that you've become very close to Ash. I suspect you would miss him if you were parted. Is that not true?"

A thunderous expression had come across Annabel's face, but for a moment Emma was more interested in Ash's. There was a look in his eyes that made him seem more familiar to her than ever. A sort of coldness, astonishing in someone so young.

"But you need Ash," said Annabel. "You've said so a dozen times. You require him as your weapon." She spoke with contempt. "You have already worked magics upon him since you took him from his mother's Court. If you give him back—"

The King leaned back in his stone seat. "I will not give him back. The Queen will see reason. It will take some time for the Black Volume to work its will upon Ash. But when it has, we will no longer need the Portal. He will be able to spread blight and destruction with his very hands. The Queen hates Shadowhunters as much as I do. Within a month, their precious land of Idris will look like this—"

He gestured at the window set in the wall. Suddenly the view through the glass changed—in fact, there was no glass. It was as if a hole had been torn in the world, and through it Emma could see a view of a blowing desert and a gray sky scorched with lightning. The sand was stained red with blood, and broken trees stood scarecrow-like against the acidic horizon.

"That's not our world," Julian murmured. "It's another dimension—like Edom—but Edom was destroyed—"

Emma couldn't stop staring. Human figures, half-covered by the sand; the white of bone. "Julian, I can see bodies—"

The King waved his hand again, and the Portal turned dark. "As Thule is now, so Idris will be."

Thule? The word was familiar. Emma frowned.

"You think you'll be able to convince the Queen to endanger her child just for power," said Annabel. "Not everyone is like you."

"But the Queen is," said the Unseelie King. "I know it, because Ash would not be the first." He grinned a skeleton grin. "Annabel Blackthorn, you have toyed with me because I have allowed it. You have no true power here."

"I know your name," Annabel gasped. "Malcolm told it to me. I can force you—"

"You will die the moment the name leaves your lips, and Ash will die after," said the King. "But because I do not wish bloodshed, I will give you one night to decide. Give me the true Black Volume, and you may remain here with Ash and be his guardian. If not, I shall join forces with the Queen instead and drive you from my lands, and you will never see Ash again."

Ash pulled away from Annabel's restraining hands. "What if *I* say no? What if I refuse?"

The King turned his red gaze on the boy. "You are a perfect candidate for the Dark Artifices," he said. "But in the end, do you truly think I would stop at harming Sebastian Morgenstern's brat?"

The name was like a blow. *Sebastian Morgenstern.* But how—

"No!" Annabel screamed. "Don't you touch him!"

"Guards," said the King, and the guards snapped to attention. "Take the woman and the boy away. I am done with them."

Julian scrambled to his feet. "We have to follow them—"

"We can't," Emma whispered. "The potion is wearing off. Look. The red light is almost gone."

Julian glanced down. The scarlet glow above his heart had dimmed to an ember.

The guards had closed about Annabel and Ash and were marching them from the chamber. Emma caught hold of Julian's hand and together they crept out from behind the boulders.

The guards were escorting Annabel and Ash out the arched doorway. For a moment, Emma and Julian paused in the center of the throne room, directly in the line of the King's view.

He was staring straight ahead of him. In the untouched side of his face, Emma thought she could see a bit of Kieran—a Kieran split down the middle, half-tortured and inhuman.

She felt Julian's hand tighten on hers. Every one of her nerves was screaming that the King could see them, that at any moment he would call for his guards, that they would die here before Emma even got a chance to lift a blade.

She told herself she would at least try to plunge her dagger into the King's heart before she died.

Julian tugged her fingers. Incredibly, he had the map in his other hand; he jerked his chin toward the arch beneath which Ash and Annabel had vanished.

There was no more time. They raced through the archway.

* * *

There was little point struggling; there were at least three faerie guards on each side of Mark, and their grip on his arms was merciless. He was dragged through the revel, still dizzy from the potion in his blood. Shapes seemed to loom up on either side of him: spinning dancers, blurred as if seen through the prism of a teardrop. The King of Cats, regarding him with glimmering tabby eyes. A row of horses, rearing away from the sparks of a fire.

He couldn't see Kieran. Kieran was somewhere behind him; Mark could hear the guards shouting at him, almost drowned out by the sounds of music and laughter. Kieran. Cristina. His heart was a cold knot of fear for both of them as he was shoved through a filthy puddle and up a set of wooden steps.

A flap of velvet canopy slapped him in the face; Mark sputtered as the guard holding him laughed. There were hands at his waist, unfastening his weapons belt.

He kicked out reflexively and was shoved to the floor. "Kneel, half-breed," snapped one of the guards. They released him, and Mark crouched where he was, on his knees, his chest throbbing with rage. Two guards stood behind him, holding spears level with the back of Mark's neck. A few feet away, Kieran was in the same position, though he was bleeding from a cut lip. His expression was set in a bitter snarl.

They were inside Oban's pavilion. The walls were heavy hanging velvet, the floor expensive rugs that had been trampled and muddied by uncountable booted feet. Wooden tables held dozens of empty and half-empty bottles of wine; some had tipped over and spilled, filling the room with the reek of alcohol.

"Well, well," said a drawling voice. Mark looked up; in front of them was a red velvet sofa, and sprawled on it was an indolent-looking young man. Hair streaked black and purple tumbled around his pointed ears, and black kohl was smudged around glittering silver eyes. He wore a silver silk doublet and hose, and white lace spilled from his cuffs. "Little brother Kieran. How nice to see you." His silver eyes flicked to Mark. "With some guy." He flicked a dismissive hand in Mark's direction and turned his smirk on Manuel. "Good work."

"I told you I saw them," Manuel said. "They were at the revel."

"I admit it never occurred to me they would be stupid enough to set foot in the Unseelie Lands," said Oban. "You win that point, Villalobos."

"They make an excellent gift," said Manuel. He stood between the guards with their spears, his arms crossed over his chest. He was grinning. "Your father will be pleased."

"My father?" Oban tapped his fingers on the arm of the sofa. "You think I should deliver Kieran to my father? He'll just kill him. Dull."

Mark darted a glance at Kieran through his eyelashes. Kieran was on his knees. He didn't look frightened of Oban, but he'd never show it if he was.

"A gift is more than just a gift," said Manuel. "It's a method of persuasion. Your father—mistakenly—thinks you weak, Prince. If you bring him Prince Kieran and the Shadowhunter half-breed, he'll realize he should take you more seriously." He lowered his voice. "We can convince him to kill the prisoners and move ahead with our plan."

Prisoners? What prisoners? Mark tensed. Could he mean Julian and Emma? But that wasn't possible. They were with the Seelie procession.

At least Cristina was safe. She had vanished, eluding the guards. The Angel knew where she was now. Mark chanced a sideways glance at Kieran: Wasn't he panicking too? Wasn't he terrified for Cristina as Mark was? He ought to be, considering the way they'd been kissing.

Oban reached for the side table and scrabbled around among the bottles stacked on top of it, looking for one with alcohol still in it. "My father does not respect me," he said. "He thinks my brothers are more worthy of the throne. Though they are not."

"I'm sure they think the same about you," Mark muttered.

Oban found a bottle and lifted it up to the light, squinting at the half inch of amber fluid still inside. "A wanted prisoner might change his mind, but it might not be enough."

"You do want to rise in your father's favor, do you not?" said Manuel.

Oban took a swig from his bottle. "Of course. Rather."

Mark had the feeling Manuel was rolling his eyes internally. "Then you need to demonstrate that he should take you seriously. The first time you went to him, he wouldn't even hear you out."

"Fatuous old bag," muttered Oban, tossing the empty bottle aside. It shattered.

"If you bring him these prisoners, he will listen to you. I will go with you—I will tell him that together we tracked them down. I will make it clear that as a representative of the Cohort, I wish to work only with you as our contact in the Unseelie Court. It will make you seem important."

"Seem?" said Oban.

Kieran made an inelegant snorting noise.

"It will make him understand how important you are," Manuel corrected smoothly. "Your father will realize the value you bring to him. The hostages are the key to a parley between Nephilim and the Unseelie Folk that has no precedent in our history. When every Shadowhunter sees you meet and achieve a mutually beneficial peace, all will realize that you and Horace Dearborn are the greatest of leaders, able to achieve the alliance your forefathers could not."

"What?" said Mark, unable to stay silent. "What are you talking about?"

"Might it not bring real war?" Oban had found another bottle. "War seems like a bad idea."

With exasperated patience, Manuel said, "There will be no war. I told you." He glanced at Kieran and then at Mark. "War is not the object here. And I think the King wants Kieran dead more than you think."

"Because the people love him," said Oban, in a maudlin tone. "They wanted him to be King. Because he was kind."

"Kindness is not a kingly quality," said Manuel. "As the people will discover when your father hangs Kieran from a gibbet high above the tower gardens."

Mark jerked backward, and nearly impaled himself on a spear. "You—"

"Kindness may not be a kingly quality, but mercy is," interrupted Kieran. "You don't have to do this, Oban. Manuel is not worth your effort, and his schemes are so many lies."

Oban sighed. "You are tediously predictable, youngest son." He dropped the bottle he was holding, and the scarlet liquid in it ran out onto the floor like blood. "I want the throne, and I shall have the throne, and Manuel will help me get it. That is all I care about. That is all that matters." A smile touched the corners of his mouth. "Unlike you, I have not come to love and pursue shadows, but only what is real."

Remember, Mark thought. *Remember that none of this is real.*

Oban flicked a hand toward the two of them as Manuel smirked almost audibly. "Chain them together and find them horses. We ride for the Unseelie Court this night."

Barnabas was already at the 101 Coffee Shop in Hollywood when Drusilla arrived. He was sitting at a tan booth and forking up a plate of delicious-looking huevos rancheros. He sported a black cowboy hat and a bolo tie that seemed to be choking him, but he looked pleased with himself.

Dru stopped to glance at her reflection in the windows that ran along one side of the diner. The other side was a kitschy rock wall;

in the corner there was a jukebox and dozens of framed photos of what Dru guessed were the owner's family and friends.

It was dark outside, and the window gave her back a clear picture of herself. Dark hair pulled up and smooth, gray business suit, classic heels (stolen from Emma's closet). She wore red lipstick and no other makeup; Kit had assured her that less was more. "You don't want to look like a clown," he'd said, tossing her powder blush in Racy Rose over his shoulder as if it were a grenade.

Somewhere out there in the shadows, Kit and Ty were watching, ready to jump to her defense if anything went wrong. Knowing that made her feel less worried. Hoisting her briefcase in her hand, she sauntered across the diner past ivory-and toffee-colored leather seats, and slid into the booth across from Barnabas.

His snake's eyes flicked up to observe her. Up close, he didn't look well. His scales were dull, and his eyes rimmed with red. "Vanessa Ashdown?"

"That's me," Dru said, setting the briefcase down on her place mat. "In the flesh."

His forked tongue slithered out of his mouth. "And plenty of it. No worries, I like a woman with curves. Most of you Shadowhunters are so bony."

Blech, Dru thought. She tapped the briefcase. "Business, Mr. Hale."

"Right." His tongue vanished, to her relief. "So, toots. You've got proof that Hypatia Vex has been passing secrets to Shadowhunters?"

"Right in here." Dru smiled and pushed the briefcase toward him.

He unsnapped it and flicked it open, then frowned. "This is money."

"Yes." She gave him a bright smile and tried not to glance around to see if anyone was coming to back her up. "It's the money we've earmarked for Hypatia in exchange for secrets."

He rolled his eyes. "Normally, I'm happy to see a big box of money, don't get me wrong. But I was kind of hoping for photos of her handing evidence to some Blackthorns."

"Why Blackthorns?" Drusilla said.

"Because," said Barnabas. "They're smarmy little rats." He sat back. "You gotta give me something better than this, Vanessa."

"Well, look closer at the money." Dru played for time. "Because, ah, it's not ordinary money."

Looking bored, Barnabas picked up a stack of twenties. Dru tensed. Kit had told her to keep Barnabas talking, but it wasn't like she could distract him by telling him the plot of *Bloody Birthday* or about the new cute thing Church had done.

"There ain't nothing special about this money," Barnabas began, and broke off as the door of the diner flew open and a tall warlock woman with dark skin and bronze hair strode into the room. She wore a glimmering pantsuit and toweringly high heels. She was followed by two other Downworlders—a muscled male werewolf and a pallid, dark-haired vampire.

"Damn," said Barnabas. "Hypatia—what—?"

"I heard you were selling secrets to Shadowhunters, Hale," said Hypatia. "Look at that—caught with your hand in the bag." She winked at Dru. The pupils of her eyes were shaped like golden stars.

"How could you?" demanded the vampire. "I thought it was all lies, Barnabas!" She sniffed and glanced at Dru. "You were really buying secrets off him? Who are you, anyway?"

"Drusilla," said Dru. "Drusilla Blackthorn."

"A Blackthorn?" said Barnabas, outraged.

"And he was definitely selling secrets," said Dru. "For instance, he just told me he dug up a copy of the Red Scrolls of Magic from under Johnny Rook's booth as soon as he died. And he's been keeping it to himself."

"Is that true?" rumbled the werewolf. "And you call yourself the head of the Shadow Market?"

"You little—" Barnabas launched himself across the table at Dru. She slid out of the booth fast and collided with someone's torso with an *oomph*. She looked up. It was Ty, a shortsword in his hand, pointed directly at Barnabas's chest.

He put one arm protectively around Dru, his gaze never wavering from the warlock. "Leave my sister alone," he said.

"That's right," said Kit. He waved from the next booth. "I forgot my weapons. But I do have this fork." He wiggled it. "You are so forked," he said to Barnabas.

"Oh, shut up," Barnabas said. But he looked defeated; the werewolf had already grabbed him, pulling his arms behind his back. Hypatia was clearing the briefcase and money off the table.

She winked her starry eyes at Ty and Dru. "Time for you Shadowhunters to go," she said. "This marks the end of your little Downworlder deal. And tell your new Inquisitor that we don't want anything to do with him or his bigoted rules. We'll go where we want, when we want."

Ty lowered his sword slowly. Kit dropped his fork, and the three of them strode out of the diner. Once on the pavement, Dru took a deep, relieved breath of air—it was a warm night, and the moon was high and glowing over Franklin Avenue. She felt shivery with excitement—she'd done it! She'd tricked a famous warlock. Pulled off a con. She was a con woman now!

"I think Hypatia meant what she said to us," Kit said, glancing back through the windows of the coffee shop. Hypatia and the other Downworlders were escorting a struggling Barnabas toward the back door. "All that stuff about telling the Inquisitor—that wasn't part of the con. That was a real message."

"As if we could get word to the Inquisitor," said Ty. He touched his hand absently to the locket at his throat. "That was good. You did a really good job, Dru."

"Yep. You kept your cool," said Kit. He glanced up and down the street. "I'd suggest we go get milk shakes or something to celebrate, but this is kind of a scary neighborhood."

"Shadowhunters don't worry about scary neighborhoods," said Dru.

"Have you learned nothing from the way Batman's parents died?" said Kit, feigning shock.

Ty smiled. And for the first time since Livvy had died, Dru laughed.

With Aline and Tavvy's help, Helen had set up a large table inside the Sanctuary. Two chairs sat behind it, and the table was covered in the accoutrements of bureaucracy: pens and blank forms that had been sent by the Clave, file folders and rubber stamps. It was all drearily mundane, in Helen's opinion.

A long line of werewolves, warlocks, vampires, and faeries stretched through the room and out the front doors. They had set up their "Registry Station" atop the Angelic Power rune etched on the floor, blocking the doors that led into the Institute.

The first Downworlder to step up to their makeshift office was a werewolf. He had an enormous mustache that reminded Helen of seventies cop movies. He was glowering. "My name is Greg—"

"Your name is Elton John," Aline said, writing it down.

"No," said the werewolf. "It's Greg. Greg Anderson."

"It's Elton John," said Aline, grabbing a stamp. "You're thirty-six and you're a chimney sweep who lives in Bel Air." She stamped the paper in red ink—REGISTERED—and handed it back.

The werewolf took the paper, blinking in puzzlement. "What are you doing?"

"It means the Clave won't be able to find you," explained Tavvy, who was sitting under the table, playing with a toy car. "But you're registered."

"Technically," said Helen, willing him to accept the ruse. If he didn't, they'd have trouble with the others.

Greg looked at the paper again. "Just my opinion," he said, "but the guy behind me looks like Humphrey Bogart."

"Humphrey it is!" said Aline, waving her stamp. "Do you want to be Humphrey Bogart?" she asked the next Downworlder, a skinny, tall warlock with a sad face and poodle ears.

"Who doesn't?" said the warlock.

Most of the Downworlders were wary as they worked their way through the rest of the line, but cooperative. There were even some smiles and thanks. They seemed to understand that Aline and Helen were attempting to undermine the system, if not why.

Aline pointed at a tall blond faerie in the line, wearing a gossamer dress. "That one's Taylor Swift."

Helen smiled as she handed a werewolf a stamped form. "How much trouble are we going to get into for this?"

"Does it matter?" said Aline. "We're going to do it anyway."

"True enough," said Helen, and reached for another form.

Take me to him. Take me.

There was quiet and silence—and then light, and a thousand sharp, pricking pains. Cristina yelped and struggled free of what felt like a tangle of briars, tumbling sideways and thumping hard onto grassy earth.

She sat up, looking ruefully down at her hands and arms, dotted with dozens of tiny pinpricks of blood. She had landed in a rosebush, which was more than a little ironic.

She got to her feet, brushing herself off. She was still in Faerie, but it seemed to be daytime here. Golden sunlight burnished a thatched-roof cottage of pale yellow stone. A turquoise-blue river ran past the small house, lined with blue and purple lupin flowers.

Cristina wasn't sure what she had expected, but it hadn't been this pastoral bliss. She dabbed gently at the blood on her hands and arms, gave up, and glanced up and down the small, winding trail that cut through the tall grass. It led from the front door of the cottage, across the meadow, and vanished into the hazy distance.

Cristina marched up to the cottage door and knocked firmly. "Adaon!" she called. "Adaon Kingson!"

The door swung open as if Adaon had been waiting on the other side. The last time Cristina had seen him, he had been decked out in the regalia of the Unseelie Court, with the broken crown insignia on his chest. Now he wore a plain linen tunic and breeches. His deep brown skin looked warm in the sunlight. It was the first time she had been able to see his resemblance to Kieran.

Maybe it was because he looked furious.

"How is it possible that you are here?" he demanded, looking around as if he couldn't believe she had come alone.

"I sought help," she said. "I was in Faerie—"

He narrowed his eyes. He seemed to be staring suspiciously at a bluebird. "Come inside immediately. It is not safe to speak outside."

The moment she was inside the cottage, Adaon closed the door and set himself to fastening a number of intricate-looking, complicated locks. "Faerie is a dangerous place right now. There are all sorts of ways you could have been tracked or followed."

They were inside a small wood-paneled entryway. An arched doorway led through to the rest of the cottage. Adaon was blocking it, arms crossed in front of his chest. He was glowering. After a moment's hesitation, Cristina held out the artifact to him. "I could not have been tracked. I used this."

If she'd hoped Adaon would look relieved, he didn't. "Where did you get that?"

"It is a family heirloom," Cristina said. "It was given freely as a gift by a family of *hadas* who an ancestor of mine aided."

Adaon scowled. "It is a token of Rhiannon. Treat it with care." He stalked out of the entryway and into a small living room, where a well-scrubbed wooden table stood in a shaft of sunlight pouring through wide, leaded windows. A small kitchen was visible: A vase on the table held a riot of colorful flowers and stacked bowls of painted pottery.

Cristina felt a bit as if she were inside the cottage of the dwarves in *Snow White*: Everything was diminutive, and Adaon seemed to tower, his head nearly scraping the ceiling. He gestured for her to sit down. She took a chair, realizing as she sat how exhausted her body was and how much she ached all over. Worry for Emma and Julian, now compounded by panic over Mark and Kieran, pounded through her like heartbeats.

"Why are you here?" Adaon demanded. He wasn't sitting. His big arms were still crossed over his chest.

"I need your help," Cristina said.

Adaon slammed a hand down on the table, making her jump. "No. I cannot give aid or help to Nephilim. I may not agree with my father on many things, but I would not go directly against his wishes by conspiring to aid a Shadowhunter."

He stood for a moment in silence. Sunlight illuminated the edges of the white lace curtains at the window. Through the glass Cristina could see a field of poppies stretching away in the distance toward glimmering cliffs, and a faint sparkle of blue water. The house smelled like sage and tea, a soft and homey scent that made the ache inside her worse.

"Do you know why I came to you?" she said.

"I do not," Adaon said grimly.

"In London, I followed Kieran from the Institute because I didn't trust him," she said. "I thought he was on his way to betray us. It turned out he was on his way to speak to you."

Adaon's frown didn't budge.

"I realized as the two of you talked that he was right to trust you, that you were the only one of his brothers who cared for him," said Cristina. "He said that you gave him Windspear. You are the only member of his family who he speaks of with any affection at all."

Adaon threw up a hand as if to ward off her words. "Enough! I don't want to hear more."

"You need to hear it."

"I do not need the Nephilim to tell me about Kieran!"

"You do," said Cristina. "Guards are taking Kieran to your father right now, as we speak. He will certainly be killed if we do nothing."

Adaon didn't move. If Cristina hadn't seen him swallow, she would have thought he was a statue. An angry, towering statue. "Helping him would be a true betrayal of my father."

"If you don't help, then it will be a true betrayal of your brother," said Cristina. "Sometimes you cannot be loyal to everyone."

Adaon leaned his big hands on the back of a chair. "Why did you come here?" he said. "Why did you bring me this news? It is possible my father will spare him. He is well liked by the people."

"You know your father will kill him for just that reason," said Cristina. Her voice shook. "Before the Hunt no one in Kieran's life ever loved or cared for him at all, save you. Are you really going to abandon him now?"

15
Turrets and Shadows

"Sebastian's son," Emma whispered. "He had a son."

They had taken shelter in a room that looked like a disused food pantry. Bare shelves lined the walls, and empty baskets littered the floor. Emma thought of the fruit and bread they had certainly once held, and tried to ignore the gnawing of her stomach. She hadn't eaten since the sandwiches the day before.

"There have always been rumors that Sebastian had an affair with the Queen," Julian said. He was sitting with his back against a wall of the pantry. His voice sounded remote, as if it were coming from the bottom of a well. He'd sounded like that since they'd left the throne room. Emma didn't know if it was a side effect of the potion or of seeing Annabel and letting her go. "But he only died five years ago."

"Time passes differently in Faerie," said Emma. "Ash seems maybe thirteen." She scowled. "He looks like Sebastian. I remember seeing Sebastian in the Institute. He was so . . ." Vicious. Cold. Inhuman. "Blond."

Julian didn't look up. His voice was like ice. "You should have let me end her."

"Julian, no." Emma rubbed at her temples; her head was aching. "You would absolutely have been killed if you tried."

"Emma—"

"No!" She dropped her hands. "I hate Annabel too. I hate her for standing there alive when Livvy's dead. I hate her for what she did. But there are more important things at stake right now than our revenge."

Julian raised his head. "You lived for revenge for years. All you thought about was revenge for your parents."

"I know. And then I got my revenge, and it did nothing for me. It left me feeling empty and cold."

"Did it?" His eyes were cold and hard as blue-green marbles.

"Yes," Emma insisted. "Also, then Malcolm came back from the dead as a sea monster, so . . ."

"So you're saying I shouldn't kill Annabel because she'll come back as a sea monster?"

"I'm just pointing out the futility of my murdering Malcolm," said Emma. "And you know who ended up killing him in the end? Annabel."

There was a long silence. Julian ran his fingers through his hair; Emma wanted to crawl across the room to him on her hands and knees, to beg him to go back to being the Julian he used to be. But maybe that was impossible. Maybe Livvy's death had fallen like a scythe between that Julian and this one, killing any possibility that he might transform, like the swan princes in the fairy tale, back into the thoughtful, considering boy she loved, with secrets in his heart and paint on his hands.

"So what are you saying?" he asked at last.

"No one would blame you for killing Annabel," said Emma. "But sometimes we have to put aside what we want right now for something bigger. You taught me that. The old you."

"Maybe," said Julian. He yanked down his sleeve, and Emma saw again what she had seen in the clearing—the peculiar rust-splashed cloth tied around his right wrist.

She put a hand on his arm, stilling his movement. "What is *that?*"

"It's Livvy's blood," he said. "I tore a strip off the shirt I was wearing when she died and tied it on my wrist. I'll take it off when I kill Annabel. Not before."

"Julian—"

He pulled his sleeve back down. "I understand what you're saying. I just don't see why I should be the one to stop."

His voice was toneless. Emma felt cold all over. It was like looking at someone bleeding from a mortal wound who didn't seem to know or understand that they were hurt.

"Anyway," Julian said. "We need to go find Ash."

I failed, Emma thought. *There was something else I should have said, something that would have convinced him, and I failed.* "Why do we need to find Ash?"

"You heard the King. Ash is the weapon. The one that Clary and Jace came to find."

"He's *part* of a weapon," Emma said. "The King is poisoning his own land, and Brocelind Forest, too. He thinks he can use Ash to make the poison even more deadly, to destroy more of Idris."

"That's the impression I got, yeah. But the King needs the Black Volume to make that second part work."

"Then aren't we better off going after the Black Volume?"

"Which one?" Julian said. "Annabel has the real one. The Queen has the copy—well, the King has it at the moment, but it's hers. That splits our goal—unless we pull Ash out of the equation." Julian's hair tumbled around his face in the darkness; Emma could see the thin scratches all over his skin where the thorns of the hedge had cut him. "Both of his bargains hinge on Ash—Annabel wants Ash, and so does the Queen. Taking Ash will buy us time and prevent the King from a making a deal."

"I'm not hurting a little kid, Julian," Emma said flatly. "If that's what you mean by 'pull Ash out of the equation,' I'm not doing it."

"We don't have to hurt him," Julian said. "Kidnapping him should work just fine."

Emma sighed. "And then what?"

"We offer Annabel a trade—the Black Volume for Ash. She'd do anything for him."

Emma wondered if she ought to point out how strange that was. She decided not to—this Julian didn't understand why anyone felt strongly about anything.

"Then we kill her and take the book," he finished.

"What about the Queen?"

"If the King doesn't have Ash, she's got no reason to trade the Black Volume, and she won't. Meanwhile we get to the falls, head back to Idris with Ash *and* the original Black Volume, and Dearborn's plan is shot. We walk into the Council with both those things and we'll be heroes. The Clave won't let the Cohort touch us."

"Ash isn't a thing," said Emma.

"The King called him a weapon," said Julian.

Emma changed tack. "We don't know how to find Ash in the tower."

"I know you saw those guards in the corridor, just like I did," Julian said. "And later in the throne room. They're Ash's guards. We know where his room is. We've seen it." His eyes were glittering with determination. "I need you with me, Emma."

"Then promise me something," she said. "Promise we'll take Ash to Jia, not Dearborn."

"Fine," said Julian. "I don't care about what happens to Sebastian Morgenstern's son."

Real Julian would have cared, Emma thought. Real Julian would have cared about any child, because he loved his own so much. He would have seen Tavvy in Ash, and Dru, and Ty, no matter who Ash's father was.

"So will you come with me?" he said.

I will, she thought. *Because someone has to protect Ash from you, and protect you from yourself.*

She rose to her feet. "I'm with you," she said.

"Hello?" Ty moved forward into the darkness of the cave, his witch-light shining in his hand. He looked like a painting to Kit, with the illumination bright on his dark hair and pale skin. "Shade? Are you here?"

Kit had his own witchlight in his pocket, but Ty's stone was casting plenty of light, picking out the cracks in the granite walls, the wooden table scored with old marks of knives and fire, the letters on its surface flaring briefly into life: *Fire wants to burn.*

They'd left Dru back at the Institute; she'd gone humming off to bed, and Kit had been pleased that they'd made her happy. She'd done well with Barnabas, too. Kit had been right: She had plenty of con artist in her.

"Shade," Ty had said the moment Drusilla was out of earshot. "We have to talk to Shade."

He'd been vibrating with excitement, his cheeks flushed, his fingers working at one of his fidget toys.

It was a clear night with a three-quarter moon, the sky alive with fast-moving clouds, blown by wind off the ocean. Ty practically ran along the edge of the water, feet soundless on the damp sand; Kit found he wasn't quite as breathless as he would have expected trying to keep up. Maybe he was turning into more of a Shadowhunter despite himself.

"Shade?" Ty called again, and this time the shadows moved and a light flared up inside the cavern. A lamp on the table had switched on, filling the chamber with illumination and shadows. Out of the deeper shadows, a grumpy voice spoke:

"Who is it? Who's bothering me?"

"Kit Herondale and Ty Blackthorn," Ty said, his witchlight flaring higher. "We need to talk to you."

There was a sigh and a shuffle. "You'd better have a good reason for waking me up." The shadows moved and resolved themselves into Shade, clambering out of a sleeping bag. He wore a pair of pin-striped pajamas and fuzzy slippers on his green feet.

"We sent you a note saying we were coming," said Kit.

Shade glared. "I was asleep. It's three in the morning."

The sleeping bag wiggled. A moment later Church crawled out, making chirping noises. He curled up on top of the bag, blinking his large yellow eyes.

"That isn't very loyal," Ty said, looking at Church sternly.

Shade yawned. "We've known each other a long time, that cat and I. We had some things to catch up on."

Kit felt the conversation getting away from him. "We did what you told us to do," he said to the yawning warlock. "We're square with the Shadow Market."

"That's right," said Ty. "Hypatia Vex is running it now and says we can come there whenever we want."

An odd expression passed over the warlock's face; interestingly, Shade did not look happy. He looked surprised and disturbed. Kit filed the fact away for future consideration.

"Then you can begin the spell," said Shade slowly. "Once you've acquired all the ingredients, of course."

"What are the ingredients?" asked Kit. "Please tell me we don't have to do Malcolm's thing with the hands of twelve murderers. I don't know twelve murderers. I don't even know twelve shoplifters."

"No." Shade had begun to pace. "Malcolm brought Annabel back the way he did because he had her body. We don't have your sister's body, so we can't use his methods."

"She wasn't my sister," murmured Kit.

"If I remember correctly, there's only one spell from the book that you can use," said Shade, still pacing.

"That's right," said Ty.

"There's really a spell?" Kit said. They both looked at him. "I just—I don't see how you can bring someone back from the dead when their body is gone."

Ty had gone tense all over. "The book says you can do it," he said. "It says it's possible."

Shade snapped his fingers, and a mug of something steaming appeared on the table. He slumped into the chair and curled his hands around it, looking grim, or as grim as a green warlock in fuzzy slippers could look. "Because there's no body, this is a highly unstable spell," he said. "You aren't the first to try it. Nothing is ever truly destroyed. That much is true. There are *ways* that the bodiless dead can be returned. Their spirit can be placed in another body, but that is a true evil, because the first body will die."

"No!" said Ty. "I don't want that. Livvy wouldn't want that."

"The body can return as a living corpse," Shade went on. "Not dead but not entirely alive. The body could come back with a corrupted mind, looking perfectly like Livvy but unable to think or speak. The disembodied spirit might return, or in some cases a Livvy from another world—like Edom—could be snatched into ours, leaving a hole behind in the world she departed."

"It seems like there aren't any good options," Kit said nervously.

"But it can work," said Ty. All the blood had drained from his face. "It *has* worked in the past. People have been brought back, perfectly."

"Unfortunately," said Shade, "yes."

Kit knew already that "yes" was all Ty would hear. "We'll get it right," Ty said. "We'll get the real Livvy back."

Kit felt the back of his neck prickle. He couldn't tell if Ty was panicking, but Kit definitely was. What in his life had he ever gotten so right that he had the nerve to volunteer for a project that absolutely couldn't go wrong?

"What are the things we need from the Market?" Ty said.

He didn't sound like he was panicking, and his calmness let Kit breathe again.

Shade sighed and drew a piece of paper toward him across the desk; he must already have scribbled on it some time before. He began to read the list out loud:

"Incense from the heart of a volcano.

Chalk powdered from the bones of a murder victim.

Blood, hair, and bone of the person to be brought over.

Myrrh grown by faeries, harvested at midnight with a silver sickle.

An object from another world."

"The person to be brought over?" Ty said. "That's Livvy, right?"

"Of course," Shade said.

"Without her body, how can we get her blood, hair, and bone?" said Kit. His mind raced along with the question: Maybe it would be impossible, maybe they couldn't get the ingredients, and there would never be a chance of getting the spell wrong and inviting disaster.

"It can be done," said Ty quietly. His fingers touched the locket at his neck briefly. "The incense, the myrrh—we can get those at the Market."

"What about an object from another world?" said Kit.

"There are a few in this dimension," said Shade. "Most are in the Spiral Labyrinth." He held up a hand. "And before you ask, no, I will not help you get one. My assistance ends with advising you."

Ty frowned. "But we'll need you to help with the spell," he said. "Shadowhunters—we can't do magic."

Kit knew what Ty meant. Warlocks were among the few who could naturally do magic in the world; magicians like his father had to find an energy source because they couldn't tap into ley lines, and energy sources—especially clean ones like the one Shade had promised them—weren't easy to get. Even if you could find someone to sell you a catalyst, Shadowhunters were forbidden by Law to buy that sort of thing, and even if Ty didn't care about breaking the Law, it would take him years to learn how to perform magic the way Johnny Rook had.

"I said I would contribute a catalyst you could use," said Shade. "You must do the rest yourselves. I will not touch necromancy."

Church meowed.

Ty picked up the list of ingredients; his eyes were deep and dark, more black than gray in the cave light. "Okay," he said. "Good enough."

He took out his witchlight and gestured for Kit to follow him; Shade rose to his feet and said something about walking them out. Kit hurried after Ty, who seemed as eager to be gone as he had been to come in the first place.

They had reached the end of the tunnel, where the rock opened out into sand and ocean, when Shade put his hand on Kit's shoulder.

"Christopher," he said. "Wait one moment."

Ty had already made his way out onto the beach. He was bent over; Kit realized he was stroking Church's fur. The cat had followed them out soundlessly and was making figure eights between Ty's legs, rubbing his head against the boy's calves.

"Watch over Tiberius," said Shade. There was something in his voice, an inflection, that made it sound as if he had learned English a long time ago. "There are many ways to be endangered by magic."

Kit glanced up in surprise. "What do you mean? We don't have to kill anybody, or create any death magic energy. Isn't that what makes necromancy wrong?"

Shade sighed. "Magic is like thermodynamics," he said. "You're always taking something from somewhere. Every act has repercussions, and this one may have repercussions you do not expect and cannot guard against. I see you think of yourself as Ty's protector." His voice gentled. "Sometimes you need to guard people against the things they want, as well as the things they fear."

Kit's heart clenched.

Out on the beach, Ty straightened up. The wind blew his hair, and he reached up his hands, unhesitating and unselfconscious, to touch the wind and the night air. His face shone like a star. In all the world, Kit had never met anyone he believed to be so incapable of evil.

"I would never let anything hurt Ty," he said. "You see, I—"

He turned to tell Shade, to explain to him how it was, how it would always be. But the warlock had disappeared.

Mark's skin burned softly where the pure iron manacles had been chained around his wrists.

Oban and his guard rode ahead on their horses; Manuel was in among them, as if it were natural for a Shadowhunter to ride among Unseelie hosts. He turned occasionally to smirk at Mark and Kieran, who walked behind the group. Manacles circled both their wrists, connected to a thick iron chain that clipped to the pommel of Oban's saddle.

It was a punishment Mark had seen before. He kept an anxious eye on Kieran in case he stumbled. A prisoner who fell would be dragged along behind Unseelie horses while the guards laughed.

Kieran was already pale with pain. The cold iron affected him much more than it did Mark; his wrists were bleeding and chafed where the iron touched them.

"They spoke of hostages," he said finally, as they reached the crest of a low hill. "Whose death are we being exchanged for?"

"We'll find out soon enough," said Mark.

"I am afraid," said Kieran, naked honesty in his voice. "Manuel Villalobos was at the Scholomance when I was hiding there. He is a terrible person. There is nothing he would not do. Most of the Cohort strike me as followers rather than leaders, even Zara. She does as her father tells her, as she has been taught, though they are teachings of hatred and cruelty. But Manuel is different. He does what he does because he wishes to cause people pain."

"Yes," said Mark. "It's what makes him dangerous. He isn't a true believer." He glanced around them; they were passing near to a patch of blight. He had started to get used to the sight of them, annihilated landscapes of ashy grass and dead trees, as if acid had been poured onto the earth from the sky. "We can trust in Cristina," he said in a near whisper. "She will be looking for help for us, even now."

"Did you notice something curious?" said Kieran. "Oban did not ask us about her. Where she might have vanished to, or who she might have sought out."

"Perhaps he was aware we did not know."

Kieran snorted. "No. Manuel did not tell him Cristina was ever there, mark my words. He would prefer Oban not be angry he had let a Shadowhunter escape."

"What is Manuel doing with Oban? No offense, but Oban doesn't seem like the brightest of your siblings."

Kieran's eyes narrowed. "He is a drunkard and a turnip."

"But an ambitious turnip."

Kieran chuckled reluctantly. "It seems to me that Manuel has stoked Oban's ambition. It is true that the Cohort cannot influence my father, but perhaps they hope to influence who the next Unseelie King might be. A weak one, that they can influence easily. Oban would be perfect for that."

They crested another hill. Mark could see the tower rise in the distance, a black thorn piercing the blue sky. He had flown over the Unseelie Tower with the Wild Hunt, but he had never been inside. He had never wanted to go. "Why would Manuel think that there would be a new Unseelie King anytime soon? Your father has been King for so long no one can remember what King Bram looked like."

Kieran glanced at the tower. A fresh burst of laughter came

from Oban and the others ahead. "Perhaps it is because the people are angry with my father. I hear things from Adaon. There are whispers of discontent. That the King has brought this blight down upon our land. That his obsession with Shadowhunters has left his people divided and impoverished. The elder faeries of Unseelie have mistrusted him since the disappearance of the First Heir. They feel that the King did not try hard enough to find her."

Mark was startled. "The First Heir was a girl? I thought that the King murdered all his female children."

Kieran didn't say anything. Mark recalled the last time they had faced the King in Faerie, when Mark had come with Emma and Julian and Cristina to save Kieran from the Lord of Shadows. Things were different now. He flashed back suddenly to the clearing, awakening to see Cristina and Kieran in each other's arms, just before the guards had come.

"Why did you kiss Cristina?" Mark said quietly. "If you did it to upset me or make me jealous, that was a terrible thing to do to her."

Kieran turned to him with surprise. "It was not to upset you or make you jealous, Mark."

"She likes you," Mark said. He had known it for some time but had never spoken the words aloud before.

Kieran flushed. "That is very strange to me. I do not deserve it."

"I am not sure I deserve her fondness either," said Mark. "Perhaps she does not bestow her heart with the care she should." He glanced down at his bleeding wrists. "Do not hurt her."

"I could not," said Kieran. "I would not. And I am sorry, Mark, if you were jealous. I had not intended that."

"It is all right," Mark said with a kind of puzzlement, as if he were surprised at the truth. "I wasn't jealous." *Not of either of you. How is that possible?*

The shadow of the tower fell over them, darkening the ground where they stood. The air seemed suddenly colder.

In front of them, the massive thorned hedge that ringed the tower rose up like a wall of spikes. White bones hung from the thorny spikes, as they had hung for hundreds of years. It had been a long, long time since a warrior had challenged the wall. And Mark could not remember ever having heard of one who had done so and lived.

"Mark," Kieran whispered.

Mark took a step forward and nearly stumbled; the chain connecting them to the horses lay limp on the ground. Oban and the others had paused in the archway of the enormous gates that were the only way through the thorn hedge.

Kieran reached for Mark and caught at his shoulder with his manacled hands. His lips were cracked and bleeding. He stared into Mark's eyes with a look of terrible pleading. Mark forgot their strange discussion about Cristina, forgot everything but Kieran's pain and his own desire to protect him.

"Mark," Kieran breathed. "I have to warn you. We will walk the path of punishment to the tower. I have seen this happen to others. It is—I cannot—"

"Kieran. It will be all right."

"No." Kieran shook his head wildly enough to make his dark-blue hair fly around his head. "My father will have lined the path to the tower with the gentry. They will scream at us. They will throw rocks and stones. It's how my father wants it. He threatened me with it after Iarlath's death. Now I am responsible for Erec's death as well. There will be no mercy for me." He choked on his words. "I am sorry you have to be here for this."

Feeling strangely calm, Mark said, "Isn't it better to have me with you?"

"No," Kieran said, and in his eyes Mark thought he saw the ocean, black and silver under the moon. Distant and untouchable. Beautiful and everlasting. "Because I love you."

The world seemed to rush away into silence. "But I thought—you said we would be done with each other."

"I am not done with you," said Kieran. "I could never be done with you, Mark Blackthorn."

Mark's whole body hummed with surprise. He barely registered it when they began to move forward again, until Kieran's grip slid from his shoulder. Reality came rushing back in, a smacking wave: He heard Kieran suck in his breath, steeling himself for the worst as they passed through the gates after Oban and the others.

Their chains rattled over the cobblestones of the path that led from the gates to the doors of the tower, an obscenely loud noise. The courtyard on either side was packed with Unseelie faeries. Some carried stones, while some held whips made of thorny vines.

Fumbling slightly, twisting his wrist against the manacles, Mark managed to take Kieran's hand in his. "We will go forward without fear," he said in a low voice. "For I am a Shadowhunter, and you are the son of a King."

Kieran threw him a grateful look. A moment later they were moving along the path, and the crowd, bearing their whips and stones, had flanked them on either side.

Mark raised his head. They would not see a Shadowhunter cringe in fear or pain. Beside him, Kieran had straightened his back; his expression was haughty, his body braced.

Braced—for blows that did not come. As Mark and Kieran walked between the rows of faeries, they stood as still as statues, their rocks unthrown, their whips unmoving.

The only sound came from Oban and his guards, their muttering rising in the silent air. Oban twisted to the side, his angry gaze raking the crowd. "Bestir yourselves, imbeciles!" he shouted. "Don't you know what you're supposed to be doing? These are murderers! They killed Iarlath! They murdered Prince Erec!"

A murmur went through the crowd, but it wasn't an angry

murmur. Mark thought he heard Erec's name spoken in anger, and Kieran's with much more gentleness; Kieran himself was looking around in great surprise.

And still the crowd did not move. Instead, as Kieran and Mark moved through and among them, voices began to rise. Mark listened incredulously as each told a story. *He gave me bread when I was starving by the side of the road. He intervened when the King's redcaps had taken my farm. He saved my husband from execution. He took responsibility for a crime my child committed. He tried to save my mother from the Riders of Mannan. And for his kindness, the King sent him to the Wild Hunt.*

Oban whipped around, his face twisted in rage. Manuel laid his hand on Oban's shoulder; he leaned in and whispered in the prince's ear. Oban subsided, looking furious.

Kieran looked at Mark in astonishment, his lips half-parted. "I do not understand," he whispered.

"They hate your father," said Mark. "But I do not think they hate you."

They had reached the steps of the tower. They paused as Oban and the others dismounted. There was a flash of movement in the crowd. A small faerie child, a girl with her hair in ribbons and bare feet, slipped from among the other fey folk and darted up to Kieran. She pressed something shyly into his hand. "For your kindness, Prince Kieran."

"What was that?" Mark asked as Kieran closed his hand around the object. But the guards had already surrounded them and were pushing them toward the doors of the tower, and Kieran did not answer.

As Diana flew with Gwyn over Brocelind, smoke furled up from the forest below like gray-and-black fingers unclosing against the sky.

The Cohort had burned the blighted areas, but haphazardly—

Diana could see the smoking stumps of trees, but the gray-black ashy land stretched out even farther than it had before, and some patches seemed untouched by fire. Diana looked on in dismay. What did the Cohort think they were doing?

They landed and Gwyn helped Diana down from Orion's back. Jia was waiting for them anxiously.

Diana ran to her. "I heard you had news about Emma and Julian. Are they all right? Have they been sent back to L.A.?"

Jia hesitated. She was looking thin and drawn, her skin papery and gray. "They have not. No."

Relief flowed through Diana: So Emma and Julian were still in Alicante. "I was so worried at the meeting," she said. "What Horace is doing to Diego and the others is unthinkable. Blaming them for crimes and sealing their mouths shut so they can't speak for themselves. It made me almost glad Emma and Julian are sequestered in that house—"

"Diana. No," Jia said. She laid a thin hand on Diana's wrist; Gwyn had come up and was listening quietly, his grizzled head tipped to one side. "A Clave member, someone loyal to me, overheard Zara talking to Manuel. She says that Horace sent Emma and Julian to Faerie on a suicide mission. I had my people check the house, and it's empty. They aren't here, Diana. They were sent to Faerie."

It was a soft explosion inside her head: rage, fury, anger at herself—she'd *known* something was wrong, had felt it. Why hadn't she trusted her instincts?

"Gwyn," she said, her voice barely recognizable in her own ears. "Take me to Faerie. Now."

Jia gripped Diana's wrist. "Diana, think. Faerie is a huge land—we don't know where they might be—"

"Gwyn and his people are hunters," said Diana. "We *will* find them. Gwyn—"

She turned to him, but he had stiffened all over, like a fox scenting hounds. "'Ware!" he cried, and whipped an ax from the scabbard on his back.

The trees rustled; Jia and Diana barely had time to draw their own weapons when the Cohort burst into the clearing, led by Zara Dearborn, brandishing a glittering sword.

A glittering sword that Diana knew. With a feeling as if she had swallowed a lump of ice, Diana recognized Cortana.

Jessica Beausejours was with Zara, along with Anush Joshi, Timothy Rockford, and Amelia Overbeck. Zara, in her Centurion uniform, grinned in triumph. "I knew it! I *knew* we would catch you conspiring with Downworlders!"

Gwyn raised an eyebrow. "There is only one Downworlder here."

Zara ignored him. "I expected no better of you, Diana Wrayburn, but Consul Penhallow? Violating the Cold Peace in your own homeland? How *could* you?"

Jia held her curved *dao* across her chest. "Spare me the dramatics, Zara," she said in clipped tones. "You don't understand what's happening, and your tantrums cause nothing but trouble."

"We're not conspiring with faeries, Zara," Diana said.

Zara spat on the ground. It was a startling gesture in its savage contempt. "How dare you deny that you are conspiring when we've caught you red-handed?"

"Zara—"

"Don't bother," Jia said to Diana. "She and the Cohort won't listen to you. They only hear what they want to hear. They accept nothing that contradicts the beliefs they already hold."

Zara turned to her followers. "Take them into custody," she said. "We will bring them to the Gard."

Gwyn threw his ax. It was a gesture so sudden that Diana leaped back in surprise; the ax sailed over the heads of the Cohort and slammed into the trunk of an oak tree. Several members of the Cohort screamed as the tree crashed over with the deafening roar of snapping branches and shattering earth.

Gwyn extended his hand, and the ax flew back into his grip. He bared his teeth at the cowering Shadowhunters. "Stay back, or I shall cut you to pieces!"

"See!" Zara had fallen to her knees when the tree had collapsed; she struggled up now, clutching Cortana tightly. "See? A conspiracy! We must fight—*Anush*!"

But Anush had fled into the bushes. The others, visibly shaken, reluctantly grouped around Zara as she took several determined steps toward Gwyn.

"What will he do?" Jia said in a quiet voice.

"He will kill them all. He's the Wild Hunt's leader, they are nothing to him."

"They are children," Jia said. "Poor Anush fled. He is only sixteen."

Diana hesitated. They *were* only children—hateful children, but Gwyn could not strike them down. It was no solution.

She ran to him, heedless of what the Cohort would think, and spoke in his ear. "Leave us," she whispered. "Please. They will take us to the Gard, but it will not be for long. You must go after Emma and Julian."

Gwyn turned to her, concern plain on his face. "But you—"

"Find them for me," Diana said. "I will be safe!" She whistled. "*Orion!*"

Orion cantered into the clearing, cutting between the Cohort and Gwyn. Gwyn clambered onto his horse's back and leaned down to kiss Diana, holding her face in his hands for a long moment.

"Be safe," he said, and Orion lifted into the sky. The Cohort were all shouting: Most had never seen anything like a steed of the Wild Hunt before. They really were children, Diana thought wearily: They still had wonder in them, mixed with their ignorance and hate.

And she could not hurt children. She stood quietly beside Jia as

Zara and Timothy relieved them of their weapons and chained their hands behind their backs.

With their invisibility potions gone, Emma and Julian had to rely on staying in the shadows, hoods up, as they crept along the corridors of the tower. Luckily, it seemed as if everyone had been summoned to some kind of event—the crowds had thinned out, and there were fewer Unseelie fey hurrying to and fro along the corridors. The guards seemed distracted as well, and no one questioned them as they slipped around the turn of a corridor and found themselves in front of the hanging tapestry with its pattern of stars.

Emma glanced around, concerned. "The guards are gone."

The corridor was, in fact, empty. Emma's nerves tingled. Something wasn't right.

"Good," Julian said. "Maybe they took a break or something."

"I don't like it," Emma said. "They wouldn't leave Ash unguarded."

"The guards might be inside the room."

"This doesn't feel right—"

"Someone's coming." Indeed, there were footsteps in the distance. Julian's face was tight with tension. "Emma, we have to move."

Against her better judgment, Emma drew a shortsword from her belt and slipped past the tapestry after Julian.

The room beyond was silent, eerily so, and empty of guards. Emma's first impression was of a place both richly decorated and very cold. A large four-poster bed carved of a single massive piece of wood dominated the space. Tapestries hung from the walls, depicting exquisite scenes of natural beauty in Faerie—forests wreathed in mist, tumbling glacial waterfalls, wildflowers growing on cliffs above the sea.

Emma could not help but think about the blight. The tapestries were stunning, a loving ode to the beauty of Faerie, but outside these walls the true Lands of Unseelie were being consumed by the blight. Had the King decorated this space? Did he see the irony of it?

Julian had placed himself by the tapestry door, his sword unsheathed. He was looking around curiously—it was hard not to notice the clothes strewn everywhere. Apparently Ash, like most teenage boys, was something of a slob. A window had been wedged open and cold air drifted through. Ash's golden crown had been dumped on the windowsill, almost as if he were daring a magpie to steal it.

Emma crept over to the bed where Ash lay, a still figure under a richly embroidered coverlet. His eyes were closed, perfect half circles fringed with silvery lashes. He looked innocent, angelic. Emma's heart went out to him—surprising, considering his resemblance to Sebastian. But it wasn't an exact duplication, she saw, stepping closer, so that her shadow fell over the bed.

"He looks a little like Clary," she whispered.

"It doesn't matter what he looks like," Julian said. "He's Sebastian's son."

He's a child, she wanted to protest, but she knew it wouldn't matter. She reached out to place a tentative hand on the boy's shoulder; as she did, she saw that there was a wide scar on the side of Ash's throat, no longer hidden by the collar of his shirt, in the shape of an X. There were odd markings on the wall behind his bed too: They looked like runes, but twisted and sinister runes, like the ones the Endarkened had worn.

A ferocious desire to protect him rose up in her, startling in both its strength and its complete lack of logic. She didn't even know this boy, she thought, but she couldn't stop herself from reaching over to shake him gently. "Ash," she whispered. "Ash, wake up. We're here to rescue you."

His eyes flew open, and she truly saw Clary in him then; they were the same color green as hers. They fixed on Emma as he sat up, reaching out a hand. They were steady and clear and a thought flashed through her head: *He could be a true leader, not like Sebastian, but like Sebastian should have been.*

Across the room, Julian was shaking his head. "Emma, no," he said. "What are you—"

Ash jerked his hand back and shouted: *"Ethna! Eochaid! Riders, help me!"*

Julian whirled toward the door, but the two Riders had already torn through the tapestry. Their bronze armor shone like blinding sunlight; Julian struck out with his blade, slashing it across the front of Eochaid's chest, but the Rider pivoted away.

Ethna's metallic hair flew around her as she launched herself at Julian with a scream of rage. He raised his sword but wasn't fast enough; she crashed into him, seizing Julian and smashing him against the wall.

Ash rolled away across the coverlet; Emma seized him and yanked him back, her fingers sinking into his shoulder. She felt as if she'd emerged from a fog: dizzy, breathless, and suddenly very, very angry. "Stop!" she shouted. "Let Julian go or I'll cut the prince's throat."

Ethna looked up with a snarl; she was standing over Julian, her blade out. He was crouched with his back against the wall, a trickle of blood running from his temple. His eyes were watchful.

"Do not be a fool," said Eochaid. "Do you not understand that your only chance to live is letting the prince go?"

Emma pressed the blade closer against Ash's throat. He was like a taut wire in her grip. *Protect Ash,* whispered a voice in the back of her head. *Ash is what matters.*

She bit down on her lip, the pain whiting out the voice in her head. "Explain yourself, Rider."

"We are in the tower," said Ethna in a tone of disgust. "We cannot slay you without the King's permission. He would be angered. But if you were threatening Ash . . ." Her look was hungry. "Then we would have no choice but to protect him."

Julian wiped blood from his face. "She's right. They can't kill us. Let Ash go, Emma."

Ash was looking fixedly at Julian. "You look like *her*," he said with surprise.

Puzzled, Emma hesitated, and Ash took the opportunity to sink his teeth into her hand. She yelled and let go of him; a circle of bleeding dents marked the curve of her thumb and forefinger. "Why?" she demanded. "You're a prisoner here. Don't you want to leave?"

Ash was crouched on the bed, an odd feral scowl on his face. He was fully dressed in breeches, a linen tunic, and boots. "In Alicante I would be the son of your most hated enemy. You would take me to my death."

"It isn't like that—" Emma began, but she didn't finish; her head flew back as Ethna delivered a stinging slap to her cheek.

"Cease your yammering," said Eochaid.

Emma turned back once to look at Ash as she and Julian were marched from the room at sword point. He stood in the middle of the chamber, looking after them; his face was blank, without Sebastian's haughtiness and cruelty—but without Clary's kindness, either. He looked like someone who had pulled off a successful chess move.

Neither Julian nor Emma spoke as they were marched along the corridors, the fey folk around them murmuring and staring. The corridors gave way soon to danker and danker hallways angling more steeply down. As the light dimmed, Emma caught a brief look at the expression of frustration and bitterness on Julian's face before the shadows clustered and she could see only moving shapes in the occasional weak illumination of green bough torches hanging on the walls.

"It seems almost a pity," said Eochaid, breaking the silence as they reached a long, serpentine hall that led to a dark hole in a distant wall. Emma could see the glimmer of guard uniforms even in the dark. "To kill these two before they can witness the destruction of the Nephilim."

"Nonsense," said Ethna curtly. "Blood for blood. They murdered our brother. Perhaps the King will let us swing the scythe that ends them."

They had reached the hole in the far wall. It was a doorway without a door, cut into a thick wall of stone. The guards on either side seemed intrigued. "More prisoners?" said the one on the left, who was lounging atop a massive wooden chest.

"Captives of the King," said Ethna in a clipped voice.

"Practically a party," said the guard, and chuckled. "Not that they stay long, mind."

Ethna rolled her eyes and hustled Emma forward with the prick of the sword between her shoulder blades. She and Julian were ushered into a wide, square room with rough-hewn stone walls. Vines grew from the ceiling, ribboning down to plunge into the hard-packed dirt floor. They wove closely together into the shape of boxes—cells, Emma realized: cells whose walls were made out of thorny vines, hard as flexible iron.

She remembered those thorns stabbing into her, and shuddered.

Ethna laughed unpleasantly. "Shiver all you want," she said. "There is no escape here, and no pity." She took Emma's weapons belt from her waist and forced her to remove the Clave's gold medallion from her throat. Emma cast Julian a panicked look—nothing would prevent them from suffering the time slippage in Faerie now.

Furious, Emma was shoved into a cell through a gap in the vines. To her relief, Julian followed a moment later. She had been afraid they would be separated and that she would go out of her mind alone. He was also weaponless. He turned to glare at the Riders as Ethna tapped the end of her sword against the cage; the vines that had parted quickly slithered and twisted together, closing up any possibility of an exit.

Ethna was grinning. The look of triumph on her face made Emma's stomach twist acidly. "Little Shadowhunters," she crooned. "What does all your angel blood avail you now?"

"Come, sister," said Eochaid, though he was smiling indulgently. "The King awaits."

Ethna spat on the ground before turning to follow her brother. Their footsteps faded away, and there was darkness and silence—cold, pressuring silence. Only a little dim illumination came from smoky torches high up on the walls.

The strength left Emma's limbs like water pouring out of a broken dam. She sank to the ground in the center of the cage, cringing away from the thorns all around her.

"Julian," she whispered. "What are we going to do?"

He dropped to his knees. She could see where goose bumps had risen all over his skin. The bloody bandage around his wrist seemed to glow like a phantom in the dark.

"I got us in here," he said. "I'll get us out."

Emma opened her mouth to protest, but no words came; it was close enough to the truth. The old Julian, her Julian, would have listened when she'd said she sensed the situation outside Ash's room wasn't right. He would have trusted her instinct. For the first time she felt something close to true mourning for that Julian, as if this Julian wasn't just temporary—as if her Julian might never come back.

"Do you care?" she said.

"You think I want to die in here?" he said. "I still have a self-preservation instinct, Emma, and that means preserving you, too. And I know—I know I'm a better Shadowhunter than I just was."

"Being a Shadowhunter isn't just in fast reflexes or strong muscles." She pressed her hand against his heart, the linen of his shirt soft against her fingers. "It's here." *Here where you're broken.*

His blue-green eyes seemed the only color in the prison; even the vines of their cell were metallic gray. "Emma—"

"It is them!" said a voice, and Emma jumped as light flared all around them. And not just any light. White-silver light, radiating from the cell opposite theirs; she could see it now, in the new illumination. Two figures stood inside, staring at them through the vines, and one of them held a glowing rune-stone in her hand.

"Witchlight," breathed Julian, rising to his feet.

"Julian? Emma?" called the same voice—familiar, and full of surprise and relief. The witchlight grew, and Emma could see the figures in the opposite cell clearly now. She bolted upright with astonishment. "It's us—it's Jace and Clary."

16
A Thousand Thrones

Oban and his guards had led Mark and Kieran blindfolded through the tower, so if there were more reactions to Kieran's presence, Mark had been unable to note them. He had, however, heard Manuel and Oban laughing about what the King was likely to do to Kieran, and to Mark as well, and he had struggled against his manacles in rage. How dare they speak that way when Kieran could hear them? Why would anyone take pleasure in such torture?

They had been led finally to a windowless stone room and left there, their hands still manacled. Oban had torn their blindfolds from them as he walked out of the room, laughing. "Look one last time upon each other before you die."

And Mark did look at Kieran now, in the dim room. Though there were no windows, light filtered down from a grating far above. The room was close, oppressive as the bottom of an elevator shaft.

"It is meant to be horrible," Kieran said, answering the question Mark had not asked. "This is where the King keeps prisoners prior to bringing them before the throne. It is meant to terrify."

"Kieran." Mark moved closer to the other boy. "It will be all right."

Kieran smiled painfully. "That is what I love about mortals," he said. "That you can say such things, for comfort, whether they be true or not."

"What did that girl give you?" Mark said. Kieran's hair was blue-black in the shadows. "The little girl, on the steps."

"A flower." Kieran's hands were bound in front of him; he opened one and showed Mark the crushed white bloom. "A white daffodil."

"Forgiveness," Mark said. Kieran looked at him in puzzlement; his education had not been flower-focused. "Flowers have their own meanings. A white daffodil means forgiveness."

Kieran let the flower fall from his hand. "I heard the words those people said as I went through the courtyard," he said. "And I do not remember."

"Do you think your father made you forget?" Mark's hands had begun to ache.

"No. I think it did not matter to me. I think I was kind because I was a prince and arrogant and careless and it suited me to be kind, but I could just as easily have been cruel. I do not remember saving a farm or a child. I was drunk on an easy life in those days. I should not be thanked or forgiven."

"Kieran—"

"And during the Hunt, I thought only of myself." White threads shot through Kieran's dark hair. He let his head fall back against the stone wall.

"No," said Mark. "You thought of me. You were kind to me."

"I wanted you," Kieran said, a hard twist to his mouth. "I was kind to you because it benefited me in the end."

Mark shook his head. "When mortals say that things will be all right, it is not only for comfort," he said. "In part it is because we do not, as faeries do, believe in an absolute truth. We bring our own truth to the world. Because I believe things will be all right, I will be less unhappy and afraid. And because you are angry at yourself, you believe that everything you have done, you have done out of selfishness."

"I have been selfish," Kieran protested. "I—"

"We are all selfish sometimes," said Mark. "And I am not saying you have nothing to atone for. Perhaps you were a selfish prince, but you were not a cruel one. You had power and you chose to use it to be kind. You could have chosen the opposite. Do not dismiss the choices you made. They were not meaningless."

"Why do you try to comfort and cheer me?" Kieran said in a dry voice, as if his throat ached. "I was angry with you when you agreed to return to your family from the Hunt—I told you none of it was real—"

"As if I did not know why you said that," said Mark. "I heard you, in the Hunt. When they whipped you, when you were tormented, you would whisper to yourself that none of it was real. As if to say the pain was all a dream. It was a gift you meant to give me—the gift of escaping agony, of retreating into a place in your mind where you were safe."

"I thought the Shadowhunters were cruel. I thought they would hurt you," said Kieran. "With you, with your family, I have learned differently. I thought I loved you in the Hunt, Mark, but that was a shadow of what I feel for you now, knowing what loving-kindness you are capable of."

The elf-bolt at his throat shone as it rose and fell with his quick breathing.

"In the Hunt, you needed me," said Kieran. "You needed me so much I never knew if you would want me, if you did not need me. Do you?"

Mark stumbled a little, moving closer to Kieran. His wrists were burning fire, but he didn't care. He pressed close to Kieran, and Kieran's bound hands caught at Mark's waist, fumbling to pull Mark closer to him. His heels lifted off the ground as he leaned into

Kieran, the two of them trying to get as close as possible, to comfort each other despite their bound hands.

Mark buried his face in the crook of Kieran's neck, breathing in his familiar scent: grass and sky. Perhaps this was the last grass and sky he would ever know.

The door to the cell swung open and a burst of light cut at Mark's eyes. He felt Kieran go tense against him.

Winter, the redcap general, stood in the doorway, his shirt and cap the color of rusty old blood, his iron-soled boots clanging on the stone floor. In his hand was a long, steel-tipped pike.

"Move apart, the both of you," he said, voice clipped. "The King will see you now."

Emma flew to the front of the cell—and remembered the thorns just in time, leaping back from touching them. Julian followed with a greater hesitation.

"Oh, thank the Angel you're here," said Emma. "I mean, not that you're here, in prison, that's bad, but—" She threw up her hands. "I'm glad to see you."

Clary chuckled wanly. "We know what you mean. I'm glad to see you, too." Her face was smudged and dirty, her red hair tied up in a knot at the back of her head. In the light of the rune-stone, Emma could see that she looked a little thin; her dirt-stained jean jacket hung loose around her shoulders. Jace, behind her, was tall and golden as ever, his eyes bright-burning in the dimness, his chin shadowed with rough beard.

"What are you doing here?" he said, dispensing with pleasantries. "Were you in Faerie? Why?"

"We were on a mission," said Julian.

Clary ducked her face down. "Please don't tell me it was to find us."

"It was to find the Black Volume of the Dead. The Inquisitor sent us."

Jace looked incredulous. "Robert sent you here?"

Emma and Julian glanced at each other. There was an awful silence.

Jace moved closer to the thorned bars of the cage that held him and Clary. "Whatever you're not telling us, don't hold it back," he said. "If something happened, you need to let us know."

Perhaps not surprisingly, it was Julian who spoke. "Robert Lightwood is dead."

The witchlight blinked out.

In the darkness, with her Night Vision rune useless, Emma could see nothing. She heard Jace make a muffled noise, and Clary whispering. Words of comfort, words of soothing—Emma was sure of it. She recognized herself, murmuring to Julian in the quiet of night.

The whispering stopped, and the witchlight flickered back on. Jace was holding it in one hand, his other wrapped tightly around one of the vines. Blood ran from between his fingers, down his arm. Emma imagined the thorns stabbing into his palm and winced.

"What about everyone else?" he said in a voice so tight it was barely human. "What about Alec?"

Emma moved closer to the front of the cell. "He's fine," she said, and filled them in as quickly as she could on what had happened, from Annabel's murder of Robert and Livvy to Horace's ascension as Inquisitor.

There was a silence when she was done, but at least Jace had let go of the vine.

"I'm so sorry about your sister," Clary said softly. "I'm sorry we weren't there."

Julian said nothing.

"There isn't anything you could have done," said Emma.

"The King is close to getting the Black Volume," said Jace. He opened and closed his bloody hand. "This is really bad news."

"But you didn't come here for that," said Julian. "You came here to find Ash. He's the weapon you're looking for, right?"

Clary nodded. "We got a tip-off from the Spiral Labyrinth that there was a weapon in Faerie that the Unseelie King had access to, something that could nullify Shadowhunter powers."

"We were sent here because of our angelic blood. Rumors of the ineffectiveness of Shadowhunter magic in the Courts were swirling; the Silent Brothers said we would be more resistant to the effects," said Jace. "We don't suffer from time slippage here, and we can use runes—or at least we could, before they took our steles away. At least we still have these." He held up the glowing witch-light, pulsing in his hand.

"So we knew we were looking for something," said Clary. "But not that it was my—that it was Ash."

"How did you figure it out?" said Emma.

"We found out pretty early on that the King had kidnapped the Seelie Queen's son," said Jace. "It's something of an open secret in the Courts. And then the first time Clary saw him—from a distance, we were captured before we ever got close—"

Clary moved restlessly inside the cell. "I knew who he was right away. He looks exactly like my brother."

Emma had heard Julian and Livvy and Mark and Dru say the words "my brother" more times than she could count. It had never sounded the way it did when Clary said it: imbued with bitterness and regret.

"And now the King has the Black Volume, which means we have hardly any time," said Jace, brushing his hand lightly across the back of Clary's neck.

"Okay," said Julian. "What exactly does the King plan to do with the Black Volume to make Ash a weapon?"

Jace lowered his voice, though Emma doubted anyone could hear them. "There are spells in the Black Volume that would imbue Ash with certain powers. The King did something like this once before—"

"Have you heard of the First Heir?" said Clary.

"Yes," Emma said. "Kieran mentioned him—or at least mentioned the story."

"It was something his brother Adaon told him." Julian was frowning. "Kieran said his father had wanted the book since the First Heir was stolen. Maybe to raise the child from the dead? But what does that have to do with Ash?"

"It's an old story," said Jace. "But as you know—all the stories are true."

"Or at least true in part." Clary smiled up at him. Emma felt a spark of longing—even in the darkness and cold of this prison, their love was undamaged. Clary turned back to Julian and Emma. "We learned that long ago the Unseelie King and the Seelie Queen decided to unite the Courts. Part of their plan involved having a child together, a child who would be heir to both Courts. But that wasn't enough for them—they wanted to create a faerie child so powerful that he could destroy the Nephilim."

"Before the child was born, they used rites and spells to give the child 'gifts,'" said Jace. "Think Sleeping Beauty but the parents are the wicked faeries."

"The child would be perfectly beautiful, a perfect leader, inspiring of perfect loyalty," said Clary. "But when the child was born, she was a girl. It had never even occurred to the King that the child wouldn't be male—being who he is, he thought the perfect leader had to be a man. The King was furious and thought that the Queen had betrayed him. The Queen, in turn, was furious that he wanted to abandon their whole plan just because the child was a girl. Then the child was kidnapped, and possibly murdered."

"No wonder—all that stuff about the King hating daughters," Emma mused.

"What do you mean 'possibly'?" said Julian.

Jace said, "We weren't able to find out what happened to that child. No one knows—the claim of the King was that she was kidnapped and murdered, but it seems likely she escaped Faerie and lived on." He shrugged. "What's clear is that Ash has mixed in him the blood of royal faeries, the blood of the Nephilim, and the blood of demons. The King believes he's the perfect candidate to finish what they began with the First Heir."

"The end of all Shadowhunters," Julian said slowly.

"The blight the King has already brought here has been taking hold slowly," Clary said. "But if the King is allowed to perform the spells he wants to on Ash, Ash will become a weapon even more powerful than the blight. We don't even know everything he'll be able to do, but he'll have the same mixture of seraphic and infernal blood that Sebastian did."

"He'd be demonic, but impervious to runes or angelic magic," said Jace. "He could bear runes, but nothing demonic could hurt him. The touch of his hands could make the blight spread like wildfire."

"The blight is already in Idris," said Emma. "Parts of Brocelind Forest have been destroyed."

"We need to get back," Clary said. She looked even paler than she had before, and younger. Emma remembered Clary on the roof at the L.A. Institute. *Knowing something awful is coming. Like a wall of darkness and blood. A shadow that spreads out over the world and blots out everything.*

"We can't wait any longer," Jace said. "We have to get out of here."

"I'm guessing that wishing to get out of here hasn't worked so far, since you're still imprisoned," said Julian.

Jace narrowed his eyes.

"Julian," Emma said. She wanted to add *sorry, he has no feelings of empathy*, but she didn't because at that moment she heard a shout, followed by a loud thump. Jace closed his hand over his witchlight, and in the near-total darkness, Emma backed away from the walls of the cage. She didn't want to accidentally walk face-first into the stabbing thorns.

There was a grinding sound as the door of the prison swung open.

"Probably guards," said Clary in a low voice.

Emma stared into the shadowy dimness. There were two figures coming toward them; she could see the gold glint of the braid on guard uniforms.

"One's carrying a sword," Emma whispered.

"They're probably coming for us," Clary said. "We've been down here longer."

"No," Julian said. Emma knew what he was thinking. Jace and Clary were valuable hostages, in their way. Emma and Julian were Shadowhunter thieves who had killed a Rider. They would not be left in the dungeons to languish. They would be beheaded quickly for the enjoyment of the Court.

"Fight back," Jace said urgently. "If they open your cell, fight back—"

Cortana, Emma thought in desperation. *Cortana!*

But nothing happened. There was no sudden and comforting weight in her hand. Only a pressure against her shoulder; Julian had moved to stand next to her. Weaponless, they faced the front of their cell. There was the sound of a gasp, then running feet—Emma raised her fists—

The smaller of the guards reached their cell and grabbed at one of the vines, then yelped in pain. A voice murmured something in a faerie language, and the torches along the walls burst into dim flame. Emma found herself staring through the tangle of vines and thorns at Cristina, wearing the livery of a faerie guard, a longsword strapped across her back.

"Emma?" Cristina breathed, her eyes wide. "What on earth are you doing here?"

* * *

Watch over Tiberius.

Kit was doing just that. Or at least he was staring at Ty, which seemed close enough. They were on the beach below the Institute; Ty had taken off his socks and shoes and was walking at the edge of the water. He glanced up at Kit, who was sitting on a rise of sand, and beckoned him closer. "The water isn't that cold!" he called. "I promise."

I believe you, Kit wanted to say. He always believed Ty. Ty wasn't a liar unless he had to be, though he was good at hiding things. He wondered what would happen if Helen asked them both straight-out if they were trying to raise Livvy from the dead.

Maybe he would be the one who told the truth. After all, he was the one who didn't really want to do it.

Kit rose slowly to his feet and walked down the beach to join Ty. The waves were breaking at least twenty feet out; by the time they reached the shoreline they were white foam and silver water. A surge splashed up and over Ty's bare feet and soaked Kit's sneakers.

Ty had been right. It wasn't all that cold.

"So tomorrow we'll go to the Shadow Market," said Ty. The moonlight played delicate shadows over his face. He seemed calm, Kit thought, and realized that it had been a long time since he hadn't felt like Ty was a tightly strung wire, thrumming by his side.

"You hated the Shadow Market in London," Kit said. "It really bothered you. The noises, and the crowd—"

Ty's gaze flicked down to Kit. "I'll wear my headphones. I'll be all right."

". . . and I don't know if we should go again so soon," Kit added. "What if Helen and Aline get suspicious?"

Ty's gray gaze darkened. "Julian told me once," he said, "that when people keep coming up with reasons not to do something, it's because they don't want to do it. Do you not want to do this? The spell, everything?"

Ty's voice sounded tight. The thrumming wire again, sharp with tension. Under the cotton of his shirt, his thin shoulders had tightened as well. The neck of his shirt was loose, the delicate line of his collarbones just visible.

Kit felt a rush of tenderness toward Ty, mixed with near panic. In other circumstances, he thought, he would just have lied. But he couldn't lie to Ty.

He splashed farther into the water, until his jeans were wet to below his knees. He turned around, the foam of the surf splashing around him. "Didn't you hear what Shade said? The Livvy we get back might not be anything like our Livvy. Your Livvy."

Ty followed him out into the water. Mist was coming down to touch the water, surrounding them in white and gray. "If we do the spell correctly, she will be. That's all. We have to do it right."

Kit could taste salt on his mouth. "I don't know . . ."

Ty reached out a hand, sweeping his arm toward the horizon, where the stars were beginning to fade into the mist. The horizon was a black line smudged with silver. "Livvy is out there," he said. "Just past where I can reach her, but I can hear her. She says my name. She wants me to bring her back. She needs me to bring her back." The corner of Ty's mouth trembled. "I don't want to do it without you. But I will."

Kit took another step into the ocean and paused. The deeper he went, the colder it got. And wasn't that the case with everything, he thought. *There are many ways to be endangered by magic.*

I could walk away, he said to himself. *I could let Ty do this on his own. But I can't tell myself that it wouldn't be the end of our friendship, because it would. I'd end up locked out of Ty's plans, just like Helen, just like Dru. Just like everyone else.*

It felt like the air was being choked out of his lungs. He spun back toward Ty. "Okay. I'll do it. We can go to the Shadow Market tomorrow."

Ty smiled. Or perhaps it would be more accurate to say that a smile broke across his face, like the sun rising. Kit stood breathless, the water receding around him, as Ty came up and put his arms around Kit's neck.

He remembered holding Ty on the roof of the Institute in London, but that had been because Ty was panicking. It had been like holding a wild animal. This was Ty hugging him because he wanted to. The soft cotton of Ty's shirt, the feeling of Ty's hair brushing against his cheek as he hid his expression from Ty by burrowing his face against the other boy's shoulder. He could hear Ty breathing. He threaded his arms around Ty, crossing his cold hands over Ty's back. When Ty leaned into him with a sigh, he felt like he'd won a race he didn't know he was running.

"Don't worry," Ty said quietly. "We're going to get her back. I promise."

That's what I'm afraid of. But Kit said nothing aloud. He held on to Ty, sick with a miserable happiness, and closed his eyes against the prying light of the moon.

"We are here to help you," said Cristina's companion. Emma recognized him, belatedly: Prince Adaon, one of the Unseelie King's sons. She had seen him the last time she was in Faerie. He was a tall faerie knight in the colors of Unseelie, handsome and dark-skinned, two daggers at his waist. He reached out to grasp the vines of their cell, which parted under his touch. Emma wriggled out through them and flung her arms around Cristina.

"Cristina," she said. "You beautiful badass, you."

Cristina smiled and patted Emma's back while Adaon freed Julian and then Jace and Clary. Jace was the last to slip through the vines. He raised an eyebrow at Julian.

"What were you saying about wishing to be rescued?" he said.

"We cannot stay here long," said Adaon. "There will come others, guards and knights alike." He glanced up and down the row of cells, frowning. "Where are they?"

"Where are who?" said Emma, letting go of Cristina reluctantly.

"Mark and Kieran," said Cristina. "Where are Mark and Kieran?"

"I came here to rescue my brother, not empty the palace's prisons of criminals," said Adaon, who Emma was beginning to think might not be the world's most jolly person.

"We're very appreciative of your efforts," said Clary. She had noticed Emma was shivering with cold. She took off her denim jacket and handed it to Emma with a gentle pat on her shoulder.

Emma slipped the jacket on, too cold and tired and hurt to protest. "But—why would Mark and Kieran be here? Why are *you* here, Cristina?"

Adaon had begun to stride up and down the line of cells, peering into each one. Cristina looked around nervously. "Mark, Kieran, and I heard that Dearborn sent you on a suicide mission," she said to Emma and Julian. "We came to help you."

"But Mark isn't with you?" said Julian, who had snapped to attention at the sound of his brother's name. "Did you get separated here? Inside the tower?"

"No. They were kidnapped on the road, by the worst of my brothers," said Adaon, who had returned from his search of the cells. "Cristina came to me for help. I knew Oban would have brought Mark and Kieran here, but I thought they would be in the prison." His mouth set in grim lines. "Oban was always overeager. He must have taken them straight to my father instead."

"You mean to the throne room?" said Emma, slightly dizzy with the suddenness with which things were happening.

"Yes," said Adaon. "To the King. They would be valuable prizes, and Oban would be eager to collect."

"They'll kill Kieran," Cristina said, a thin thread of panic in her voice. "He already escaped execution once. They'll kill Mark, too."

"Then we'd better get there and prevent it," said Jace. Under the dirt and the beard, he was starting to look more like the Jace Emma had always known, the one she had once wanted to be like—the best warrior of all the Shadowhunters. "Now."

Adaon gave him a scornful look. "It's too dangerous for you, Nephilim."

"You came here for your brother," Julian said, his eyes blazing. "We're going after mine. If you want to stop us, you'll have to use force."

"We should all go together," Clary said. "The more of us there are, the more easily we can defeat the King."

"But you are powerless here, Nephilim," said Adaon.

"No," Jace said, and the witchlight blazed up in his hand, light spearing through his fingers. They all stood bathed in its white light. Cristina stared with her mouth open; Adaon betrayed shock the way faeries usually did, by moving one or two facial muscles slightly.

"Very well," he said coolly. "But I will not risk being caught by the guards wandering the tower openly, like fools. All of you walk before me. You will behave as my prisoners now."

"You want us to act like prisoners being marched to the King?" said Julian, who didn't look delighted at the thought.

"I want you to look afraid," said Adaon, drawing his sword and motioning for them to get in front of him. "Because you should be."

Diana had expected to be locked in a cell in the Gard's prisons, but instead she was brought to a surprisingly luxurious room. A Turkish rug covered the floor and a fire burned high in a carved stone fireplace. Deep velvet armchairs were pulled up to the fire; she sat in one, stiff with tension, and stared out the picture window at the rooftops of Idris.

Her mind was full of Gwyn, and of Emma and Julian. What if she had sent Gwyn into danger? Why had she assumed he would travel to Faerie to find two Shadowhunters only because she had asked?

As for Emma and Julian, two words circled in her head like sharks, over and over.

Suicide mission.

Horace Dearborn entered, carrying a silver tray with a tea service on it. *Now I've seen it all,* Diana thought as he sat down and settled the tray on a small table between them.

"Diana Wrayburn," he said. "I've been meaning to have a private conversation with you for a long time."

"You could have invited me to the Gard at any time. You didn't need to have me arrested in the woods."

He sighed deeply. "I'm sorry it had to happen like that, but you were consorting with faeries and breaking the Cold Peace. Understand, I like a woman with spirit." His gaze slid over her in a way that made her feel like shuddering.

She crossed her arms over her chest. "Where's Jia?"

Horace picked up the teapot and began to pour. Every move was measured and calm. "By the will of the Council, the Consul is under house arrest for the time being, until her connection with faeries is investigated."

It wasn't really a surprise, but it still felt like a blow. "Don't tell me. Her trial will be held as soon as the Mortal Sword is 'reforged,'" Diana said bitterly.

He bobbed his head enthusiastically. "Exactly, exactly." He set the teapot down. "An unfortunate situation. And one you could find yourself in—unless you're willing to make a bargain with me."

"What kind of bargain?"

He handed her a teacup; mechanically, Diana took it. "The next Council meeting will be a difficult one, as the Clave is brought to understand that future decisions must be arrived at without the Consul. A transition of power is always difficult, wouldn't you say?"

Diana stared at him stonily.

"Let me be clear," Horace said, and though his expression was easy and friendly, there was no friendliness in his eyes. "Take my side at the next Council meeting. You have influence over people. The L.A. Institute, the New York Institute—many Institutes will listen to you. If you back me as the next Consul, a replacement for Penhallow, so will they."

"People listen to me because I don't compromise my values," Diana said. "They know when I say something, I believe it. I could never believe you would make a good Consul."

"Is that so?" The false friendliness had vanished from his face. "Do you think I care about your *values*, Diana Wrayburn? You'll stand by my side, because if you don't, I will reveal your secret to the Clave."

Diana's throat tightened. "What secret?"

Horace rose to his feet, his expression thunderous. "For all your talk of values, I know you have a secret. I know you've refused to become head of the Los Angeles Institute all these years—letting a madman run it—I *know* you carry a shadow with you, Diana Wrayburn, and I know what it is. I know you submitted yourself to mundane medical treatment in Bangkok."

Stunned and furious, Diana was silent. How did he know? Her mind raced: The Clave considered a Shadowhunter who let mundane doctors look at their blood, learn their secrets, a traitor. Never mind that Catarina had covered up all her unusual test results. Horace would blame her anyway.

"And let me tell you this," said Horace. "I will use that information to the fullest unless you do as I say. You will be torn from those Blackthorns you love so dearly. Imprisoned, perhaps, alongside other traitors."

"Unless what?" Diana said dully.

"Unless you agree to stand by my side at the next meeting and declare that Jia is incompetent and that I should be the next Consul. Do you understand?"

Diana felt as if she were seeing herself through the wrong end of a telescope, a tiny figure with Horace looming vastly over her. "I understand."

"And do you agree to throw your support behind the Cohort?"

"Yes." She got to her feet. She was very conscious of her torn and dirty clothes—the Cohort had not been gentle with her or Jia, though they had surrendered quietly.

Horace opened his mouth, perhaps to call for the guards to take her away. Moving more swiftly than she would have thought possible, Diana seized the Inquisitor's sword from the belt at his waist and swung it.

Horace screamed. He staggered back, still screaming, and fell to his knees; there was blood all over his robes. His arm was hanging at a strange angle.

Guards burst into the room, but Diana had already run to the window and thrown it open. She hurled herself onto the roof, skidding nearly to the edge before she arrested her fall by catching at the slate tiles.

The guards were at the window. She scrambled to her feet and raced across the roof, looking for an overhang she could swing down from. A shadow passed across the moon, obscuring the demon towers. She heard the sound of hoofbeats, and she knew.

As the guards crawled through the window, she hurled herself from the roof.

"Diana!" Gwyn banked Orion, turned, reached out to catch her. She landed awkwardly, hurling her arms around his neck. Strong hands wrapped her waist; she glanced back once and saw the pale

faces of the guards watching from the roof of the Gard as they sailed into the night.

Dru flipped off the TV in the middle of *The Deadly Bees*, which was unusual because it was one of her favorite bad movies. She'd even bought a pair of gold bee earrings at Venice Beach once so she could wear them while she watched the death-by-stinger scenes.

She was too restless to sit still, though. The excitement she'd felt outside the 101 Coffee Shop still prickled the back of her neck. It had been so much *fun* being teamed up with Kit and Ty, laughing with them, in on their plans.

She swung her legs off the sofa and headed barefoot out into the hallway. She'd painted the toenails on one foot acid green, but she didn't feel like sticking around to do the other one. She felt like finding Livvy and curling up with her on her bed, laughing at out-of-date mundane magazines.

The pain of remembering Livvy changed from moment to moment; sometimes a dull, aching one, sometimes a sharp flash as of being stuck with a hot needle. If Julian or Emma were here, she could have talked to them about it, or even Mark. As she passed the big staircase leading down to the entryway, she could hear the sound of voices from the Sanctuary. Helen's, friendly and calm, and Aline's, sharp and authoritative. She wondered if she would have gone to either of them even if they hadn't been so busy. Dru couldn't really imagine it.

She thought of tonight, though, giggling in the back of the car with Kit and Ty, and the desert wind in her hair. It carried the smell of white oleander even in the center of Hollywood. The night had filled the gnawing urge to *do something* inside her that she hadn't even realized was there.

She reached the twins' bedrooms. Ty and Livvy had always had bedrooms directly across from each other; the door of Livvy's room was shut tight and had been since they'd returned from Idris.

Dru laid her hand on it, as if she could feel her sister's heartbeat through the wood. Livvy had painted her door red once, and the flaking paint was rough against Dru's fingers.

In a horror movie, Dru thought, this was when Livvy would burst out half-rotted, clawing at Dru with her dead hands. The idea didn't frighten her at all. Maybe that was why she liked horror movies, Dru thought; the dead never stayed dead, and those left behind were too busy wandering unwisely around in the woods to have time to grieve or feel loss.

She left Livvy's door and went over to Ty's. She knocked, but there was music playing in the room and she couldn't hear a reply. She pushed the door open and froze.

The radio was on, Chopin blasting, but Ty wasn't there. The space was freezing. All the windows were wide open. Dru almost tripped getting across the room to slam the largest window shut. She looked down and saw that Ty's books were scattered over the floor, no longer in neat rows determined by subject and color. His desk chair lay in pieces, his clothes were scattered everywhere, and there were smears of dried blood on his sheets and pillowcases.

Ty. Oh, Ty.

Dru closed the door as hastily as she could without slamming it, and hurried off down the hallway as if a monster from one of her old movies were chasing her.

They stopped outside the prison, where the dead body of the guard lay draped over the wooden chest Emma had noticed earlier. Adaon grimaced and used the tip of his boot to shove the guard's body aside. It hit the bloodstained flagstones with a thump. To Emma's puzzlement, Adaon knelt and shoved the chest open, the hinges groaning and squeaking.

Her puzzlement vanished quickly. The chest was full of

weapons—longswords, daggers, bows. Emma recognized the sword the Riders had taken from her, and Julian's as well. She craned her neck to stare, but she didn't see the medallion anywhere among the confiscated items.

Adaon seized up a number of swords. Jace held out his hand for one.

"Come to papa," he crooned.

"I can't believe you have a beard," Emma noted, momentarily diverted.

Jace touched his bristly cheek. "Well, it has been a week, at least. I expect it makes me look manly, like a burnished god."

"I hate it," said Emma.

"I like it," said Clary loyally.

"I don't believe you," said Emma. She stuck out her hand toward Adaon. "Give me my sword. Jace can use it to shave."

Adaon glared at all of them. "You shall bear no blades. You cannot be armed if you are meant to be prisoners. I will carry the swords." He swung them up over his shoulder as if they were a bunch of kindling. "Now, come."

They marched ahead of Adaon, through the now-familiar dank underground corridors. Julian was silent, lost in thought. What did he feel? Emma wondered. He loved his family, still, but he had said it was different now. Did that mean he wasn't terrified for Mark?

Emma moved closer to Cristina. "How did you end up finding Adaon?" she whispered. "Did you just click your ruby heels together and demand to be taken to the Unseelie King's hottest son?"

Cristina rolled her eyes. "I saw Adaon in London, with Kieran," she whispered. "He seemed to care about Kieran. I took a chance."

"And how did you get to him?"

"I'll tell you later. And he is not the hottest Unseelie prince. Kieran is the hottest," Cristina said, and blushed beet red.

Emma eyed Adaon's muscles, which were bunching spectacularly under his tunic as he balanced the swords. "I thought Kieran was at the Scholomance?"

Cristina sighed. "You missed a lot. I will tell you everything, if we—"

"Survive?" Emma said. "Yeah. I have a lot to tell you, too."

"Be quiet!" snapped Adaon. "Enough chatter, prisoners!"

They had emerged from the underground tunnels into the lower levels of the tower. Seelie and Unseelie faeries streamed by, hurrying to and fro. A passing redcap gave Adaon a broad wink.

"Good work, Prince," he growled. "Round up those Nephilim!"

"Thank you," said Adaon. "They're very rowdy."

He glared at Cristina and Emma.

"Still think he's hot?" Cristina muttered.

"Possibly more so," whispered Emma. She felt an insane urge to giggle, despite the awful situation. She was just so happy to see Cristina again. "We're going to get through this, and we're going to get back home, and we're going to tell each other everything."

"That is enough. The two of you, move apart," Adaon snapped, and Emma sheepishly went to walk next to Clary. They had reached the less crowded, more residential part of the tower, with its rows of richly decorated doors.

Clary looked exhausted, her clothes stained with blood and dirt.

"How did you get caught?" Emma murmured, keeping a weather eye on Adaon.

"The Riders of Mannan," said Clary in a low voice. "They've been set the task of guarding Ash. We tried to fight them off, but they're more powerful here than they are in our world." She glanced sideways at Emma. "I heard you killed one of them. That's pretty impressive."

"I think it was Cortana, not me."

"Don't underestimate the power of the right blade," said Clary. "I miss Heosphoros sometimes. I miss the feel of it in my hand."

Heosphoros, like Cortana, had been forged by the legendary weapon-maker Wayland the Smith. Every schoolchild knew Clary had carried the sword into Edom and slain Sebastian Morgenstern with it, and that it had been destroyed in the resulting conflagration.

Was Clary thinking about Sebastian? Without being able to stop herself, Emma whispered, "I don't think Ash has to be like his father. He's still a little kid. He could grow up better—kinder."

Clary's smile was sad. "So he got to you, too."

"What?"

"'A perfect leader, inspiring of perfect loyalty,'" Clary said. "The King has already done things to Ash, using his blood, I think, to make him like the First Heir. When you talked to him, you wanted to follow him and protect him, didn't you?"

Emma blanched. "I did, but—"

"Prince Adaon!" called a rough voice. Emma looked up to see that they stood in front of the rows of redcaps guarding the throne room. The leader of them—the one with the bloodiest, reddest cap and uniform—was looking at Adaon with some surprise. "What is this?"

"Prisoners for the King," Adaon barked.

"These were caught a week hence." The redcap pointed at Jace and Clary.

"Aye, but I discovered these others in the prison, attempting to free them." Adaon indicated Cristina, Julian, and Emma. "They are Nephilim spies. They claim they have information for the King, which they would trade for their miserable, wormlike lives."

"Wormlike?" Julian muttered. "Really?"

"Hold here a moment," said the redcaps' leader. He ducked through the archway. A moment later he had returned, a faint smirk on his face. "Prince Adaon, pass through. Your father would see you, and prayed me give you the expectation of a familial reunion."

A familial reunion. The King could just mean himself, of course. But he could also mean Kieran—and Mark.

Julian had reacted too, if silently. His hand tightened as if he could grip an imaginary blade, and his eyes fixed on the dark archway.

"Thank you, General Winter," said Adaon, and began to lead them all forward.

This time they weren't walking into the throne room invisible to all eyes. This time they would be seen. Emma's throat was dry, her heart pounding.

Unlike the Seelie Queen's ever-changing throne room, the inner sanctum of the King was unaltered. The massive Portal still covered one wall. It showed a blowing desert landscape, where trees poked out of the ground like skeleton hands clawing for air. The yellow-bright desert light lent an unnatural tint to the room, as if they stood in the light of invisible flames.

The King was upon his throne, his one eye blazing red. In front of him were Mark and Kieran, surrounded by redcaps. Mark's hands were manacled together; Kieran knelt, his bound wrists connected to a metal chain sunk into the stone floor. When they jerked around to see who had come in, shock and relief flooded across Mark's face, followed by horror. There was a bloody cut across Kieran's forehead.

His lips formed a single word. *Cristina.*

Cristina gave a ragged gasp. Emma reached to catch her friend's wrist, but she was frozen in place.

It was Julian who bolted forward, his gaze fixed on Mark. Adaon caught him with his free arm and yanked him back. Emma remembered what Julian had said about the atavistic need to protect Ty. It seemed he felt it for his other siblings too: He was still struggling as Adaon turned and said something to Jace. The Strength rune on Jace's forearm flashed as he flung an arm around Julian's chest, immobilizing him.

"Keep him back!" Winter, the redcap general, pointed the tip of his pikestaff at Julian. More redcaps had streamed in to stand between Adaon's captives and the King, a thin crimson line.

Julian's body was a taut line of tension and hate as he stared at the King, who was grinning his odd, half-skeletal grin. "Well done, Adaon," the King said. "I hear you foiled an attempt to escape our prisons."

Mark's shoulders slumped. Kieran gazed at his father with loathing.

"Look your fill, my son," the King said to Kieran. "Your friends are all my prisoners. There is no hope for you." He turned. "Let me see them, Adaon."

With the tip of his sword, Adaon urged Emma and the others closer to the throne. Emma felt her chest tighten, remembering the last time she had stood before the King of Unseelie, how he had looked into her heart somehow and seen what she had most wanted, and given it to her as a dose of poison.

"You," said the King, his eyes on Emma. "You fought my champion."

"And she won," said Cristina proudly, her back straight.

The King ignored her. "And you slew a Rider, my Fal. Interesting." He turned to Julian. "You disrupted my Court and took my son hostage. His blood is on your hands." Lastly, he gazed at Jace and Clary. "Because of you we suffer the Cold Peace."

Adaon cleared his throat. "Then why are they still alive, Father? Why have you not killed them?"

"Not helpful," Jace muttered. He had let go of Julian, who stood poised like a runner waiting for the starting gun.

"Leverage against the Clave," said the King, caressing the arm of his throne. The stone was carved with a pattern of screaming faces. "To us they are enemies. To the Clave, they are heroes. It is ever the way with war."

"But do we not seek an end to the Cold Peace?" said Adaon. "If we return these prisoners to the Clave, we could reopen negotiations. Find common ground. They will see that we are not all bloodthirsty murderers, as they believe."

The King was silent for a moment. He was expressionless, but there was a look of apprehension on Kieran's face that Emma didn't like.

At last the King smiled. "Adaon, you are truly the best of my sons. In your heart you long for peace, and peace we shall have—when the Nephilim realize we have a weapon that can destroy them all."

"Ash," Emma whispered.

She hadn't even meant to speak aloud, but the King heard. His ghastly face turned toward her. In the depths of his cavernous eye sockets, pinpoint lights gleamed.

"Come here," he said.

Julian made a noise of protest—or maybe it was something else; Emma couldn't tell. He was biting his lip hard, blood running down his chin. He didn't seem to notice, though, and he did nothing to stop her as she turned to go toward the King. She wondered if he even knew about the blood.

She approached the throne, moving past the line of redcaps. She felt utterly naked without a weapon in her hand. She hadn't felt so vulnerable since Iarlath had whipped her against the quickbeam tree.

The King thrust out a hand. "Stop," he said, and Emma stopped. There was enough adrenaline coursing through her that she felt a little drunk. She wanted nothing more than to fling herself at the King, tear at him, punch and kick him. But she knew that if she tried, she would be dead in an instant. The redcaps were everywhere.

"One of you I will choose to return to the Clave as my messenger," said the King. "It could be you."

Emma raised her chin. "I don't want to carry your messages."

The King chuckled. "I didn't want you to kill one of my Riders, but you did. Perhaps this shall be your punishment."

"Punish me by keeping me here," said Emma. "Let the others go."

"A noble, but stupid, attempt at a ploy," said the King. "Child, all the wisdom of the Nephilim could fit into one acorn in the hand of a faerie. You are a young and foolish people and in your foolishness, you will die." He leaned forward, the pinpoint gleaming in his right eye blooming into a circle of flame. "How do you know of Ash?"

"No! *No! Leave him alone!*" Emma whirled; a woman's scream lanced through the room like the sweep of a sharp blade. She felt herself tense further; Ethna and Eochaid had stalked into the room, marching Ash between them. He was without his gold crown and looked sulky and angry.

Rushing along behind him was Annabel, crying out. "Stop! Haven't you done enough? Stop, I tell you! Ash is my charge—"

She saw Emma and froze. Her eyes darted toward Adaon, lighting on Julian, who stared back at her with blazing hatred. Jace was gripping his shoulder again.

She seemed to shrink into her clothes—a gray linen dress and woolen jacket. Her left hand was a claw that clutched the true Black Volume.

"No," she moaned. "No, no, I didn't mean it. I didn't mean to do it."

Emma heard a deep growl. A moment later she realized it was Mark, his chains rattling. Annabel gasped, recognizing him. She staggered back as one of the redcaps darted toward Mark, pike raised.

Mark backed up—but he wasn't retreating, Emma saw, only loosening the chains that bound his wrists. He spun, flinging the chains around the redcap's neck; the pike crashed to the ground as he seized the length of chain and jerked, hard.

The guard was flung backward, hurtling into his fellow redcaps. They all stumbled. Mark stood poised and breathing hard, his eyes fierce and hard as glass. Winter gazed at him and Kieran with a considering look.

"Shall I kill him for you, liege?" said Winter.

The King shook his head, clearly annoyed. "Have him beaten to his bones later. Redcaps, be more wary of the prisoners." He sneered. "They bite."

Annabel was still moaning softly. She cast a terrified look at Emma, Julian, and Mark—which was ridiculous, Emma thought, as they were all obviously prisoners—and a longing one at Ash.

Perfect loyalty, Emma thought. No wonder Annabel had attached herself so swiftly and tightly to Ash.

The King snapped his fingers at Emma. "Return to Adaon, girl."

Emma bristled but said nothing. She sauntered back across the room to Adaon and the others, refusing to give the King the satisfaction of hurrying.

Emma reached the rest of the group just as Annabel gave another whimpering scream. Emma pushed in next to Julian, taking his arm. His muscles jumped under her touch. She wrapped her hand around his forearm and Jace stepped away from them, giving them space.

Emma could feel the shape of the bloody rag tied around Julian's forearm under her fingers. *Remember what Livvy would want*, she thought. *Don't get yourself killed.*

The King turned to Eochaid. "Give Ash your sword, Rider."

Eochaid reeled back, clearly stunned. He turned toward Ethna, but she shook her head, her bronze hair spilling over her shoulders. Her message was clear: *Do it*.

They watched as Eochaid handed over his gleaming bronze-gold sword. It was far too big for Ash, who took it with the grip of someone who was used to handling weapons, but not ones this big and heavy. He stared at the King with shocked eyes.

"Cut Kieran's throat, Ash Morgenstern," said the King.

He isn't even pretending, Emma thought. *He doesn't care if we know exactly who Ash is or not.*

"No!" cried Mark. He lunged toward Ash and Kieran, but the redcaps cut him off. They were incredibly quick, and angry now—he had hurt one of their own.

Clary gasped. Emma could hear Cristina whispering frantically beside her, though not the individual words. Kieran stayed where he was, gazing flatly into the distance as if the King hadn't spoken.

"Why?" said Ash. His voice shook. Emma wondered if it was real or faked for sympathy.

"You must spill royal blood," said the King, "and Kieran's is the most expendable."

"*You are a bastard!*" Mark shouted, struggling against his manacles and the grip of the redcaps.

"This is too much," Annabel cried. "He's just a child."

"Which is why this must be done now," said the King. "The Dark Artifices would kill an older child." He leaned forward to look Ash in the face, a parody of a concerned adult. "Kieran will die regardless," he said, "whether your hand wields the blade or not. And if you do not do it, he will die slowly, in howling pain."

Kieran's gaze tracked slowly across the room—but not toward Ash. He looked at Cristina, who was gazing helplessly at him, and then at Mark, struggling in the redcaps' grip.

He smiled.

Ash took a step forward. The sword hung loose in his hand and he was biting his lip. At last Kieran glanced at him.

"Do what you must, child," he said, his voice kind and quiet. "I know what it is to be given no good choice by the King of the Unseelie Court."

"Ungrateful whelp!" barked the King, sneering at Kieran. "Ash—*now!*"

Emma looked wildly toward Julian and the others. Adaon

couldn't help them; there were too many redcaps, and the Riders were impossible to fight—

More redcaps spilled into the room. It took Emma a moment to realize they were running. Fleeing in terror from the storm that followed—a slender figure blazing in scarlet and gold, with red hair flowing around her like spilled blood.

The Seelie Queen.

An expression of surprise crossed the Unseelie King's face, followed swiftly by rage. Ash dropped the sword he was holding with a clatter, backing away from Kieran as the Queen approached.

Emma had never seen the Seelie Queen like this. Her eyes were brilliant, blazing with unfaerie-like emotion. She was like a tidal wave, rushing toward her son.

"*No!*" Annabel's screech was almost inhuman. Thrusting the Black Volume into her jacket, she bolted toward Ash, her arms held out.

The Seelie Queen turned in one smooth motion and flung out her hand; Annabel sailed into the air and slammed into the rock wall of the chamber. She slid to the floor, gasping for breath.

She had given the Riders time, though, to gather around Ash. The Queen strode toward them, her face radiant with power and rage.

"You cannot touch him," said Ethna, her voice shimmering with a metallic hum. "He belongs to the King."

"He is my *son*," said the Queen with contempt. Her gaze flickered between the two Riders. "You are of the oldest magic, the magic of the elements. You deserve better than to lick the boots of the Unseelie King like dogs."

She tore her gaze from Ash and stalked up to the King, light flickering in her hair like tiny flames. "You," she said. "Deceiver. Your words of an alliance were so many dried leaves blown on the empty air."

The King set the copy of the Black Volume on the arm of his

throne and rose to his feet. Emma felt a bolt of wonder go down her spine. The King and Queen of Faerie, facing off before her. It was like a scene out of legend.

Her fingers itched almost unbearably for a sword.

"I do what I do because I must," said the King. "No one else has the strength to do it! The Nephilim are our single greatest enemy. They always have been. Yet you would make treaties with them, seek peace with them, live alongside them." He sneered. "Give your *body* to them."

Emma's mouth dropped open. *So rude*, she mouthed at Cristina.

The Queen straightened her back. She was still thin and wan, but the power of her Queenship seemed to radiate through her like light through a lamp. "You had your chance with our child, and because you did not believe a woman could be strong, you threw it away. I will not give you another of my children for your careless slaughter!"

The First Heir, Emma thought. *So it's true.*

There was a murmur of shock in the room—not from the human prisoners, but from the Riders and redcaps. A dark flush of rage went over the King's face. He flung out his arm, sheathed to the elbow in a golden gauntlet, toward the roiling Portal on the north wall.

"Gaze upon this Portal, glorious Queen," he said through his teeth, and the image in the Portal began to change. Where before the desert landscape had been deserted, it was possible now to see darting figures among the poison-colored whirls of sand. The sky above the landscape had turned to a scorched rust and gold.

Emma heard Clary make a strange choking noise.

"I have torn a hole through to another world," said the King. "A world whose very substance is poisonous to Nephilim. Already our lands are protected by its earth, and already the poison begins to spread in Idris."

"It's not the ley lines," Cristina whispered. "It's the blight."

They spun to stare at the Portal. The scene had changed again. It now showed the same desert in the aftermath of a battle. Blood stained the sand red. Bodies were strewn everywhere, twisted and blackened by the sun. Faint screams and wailing could be heard, dim as the memory of something horrible.

Jace whirled on the King. "What is this? What is this world? What have you done?"

Clary's hand circled Emma's wrist, gripping tightly. Her voice was a bare whisper. *"That's me."*

Emma stared through the Portal. Wind blew the sand in harsh gusts, uncovering a body in black Shadowhunter gear, the chest torn open and white bone showing. A spill of red hair threaded through the sand, mixing with blood.

"That was my dream," Clary whispered. Her voice was choked with tears. Emma stood frozen, staring at Clary's dead body. "*That's* what I saw."

The sand blew again, and Clary's body vanished from view just as Jace turned back around. "What world is this?" he demanded.

"Pray you never have to find out," said the King. "The land of Thule is death, and it will rain down death in your world. In Ash's hands it will be the greatest weapon ever known."

"And what will be the cost to Ash?" demanded the Queen. "What will be the cost to *him*? Already you have placed spells upon him. Already you have bled him. You wear his blood around your throat! Deny it, if you can!"

Emma stared at the vial around the King's throat: She had thought it was a scarlet potion. It was not. She remembered the scar on Ash's throat and felt sick.

The King chuckled. "I have no wish to deny it. His blood is unique—Nephilim blood and demonic blood, mixed with the blood of the fey. I draw power from it, though only a fraction of the power Ash could have if you allow me to keep the Black Volume."

The Queen's face twisted. "You are bound by your oath to return it to me, King—"

The King tensed; Emma didn't understand as much about faeries as Cristina did, but she knew that if the King had sworn he would return the book to the Queen at dawn, he would have no choice but to do it. "It will bring us both indescribable power. Just let me show you—"

"No!" A streak of gray linen and dark hair shot across the room and caught hold of Ash, whirling him off his feet.

Ash cried out as Annabel seized him. She flew with him across the room, Ash's wrist gripped tightly in her hand. The Riders rushed after her, the redcaps circling from the door. Whirling like a trapped rabbit, she bared her teeth, Ash's wrist still caught in hers.

"I will speak your name!" she shrieked at the King, and he froze. "In front of all these people! Even if you kill me, they will all have heard the word! Now tell them to stand down! They must stand down!"

The King made a choking sound. As the Queen stared in disbelief, he clenched his fists so tightly that his gauntlets bent and shattered. Their metal stabbed into his skin and blood bloomed around the jagged edges.

"She knows your name?" the Queen demanded, her voice rising. "That Nephilim *knows your name?*"

"Stand down, Riders," the King said in a voice that sounded as if he were being strangled. "Stand down, all of you!"

The Riders and redcaps froze. Realizing what was happening, the Queen shrieked and ran toward Annabel, raising her hands. But she was too late. Throwing her arms around Ash, Annabel hurled herself backward through the Portal.

There was a sound as of thick fabric tearing. The Portal stretched apart and closed over Annabel and Ash. The Queen skidded to a stop, twisting her body to avoid crashing through the Portal.

Julian sucked in his breath. The image in the Portal had

changed—now they could see Annabel and Ash standing in the broken wasteland, sand swirling about them. The Queen screamed, holding out her hands as if she could touch Ash, could enfold him in her arms.

For a moment Emma almost pitied her.

The sand whirled again, and Ash and Annabel vanished from view. The King slumped down on his throne, his face in his hands.

The Queen spun away from the Portal, striding toward the throne. Grief and rage were etched onto her features. "You have done the second of my children to his death, Lord of Shadows," she said. "There shall never be another."

"Enough of your foolishness!" the King snapped. "I am the one who sacrificed for our child!" He indicated the ruin of his face, the glimmer of white bone where flesh should be. "Your children were and always have been nothing but ornaments to your vanity!"

The Queen screamed something in a language Emma didn't understand and flung herself at the King, drawing a jeweled dagger from her bodice.

"Guards!" the King shouted. "Kill her!"

But the redcaps had frozen, staring in shock at the Queen as she brought the dagger down. The King threw up an arm to defend himself. He roared in pain as the knife sank into his shoulder, and blood splattered the ground below the throne.

It seemed to spur the redcaps into action. They raced forward to seize the Queen, who turned on them in fury. Even the Riders were staring.

"*Now,*" Adaon said.

He moved lightning fast, flinging the swords he held into the eager hands of the Shadowhunters who surrounded him. Emma caught one out of the air and raced toward Mark and Kieran, Julian and Cristina on either side of her.

Her nerves caught fire as the redcaps, realizing what was going on, rushed at the advancing Nephilim. She had hated every moment of standing still; as one redcap lunged at her she leaped for the nearest boulder, caromed off it, and used the force of her rebound to sever another's head as she landed. Blood sprayed, blackish red.

The King's face suffused with blood as he saw what his son was doing. "*Adaon!*" he bellowed, the sound like a roar, but Adaon was already racing toward Mark and Kieran, knocking redcaps aside with savage blows from his broadsword.

That's right, Emma thought with a savage pleasure, *every one of your sons hates you, King.*

She spun to engage another redcap, her blade clashing against his iron pikestaff. Jace and Clary were battling more redcaps. Julian and Cristina were behind Adaon, pushing toward Kieran and Mark, who were surrounded by guards.

"Riders!" the King cried, spittle flying from his lips. "Stop him! *Stop Adaon!*"

Eochaid sprang, leaping over the heads of a group of redcaps to land in front of Adaon. The prince's broadsword moved with incredible speed, parrying Eochaid's blade. Adaon shouted at Cristina and Julian to get to Mark and Kieran, and turned back to Eochaid just as Ethna strode up to them, her sword drawn.

Emma ducked low, cutting at the redcap's legs; she said a silent prayer of thanks for Isabelle's bracelet, powering her blows as her own body weakened. The guard went down in a welter of blood as Jace raced to Adaon's side. His sword slammed against Ethna's with a ringing clang.

And Emma remembered why she had always wanted to be Jace Herondale when she was a kid. His sword flew around him like sunlight dancing off water, and for several moments he drove Ethna back, while Adaon pressed Eochaid, driving him farther away from the throne and from Kieran and Mark.

Clary leaped over a boulder, landing beside Emma; she was

panting and her sword was drenched in blood. "We have to hold the redcaps off," she said. "Come with me!"

Emma darted after her, slashing at guards as she went. A group of redcaps including General Winter had surrounded Cristina and Julian, preventing them from getting near Kieran and Mark.

Emma sprang for the rough wall of the throne room. She scrambled up one-handed, looking down on the chaos below. The Queen and King were battling back and forth before the throne. Adaon and Jace were holding their own against the Riders, though Adaon had a long cut across one shoulder that was bleeding freely. And Clary was spinning, quick and fast, jabbing at the redcap guards and then darting back out of reach with startling swiftness.

Emma flung herself off the wall, air rushing past her as she flipped and twisted, landing boots-first and sending Winter sprawling. The other redcaps rushed her and she swung her blade in an arc, slicing the tips from their pikestaffs. She sprang away from Winter and advanced on the other guards, her sword arcing in the air. "I slew Fal the Rider," she said in her most menacing voice. "I will slay you, too."

They paled markedly. Several fell back, as behind them Julian and Cristina rushed to Mark and to Kieran. Julian hauled Mark to his feet, bringing his sword down to sever the chain that connected Mark's wrists. They swung free, each one still bearing an iron wristband.

Mark caught hold of his brother with his manacled arms and hugged him quickly, fiercely. Emma's eyes prickled but there was no time to look at them; she spun and kicked and slashed, the world a chaos of silver and ice and blood.

Emma heard Cristina call her name.

Ice turned to fire. She ran toward the sound, leaping over toppled rocks, and found Cristina standing with a shattered blade in her hand. Kieran was still kneeling, pieces of the broken sword scattered around the chain that bound his wrists to the earth.

"Emma, please—" Cristina began, but Emma was already bringing her blade down. It wasn't Cortana, but it held; the chain shattered and Kieran leaped to his feet. Cristina seized him by the arm.

"We must go," she said, her eyes frantic. "I can use the artifact to return us—"

"Call everyone to you," Emma said. She pressed her sword into Cristina's hand. "I need to get the copy of the Black Volume."

Cristina tried to shove the sword back at Emma. "What? *Where?*"

But Emma was already running, kicking off the uneven floor to hurl herself at the steps to the throne. She heard the King bellow; she heard Julian cry out her name. She had reached the top of the steps. The throne loomed up before her, dark and granite, the printer-bound pages of the Black Volume resting on a great stone arm.

Emma seized the book and spun around just in time to hear Adaon cry out, a hoarse shout of pain. Eochaid had him trapped against the side of a massive boulder. The front of Adaon's tunic was soaked with blood, and Eochaid's sword kissed his throat.

"Shall I slay him, King?" Eochaid said in a gloating voice. Most of the bystanders in the room had frozen. Cristina had her hand over her mouth; she was the one who had brought Adaon here, after all. Even the redcaps were staring. "Your traitor son? Shall I end his life?"

The Queen began to laugh. Redcaps had caught her by the arms, but she was still smiling her strange, catlike smile. "Oh, my lord," she said. "Is there a one of your sons that does not hate your name?"

The King bared his teeth. "Cut his throat," he said to Eochaid.

Adaon's muscles tensed. Emma's brain worked frantically—she saw Kieran start forward, but there was no way he could reach

Adaon in time—Eochaid raised his blade like an executioner, his other arm braced against Adaon's chest—

There was a horrible choking cry. *Adaon*, Emma thought wildly, stumbling down the steps, but no, Eochaid was turning away from his captive, his sword still raised, his face contorted in surprise.

The King was sinking to his knees, blood running freely down the front of his rich doublet. Kieran's hand was still raised in the air. Something protruded from the King's throat—a sliver of what looked almost like glass. . . .

The elf-bolt arrowhead, Emma realized with a start. Kieran had flung his necklace at the King with incredible force.

Eochaid and Ethna rushed toward the King, their gleaming swords in hand, their faces pictures of dismay. Adaon, too, walked toward his father. Kieran did not move. He was leaning heavily on Cristina's shoulder, his face expressionless.

Kneeling, the King clawed at his throat. To Emma's shock, he seemed to be weakening—his hand scrabbled at the embedded elf-bolt, and then fell to his side, hanging uselessly.

Adaon looked down at him. "Father," he said in a low voice. "Forgive me."

Ethna's face contorted into a mask. Jace and Clary, both bloody and filthy, were staring in amazement. Distantly, Emma knew she was seeing something remarkable. The dying of a King who had ruled for a thousand years.

Ethna whirled to glare at Kieran. "Kinslayer!" she cried. "Patricide!"

"He was trying to save Adaon!" Mark shouted back. "Are you blind, Rider?"

"Because he wants to be King," snarled Eochaid. "Because he wants the throne!"

The Queen began to laugh. She drew free of the redcaps who had held her as if their touch were no more than spiderwebs, though several fell screaming to the floor, their palms burned and blackened, their fingers snapped.

"Already they scavenge for your throne like dogs worrying at a bone," she said to the King, as blood ran out of the corners of his mouth and his eyes rolled up to the whites.

She seized Adaon by the arm. He cried out in shock and pain; the Queen's hair whipped around them both as she grinned down at the King.

"You took my son," she said. "Now I take yours."

She vanished, and Adaon vanished with her. The King gave a cry and fell to the ground, scrabbling at the earth with gauntleted hands. His crown tumbled from his head and struck the stone floor as he choked out garbled words. Perhaps he was trying to say the Queen's name, perhaps Adaon's. Perhaps even Kieran's. Emma would never know. The King's body stiffened and slumped, and both Eochaid and Ethna cried out.

He had gone still. But his blood continued to run out around him, snaking across the floor in rivulets. The redcaps were scrambling back from the King's body, their faces masks of horror.

Winter lowered the pikestaff he had been aiming at Emma. "The King is dead! King Arawn is dead!" he cried, and Emma realized it must be true: It was safe to speak the King's true name now that he was no longer alive.

The redcaps fled—save Winter, who held his ground—pouring out of the throne room in a river of crimson. Cristina was shouting for the other Shadowhunters; she held Mark by one hand, and he gripped a stunned-looking Kieran. Jace and Clary were scrambling over a pile of boulders to get to them. Julian was only yards away; Emma began to run as the King's body burst into flames.

She cast one look back over her shoulder. The King was burning and so was the ground everywhere his blood had spilled—small fires and larger ones, burning fierce and hot, consuming the stone floor as if it were kindling. The King's body had already vanished behind a sheet of flames.

A figure reared up out of the smoke, cutting Emma off.

It was Ethna. She gleamed all over like a weapon, her bronze armor unsmudged, her metallic eyes gleaming with bloodlust. "My oath to the King died with him," she said, baring her teeth. "Your life is forfeit now, murderer!"

She lunged at Emma. Emma's sword was gone; she flung up the copy of the Black Volume, and Ethna's sword plunged into it. Ethna flung it aside in disgust; the shredded remains of the book landed on the burning ground, its pages bursting into flames.

Emma could hear Clary calling out to her, and the others, shouting for her to come quickly. She realized with a sinking heart that they must not be able to see her; they wouldn't know she needed help, they wouldn't know—

Ethna's blade flew through the air, bronze cutting through smoke. Emma twisted aside and fell to the ground, rolling to avoid the slashing blows that followed. Each time Ethna's blade barely missed her, it cut a deep gouge into the stone floor.

It was getting harder for Emma to breathe. She scrambled to her knees, only to have Ethna plant a booted foot in her shoulder. She shoved, and Emma sprawled backward, hitting the ground hard.

"Die on your back, bitch," Ethna said, raising her sword high.

Emma flung her hands out as if they could ward off the blade. Ethna laughed, swung down—

And toppled sideways. Emma scrambled upright, choking on smoke and disbelief.

Julian.

He had thrown himself onto Ethna and was kneeling on her back, stabbing her over and over with something clutched in his fist. Emma realized with a shock that it was the iron figurine that Simon had given to him. Ethna was screaming, trying to writhe away from the iron. Emma whirled around: The room was blazing with fire, the boulders glowing like red-hot coals. Hot pain stabbed her side; a coal had landed on the sleeve of her jacket. She yanked it off furiously and stomped on it, putting the fire out. *Sorry, Clary.*

She thought she could still see the dim figures of the others through the smoke. The surface of the Portal seemed to ripple like melting glass.

"Julian!" she screamed, and held out her hand. "Leave her! We have to get to the others!"

He looked up, his eyes wild with rage, and Ethna wrenched away from him with a yelp of anger and pain. Julian landed on his feet, already racing toward Emma. Together they fled toward the sound of Cristina's voice, rising and desperate, shouting their names. Emma thought she could hear Mark, too, and the others—

A sheet of flame blazed up from the ground, knocking them backward. They swung around, looking for a way around it, and Emma gasped: Ethna and Eochaid were striding toward them, Ethna bloodied and glaring, Eochaid gleaming and deadly.

The Riders were at the heart of their power. Emma and Julian were starving, exhausted, and weakened. Emma's heart sank.

"Cristina!" she screamed. "Go! Go! *Get out of here!*"

Julian caught hold of her wrist. "There's only one way."

His eyes flicked toward the wall—she tensed, then nodded—and the two of them took off running, just as the Riders began to raise their blades.

Emma heard them cry out in confusion and disappointed bloodlust. She didn't care; the Portal was looming up in front of her like the dark window of a high-rise building, all shadow and gleam.

She reached it and leaped, Julian's hand in hers, and together they sailed through the Portal.

* * *

Diego wasn't sure how long he'd been in the barren stone cell. There were no windows, no sense of time passing. He knew Rayan and Divya were in the same prison, but the thick stone walls of the cells kept them from being able to shout or call to each other.

It was almost a relief when there were footsteps in the corridor and—instead of the usual guard who came twice a day with a plate of bland food—Zara appeared, resplendent in Centurion gear. He would have thought she would be smirking, but she was oddly expressionless. Cortana was strapped to her side, and she caressed its hilt absently as she looked at him through the bars, as if she were stroking the head of a dog.

"My dear fiancé," she said. "How are you finding the accommodations? Not too cold and unwelcoming?"

He said nothing. The rune of Quietude the Cohort had put on him had been removed almost immediately after the meeting, but that didn't mean he had anything to talk to Zara about.

"And to think," she went on. "If you'd played your cards a little differently, you might have been living in the Gard tower with me."

"And that *wouldn't* have been cold and unwelcoming?" spat Diego. "Living with someone I hate?"

She flinched a little. Diego was surprised. Surely she knew they hated each other?

"You have no right or reason to hate *me*," she said. "I'm the one who was betrayed. You were a convenient marriage prospect. Now you're a traitor. It would shame me to marry you."

Diego let his head fall back against the wall. "Good," he said wearily. "You have taken everything from me. At least I no longer have to pretend to love you."

Her lips tightened. "I know you never intended to go through with the marriage. You were just trying to buy time for your vigilante brother. Still—I'll make you a deal. You claim Jaime still has the faerie artifact. We want it. It should be in government hands."

Her lips twisted into an ugly smirk. "If you tell us where to find it, I'll pardon you."

"I haven't the vaguest idea," said Diego. "And carrying that sword around won't make you Emma Carstairs."

She glared at him. "You shouldn't have said that. *Or* the thing about how I've taken everything from you already. You still have a lot left to lose." She turned her head. "Milo? Bring the second prisoner forward."

There was a blur of movement in the shadowy corridor, and the cell door opened. Diego strained forward as a dark figure was hurled into the cell alongside him.

Milo slammed the door shut and locked it as the new arrival groaned and sat up. Diego's heart turned over in his chest. Even bruised and bloody, with his lip cut and a burn scar on his cheek, he would recognize his younger brother anywhere.

"Jaime," he breathed.

"He seems to know no more about the artifact than you do," said Zara. "But then, without the Mortal Sword, we can't make him tell the truth. So we have to fall back on more old-fashioned methods of dealing with liars and traitors." She traced the hilt of Cortana with loving fingertips. "I'm sure you know what I mean."

"Jaime," Diego said again. The ceiling was too low for him to stand up; he crawled across the floor to his brother, pulling Jaime against him.

Jaime, half-conscious, lolled against his shoulder, his eyes almost slitted shut. His clothes were torn and wet with blood. Diego felt a cold fear at his heart: What wounds lay underneath?

"Hola, hermano," Jaime whispered.

"During his discussions with the Inquisitor about the location of the artifact, your brother became overexcited. He needed to be subdued." Now Zara did smile. "The guards accidentally, shall we say, injured him. It would be a shame if his injuries were to become infected or if he were to die because he lacked proper medical care."

"Give me a stele," hissed Diego. He had never hated anyone more than he hated Zara in that moment. "He needs an *iratze*."

"Give me the artifact," said Zara. "And he can have one."

Diego said nothing. He had no idea where the Eternidad was, the heirloom that Jaime had suffered so much to protect. He held his brother tighter, his lips pressed together. He would not beg Zara for mercy.

"No?" she preened. "As you like. Perhaps when your brother is screaming with fever you will feel differently. Call upon me, Diego dear, if you ever change your mind."

Manuel strode into the throne room, smirking, Oban on his heels.

Manuel couldn't help the smirking; as he sometimes told people, it was just the natural expression of his face. It was true that he also liked chaos, though, and right now, there was chaos aplenty to please him.

The throne room looked charred, the rock walls and floor smeared with black ash. The place reeked of blood and sulfur. Bodies of redcaps were strewn on the floor, one covered by an expensive-looking tapestry. On a far wall, the shrinking Portal showed a beach at night, under a red moon.

Oban clicked his tongue, which Manuel had learned was the faerie equivalent of letting out a low whistle. "What happened in here? It looks like the aftermath of one of my more famous parties."

Manuel poked at the tapestry-covered mound with his toe.

"And the fields outside are full of fleeing Seelie fey, now that their Queen is gone," Oban went on. "Manuel, I demand an explanation. Where is my father?"

Winter, the somber redcap leader, came over to them. He was streaked with blood and ash. "Prince," he said. "Your father lies here."

He indicated the mound Manuel was poking with his toe.

Manuel bent over and yanked the tapestry back. The thing beneath did not look human, or fey, or as if it had ever lived at all. It was the blackened, crumbling outline of a man drawn in ash, its face a rictus. Something gleamed at its throat.

Manuel knelt to take it. An etched glass vial of scarlet liquid. *Interesting*. He placed it in his jacket pocket.

"What's that?" said Oban. For a moment Manuel felt a spark of worry that Oban had chosen to take an interest in something important. Fortunately, it was not the case—Oban had caught sight of a gleaming elf-bolt necklace among his father's remains. He bent to grab the shining thing, letting it dangle from his fingers. "Kieran?" he said incredulously. "*Kieran* killed our father?"

"Does it matter?" said Manuel in a low voice. "The old man is dead. That is good news."

It was indeed. The previous King had been an uneasy ally, if one could call him an ally at all. Though the Cohort had helped him spread the blight in Idris and that had pleased him, he had never trusted them or interested himself in their greater plans. Nor had he warned them of his intention to seize the Black Volume, an event which had irritated Horace greatly.

Oban would be different. He would trust those who had put him in power.

He was a fool.

"It might give Kieran claim to the throne if it were known," said Oban, his slack, handsome face darkening. "Who saw the King slain? What of Kieran's Nephilim companions?"

"My redcaps saw, but they will not speak," said Winter as Oban moved to the throne. The King's crown rested on its seat, gleaming dully. "Prince Kieran has fled with most of the Nephilim to the human world."

Oban's face tightened. "Where he might brag of slaying our father?"

"I don't think he will do that," said General Winter. A look of relief crossed Oban's face. He did tend to respond like putty to anyone in authority, Manuel thought. "He seems to love dearly those Nephilim he has befriended, and they him. I do not think he wants the throne, or would endanger them."

"We will keep a watch out," said Oban. "Where is Adaon?"

"Adaon was taken prisoner by the Seelie Queen."

"Adaon taken prisoner?" asked Oban, and when Winter nodded, he laughed and tumbled into the throne's seat. "And what of the Queen's son, the brat?"

"Gone with the undead witch, through the Portal," said Winter. "It does not seem likely they will survive long."

"Well, the kingdom cannot go on without a ruler. It seems my destiny has found me." Oban handed the crown to Winter. "Crown me."

With the death of the King, the Portal was disappearing. It was now the size of a porthole on a boat. Through the small circle, Manuel could see a dead city, ruined towers and broken roads. Something lay in a heap on the floor near the Portal, among the signs of a fight. Manuel stopped to pick it up; it was a bloody jean jacket.

He frowned, turning it over in his hands. It was a small jacket, a girl's, slashed and bloody, one sleeve partially burned. He slipped his fingers into the breast pocket and withdrew a ring stamped with butterflies.

Fairchild.

Manuel returned to Oban just as Winter placed the crown on the prince's head, looking extremely uncomfortable.

Manuel shook the jacket in Winter's direction. "You said *most* of the Nephilim returned to the human world. What happened to the girl who wore this? The girl and the boy, the Nephilim prisoners?"

"They went through the Portal." Winter gestured toward it. "They are as good as dead. That land is poison, especially to those such as they." He stepped back from Oban. "You are King now, sire."

Oban touched the crown on his head and laughed. "Bring wine, Winter! I am parched! Empty the cellars! The most beautiful maidens and youths of the Court, bring them to me! Today is a great day!"

Manuel smiled down at the bloody jacket. "Yes. Today is indeed a day for celebration."

PART TWO

Thule

I had a dream, which was not all a dream.
The bright sun was extinguish'd, and the stars
Did wander darkling in the eternal space,
Rayless, and pathless, and the icy earth
Swung blind and blackening in the moonless air;
Morn came and went—and came, and brought no day,
And men forgot their passions in the dread
Of this their desolation; and all hearts
Were chill'd into a selfish prayer for light.

—Lord Byron, "Darkness"

17

In a Strange City

It wasn't a desert. It was a beach.

The blackness of the Portal had been like nothing Julian had ever experienced before. No light, sound, or movement, only the stomach-dropping feeling of having tumbled down an elevator shaft. When the world returned at last, it was a silent explosion rushing toward him. Reborn into sound and movement, he hit the ground hard, sand spraying up around him.

He rolled to his side, heart pounding. He had lost hold of Emma's hand somewhere in the hurtling darkness, but there she was, struggling to her knees beside him. Her faerie clothes were shredded and bloodstained, but she seemed unharmed.

A gasping pain went through him, sharp as an arrow. It took him a moment to recognize it as relief.

Emma was scrambling to her feet, brushing herself off. Julian rose dizzily; they were on a wide, familiar-looking beach at night, dotted with half-eroded rock formations. Bluffs rose behind them, rickety wooden stairs twisting down their faces to connect the road above with the sand.

Music was playing, loud and jarring. The far end of the beach was thronged with people, none of whom seemed to have noticed their abrupt arrival. It was a peculiar crowd—a mix of humans, vampires, and even a few faeries dotted here and there, garbed in black and metal. Julian squinted but couldn't make out details.

Emma touched the Night Vision rune on her own arm and frowned at him. "My runes aren't working," she whispered. "Same as in Faerie."

Julian shook his head as if to say, *I don't know what's going on.* He started as something sharp prickled his side—glancing down, he realized his phone had been smashed to pieces. Jagged bits of plastic stuck into his skin. He dropped the phone with a wince—it would be no use to anyone now.

He glanced around. The sky was heavily clouded, and a blood-red moon cast a dull glow across the sand. "I know this beach," he said. The rock formations were familiar, the curve of the shoreline, the shape of the waves—though the color of the ocean water was ink black, and where it broke against the shoreline it left edgings of black lace.

Emma touched his shoulder. "Julian? We need to make a plan."

She was gray with fatigue, shadows smudged under her deep brown eyes. Her golden hair fell in thick tangles around her shoulders. Emotion exploded inside Julian. Pain, love, panic, grief, and yearning poured through him like blood from a wound whose sutures had torn open.

He staggered away from Emma and crumpled against a rock, his stomach heaving violently as it emptied itself of bitter bile. When his body had stopped spasming, he wiped his mouth, scrubbed his hands with sand, and returned to where Emma had partly climbed one of the rock formations. Sea stacks, they were called, or something like that.

He clenched his hands. His emotions roiled like a hurricane tide, pressing at the inside of his skull, and in response his mind seemed to be running all over the place, catching at random pieces of information and tossing them up like roadblocks.

Focus, he told himself, and bit at his lip until the pain cleared his head. He could taste blood.

Emma was halfway up the sea stack, staring toward the south. "This is really, really weird."

"Weird how?" He was surprised by how normal he sounded. In the distance, two figures passed by—both vampires, one a girl with long brown hair. They both waved at him casually. What the hell was going on?

She jumped down. "Are you okay?" she asked, pushing back her hair.

"I think it was the trip through the Portal," he lied. Whatever was going on with him, it wasn't that.

"Look at this." Emma had somehow managed to hang on to her phone through all their travails. She flicked through to show Julian the photo she'd taken from the sea stack.

It was dark, but he immediately recognized the shoreline, and in the distance the ruins of the Santa Monica Pier. The Ferris wheel had been tipped over, a crushed hunk of metal. Dark shapes wheeled in the sky above. They were definitely not birds.

Emma swallowed hard. "This is Los Angeles, Julian. This is right near the Institute."

"But the King said this was Thule—he said it was a world that was poisonous to Nephilim—"

He broke off in horror. At the opposite end of the beach from the crowd, two long columns of human figures were marching in neat military formation. As they grew closer, Julian caught sight of a flash of scarlet gear.

He and Emma dived behind the nearest rock formation, pressing themselves flat against it. They could see the marchers getting closer. The throng at the other end of the beach had started to move toward them as well, and the music had vanished. There was only the sound of the crashing waves, the wind, and marching feet.

"Endarkened," Emma breathed as they drew closer. During the Dark War, Sebastian Morgenstern had kidnapped hundreds of Shadowhunters and controlled them using his own version of the Mortal Cup. They had been called the Endarkened, and they had been recognizable by the scarlet gear they wore.

Julian's father had been one of them, until Julian had killed him. He still dreamed about it.

"But the Endarkened are all dead," Julian said in a distant, mechanical tone. "They died when Sebastian died."

"In our world." Emma turned to him. "Julian, we know what this is. We just don't want it to be the truth. This is—Thule is—a version of our own world. Something must have happened differently in the past here—something that put this world on an alternate path. Like Edom."

Julian knew she was right; he had known it since he recognized the pier. He shoved back thoughts of his own family, his father. He couldn't think about that right now.

The columns of marching Endarkened had given way to a cluster of guards holding banners. Each banner bore the sigil of a star inside a circle.

"By the Angel," Emma whispered. She pressed her hand against her mouth.

Morgenstern. The morning star.

Behind the flag bearers walked Sebastian.

He looked older than he had the last time Julian had seen him, a teenage boy with hair like white ice, powered by hatred and poison. He looked to be in his midtwenties now, still slim and boyish, but with a harder cast to his face. The features that had been gently edged were sharp as glass now, and his black eyes burned. Phaesphoros, the Morgenstern sword, was slung over his shoulder in a scabbard worked with a design of stars and flames.

Walking just behind him was Jace Herondale.

It was a harder and stranger blow. They had just left Jace, fighting by their side in the Unseelie Court, weary and tired but still fierce and protective. This Jace looked to be about the same age as that one; he was strongly muscled all over, his golden hair tousled, his face as handsome as ever. But there was a dead, dark light in his golden eyes. A sullen ferocity that Julian associated with the Cohort and their ilk, those who attacked rather than those who protected.

Behind them came a woman with gray-brown hair Julian recognized as Amatis Graymark, Luke's sister. She had been one of the first and fiercest of Sebastian's Endarkened, and that seemed true here as well. Her face was deeply lined, her mouth grimly set. She pushed a prisoner ahead of her—someone dressed in Shadowhunter black, a strip of rough canvas wrapped around and around their head, obscuring their features.

"Come!" Sebastian cried, and some invisible force amplified his voice so that it boomed up and down the beach. "Endarkened, guests, gather around. We are here to celebrate the capture and execution of a significant traitor. One who has turned against the light of the Star."

There was a roar of excitement. The crowd began to gather into a loose rectangle, with Sebastian and his guards at the south end of it. Julian saw Jace lean over to say something to Sebastian, and Sebastian laughed with an easy camaraderie that sent a chill down Julian's spine. Jace wore a gray suit jacket, not a scarlet uniform—so he wasn't Endarkened, then? His gaze flicked around the crowd; other than Amatis, he recognized several Shadowhunters he had known vaguely from the Los Angeles Conclave—he saw the young-looking vampire girl who had waved at him before, giggling and talking to Anselm Nightshade—

And he saw Emma.

It was clearly Emma. He would have known Emma anywhere, in any costume, in any darkness or light. The bloody moonlight spilled onto her pale hair; she wore a red dress with no back, and her skin was smooth and free of runes. She was talking to a tall boy who was mostly in shadow, but Julian barely looked at him: He was looking at her, his Emma, beautiful and alive and safe and—

She laughed and reached her arms up. The tall young man threaded his hands into Emma's hair and she kissed him.

It hit him with the force of a train. Jealousy: white-hot, boiling, venomous. It was all Julian could do to stay behind the rock as the boy's hands trailed down Emma's bare back.

He shook with the force of his feeling. Emotion tore at him, threatened to overwhelm him and drive him to his knees. Hot waves of jealousy mixed with desperate longing. Those ought to be his hands on Emma's hair, her skin.

He turned his head to the side, gasping. His shirt was stuck to his body with sweat. Emma—the real Emma—still pressed up against the rock beside him, looked at him with alarm. "Julian, what's wrong?"

His heartbeat had already begun to slow. *This* was his Emma. The other was a fake, a simulacrum. "Look," he whispered, and gestured.

Emma followed his gaze, and blushed. "Oh. That's *us*?"

Julian stared around the rock again. Emma and the boy had pulled apart, and how had he not seen it? It was like looking into a mirror that showed you what you might look like in a few years. There he was, Blackthorn hair and eyes, sea-glass bracelet, dressed in red and black. Julian stared as the other him drew the other Emma closer and kissed her again.

It definitely wasn't a first kiss, or even a second one. Other Julian's fingers trailed down Other Emma's back, obviously luxuriating in the feel of her bare skin. His hands found her satin-covered hips and splayed over them, pulling her body closer; she raised a leg and hooked it over his hip, letting her head fall back so he could press his lips to her throat.

Other Julian was a very confident kisser, apparently.

"This is the worst," said Emma. "Not only are we apparently Endarkened in this world, we're huge on PDA."

"The other Endarkened probably can't stand us," said Julian. "Emma, this seems recent. This world couldn't have split from ours that long ago—"

"Silence!" Sebastian's voice echoed up and down the beach and the crowd hushed. Alternate Emma and Julian stopped kissing, which was a relief. "Jace, put the traitor on her knees."

So it was a woman. Julian watched with a twisting feeling in his empty stomach as Jace shoved the prisoner to her knees and began slowly to unwind her blindfold.

"Ash!" Sebastian called. "Ash, come watch, my child, and learn!"

Julian felt Emma freeze up in shock beside him. There was a stir among the guards, and from among them appeared Ash Morgenstern, his expression rigid.

He had changed more since the last time they'd seen him than either Jace or Sebastian had. He had gone from thirteen to what Emma would have guessed was seventeen; he was no longer a skinny kid but a boy on the cusp of adulthood, tall and broad-shouldered. His white-blond hair had been cut short and he wasn't wearing Endarkened red—just an ordinary white thermal shirt and jeans.

He still had the X-shaped scar on his throat, though. It was unmistakable, even at this distance.

Ash crossed his arms over his chest. "I'm here, Father," he said blandly, and it struck Julian how peculiar it was, this boy calling someone who looked five years older than he did "Father."

"This is our world's Ash," Julian said. "The one Annabel brought through the Portal."

Emma nodded. "His scar. I saw."

Jace drew the last of the coverings away from the kneeling woman's face. Emma flinched back as if struck.

It was Maryse Lightwood.

Her hair had been cut very short, and her face was haggard. Ash watched expressionless as she gazed around her in silent horror. A silver chain dangled around his throat; Julian didn't recall him having it in Faerie. How many years had elapsed for him here between his escape into the Portal and Emma and Julian's arrival in Thule?

"Maryse Lightwood," said Sebastian, pacing in a slow circle around her. Emma hadn't moved or made a sound since her initial flinch. Julian wondered if she was remembering Maryse in their world—grieving at the side of her former husband's pyre, but surrounded by her children, her grandchildren. . . .

Emma must be wondering about her own parents, he realized with a jolt. Wondering if they were alive in this world. But she hadn't said a word.

"You stand accused of aiding and assisting rebels against the cause of the Fallen Star. Now, we know you did it, so we're not having a trial, because we're against those anyway. But you—you committed the greatest treason of all. You tried to break the bond between two brothers. Jace and I are brothers. You are not his mother. The only family he has is me."

"Oh my God," Emma whispered. "This is that weird bond they had—when Sebastian possessed Jace, remember? So *that* happened in this world. . . ."

"I killed my own mother, Lilith, for Jace," said Sebastian. "Now he will kill his mother for me."

Jace unsheathed the sword at his waist. It had a long, wicked silver blade that glimmered red in the moonlight. Julian thought again of the Jace in their world: laughing, joking, animated. It seemed like something more than possession was at work here. Like this Jace was dead inside.

Sebastian's lips were turned up at the corners; he was smiling, but it wasn't a very human smile. "Any last words, Maryse?"

Maryse twisted around so that she was looking up at Jace. The tense lines of her face seemed to relax, and for a moment, Julian saw John Carstairs looking at Emma, or his own mother looking at him, that mixture of love for what is and sorrow for what cannot be kept. . . .

"Do you remember, Jace?" she said. "That song I used to sing to you when you were a boy." She began to sing, her voice high and wavering.

À la claire fontaine
m'en allant promener
J'ai trouvé l'eau si belle
que je m'y suis baigné.
Il y a longtemps que je t'aime,
jamais je ne t'oublierai.

Julian only knew enough French to translate a few words. *I have loved you for a long time. I will never forget you.*

"*Il y a longtemps que je t'aime—*" Maryse sang, her voice rising, quavering at the highest note—

Ash was gripping his own elbows tightly. He turned his head aside, just at the moment that Jace brought the sword down and across, severing Maryse's head from her body. White bone, red blood; her body crumpled to the sand, her head rolling to lie cheek down, open-eyed. She still seemed to be staring at Jace.

Blood had splattered Ash's face, his shirt. The crowd was clapping and cheering. Jace bent to clean his sword on the sand as Sebastian strolled over to Ash, his smile turning from inhuman to something else. Something possessive.

"I hope that was a learning experience," he said to Ash.

"I learned not to wear white to an execution," said Ash, brushing his hand down the front of his shirt; it left red smears behind. "Useful."

"Once we have the Mortal Instruments in hand, you'll see a lot more death, Ash." Sebastian chuckled and once again raised his voice. "Feeding time," he announced, and the words rang up and down the beach. There was a scream inside Julian's head, clawing to get out; he glanced at Emma and saw the same scream in her eyes. Maybe it belonged to them both.

She grabbed his wrist with enough force to grind the small bones together. "We have to go. We have to get away."

Her words tumbled over each other; Julian didn't even have time to agree. As the vampires closed in on Maryse's body, they ran for the bluffs, keeping low. The night was filled with a cacophony of shrieks and howls and the air carried the coppery tinge of blood. Emma was whispering, "*No, no, no,*" under her breath, even as she hit the bottom of a rickety wooden staircase and bolted up it in a crouching run. Julian followed, doing his best not to look back.

The stairs shook underfoot but held; the top of the bluffs was in sight. Emma reached the end of the stairs—and cried out as she was whisked out of sight.

Julian's vision went white. He had no awareness of climbing the rest of the steps; he was simply at the top of the bluffs—familiar highway, rows of parked cars, sand and grass underfoot—and there was Emma, held in the grip of a tall, redheaded boy whose familiar face smacked Julian like a punch in the gut.

"Cameron?" Julian said, incredulous. "Cameron Ashdown?"

Cameron looked about nineteen or twenty. His thick red hair was cut military short. He was whipcord lean, wearing a tan T-shirt and camo pants, a Sam Browne belt slung diagonally over his shoulder. There was a pistol thrust through it.

His face twisted in disgust. "Both of you together. I might have guessed."

Julian took a step forward. "Let her go, you Endarkened piece of—"

Cameron's eyes rounded with almost comical surprise, and Emma took advantage of the moment to kick backward savagely, twisting her body to deliver several quick punches to his side. She spun away from him as he gagged, but he'd already gotten the pistol out of its holster.

He pointed it at both of them. Shadowhunters didn't use guns, but Julian could tell just by the way he held it that *this* Cameron Ashdown knew them well.

If Cameron shot, Julian thought, there might be time for him to throw himself in front of Emma. He'd take the bullet, even if he hated the idea of leaving her here alone. . . .

Cameron raised his voice. "Livia!" he called. "You're going to want to see this."

Julian's chest turned to ice. He imagined he was still breathing, he must be or he'd die, but he couldn't feel it, couldn't feel the blood in his body or the pulse of his breath or the beat of his heart. He only saw her, appearing from between two cars: She walked toward them casually, her long dark Blackthorn hair blowing in the wind off the sea.

Livvy.

She looked about seventeen. She wore black leather pants with a bullet belt slung around her waist and a gray tank top with holes in it over a mesh shirt. Her boots were thick-soled with a dozen buckles. On her wrists were D-ring canvas bracelets with short throwing knives shoved under the straps. A scar—one of many—cut across her face, from the top of her left temple, across her eye, to the middle of her cheek. She carried a shotgun, and as she walked toward them, she raised it effortlessly and pointed it directly at Julian.

"It's them," Cameron said. "Don't know what they're doing away from the other Endarkened."

"Who cares?" Livvy said. "I'm gonna kill them, and they'd thank me for it if they still had souls."

Julian threw up his hands. Joy at seeing her, uncontrollable and dizzying, warred with panic. "Livvy, it's *us*—"

"Don't even *try*," she spat. She pumped the shotgun expertly. "I'd tell you to pray, but the Angel is dead."

"Look—" Emma started, and Livvy began to swing the gun toward her; Julian took a step toward his sister, and then Cameron, who Julian had almost forgotten was there, said:

"*Wait.*"

Livvy froze. "This had better be good, Cam."

Cameron pointed at Julian. "His collar's torn—" He shook his head impatiently. "Show her," he said to Julian.

"*Your rune,*" Emma whispered, and Julian, realization bursting brightly behind his eyes, yanked his collar down to show Livvy the rune on his chest. Though Julian's impermanent runes—Night Vision, Stealth, Sure-Strike—had been fading to gray since they'd entered Faerie, his *parabatai* rune stood out black and clear.

Livvy froze.

"The Endarkened can't bear Nephilim runes," said Julian. "You know that, Livvy."

"I know you think we're Emma and Julian, the Endarkened version," said Emma. "But we've seen them. They're down on the beach." She pointed. "Seriously. *Look.*"

A flicker of doubt crossed Livvy's face. "Cameron. Go look."

Cameron went to the edge of the bluffs and peered down through a pair of binoculars. Julian held his breath; he could tell Emma was holding hers as well.

"Yeah, they're there," Cameron said after a long pause. "And they're making out. Gross."

"They were always doing that before they were Endarkened," said Livvy. "Some things never change."

Emma raised her left hand to show her Voyance rune. "We're Shadowhunters. We know you, Livvy, and we love you—"

"*Stop,*" Livvy said fiercely. "Fine, maybe you're not the Endarkened, but this could still be some kind of demonic shape-changing—"

"These are *angelic* runes," said Julian. "We're not demons—"

"Then *who are you?*" Livvy cried, and her voice echoed with an awful hopelessness, a loneliness as dark and bottomless as a well. "Who am I supposed to think you are?"

"We're still us," Emma said. "Jules and Emma. We're from another world. One where Sebastian is not in charge. One with runes."

Livvy stared at her blankly.

"Liv," said Cameron, lowering his binoculars. "The party on the beach is starting to break up. They'll be climbing up here any second. What are we doing?"

Livvy hesitated, but only for a second. Julian guessed that a lot of free time to make decisions wasn't a luxury this version of his sister had. "Let's take them back to the Bradbury," she said. "Maybe Diana will be back. She's seen a lot—she might have some idea what's going on here."

"Diana? Diana Wrayburn?" said Emma with relief. "Yes, take us to Diana, *please.*"

Cameron and Livvy exchanged a look of complete bafflement.

"All right, fine," Livvy said finally. She gestured toward a black Jeep Wrangler with tinted windows parked along the side of the highway. "Get in the car, both of you, backseat. And don't even consider trying anything funny. I'll blow your heads right off."

Livvy was riding shotgun, which meant she was sitting in the passenger seat with an actual shotgun slung across her lap. Beside her, Cameron drove with a sharp efficiency that was entirely at odds with the hapless, slightly lazy Cameron Emma knew in her own world. He navigated the car effortlessly around the massive potholes that pocked the asphalt of the Pacific Coast Highway like dings in the side of an old car.

Julian was silent, staring out his window with an appalled fascination. There was little to see, except the ruined road swept by their headlights, but the darkness itself was startling. The absence of streetlights, road signs, and illuminated windows lining the road was shocking in itself, like looking at a face missing its eyes.

Light finally evolved out of the darkness as they reached the end of the highway, where a tunnel connected it to the 10 freeway. On their right was the Santa Monica Pier, the familiar jetty now in ruins as if a giant had hacked at it with an ax. Chunks of wood and concrete lay tumbled and jagged in the water. Only the old carousel was untouched. It was lit up, atonal music pouring from its speakers. Clinging to the backs of the old-fashioned painted ponies were shadowy, inhuman shapes, their chittering giggles carried on the night air. The faces of the ponies appeared to be twisted into tormented, shrieking masks.

Emma looked away, glad when the car went into the tunnel, cutting off her view of the merry-go-round.

"The pier is one of the first places that the hellbeasts staked out," Cameron said, glancing into the backseat. "Who knew that demons liked amusement parks?"

Emma cleared her throat. "Mad for funnel cakes?"

Cameron laughed dryly. "Same old Emma. Sarcastic in the face of adversity."

Livvy darted a sharp look at him.

"I guess we shouldn't ask about Disneyland," said Julian in a flat voice.

Julian probably hadn't expected Cameron and Livvy to laugh, but the way they both tensed suggested that something really terrible had happened at Disneyland. Emma decided not to pursue it.

There were bigger questions. "When did all this happen?" she said.

"Just after the Dark War," said Livvy. "When Sebastian won."

"So he still attacked all the Institutes?" Emma asked. She hadn't wanted to think about it, hadn't wanted to court even the tiny possibility that her parents might be alive in this world, but she couldn't help the catch of hope in her voice. "Los Angeles, too?"

"Yes," said Livvy. Her voice was flat. "Your parents were killed. Our father was Endarkened."

Emma flinched. She'd known there was no real hope, but it still hurt. And Julian must have wondered about his father, she knew. She wanted to reach out a hand to him, but the memory of the emotionless Julian of the past week held her back.

"In our world, those things happened too," said Julian, after a long pause. "But we won the war."

"Sebastian died," said Emma. "Clary killed him."

"Clary Fairchild?" said Cameron. His voice was thick with doubt. "She was murdered by the demon Lilith at the Battle of the Burren."

"No," said Emma stubbornly. "Clary and her friends won at the Battle of the Burren. There are paintings of it. She rescued Jace with the sword Glorious and they tracked Sebastian down in Edom; he never won—"

Livvy tapped her short fingernails on the barrel of her gun. "Nice story. So you're claiming you come from a place where Sebastian is dead, demons aren't roaming the streets, and Shadowhunters still have angelic power?"

"Yes," Emma said.

Livvy turned to look at her. The scar that cut across her eye was an angry red in the scarlet moonlight. "Well, if it's so great there, what are you doing here?"

"It wasn't a planned vacation. Not everything in our world is perfect," Emma said. "Far from it, really."

She glanced at Julian and to her surprise found him looking back at her, matching her searching glance with his own. An echo of their old instant communication flared—*Should we tell Livvy that she's dead in our world?*

Emma shook her head slightly. Livvy didn't believe them about anything yet. That piece of information wouldn't help.

"Gotta get off," said Cameron. There were a few lights out here, illuminating patches of highway, and Emma could see the occasional illumination dotting the flat plain of the city beyond. It didn't look anything like Los Angeles at night, though. The diamond chains of white light were gone, replaced by irregular spots of brightness. A fire burned somewhere on a distant hill.

In front of them, a massive crack divided the highway, as if someone had sliced neatly through the concrete. Cameron swung away from the rift, taking the nearest off-ramp. He dimmed the headlights as they hit the streets, and cruised at a slow speed through a residential neighborhood.

It was an unremarkable L.A. street lined with one-level ranch houses. Most of them were boarded up, the curtains pulled, only tiny glimpses of light visible within. Many were completely dark, and a few of those showed signs of forced entry—doors torn off at the hinges, bloodstains smearing the white stucco walls. Along the curb were a few abandoned cars with their trunks still open as though the people who owned them had been . . . taken away . . . while trying to make a break for it.

Saddest of all were the signs that children had once lived here: a torn-apart jungle gym, a bent tricycle lying in the middle of a driveway. A ghostly swing set pushed by the breeze.

A curve in the road loomed in front of them. As Cameron swung the car around, the headlights picked out a strange sight. A family—two parents and two children, a boy and a girl—were sitting at a picnic table on their lawn. They were eating in silence from plates of grilled meat, coleslaw, and potato salad. They were all deathly pale.

Emma swung around to stare as they receded into the distance. "What is going on with them?"

"Forsworn," said Livvy, curling her lip with distaste. "They're mundanes who are loyal to Sebastian. He runs the Institutes now and protects mundanes who swear allegiance to him. Half the remaining mundanes in the world are Forsworn."

"What about the other half?" said Julian.

"Rebels. Freedom fighters. You can either be one or the other."

"You're rebels?" Emma said.

Cameron laughed and looked fondly at Livvy. "Livia isn't just a rebel. She's the baddest badass rebel of them all."

He stroked the back of Livvy's neck gently. Emma hoped Julian's head wouldn't blow right off. Livvy clearly wasn't fifteen anymore, but she was still Julian's little sister, sort of. Hastily, Emma said, "Shadowhunters and mundanes are united as a rebellion? What about Downworlders?"

"There are no Shadowhunters anymore," Livvy said. She held up her right hand. There was no Voyance rune on the back. If Emma squinted, she thought she could glimpse the faint scar where it had once been: a shadow of a shadow. "The power of the Angel is broken. Steles don't work, runes fade like ghosts. Sebastian Morgenstern went from Institute to Institute and killed everyone who wouldn't pledge their loyalty to him. He opened the world to demons and they salted the earth with demon poisons and shattered the glass towers. Idris was overrun and the Adamant Citadel was destroyed. Angelic magic doesn't work. Demonic magic is the only magic there is." She tightened her hands on her shotgun. "Most of those who were once Shadowhunters are Endarkened now."

A world without Shadowhunters. A world without angels. They had left the residential neighborhood behind and were rolling down what Emma guessed might be Sunset Boulevard. It was hard to tell with the street signs gone. There were other cars on the road, finally, and even a slight slowdown in traffic. Emma glanced to the side and saw a pallid vampire behind the wheel of a Subaru in the next lane. He glanced at her and winked.

"We're coming to a checkpoint," Cameron said.

"Let us handle this," said Livvy. "Don't talk."

The car slowed to a crawl; up ahead Emma could see striped barriers. Most of the buildings along the boulevard were ruined shells. They had drawn up alongside one whose crumbling walls circled a mostly intact courtyard that had clearly once been the lobby of an office building. Demons were clustered everywhere: on piles of overturned furniture, clambering on the shattered walls, feeding from metal troughs of dark sticky stuff that might be blood. In the center of the room was a pole with a woman in a white dress tied to it, blood seeping through her dress. Her head lolled to the side as if she'd fainted.

Emma started to undo her seat belt. "We have to do something."

"No!" Livvy said sharply. "You'll get killed, and you'll get us killed too. We can't protect the world like that anymore."

"I'm not afraid," Emma said.

Livvy shot her a white-hot look of anger. "You should be."

"Checkpoint," snapped Cameron, and the car shot forward and stopped at the barriers. Cam lowered the driver's-side window, and Emma nearly jumped out of her seat as an eyeless demon with a wrinkled head like an old grape leaned into the car. It wore a high-collared gray uniform, and though it had no nose or eyes, it did have a mouth that stretched across its face.

"Credentials," it hissed.

Cameron jerked down his sleeve and stuck out his left hand, baring his wrist. Emma caught a glimpse of a mark on his inner wrist, above his pulse point, just as the demon extruded a gray raspy tongue that looked like a long, dead worm and licked Cameron's wrist.

Please, Emma thought, *do not let me puke in the back of this car. I remember this car. I made out with Cameron in the back of this car. Oh God, that demon licked his wrist. The whole car stinks like demon flesh.*

Something covered her hand, something warm and reassuring. She blinked. Julian had wrapped his fingers around hers. The surprise brought her back to herself sharply.

"Ah, Mr. Ashdown," the demon said. "I didn't realize. Have a pleasant evening." It drew back, and Cameron hit the gas. They had driven several blocks before anyone spoke.

"What was that thing with—" Julian began.

"The tongue! I know!" Emma said. "What the hell?"

"—the demon calling you Mr. Ashdown?" Julian finished.

"My family are Forsworn—loyal to the Fallen Star," said Cam shortly. "They run the Institute here for Sebastian. Members of the Legion of the Star are marked with special tattoos."

Livvy showed them the inside of her right wrist, where a design was marked, a star inside a circle. The same sigil that had been on Sebastian's banners earlier. "Mine is forged. That's why Cameron is driving," Livvy said. She glanced at him with wry fondness. "His family doesn't know he's not loyal to the Star."

"I can't say I'm astonished Paige and Vanessa turned out to be traitors," said Emma, and she saw Livvy flick her an odd glance. Surprise she knew who Paige and Vanessa were? Agreement? Emma wasn't sure.

They had reached downtown L.A., an area that had been pretty thick with demon activity even in the regular world. Here the streets were surprisingly crowded—Emma saw vampires and faeries walking around freely, and even a repurposed convenience store advertising blood milk shakes in the window. A group of large cats scuttled by, and as they turned their heads Emma saw they had the faces of human babies. No one on the sidewalk gave them a second glance.

"So Downworlders," Julian said. "How do they fit in here?"

"You don't want to know," Livvy said.

"We do," said Emma. "We know warlocks—we could try to get in touch with them here, get help—"

"Warlocks?" Livvy snapped. "There are no warlocks. Once Sebastian opened the world to hellbeasts, the warlocks started to get sick. Some died, and as for the rest, their humanity degraded. They turned into demons."

"Into *demons?*" Emma said. "All the way?"

"What about Magnus?" said Julian. "Magnus Bane?"

Emma felt a chill run over her. So far they hadn't asked after the welfare of anyone they knew. She suspected both of them found the prospect terrifying.

"Magnus Bane was one of the first great tragedies," said Livvy as if she were reciting an old story everyone knew. "Bane realized he was turning into a demon. He begged his boyfriend, Alexander Lightwood, to kill him. Alec did, and then turned the sword on himself. Their bodies were found together in the ruins of New York."

Julian had gone whiter than paper. Emma put her head down, feeling like she might faint.

Magnus and Alec, who had always been a symbol of all that was good, so horribly gone.

"So that's warlocks," said Livvy. "The Fair Folk are allied with Sebastian and mostly they live in the protected realms of Faerie, though some like to visit our world, do a little mischief. You know."

"I don't think we do," Julian said. "The realms of Faerie are protected?"

"The faeries were Sebastian's allies during the Dark War," said Livvy. "They lost a lot of warriors. The Seelie Queen herself was killed. Sebastian rewarded them after the war by giving them what they wanted—isolation. Entrances to Faerie are walled off from this world, and any human or even Endarkened who threatens one of the few faeries remaining in Thule is severely punished."

"The Seelie Queen never had a—a child?" Julian asked.

"She died without children," said Livvy. "The Unseelie King has united both Courts and rules over everything there now. His heir is Prince Erec, or at least that's what we last heard. Not a lot of news from Faerie gets out."

So there was no second Ash in this world, Emma thought. Probably good, since one Ash seemed like more than enough.

"As for the werewolves, the packs are all scattered," said Cameron. "You've got some lone wolves, some who've thrown their lot in with Sebastian, some are rebels with us, most were killed. Vampires are doing a bit better because demons don't like to eat them as much—they're already dead."

"There are a few vampire cults that have joined up with Sebastian," said Livvy. "They worship him and believe that when they eat everyone in Thule, he will lead them through to a world of more people with more blood."

"Raphael Santiago says they're idiots, and when all the people are gone, they'll starve," said Cameron.

"Raphael Santiago is still alive? In our world he's dead," said Julian.

"Well, there's one point for Thule," said Livvy with a crooked smile. "When we get to the building you'll see—"

She broke off as a human came pelting out of an alley. A teenage boy, filthy and skinny to the point of starvation, hair hanging in matted clumps. His clothes were dirty, a ragged pack dangling from one arm.

Livvy tensed. "Unsworn human," she said. "Demons can hunt them for sport. Cam—"

"Livvy, we shouldn't," Cameron said.

"Pull over!" Livvy snapped. Cameron slammed on the brakes, throwing them all forward; Julian was up and out of his seat, throwing his arm out to catch Livvy by the shoulder and prevent her from bumping her head.

She shot him a startled look. Then she was shaking him off and powering down her window, leaning out to shout to the boy. "Over here!"

The boy changed course and raced toward them. Behind him, something appeared at the mouth of the alley. Something that looked as if it were made of shadows and ragged black wings. It dived toward him at incredible speed and Livvy swore. "He's not going to make it."

"He might," Cameron said. "Ten bucks."

"What the hell?" Emma said. She reached for the handle of her door and shoved it open—Julian grabbed her by the sleeve of her tunic, yanking her back—and the ragged shadow was on the boy like a hawk on a mouse. He gave one terrified shriek as it seized him, and they both shot up into the air, disappearing into the ashy sky.

Cam hit the gas; a few passersby were staring at them. Emma was breathing hard. Mundanes weren't supposed to be killed by demons. Shadowhunters were supposed to be able to help.

But there were no Shadowhunters here.

"You owe me four thousand dollars, Cam," Livvy said tonelessly.

"Yeah," said Cameron. "I'll repay you as soon as the international banking system is reestablished."

"What about our family?" Julian said abruptly. He let go of Emma's sleeve; she'd almost forgotten he was holding on to her. "Are any of them here, Livia?"

Livvy's mouth flattened into a tense line. "I'm still not convinced you're Julian," she said. "And my family is my business."

They turned abruptly off the street, and for a moment Emma thought they were going to plow into the side of a familiar brown brick structure: the famous downtown Bradbury Building, surprisingly still standing. At what felt like the last minute, a sheet of bricks and sandstone rose up out of the way and they pulled into a cavernous dark space.

A garage. They piled out of the car, and Cameron went over to chat with a girl in camo pants and a black tank top who was turning a metal crank that slid the garage door closed. It was a massive slab of brick and metal operated by a cleverly jointed set of gears.

"We're on our own generator here," said Livvy. "And we do a lot of stuff by hand. We don't need the Forsworn tracing us by our electricity usage." She tossed her shotgun back into the car. "Come on."

They followed her to a door that led into a spacious entryway. It was clear they were inside a large office building. The walls were brick and marble, the floor tiled, and above her she could see an intricate maze of catwalks, metal staircases, and the glint of old ironwork.

Livvy narrowed her eyes at both of them. "Okay," she said slowly.

"Okay, what?" said Emma.

"You just passed through a corridor whose walls were packed with salt, gold, and cold iron," Livvy said. "A crazy old millionaire built this place. He believed in ghosts and he stuffed the building with everything that's meant to repel the supernatural. Some of it does still work."

The door behind them banged. Cameron had returned. "Divya says Diana's not back yet," he said. "You want me to take these two upstairs to wait?"

"Yeah." Livvy rubbed the back of her hand across her forehead tiredly. "They made it in here. Maybe they are harmless."

"You mean maybe I'm really your brother," said Julian.

Livvy's back stiffened. "I didn't say that." She gestured at Cameron. "Take them to one of the newbie rooms. Make sure there are guards on the floor."

Without another word, she turned and walked away, heading for one of the iron staircases. Julian exhaled sharply, staring after her. Emma couldn't help it; her heart ached at his expression. He looked as if he were being crushed from the inside out. The image of him cradling his sister's body as she bled out in the Council Hall rose like a nightmare behind her eyes.

She caught up with Livvy in the stairwell; Livvy turned to her, and the scars on her face cut at Emma again as if she could feel the pain of getting them. "Seriously?" Livvy said. "What do you want?"

"Come on, Livvy," said Emma, and Livvy raised her eyebrows. "You know it's really Julian. In your heart, you know. In the car he tried to protect you from bumping your head, just like he always has; he can't help himself. Nobody could act that, or fake it."

Livvy tensed. "You don't understand. I can't—"

"Take this." Emma shoved her phone into Livvy's hands. Livvy stared at it as if she'd never seen an iPhone before. Then she shook her head.

"You might be surprised to hear this, but we don't really get much cell reception here," she said.

"Cute," said Emma. "I want you to look at the photos." She jabbed at the phone with a shaking finger. "Pictures of the last five years. Look—here's Dru." She heard Livvy suck in her breath. "And Mark at the beach, and here's Helen and Aline's wedding. And Ty, last month—"

Livvy made a half-choked noise. "Ty is alive in your world?"

Emma froze. "Yes," she whispered. "Yes, of course he is."

Livvy tightened her hand on the phone. She turned and fled up the stairs, her boots clanging against the iron framework. But not before Emma saw that her eyes were shining with tears.

18
Hell Rising

As Julian and Emma followed Cameron through the Bradbury lobby, they passed several other groups of Livvy's rebels. That was what Julian was calling them in his mind, anyway. These were Livvy's people; she was clearly important here. He felt proud of her at the same time that he felt a thousand other emotions tearing through him—joy, despair, horror, fear, grief, and love and hope. They battered at him like the sea at high tide.

And yearning, too. A yearning for Emma that felt like knives in his blood. When she spoke, he couldn't stop staring at her mouth, the way her top lip curved like a perfectly made bow. Was this why he'd begged Magnus to turn his feelings for her off? He couldn't remember if it had been like this before, or if now was worse. He was drowning.

"Look," Emma whispered, touching his arm, and his skin burned where she touched him and, *Stop*, he told himself fiercely. *Stop*. "It's Maia Roberts and Bat Velasquez."

Thankful for the distraction, Julian glanced over to see the girl who was the werewolf representative to the Council in his reality. Her hair was in two thick braids, and she was descending a set of stairs next to a handsome, scarred boy who Julian recognized as her boyfriend. Like Livvy, their clothes looked like they'd been scrounged from an army-navy store. Military jackets, camo, boots, and bullet belts.

There were a lot of bullets in this world. The front doors of the building had been boarded up, the boards glopped with cement to hold them in place. Rows of nails next to the doors held guns of all shapes and sizes; boxes of ammo were stacked on the floor. On the wall nearby someone had written ANGELS AND MINISTERS OF GRACE DEFEND US in red paint.

They followed Cameron up another set of wood-and-iron stairs. The inside of the building had probably been breathtakingly beautiful once, when light had streamed in through the windows and the glass roof overhead. Even now it was striking, though the windows and roof were boarded over, the terra-cotta walls cracked. Electric lights burned sodium yellow, and the web of stairs and catwalks angled blackly through the twilight gloom as they passed rebel guards armed with pistols.

"Lot of guns," said Emma, a little dubiously, as they reached the top floor.

"Bullets don't work on demons, but they'll still take down a bad vamp or an Endarkened," said Cameron. They were passing along a walkway. Beyond the iron balustrade on the left side was the yawning darkness of the atrium; the right wall was lined with doors. "There used to be a branch of the LAPD in this building, you know, back when there were police. Demons took them out in minutes, but they left behind plenty of Glocks." He paused. "Here we are."

He pushed open a plain wooden door and flicked on the light. Julian followed Emma into the room: It had clearly once been an office, repurposed into a bedroom. *Newbie rooms*, Livvy had said. There was a desk and an open wardrobe where a motley collection of clothes hung. The walls were pale stucco and warm old wood, and through a doorway Julian could glimpse a small tiled bathroom.

Someone seemed to have taken the time to try to make the place look a little nice—a sheet of metal covered the single window, but it had been painted a dark blue dotted with small yellow stars, and there was a colorful blanket on the bed.

"Sorry the bed's not bigger," said Cameron. "We don't get too many couples. There are condoms in the nightstand drawer, too."

He said it matter-of-factly. Emma blushed. Julian tried to stay expressionless.

"Someone will bring you some food," Cameron added. "There are energy bars and Gatorade in the wardrobe if you can't wait. Don't try to leave the room—there are guards all over." He hesitated in the doorway. "And, uh, welcome," he added, a little awkwardly, and left.

Emma wasted no time in raiding the wardrobe for energy bars, and turned up a small bag of potato chips as a bonus. "You want half?" she asked, tossing Julian a bar and holding up the chips.

"No." He knew he should be ravenous. He could barely remember the last time they'd eaten. But he actually felt a little sick. He was alone with Emma now, and it was overwhelming.

"If Ash is here, where's Annabel?" she said. "They came through the Portal together."

"She could be anywhere in Thule," Julian said. "Even if she figured out a way to return to our world, I doubt she'd leave Ash."

Emma sighed. "Speaking of which, I guess we should talk about how we try to get home. It can't be impossible. If we could get into Faerie somehow—there might be someone there, someone who can do magic—"

"Didn't Livvy say the entrances to Faerie were walled off?"

"We've made it through walls before," Emma said quietly, and he knew she was thinking, as he was, of the thorns around the Unseelie Tower.

"I know." Julian couldn't stop staring at her. They were both filthy, both bloody and hungry and exhausted. But against the darkness and chaos of this world, his Emma burned brighter than ever.

"Why are you looking at me like that?" she said. She tossed the empty chip bag into a metal wastebasket. "Eat your energy bar, Julian."

He peeled the wrapper off, clearing his throat. "I should probably sleep on the floor."

She stopped pacing. "If you want," she said. "I guess in this world we were always a couple. Not *parabatai*. I mean, that makes sense. If the Dark War hadn't turned out like it did, we never would have . . ."

"How long were we even together here, before we were Endarkened?" Julian said.

"Maybe Livvy will tell us. I mean, I know she's not really Livvy. Not our Livvy. She's Livvy that could have been."

"She's alive," Julian said. He stared down at his energy bar. The thought of eating it made him nauseous. "And she's been through hell. And I wasn't here to protect her."

Emma's brown eyes were dark and direct. "Do you care?"

He met her gaze, and for the first time in what felt like forever, he could feel what she was feeling, as he'd been able to for so long. He felt her wariness, her bone-deep hurt, and he knew he'd been the one to hurt her. He'd rejected her over and over, pushed her away, told her he felt nothing.

"Emma." His voice was scratchy. "The spell—it's broken."

"What?"

"When Livvy and Cameron said there was no magic here, they meant it. The spell Magnus put on me, it's not working here. I can feel things again."

Emma just stared. "You mean about me?"

"Yeah." When she didn't move, Julian took a step forward and put his arms around her. She stood as stiffly as a wooden carving, her arms at her sides. It was like hugging a statue. "I feel everything," he said desperately. "I feel like I did before."

She pulled away from him. "Well, maybe I don't."

"Emma—" He didn't move toward her. She deserved her space. She deserved whatever she wanted. She must have dammed up so many words while he'd been under the spell, words it would have been completely pointless to say to his emotionless self. He could only imagine the control it must have taken. "What do you mean?"

"You hurt me," Emma said. "You hurt me a lot." She took a shuddering breath. "I know you did it because of a spell, but you had that spell cast on yourself without thinking about how it would affect me or your family or your role as a Shadowhunter. And I hate to tell you all this now, because we're in this terrible place and you just found out your sister is alive, sort of, and she looks kind of like Mad Max, which is cool actually, but this is the only place I can tell you, because when we get home—if we ever get home—you won't care." She paused, breathing as if she'd been running. "Okay. Fine. I'm going to take a shower. If you even think about following me into the bathroom to talk, I'll shoot you."

"You don't have a gun," Julian pointed out. It wasn't a helpful thing to say—Emma stalked into the bathroom and slammed the door behind her. A moment later, there was the sound of running water.

Julian sank down onto the bed. After having his soul wrapped in cotton wool for so long, the new rawness of emotion felt like razor wire cutting into his heart every time it expanded with a breath.

But it wasn't just pain. There was the bright current of joy that was seeing Livvy, hearing her voice. Of pride in watching Emma burn like fire in the Arctic, like the northern lights.

A voice seemed to ring in his head, clear as a bell; it was the Seelie Queen's voice.

Have you ever wondered how we lure mortals to live amongst faeries and serve us, son of thorns? We choose those who have lost something and promise them that which humans desire most of all, a cessation to their grief and suffering. Little do they know that once they enter our Lands, they are in the cage and will never again feel happiness.

You are in that cage, boy.

The Queen was deceitful, but sometimes right. Grief could be like a wolf tearing your insides, and you would do anything to make it stop. He remembered his despair as he looked in the mirror in Alicante and knew that he had lost Livvy and would soon lose Emma, too. He had gone to Magnus like a shipwrecked man struggling onto a lonely rock, knowing he might die the next day of heat or thirst, but desperate to escape the tempest.

And then the tempest had been gone. He had been in the eye of the hurricane, the storm around him, but he had been untouched. It had felt like a cessation to suffering. Only now did he recognize what he couldn't see before: that he had been going through life with a black hole at the center of him, a space like the emptiness between Portals.

Even at the moments when an emotion was so strong it seemed to pierce the veil, he had felt it at a sort of colorless, glassy remove—Ty atop Livvy's pyre, Emma as the thorns of the hedge tore at her. He could see her now, all black and white, the only spots of color where the blood had been drawn.

There was a knock on the door. Julian's throat was too tight for him to speak, but it didn't seem to matter: Cameron Ashdown barged in anyway, carrying a pile of clothes. He dumped them into the wardrobe, went back to the hallway, and returned with a box of canned food, toothpaste, soap, and other basics. Dropping it on the desk, he rolled his shoulders back with an exaggerated sigh. "Jeans and turtlenecks, gloves and boots. If you go back outside, cover up as much as you can to hide your runes. There's concealer, too, if you want to get fancy. Need anything else?"

Julian gave him a long look. "Yeah," he said finally. "Actually, I do."

Cameron had only just gone off muttering when Julian heard the water in the bathroom switch off. A moment later Emma appeared, wrapped in a towel, cheeks pink and glowing. Had she always looked like that? Such intense colors, the gold of her hair, black Marks against pale skin, the soft brown of her eyes—

"I'm sorry," he said as she reached for the clothes on the bed. She froze. "I'm only just starting to understand how sorry I am."

She went into the bathroom and came out a moment later dressed in black cargo pants and a green tank top. The permanent Marks twining her arms looked stark and startling, a reminder that no one else here had them. "Whoever was eyeballing our sizes has way overestimated my attributes," she said, buckling her belt. "The bra they gave me is huge. I could wear it as a hat."

Cameron barged back in without knocking again. "Got what you asked for," he said, and dumped a pile of pencils and a Canson sketch pad into Julian's lap. "Have to admit, it's a first. Most newbies ask for chocolate."

"Do you have chocolate?" Emma said.

"No," said Cameron, and stomped back out of the room. Emma watched him go with a bemused expression.

"I really like this new Cameron," she said. "Who knew he had it in him to be such a badass? He was such a nice guy, but . . ."

"He always had kind of a secret side," Julian said. He wondered if there was something about suddenly getting his emotions back that meant he didn't feel like covering things up. Maybe he'd regret it later. "A while ago, he approached Diana, because he was pretty sure Anselm Nightshade was murdering werewolf children. He couldn't prove it, but he had some good reasons for thinking it. His family kept telling him to drop it, that Nightshade had powerful friends. So he brought it to us—to the Institute."

"That's why you had Nightshade arrested," said Emma, realizing. "You wanted the Clave to be able to search his house."

"Diana told me they found a basement full of bones," said Julian. "Werewolf children, just like Cameron said. They tested the stuff in the restaurant and there was death magic all over the place. Cameron was right, and he stood up to his family, in his own way. And he did it for Downworlders that he didn't know."

"You never said anything," Emma said. "Not about Cameron, or about you—why you really got Anselm arrested. There are people who still blame you."

He gave her a rueful smile. "Sometimes you have to let people blame you. When the only other option is letting bad things happen, it doesn't matter what people think."

She didn't reply. When he glanced over at her, she looked as if she'd forgotten all about Cameron and Nightshade. Her eyes were wide and luminous as she reached out to touch a few of the Prismacolors that had rolled onto the bed.

"You asked for art supplies?" she whispered.

Julian looked down at his hands. "All this time, since the spell, I've been walking around missing the whole center of myself, but the thing is—I didn't even notice. Not consciously. But I felt it. I was living in black and white and now the color is back." He exhaled. "I'm saying it all wrong."

"No," Emma said, "I think I get it. You mean that the part of you that feels is also the part of you that creates things."

"They always say faeries steal human children because they can't make art or music of their own. Neither can warlocks or vampires. It requires mortality to make art. The knowledge of death, of things limited. There is fire inside us, Emma, and as it blazes, it burns us, and the burning causes pain—but without its light, I cannot see to draw."

"Then draw now," she said, her voice husky. She pressed several pencils into his open hand and began to turn away.

"I'm sorry," he said again. "I shouldn't burden you."

"You're not burdening me," she said, still facing away. "You're reminding me why I love you."

The words caught at his heart, sharp with a painful joy.

"You're not off the hook, though," she added, and went over to the wardrobe. He left her alone to rifle through the pairs of socks and shoes, looking for something that might fit. He wanted to talk to her—talk to her forever, about everything—but that had to be at her discretion. Not his.

Instead he put pencil to paper and let his imagination go, let the images that rose up inside him and captured his brain flow out in Alicante silver and Seelie green, in Unseelie black and blood red. He drew the King on his throne, pale and powerful and unhappy. He drew Annabel holding Ash's hand. He drew Emma with Cortana, surrounded by thorns. He drew Drusilla, all in black, a murder of crows circling behind her.

He was conscious that Emma had come to lie down beside him and was watching him with quiet curiosity, her head propped on her arm. She was half-asleep, lips parted, when the door banged open again. Julian threw the sketchbook down. "Look, Cameron—"

But it wasn't Cameron. It was Livvy.

She had taken off her Sam Browne ammo belt, but otherwise looked much the same. In the brighter light of the bedroom, Julian could see the shadows smudged under her eyes. "Cameron said you asked for a sketch pad and pencils," she said in a near whisper.

Julian didn't move. He half felt as if any movement would spook her, as if he were trying to lure a nervous forest creature closer. "Do you want to see?"

Julian held out the sketch pad; she took it and flipped through it, slowly and then faster. Emma was sitting up now, clutching one of the pillows.

Livvy thrust the sketch pad back at Julian. She was looking down; he couldn't see her face, only twin fringes of dark lashes. He felt a twinge of disappointment. *She doesn't believe me; the pictures meant nothing to her. I'm nothing to her.*

"No one draws like my brother," she said, taking a deep breath and letting it out slowly. She lifted her head and looked directly at

Julian with a sort of bewilderment that was half hurt, half hope. "But you do."

"You remember when I tried to teach you to draw, when you were nine?" said Julian. "And you snapped all my pencils?"

Something almost like a smile touched the edge of Livvy's mouth. For a moment, she was familiar Livvy, despite the scars and black leather. A second later it was as if a mask had passed across her face, and she was a different Livia, a rebel leader, a scarred warrior. "You don't need to try to convince me anymore," she said. She turned away, her movements precise and military. "Finish getting cleaned up. I'll meet you two in the main office in an hour."

"Did we ever date in this world?" Emma said. "You know, you and me."

Cameron nearly fell down several metal steps. They were in the maze of stairs and catwalks that crisscrossed the inside of the Bradbury Building. "Of course not!"

Emma felt mildly stung. She knew it wasn't a big deal, considering, but sometimes you wanted to focus on something trivial to take your mind off the apocalypse. Cameron in her world had been almost embarrassingly devoted, always coming back after they broke up, sending love notes and flowers and sad llama pictures.

"You were always with Julian," Cameron added. "Aren't you together in your world?"

"I'm right here," Julian said in the deceptively mild tone that meant he was annoyed.

"I mean, yes," Emma said. "At least, we're on and off. Sometimes very on, sometimes very off. You and I dated briefly, is all."

"We don't really have time for that kind of personal drama here," Cameron said. "It's hard to focus on your love life when giant spiders are chasing you."

Cameron was pretty funny here, Emma thought. If he'd been this amusing at home, their relationship might have lasted longer.

"When you say 'giant,' how giant exactly?" she said. "Bigger than Dumpsters?"

"Not the babies," Cameron said, and gave them a horrible smile. "We're here—go on in, and don't tell Livvy we dated in your world, because it's weird."

They found Livvy in another repurposed office—this one had clearly once been more of a loft, big and airy and probably full of light before the windows had been covered. Strips of brick alternated with polished wood on the walls, and dozens of vintage fruit labels advertising California apples, pears, and oranges hung between the boarded-up windows. A group of four sleek, modern couches formed a square around a glass coffee table. Livvy was lounging on one of the couches, drinking a glass of something dark brown.

"That's not alcohol, is it?" Julian sounded appalled. "You shouldn't be drinking."

"You'll be drinking tomorrow," Livvy said, and pointed at a bottle of Jack Daniel's on the glass table. "Just saying." She waved a hand. "Sit down."

They settled themselves on the couch opposite her. There was a fireplace in the room too, but the grate had been plugged with metal some time ago. Someone with a sense of humor had painted flames on the metal. It was too bad. Emma would have liked a fire. It would have felt like something natural.

Livvy turned her glass around in her scarred hands. "So I believe you," she said. "You are who you say you are. Which means I know what you want to ask me."

"Yeah," Julian said. He cleared his throat. "Mark?" he said. "Ty? Helen, and Dru—"

"But you also probably want to get out of here," Livvy interrupted. "Since you ended up here by accident and your world sounds like a much better place."

"We have to leave," Emma said. "There are people at home who could be hurt or even killed if we don't come back—"

"But we want to take you with us," Julian said. Emma had known he was going to say it; they hadn't discussed it, but it had never been a question. Of course Julian would want Livvy to come back with them.

Livvy gave a long, slow nod. "Right," she said. "Do you have a reason to think that there's any way you can get back at all? Interdimensional travel isn't exactly easy."

"We'd only just started to discuss it," Emma said. "But we'll think of something." She spoke with more confidence than she felt.

Livvy held up a hand. "If there's any chance you can get away, are you really sure that you want to know what happened to—to everyone? Because I wish every single day that I didn't."

Without taking his eyes off Livvy, Julian said, "What I wish is that I could've been here for you."

Livvy's gaze was distant. "You were, I guess. Both of you." She pulled her knees up under her. "You saved our lives when you sacrificed yourselves to get us out of Manhattan the day it fell."

Emma shivered. "New York? Why were we in New York?"

"The Battle of the Burren was when everything went wrong," said Livvy. "Clary was there, Alec and Isabelle Lightwood, Magnus Bane—and Helen and Aline, of course. They were winning. Jace was under Sebastian's thrall, but Clary was wielding Glorious, the sword of the Angel of Paradise. She was about to break him free when Lilith appeared. She cast the sword into Hell and cut Clary down. Helen and the others were lucky to escape with their lives.

"That was Sebastian's great victory. After that he joined forces with the Fair Folk. They stormed Alicante while we hid in the Hall of Accords. The Shadowhunters fought—our father fought—but Sebastian was too powerful. As Alicante fell to his forces, a group of warlocks opened up a Portal for the children. Just people under fifteen. We had to leave Helen and Mark behind. Dru was screaming as they ripped her out of Helen's arms and drove us through the Portal to Manhattan.

"Catarina Loss and Magnus Bane had set up a temporary shelter there. The war raged on in Idris. We got a message from Helen. Mark had been taken by the Fair Folk. She didn't know what they would do to him. I still don't know. I hope he's in Faerie and it's green and bright and he's forgotten all of us."

"He hasn't," Julian said in a low voice. "Mark doesn't forget."

Livvy just blinked, fast, as if her eyes stung. "Helen and Aline hung on, fighting. Sometimes we got a fire-message from them. We heard that strange gray patches started to appear in Brocelind Forest. They called them the 'blight.' They turned out to be doorways for demons."

"Doorways for demons?" Emma demanded, sitting up straight, but Livvy was caught up in her story, turning her glass over and over in her hands so fast Emma was surprised it hadn't started sparking.

"Demons flooded into Idris. The Fair Folk and Endarkened drove the Shadowhunters out of Alicante, and the demons finished them off. We were in New York when we learned Idris had fallen. Everyone wanted to know the names of the dead, but there was no information. We couldn't find out what had happened to Helen and Aline, if they'd lived or been Endarkened—we didn't know.

"We did know we wouldn't be safe for long. Sebastian didn't care about keeping secrets from the human world. He wanted to burn it all down. Demons began to appear everywhere, running rampant, slaughtering humans in the streets. The blight spread, appearing all over the world. It poisoned everything it touched and the warlocks started to sicken.

"After two months the shelter was destroyed. The streets were full of monsters, and the warlocks were getting sicker and sicker. The more powerful they were, the more magic they'd used, the quicker they got sick and the more likely they were to turn into demons. Catarina fled so she wouldn't hurt anyone. You heard what happened to Alec and Magnus. The shelter collapsed and the kids spilled into the streets." She looked at Julian. "It was winter. We had nowhere to go. But you kept us together. You said, at all costs, we stay together. We live because we're together. We *never* leave each other."

Julian cleared his throat. "That sounds right."

Livvy's eyes bored into him. "Before she left, Catarina Loss arranged for a bunch of trains to take Shadowhunter and Downworlder kids across the country. The demons were spreading east to west, and the rumor was that California was pretty clear. We left from White Plains station—we walked all night, and you carried Tavvy. He was so hungry. We were all hungry. You kept trying to give us your food, especially Ty. We got to the station and the last train was leaving. That's when we saw them. The Endarkened. They came for us in their red gear, like a rain of blood. They were going to kill us all before we got on that train.

"You didn't even kiss us good-bye," Livvy said, her voice remote. "You just shoved us toward the trains. You shouted at us to get on, told me to look after the younger ones. And you went for the Endarkened with your swords out. We could see you fighting them as the train pulled out—just the two of you and fifty Endarkened, in the snow."

At least we went down protecting them, Emma thought. It was cold comfort.

"And then there were four," Livvy said, and reached for the whiskey bottle. "Me and Ty, Dru and Tavvy. I did what you said. I looked after them. The trains inched through the winter. We met Cameron somewhere around Chicago—we'd all started going from train to train by then, trading food for matches, that sort of thing. Cameron said we should go to L.A., that his sister was there and she said things were okay.

"Of course when we hit Union Station, it turned out Paige Ashdown had joined the Legion of the Star. That's what they were calling themselves. Traitors, we called them. She was standing there grinning bloody murder with a dozen Endarkened around her. Cameron gave me a shove, and Ty and I ran. We were dragging Dru and Tavvy with us. They were crying and screaming. They'd thought they were coming home.

"I don't think we realized until then how bad things had gotten. Demons hunted unsworn humans through the streets, and there was nothing we could do. Our Marks were fading. We were getting weaker every day. Runes and seraph blades didn't work. We had nothing to fight demons with, so we hid. Like cowards."

"By the Angel, Livvy, you can't have been expected to do anything else. You were *ten*," Emma said.

"No one says 'By the Angel' anymore." Livvy poured out a measure of Jack Daniel's and recapped the bottle. "At least it wasn't cold. I remembered what you'd said, Jules, to take care of the younger ones. Ty isn't—he wasn't—really younger than me, but he was shattered. His whole heart was broken when we lost you. He loved you so much, Jules."

Julian didn't speak. He was pale as the snow in Livvy's story. Emma slid her hand across the couch, touched her fingers to his. They were icy. This world was the pure distilled essence of his nightmares, Emma thought. A place where his siblings had been ripped from him, where he couldn't protect them as the world fell down around them in darkness and flame.

"We slept in alleys, in the abandoned houses of murdered humans," Livvy said. "We scrounged for food in supermarkets. We never stayed in the same place for more than two nights. Tavvy screamed himself to sleep in my arms every night, but we were careful. I thought we were careful. We slept inside rings of salt and iron. I tried, but . . ." She took a swallow of whiskey. Emma would have choked; Livvy seemed used to it. "One night we were sleeping on the street. In the ruins of the Grove. There were still stores with food and clothes there. I'd surrounded us with salt, but a Shinagami demon came from above—it was a fast blur with wings and talons like knives. It snatched Tavvy away from me—we were both screaming." She took a ragged breath. "There was this stupid ornamental fountain. Ty jumped up onto the side and attacked the Shinagami with a throwing knife. I think he hit it, but without runes, there's just—you *can't hurt them.* It was still holding Tavvy. It just turned around and slashed out with a talon and cut Ty-Ty's throat." She didn't seem to notice or care that she'd called him by his baby name. She was gripping her glass tightly, her eyes blank and haunted. "My Ty, he fell into the fountain and it was all water and blood. The Shinagami was gone. Tavvy was gone. I hauled Ty out, but he was dead in my arms."

Dead in my arms. Emma tightened her grip on Julian's hand, seeing him on the Council Hall dais, holding Livvy as the life and the blood went out of her.

"I kissed him. I told him I loved him. And I went and got a jug of gasoline and burned his body so the demons wouldn't find it." Livvy's mouth twisted. "And then it was just me and Dru."

"Livia . . ." Julian leaned forward, but his sister held up a hand as if to ward off whatever he was going to say next.

"Let me finish," she said. "I've gotten this far." She took another drink and closed her eyes. "After that, Dru stopped talking. I told her we were going to go to the Institute and get help. She didn't say anything. I knew there wasn't any help there. But I thought maybe we could join the Legion of the Star—I didn't care anymore. We were walking along the highway when a car pulled up. It was Cameron.

"He could see we were bloody and starving. And that there were only two of us. He didn't ask questions. He told us about this place, the Bradbury Building. He was tapped into the resistance. It was tiny then, but there were two ex-Shadowhunters who had once hunted a demon here. They said it was an old, strong building full of salt and iron, easy to lock down. Plus because of the LAPD leasing space, there was a stockpile of weapons here.

"We joined up with the others and helped them break in. Even Dru helped, though she still wasn't talking. We started to reinforce the building and spread the word that those resisting Sebastian were welcome here. People came from New York, from Canada and Mexico, from all over. We slowly built up the population, made a haven for refugees."

"So Dru is still—?" Emma began eagerly, but Livvy went on.

"Two years ago she went out with a scouting party. Never came back. It happens all the time."

"Did you look for her?" Julian said.

Livvy turned a flat gaze on him. "We don't go after people here," she said. "We don't do rescue missions. They get more people killed. If I disappeared, I wouldn't expect anyone to come after me. I'd hope they wouldn't be that stupid." She set her glass down. "Anyway, now you know. That's the story."

They stared at each other, the three of them, for a long moment. Then Julian stood up. He went around the table and lifted Livvy up and hugged her, so tightly that Emma saw her gasp in surprise.

Don't push him away, she thought, *please, don't*.

Livvy didn't. She squeezed her eyes shut and grabbed onto Julian. They stood hugging each other for a long moment like two drowning people clinging to the same life raft. Livvy pressed her face against Julian's shoulder and gave a single, dry sob.

Emma stumbled to her feet and over to them, not inserting herself into the hug but gently stroking Livvy's hair. Livvy raised her head from Julian's shoulder and offered her a tiny smile.

"We're going to get back to our world," Julian said. "Ty is alive there. Everyone's alive there. We'll take you with us. You belong there, not here."

Emma waited for Livvy to ask about her own fate in their world, but she didn't. Instead she pulled a little away from Julian and shook her head—not angrily, but with immense sadness. "There are things I have to do here," she said. "It's not like we're just walled up here waiting to die. We're *fighting*, Jules."

"Jesus, Livs," he said in a half-broken voice. "It's so dangerous—"

"I know," she said, and patted his face lightly, the way she had sometimes when she was a very little girl, as if the familiar shape of his features was reassuring. Then she stepped away, breaking the hug. She smoothed her hair back and said, "I didn't tell you about the Silent Brothers."

"The Silent Brothers?" Emma was puzzled.

"When Idris fell, the Silent Brothers were killed, but before they died they sealed the Silent City, with the Mortal Cup and Mortal Sword inside it. No one could get in. Not even Sebastian. And he wants to, desperately."

"Why does he want the Mortal Instruments?" said Julian.

"He has a version of the Cup that controls the Endarkened," said Livvy. "But he wants to master *us*. He thinks if he can get the Mortal Instruments together, he can control what remains of the Nephilim—turn us from rebels into slaves."

"Sebastian said something on the beach," Emma recalled, "about the Mortal Instruments."

"We have people on the inside, like Cameron," said Livvy. "The rumor is that Sebastian is getting closer to figuring out a way into the City." She hesitated. "That would be the end of us. All we can do is hope he doesn't make it, or that the progress is slow. We can't stop him."

Emma and Julian stared at each other. "What if we could find a warlock?" Emma suggested. "Someone who could help *you* get into the Silent City first?"

Livvy hesitated. "I like your enthusiasm," she said. "But the warlocks are all dead or demons."

"Hear me out," Emma said. She was thinking of Cristina, in the Unseelie Court: *It's not the ley lines. It's the blight.* "You were talking about how the demons came into Idris through patches of blight. We have those in our world too, though demons aren't coming through yet. And our warlocks are also getting sick—the oldest and most powerful first. They're not turning into demons—not yet, anyway—but the illness is the same."

"And?" Julian said. He was looking at her with thoughtful respect. Emma had always been praised for her fighting skills, but only Julian had been there to reassure her she was smart and capable, too. She realized suddenly how much she'd missed that.

"In our world, there's one warlock who is immune to the sickness," said Emma. "Tessa Gray. If she's immune here, too, she might be able to help us."

Livvy was staring. "There are rumors of the Last Warlock, but I've never seen Tessa here in Los Angeles. I don't even know if she's still alive."

"I have a way to contact her." Emma held up her hand. "This ring. Maybe it will work here. It's worth a shot."

Livvy looked from the ring to Emma. She spoke slowly. "I remember that ring. You used to wear it. Brother Zachariah gave it to you while we were in Manhattan, but it was lost when you—when Emma was lost."

A spark of hope flared in Emma's heart. "He gave it to me in my world too," she said. "It could work here if Tessa still has the other one."

Livvy didn't say anything. Emma had a feeling she'd long ago given up believing things were worth a shot.

"Let me just try," Emma said, and swung her left hand hard against one of the concrete pillars. The glass bauble in the ring smashed, and the metal of the ring darkened, suddenly splotched with markings like rust or blood. The prongs that had held the glass disappeared—the ring was now just a metal band.

Livvy exhaled. "Real magic," she said. "I haven't seen that in a long time."

"Seems like a good sign," said Julian. "If Tessa is still here, she might have powers that still work."

It seemed like a spiderweb-thin string to hang hope on, Emma thought. But what else did they have?

Livvy went over to one of the desks and returned with Emma's phone. "Here you go," she said a little reluctantly.

"Keep it if you want it," Emma said; she knew Julian was looking at her, his eyebrows raised in surprise. "Really—"

"The battery's dying anyway," Livvy said, but there was something else in her voice, something that said it hurt to look at the pictures of a life that had been taken from her. "Ty grew up so handsome," she added. "The girls must be all over him. Or the boys," she added with a sideways smile that faded quickly. "Anyway. You take it."

Emma put the phone into her pocket. As Livvy turned away, Emma thought she caught sight of the edge of a black Mark just under the collar of Livvy's T-shirt. She blinked—weren't there no Marks here?

It looked like the curlicue of a mourning rune.

Livvy flopped back down on the couch. "Well, there's no point waiting here," she said. "It'll just make us tense. You guys go and get some sleep. If nothing happens by tomorrow afternoon, we can regroup."

Emma and Julian made for the exit. At the door, Julian hesitated. "I was wondering," he said. "Is this place any better by daylight?"

Livvy had been studying her hands, with their patterns of scars.

She raised her eyes and for a moment they blazed, familiar Blackthorn blue.

"Just you wait," she said.

Pajamas didn't seem to be a thing in Thule. After showering, Julian sat on the bed in a pair of sweatpants and a T-shirt, staring at the painted metal window with its false silver stars. He was thinking of Mark. When Mark had been a captive of the Wild Hunt, every night he had counted out his brothers' and sisters' names on the points of light wheeling above.

In Thule you couldn't see the stars. What had Livvy done? How had she remembered them all? Or had it been less painful to try to forget? Mark had thought his siblings were alive and happy without him. Livvy knew they were dead or in thrall. Which was worse?

"She didn't ask," he said as Emma came out of the bathroom in her tank top and a pair of boxer briefs. "Livvy—she didn't ask about our world. Nothing at all."

Emma sank onto the bed beside him. She had pulled her hair back in a braid; he could feel the warmth of her and smell the soap on her skin. His insides tightened. "Can you blame her? Our world's not perfect. But it isn't *this*. It isn't a whole world of birthdays she missed, and growing up she didn't get to see, and comfort she never got."

"She's alive here, though," Julian said.

"Julian." Emma touched his face lightly. He wanted to lean into the touch but held himself back with a body-tensing effort. "She's *surviving* here."

"And there's a difference?"

She gave him a long look before dropping her hand and settling back against the pillows. "You know there is."

She lay on her side, tendrils of pale hair escaping from her braid, gold against the white pillows. Her eyes were the color of polished wood, her body curved like a violin. Julian wanted to grab his sketch pad, to draw her, the way he always had when his feelings for her grew too intense. His heart exploding paint and colors because he could not speak the words.

"Do you want me to sleep on the floor?" he asked. His voice was husky. Nothing he could do about that.

She shook her head, still looking at him with those enormous eyes. "I was thinking," she said. "If Shadowhunter magic is gone here . . . If seraph blades don't work, or angelic magic . . ."

"Then our *parabatai* bond is probably broken," he finished. "I thought of that too."

"But we can't be sure," she said. "I mean, I guess we could try to do something, to make something happen, the way we burned that church. . . ."

"Probably not a good idea to experiment with arson." Julian could feel his heart beating. Emma was leaning closer to him. He could see the smooth curve of her collarbone, the place where her tanned skin grew paler. He dragged his gaze away.

"We could try the other thing," she said. "You know. Kissing."

"Emma—"

"I feel it when we kiss." Her pupils were enormous. "I know you do too. The bond."

It was like having helium pumped into his blood. He felt light as air. "You're sure? You absolutely want this?"

"Yeah." She settled back farther into the pillows. She was looking up at him now, her stubborn chin tilted up, her elbows on the bed. Her legs sprawled out, long and glorious. He slid closer to her. He could see her pulse beating in her throat. Her lips parted, her voice low: "I want this."

He moved over her, not touching her yet, his body a whisper from hers. He saw her eyes darken. She wriggled under him, her legs sliding against his.

"Emma," he rasped. "What happened to that bra? You know, the enormous one?"

She grinned. "I went without."

The air in the room felt suddenly superheated. Julian tried to breathe normally, despite knowing that if he slid his hands up under Emma's tank top he would encounter only soft skin and bare curves.

But she hadn't asked him to do that. She'd asked for a kiss. He propped himself over her, a hand on either side of her head. Slowly, he lowered himself: exquisitely slowly, until their mouths were an inch apart. He could feel her warm breath against his face. Still, their bodies were barely touching. She moved restlessly under him, her fingers digging into the coverlet.

"Kiss me," she murmured, and he bent to brush his lips over hers—just a brush, the lightest of touches. She chased his lips with her own; he turned his face to the side, tracing the same warm, light touch along her jaw, her cheek. When he reached her mouth again she was gasping, her eyes half-closed. He drew her lower lip into his mouth, running his tongue along it, tracing the curve, the sensitive corners.

She gasped again, pressing her back deeper into the cushions, her body arching. He felt her breasts brush against his chest, sending a shot of heat directly to his groin. He dug his fingers into the mattress, willing himself to keep control. To give her only and exactly what she'd asked for.

A kiss.

He sucked and licked at her bottom lip, traced the bow shape of the upper. Licked along the seam of the two until her lips parted and he sealed his mouth to hers, all heat and wetness and the taste of her, mint and tea. She wrapped her hands around his biceps, arching up against him as they kissed on and on. Her body was soft and warm; she was moaning into his mouth, dragging her heels up the backs of his calves, her hands sliding to his shirt, fingers curling under—

She broke away. She was breathing as if she'd been running a marathon, her lips damp and pink from kissing, her cheeks flaming. "Holy f—" she began, then coughed and blushed. "Have you been *practicing*?"

"No," Julian said. He was proud of himself for managing an entire syllable. He decided to try out a sentence. "I have not."

"Okay," Emma breathed. "Okay. No one's on fire, no *parabatai* weirdness in evidence. That's about as much testing as I'm up for right now."

Julian rolled carefully onto his side. "But I can still sleep on the bed, right?"

Her lips curled into a smile. "I think you've earned that, yeah."

"I can scooch all the way to the edge," he offered.

"Don't push it, Julian," she said, and rolled against him, her body curling into his. He put his arms tentatively around her, and she burrowed closer, closing her eyes.

"Emma?" he said.

No answer.

He couldn't believe it. She was asleep. Breathing softly and regularly, her small cold nose pressed into his collarbone. She was asleep, and he felt like his whole body was burning up. The shuddering waves of pleasure and desire that had rolled over him just from kissing her still stunned him.

That had felt good. Almost euphorically good. And not just because of what had bloomed inside his own cells, his own skin. It had been Emma, the noises she'd made, the way she'd touched him. It wasn't the *parabatai* bond, but it was *their* bond. It was the pleasure he'd given her, mirrored back at him a thousandfold. It was everything he hadn't been able to feel since the spell.

The Queen's voice came, unwanted, silvery as a bell and flawed with malice:

You are in the cage, boy.

He shivered and drew Emma closer.

19
The Jewelled Dead

Emma dreamed of fire and thunder, and was woken by the sound of splintering wood. At least, it *sounded* like the wood was splintering. When she sat up, groggy and confused, Julian's arm still around her waist, she realized it was someone knocking very, very hard at the bedroom door.

Julian moved, groaning softly in his sleep; Emma extricated herself and padded over to throw the door open, expecting Cameron or Livvy.

It was Diana.

The sight of her acted like a shot of caffeine. She was all in black, from her black motorcycle boots to her leather pants and jacket. Her hair was secured in a tight, curly ponytail at the back of her head. She looked intimidating, but Emma didn't care much: She gave a little yelp and threw her arms around Diana, who made a loud noise of surprise.

"Whoa there, stranger," she said. "What's going on?"

"Sorry." Julian had appeared and gently peeled Emma away. "In our world, you're our tutor."

"Oh, right. Your alternate dimension. Livvy told me about it when I got back from my pharmacy run." Diana raised her eyebrows. "Wild."

"Do you not know us at all here?" Emma asked with some disappointment.

"Not since you were little kids. I saw you in the Accords Hall during the Dark War, before they Portaled all the children away. You were good little fighters," she added. "Then I heard you got Endarkened. I didn't expect I'd see you again unless you were pointing the business end of a gun at me."

"Well," Emma said. "Good surprise, huh?"

Diana looked darkly amused. "Come on. You can tell me what I'm like in your world while I take you to the lobby."

They threw on clothes—boots, long-sleeved shirts, bomber jackets. Emma wondered where the rebels got their supplies. Her black pants felt like they were made out of canvas or something else similarly thick and itchy. The boots were cool, though, and she had to admit she liked the way Julian wore his faded shirt and army pants. They clung to his lean, muscular body in a way that made her try not to think about the previous night.

As they left the room, Julian tore a page from his sketchbook and tucked it into his jacket pocket. "For luck," he said.

They joined Diana in the hallway, their boots clomping loudly on the polished wood. "In our world," Emma said, as they headed down a set of stairs, "you're dating a faerie."

Diana frowned. "A faerie? Why would I be dating a traitor?"

"Things are a little more complicated at home."

"Things are pretty complicated here, kid," Diana said as they reached the ground floor. "Come on through."

They passed under a brick archway and into a massive room full of furniture that looked as if it had been scrounged from different offices. There were modern steel-and-leather couches, and vintage patchwork and velvet ones. Armchairs made of cotton and chintz, some in good shape and some torn up; cheap chipboard tables on metal legs, laid end to end to create a sort of boardroom effect.

There was a crowd in the room: Emma saw Livvy and Cameron, Bat and Maia, and a few familiar faces—Divya Joshi and Rayan Maduabuchi, one or two of the older Los Angeles Conclave members. They were all staring at the east wall of the room—ordinary brick and sandstone, it was currently burning with huge, fiery letters, reaching from one end of the wall to the other.

SEEK CHURCH.

"Do you understand it?" Diana said. "Nobody here does. Churches aren't doing well in this world. They're all deconsecrated and full of demons."

"Everyone's so quiet," Emma said, whispering herself. "Are they—scared?"

"Not really," said Diana. "I think it's just been so long since any of us have seen magic."

Livvy pushed her way through the crowd toward them, leaving Cameron behind. "Is this from Tessa Gray?" she demanded, eyes wide, as she reached them. "Is this a response to that summons? Did it *work?*"

"Yeah," Julian said. "I'm pretty sure that's exactly what this is. Tessa wants us to come to her."

"Not too trusting," said Diana. "She must have some sense."

"But the church part?" Livvy looked puzzled. "What church does she mean?"

"She means a cat," said Julian.

"And please don't say all the cats are dead," said Emma. "I'm not sure I can cope with feline death on a massive scale."

"Cats actually do okay here," said Diana. "They're a little demony themselves."

Livvy waved her hands. "Can we stick to specifics? What do you mean, a cat?"

"An unusual cat," said Julian. "His name's Church. He belonged to Jem Carstairs once, and he used to live with us in the Institute after the Dark War."

"We can't go to the Institute," said Emma. "It's full of evil Ashdowns."

"Yeah, but Church was a wandering cat—you remember," Julian said. "He didn't really live in the Institute with us. He padded around on the beach and stopped by whenever he felt like it. And he led us where he wanted us to go. If we find Church—he could lead us to Tessa."

"Tessa and Brother Zachariah did have a foul-tempered cat with them in New York, after the war," said Livvy.

"I'll go with you to the beach," Diana said.

"That means you have to cross the whole city in daylight," Livvy said. "I don't like it."

"Would it be safer to go at night?" said Julian.

"No, that's even worse," Livvy said.

"Hey," said a soft voice.

Emma turned to see a boy with wavy hair and light brown skin looking at them with a mixture of annoyance and—no, it was mostly just annoyance.

"Raphael Santiago?" she said.

She recognized him from the Dark War, from pictures in history books about its heroes. Emma had always thought that Raphael, who had made his famous sacrifice to save Magnus Bane's life, had an angelic face. The crown of curls, the cross scar at his throat, and the wide eyes in the child-round face were the same. She had not expected the sardonic expression overlaying all that.

"I know who you are," Emma said.

He didn't look impressed. "I know who you are too. You're those Endarkened who always make a disgusting display of yourselves. I realize you are evil, but why can't you be more discreet?"

"That's really not us," said Julian. "Those are different people."

"So you say," said Raphael. "This is a stupid plan and you are all going to die. I see all the Angel's gifts are truly gone, leaving only the Nephilim gift of remarkable short-sightedness. Out of the demonic frying pan, right back into the demonic frying pan."

"Are you saying we shouldn't answer Tessa's summons?" said Emma, who was starting to get annoyed.

"Raphael's just in a bad mood," said Livvy. She ruffled Raphael's curly hair. "Aren't you in a bad mood?" she cooed.

Raphael glared daggers at her. Livvy smiled.

"I didn't say you should or shouldn't do anything," Raphael snapped. "Go ahead and look for Tessa. But you might want my help. You're a lot more likely to make it across the city if you have transportation. But my help's not for free."

"Annoyingly, everything he says is true," Livvy admitted.

"Okay," said Julian. "What do you want, vampire?"

"Information," said Raphael. "In your world, is my city still standing? New York."

Julian nodded.

"Am I alive?" Raphael said.

"No," said Emma. There didn't seem to be any point in beating around the bush.

Raphael paused only for a moment. "Then who is the leader of the New York vampire clan there?" said Raphael.

"Lily Chen," Emma said.

Raphael smiled, surprising her. It was a real smile, with real fondness in it. Emma felt herself soften. "In our world, you're a hero. You sacrificed your life so Magnus could live," she said.

Raphael looked horrified. "Tell me you're not talking about Magnus Bane. Tell me you're talking about a much cooler Magnus. I would never do that. If I did do that, I would never want anybody to talk about it. I cannot believe Magnus would shame me by talking about that."

Julian's mouth twitched at the corner. "He named his child for you. Rafael Santiago Lightwood-Bane."

"That is revolting. So everybody knows? I am so embarrassed," said Raphael. He looked at Diana. "Under a tarp in the garage are several of my motorcycles. Take two of them. Do not crash them or I will be very angry."

"Noted," said Diana. "We'll have them back by nightfall."

"Shouldn't you be asleep, Raphael?" said Emma, suddenly struck. "You're a vampire. It's daytime."

Raphael smiled coldly. "Oh, little Shadowhunter," he said. "Wait until you see the sun."

They found the motorcycles in the garage, as Raphael had said they would, and Divya opened the metal door so they could wheel the cycles onto the street. She closed it up quickly after them, and to the sound of the clanging and whirring of gears, Julian looked up and saw the sky.

His first thought was that he should step in front of Emma, protect her somehow from the ruins of the sun. His second was a fragmented memory of a piece of poetry his uncle had taught him. *Morn came and went—and came, and brought no day.*

The sun was a red-black cinder, glowing dully against a bank of streaky clouds. It cast an ugly light—a reddish-brown light, as if they were seeing the world through blood-tinted water. The air was thick and carried the taste of dirt and copper on it.

They were on what Julian guessed was West Broadway, the street much less crowded than it had been the night before. The occasional shadow slunk in and out of the gaps between buildings, and the convenience store offering blood milk shakes was, surprisingly, open. Something was sitting behind the counter, reading an old magazine, but it wasn't shaped like a human being.

Trash blew up and down the mostly empty street, carried on the heated wind. This kind of weather came sometimes in Los Angeles, when the wind blew from the desert. Los Angelenos called them "devil winds" or "murder winds." Maybe they came all the time in Thule.

"You ready?" said Diana, throwing one leg over her cycle and gesturing to the second one.

Julian had never ridden a motorcycle. He was willing to have a whack at it, but Emma had already climbed on. She zipped up the leather jacket she'd taken from the wardrobe and crooked a finger at Julian. "Mark showed me how to ride one of these," she said. "Remember?"

Julian remembered. He remembered how jealous of Mark he'd been too—Mark, who could flirt with Emma casually. Who could kiss her, embrace her, while Julian had to treat her like a bomb that would explode if he touched her. If they touched each other.

But not here, he reminded himself. This might be hell, but they weren't *parabatai* here. He settled himself on the cycle behind Emma and slipped his arms around her waist. She had a Glock thrust through her belt, just like he did.

She reached down to brush her fingers across his clasped hands where they rested above her belt. He ducked his head and kissed the back of her neck.

She shivered.

"Enough, you guys," Diana said. "Let's go."

She took off and Emma started up their own cycle, pulling in the clutch while holding down the start button. The engine revved with a loud noise and they were hurtling after Diana down the deserted street. Diana gunned her cycle toward a hill; Emma crouched down low, and Julian did the same. "Hold on," Emma shouted into the wind, and their cycle lifted off the ground, angling into the air. The ground fell away below them, and they were soaring, Diana beside them. Julian couldn't help thinking of the Wild Hunt, of flying through the air above a sleeping England, riding a path of wind and stars.

But this was different. From above, they could see the utter destruction of the city clearly. The sky was filled with wheeling dark figures—other airborne motorcycles, and demons abroad at daylight, protected by the dim sun and the thick cover of clouds. Fires burned at intervals, smoke swirling up from the Miracle Mile. The streets around Beverly Hills had been dammed up and flooded, forming a sort of moat around Bel Air, and as they soared over it, Julian gazed down into the churning water. A massive sea monster, hideous and humped, was pulling its way along the moat by its tentacles. It threw back its head and howled, and Julian glimpsed a black, yawning mouth, studded with teeth like a great white shark's.

They soared over Wilshire, which had become a boulevard of horrors. Julian glimpsed a human musician dangling from puppet strings made of his own nerves and blood vessels, being forced to play a mandolin even as he screamed in agony. A demon lounged at a covered table where xylophones of human ribs were for sale, another—a massive one-eyed serpent—coiled around a "lemonade" stand where vampires stepped up for a wedge of lemon and a bite of a screaming, terrified human.

Julian closed his eyes.

When he opened them again, they were flying north over the highway by the sea. At least here it was mostly deserted, though they could see down into the ruins of the once-wealthy houses that had lined the shores of Malibu. They were overgrown now, their swimming pools empty or full of black water. Even the ocean looked different. In the dim daylight the water was black and churning, without fish or seaweed to be seen.

He felt Emma tense. Her words were torn away by the wind, but he caught enough of them to understand. "Julian—the *Institute*."

He glanced to the east. There it was, their Institute, glass and stone and steel, rising from the scrub grass of the Santa Monica Mountains. His heart lurched with yearning. It seemed so familiar, even under the red-orange hell glow of the dying sun.

But no—two flags flew from the Institute's roof. One showed the star-in-circle symbol of Sebastian, and the other the family crest of the Ashdowns: an ash tree surrounded by leaves.

He was glad when Emma swung the cycle around and the Institute was no longer in view.

Diana was ahead of them, her cycle descending toward the beach. She landed with a few puffs of sand and turned to watch as Emma and Julian lurched down after her with considerable less grace. They hit the sand with enough force to snap Julian's teeth sharply together.

"Ouch," he said.

Emma swung around, her cheeks pink, her hair windblown. "You think you could do better?"

"No," he said, and kissed her cheek.

Her face turned a darker pink, and Diana made an exasperated noise. "You two are almost as bad as the Endarkened versions of yourselves. Now, come on—we have to hide these cycles."

As Julian rolled their cycle under a rock overhang, he realized he didn't mind Diana's teasing at all. He hadn't minded Cameron's teasing about the bed, either. It was all a reminder that here, he and Emma had a completely normal relationship—nothing secret, nothing forbidden. Nothing dangerous.

It was perhaps the only thing in Thule that *was* ordinary, but in this world without angels, it felt like a blessing.

"Well, here we are," Diana said, once the cycles were hidden. "Looking for a cat on a beach."

"Church usually comes to us," said Julian, glancing around. "It looks—almost ordinary here."

"I wouldn't go in the water," said Diana darkly. "But yeah, Sebastian seems to like the beach. Mostly he leaves it alone and uses it for ceremonies and executions."

Emma began to make cooing, clicking kitty-come-here noises.

"Don't blame me if you summon a cat demon," said Diana. She stretched, the joints in her wrists popping audibly. "A week to get back from Mexico City, and now this, two days after I get home," she said, half to herself. "I really thought I might get a chance to rest. Silly me."

Emma whirled around. "Mexico City?" she demanded. "Did you—do you know if Cristina Mendoza Rosales is all right?"

"Cristina Rosales? The Rose of Mexico?" Diana said, looking surprised. "Because of her, Mexico City is one of the few Shadowhunter strongholds left. I mean, there's no angelic magic, but they patrol, they keep the demons down. The Rosales family are a resistance legend."

"I knew it," Emma said. She wiped hastily at her damp face. "I *knew* it."

"Are there other pockets? Places people are resisting?" Julian said.

"Livvy's doing what she can here," said Diana somewhat pointedly. "There'd be a lot more dead if not for her. We hear things about Jerusalem—Singapore—Sri Lanka. Oh, and Bangkok, which doesn't surprise me. I know that city pretty well since I transitioned there."

Emma looked puzzled. "What do you mean, transitioned?"

"I'm transgender," Diana said, puzzled. "You must know that if you knew me in your world."

"Right," Julian said hastily. "We just didn't know about the Bangkok thing."

Diana looked even more puzzled. "But when I—" She broke off. "Is that what I think it is?"

She pointed. Sitting on top of a nearby boulder was a cat. Not just any cat—an angry-looking blue Persian cat with an aggressively fluffed-out tail.

"Church!" Emma scooped him up in her arms, and Church did what he usually did. He went limp.

"Is that cat dead?" Diana demanded.

"No, he isn't," Emma cooed, and kissed his furry face. Church went limper. "He just hates affection."

Diana shook her head. She seemed completely unaffected by having told them something that in their world was a secret she had guarded. Guilt and annoyance with himself were rising inside Julian; he tried to shove them down. Now wasn't the time, nor would it be right to burden this Diana with his feelings.

"I wuv you," Emma said to Church. "I wuv you very much."

Church wiggled out of her grasp and meowed. He padded toward Julian, meowed again, and then turned to frisk away along the beach.

"He wants us to follow him," Julian said, clomping after Church. His enormous boots were a pain when it came to walking on sand. He heard Diana mutter something about how if she'd wanted to run around after deranged animals, she would have volunteered for the zoo patrol, but she headed after them anyway.

They trailed Church along the inner bluffs until they reached a path that led to a hole in the cliff face. Julian knew it well. When you grew up on the beach, you explored every rock, arch, cove, and cave. This one led to an impressive but empty cave, if he recalled correctly. He and Emma had once dragged a table in there and held meetings before they'd gotten bored with having a secret society with only two people in it.

Church scrambled up to the entrance of the cave and meowed loudly. There was a grinding sound like stone moving aside, and a figure stepped out of the shadows.

It was a man with dark hair, in long parchment robes. His cheeks were scarred, his eyes dark, full of wisdom and sorrow.

"Jem!" Emma screamed, and began to run up the path, her face shining with eagerness.

Jem held up his hand. His palms were scarred with runes, and Julian ached to see them—runes, in this runeless place. Insight. Quietude. Courage.

And then Jem began to change. Diana swore and yanked a pistol from her belt as a ripple went over Jem's features and the parchment robes slid to the ground. His hair lightened and tumbled, long and waving, to the middle of his back; his eyes turned gray and long-lashed, his figure curved and feminine inside a plain gray dress.

Diana cocked the pistol. "Who are you?"

Emma had stopped in the middle of the path. She blinked back tears and said, "This is her. The Last Warlock. This is Tessa Gray."

Tessa had set the inside of the cave up as cozily as possible. There was a small fireplace, whose smoke went up a flue built into the rocks. The stone floor was brushed clean and dotted with carpets; there was a small sleeping annex and multiple chairs covered in cushions and soft pillows. There was even a little kitchen with a small range, a refrigerator humming along without being plugged into anything, and a wooden table already set with teacups and a loaf of warm sweet bread.

Realizing she hadn't had breakfast, Emma wondered if it would be a faux pas to leap on the bread and devour it. Probably.

"Sit down and eat," Tessa said, as if reading her mind. As they settled around the table, Church climbed into Emma's lap, rolled onto his back, and promptly fell asleep with his feet in the air.

Diana tore off a hunk of the bread and stuffed it in her mouth. She closed her eyes in bliss. "Oh. My. God."

Emma decided that was her cue. For the next minute, she shut out the world around her and entered a blissful carb coma. The last time she'd eaten real food was in that clearing with Julian, and this was warm and home-cooked and felt like the taste of hope.

When she opened her eyes, she realized Julian hadn't even taken a bite yet. He was looking at Tessa—that Julian look that seemed completely innocent but actually meant he was taking someone's measure, assessing their weaknesses, and deciding if he trusted them.

It was pretty hot, actually. Emma sucked a piece of sugar off her thumb and tried not to smile to herself.

"You must be wondering who we are," he said as Tessa poured their tea.

"No." Tessa set the teapot down and took a seat, wrapping a shawl around her shoulders. "I know who you are. You are Emma Carstairs and Julian Blackthorn, but not the ones from this world."

"You already know that?" said Diana in surprise.

"I see as a warlock sees," said Tessa. "I know they do not belong here." She indicated Julian and Emma. "And I have seen, a little, into other worlds—into their world in particular. It is closer to this one than we might like to think."

"What do you mean?" Julian said. "They seem pretty different to me."

"There are stress points in history," said Tessa. "Places where a great deal of chance is at play. Battles, peace treaties, marriages. That sort of thing. That's where timelines are likely to split. Our two timelines split at the Battle of the Burren. In your world, the demon Lilith was too weak to render Sebastian Morgenstern much help. In Thule, another demon gave aid and strength to Lilith. She was able to kill Clary Fairchild, and that's where our timelines split—only seven years ago."

"So this is what our world would be like without Clary," said Emma, remembering all the times she'd heard people—mostly men—say that Clary wasn't a hero, that she hadn't done much that deserved to be praised, that she was selfish, even worthless, just a girl who'd been in the right places at the right times.

"Yes," said Tessa. "Interesting, isn't it? I gather that in your world, Jace Herondale is a hero. Here he is a monster second only to Sebastian."

"Doesn't he even care that Sebastian let Lilith kill Clary?" demanded Emma. "Even when Jace was in thrall to Sebastian in our world, he loved Clary."

"Sebastian claims the death of Clary was not what he wanted," said Tessa. "He says he murdered Lilith as revenge for her taking of Clary's life."

"Not sure anyone believes that but Jace," said Diana.

"He's the only one who has to," said Tessa. She ran her finger around the rim of her teacup. "I must apologize for testing you," she said abruptly. "I appeared as Jem when you arrived because I knew that the real Emma Carstairs would be delighted to see him, while anyone aligned with Sebastian would be horrified at the sight of a Silent Brother."

"Jem . . . ?" Emma whispered. She knew what Livvy had said, that all the Brothers were gone, but still she had hoped.

Tessa didn't look up. "He died in the attempt to seal the Silent City. It was successful, but he gave his life to hold off Sebastian's Endarkened as the Brothers made their last stand to protect the Mortal Instruments."

"I'm sorry," Julian said. Emma remembered Tessa and Jem in her own world, eyes only for each other.

Tessa cleared her throat. "Sebastian already has possession of the Mortal Mirror—Lake Lyn. It is surrounded by demons, ten thousand strong. None can go anywhere near it."

"Why is he guarding the lake so fiercely?" said Emma. "If no one can get to any of the Mortal Instruments—"

"As the warlocks were sickening, we found that the water of Lake Lyn could neutralize the blight that was eating through our world. We raced there to collect the water. But by the time we arrived at the lake, Sebastian had surrounded it with countless demons."

Emma and Julian exchanged a look. "With the blight gone, would the warlocks have been cured?"

"We believe so," said Tessa. "We had a small amount of the water and used it to cure the blight around the Spiral Labyrinth. We even gave it to some warlocks, mixed with ordinary water, and they began to improve. But it simply wasn't enough. The warlocks began to sicken and turn again. We could not save them."

Emma's heart thumped. If the water of Lake Lyn had neutralized some of the blight here in Thule—if it had helped the warlocks, even as this world was turning to demonic poison all around them—surely the water of their own Lake Lyn, in their own world, might be a cure?

They needed to get home more desperately than ever. But first—

"We need your help," Emma said. "That's why we called on you."

"I guessed that." Tessa rested her chin in her hand. She looked young, no more than twenty, though Emma knew she was over a hundred. "Is it that you want to get back to your world?"

"It's not just that," Julian said. "We need to get into the Silent City. We have to get to the Mortal Cup and the Mortal Sword before Sebastian does."

"And then what?" Tessa said.

"And then we destroy them so Sebastian can't use them," said Emma.

Tessa raised her eyebrows. "Destroy the Mortal Instruments? They're very nearly indestructible."

Emma thought of the Mortal Sword shattering under Cortana's blade. "If you open up a Portal back to our world, we can take them through with us. Sebastian will never be able to find them."

"If it was that simple," Tessa said sharply, "I would have already opened a Portal, leaped through it, and taken the Cup and Sword with me. To open a Portal between worlds—that is complex, powerful magic, far beyond most warlocks. I can see into your world, but I cannot reach it."

"But you can get into the Silent City, right?" said Emma.

"I believe so, though I have not tried," said Tessa. "I thought the Sword and the Cup were safe there. The Silent Brothers died to protect the Instruments and to remove them would have left them vulnerable to Sebastian. Yet now he is close to breaking the seal on the doors." She frowned. "If you can truly bring the Instruments back to your world then they would be safer there. But without the knowledge that a Portal can be opened, there is another way to end the threat."

"What do you mean?" said Julian. "There's nothing we could do with the Sword or Cup here, besides demonic magic."

"People used to say that the Mortal Sword could kill Sebastian," said Diana, her gaze sharp. "But that's not true, is it? I was at the last battle of Idris. I saw Isabelle Lightwood take up the Mortal Sword and deal Sebastian an incredible blow. He wasn't even nicked. He struck her down instead."

"*Ave atque vale*, Isabelle Lightwood." Tessa closed her eyes. "You have to understand. By then the invulnerability granted to Sebastian by Lilith had grown so strong no warrior of this earth could slay him. But there is something most do not know. Even Sebastian does not know it." She opened her eyes. "He is tied to Thule, and Thule to him. A warrior *of this world* cannot slay him with the Sword. But the Silent Brothers knew that did not hold true for a warrior who was not of Thule. They locked the Sword away, hoping for a day when a warrior would arrive from Heaven and end Sebastian's reign."

For a long moment, she gazed intently at Emma and Julian.

"We're not from Heaven," Emma said. "Despite what some bad pickup lines I've heard over the years might have you believe."

"Seems like Heaven compared to here," said Diana.

"We can't wait forever to be rescued by angels," Tessa said. "This is a gift, you being here."

"Let's be clear." Julian took a bite of bread. His face was expressionless but Emma could read his eyes, knew the gears were whirling in his brain. "You're asking us to kill Sebastian."

"I have to ask," Tessa said. "I have to make Jem's sacrifice mean something."

"In our world," Julian said, "the bond between Jace and Sebastian meant that killing Jace would destroy Sebastian, and the other way around as well. If we—"

Tessa shook her head. "There was a point at which that was true here, when Sebastian believed it protected him from the Clave. There is no Clave now, nor does that aspect of their bond remain."

"I get it," said Emma. "But with how far gone this world is—would just killing Sebastian make that much of a difference?"

Tessa leaned back in her chair. "In your world, what happened when Sebastian died?"

"It was the end of the Endarkened," Emma said, though she had a feeling Tessa already knew that.

"That would give us a fighting chance," Tessa said. "Sebastian can't do everything himself. He leaves most of the dirty work to the Endarkened and the Forsworn." She glanced at Diana. "I know you agree."

"Maybe," Diana said. "But going after Sebastian seems like a suicide mission."

"I wouldn't ask if there were any other choices," Tessa said quietly. She turned to Emma and Julian. "As you've requested, I will break the seal and open the Silent City for you. And I will do whatever I can to get you home. All I ask is that if you get a chance, an opening—you kill Sebastian."

Emma looked across the table at Julian. In his clear blue-green eyes she could see both his desire to agree to what Tessa was asking and his fear that it would put her, Emma, in danger.

"I know Thule isn't your world, but it's only a breath away,"

Tessa said. "If I could save the Jem who lives in your world, I would. And now you have a chance to save your sister here."

In Tessa's voice, Emma heard that she understood that the Livvy in their world was dead.

"She is safe in the Bradbury, but for how long? How safe are any of us? Any safety is temporary as long as Sebastian lives."

Ignoring Church's indignant meow, Emma reached across the table and put her hand over Julian's. *Don't fear for me*, parabatai, she thought. *This is a chance for both of us. For you to save Livvy as you could not in our world, and for me to avenge my parents, as I could not either.*

"We'll do it," she said, and Julian's eyes blazed like tinder set alight. "Of course we will. Just tell us what we have to do."

As they climbed onto the cycles, Diana warned them they'd be driving back on surface streets, not flying—the closer it got to nightfall, she said, the more full the skies were of demons. Even the vampires stayed out of the air after dark.

Emma was surprised to discover Diana had woken them up later in the day than she'd thought. The nuances of morning light, afternoon light, and evening light were lost here: There was only the dying sun and the blood moon. As their motorcycles raced along the Pacific Coast Highway, the moon rose sluggishly, barely illuminating the road ahead. Instead of sparkling on top of the waves, the moonlight turned the water an even more poisonous color—no longer Blackthorn blue-green, but ashy black.

Emma was glad for the warmth of Julian's arms around her as they turned off the highway and onto Wilshire. To be this close to all that was ruined was painful. She knew these streets. She had been to this supermarket to pick up cereal for Tavvy: It was a ruin of smashed wood and broken beams now, where a few unsworn humans huddled around watch fires, their faces haggard with desperation and hunger. And there had been a candy store on this corner, where now a demon proprietor stood watch over rows of glass tanks in which drowned bodies floated. Every once in a while he would plunge a ladle into one of the tanks, pour some of the viscous water into a bowl, and sell it to a demonic passerby.

How long could Thule go on like this? Emma wondered as they rolled along the Miracle Mile. The tall office buildings here stood empty, their windows shattered. The streets were deserted. Humans were being hunted to extinction, and just like Raphael, she doubted Sebastian had another world full of fresh blood and meat up his sleeve. What happened when they were all gone? Did the demons turn on the Endarkened? On the vampires? Would they move on to another world, leaving Sebastian to rule over emptiness?

"Slow down," Julian said in her ear, and she realized that while she'd been musing, they'd reached a crowded and well-lit section of street. "Checkpoint."

She swore silently and pulled in behind Diana. The area was buzzing—Endarkened wandered up and down the street, and the bars and restaurants here were basically intact, some of them lit up blue and green and acid yellow. Emma could even hear atonal, wailing music.

There were black-and-white barriers up in front of them, blocking the road. A two-legged lizard demon with a circle of black spider's eyes ringing its scaled head loped out of a small booth and over to Diana.

"I'm not letting some demon lick me," muttered Emma. "It's not happening."

"I'm pretty sure it was just licking Cameron to make sure his tattoo was real."

"Sure," said Emma. "That's its story."

Diana turned around on her bike and gave them a tight, artificial grin. Emma's heart started to beat faster. She didn't like the look of that smile.

The lizard demon loped toward them. It was massive, at least nine feet tall and half again as wide. It seemed to be wearing a police uniform, though Emma had no idea where it had gotten one that would fit.

"The boss has been looking for you all day," it slurred. Emma guessed its mouth wasn't really shaped for human speech. "Where you been?"

"The boss?" Emma echoed.

Fortunately, the lizard was too stupid to be suspicious. "The Fallen Star," it slurred. "Sebastian Morgenstern. He wants to talk to you both."

20
The Hours Are Breathing

Sebastian wants to talk to us? **Emma thought with horror, and** then, with a duller pang of realization: *It thinks we're the Endarkened versions of ourselves.* Well, that explained Diana's expression.

Julian's fingers gripped Emma's arm tightly. He slid casually off the cycle. "Okay," he said. "Where's the boss at?"

The lizard demon drew a paper bag out of its breast pocket. The bag seemed to be full of wriggling spiders. It popped one into its mouth and chewed while Emma's stomach lurched.

"In the old nightclub," it said around a crunchy mouthful of spider, and pointed toward a black glass-and-steel low-slung building. A dull red carpet was spread out on the pavement in front of the entrance. "Go. I watch your motorcycle."

Emma slid off the cycle, feeling as if ice had invaded her veins. Neither she nor Julian looked at each other; somehow both of them were crossing the street, striding along next to each other as if nothing unusual were happening.

Sebastian knows who we really are, Emma thought. *He knows, and he's going to kill us.*

She kept walking. They reached the pavement, and she heard

the roar of a motorcycle starting up; she turned to see Diana speeding away from the checkpoint. She knew why Diana had needed to go, and didn't blame her, but the sight still sent a cold stab through her chest: They were alone.

The nightclub was guarded by Iblis demons, who gave them a casual once-over and let them pass through the doors into a narrow corridor lined with mirrors. Emma could see her own reflection: She looked starkly pale, her mouth a tight line. That was bad. She had to relax. Julian, beside her, looked calm and collected, his hair ruffled from the motorcycle but otherwise nothing out of place.

He took her hand as the corridor opened up into a massive room. Warmth seemed to flow from him, through Emma's hand, into her veins; she took a deep, harsh breath as a wave of cold air smacked into them.

The nightclub was silvery-white and black, a dark fairyland of ice. A long bar carved from a block of ice ran along one wall. Cascades of frozen water, polar blue and arctic green, spilled from the ceiling, turning the dance floor into a labyrinth of glimmering sheets.

Julian's hand tightened on Emma's. She glanced down; the floor underneath them was solid ice, and beneath the ice she could see the shadows of trapped bodies—here the shape of a hand, there a screaming, frozen face. Her chest tightened. *We are walking on the bodies of the dead,* she thought.

Julian glanced sideways at her, shook his head slightly as if to say, *We can't think about that right now.*

Compartmentalizing, she thought as they headed toward a roped-off area at the back of the club. That was how Julian got through things. Pushing down thoughts, walling them off, living in the moment of the act that had become his reality.

She did her best to shove the thoughts of the dead away as they ducked under the ropes and found themselves in an area full of couches and chairs upholstered in ice-blue velvet. Sprawled in the largest armchair was Sebastian.

Up close, he was clearly older than the boy Emma remembered from her world. He was broader, his jaw more square, his eyes tar black. He wore a crisp black designer suit with a pattern of roses on the lapels, a thick fur coat draped over it. His ice-white hair mixed with the pale gold fur; if Emma hadn't known who he was and hated him, she would have thought he was beautiful, a wintry prince.

Standing beside him, his fingers resting lightly on the back of Sebastian's chair, was Jace. He too wore a black suit, and when he turned slightly, Emma saw the strap of a holster beneath it. There were leather gauntlets on his wrists, under the sharp cuffs of his jacket. She would have bet he was carrying several knives.

Is he Sebastian's bodyguard? she wondered. *Does it amuse Sebastian to keep one of the Clave's heroes as a sort of pet, bound to his side?*

And then there was Ash. Wearing jeans and a T-shirt, sprawled in a chair some distance away with an electronic device in his hands, he seemed to be playing a video game. The light from the game came and went, illuminating his sharp-featured face, the points of his ears.

Sebastian's cold gaze swept over Emma and Julian. Emma felt her whole body tense. She knew their runes were covered by fabric and concealer, but she still felt as if Sebastian could see right through her. As if he'd know immediately they weren't Endarkened.

"If it isn't the two lovebirds," he drawled. He glanced at Emma. "I haven't really seen your face before. Your friend here's been too busy sucking it."

Julian replied in a flat monotone. "Sorry to have annoyed you, sir."

"It doesn't annoy me," Sebastian said. "Just an observation." He settled back in his chair. "I prefer redheads myself."

A flicker of something went over Jace's face. It was gone too quickly for Emma to guess at its meaning. Ash looked up, though, and Emma tensed. If Ash recognized them . . .

He glanced back down at his game, his expression evincing no interest.

Emma was finding it hard not to shiver. The cold was intense, and Sebastian's gaze colder still. He templed his fingers under his chin. "Rumors have been swirling," he said, "that a certain Livia Blackthorn is raising a pathetic little rebellion downtown."

Emma's stomach lurched.

"She's nothing to us," Julian said quickly. He sounded like he meant it too.

"Of course not," said Sebastian. "But you were once her brother and her friend. Humans are regrettably sentimental. She might be tricked into trusting you."

"Livvy would never trust a pair of Endarkened," Emma said, and froze. It was the wrong thing to say.

Jace's golden eyes narrowed with suspicion. He began to speak, but Sebastian cut him off with a dismissive wave. "Not now, Jace."

Jace's expression went blank. He turned away from Sebastian and went to Ash, leaning over the back of his chair to point out something on his game screen. Ash nodded.

It would almost have looked like a sweet brotherly moment if it hadn't been so screwed up and awful. If the chandelier overhead hadn't been made of frozen human arms, each one gripping a torch that spat demonic light. If Emma could forget the faces beneath the floor.

"What Emma means is that Livvy's always been cunning," said Julian. "In a low sort of way."

"Interesting," said Sebastian. "I tend to approve of low cunning, though not when directed at me, of course."

"We know her very well," said Julian. "I'm sure we can suss out her little rebellion's location without much trouble."

Sebastian smirked. "I like your confidence," he said. "You wouldn't believe what I—" He broke off with a frown. "Is that damn dog barking again?"

It *was* a dog barking. A few seconds later, a black-and-white terrier bounded into the room on the end of a long leash. At the other end of the leash was a woman with long dark hair.

It was Annabel Blackthorn.

She wore a red dress without sleeves, though she must have been freezing in the cold air. Her skin was dead white.

Seeing Emma and Julian, she went even whiter. Her grip tightened on the dog's leash.

Adrenaline spilled through Emma's veins. Annabel was going to spill, she was going to turn them in. She had no reason not to. And then Sebastian would kill them. *I swear,* Emma thought, *I will find a way to make him bleed before I die.*

I will find a way to make them both bleed.

"I'm sorry," Annabel said petulantly. "He wanted to see Ash. Didn't you, Malcolm?"

Even Julian's expression flickered at that. Emma watched in horror as Annabel bent down to rub the dog's ears. It looked up at her with wide lavender eyes and barked again.

Malcolm Fade, High Warlock of Los Angeles, was now a demon terrier.

"Get your nasty familiar out of here," Sebastian snapped. "I'm doing business. If Ash needs something, he'll call on you, Annabel. He's practically a grown man. He no longer requires a nursemaid."

"Everyone needs a mother," Annabel said. "Don't you, Ash?"

Ash said nothing. He was immersed in his game. With an irritated sigh, Annabel stalked out of the room, Malcolm trotting behind her.

"As I was saying." Sebastian's face was tight with annoyance. "Annabel is one of my best torturers—you wouldn't believe the creative skill she can display with a single knife and a Shadowhunter—but like the rest of those around me, she is too vulnerable to her emotions. I don't know why people don't just understand what's best for them."

"If they did, they wouldn't need leaders," said Julian. "Like you."

Sebastian gave him a considering look. "I suppose that's true. But it is like a weight of responsibility. Crushing me. You understand."

"Let us seek out Livia for you," Julian said. "We'll go take care of the threat and bring you back her head."

Sebastian looked pleased. He glanced at Emma. "You don't talk much, do you?"

I can't, Emma thought. *I can't stand here and lie and pretend like Julian. I can't.*

But the warmth of Julian's hand was still in hers, the strength of their bond—even when it was no longer magical—lifting her chin, setting her jaw hard. She took her hand out of Julian's and slowly, deliberately, cracked her knuckles.

"I prefer killing," she said. "'Say it with bullets,' that's my motto."

Sebastian actually laughed, and for a moment Emma remembered Clary on the roof of the Institute, talking about a green-eyed brother who had never existed, but could have. Maybe in some other world, a better one than Thule.

"Very well," Sebastian said. "You will be well rewarded if you succeed in this. There might even be a Bel Air house in it for you. Especially if you find any pretty redheads among the rebels and bring them back for Jace and me to play with." He grinned. "Run along now, before you freeze to death."

He flicked a dismissive gesture at them. There was a force behind it—Emma felt herself spun around as if by a hand on her shoulder. She nearly staggered, regained her footing, and found they were almost at the doors of the club. She didn't even remember passing the mirrors.

Then they were out on the street, and she was gasping in lungfuls of the hot, dirty air, the warmth of the humid night suddenly welcome. They reclaimed their motorcycle from the lizard guard and rode several blocks without speaking a word until Julian leaned forward and said, through gritted teeth, "Pull over."

The block they were on was nearly deserted, the streetlights smashed and the pavement dark. As soon as Emma pulled to a stop, Julian swung himself off the cycle and staggered over to the storefront of a destroyed Starbucks. Emma could hear him throwing up in the shadows. Her stomach tightened in sympathy. She wanted to go to him but was afraid to leave the cycle. It was their only way back to the Bradbury. Without it they were dead.

When Julian returned, his face smudged with shadow and bruises, Emma handed him a bottle of water.

"You were amazing in the nightclub," she said.

He took a swig from the bottle. "I felt like I was being torn apart inside," he said matter-of-factly. "To stand there and say those things about Livvy—to call that bastard monster 'sir'—to keep from ripping Annabel limb from limb—"

"Do it now, then," said a voice from the shadows. "Rip me apart, if you can."

Emma's Glock was already out as she turned, lowering it to point directly at the pale woman in the shadows. Her red dress was a smear of blood against the night.

Annabel's colorless lips curled into a smile. "That gun won't hurt me," she said. "And the shot, the screams, will bring the Endarkened running. Chance it if you wish. I wouldn't."

Julian dropped the bottle. Water splashed over his boots. Emma prayed he wouldn't launch himself at Annabel; his hands were shaking. "We can hurt you," he said. "We can make you bleed."

It was so close to what Emma herself had thought inside the nightclub that she was taken aback for a moment.

"The Endarkened will come," Annabel said. "All I have to do is scream." Her Marks had faded, just like all the other Shadowhunters'; her skin was pale as milk, without a single design. Emma was startled by how calm she seemed. How sane. But then, several years had passed here, for her. "I knew who you were the moment I saw you. You look just as you did in the Unseelie Court. The marks of the battle on your faces haven't even healed."

"Then why didn't you tell Sebastian?" Emma spat. "If you wanted to get rid of us—"

"I don't want to get rid of you. I want to make a deal with you."

Julian yanked up his right sleeve with enough force to tear the fabric. There on his wrist was the rag he had worn all through Faerie, still crusted with dried blood. "This is my sister's blood," he ground out. "Blood *you* spilled. Why would I ever want to make a deal with you?"

Annabel looked unmoved at the sight of Livvy's blood. "Because you want to get home," she said. "Because you can't stop thinking of what could be happening to the rest of your family. I am still possessed of powerful dark magics, you know. The Black Volume works even better here. I can open a Portal to take you home. I'm the only one in this world who can."

"Why would you do that for us?" said Emma.

Annabel gave an odd little smile. In her red dress, she seemed to float suspended like a drop of blood in water. "The Inquisitor sent you into Faerie to die," she said. "The Clave despises you and wants you dead. All because you wanted to protect what you loved. How would I not understand what that's like?"

This, Emma felt, was pretty twisted logic. Julian, though, was staring at Annabel as if she were a nightmare he could not look away from.

"You enspelled yourself," Annabel went on, her gaze fixed on Julian. "To feel nothing. I sensed the spell when I saw you in Faerie. I saw it, and I felt *joy*." She twirled, her red skirt spinning out around her. "You made yourself like Malcolm. He cut himself away from emotions to get me back."

"No," Emma said, unable to bear the look on Julian's face. "He tried to get you back because he *loved you*. Because he *felt* emotions."

"Maybe at first." Annabel stopped twirling. "But it was no longer the case by the time he raised me, was it? He had kept me trapped and tortured all those years, so he could bring me back for *him*, not for *me*. That is not love, to sacrifice your beloved's happiness for your own needs. By the time he was able to get me back, he was so divorced from the world that he cared about his goal more than he cared about the kinds of love that matter. A thing that was true and pure and beautiful became corrupt and evil." She smiled, and her teeth shone like underwater pearls. "Once you no longer feel empathy, you become a monster. You may not be under the spell here, Julian Blackthorn, but what about when you return? What will you do then, when you cannot bear to feel what you feel?"

"Shut *up*," Emma said through her teeth. "You don't understand anything." She turned to Julian. "Let's get away from here."

But Julian was still staring at Annabel. "You want something," he said in a deadly flat voice. "What?"

"Ah." Annabel was still smiling. "When I open the Portal, take Ash with you. He is in danger."

"*Ash?*" Julian repeated, incredulous.

"Ash seems to be doing fine here," said Emma, lowering her Glock. "I mean, maybe he's getting bored with his video game selection since, you know, Sebastian killed all the people who make video games. Or he could be running out of batteries. But I'm not sure that qualifies as *danger*."

Annabel's face darkened. "He is too good for this place," she said. "And more than that—when we first found ourselves here, I brought him to Sebastian. I believed Sebastian would take care of

Ash because he is his father. And for a time, he did. But rumors are circulating that the energy drain of maintaining so many Endarkened is slowly tearing Sebastian apart. The life forces of the Endarkened are poisoned. Useless. But Ash's is not. I believe eventually he will kill Ash and use his considerable life force to rejuvenate himself."

"No one's safe, huh?" said Julian. He sounded distinctly unimpressed.

"This is a good world for me," said Annabel. "I hate the Nephilim, and I am powerful enough to be safe from demons."

"And Sebastian lets you torture Nephilim," Emma said.

"Indeed. I visit upon them the wounds that were once visited upon me by the Council." There was no emotion in her voice, not even a faint hint of gloating, only a deadly dullness that was even worse. "But it is not a good place for Ash. We cannot hide—Sebastian would hunt him down anywhere. He will be better off in your world."

"Then why don't you take him there yourself?" said Emma.

"I would if I could. It sickens me to be parted from him," Annabel said. "I have given all my life these years to his care. "

Perfect loyalty, Emma thought. Was it that loyalty that had made Annabel so haggard, so sick-looking? Always putting Ash before herself, following him from place to place, ready to die for him at any moment, and never really knowing why?

"But in your world," Annabel went on, "I would be hunted, and torn from Ash. He would have no one to protect him. This way, he will have you."

"You seem to have a lot of trust in us," said Julian, "given that you know we hate you."

"But you don't hate Ash," Annabel said. "He is innocent, and you have always protected the innocent. It is what you *do*." She smiled, a knowing smile, as if she felt in her heart that she had caught them in a net. "Besides. You are desperate to get home, and desperation always has a price. So how about it, Nephilim? Do we have a deal?"

Ash scooped the piece of paper that had fallen from Julian Blackthorn's jacket off the floor of the nightclub. He was careful not to let Sebastian see him do it. He'd been in Thule long enough to know that it was never a good idea to catch Sebastian's attention unawares.

Not that Sebastian was always cruel. He was generous in fits and starts, when he remembered Ash existed. He'd hand him weapons or games he found in raids on rebel homes. He ensured that Ash dressed nicely, since he considered Ash a reflection of himself. Jace was the only one who was ever actually kind, though, seeming to find in Ash somewhere to put the frustrated, bottled-up feelings he still carried for Clary Fairchild and Alexander and Isabelle Lightwood.

And then there was Annabel. But Ash didn't want to think about Annabel.

Ash unfolded the paper. A jolt went through his body. He turned away quickly so that Jace and Sebastian, deep in conversation, wouldn't see his expression.

It was *her*, the strange human girl he'd once seen in the Unseelie weapons room. Dark hair, eyes the color of the sky he only partially remembered. A murder of crows circled in the sky behind her. Not a photograph, but a drawing, done with a wistful hand, a sense of love and longing emanating from the page. A name was scribbled in a corner: *Drusilla Blackthorn*.

Drusilla. She looked lonely, Ash thought, but determined as well, as if a hope lived behind those summer-blue eyes, a hope that could not be quenched by loss, a hope too strong to feel despair.

Ash's heart was pounding, though he could not have said why. Hastily, he folded the drawing and thrust it into his pocket.

* * *

Diana was waiting for them outside the Bradbury, leaning against the closed garage door with a shotgun over her shoulder. She lowered the weapon with a look of visible relief as Emma and Julian's motorcycle puttered to a stop in front of her.

"I knew you'd make it," she said as Julian swung himself off the bike.

"Aw," said Emma, dismounting. "You were worried about us!"

Diana tapped on the garage door with the tip of her shotgun. She said something to Emma that was lost in the grinding of the gears as the door opened.

Julian watched Emma answer Diana with a smile and wondered how she did it. Somehow Emma could always find lightness or a joke even under the greatest stress. Maybe it was the same way he could stand in front of Sebastian and pretend to be the Endarkened version of himself without even feeling his hands shake. That started only when it was over.

"I'm sorry I had to take off," Diana said once the door was shut and bolted and their bike stowed back under Raphael's tarp. "If I'd stuck around and you'd been caught—"

"There's nothing you could have done for us," said Julian. "And they would have killed you, once they figured out who we really were."

"At least this way someone was bringing the news about Tessa back to Livvy. We get it," Emma added. "Have you told her yet?"

"I was waiting for you." She grinned sideways. "And I didn't want to have to tell Livvy I'd lost her brother."

Her brother. The words were like dream words, half-true, however Julian might want them to be fully real.

"So what did Sebastian want from you?" Diana asked as she let them back into the building. They must have come in very late the night before, Julian realized—at this hour, the corridors were still full of people, hurrying back and forth. They passed the open door of a pantry, full of canned and jarred goods. The kitchen was probably nearby; the air smelled like tomato soup.

"He offered us a house in Bel Air," said Emma.

Diana clucked her tongue. "Fancy. Bel Air is where Sebastian lives, and the more favored Endarkened. The moat protects it."

"The one made of giant bones?" said Julian.

"Yeah, that moat," said Diana. They'd reached the door of Livvy's office; Diana bumped it open with her hip and ushered them inside.

Somehow Julian had thought Livvy would be alone, waiting for them, but she wasn't. She was standing at one of the long architectural tables with Bat and Maia, looking at a map of Los Angeles. Cameron was pacing up and down the room.

Livvy looked up as the door opened, and relief washed across her face. For a moment Julian was watching a small Livvy at the beach, trapped on a rock by the tide, the same look of desperate relief on her face when he came to pick her up and carry her back to shore.

But this Livvy was not the same little girl. She was not a little girl at all. She covered the look of relief quickly. "Glad you're back," she said. "Any luck?"

Julian filled them in on the meeting with Tessa—leaving out, for now, the part where she'd asked them to kill Sebastian—while Emma went to the coffeemaker in the corner and collected hot coffee for them both. It was bitter and black and stung when he swallowed it.

"I guess I owe you five thousand bucks," Cameron said to Livvy when Julian was done. "I didn't think Tessa was still alive, much less that she'd be able to get us into the Silent City."

"This is great news," Maia said. She was leaning back against the edge of the map table. One hand was casually looped around her opposing elbow, and Julian could glimpse a tattoo of a lily on Maia's forearm. "We should start a strategy session. Assign groups.

Some can circle the entrance to the Silent City, some can be on sniper watch, some can guard the warlock, some—"

"There's also some bad news," Julian said. "On the way back from the beach we were stopped at a checkpoint. Sebastian wanted to see us."

Livvy tensed all over. "What? Why?"

"He thought we were the Endarkened versions of ourselves. Emma and Julian from this world," Emma said.

"He knows you've got something going on here downtown," said Julian. "He even knows your name, Livvy."

There was a moment of grim silence.

"I told her to go by a nickname like 'The Masked Avenger,' but she wouldn't listen to me," said Bat with a forced smile.

"Ah," said Emma. "Laughing in the face of danger. I approve."

Livvy pinched the bridge of her nose. "That means we don't have any time to lose. Can you get in touch with Tessa?"

"Now that we know where she is, anyone can borrow my bike and bring her a message," said Diana. "It's no problem."

"We should do this during the day. Too many demons at night," Livvy added.

"I guess that gives us a little time," Diana said.

Cameron put his hand on Livvy's shoulder. It gave Julian an odd feeling—he had been so jealous of Cameron in their own world, of the way that he and Emma behaved together when they were dating. They had everything he and Emma never would—the ability to casually touch one another, to kiss in public. Now this Cameron was Livvy's boyfriend, sparking Julian's protectiveness rather than his jealousy. He had to admit grudgingly, though, that it seemed like Cameron had been a pretty good boyfriend. He was kind, despite his awful family, and obviously thought the sun rose and set on Livvy.

As well he should.

"Come look at the map," said Maia, and they all gathered

around. She ran a bronze-ringed finger across the paper, indicating their location. "Here's us. Here's the entrance to the Silent City. It's just a few blocks away, so we can walk over, but we probably ought to pose as Endarkened."

"We'll go at dawn for the lowest demonic activity," said Livvy. "As for Tessa Gray—"

"All we have to do is let her know when and she'll meet us at the Silent City entrance," said Julian. "Is it where it is in our world? Angels Flight?"

Bat looked surprised. "Yeah. It's the same."

Angels Flight was a narrow-gauge railway that climbed Bunker Hill in downtown L.A., its track seeming to reach up into the sky. Julian had visited it only in its capacity as the entrance to the Silent City once.

"Okay." Maia clapped her hands together. "Everyone's going to be in the mess hall for dinner, so let's go put together some teams."

"You get to argue with Raphael," said Bat.

Maia rolled her eyes. "Sure. He always says he's not going to cooperate and then coughs up a bunch of vamp fighters at the last minute."

"I'll handle the wolf contingent," said Bat.

Diana threw up her hands. "And I'll rally everybody else. How many do we need? Thirty, maybe? Too big a crowd will bring attention we don't need—"

"Guys," Livvy said, looking across the map table at Julian. "I'd like to talk to my brother alone, if you don't mind."

"Oh, sure," Maia said. "No problem. See you in a couple."

She headed out with Bat. Cameron kissed Livvy on the cheek. "See you later."

"I'll be on weapons," Diana said, heading for the door.

Emma met Julian's eyes. "Weapons sound great," she said. "I'll go with Diana."

As soon as the door closed behind them, Livvy went over to one of the long couches and sat down. She looked at Julian with her direct gaze, so much like his Livvy's, save for the scar across her eye. "Jules," she said. "What are you not telling me? There's something you're not telling me."

Julian leaned back against the long table. He spoke carefully. "What makes you think that?"

"Because you told us how to break into the Silent City and get the Mortal Instruments, but you didn't say you'd found out how to destroy them. I know you wouldn't suggest we keep them—once we have them, we'll be major targets for Sebastian."

"We're planning to take them back to our world," Julian said. "Sebastian won't find them there."

"Okay," Livvy said slowly. "So Tessa Gray can open a Portal for you to get back home?"

"No." Julian flexed his hands; his skin felt tight. "Not exactly."

Livvy snapped her fingers. "And here's the part you were leaving out. What?"

"Do you know a woman named Annabel?" Julian asked. "She's from our world, but you might have seen her with Sebastian here. Long dark hair—?"

"That necromancer who showed up with Sebastian's kid? Her name is Annabel?" Livvy whistled. "They don't call her that here. The Legion of the Star calls her the Queen of Air and Darkness."

"That's from an old poem," Julian said, looking thoughtful.

"So that means Ash Morgenstern is from your world too," said Livvy.

"Yes. In fact, he's from Faerie in our world. We all came through the same Portal, but it delivered them here about five years ago, I'm guessing. Two years after the Battle of the Burren. I suspect they went straight to Sebastian. She knew he was Sebastian's son, and since Sebastian's alive here, and in charge . . ."

"I think I'm getting a headache." Livvy rubbed her temples. "Faerie, huh? I guess that explains why Ash is so close in age to his 'father.'"

Julian nodded. "Time in the Undying Lands is superweird. I don't pretend to understand it." He raked a hand through his hair. "The thing is—Annabel offered me a deal."

"What kind of deal?" said Livvy warily.

"She's a powerful magician," Julian said. He spoke with immense deliberation. There was no need to tell Livvy that Annabel was a Blackthorn. It would bring more questions—ones he didn't want to answer. "Because she took the Black Volume from our world, she can open a Portal to get back to it. She offered to open one for us."

"Why would she offer to do that for you if she's one of Sebastian's minions?"

"She doesn't care about Sebastian. She only cares about Ash, and she's afraid for him. She's offering to send us back if we take him with us."

"She probably isn't wrong to be worried. Sebastian ruins everyone close to him." Livvy pulled her legs up under her. "Do you trust this Annabel?"

"I hate her," Julian said, before he could stop himself. He saw Livvy's eyes widen and forced himself to go on more calmly. "But I trust her feelings for Ash are real. He has a certain influence over people."

"That's interesting." Livvy's gaze was slightly unfocused. "Dru saw him a couple years ago. At an execution, like the one you saw on the beach. She kept talking about him afterward, about how he didn't seem like he really wanted to be there." She tucked a piece of hair behind her ear. "Did you—if you go through the Portal, do you still want me to come with you?"

"Of course I do," Julian said. "It's part of the reason I didn't turn Annabel down. I want to get you out of here."

Livvy bit her lip. "What about the me that exists in your world? Won't that get confusing?"

Julian said nothing; he had expected this, and yet he still had no answer. He watched her face change, settling into lines of certainty and resignation, and felt a piece of his heart wither.

"I'm dead, aren't I?" Livvy's voice was steady. "I'm dead in your world. I can tell by the way you look at me."

"Yeah." Julian was shivering as if he were cold, though the air was hot and still. "It was my fault, Livs. You—"

"Don't." She stood up and crossed the room to him, placing her hands flat against his chest as if she meant to push him. "You didn't do anything to hurt me, Jules. I know you too well for you to convince me of that. You forget, in this world, you sacrificed yourself for me." Her Blackthorn eyes were wide and shimmering and tearless. "I'm sorry we lost each other in your world. I'd like to think somewhere we're intact. All of us together." She took a step back from him. "Let me show you something."

His throat was too raw for him to speak. He watched as she turned around, her back to him, and pulled off her sweatshirt. Under it she wore a white tank top. It did nothing to hide the massive tattoo that stretched across her back like wings: a mourning rune, spreading from the base of her neck to the middle of her spine, its edges touching her shoulders.

His voice cracked. "For Ty."

She bent down and retrieved her sweatshirt, pulling it back on to hide the rune. When she turned back to look at him, her eyes were glittering. "For all of you," she said.

"Come back home with me," Julian whispered. "Livvy—"

She sighed. "I can tell you want my permission to make this deal with the necromancer, Jules. I can tell you think it would make this an easier and better choice. But I can't do that." She shook her head. "In Thule, terrible choices are all we have. This one is yours to make."

* * *

At the weapons supply closet, Emma waded in happily; she'd never been that interested in guns—they didn't work on demons, so Shadowhunters didn't use them—but there were plenty of other items of localized destruction. She thrust a handful of throwing knives through her belt and headed for a table of daggers.

Diana leaned against the wall and watched her with weary amusement. "In your world," she said, "you were *parabatai*?"

Emma paused, a blade in her hand. "We were."

"I wouldn't mention that too much if I were you," said Diana. "People here don't really like to think about *parabatai*."

"Why not?"

Diana sighed. "As Sebastian gained control of the world, and it became darker and more desperate, *parabatai* changed. It happened overnight, unlike the change of the warlocks. One day the world awoke to find that those who were *parabatai* had become monsters."

Emma almost dropped the knife. "They became evil?"

"Monsters," repeated Diana. "Their runes began to burn like fire, as if they had fire in their veins instead of blood. People said that the blades of those who fought them shattered in their hands. Black lines spread over their bodies and they became monstrous—physically monstrous. I never saw it happen, mind you—I heard this all third-hand. Stories about ruthless, massive shining creatures, tearing cities apart. Sebastian had to release thousands of demons to take them down. A lot of mundanes and Shadowhunters died."

"But why would that happen?" Emma whispered, her throat suddenly dry.

"Probably the same reason the warlocks turned into demons. The world turning twisted and demonic. No one knows, really."

"Are you worried that'll happen to us?" Emma asked. She was blindly picking up more weapons, not really looking at what she was taking anymore. "That we could change here?"

"No chance of that," Diana said. "Once the angelic magic had stopped working completely, the few *parabatai* who'd survived were fine. Their bonds broke and they didn't change."

Emma nodded. "I can feel that my bond with Julian is broken here."

"Yeah. There are no more Shadowhunters, so there are no more *parabatai*. Still, like I said, I wouldn't mention it to people. Your runes will end up fading soon enough. You know. If you stay here."

"If we stay here," Emma echoed, a little faintly. Her head was spinning. "Right. I think I should go back now. Julian might be wondering where I am."

"I see you've been decorating," Julian said when he came into the bedroom. He looked tired but alert, his chocolate-brown hair still tousled from the bike ride.

Emma glanced around—she'd liberated a startling number of weapons from the supply closet downstairs. There was a pile of daggers and throwing knives in one corner, one of swords in another, and another of LAPD-issue guns: Glocks and Berettas, mostly. "Thanks," she said. "The theme is Stuff That Can Kill You."

Julian laughed and went into the bathroom; she heard the sink water running as he brushed his teeth. She'd borrowed one of the men's button-down shirts they'd given Julian and was wearing it like a nightshirt over her underwear: not, she thought, the sexiest of all pajama options, but it was comfortable.

Emma curled her legs up under her and resisted the urge to ask Julian if he was all right. After she'd gotten back from her expedition with Diana, she'd waited for Julian with growing anxiety. This was a world that could hurt them in a lot of ways. They could be slaughtered by demons or hunted down by Endarkened. And if they'd arrived earlier, apparently, they could have turned into monsters and destroyed a city.

There is a corruption at the heart of the bond of parabatai. *A poison. A darkness in it that mirrors its goodness. There is a reason* parabatai *cannot fall in love, and it is monstrous beyond all you could imagine.*

She shook her head. She wouldn't listen to the lying words of the Queen. Everything in Thule was twisted and monstrous—of course the *parabatai* bond would not have been spared.

More real and dangerous was the shadow of heartbreak around every corner. She knew how badly Julian wanted this Livvy to come back to their world with them, but she had seen Livvy's expression when he'd asked, and she wondered.

When he came back to the bedroom, his hair and T-shirt were damp, and he looked slightly more awake. She guessed he'd splashed water on his face. "Did they have crossbows?" he asked, examining the pile of swords. He picked one up and examined it, the blade refracting light as he turned it this way and that.

Butterflies fluttered in Emma's stomach. Only a few, but there was something about watching Julian be a *Shadowhunter*, be the warrior she had watched him grow into. The muscles moved smoothly in his arm and shoulder as he manipulated the blade and set it back down again, a considering look on his face.

Emma hoped her cheeks weren't pink. "I got you one. It's in the wardrobe."

He went to check. "If we make it to the Silent City without any Endarkened or demons noticing, we might not have to use any of these."

"Diana always said the best weapons were kept in great shape for use but never needed to be used," said Emma. "Of course I never really knew what she was talking about."

"Obviously." He smiled, but it didn't reach his eyes. "Emma, I need to tell you something."

She pushed herself upright against the headboard of the bed. Her heart skipped a beat, but she tried to keep her expression calm and welcoming. Julian wasn't great at opening up even when he *had* emotions; still, she'd missed their sharing of each other's secrets and burdens more than anything else when he'd been under the spell.

He sat down on the edge of the bed and looked up at the ceiling. "I didn't tell Livvy about Tessa asking us to kill Sebastian," he said.

"Sure," Emma said. "If we can't get into the Silent City and get the Mortal Instruments, it'll never matter anyway. Why freak her out early?"

"But I did tell her that if we got the Sword and the Cup, we'd bring them back with us. To protect them."

Emma waited. She wasn't sure where Julian was going with this.

"When we were in the Seelie Court," Julian said, "just this last time—when I talked to the Queen—she told me how it would be possible to break all *parabatai* bonds at once."

Emma gripped the covers. "Yes. And you told me it was impossible."

His eyes were windows to an ocean that no longer existed in this world. "We did what she asked," he said. "We brought her the Black Volume. So she told me, because she thought it would be funny. You see, there's only one way to do it. You have to destroy the first recorded *parabatai* rune, which is kept in the Silent City. And you have to do it with the Mortal Sword."

"And in our world, the Sword is shattered," Emma said. It made sense, in a twisted way: She could imagine the Queen's delight in delivering that news.

"I didn't tell you because I thought it didn't matter," he said. "It was never going to be possible. The Sword was broken."

"And you didn't tell me because of the spell," she said, gently. "You didn't feel like you had to."

"Yeah," he said. He took a shuddering breath. "But now we're talking about bringing this sword back to our world, and I know it's a million-in-one shot, but it could be possible—I mean, we could be looking at that choice. I could be."

There were a million things Emma wanted to say. *You promised you wouldn't* and *it would be a terrible thing to do* trembled on the tip of her tongue. She remembered the moral surety she'd felt when Julian had first told her the Queen had dangled this temptation in front of him.

But it was hard after Livvy's death to have moral surety about anything.

"I asked Magnus to put that spell on me because I was terrified," Julian said. "I imagined us turning into monsters. Destroying everything we loved. I still had Livvy's blood under my fingernails." His voice shook. "But there's something else I'm just as afraid of, and that's why the Queen's voice keeps echoing in my mind."

Emma looked at him, waiting.

"Losing you," he said. "You're the only person I've ever loved like this, and I know you're the only person I ever will. And I'm not myself without you, Emma. Once you dissolve dye in water, you can't take it back out. It's like that. I can't take you out of me. It means cutting out my heart, and I don't like myself without my heart. I know that now."

"Julian," Emma whispered.

"I'm not going to do it," he said. "I'm not going to use the Sword. I can't cause other people pain like the pain I've felt. But if we do get home, and we have the Sword, I think we need to trade it to the Inquisitor for exile. I think we don't have another choice."

"True exile?" Emma said. "They'll separate us from the kids, Julian, they'll separate you—"

"I know," he said. "There was a time I thought there could be nothing worse. But I realize now I was wrong. I held Livvy while she died, and that was worse. What happened to Livvy here—losing all of us—that's unimaginably worse. I asked myself whether I would rather go through what Mark went through—being cut off from his family but thinking of them as well and happy—or what Livvy went through here, knowing her brothers and sisters were dead. It's no question. I'd rather they were safe and alive even if I couldn't be with them."

"I don't know, Julian—"

His expression was nakedly vulnerable. "Unless you don't feel that way about me anymore," he said. "If you'd stopped loving me while I was under the spell, I wouldn't blame you."

"I guess that would solve our problem," she said without thinking. Julian flinched.

Emma crawled hastily across the bed toward him. She knelt in the center of the coverlet and reached to touch his shoulder. He turned his head to look at her, wincing a little, as if he were looking at the sun.

"Julian," she said. "I was angry at you. I *missed* you. But I didn't stop loving you." She brushed the back of her hand lightly against his cheek. "As long as you exist and I exist, I will love you."

"Emma." He moved to kneel on the bed opposite her. She was a head shorter than him in this position. He touched her hair, drawing it forward over her shoulder. His eyes were shadow dark. "I don't know what will happen when we get back," he said. "I don't know if asking for exile from Dearborn will work. I don't know if we'll be separated. But if we are, I'll think of what you just said and it will carry me through whatever happens. In the dark, in the shadows, in the times when I am alone, I will remember."

Her eyes stung. "I can say it again."

"No need." He touched her cheek lightly. "I'll always remember what you looked like when you said it."

"Then I wish I'd worn something a little sexier," she said with a shaky laugh.

His eyes darkened—that desire-darkening that only she ever

got to see. "Believe me, there is nothing hotter than you in one of my shirts," he said. He touched the collar of the shirt lightly. Goose bumps exploded across her skin. His voice was low and rough. "I've always wanted you. Even when I didn't know it."

"Even during our *parabatai* ceremony?"

She half-expected him to laugh, but instead his finger traced the material of her shirt, along her collarbone to the notch at the base of her throat. "Especially then."

"Julian . . ."

"Entreat me not to leave thee," he whispered, *"or to return from following after thee."* He flicked open the top button of her shirt, baring a small patch of skin. He looked up at her and she nodded, dry-mouthed: *Yes, I want this, yes.*

"Whither thou goest, I will go." His fingers glided downward. Another button flicked open. The swell of her breasts was visible; his pupils expanded, darkened.

There was something heretical about it, something that carried the frisson of the ultimately forbidden. The words of the *parabatai* ceremony were not meant to convey desire. Yet every word shivered through Emma's nerves, as if the wings of angels brushed her skin.

She reached for his shirt, drew it up over his head. Smoothed her hands down his chest to the dip of his waist, the ridged muscles in his abdomen. Traced each scar. *"And where thou lodgest, I will lodge."*

His fingers found another button, and another. Her shirt fell open with a whisper of cloth. Slowly, he pushed it off her shoulders, letting it slip down her arms. His eyes were ravenous but his hands were gentle; he stroked her bare shoulders and bent to kiss the places the shirt had revealed, tracing a path between her breasts as she arched backward in his arms. He murmured against her skin. *"Thy people shall be my people. Thy God, my God."*

She tumbled backward, pulling Julian on top of her. His weight pressed her down into the softness of the bed. He curled his hands beneath her body and kissed her long and slow. She traced her fingers through his hair as she had always loved to do, the silky curls tickling her palms.

They shed their clothes unhurriedly. Each new piece of skin revealed was cause for another reverent touch, another slow kiss. "*Whither thou diest, will I die,*" Julian whispered against her mouth.

She unbuckled his jeans and he kicked them away. She could feel him hard against her, but there was no haste: His fingers traced the curves of her, the dips and hollows of her body, as if he were describing a portrait of her in gilt and ivory with each brush of his hands.

She wrapped her legs around him to keep him close to her. His lips grazed her cheek, her hair, as he moved inside her; his gaze never broke with hers, drawing them both upward. They rose as one in fire and sparks, every moment brighter; and when at last they broke and fell together, they were stars collapsing in gold and glory.

Afterward, Emma curled into and against Julian, breathless. He was flushed, sheened with sweat, as he gathered her hair in one hand, winding it through his fingers. "*If aught but death part thee and me*, Emma," he said, and pressed his lips to the strands.

Emma closed her eyes as she whispered, "Julian. Julian. *If aught but death part thee and me.*"

Julian sat on the edge of the bed, looking into the darkness.

His heart was full of Emma, but his mind was in turmoil. He was glad he had told her the truth about the Queen's words, about his determination to seek exile. He had meant to say more.

As long as you exist and I exist, I will love you. The words had filled his heart and broken it. The danger of loving Emma had become like a battle scar: a source of pride, a memory of pain. He hadn't been able to say the rest: *But what if the spell comes back when we go home? What if I stop understanding what it means to love you?*

She had been so brave, his Emma, and so beautiful, and he had wanted her so badly his hands had been shaking as he unbuttoned her shirt, as he reached into the nightstand drawer. She was asleep now, the blankets drawn up around her, her shoulder a pale crescent moon. And he was sitting on the edge of the bed, holding the jeweled dagger Emma had brought up earlier from the weapons closet downstairs.

He turned it over in his hand. It was small, with a sharp blade, and red stones in the pommel. He could hear the Queen's voice in his head. *In the Land of Faerie, as mortals feel no sorrow, neither can they feel joy.*

He thought of the way he and Emma had always written on each other's skin with their fingers, spelling words no one else could hear.

He thought of the great hollow that he had carried around inside him after the spell, without knowing he carried it, like a mundane possessed by a demon that clung to his back and fed on his soul, never knowing where the misery came from.

Once you no longer feel empathy, you become a monster. You may not be under the spell here, Julian Blackthorn, but what about when you return? What will you do then, when you cannot bear to feel what you feel?

He stretched out his arm and brought the blade down.

21
No Rays from Heaven

Diana came at dawn and pounded on their door. Emma woke groggy, her hair tangled and her lips sore. She rolled over to find Julian lying on his side, fully dressed in a long-sleeved black shirt and army-green pants. He looked freshly showered, his hair too wet to be curly, his mouth tasting like toothpaste when she leaned over to kiss him. Had he even slept at all?

She staggered off to shower and dress. With every piece of clothing she put on, she felt another layer of anticipation, waking her up more surely than caffeine or sugar ever could. Long-sleeved shirt. Padded vest. Canvas pants. Thick-soled boots. Daggers and *chigiriki* through her belt, throwing stars in her pockets, a longsword in a scabbard on her back. She bound her hair into a braid and, with some reluctance, picked up a gun and tucked it into the holster attached to her belt.

"Done," she announced.

Julian was leaning against the wall by the door, one booted foot braced behind him. He flicked a piece of hair out of his eyes. "I've been ready for hours," he said.

Emma threw a pillow at him.

It was nice to have their banter back, she thought, as they

headed downstairs. Strange how humor and the ability to joke were tied to emotions; a Julian who didn't feel was a Julian whose humor was a dark and bitter one.

The mess hall was crowded and smelled like coffee. Werewolves, vampires, and former Shadowhunters sat at long tables, eating and drinking from chipped and mismatched bowls and mugs. It was an oddly unified scene, Emma thought. She couldn't imagine a situation in her world where a big group of Shadowhunters and Downworlders would be seated together for a casual meal. Maybe Alec and Magnus's Downworlder-Shadowhunter Alliance ate together, but she had to admit she knew shamefully little about them.

"Hey." It was Maia, showing them to a long table where Bat and Cameron were sitting. Two bowls of oatmeal and mugs of coffee had been put out for them. Emma glared at the coffee as she sat down. Even in Thule, everyone assumed she drank the stuff.

"Eat," said Maia, sliding into a chair next to Bat. "We all need the energy."

"Where's Livvy?" said Julian, taking a bite of oatmeal.

"Over there." Cameron pointed with his spoon. "Running around putting out fires as usual."

Emma tried the oatmeal. It tasted like cooked paper.

"Here." Maia handed her a small chipped bowl. "Cinnamon. Makes it taste better."

As Emma took the bowl, she noticed that there were other tattoos on Maia's arm alongside the lily—a fletched arrow, a lick of blue flame, and a sage leaf.

"Do those mean something?" she asked. Julian was chatting with Cameron, something Emma couldn't have imagined happening in her world. She was a little surprised it was happening here. "Your tattoos, I mean."

Maia touched the small illustrations with light fingers. "They honor my fallen friends," she said quietly. "The sage leaf is for Clary. The arrow and flame are for Alec and Magnus. The lily . . ."

"Lily Chen," Emma said, thinking of Raphael's expression when she'd said Lily's name.

"Yes," Maia said. "We became friends in New York after the Battle of the Burren."

"I'm so sorry about your friends."

Maia sat back. "Don't be sorry, Emma Carstairs," she said. "You and Julian have brought us hope. This—today—this is the first move we've made against Sebastian, the first thing we've done that hasn't been just about surviving. So thank you for that."

The backs of Emma's eyes stung. She looked down and took another bite of oatmeal. Maia was right—it was better with cinnamon.

"Do you not want your coffee?" Diana said, appearing at their table. She was dressed entirely in black from head to toe, two bullet belts lashed around her waist. "I'll drink it."

Emma shuddered. "Take it away. I'd be grateful."

A group of people dressed in black like Diana, carrying guns, marched out the door in formation. "Snipers," Diana said. "They'll be covering us from above."

"Diana, we will be going on ahead now," said Raphael, appearing out of nowhere in that irritating way vampires had. He hadn't bothered with any kind of military clothes; he wore jeans and a T-shirt and looked about fifteen.

"You're scouting?" Emma said.

"That's my excuse for not traveling with you humans, yes," said Raphael.

It was somewhat mysterious, Emma thought, that Magnus and Alec had liked this guy enough to name their kid after him. "But I was so looking forward to playing I Spy," she said.

"You would have lost," said Raphael. "Vampires excel at I Spy."

As he stalked away, he paused to talk to someone. Livvy. She patted him on the shoulder, and to Emma's surprise he didn't glare—he nodded, an almost friendly nod, and went to join his group of vampire scouts. They headed out the door as Livvy approached Emma and Julian's table.

"Everybody's ready," she said. She looked a lot like she had when they'd first seen her in Thule. Tough and ready for anything. Her hair was pulled back into a tight ponytail; she bent over to kiss Cameron on the cheek and patted Julian's shoulder. "Jules, you and Emma come with me. We've got fog today."

"Fog doesn't seem so bad," Emma said.

Livvy sighed. "You'll see."

Emma did see. Fog in Thule was like everything else in Thule: surprisingly horrible.

They left the Bradbury in a small group: Emma, Julian, Livvy, Cameron, Bat, Maia, Divya, Rayan, and a few other rebels Emma didn't know by name. And the fog had hit them like a wall: thick columns of mist rising from the ground and drifting through the air, turning everything more than a few feet ahead into a blur. It smelled like burning, like the smoke from a deep fire.

"It'll make your eyes sting, and your throat, too, but it doesn't hurt you," Livvy said as they split up into smaller groups, spreading out across Broadway. "Sucks for the snipers, though. No visibility."

She was walking with Emma and Julian in the gutter next to the pavement. They followed Livvy, since she seemed to know where she was going. The fog cut the dim light of the dying sun almost completely; Livvy had taken out a flashlight and was aiming the beam into the mist ahead.

"At least there won't be any cars," Livvy said. "Sometimes the Endarkened try to run you over if they think you're unsworn. But no one drives around in the fog."

"Does it ever rain?" asked Emma.

"Believe me," said Livvy, "you do not want to be here when it rains."

Her tone suggested both that Emma shouldn't inquire further and that it probably rained knives or rabid frogs.

The white fog seemed to shroud sound as well as sight. They padded along, their footsteps muffled, following Livvy's flashlight beam. Julian seemed lost in thought; Livvy glanced at him, and then at Emma. "I have something I want you to take," she said in a voice so low Emma had to lean in to hear it. "It's a letter I wrote for Ty."

She slipped the envelope into Emma's hand; Emma tucked it into her inside pocket after glancing at the scrawled name on the envelope. *Tiberius.*

"Okay." Emma looked straight ahead. "But if you aren't coming back through the Portal with us, you have to tell Julian."

"The Portal's not really a sure thing, is it?" Livvy said mildly.

"We're going to get back," Emma said. "Somehow."

Livvy inclined her head, acknowledging Emma's determination. "I haven't made up my mind yet."

"Look," Julian said. He seemed to sharpen around the edges as he came closer to them, no longer blurred by the fog. "We're there."

Angels Flight loomed up above them, its bulk cutting through the mist. The railway itself had been fenced off long ago, back when people cared about things like safety, but the fencing had been trampled down, and torn strips of chain link lay scattered on the pavement. Two wooden trolley cars lay on their sides halfway up the hill, toppled from the tracks like broken toys. An ornate orange-and-black archway with the words ANGELS FLIGHT towered over the railway entrance.

Standing in front of one of the pillars holding up the archway was Tessa.

She wasn't disguised as Jem today. Nor was she dressed like a

Shadowhunter or a Silent Brother. She wore a plain black dress, her hair loose and straight. She looked about Clary's age.

"You're here," she said.

Livvy had stopped in her tracks; she held out a hand indicating Julian and Emma should stop as well. She flicked off her flashlight as several dozen figures emerged from the mist. Emma tensed, then relaxed as she recognized them—Diana. Bat. Cameron. Raphael. Maia. And dozens more rebels, clad in black and green.

They stood in silence in two long rows. Military formation. None of them moved.

Tessa looked at Livvy wonderingly. "Are all of these people your people?"

"Yes," Livvy said. She was regarding Tessa with a mix of distrust and hope. "These are my people."

Tessa smiled, a sudden and wonderful smile. "You've done well, Livia Blackthorn. You've honored your family name."

Livvy seemed taken aback. "My family?"

"Long have there been Blackthorns," said Tessa, "and long have they lived with honor. I see much honor here." She glanced in the direction of the rebels, and then turned—seeming unconcerned with the show of force at her back—and raised her hands in front of her.

There was indrawn breath from the rebels as Tessa's fingers sparked with yellow fire. A door—two doors—evolved under her hands, filling the archway. Each was a massive slab of stone. Across them both had been crudely carved a phrase in Latin. *Nescis quid serus vesper vehat.*

"Who knows what nightfall brings?" Julian translated, and a shiver went up Emma's spine.

Tessa brushed the yellow flames of her fingers across the doors, and a loud grinding sound cut through the muffling fog. The doors shuddered and began to slide apart, dust showering down from years of disuse.

A hollow, booming cry echoed from the darkness as the doors slid open completely. Deep blackness was all that was visible beyond the entrance: Emma could not see the stairs she knew led down into the Silent City. She could see only shadow.

Emma and Julian stepped forward, Emma peering into the blackness of the Silent City's entrance, just as Tessa sank to the ground.

They darted to her side. She pushed herself upright against a pillar, her face as white as the mist. "I'm all right, I'm all right," she said, though up close, the sides of her mouth and eyes were threaded with scarlet, as if the small blood vessels there had burst with strain. "We should hurry. It isn't wise to leave the Silent City open—"

She tried to struggle to her feet and sank back down again with a gasp.

Livvy handed her flashlight to Emma and knelt down beside Tessa. "Cameron! Diana! Go with Emma and Jules into the Bone City. Maia, I need a medic."

There was a flurry of activity. As Cameron and Diana came to join them, Emma tried to argue that she should be the one to stay with Tessa, but Livvy was adamant. "You did the *parabatai* ceremony," she said. "You know the Silent City. There's no reason its architecture here should be any different."

"Hurry," Tessa said again as Maia bent down beside her with a first-aid kit. "The Instruments are in the Star Chamber." She coughed. "Go!"

Emma flipped Livvy's flashlight on and darted through the entrance of the City, Julian beside her, Cameron and Diana taking the rear. The noise of the street above vanished almost immediately, muffled by the fog and the heavy stone walls. The Silent City was more silent than it had ever been, she thought. The beam of the flashlight bounced off the walls, illuminating chipped stone, and, as they made their way deeper underground, polished white and yellow bone.

Livvy had been right. The architecture of the Silent City was the same here. Julian walked alongside Emma, reminding her of the last time they'd been to this place together, at their *parabatai* ceremony. The city had smelled old then, like bones and dust and stone, but it had been a living and inhabited place. Now it smelled of stale air, disuse, and death.

It was not *her* City of Bones, of course. But she had been taught from childhood that all Cities were one City; there were different entrances but only one stronghold. As they passed through the arched rooms of mausoleums, Emma could not help but think: *Never will more warriors be added to this army; never will more ashes help to build the City of Bones.*

They ducked through a tunnel that opened into a square pavilion. Spires of carved bone occupied each corner. Squares of marble like a checkerboard, bronze and red, made up the floor; in the center was the mosaic that gave the room its name, a parabolic design of silver stars.

A black basalt table ran along one wall. Laid out atop it were two objects: a cup and a sword. The Cup was gold, with a ruby-studded rim; the sword was a heavy dark silver, with a hilt in the shape of angel wings.

Emma knew them both. Every Shadowhunter did, from a thousand paintings and tapestries and illustrations in history books. She noticed, with a strange detached surprise, that neither the Cup nor the Sword had gathered any dust.

Cameron inhaled sharply. "I never thought I'd actually *see* them again. Not after the War."

"Give me the flashlight," Diana said, reaching out her hand to Emma. "Go on, you two."

Emma handed over the light, and she and Julian approached

the table. Julian picked up the Cup and tucked it through the strap of the Sam Browne belt across his chest, then zipped his jacket up over it. It took Emma a moment longer to steel herself to pick up the sword. Her last sight of it had been in Annabel's hand as Annabel had cut down Robert Lightwood and plunged the shards of the sword into Livvy's chest.

But this was another sword: unbloodied, unbroken. She took hold of the grip and switched it with the longsword on her back; the Mortal Sword was a heavy weight against her spine, and she remembered what the Queen had said: that the Nephilim had once been giants on the earth, with the strength of a thousand men.

"We'd better go," Diana said. "Like the warlock said, better not to leave this place open too long."

Cameron looked around with a shiver of distaste. "Can't get out of here too soon for me."

As they passed through the City, the beam of the flashlight danced off the semiprecious stones embedded in the archways of bone. They gleamed in a way that made Emma sad: What was the point of beauty nobody saw? They reached a tunnel and she realized with relief they must be getting close to the stairs and the surface: She could hear the wind, the sound of a car backfiring—

She stiffened. *Nobody drives in the fog.*

"What's that noise?" she said.

They all jerked to attention. The sound came again, and this time Cameron paled.

"Gunshots," Diana said, sliding a gun out of the holster on her hip.

"Livvy." Cameron began to run; he'd gone a few feet when figures loomed up out of the shadows, figures of smoke and scarlet. A silver blade slashed out of the darkness.

"Endarkened!" Julian shouted.

Emma's longsword was already in her left hand; she raced forward, seizing a *bo-shuriken* out of her belt and hurling it toward one of the figures in red. They staggered back, a spray of blood painting the wall behind them.

An Endarkened woman with long brown hair lunged toward her. Cameron was struggling with one at the foot of a set of stairs. A shot rang out, echoing in Emma's ears; the Endarkened fell like a rock. Emma glanced back to see Julian lowering a pistol, his expression stony. Smoke still curled from the muzzle.

"Go!" Diana dropped the flashlight, shoved Emma from behind, and took aim. *"Get to Livvy! Get to the others!"*

The implication was clear: Get the Cup and Sword away from the Endarkened. Emma took off, longsword in hand, laying about her in double arcs of slashing blows; she saw Cameron struggling with an Endarkened she recognized as Dane Larkspear. Rotten in one world, rotten in another, she thought, as Cameron kicked Dane's legs out from under him.

There were more Endarkened coming, though, from one of the other tunnels. She heard Julian shout, and then they were rocketing up the stairs, Emma with her sword and Julian with his gun. They burst out of the entrance to the Silent City—

And into the middle of a horrible tableau.

Fog was still curling everywhere, white strands like the web of an enormous spider. But Emma could see what she needed to see. Dozens of Livvy's rebels knelt in silence, hands behind their heads. Behind them stood long rows of Endarkened armed with bayonets and machine guns. Tessa was still slumped against the pillar of the archway, but it was Raphael holding her now, and with surprising care.

Livvy was on her feet, in the center of the group of Endarkened and rebels. She was on her feet because Julian—a taller, older, bigger Julian, with a bleak, deadly grin, dressed all in red—was standing behind her, one arm lashed around her throat. His free hand held a pistol to her temple.

Behind him stood Sebastian, in another expensive dark suit, and with Sebastian, flanking him, were Jace and Ash. Ash was weaponless, but Jace carried a sword that Emma recognized: Heosphoros, which in her world had been Clary's. It was a beautiful sword, its cross-guard gold and obsidian, the dark silver blade stamped with black stars.

Everything seemed to slow to a crawl. Emma heard Julian's breath rattle in his throat; he stopped dead, as if he had been turned to stone.

"Julian Blackthorn," Sebastian said, and the white mist curling around him was the color of his hair, of Ash's hair. Two winter princes. "Did you *really* think I'd be fooled by your poor performance in the nightclub?"

"Annabel," Julian said, his voice hoarse, and Emma knew what he was thinking: Annabel must have betrayed them, Annabel, who knew who they really were.

Sebastian's brow furrowed. "What about Annabel?"

Ash shook his head slightly. It was a tiny movement, a minuscule negation, but Emma saw it, and she was fairly sure Julian had seen it too. *No,* he was saying. *Annabel didn't betray you.*

But why would Ash—?

"Drop your gun," Sebastian said, and Julian did, tossing it into the fog. Sebastian had barely looked at Emma; now he turned his lazy, contemptuous gaze in her direction. "And you. Drop that cheap sword."

Emma dropped the longsword with a clang. Had he not seen the Mortal Sword strapped across her back?

"You have the sun in your skin," Sebastian said. "That alone would have told me you weren't from Thule. And thanks to Ash, I know the story of your world. I knew of the Portal. I've been wondering all this time if one of you would stumble through it. I knew you'd go straight for the Mortal Instruments to hide them from me. All I had to do was post some guards here and wait for the tip-off."

He grinned like a jaguar. "Now hand over the Mortal Instruments, or Julian here will blow your sister's head off."

The real Julian looked at Livvy. Emma was screaming inside: *He can't watch her die again, not again, nobody could live through that twice.*

Livvy's gaze was steady on her brother's. There was no fear in her expression.

"You won't let her live," Julian said. "No matter what I do, you'll kill her."

Sebastian grinned a little wider. "You'll have to wait and see."

"All right," Julian said. His shoulders slumped. "I'm reaching for the Cup," he said, holding up one hand as the other unzipped his jacket. Emma watched him in dismay as he reached inside. "I'm going to hold it out to you—"

He drew his hand out from his jacket; he was holding a throwing knife, small and sharp with red stones in the hilt; Emma barely had time to recognize it before he had flung it. It whipped through the air, grazing Livvy's cheek and sinking deeply into the eye of the Endarkened Julian who held her.

He didn't even scream. He fell back, hitting the pavement with a thud, his pistol rolling out of his open hand; Sebastian shouted but Livvy was already gone, ducking and rolling into the mist.

Emma drew the Mortal Sword and charged, directly at Sebastian.

The world exploded into chaos. Sebastian yelled for his Endarkened and they came running, abandoning the rebels to throw themselves between Emma and their leader. Jace lunged at Emma, pushing Ash behind him, but Julian was already there; he had caught up the fallen longsword and it clanged, hard, against Heosphoros as he drove Jace back, away from Emma.

Emma slashed out at the nearest Endarkened with the Mortal Sword. Its heaviness had turned to light in her grip; it sang as she wielded it as only Cortana had sung in her hand before, and suddenly she remembered its name: Maellartach. An Endarkened with close-cropped blond hair aimed a pistol at her; the bullet clanged off the blade of Maellartach. The Endarkened gaped at her and Emma drove the Mortal Sword into his chest, flinging him backward with such force that he took another Endarkened down with him as he fell.

She heard someone cry out; it was Livvy, leaping into the fray. She ducked, rolled, and shot, taking out an Endarkened who was charging at Bat. The sounds of battle echoed like dull thunder off the walls of mist that curled and slid around them.

Maellartach was a silver blur in Emma's hand, turning away blades and bullets as she inched closer to Sebastian. She saw Bat move toward Ash, bayonet in hand. Ash wasn't moving; he was standing watching the chaos like an onlooker at the theater.

"Put your hands behind your back," Bat said, and Ash glanced over at him with a frown, as if he were a rude guest who had interrupted a play. Bat raised the bayonet. "Look, kid, you'd better—"

Ash fixed Bat with a steady green gaze. "You don't want to do that," he said.

Bat froze, gripping his weapon. Ash turned and walked away—not hurrying, almost *sauntering*, really—and vanished into the fog.

"Bat! Look *out*!" Maia shouted, and Bat spun to plunge his bayonet into the body of an advancing Endarkened warrior.

And then came the scream. A howl of agony so shrill and intense, it pierced the fog. A woman in Endarkened gear flew across the square, her hair unfurling behind her like a banner spun out of gold, and threw herself across the dead body of this world's Julian Blackthorn.

Emma knew it was herself; the herself of Thule, clutching at the body of her dead partner, sobbing against his chest, her fingers clawing his blood-wet clothes. She screamed over and over, each a sharp, short howl, like a car alarm going off on an empty street.

Emma couldn't help staring, and Julian—her own Julian—

jerked in surprise and spun to look—recognizing the sound of Emma's voice, she guessed. The split-second break in his attention left an opening for Jace, who lunged forward with Heosphoros; Julian, twisting to the side, just barely avoided the blade, but stumbled; Jace swept his feet out from under him and he went down.

No. Emma spun around, reversing course, but if Jace brought the sword down, there was no way she'd get there in time—

A plume of yellow flame shot between Jace and Julian. Julian scrambled back as Jace turned to stare; Raphael was holding Tessa upright, and her hand was stretched out, yellow fire still dancing at her fingertips. She looked frayed and exhausted, but her eyes were dark with sorrow as they fixed on Jace.

It was an odd, frozen moment, the kind that sometimes happened in the midst of battle. It was broken by a figure stumbling from the entrance to the Silent City—Diana, bloodstained and panting, but alive. Emma's heart leaped with relief.

Sebastian's eyes narrowed. "Go into the City!" he shouted. "Find everything! Spell books! Records! Bring it all to me!"

Tessa gasped. "No—the destruction he could wreak—"

Jace immediately turned away from Julian, as if he'd forgotten he was there. "Endarkened," he called. His voice was deep and flat, without tone or emotion. "Come to me."

Emma turned to run toward the City entrance; she could hear Sebastian laughing. Julian had sprung to his feet and was beside her; Livvy spun, kicked at an Endarkened, and ran toward Tessa and the others. "Shut the doors! *Shut the doors!*"

"No!" Diana looked wildly around the scene of carnage. "Cameron's still in there!"

Julian turned toward Tessa. "What can we do?"

"I can shut the doors, but you must understand that I cannot open them again," Tessa said. "Cameron will be trapped."

A look of agony passed across Livvy's face. Jace and the other Endarkened were moving toward them; there were seconds to spare.

The agony didn't leave Livvy's eyes, but her jaw hardened. In that moment, she had never looked more like Julian. "Close the doors," she said.

"Stop the warlock!" Sebastian cried. "Stop her—"

He broke off with a howl. Maia, behind him, had plunged a sword into his side. The blade drove into him, smeared with blackish blood. He barely seemed to notice.

"Tessa—" Emma began, and she didn't know what she planned to say, whether she planned to ask Tessa if she had the strength to close the doors, whether she intended to tell her to do it or not to do it. Tessa moved before she could finish her sentence, raising her slender arms, murmuring words Emma would always try to remember and always find sliding out of her mind.

Golden sparks flew from Tessa's fingers, illuminating the archway. The doors began to slide closed, grinding and rattling. Sebastian yelled with rage and grabbed the sword protruding from his side. He yanked it free and flung it at Maia, who threw herself to the ground to avoid being struck.

"Stop!" he shouted, striding toward the entrance to the City. "Stop *now*—"

The doors slammed shut with an echo that reverberated through the fog. Emma looked at Tessa, who gave her a sweet, sad smile. Blood was running from the corners of Tessa's mouth, from her split fingernails.

"No," said Raphael. He had been so quiet, Emma had almost forgotten he was there. "Tessa—"

Tessa Gray burst into flame. It was not as if she had caught fire, not really; in between one moment and the next, she *became* fire, became a glowing pillar of conflagration. The burning light was white and gold: It cut through the mist, illuminating the world.

Raphael fell back, an arm across his face to shield himself from the light. In the brilliance, Emma could see sharp details: the cut across Livvy's face where Julian's blade had grazed her, the tears in Diana's eyes, the rage on Sebastian's face as he stared at the shut doors, the fear of the Endarkened as they cringed away from the light.

"Cowards! The light cannot hurt you!" Sebastian shouted. "Fight on!"

"We have to get back to the Bradbury," Livia said desperately. "We have to get out of here."

"Livvy," Julian said. "We can't lead them back to your headquarters. We have to deal with them now."

"And there's only one way to do that," Emma said. She tightened her grip on the Mortal Sword and started toward Sebastian.

She was burning with a new fury, filling her, sustaining her. *Cameron. Tessa.* She thought of Livvy, having lost someone else she loved. And she launched herself at Sebastian, the Mortal Sword curving through the air like a whip made of fire and gold.

Sebastian growled. Phaesphoros leaped into his hand, and he strode toward Emma. Fury seemed to dance around him like sparks. "You think to strike me down with the Mortal Sword," he said. "Isabelle Lightwood tried that, and now she molders in a grave in Idris."

"What if I cut your head off?" Emma taunted. "Do you keep on being the dickweed ruler of this planet in two different pieces?"

Sebastian spun, the Morgenstern sword a black-and-silver blur. Emma leaped, the sword slashing under her feet. She landed on a toppled fire hydrant. "Go ahead and try," Sebastian said in a bored voice. "Others have; I cannot be killed. I will tire you out, girl, and cut you into puzzle pieces to amuse the demons."

The clash of battle was all around them. Tessa's fire was dimming, and in the clamor of the mist, Emma could just see Julian, battling Jace. Julian had taken one of the Endarkened's swords and was fighting defensively, as Diana had taught them when their opponent was stronger than they were.

Livvy was fighting Endarkened with a new anger and energy. So was Raphael. As Emma flicked her glance toward the others, she saw Raphael seize a red-haired Endarkened woman and tear her throat out with his teeth.

And then she saw it: a glow in the distance. A whirling, spinning illumination she knew well: the light of a Portal.

Emma leaped down off the fire hydrant and pressed her attack; Sebastian actually fell back for a moment in surprise before he recovered and struck back even harder. The blade hummed in Emma's hand as her heart beat out two words: *distract him, distract him.*

Phaesphorus slammed against Maellartach. Sebastian bared his teeth in a grin that was nothing like a real grin. Emma wondered if he'd once been able to fake a human smile and forgotten how. She thought of the way Clary spoke of him, of someone who had been lost long before he died.

A sharp pain cut through her. Sebastian's sword had scored the front of her left thigh; blood stained the rip in her canvas pants. He grinned again and kicked her wound, violently; the pain whited out her vision and she felt herself tilt. She hit the ground with a crack that she was fairly sure was her collarbone snapping.

"You begin to bore me," Sebastian said, prowling above her like a cat. Her vision was blurry with pain, but she could see the Portal light growing stronger. The air seemed to shimmer. In the distance, she could still hear the other Emma sobbing.

"Other worlds," he mused. "Why should I care about some other world when I rule this one? What should some other world mean to me?"

"Do you want to know how you died there?" Emma said. The pain of her broken bone seared through her. She could hear battle all around her, hear Julian and Jace fighting. She fought to keep from fainting. The longer she distracted Sebastian, the better.

"You want to live forever in this world," she said. "Don't you want to know how you died in our world? Maybe it could happen here, too. Ash wouldn't know about it. Neither would Annabel. But I do."

He lowered Phaesphoros and let the tip of it nick her collarbone. Emma almost screamed from the pain. "Tell me."

"Clary killed you," Emma said, and saw his eyes fly wide open. "With heavenly fire. It burned out everything that was evil in you, and there wasn't enough left to live for long. But you died in your mother's arms, and your sister cried over you. In the club yesterday you talked about the weight on you, crushing you. In our world, your last words were 'I've never felt so light.'"

His face twisted. For a moment there was fear there, in his eyes, and more than fear—regret, perhaps, even pain.

"You *lie*," he hissed, sliding the tip of his sword down to her sternum, where a stabbing blow would sever her abdominal aorta. She would bleed out in agony. "Tell me it isn't the truth. *Tell me!*"

His hand tightened on the blade.

There was a blur behind him, a flurry of wings, and something struck him hard, a blow to the shoulder that made him stagger sideways. Emma saw Sebastian whirl around, a look of fury on his face. "*Ash!* What are you doing?"

Emma's mouth dropped open in surprise. It *was* Ash—and from his back extended a pair of wings. For Emma, who had been raised all her life on images of Raziel, it was like a blow: She pushed herself up on her elbows, staring.

They were angel's wings, and yet they weren't. They were black, tipped with silver; they shimmered like the night sky. She guessed they were wider than the span of his outstretched arms.

They were beautiful, the most beautiful thing she had seen in Thule.

"No," Ash said calmly, looking at his father, and plucked the sword from Sebastian's hand. He stepped back, and Emma rolled to her feet, her collarbone screaming in pain, and thrust the Mortal Sword into Sebastian's chest.

She yanked it free, feeling the blade scrape against the bone of his rib cage, prepared to thrust again, to cut him to pieces—

As she drew the sword back, he shuddered. He hadn't made a sound when she stabbed him; now his mouth opened, and black blood cascaded over his lower lip and chin as his eyes rolled back. Emma could hear the Endarkened screaming. His skin began to split and burn.

He threw his head back in a silent scream and burst apart into ashes, the way demons vanished in Emma's world.

The screaming of Thule Emma cut off abruptly. She sprawled lifeless over her Julian's body. One by one, the other Endarkened began to fall, crumpling at the feet of the rebels they were fighting.

Jace gave a cry and fell to his knees. Behind him Emma could see the illumination of the Portal, open now and blazing with blue light.

"Jace," she whispered, and moved to go toward him.

Ash stepped in front of her.

"I wouldn't," he said. He spoke in that same eerily calm voice in which he had said to his father, *No*. "He's been under Sebastian's control too long. He isn't what you think. He can't go back."

She swung her sword up to point at Ash, close to nausea from the pain of her broken collarbone. Ash looked back at her, unflinching.

"Why did you do that?" she demanded. "Betray Sebastian. Why?"

"He was going to kill me," Ash said. He had a low voice, slightly husky, not the boy's voice he'd had in the Unseelie Court. "Besides, I liked your speech about Clary. It was interesting."

Julian had turned away from Jace, who still knelt on the ground, staring down at the sword in his hands. Julian moved toward Emma as Livvy stared; she was slashed with wounds but still standing, and her rebels were approaching to circle around her. They wore expressions of shock and disbelief.

A scream cut through the eerie silence of dead Endarkened and stunned warriors. A scream that Emma knew well.

"Don't hurt him!" Annabel cried. She raced toward Ash, her hands outstretched. She wore her red gown, and her feet were bare as she ran.

She seized hold of Ash's arm and began to drag him toward the Portal.

Emma broke from her frozen state and began to run toward Julian as he moved to stand in front of the Portal. His sword flashed out as he raised it, just as Ash pulled hard against Annabel's grip. He was shouting at her that he didn't want to go, not without Jace.

Annabel was strong; Emma knew how strong. But it appeared that Ash was stronger. He yanked free of her grip and began to run toward Jace.

The light of the Portal had begun to dim. Was Annabel closing it, or was it dying on its own, naturally? Either way, Emma's heart kicked into high gear, slamming against her rib cage. She leaped over the body of an Endarkened and came down on the other side just as Annabel whirled on her.

"Stay back!" Annabel shouted. "Neither of you can enter the Portal! Not without Ash!"

Ash turned to look at the sound of his name; he was kneeling beside Jace, his hand on Jace's shoulder. Ash's face was twisted with what looked like grief.

Annabel began to advance on Emma. Her face was frighteningly blank, the way it had been that day on the dais. The day she'd thrust the Mortal Sword into Livvy's heart and stopped it forever.

Behind Annabel, Julian lifted his free hand. Emma knew immediately what he meant, what he wanted.

She raised the Mortal Sword, gritting her teeth in pain, and threw it.

It flashed past Annabel; Julian cast his own sword aside and caught it out of the air. He swung its still-bloodied blade in a curving arc, slicing through Annabel's spine.

Annabel gave a terrible, inhuman shriek, like the shriek of a fisher cat. She spun like a malfunctioning top, and Julian rammed the Mortal Sword into her chest, just as she'd done to Livvy.

He pulled the blade free, her blood dripping over his clenched fist, spattering his skin. He stood like a statue, gripping the Mortal Sword as Annabel collapsed to the ground like a marionette with its strings cut.

She lay on her back, her face upturned, a pool of scarlet beginning to spread around her, mixing with the torn frills of her red dress. Her hands, knotted into claws at her sides, relaxed in death; her bare feet were dark scarlet, as if she were wearing slippers made of blood.

Julian looked down at her body. Her eyes—still Blackthorn blue—were already beginning to film over.

"Queen of Air and Darkness," he said in a low voice. "I will never be like Malcolm."

Emma took a long, ragged breath as Julian handed her back the Mortal Sword. Then he tore the bloodied rag from his wrist and cast it down beside Annabel's body.

Her blood began to soak into it, mixing with Livvy's.

Before Emma could speak, she heard Ash cry out. Whether it was a cry of pain or triumph, she couldn't tell. He was still kneeling beside Jace.

Julian held out his hand. "Ash!" he cried. "Come with us! I swear we'll take care of you!"

Ash looked at him for a long moment with steady, unreadable

green eyes. Then he shook his head. His wings beat darkly against the air; catching hold of Jace, he sailed upward, both of them vanishing into the cloudy sky.

Julian lowered his hand, his face troubled, but Livvy was already running toward him, her face white with distress. "Jules! Emma! The Portal!"

Emma swung around; the Portal had dimmed even further, its light wavering. Livvy reached Julian and he slung an arm around her, hugging her tight against his side.

"We have to go," he said. "The Portal's fading—it'll only hang on for a few minutes now Annabel's gone."

Livvy pressed her face into Julian's shoulder and, for a moment, hugged him incredibly tightly. When she let go, her face was shining with tears. "Go," she whispered.

"Come with us," Julian said.

"No, Julian. You know I can't," Livvy said. "My people finally have a chance. You gave us a chance. I'm grateful, but I can't have Cameron die for the safety of a world that I'm willing to run away from."

Emma was afraid Julian would protest. He didn't. Maybe he'd been more prepared for this than she'd thought. He reached into his jacket and pulled out the Cup; it gleamed dull gold in the Portal light—the blue light of a sky with a real sun. "Take this." He pressed it into Livvy's hands. "With it, perhaps the Nephilim can be reborn here."

Livvy cradled it in her fingers. "I may never be able to use this."

"But you might," Emma said. "Take it."

"And let me give you one last thing," Julian said. He bent and whispered in Livvy's ear. Her eyes went wide.

"Go!" someone shouted; it was Raphael, who along with Diana, Bat, and Maia, was watching them. "You stupid humans, go before it is too late!"

Julian and Livvy looked at each other one last time. When he turned away, Emma thought she could hear the sound of his heart tearing itself apart: One piece would always be here, in Thule, with Livvy.

"Go!" Raphael shouted again; the Portal had narrowed to a gap smaller than a doorway. "And tell Magnus and Alec to rename their child!"

Emma slid her hand into Julian's. Her other hand gripped the Mortal Sword. Julian looked down at her; in the sunlight of the Portal, his eyes were sea-blue.

"See you on the other side," he whispered, and together they stepped through.

22

THE WORST AND THE BEST

The Silent City was empty, full of the echoes of past dreams and whispers. *The torches in the walls were lit, casting a golden glow over the spires of bone and mausoleums of rhodolite and white agate.*

Emma walked unhurried among the bones of the dead. She knew she should be anxious, perhaps hurrying, but she couldn't remember why, or what she was seeking. She knew she was wearing gear—battle gear, black and silver as a starry sky. Her boots echoing on the marble were the only sound in the City.

She passed through a familiar room with a high, domed ceiling. Marble of all colors flowed together in patterns too intricate for the eye to follow. On the floor were two interlocking circles: This was where she and Julian had become parabatai.

Beyond that room was the Star Chamber. The parabolic stars glimmered on the floor; the Mortal Sword hung point-down behind the basalt Judges' Bar, as if waiting for her. She took hold of it and found it featherlight. Crossing the room, she stepped into the square of the Speaking Stars.

"Emma! Emma, it's me, Cristina." A cool hand was holding hers. She was tossing and turning; there was a searing pain at her throat.

"Cristina," she whispered, her lips dry and cracked. "Hide the Sword. Please, please, hide it."

There was a click. The floor beneath her opened along an invisible seam, two slabs of marble rolling smoothly apart. Revealed beneath them was a square compartment containing a stone tablet, on which was painted a crude parabatai *rune. It was neither fine work nor beautiful, but it radiated power.*

Gripping the hilt of Maellartach, Emma brought it down, point first. The blade split the tablet apart and Emma staggered back in a cloud of dust and power.

It is severed, *she thought.* The bond is severed.

She felt no joy and no relief. Only fear as a whispering voice called her name: "Emma, Emma, how could you?"

She turned to see Jem in his Silent Brother robes. A red stain was spreading slowly across his chest. She cried out as he fell. . . .

"Emma, talk to me. You're going to be all right. Julian's going to be all right." Cristina sounded on the verge of tears.

Emma knew she was in a bed, but it felt as if huge manacles had chained down her arms and legs. They were so heavy. Voices rose and fell around her: She recognized Mark's voice, and Helen's.

"What happened to them?" Helen said. "They appeared just a few moments after you, but in totally different clothing. I don't understand."

"Neither do I." Mark sounded wretched. Emma felt his hand brush her hair. "Emma, where have you been?"

Emma stood before the silver mirror. She saw herself reflected back: pale hair, runed skin, all familiar, but her eyes were the dull red of the moon in Thule.

Then she was falling, falling through the water. She saw the great monsters of the deep, shark-finned and serpentine-toothed, and then she saw Ash rise up through the water with his black wings gleaming silver and gold, and the monsters fell back from him in fear. . . .

She woke with a hoarse cry, struggling against the seaweed that dragged her down, into deeper water—she realized she was struggling against sheets that were wound around her, and sagged back, gasping for breath. Hands were on her shoulders, then brushing back her hair; a soft voice was saying her name.

"Emma," Cristina said. "Emma, it's all right. You've been dreaming."

Emma opened her eyes. She was in her room in the Institute; blue paint, familiar mural on the wall of swallows in flight over castle towers, sunlight spilling through an open window. She could hear the sounds of the sea, of music playing in another room.

"Cristina," Emma whispered. "I'm so glad it's you."

Cristina made a hiccuping noise and threw her arms around Emma, hugging her tightly. "I'm so sorry," she said. "I'm *so* sorry we left Faerie without you, it's all I've been able to think about. I should never, *never* have left you—"

As if from a great distance, Emma remembered the Unseelie Court. How the flames had cut them off from Cristina and the others, how she had nodded at her, giving her permission to save herself, the others. "Tina!" she exclaimed, patting her friend on the back. Her voice was hoarse, her throat oddly sore. "It's all right, I told you to go."

Cristina sat back, her nose and eyes pink. "But where did you go? And why did you keep calling me the Rose of Mexico?" She wrinkled up her forehead in puzzlement.

Emma made a noise that was half laugh, half gasp. "I have a *lot* to tell you," she said. "But first, I just have to know"—she caught Cristina's hand—"is everyone alive? Julian, all the others—"

"Of course!" Cristina looked horrified. "Everyone's alive. Everyone."

Emma squeezed Cristina's hand and let go. "What has the blight done to Magnus? Are we too late?"

"It's odd that you should ask. Alec and Magnus arrived here yesterday." Cristina hesitated. "Magnus isn't doing well at all. He's very ill. We've been in contact with the Spiral Labyrinth—"

"But they still think it's the ley lines." Emma started to swing her legs out of the bed. A wave of dizziness swamped her, and she braced herself against the pillows, breathing hard.

"No, no, they don't. I realized it was the blight in Faerie. Emma, don't try to get up—"

"What about Diana?" Emma demanded. "She was in Idris—"

"She isn't anymore." Cristina looked grim. "That's another long story. But she's fine."

"Emma!" The door burst open and Helen flew in, all disarrayed fair hair and anxious eyes. She flew to hug Emma, and Emma felt another wave of dizziness go over her: She thought of Thule, and how Helen had been separated from her family forever there. She would never forgive the Clave for exiling Helen to Wrangel Island, but at least she was back. At least this was a world where it was possible to be lost and then return.

Helen hugged Emma until she waved her arms to indicate that she needed oxygen. Cristina fussed as Emma once against tried to get up and succeeded in propping herself against the pillows just as Aline, Dru, Tavvy, Jace, and Clary crowded in.

"Emma!" Tavvy exclaimed, having no time for sickroom protocols, and jumped up onto the bed. Emma hugged him gently and ruffled his hair while the others gathered around; she heard Jace ask Cristina if Emma had been talking and whether she seemed coherent.

"You shaved," she said, pointing at him. "It's a big improvement."

There was a scrum of hugging and exclaiming; Clary came last and smiled down at Emma the same way she'd once smiled at her outside the Council Hall, the first time they'd ever met, when Clary had helped dispel the fears of a terrified child.

"I knew you'd be all right," Clary said, her voice pitched so low only Emma could hear her.

There was a knock on the door, which barely opened into the crowded room. Emma felt a flare like a match tip against her left arm, and realized with a shock of joy what it was, just as Julian stepped into the room, leaning on Mark's shoulder.

Her *parabatai* rune. It felt like forever since it had sparked with life. Her eyes met Julian's and for a moment she was unaware of anything else: just that Julian was there, that he was all right, that there were bandages on his left arm and visible under his T-shirt but it didn't matter, he was *alive*.

"He just woke up about an hour ago," Mark said as the others beamed at Julian. "He's been asking for you, Emma."

Aline clapped her hands together. "Okay, now that we've gotten the hugging and stuff out of the way, where *were* you two?" She indicated Emma and Julian with an accusatory wave of her hand. "Do you know how terrified we were when Mark and Cristina and the others suddenly appeared and you weren't with them, and then you suddenly popped out of nowhere all beaten up and wearing strange clothes?" She gestured to Emma's night table, where her Thule clothes lay neatly folded.

"I . . . ," Emma began, and broke off as Aline marched out of the room. "Is she mad?"

"Worried," Helen said diplomatically. "We all were. Emma, you had a broken collarbone, and Julian had broken ribs. They should be better now—it's been three days." The exhaustion and worry of those three days told in the dark circles beneath her eyes.

"And you were incoherent," said Jace. "Julian was out cold at first, but you kept shouting about demons and black skies and a dead sun. Like you'd been to Edom." Jace's eyes were narrowed. He wasn't far off, Emma thought; Jace could be silly when he felt like it, but he was smart.

Aline stomped back into the room. She had quite a stomp for a woman who was built along delicate lines. "Also, what is *this?*" she demanded, holding up the Mortal Sword.

Tavvy made a delighted noise. "I know that one! It's the Mortal Sword!"

"No, the Mortal Sword is broken," Dru said. "That's got to be something else." She frowned. "What *is* it, Jules?"

"It's the Mortal Sword," Julian said. "But we have to keep its existence here an absolute secret."

Another hubbub broke out. Someone pounded on the door; it turned out Kit and Ty were in the corridor. They'd been downstairs with Kieran, Alec, and Magnus and had just found out Emma was awake. Cristina scolded everyone in Spanish for making noise, and Jace wanted to hold the Mortal Sword, and Julian indicated to Mark that he could stand on his own, and Aline stuck her head into the hallway to say something to Ty and Kit, and Emma looked at Julian, who was looking directly back at her.

"All right, *stop*," Emma said, throwing her hands up. "Give me and Julian a second alone to talk. Then we'll tell you everything." She frowned. "But not in my bedroom. It's crowded and giving me privacy issues."

"The library," Clary said. "I'll help set it up, and get you some food. You must be starving, even though we gave you a few of these." She tapped the Nourishment rune on Emma's arm. "Okay, come on, clear the room. . . ."

"Give Ty a hug for me," Emma said to Tavvy as he hopped down. He looked dubious about the transference of hugs, but filed out with everyone else.

And then the room was quiet and empty except for Emma and Julian. She slid out of bed, and this time she managed to stand without dizziness. She felt the slight twinge of her rune and thought: *It's because Julian's here, I'm drawing strength from him.*

"Do you feel it?" she said, touching her left bicep. "The *parabatai* rune?"

"I don't feel much," he said, and Emma's heart sank. She'd known it, really, from the moment he'd walked in, but she hadn't realized how much hope she still had hanging on the idea that somehow, the spell might have been broken.

"Turn around," she said dully. "I have to get dressed."

Julian raised his eyebrows. "I *have* seen it all before, you know."

"Which does not entitle you to further viewing privileges," said Emma. "Turn. Around."

Julian turned around. Emma fished into her closet for the least Thule-esque clothes she had and eventually fished out a flowered dress and vintage sandals. She changed, watching Julian as he watched the wall.

"So just to be clear, the spell is back," she said once the dress was on. Quietly, she picked up the vest she'd worn in Thule, took Livvy's letter, and transferred it to the pocket of her dress.

"Yes," he said, and she felt the word like a needle in her heart. "I had some dreams, dreams with emotions in them, but by the time I woke up . . . they faded. I know that I felt, even how I felt, but I can't *feel* it. It's like knowing I had a wound, but I can't remember what the pain was like."

Emma kicked her feet into her sandals and twisted her hair up into a knot. She suspected she probably looked pallid and horrible, but did it matter? Julian was the only person she wanted to impress, and he didn't care.

"Turn around," she said, and he turned. He looked grimmer than she would have thought, as if the spell being unbroken was bitter to him, too. "So what are you going to do?"

"Come here," he said, and she came close to him with a little reluctance as he began to unwind the bandages on his arm. It was hard not to remember the way he'd spoken to her in Thule, the way he'd placed each bit of himself, his hope and yearning and desire and fear, in her hands.

I'm not myself without you, Emma. Once you dissolve dye in water, you can't take it back out. It's like that. I can't take you out of me. It means cutting out my heart, and I don't like myself without my heart.

The bandages came free and he extended his forearm to her. She sucked in her breath. "Who did this?" she demanded.

"I did," he said. "Before we left Thule."

Across the skin of his inner arm, he had cut words: words that had healed now, into red-black scars.

YOU ARE IN THE CAGE.

"Do you know what this means?" he said. "Why I did this?"

Her heart felt like it was breaking into a thousand pieces. "I do," she said. "Do you?"

Someone knocked on the door; Julian jumped back and began hurriedly rewrapping his arm.

"What's up?" Emma called. "We're almost ready."

"I just wanted to tell you to come down," Mark said. "We are all eager to hear your story, and I've made my famous doughnut sandwiches."

"I'm not sure 'Tavvy likes them' is exactly what most people mean when they say 'famous,'" Emma said.

Julian, her Julian, would have laughed. This Julian just said, "We'd better go," and walked past her to the door.

At first Cristina thought Kieran's hair had turned white from shock or annoyance. It took a few minutes for her to realize it was powdered sugar.

They were in the kitchen, helping Mark as he put together plates of apples and cheese and "doughnut sandwiches"—truly horrible concoctions involving doughnuts cut in half and filled with peanut butter, honey, and jelly.

Kieran liked the honey, though. He licked some off his fingers and started to peel an apple with a small, sharp knife.

"Guácala." Cristina laughed. "Gross! Wash your hands after you lick them."

"We never washed our hands in the Hunt," said Kieran, sucking honey from his finger in a way that made Cristina's stomach feel fluttery.

"That's true. We didn't," Mark agreed, slicing a doughnut in half and sending up another cloud of powdered sugar.

"That is because you lived like savages," said Cristina. "Go wash your hands!" She steered Kieran to the sink, whose taps still confused him, and went over to dust sugar off the back of Mark's shirt.

He turned to smile at her, and her stomach flipped again. Feeling very odd, she left Mark and went back to cutting cheese into small cubes as Kieran and Mark squabbled fondly about whether or not it was disgusting to eat sugar directly out of the box.

There was something about being with both of them that was sweetly, calmly domestic in a way she hadn't felt since she'd left home. Which was odd, because there was nothing ordinary at all about either Mark or Kieran and nothing normal about how she felt about the two of them.

She had, in fact, hardly seen either of them since they'd returned from Faerie. She'd spent her time in Emma's room, worried that Emma would wake up and she wouldn't be there. She'd slept on a mattress next to the bed, though she hadn't slept all that much; Emma had tossed restlessly night and day and called out over and over: for Livvy, for Dru and Ty and Mark, for her parents, and most often, for Julian.

That was another reason Cristina wanted to be in the room with Emma, one she had not admitted to anyone. In her incoherent state, Emma was calling out to Julian that she loved him, for him to come and hold her. Any of those statements might be written off as the love felt between *parabatai*—but then again, they might not be.

As a keeper of Emma and Julian's secret, Cristina felt she owed it to them both to protect Emma's unconscious confidences.

She knew Mark felt the same: He'd been with Julian, though he reported that Julian cried out much less. It was one of the few things Mark had said to her since they'd gotten back from Faerie. She'd been avoiding both Mark and Kieran deliberately—Diego and Jaime were in prison, the Consul was under house arrest, the Dearborns were still in power, and Emma and Julian were unconscious; she was far too frayed to deal with her mess of a love life at the moment.

She hadn't realized till this moment quite how much she'd missed them.

"Hello!" It was Tavvy, bouncing into the kitchen. He'd been subdued the last few days while Julian had been sick, but he'd recovered with the admirable elasticity of children. "I'm supposed to carry sandwiches," he added with the air of someone who has been given a task of great importance.

Mark gave him a plate of the doughnuts, and another to Kieran, who shepherded Tavvy out of the room in the manner of one growing used to being surrounded by a large family.

"I wish I'd had a camera," Cristina said after they left. "A photograph of a haughty prince of Faerie carrying a plate of terrible doughnut sandwiches would be quite a memento."

"My sandwiches are not terrible." Mark leaned back against the counter with an easy grace. In blue jeans and a T-shirt, he looked entirely human—if you didn't note his sharply pointed ears. "You really care about him, don't you?"

"About Kieran?" Cristina felt her pulse speed up: with nerves and with closeness to Mark. They had spoken only of surface things for days. The intimacy of discussing their actual feelings was making her heart race. "Yes. I—I mean, you know that, don't you?" She felt herself blush. "You saw us kiss."

"I did," Mark said. "I did not know what it meant to you, nor to Kieran, either." He looked thoughtful. "It is easy to be carried away in Faerie. I wanted to reassure you I was not angry or jealous. I am truly not, Cristina."

"All right," she said awkwardly. "Thank you."

But what did it mean that he wasn't angry or jealous? If what had happened with her and Kieran in Faerie had happened among Shadowhunters, she would have considered it a declaration of interest. And would have worried that Mark was upset. But it hadn't been, had it? It might have meant nothing more to Kieran than a handshake.

She trailed a hand along the smooth top of the counter. She could not help but remember a conversation she had had with Mark once, here in the Institute. It felt so long ago. It came back to her like a lucid dream:

There was nothing rehearsed about the look Mark gave her then. "I meant it when I said you were beautiful. I want you, and Kieran would not mind—"

"You want me?"

"Yes," Mark said simply, and Cristina looked away, suddenly very aware of how close his body was to hers. Of the shape of his shoulders under his jacket. He was lovely as faeries were lovely, with a sort of unearthliness, as quicksilver as moonlight on water. He didn't seem quite touchable, but she had seen him kiss Kieran and knew better. "You do not want to be wanted?"

In another time, the time before, Cristina would have blushed. "It is not the sort of compliment mortal women enjoy."

"But why not?" said Mark.

"Because it makes it sound like I am a thing you want to use. And when you say Kieran would not mind, you make it sound as if he would not mind because I do not matter."

"That is very human," he said. "To be jealous of a body but not a heart."

"You see, I do not want a body without a heart," she said.

A body without a heart.

She could have both Mark and Kieran now, in the way that Mark had suggested so long ago—she could kiss them, and be with them, and bid them good-bye when they left her, because they would.

"Cristina," Mark said. "Are you all right? You seem—sad. I would have hoped to reassure you." He touched the side of her face lightly, his fingers tracing the shape of her cheekbone.

I don't want to talk about this, Cristina thought. They had spent three days speaking of nothing important save Emma and Julian. Those three days and the peace of them felt delicate, as if too much discussion of reality and its harshness might shatter everything.

"We don't have time to talk now," she said. "Perhaps later—"

"Then let me say one thing." Mark spoke quietly. "I have been long torn between two worlds. I thought I was a Shadowhunter, told myself I was only that. But I have realized my ties to Faerie are stronger than I thought. I cannot leave half my blood, half my heart, in either world. I dream it might be possible to have both, but I know it cannot be."

Cristina turned away so as not to see the look on his face. Mark would choose Faerie, she knew. Mark would choose Kieran. They had their history together, a great love in the past. They were both faeries, and though she had studied Faerie and yearned toward it with all her heart, it was not the same. They would be together because they belonged together, because they were beautiful together, and there would be pain for her when she lost them both.

But that was the way for mortals who loved the folk of Faerie. They always paid a heavy price.

It was, Emma discovered, not actually possible to hate a doughnut sandwich. Even if her arteries might pay for it someday down the line. She ate three.

Mark had placed them with care on platters, which sat in the middle of one of the big library tables—something about the desire to please in the gesture touched Emma's heart.

Everyone else was crowded around the long table, including Kieran, who sat quietly, his face blank, beside Mark. He wore a simple black shirt and linen pants; he looked nothing like he had the last time Emma had seen him, in the Unseelie Court, covered in blood and dirt, his face twisted with rage.

Magnus looked different than he had the last time she'd seen him, too. And not in a good way. He had come down to the library leaning heavily on Alec, his face gray and tight, sharply drawn with pain. He lay on a long couch by the table, a blanket around his shoulders. Despite the blanket and the warm weather, he shivered often. Every time he did, Alec would bend down over him and smooth his hair back or draw the blankets up more tightly over his shoulders.

And every time Alec did, Jace—sitting across the table, beside Clary—would tense, his hands curling into useless fists. Because that was what being *parabatai* meant, Emma knew. Feeling someone else's pain as if it was your own.

Magnus kept his eyes closed while Emma told the story of Thule, Julian interjecting quietly when she forgot a detail or glossed over something he thought was necessary. He didn't push her, though, at the harder parts—when she had to talk about how Alec and Magnus had died or about Isabelle's last stand with the Mortal Sword. About Clary's death at Lilith's hands.

And about Jace. His eyes widened incredulously when Emma spoke of the Jace who lived in Thule, who had been bound to Sebastian for so long he would never be free. Emma saw Clary reach over to grip his hand tightly, her eyes shining with tears the way they hadn't when her own death had been described.

But the worst, of course, was describing Livvy. Because while the other stories were horrors, knowing about Livvy in Thule reminded them that there was a horror story in this world that they could neither change nor reverse.

Dru, who had insisted on sitting at the table with everyone else, said nothing when they described Livvy, but tears streaked silently down her cheeks. Mark went ashen. And Ty—who looked thinner than Emma remembered him, bitten down like a ragged fingernail—made no sound either. Kit, who was sitting beside him, tentatively put his hand over Ty's where it lay on the table; Ty didn't react, though he didn't draw away from Kit either.

Emma went on, because she had no choice but to go on. Her throat was aching badly by the time she finished; gray-faced, Cristina pushed a glass of water toward her and she took it gratefully.

A silence had fallen. No one seemed to know what to say. The only sound was the faint tinny chime of the music coming from Tavvy's headphones as he played with a train set in the corner—they were Ty's headphones, really, but he'd put them gently on Tavvy's head before Emma had started talking.

"Poor Ash," Clary said. She was very pale. "He was—my nephew. I mean, my brother was a monster, but . . ."

"Ash saved me," said Emma. "He saved my life. And he said it was because he liked something I said about you. But he stayed because he wanted to stay in Thule. We offered to bring him back. He didn't want to come."

Clary smiled tightly, her eyes sparkling with tears. "Thank you."

"Okay, let's talk about the important part." Magnus turned to Alec with a furious look on his face. "You *killed yourself*? Why would you do that?"

Alec looked startled. "That wasn't me," he pointed out. "It's an alternate universe, Magnus!"

Magnus grabbed Alec by the front of his shirt. "If I die, you are not allowed to do *anything* like that! Who would take care of our kids? How could you do that to them?"

"We never had kids in that world!" Alec protested.

"Where *are* Rafe and Max?" Emma whispered to Cristina.

"Simon and Isabelle are looking after them in New York. Alec checks in every day to see if Max is getting sick, but he seems fine so far," Cristina whispered back.

"You are *not allowed* to hurt yourself, under any circumstances," Magnus said, his voice gruff. "Do you understand that, Alexander?"

"I would never," Alec said softly, stroking Magnus's cheek. Magnus clasped Alec's hand against his face. "Never."

They all looked away, letting Magnus and Alec have their moment in privacy.

"I see why you clawed at me when I tried to lift you up," Jace said to Emma. His golden eyes were dark with a regret she could only begin to understand. "When you first came through the Portal. You were lying on the ground, and I—you were bleeding, and I thought I should carry you to the infirmary, but you clawed at me and screamed like I was a monster."

"I don't remember it," Emma said honestly. "Jace, I know you're a completely different person than *him*, even if he did look like you. You can't feel bad or responsible for what someone who wasn't you did." She turned to look at the rest of the table. "The Thule versions of us aren't really us," she added. "If you think of them as copies of you, it'll drive you crazy."

"That Livvy," said Ty. "She isn't mine. She isn't my Livvy."

Kit gave him a quick, startled look. The other Blackthorns looked puzzled, but—though Julian raised his hand, then lowered it again, as if he meant to protest—no one spoke.

Perhaps it *was* better for Ty to know and to understand that the Livvy in Thule wasn't the same Livvy he'd lost. Still, Emma thought of the letter, now in her pocket, and felt its weight as if it were made of iron rather than paper and ink.

"It is terrible to believe that there can be such darkness so close to our own world," Mark said in a low voice. "That we evaded this future by such a thin margin."

"It wasn't just chance, Mark," said Helen. "It was because we had Clary, because we had Jace, because we had good people working together to make things right."

"We have good people now," Magnus said. "I have seen good people fall and fail in the past."

"Magnus, you and Alec came here because you thought you might learn how to cure yourself," Helen began.

"Because Catarina told us to," Magnus corrected. "Believe me, I don't just pop out to California for my health under normal circumstances."

"There's nothing normal about any of this," said Emma.

"Please," Helen said. "I know this was an awful story, and we're all upset, but we have to focus."

"Wait a second," Magnus said. "Does this mean Max is turning into a tiny little demon? Do you know how many preschool waiting lists he's on? He'll never get into the Little Red School House now."

Aline threw a lamp. No one was expecting it, and the result was quite spectacular: It shattered against one of the dormer windows, and pieces of ceramic flew everywhere.

She stood up, dusting off her hands. "Everyone, BE QUIET AND LISTEN TO MY WIFE," she said. "Magnus, I know you make jokes when you're scared. I remember Rome." She gave him a surprisingly sweet smile. "But we have to focus." She turned to Helen. "Go on, honey. You're doing great."

She sat back down and folded her hands.

"She definitely has a temper," Emma whispered to Cristina. "I like it."

"Remind me to tell you about the frittata," Cristina whispered back.

"The important thing here," said Helen, "is the blight. We didn't realize how important it was—that the blighted areas will become doorways for demons. That our warlocks"—she looked at Magnus—"will turn *into* demons. We have to close up these doorways and destroy the blight, and we can't expect any help from Idris."

"Why?" said Julian. "What's going on? What about Jia?"

"She's under house arrest in Idris," Aline said quietly. "Horace is claiming he caught her meeting with faeries in Brocelind. She and Diana were arrested together, but Diana escaped."

"We heard about some of this from Diana," said Clary. "After she escaped from Idris, Gwyn brought her here and she filled us in on what happened to her in Alicante."

"Why isn't she still here?" asked Emma. "Why did she leave?"

"Look at this." Mark pushed a piece of paper across the table; Julian and Emma leaned in to read it together.

It was a message from the Clave. It said that Diana Wrayburn was missing, believed to be under the influence of faeries. All Institutes should be on the lookout for her, for her own good, and alert the Inquisitor as soon as she was spotted.

"It's all nonsense," said Aline. "My father says they're afraid of Diana's influence and didn't want to just name her as a traitor. They're even lying about what happened to the Inquisitor. They're claiming he lost his arm in a battle with Downworlders when they were clearing them out of Idris."

"His *arm?*" echoed Emma, bewildered.

"Diana cut the Inquisitor's arm off," said Jace.

Emma upset her glass of water. "She did *what?*"

"He was threatening her," said Clary grimly. "If Gwyn hadn't been around to get her out of Alicante, I don't know what would have happened."

"It was badass," said Jace.

"Well, good for her," said Emma. "That definitely calls for a large tapestry one of these days."

"Fifty bucks says the Inquisitor develops a high-tech robot arm that shoots laser beams," said Kit. Everyone looked at him. "It always happens in movies," he explained.

"We're Shadowhunters," said Julian. "We're not high-tech."

He sat back in his chair. Emma could see the bandages under his sleeve when he moved.

YOU ARE IN THE CAGE.

She shivered.

"We wanted Diana to stay here with us, but she thought that would make us a target," said Helen. "She went to hide out with Gwyn, though she's meant to check back in a few days."

Emma privately hoped Diana and Gwyn were having a fabulous romantic time in a treetop or something. Diana deserved it.

"It's awful all over," said Alec. "The Downworlder registry is almost complete—with, of course, some notable exceptions." He indicated Helen and Aline with a nod.

"Quite a few Downworlders have managed to escape the Registry, *moi* included," said Magnus. "Alec threatened to kill me if I even considered putting my name on some sinister list of the Cohort's undesirables."

"There was no actual threatening," said Alec, in case anyone was wondering.

"Well, all Downworlders have been removed from Idris, including the ones who were teachers at Shadowhunter Academy," Mark said.

"Rumors are running wild among Downworlders of sneak attacks by Shadowhunters. It's like the bad old days before the Accords," Magnus said.

"The Iron Sisters have cut off communication with the Cohort," said Aline. "The Silent Brothers haven't said anything yet, but there was a statement from the Iron Sisters that they didn't accept Horace's authority. Horace is furious and keeps hounding them, especially because they have the shards of the Mortal Sword."

"There's more," said Cristina. "Diego, Divya, and Rayan have been arrested, along with many others." Her voice was strained.

"They're throwing everyone in prison who disagrees with them," said Aline.

In a small voice, Dru said, "Jaime went to try to save his brother, but he wound up in prison too. We heard about it from Patrick Penhallow."

Emma looked at Cristina, who was biting her lip unhappily.

"Since we have no help from the Clave, and perhaps active opposition, what do we do?" Julian said.

"We do what Tessa told you to do in Thule," said Magnus. "I trust Tessa; I always have. Just as you trusted Livvy when you found her in Thule. They might not be exact copies of us, these alternate selves, but they are not so different, either."

"So we pour some of the water of Lake Lyn on the blighted areas, and save some to cure the warlocks," said Helen. "The big problem being how we get to Lake Lyn past the Cohort guards who are all over Idris. And then how we get back out—"

"I will do it," Magnus said, sitting up. The blanket fell loosely around him. "I will—"

"No!" Alec said sharply. "You are not risking yourself, Magnus, not in your condition."

Magnus opened his mouth to object. Clary leaned across the table, her eyes entreating. "Please, Magnus. You've helped us so many times. Let us help you."

"How?" Magnus said gruffly.

Jace rose to his feet. "We'll go to Idris."

Clary stood up too; she only reached to Jace's bicep, but her determination was clear. "I can create Portals. We can't get into

Alicante, but we don't need to—just into Idris. We'll go to Lake Lyn, then Brocelind, and get back as fast as we can. We'll go as many times as we need to so we can get enough water."

"There are guards patrolling all over Idris," said Helen. "You'll need to be armed and prepared."

"Then we'll start getting armed now." Jace winked at Magnus. "Prepare to be helped, warlock, whether you like it or not."

"Not," Magnus grumbled, subsiding into his blanket, but he was smiling. And the look Alec gave Jace and Clary was more eloquent than any speech.

"Wait." Aline held up a hand. She was shuffling through a pile of papers on the table. "I've got the schedules of the patrols here. They're sweeping different locations in Idris to make sure they're 'clear' of Downworlders." She spoke the words with distaste. "They're doing Lake Lyn today and tonight." She looked up. "You can't go now."

"We can deal with some guards," Jace said.

"No," said Magnus. "It's too dangerous. You could deal with ten guards, or twenty, but this is going to be fifty or a hundred—"

"A hundred," said Helen, looking over Aline's shoulder. "At least."

"I won't let you take the risk," Magnus said. "I'll wear myself out using my magic to drag you back."

"*Magnus.*" Clary sounded appalled.

"What does the schedule say?" asked Julian. "When can they go?"

"Tomorrow, dawn," said Aline. "They should have dispersed by then." She set the papers down. "I know it's not ideal, but it's what we need to do. We'll spend today setting up and getting you ready. Making sure everything goes without a hitch."

There was a general hubbub as everyone offered to pitch in, claiming one responsibility or another: Emma and Cristina were going to talk to Catarina about the possible cure, Mark and Julian were going to check maps of Brocelind to find where the areas of blight were, Clary and Jace were going to gather up their gear and weapons, and Helen and Aline were going to try to find out exactly when the patrol would be moving from Lake Lyn to Brocelind Forest. Ty and Kit, meanwhile, would start putting together lists of local warlocks who might need lake water when it was retrieved.

As everyone gathered up their things, Ty went over to the corner where Tavvy was playing and knelt down to hand him a small train. Amid the confusion, Emma slipped after him. He appeared to have offered the train as a trade for his headphones.

"Ty," Emma said, crouching down. Tavvy was busy turning trains upside down. "I have to give you something."

"What kind of thing?" He sounded puzzled.

She hesitated and then drew the envelope from her pocket. "It's a letter," she said. "From the Livvy in the other dimension—in Thule. We told her about you and she wanted to write something for you to read. I haven't looked at it," she added. "It's just for you."

Ty stood up. He was graceful as a hollow-boned bird and looked as light and fragile. "She's not my Livvy."

"I know," Emma said. She couldn't stop looking at his hands—his knuckles were raw and red. Her Julian would have noticed that already and been moving heaven and earth to find out what happened. "And you don't have to read it. But it's yours, and I think you should have it." She paused. "After all, it did come from a pretty long way away."

A look passed over his face that she couldn't quite decipher; he took it, though, and folded it up inside his jacket.

"Thanks," he said, and went across the room to join Kit in the DOWNWORLDERS—WARLOCKS section, where Kit was struggling with several heavy books.

"Don't," she heard Cristina say, and looked around in surprise. She didn't see Cristina anywhere, but that had definitely been her voice. She glanced around; Tavvy was absorbed with his train and everyone else was hurrying to and fro. "Kieran. I know you are worried for Adaon, but you didn't speak a word through the whole meeting."

Oh dear, Emma thought. She realized that Cristina's voice was coming from the other side of a bookcase, and that Cristina and Kieran had no idea she was there. If she tried to leave, though, they'd know immediately.

"These are Shadowhunter politics," Kieran said. There was something in his voice, Emma thought. Something different. "It is not something I understand. It is not my fight."

"It *is* your fight," Cristina replied. Emma had rarely heard her speak with such intensity. "You fight for what you love. We all do." She hesitated. "Your heart is hidden, but I know you love Mark. I know you love Faerie. Fight for that, Kieran."

"Cristina—" Kieran began, but Cristina had already hurried away; she emerged from her side of the bookcase and saw Emma immediately. She looked surprised, then guilty, and hurried quickly from the room.

Kieran started to follow but stopped halfway across the room and leaned his hands on the table, bowing his head.

Emma started to edge out from behind the bookcase, hoping to creep to the door unnoticed. She should have known better than to try to sneak by a faerie, she realized ruefully; Kieran looked up at the first tap of her shoes on the polished wood floor. "Emma?"

"Just going," she said. "Don't mind me."

"But I wish to mind you," he said, coming out from behind the table. He was all graceful angles, pallor and darkness. Emma supposed she could see what drew Cristina to him. "I have had cause to understand how much pain I brought to you, when you were whipped by Iarlath," he said. "I never desired that outcome, yet I did cause it. I cannot change that, but I can offer my sincere regrets and swear myself to accomplish any task that you set me."

Emma had not been expecting this. "Any task? Like, you would be willing to learn to hula dance?"

"Is that a torture of your people?" said Kieran. "Then yes, I would submit to it, for your sake."

Sadly Emma put aside the thought of Kieran in a grass skirt. "You fought on our side in the Unseelie Court," she said. "You brought Mark and Cristina back safely with you, and they mean everything to me. You've proven yourself a true friend, Kieran. You have my forgiveness and you don't need to do anything else to earn it."

He actually blushed, the touch of color warming his pale cheeks. "That is not what a faerie would say."

"It's what I say," Emma said cheerfully.

Kieran strode toward the door, where he paused and turned to her. "I have known how Cristina loves you, and I understand why. If you had been born a faerie, you would be a great knight of the Court. You are one of the bravest people I have ever known."

Emma stammered a thank-you, but Kieran was already gone, like a shadow melting into the forest. She stared after him, realizing what it was she'd heard earlier in the way he said Cristina's name, as if it were a torment that he adored: She had never heard him speak any name but Mark's that way before.

"Is there anything you want to talk to me about?" Magnus asked as Julian prepared to leave the library.

He'd thought Magnus was asleep—he was leaning back on his couch, his eyes closed. There were deep shadows beneath them, the kind that came from multiple sleepless nights.

"No." Julian tensed all over. He thought of the words cut onto the skin of his arm. He knew if he showed them to Magnus, the warlock would want to take the spell off him immediately, and Magnus was too weak for that. The effort might kill him.

He also knew his reaction to the thought of Magnus dying was off-kilter and wrong. It was dulled down, flattened. He didn't want Magnus to die, but he knew he should feel more than *not wanting*, just as he should have felt more than flat relief at being reunited with his siblings.

And he knew he should feel more when he saw Emma. It was as if a white space of nothingness had been cut out all around her and when he stepped into it, everything went blank. It was difficult to even speak. It was worse than it had been before, he thought. Somehow, his emotions were even more damped down than they had been before Thule.

He felt despair, but it was dull and distant too. It made him want to grip the blade of a knife just to feel anything at all.

"I suppose you wouldn't," Magnus said. "Given that you probably don't feel much." His cat eyes glittered. "I shouldn't have put that spell on you. I regret it."

"Don't," Julian said, and he wasn't sure if he meant *don't say that to me* or *don't regret it*. His emotions were too distant for him to reach. He did know he wanted to stop talking to Magnus now, and he went out into the corridor, tense and breathless.

"Jules!" He turned around and saw Ty, coming toward him along the hallway. The distant part of himself said Ty looked—different. His mind scrambled for the words "bruised/hurt/fragile" and couldn't hold them. "Can I talk to you?"

Askew, he thought. *He looks atypical for Ty*. He stopped trying to find words and followed Ty into one of the vacant bedrooms along the hall, where Ty closed the door behind them, turned around, and threw his arms around Julian without a word of warning.

It was awful.

Not because being hugged by Ty was awful. It was nice, as much as Julian could sense that it was nice: His brain said *this is your blood, your family*, and his arms went up automatically to hug

Ty back. His brother was fragile in his arms, all soft hair and sharp bones, as if he were made out of seashells and dandelion fluff and strung together with fine silk thread.

"I'm glad you're back," Ty said in a muffled voice. He'd pressed his head against Julian's shoulder, and his headphones had tilted sideways. Ty reached up automatically to right them. "I was afraid we'd never all be back together again."

"But we are back together," Julian said.

Ty leaned back a little, his hands gripping the front of Julian's jacket. "I want you to know I'm sorry," he said, in the rushed tones of someone who had practiced a speech for a long time. "At Livvy's funeral I climbed the pyre and you cut up your hands coming after me, and I thought maybe you left because you didn't want to deal with me."

Something in Julian's head was screaming. Screaming that he loved his little brother more than he loved almost anything else on earth. Screaming that Ty rarely reached out like this, rarely initiated physical contact with Julian like this. A Julian who felt very far away was scrambling desperately, wanting to react correctly, wanting to give Ty what he needed so he could recover from Livvy's death and not be wrecked or lost.

But it was like pounding on soundproofed glass. The Julian he was now couldn't hear. The silence of his heart was almost as profound as the silence he felt around Emma.

"That's not it," he said. "I mean, that wasn't it. We left because of the Inquisitor." Distant Julian was bruising his hands slamming them against the glass. This Julian struggled for words and said, "It's not your fault."

"Okay," Ty said. "I have a plan. A plan to fix everything."

"Good," Julian said, and Ty looked surprised, but he didn't see it. He was scrambling to hold on, to try to find the right words, the feeling words to say to Ty, who had thought Julian had gone away because he was angry. "I'm sure you have a great plan. I trust you."

He let go of Ty and turned toward the door. Better to be done than to risk saying the wrong thing. He would be all right as soon as the spell was off him. He could talk to Ty then.

"Jules . . . ?" Ty said. He stood uncertainly by the arm of the sofa, fiddling with the cord of his headphones. "Do you want to know . . . ?"

"It's great that you're doing better, Ty," Julian said, not looking at Ty's face, his eloquently moving hands.

It was only a few seconds, but by the time Julian made it out into the hallway he was breathing as hard as if he had escaped from a monster.

23
That Winds May Be

Diego was starting to be seriously worried about Jaime.

It was hard to tell how many days the brothers had been in the Gard's prisons. They could hear only murmurs from the other cells: The thick stone walls muffled noise deliberately to prevent communication among the prisoners. They hadn't seen Zara again either. The only people who came to their cell were the guards who brought occasional meals.

Sometimes Diego would beg the guards—dressed in the dark blue and gold of Gard Watchmen—to bring him a stele or medicine for his brother, but they always ignored him. He thought bitterly that it was exactly Dearborn's kind of clever to make sure the Watchmen who worked in the Gard were suborned to the Cohort's cause.

Jaime moved restlessly on the pile of clothes and straw Diego had managed to cobble together as a bed. He'd donated his own sweater and sat shivering in his light undershirt. Still, he wished there was more he could do. Jaime was flushed, his skin tight-looking and shiny with fever.

"I swear I saw her last night," he murmured.

"Who?" said Diego. He sat with his back to the cold stone wall, close enough to touch his brother if Jaime needed him. "Zara?"

Jaime's eyes were closed. "The Consul. She was wearing her robes. She looked at me and she shook her head. Like she thought I shouldn't be in here."

You shouldn't. You're barely seventeen. Diego had done what he could to clean Jaime up after Zara had dumped him in the cell. Most of his wounds were shallow cuts, and he had two broken fingers—but there was one deep, dangerous wound in his shoulder. Over the past days, it had puffed up and turned red. Diego felt impotently rageful—Shadowhunters didn't die of infections. They were healed by *iratzes* or they died in battle, in a blaze of glory. Not like this, of fever, on a bed of rags and straw.

Jaime smiled his crooked smile. "Don't feel sorry for me," he said. "You got the worse end of the deal. I got to run all over the world with the Eternidad. You had to romance Zara."

"Jaime—"

Jaime wheezed a cough. "I hope you pulled out one of your famous Diego Rosales moves, like winning her a big stuffed animal at a carnival."

"Jaime, we must be serious."

Jaime's wide dark eyes opened. "My dying wish is that we *not* be serious."

Diego sat up angrily. "You are not dying! And we need to talk about Cristina."

That got Jaime's attention. He struggled into a sitting position. "I *have* been thinking about Cristina. Zara doesn't know that she has the Eternidad—the heirloom—and there is no reason for her ever to know."

"We could try to figure out a way to warn Cristina. Tell her to abandon the heirloom somewhere—give it to someone else—it would give her a head start—"

"No." Jaime's eyes glimmered with fever. "Absolutely not. If we told Zara that Cristina had it, she'd torture Cristina to get the information just like she tortured me. Even if it had been thrown into the depths of the ocean, Zara wouldn't care—she would torture Cristina regardless. Zara can't know who has it."

"What if we told Cristina to give it to Zara?" Diego said slowly.

"We can't. Would you really want the Cohort to get their hands on it? We don't even understand everything it does." He reached out and took Diego's hand in his fever-hot one. His fingers felt as thin as they had when he was ten. "I will be okay," he said. "Please. Do not do any of these things for me."

There was a clang as Zara appeared in the corridor, followed by the hunched figure of Anush Joshi. Cortana glimmered at her hip. The sight annoyed Diego: A blade like Cortana should be worn strapped to the back. Zara cared more about showing off the sword than she did about having such a special weapon.

Anush carried a tray with two bowls of the usual glop on it. Kneeling, he slid it through the low gap in the bottom of the cell door.

How can someone as wonderful as Divya have such a terrible cousin? Diego thought.

"That's right, Anush," Zara said, prowling around her companion. "This is your punishment for deserting us in the forest—bringing slop to our worst, smelliest prisoners." She sneered at Diego. "Your brother doesn't look too good. Feverish, I think. Changed your mind yet?"

"Nobody's changed their mind, Zara," Jaime said.

Zara ignored him, looking at Diego. He could tell her what she wanted to know and trade Jaime's safety for the heirloom. The part of him that was a big brother, that had always protected Jaime, entreated him to do it.

But strangely, in the moment, he remembered Kieran saying: *You decide you will find a solution when the time comes, but when the worst happens, you find yourself unprepared.*

He could save Jaime in the moment, but he understood Zara well enough to know that that wouldn't mean Jaime and Diego would walk free.

If the Cohort got their way, no one would ever walk free again.

"Jaime is correct," Diego said. "No one has changed their mind."

Zara rolled her eyes. "Fine. I'll see you later."

She stalked away, Anush hurrying like a dispirited shadow in her wake.

Emma sat beside Cristina on the office desk and drank in the view. The walls were glass, and through them she could see the ocean on one side and the mountains on the other. It felt as if the colors of the world had been restored to her, after the darkness of Thule. The sea seemed to sing blues and silvers, golds and greens. The desert, too, glowed with green bright and dull, rich terra-cotta sand and dirt, and deep purple shadows between the hills.

Cristina took a small vial out of her pocket, made of thick blue glass. She unstoppered it and held it up to the light.

Nothing happened. Emma looked at Cristina sideways.

"It always takes a bit of time," Cristina said reassuringly.

"I heard you in the Unseelie Court," Emma said. "You said that it wasn't the ley lines—that it was the blight. You figured it out, didn't you? What was causing the warlocks' sickness?"

Cristina turned the vial around. "I suspected it, but I wasn't totally sure. I knew the blight in Brocelind was the same as the blight in Faerie, but when I realized the King was causing them both—that he *wanted* to poison our world—I realized it might be what was hurting the warlocks."

"And Catarina knows?"

"I told her when we got back. She said she'd look into it—"

Smoke began to stream out of the vial, gray-white and opaque. It slowly shaped itself into a slightly distorted scene, wavering at the edges: They were looking at Tessa in a loose blue dress, a stone wall visible behind her.

"Tessa?" Emma said.

"Tessa!" Cristina said. "Is Catarina there as well?"

Tessa tried to smile, but it wavered. "Last night Catarina fell into a sleep that we haven't been able to wake her from. She is—very ill."

Cristina murmured in sympathy. Emma couldn't stop staring at Tessa. She looked so different—not older or younger, but more alive. She had not realized how much Thule Tessa's emotions had seemed deadened, as if she had long ago given up on having them.

And this Tessa, Emma remembered, was pregnant. It wasn't visible yet, though Tessa did rest one hand with light protectiveness on her belly as she spoke.

"Before Catarina fell into unconsciousness," Tessa said, "she told me that she thought Cristina was right about the blight. We have some samples of it here, and we've been studying them, but I fear we will be too late to save Magnus and Catarina—and so many others." Her eyes were bright with tears.

Emma sprang to reassure her. "We think we might have the answer," she said, and scrambled to tell her story again, ending it on her meeting with Tessa in the cave. There seemed no reason to tell her now what had come after that.

"*I* told you this?" Tessa seemed astonished. "A me that you encountered in another world?"

"I know it sounds hard to believe. You were living in that cave, the big one up by Staircase Beach. You had Church with you."

"That does sound right." Tessa seemed dazed. "What's the plan? I can help you, though there are few other warlocks well enough to join me—"

"No, it's all right," Cristina said. "Jace and Clary are going."

Tessa frowned. "That seems dangerous."

"Aline found a time tomorrow when she thinks there won't be

guards at Lake Lyn," said Cristina. "They're going to leave at dawn."

"I suppose danger can never be avoided for Nephilim," said Tessa. She glanced at Cristina. "Could Emma and I speak for a moment alone, please?"

Cristina blinked in surprise, then hopped down from the desk. "Of course." She bumped Emma's shoulder companionably as she headed out the door, and then Emma was alone in the office with a wavering but determined-looking Tessa.

"Emma," Tessa said as soon as the door had shut behind Cristina. "I wanted to talk to you about Kit Herondale."

Kit picked his way across the sand, his sneakers already wet where the incoming tide had caught him unawares.

It was the first time he'd been down to the beach near the Institute without Ty. He felt almost guilty, though when he'd told Ty he was taking a walk, Ty had just nodded and said he'd see him later—Kit knew Ty wanted to talk to Julian, and he didn't want to interrupt anyway.

There was something restful about this space, where the sea met the shore. Kit had learned long ago in the Shadow Market that there were "in-between" spaces in the world where it was easier to do certain kinds of magic: the middle of bridges, caves between the earth and the underworld, borderlands between the Seelie and Unseelie Courts. And the Shadow Market itself, between Downworld and the mundane.

The tide line was a place like that, and because of that it felt like home. It reminded him of an old song he remembered someone singing to him. It must have been his father, though he always remembered it in a woman's voice.

Tell him to buy me an acre of land,
Parsley, sage, rosemary, and thyme;

Between the salt water and the sea sand,
Then he shall be a true love of mine.

"That's a very, very old song," said a voice. Kit almost tumbled off the rock he'd been clambering over. The sky was deep blue, studded with white clouds, and standing above him on a heap of rocks was Shade. He wore a ragged navy suit with a stitched collar and cuffs, his green skin a stark contrast. "How do you know it?"

Kit, who hadn't even realized he'd been humming the tune, shrugged. Shade had left off his usual hood. His green face was lined and good-humored, his hair curly and white. Small horns protruded from his temples, curling inward like seashells. Something about him struck Kit as a little odd. "Heard it in the Market."

"What are you doing out and about without your shadow?"

"Ty's not my shadow," said Kit crossly.

"My apologies. I suppose you're his." Shade's eyes were solemn. "Have you come to tell me of the progress you've made in your foolish plan to raise his sister from the dead?"

It wasn't why Kit had come down here, but he found himself telling Shade anyway, about Emma and Julian's return (though he made no mention of Thule) and the visits they'd made to the Shadow Market in the ensuing chaos, no one noticing they were gone. Julian, usually the most eagle-eyed older brother in the world, had been unconscious, and even today he'd seemed unfocused and groggy.

"You've done better than I thought you would," Shade said grudgingly, looking out to sea. "Still. You've mostly gotten the easy stuff. There's still some objects that ought to trip you up."

"You sound like you want us to fail," said Kit.

"Of course I do!" Shade barked. "You shouldn't be messing around with necromancy! It never does anyone any good!"

Kit backed up until his heels hit the surf. "Then why *are* you helping us?"

"Look, there's a reason I'm here," said Shade. "Yeah, Hypatia passed on Tiberius's message to me, but I was headed to the cave anyway to keep an eye on you."

"On me?"

"Yes, you. Did you really think I was sticking around and helping you with your dumb necromancy just as a favor to Hypatia? We're not that close. Jem's the one who asked me to look out for you. The whole Carstairs owe the Herondales business. You know."

It was weird to Kit, the idea that someone would be worried about protecting him just because of his last name. "Okay, but why are you helping us with the spell stuff?"

"Because I said I would protect you, and I will. Your Ty is stubborn like the Blackthorns are all stubborn, and you're even stubborner. If I didn't help you two, some other warlock would, someone who didn't care if you both got hurt. And no, I haven't told anyone about it."

"A lot of the other warlocks are sick," Kit said, realizing that this was what had seemed odd about Shade. He didn't look even a little bit ill.

"And I might get sick too, eventually, but there will always be unscrupulous magic-users—what *are* you looking all cross-eyed about, boy?"

"I guess I was thinking that you didn't know they found a cure for the warlock plague," said Kit. "Up at the Institute."

It was the first time he had ever seen the warlock look genuinely surprised. "The Nephilim? Found a cure for the *warlock* illness?"

Kit thought back on the way he'd been introduced to the idea of Shadowhunters. Not as people but as a vicious, holier-than-thou army of true believers. As if they were all like Horace Dearborn, and none were like Julian Blackthorn or Cristina Rosales. Or like Alec Lightwood, patiently holding a glass of water with a straw in it so his sick warlock boyfriend could drink.

"Yes," he said. "Jace and Clary are going to retrieve it. I'll make sure you get some."

Shade's face twisted, and he turned so Kit couldn't see his expression. "If you insist," he said gruffly. "But make sure Catarina Loss gets it first, and Magnus Bane. I've got some protections. I'll be fine for a good long while."

"Magnus will be the first to get it, don't worry," said Kit. "He's at the Institute now."

At that Shade spun back around. "Magnus is here?" He glanced up at the Institute where it gleamed like a legendary castle on a hill. "When he's well, tell him I'm in the Staircase Beach cave," he said. "Tell him Ragnor says hello."

Ragnor Shade? Whatever force blessed people with good names had passed this poor guy over, Kit thought.

He turned to head back up the path from the beach to the highway. The sand stretched out before him in a shimmering crescent, the tide line touched with silver.

"Christopher," said Shade, and Kit paused, surprised at the sound of the name hardly anyone ever called him. "Your father," Shade began, and hesitated. "Your father wasn't a Herondale."

Kit froze. In that moment, he had a sudden terror that it had all been a mistake: He *wasn't* a Shadowhunter, he didn't belong here, he would be taken away from all of it, from Ty, from everyone—

"Your mother," said Shade. "She was the Herondale. And an unusual one. You want to look into your mother."

Relief punched through Kit like a blow. A few weeks ago he would have been delighted to have been told he wasn't Nephilim. Now it seemed like the worst fate he could imagine. "What was her name?" he said. "Shade! What was my mother's name?"

But the warlock had jumped down from his rock and was walking away; the sound of the waves and tide swallowed up Kit's words, and Shade didn't turn around.

* * *

Killer dolls, sinister woodsmen, eyeless ghouls, and graveyards full of mist. Dru would have listed those as her top favorite things about *Asylum: Frozen Fear*, but they didn't seem to interest Kieran much. He sprawled on the other side of the couch, gazing moodily into space even when people on screen started screaming.

"This is my favorite part," said Dru, part of her mind on nibbling popcorn, the other part on whether or not Kieran was imagining himself in a different, peaceful place, maybe a beach. She didn't quite know how she'd inherited him after the meeting, just that they seemed to be the two people who hadn't been given a task to do. She'd escaped to the den, and a few moments later Kieran had appeared, flopped down on the sofa, and picked up a calendar of fluffy cats that someone—okay, her—had left around. "The bit where he steps on the voodoo doll and it explodes into blood and—"

"This manner of marking the passage of time is a marvel," said Kieran. "When you are done with one kitten, then there is another kitten. By the next winter solstice, you will have seen twelve full kittens! One of them is in a glass!"

"In December there are three kittens in a basket," Dru said. "But you should really watch the movie—"

Kieran set the calendar down and gazed at the screen in some puzzlement. Then he sighed. "I just don't understand," he said. "I love them both, but it seems as if they cannot understand that. As if it is a torment or an insult."

Dru hit the mute button and put down the remote. Finally, she thought, someone was talking to her like an adult. Admittedly, Kieran wasn't making a lot of sense, but still.

"Shadowhunters are slow to love," she said, "but once we love, we love forever."

It was something she remembered Helen having said to her once, maybe at her wedding.

Kieran blinked and focused in on her, as if she'd said something clever. "Yes," he said. "Yes, that is true. I must trust in Mark's love. But Cristina—she has never said she loves me. And they both feel so far away just now."

"Everyone feels far away just now," Dru said, thinking of how lonely the past few days had been. "But that's because they're worried. When they get worried, they pull inside themselves and sometimes they forget that you're there." She glanced down at her popcorn. "But it doesn't mean they don't care."

Kieran leaned an elbow on his knee. "So what do I do, Drusilla?"

"Um," Drusilla said. "Don't remain silent about what you want, or you may never get it."

"You are very wise," Kieran said gravely.

"Well," said Dru. "I actually saw that on a mug."

"Mugs in this world are very wise." Dru wasn't entirely sure if Kieran was smiling or not, but by the way he sat back and crossed his arms, she sensed he was done with questions. She turned the TV volume back on.

Emma pulled out the pushpins, carefully taking down the different-colored string, the old newspaper clippings, the photos curling at the edges. Each one representing a clue, or what she'd thought was a clue, to the secret of her parents' deaths: Who had killed them? Why had they died as they had?

Now Emma knew the answers. She had asked Julian some time ago what she should do with all the evidence she'd collected, but he'd indicated that it was her decision. He'd always called it her Wall of Crazy, but in a lot of ways Emma thought of it as a wall of sanity, because creating it had kept her sane during a time where she'd felt helpless, overwhelmed with missing her parents and the sure support of their love.

This was for you, Mom and Dad, she thought, dumping the last of the photos into shoe boxes. *I know what happened to you now, and the person who killed you is dead. Maybe that makes a difference. Maybe not. I know it doesn't mean I miss you any less.*

She wondered if she should say more. That revenge wasn't the panacea she had hoped for. That in fact she was a little frightened of it now: She knew how powerful it was, how it drove you. In Thule she had seen how the vengefulness of an abandoned, angry boy had burned down the world. But it hadn't made Sebastian happy. Revenge had only made Sebastian in Thule miserable, though he had conquered all he saw.

There was a knock on the door. Emma shoved the boxes into her closet and went to answer it. To her surprise, it was Julian. She would have thought he would have been downstairs with the others. They'd had a big dinner in the library—delivery Thai food—and everyone was there, reminiscing and joking, Magnus dozing gently in Alec's arms while they both sprawled on the couch. It was almost as if Jace and Clary didn't have to leave on a dangerous mission at dawn, but that was the Shadowhunter way. There were always missions. There was always a dangerous dawn.

Emma had wanted to be with them, but to be around Julian and other people when he was like this hurt. It hurt to look at him, and to conceal what she knew, and to wonder if others noticed, and if so, what they thought.

Julian went to lean against the windowsill. The stars were just coming out, pinpointing the sky with scraps of light.

"I think I messed things up with Ty," he said. "He wanted to talk to me, and I don't think I responded the right way."

Emma brushed off her knees. She was wearing a pale green vintage nightgown that doubled as a dress. "What did he want to talk to you about?"

A few loose curls of dark chocolate hair tumbled over Julian's forehead. He was still beautiful, Emma thought. It didn't make any difference what she *knew*; she ached at the sight of his painter's hands, strong and articulate, the soft darkness of his hair, the cupid's bow of his lip, the color of his eyes. The way he moved, his artist's grace, the things about him that whispered *Julian* to her. "I don't know," he said. "I didn't understand it. I *would* have understood it—I know I would have—if it weren't for the spell."

"You went up on that pyre for him," she said.

"I know—I told you, it was like a survival instinct, something I had no control over. But this isn't a matter of living and dying. It's emotions. And so my mind won't process them."

Emotions can be matters of living and dying. Emma pointed to her closet. "Do you know why I took all that down?"

Julian's brow furrowed. "You're done with it," he said. "You found out who killed your parents. You don't need that stuff anymore."

"Yes and no, I guess."

"If everything goes well, hopefully Magnus can take the spell off me tomorrow, or the day after," said Julian. "It depends how fast the cure works."

"You could have talked to him about it already," Emma said, moving to lean against the sill beside Julian. It reminded her of past, better times, when they'd both sit on the sill and read, or Julian would draw, silent and content for hours at a time. "Why wait?"

"I can't tell him all of it," Julian said. "I can't show him what I wrote on my arm—he'd want to take the spell off right away, and he's not strong enough. It could kill him."

Emma turned to him in surprise. "That's empathy, Julian. That's you understanding what Magnus might feel. That's good, right?"

"Maybe," he said. "There's something I've been doing when I'm not sure about how to handle something emotional. I try to imagine what *you* would do. What you would take into account. The conversation with Ty went too fast for me to do it, but it does help."

"What *I* would do?"

"It all breaks apart when I'm with you, of course," he said. "I can't think of what you would want me to do about you, or around you. I can't see you through your own eyes. I can't even see *me* through your eyes." He touched her bare arm lightly, where her *parabatai* rune was, tracing its edges.

She could see his reflection in the window: another Julian with the same sharp profile, the same shadowed lashes. "You have a talent, Emma," he said. "A goodness that makes people happy. You assume people are not just capable of their best but that they want to be their best. You assume the same about me." Emma tried to breathe normally. The feeling of his fingers on her rune was making her body tremble. "You believe in me more than I believe in myself."

His fingers traced a path down her bare arm, to her wrist, and back up. They were light and clever fingers; he touched her as if he were sketching her body, tracing the lines of her collarbones. Grazing the notch at the base of her throat. Gliding down to run along the neckline of her dress, just grazing the upper curve of her breasts.

Emma shivered. She could lose herself in this sensation, she knew, could drown in it and forget, shield herself behind it. "If you're going to do that," she said, "you should kiss me."

He folded her into his arms. His mouth on hers was warm and soft, a gentle kiss deepening into heat. Her hands moved over his body, the feel of it now familiar to her: the smooth muscles under his T-shirt, the roughness of scars, the delicacy of shoulder blades, the curving hollow of his spine. He murmured that she was beautiful, that he wanted her, that he always had.

Her heart was beating its way out of her chest; every one of her cells was telling her that this was Julian, her Julian, that he felt, tasted, breathed the same and that she loved him.

"This is perfect," he whispered against her mouth. "This is how we can be together and not hurt anyone."

Her body screamed at her not to react, just to go along with it.

But her mind betrayed her. "What do you mean, exactly?"

He looked at her with his dark hair half in his face. She wanted to pull him to her and cover his mouth with more kisses; she wanted to close her eyes and forget anything was wrong.

But she had never had to close her eyes with Julian before.

"It's the emotions that matter, not the act," he said. "If I'm not in love with you, we can do this, be together physically, and it won't matter to the curse."

If I'm not in love with you.

She stepped away from him. It felt as if she were tearing her own skin open, as if she would look down and see blood seeping from the wounds where she had ripped herself away from him.

"I can't," she said. "When you get your feelings back, we'll both regret that we did this when you didn't care."

He looked puzzled. "I want you just as much as I ever did. That hasn't changed."

She felt suddenly weary. "I believe you. You just told me you wanted me. That I was beautiful. But you didn't say you loved me. You've always said that before."

There was a brief flicker in his eyes. "I'm not the same person. I can't say I feel things I don't understand."

"Well, I want the same person," she said. "I want Julian Blackthorn. *My* Julian Blackthorn."

He reached to touch her face. She stepped back, away from him—not because she disliked his touch, but because she liked it too much. Her body didn't know the difference between this Julian and the one she needed.

"So who am I to you, then?" he asked, dropping his hand.

"You are the person I have to protect until my Julian comes back to live inside you again," she said. "I don't want *this.* I want the Julian I love. You might be in the cage, Jules, but as long as you are like this, *I am in the cage with you.*"

* * *

Morning came as it always did, with sunshine and the annoying chirping of birds. Emma staggered out of her bedroom with her head pounding and discovered Cristina lurking in the hallway outside her door. She was holding a mug of coffee and wearing a pretty peach sweater with pearls around the collar.

Emma had slept only about three hours after Julian had left her room, and they'd been a bad three hours at that. When she slammed the bedroom door behind her, Cristina jumped nervously into the air.

"How much coffee have you *had*?" Emma asked. She pulled her hair up and secured it with a yellow daisy-printed cloth band.

"This is my third. I feel like a hummingbird." Cristina waved the mug and fell into step beside Emma as they headed to the kitchen. "I need to talk to you, Emma."

"Why?" Emma said warily.

"My love life is a disaster," said Cristina. "*Qué lío.*"

"Oh good," Emma said. "I was afraid it was going to be something about politics."

Cristina looked tragic. "I kissed Kieran."

"What? Where?" Emma demanded, almost falling down the steps.

"In Faerie," Cristina wailed.

"Actually, I meant, like, on the cheek or what?"

"No," Cristina said. "A real kiss. With *mouths*."

"How was it?" Emma was fascinated. She couldn't picture kissing Kieran. He always seemed so cold and so removed. He was certainly beautiful, but the way a statue was beautiful, not a person.

Cristina blushed all over her face and neck. "It was lovely," she said in a small voice. "Gentle and as if he cared very much for me."

That was even stranger. However, Emma felt, the point was to strive to be supportive of Cristina. She would rather Cristina was with Mark, of course, but Mark had been mucking about rather, and there was that binding spell. . . . "Well," said Emma. "What happens in Faerie stays in Faerie, I guess?"

"If you mean I shouldn't tell Mark, he knows," said Cristina. "And if you are going to ask if I want to be with Mark alone, I cannot answer that, either. I do not know what I want."

"What about how Mark and Kieran feel about each other?" said Emma. "Is it still romantic?"

"I think they love each other in a way I cannot touch," said Cristina, and there was a sadness in her voice that made Emma want to stop dead in the middle of the hallway and put her arms around her friend. But they'd already reached the kitchen. It was crowded with people—Emma could smell coffee but not food cooking. The table was bare, the kitchen range cold. Julian and Helen, along with Mark and Kieran, were crowded around the table, where Clary and Jace sat, all of them looking with disbelief down at a piece of official-looking paper.

Emma stopped dead, Cristina wide-eyed beside her. "We thought—did you already go to Idris and come back? I thought you had to leave at dawn?" Emma said.

Jace glanced up. "We never left," he said. Clary was still staring at the paper she held, her face white and stunned.

"Was a there a problem?" Emma asked anxiously.

"You might say that." Jace's tone was light, but his golden eyes were stormy. He tapped the paper. "It's a message from the Clave. According to this, Clary and I are dead."

Zara always chose the same chair in the Inquisitor's office. Manuel suspected it was because she liked to sit beneath the portrait of herself, so that people would be forced to gaze at two Zaras, and not just one.

"Reports have been coming in all day," said Zara, twirling one of her braids. "Institutes are responding with outrage to the news of Jace and Clary's death at Faerie hands."

"As we expected," said Horace, shifting in his chair with a grunt of pain. It annoyed Manuel that Horace was still complaining about his arm, a mass of white bandages below the stump of his elbow. Surely the *iratzes* would have healed the cut, and Horace had only himself to blame for letting the Wrayburn bitch get the better of him.

Manuel detested Horace. But then, Manuel detested true believers in general. He couldn't have given less of a damn whether there were Downworlders in Alicante or faeries in Brocelind Forest or werewolves in his bathtub. Prejudice against Downworlders struck him as boring and unnecessary. The only thing it was useful for was making people afraid.

When people were afraid, they would do anything you wanted if they thought it would make them safe again. When Horace spoke of reclaiming the past glory of the Nephilim, and the crowds cheered, Manuel knew what they were truly cheering for, and it was not glory. It was a cessation of fear. The fear they had felt since the Dark War had made them understand that they were not invincible.

Once, they believed, they had been invincible. They had stood with their boots on the necks of Downworlders and demons, and they had straddled the world. Now they recalled the burning bodies in Angel Square, and they were afraid.

And fear was useful. Fear could be manipulated into more power. And power was all Manuel cared about, in the end.

"Have we heard anything from the Los Angeles Institute?" Horace asked, lounging behind his large desk. "We know from Faerie that the Blackthorns and their companions returned home. But what do they know?"

What do they know? Horace and Zara had wondered the same

when Dane's body had come back to them, nearly dismembered. Dane had been a fool, creeping away from Oban's camp in the middle of the night to seek the glory of retrieving the Black Volume on his own. (And he'd taken their time slippage medallion with him, which had meant that Manuel had discovered he'd lost a day or two when he'd returned to Idris.) Manuel suspected there was a longsword wound under those kelpie bites, but he didn't mention it to the Dearborns. They saw what they wanted to see, and if Emma and Julian knew that Horace had set an assassin on their trail, it wouldn't matter for much longer.

"About Clary and Jace?" Manuel said. "I'm sure they know that they disappeared through the Portal into Thule. It would be impossible to get them back, though. Time has passed, the Portal has closed, and Oban assured me Thule is a deadly place. By now they will be bones bleaching in the sand of another world."

"The Blackthorns and that Emma wouldn't dare say anything against us anyway," said Zara. "We still hold their secret in the palms of our hands." She touched Cortana's hilt. "Besides, nothing of theirs will be *theirs* for much longer, not even the Institute. A few others may stand against us: Mexico City, Buenos Aires, Mumbai. But we will deal with them all."

Zara was also a true believer, Manuel thought with some distaste. She was a stick and a bore and he had never believed Diego Rocio Rosales actually saw anything in her; on balance, he seemed to have turned out to be right. He suspected Diego was languishing in jail as much for rejecting Zara as for helping some idiot faerie run away from the Scholomance.

Horace turned to Manuel. "What about your phase of the plan, Villalobos?"

"Everything is in order. The Unseelie forces are massing under King Oban. When they arrive at the walls of Alicante, we will ride out to show our willingness to parley with them on the Imperishable

Fields. We will make sure all Shadowhunters in Alicante see us. After this charade, we will return to the Council and tell them that the fey have surrendered. The Cold Peace will be over, and in return for their willingness to help us, all entrances to Faerie will be sealed off with wards. It will be made off-limits to Shadowhunters."

"Very good," said Horace. "But with the Portal to Thule closing, where does that leave us with the blight?"

"Exactly where we want to be," Manuel said. He was pleased—pretending they wished to destroy the blight with fire had been his idea. He'd known it wouldn't work, and the failure would leave the Nephilim more frightened than before. "The poison has spread far enough for our purposes. The Clave all know of the blight now, and fear what it will do."

"And fear will make them agreeable," said Horace. "Zara?"

"The warlocks are growing sicker," Zara said with relish. "No reported transformations yet, but many Institutes have taken in warlocks in an effort to heal them. Once they turn into demons, you can imagine the bloody chaos that will ensue."

"Which should make it easy to enact martial law and rid ourselves of the rest of the warlocks," said Horace.

The fact that the blight would serve not just to frighten Shadowhunters but also to harm warlocks had always been seen as a plus by Horace, though Manuel saw little point in an exercise that would seriously limit the Shadowhunters' ability to do things like open Portals and heal unusual illnesses. That was the problem with true believers. They were never practical. Ah well. Some warlocks would probably survive, he reasoned. Once all the Cohort's demands were met, they could afford to be generous and destroy the blight for good. It wasn't as if Horace was fond of the blight, or its propensity to deaden angelic magic. It was simply a useful tool, as the Larkspears had been.

"Are you not worried that the transformed warlocks will get out of control and slaughter Shadowhunters? Even mundanes?"

"I am not," said Horace. "A properly trained Shadowhunter should be able to handle a warlock turned demon. If they cannot, then we have done our society a favor in culling them."

"My question is whether Oban can be trusted," said Zara, curling her lip. "He is a faerie, after all."

"He can," said Manuel. "He is far more malleable than his father was. He wants his kingdom, and we want ours. And if we bring him Prince Kieran's head as promised, he will be very pleased indeed."

Horace sighed. "If only these arrangements did not have to be secret. The whole of the Clave should glory in the rightness of our plan."

"But they don't like faeries, Papa," said Zara, who was, as always, incredibly literal. "They wouldn't like making deals with them or encouraging them to bring the blight into Idris, even if it was for a worthy cause. It *is* illegal to work with demonic magic—though I know it's necessary," she added hastily. "I wish Samantha and Dane were still around. Then we could talk to *them*."

Manuel thought with little interest of Dane, undone by his own stupidity, and of Samantha, currently raving her head off in the Basilias. He doubted either of them would have been much help even in their former states.

"It is a lonely burden, daughter, to be the ones tasked with doing the right thing," said Horace pompously.

Zara got up from her chair and patted his shoulder. "Poor Papa. Do you want to look into the scrying mirror one more time? It always cheers you up."

Manuel sat up in his chair. The scrying mirror was one of the few things he didn't find boring. Oban had magicked it to reflect the fields before the Unseelie Tower.

Zara held the mirror up so that the light from the demon towers sparked off its silver handle. She gave a little squeal as the glass turned clear, and through it they saw the green fields of Unseelie and the anthracite tower. Lined up in front of the tower were row upon row of Unseelie warriors, so many that the view of them filled the scene even as the rows diminished into the distance: an army without limit, without end. Their swords shone in the sunlight like a vast field planted with razor-sharp blades.

"What do you think?" said Horace with pride, as if he himself had put together the army. "Spectacular, isn't it, Annabel?"

The woman with the long dark-brown hair, sitting silently in the corner of the room, nodded calmly. She wore clothes that matched the ones she had worn that bloody day in the Council Hall; Zara had dredged up near-exact copies, but it was Manuel who had first thought of deploying them, as if they were themselves a weapon.

There were few things stronger than fear. Since the Council meeting, the Shadowhunters had been terrified of Annabel Blackthorn. If she appeared before them, they would cower behind Horace. His ability to protect them would be all they cared about.

And when it came to Julian Blackthorn and the rest of his irritating family, there would be more than just fear. There would be rage. Hatred. All emotions the Cohort could exploit.

Horace gave a nervous laugh and turned back to studying the mirror.

Hidden by the lengthening shadows, Manuel grinned savagely. Absolutely nobody was prepared for what was coming.

Just the way he liked it.

24
The Long Night-Time

Aline Penhallow, Head of the Los Angeles Institute:
White banners of mourning fly over our capital city today, and green flags to speed the healing of our hearts.

Heroes of the Dark War Jonathan Herondale and Clarissa Fairchild have been slain by Unseelie hands. They were on a mission for the Clave, and their deaths will be celebrated as the deaths of heroes. Their bodies have not yet been recovered.

Such a brutal breakage of the Cold Peace must be reckoned with. Starting this morning, at sunrise in Alicante, we shall consider ourselves in a state of War with Faerie-kind. Members of the Council will reach out to the Court to seek parley and reparations. If a faerie is seen outside their Lands, you are free to capture them and bring them to Alicante for questioning. If you must slay the faerie in question, you will not be in breach of the Accords.

Faeries are cunning, but we will prevail and avenge our fallen heroes. As always in a state of War, individual Shadowhunters are expected to return to Idris to report for duty within forty-eight hours. Please notify the Clave of your travel plans as Portal activity into Idris will be monitored.

Horace Dearborn, Inquisitor
NB: As our Consul, Jia Penhallow, is suspected of involvement with faeries, she is being held in the Gard tower until such time as she can be questioned.

"Jia?" Emma said in disbelief. "They *jailed* the Consul?"

"Aline is trying to reach Patrick," said Helen in a low voice. "House arrest is one thing, but this is another. Aline's frantic."

"Who knows you're alive?" Alec demanded, turning to Jace. "Who knows that what's in this letter isn't true?"

Jace looked startled. "The people in this house. Magnus—where is Magnus?"

"Sleeping," Alec said. "So, besides us?"

"Simon and Izzy. Mom. Maia and Bat. That's all." He swiveled around in his chair. "Why? Do you think we should go to Alicante? Expose their lies?"

"No," Julian said. His voice was quiet but firm. "You can't do that."

"Why not?" Helen said.

"Because this isn't a mistake," said Julian. "This is a false flag operation. They believe you're dead—they wouldn't risk this if they didn't—and they're pinning the blame on Faerie to encourage a war."

"Why would anyone want war?" said Helen. "Didn't they see what the last one did?"

"People seize power in wars," said Julian. "If they make faeries the enemy, they can make themselves the heroes. Everyone will forget the complaints they had about the current Council. They'll unite behind them in a common cause. A war can begin with a single death. Here they have two—and both are famous, heroes to the Clave."

Both Jace and Clary looked uncomfortable.

"I see a flaw in this plan," said Jace. "They still have to fight and win a war."

"Maybe," said Julian. "Maybe not. It depends what their plan is."

"I see another flaw," said Clary. "We're not actually dead. It's pretty cocky of them to think they can get away with pretending we are."

"I think they believe it," said Emma. "The fight in the Court was chaos. They probably don't realize who went through the Portal into Thule and who didn't. And who knows what Manuel told them. He likes to bend the truth anyway, and without the Mortal Sword, he can bend away. I bet he wants a war."

"But surely the Council won't truly support the idea of a war with Faerie," said Clary. "Or do you really think the whole Council is lost to us?"

Emma was surprised; Clary was looking at Julian as if she were deeply invested in his answer, though she was five years older. It was strange to think Julian's sharp brilliance didn't just belong to her, to his family.

"Enough of them are," said Julian. "Enough of them have already gotten behind the Cohort and this message. Otherwise they wouldn't be demanding we all return to Alicante in two days."

"But we're not going to do that," said Mark. "We cannot go back to Alicante now. It is under the Cohort's control."

"And last time we were there, Horace sent us on a suicide mission," Emma pointed out. "I don't think we'd all be safe in Idris." It was a sobering thought—Idris was their homeland, meant to be the safest place in the world for Shadowhunters.

"We're not going," Helen said. "Not only would it be unsafe but it would mean abandoning the warlocks to the ravages of the blight."

"But Jace and Clary can't go to Lake Lyn," said Alec. His black hair was standing up in a ruffled mess, and his hands were tightened into fists. "All Portal activity is being monitored."

"That's why you didn't leave at dawn," Emma said, wondering how long Clary and Jace had been sitting here, staring at the letter in horror.

"But there has to be some way," Jace said, gazing at Alec with desperation. "Clary and I can travel overland, or—"

"You can't," Emma interrupted. "There are pieces of this I don't understand, but I can tell you one thing. The Cohort is using your deaths to get what they want. If the two of you go to Alicante and the Cohort hears about it, even a whisper, they'll put everything they've got into killing you."

"Emma's right," said Julian. "They have to keep believing you're dead."

"Then I'll go," Alec said. "Clary can make me a Portal to somewhere near Idris and I can cross the border on foot—"

"Alec, no. Magnus needs you here," Clary said. "Besides, you're the head of the Downworlder-Shadowhunter Alliance. The Cohort would love to get their hands on you."

Kieran rose to his feet. "None of you can go," he said. "What you Nephilim lack is subtlety. You would go galloping into Idris, bringing disaster down on all of us. Meanwhile, faeries can slip into Idris as swift as a shadow and bring back what you need."

"Faeries?" Jace raised an eyebrow. "You seem to be one faerie. Maybe two if you count half of Helen and half of Mark."

Kieran looked annoyed.

"Faeries are forbidden to even set foot on the soil of Idris," said Alec. "There are probably wards up, and sensors—"

"Isn't it convenient that there are faerie steeds who fly," Kieran said, "and riders who ride those steeds, and that I am one?"

"This is kind of a rude way of offering help," said Jace, and caught Clary's eye. "But I'm all in," he added. "Are you offering to fly into Idris and collect the water?"

Kieran had begun to pace. His dark hair had turned deep blue, threaded with white strands. "You will need more than one faerie. You will need a legion. Those who can fly into Idris, collect the water, destroy the blight, and bring the cure to warlocks all over the world. You need the Wild Hunt."

"The Hunt?" said Mark. "Even with Gwyn as a friend of Diana's, I do not think the Hunt would do this for Nephilim."

Kieran drew himself up. For the first time, Emma saw some of his father in his stance and in the set of his jaw. "I am a prince of Faerie, and a Hunter," he said. "I killed the Unseelie King with my own hands. I believe they will do it for me."

On the roof, Kit could hear voices floating up from the kitchen below—raised and frantic voices. He couldn't hear what they were talking about, though.

"A letter from Livvy," he said, turning around to look at Ty. The other boy was sitting at the roof's edge, his legs dangling over the side. Kit hated how close Ty was willing to get to the edges of things: Sometimes it seemed like he had no sense of spatial danger, the reality of what would happen if he fell. "The other Livvy, in the other universe."

Ty nodded. His too-long hair fell into his eyes, and he pushed it back impatiently. He was wearing a white sweater with holes in the cuffs that he'd pushed his thumbs through, as if he were hooking the sleeves on. "Emma gave it to me. I wondered if you wanted to read it."

"Yes," Kit said. "I do."

Ty held it out to him and Kit took the light envelope, looked at the scrawl on the cover. *Tiberius.* Did it look like Livvy's handwriting? He wasn't sure. He didn't remember studying her handwriting; he knew he was forgetting the sound of her voice.

The sun was beating down on the roof, making Ty's gold locket spark. Kit opened the letter and began to read.

Ty,
I've thought so many times about what I would say to you if you reappeared suddenly. If I was walking along the street and you popped out of thin air, walking along beside me like you always used to, with your hands in your pockets and your head tilted back.

Mom used to say you walked celestially, looking up

at the sky as if you were scanning the clouds for angels. Do you remember that?

In your world I am ashes, I am ancestors, my memories and hopes and dreams have gone to build the City of Bones. In your world, I am lucky, because I do not have to live in a world without you. But in this world, I am you. I am the twinless twin. So I can tell you this:

When your twin leaves the earth you live on, it never turns the same way again: the weight of their soul is gone, and everything is off balance. The world rocks under your feet like an unquiet sea. I can't tell you it gets easier. But it does get steadier; you learn how to live with the new rocking of the new earth, the way sailors gain sea legs. You learn. I promise.

I know you're not exactly the Ty I had in this world, my brilliant, beautiful brother. But I know from Julian that you are beautiful and brilliant too. I know that you are loved. I hope that you are happy. Please be happy. You deserve it so much.

I want to ask if you remember the way we used to whisper words to each other in the dark: star, twin, glass. But I'll never know your answer. So I'll whisper to myself as I fold this letter up and slide it into the envelope, hoping against hope it will somehow reach you. I whisper your name, Ty. I whisper the most important thing:

I love you. I love you. I love you.

Livvy

When Kit lowered the letter, the whole world looked a little too sharp and bright, as if he were seeing it through a magnifying glass. His throat hurt. "What—what do you think?"

I love you, I love you, I love you

Let him hear it, let him believe it and let go.

"I think . . ." Ty reached up for the letter and folded it back into his jacket pocket. "I think this isn't my Livvy. I'm sure she's a good person, but she isn't mine."

Kit sat down, a little suddenly. "What do you mean?"

Ty gazed out at the ocean, at its steady incursion and recession. "My Livvy would want to come back to me. This one didn't. It would be interesting to meet this Livvy, but it's probably good that she didn't come back with Emma and Jules, because then we couldn't bring back the right Livvy."

"No," Kit said. "No, you don't get it. It's not that she didn't want to come back. She's needed there. I'm sure she would have wanted to be with her family if she could. Imagine having to bear that loss—"

"I don't want to." Ty cut him off sharply. "I know she feels bad. I'm really sorry for her. I am." He had taken a piece of thread from his pocket and was worrying at it with nervous hands. "But that's not why I brought you the letter. You know what it is?"

"I guess I don't," Kit said.

"It's the last thing we need for the spell," Ty said. "It's an object from another dimension."

Kit felt as if he were on a roller coaster that had suddenly, precipitously, dropped. He was about to say something when Ty made a soft sound of wonder; he tilted his head back as above them flew a black-and-gray horse and a brown one, their hooves trailing gold and silver vapor. They both watched in silence as the horses landed on the grass in front of the Institute.

One of the riders was a familiar woman in a black dress. Diana. The other was Gwyn ap Nudd, leader of the Wild Hunt. They both watched in astonishment as Gwyn dismounted before going to help Diana down.

* * *

Dru clambered up onto the roof. Ty and Kit were already there, standing disturbingly close to the roof's edge. She wasn't surprised; she'd figured out a long time ago that whenever they wanted to talk in private, they disappeared up here, the way Emma and Julian used to when they were younger.

She hadn't really talked to either of them since the time she'd gone into Ty's room. She didn't know what to say. Everyone else in the family—Helen, Mark—was talking about how well Ty was recovering, how strong he was being, how he was holding up in the face of Livvy's death.

But she had seen his room torn apart and the blood on his pillowcases. It had made her look more closely at him—at how thin he was, and the scrapes across his knuckles.

After their father had died, Ty had gone through a phase of biting at his own hands. He would wake up in the night having gnawed the skin over his knuckles. She guessed he was doing that again, and that was why there was blood on his pillows. Helen and Mark couldn't recognize it; they hadn't been there years ago. Livvy would have known. Julian would have known, but he had only just gotten home. And besides, talking to anyone about it seemed like a betrayal of Ty.

The story of Thule haunted her, too—a world in which Ty was dead. In which she herself was missing. In which the Blackthorns were no longer a family. A world where Sebastian Morgenstern had ruled. Even the name Ash haunted her, as if she'd heard it before, though she had no memory of having done so. The idea of Thule was a dark nightmare, reminding her of the fragility of the bonds that held her to her family. The last thing she wanted to do was upset Ty.

And so she'd avoided him, and Kit by consequence since they were always together. They didn't own the roof, though. She stomped over to where they were standing, making plenty of noise so she wouldn't surprise them.

They didn't seem bothered to see her. "Gwyn and Diana are here," said Kit. When he'd come to them, he had looked a bit pale, as if he'd spent most of his time indoors and at night markets. Now he had color—the beginnings of a tan and flushed cheeks. He looked more like Jace, especially as his hair had grown out and started to curl.

"I know." She joined them at the roof's edge. "They're going to Idris. They're going to get the water from Lake Lyn."

She filled them in quickly, pleased to be the one who had news for a change. Kieran had come out of the Institute and was walking across the grass toward Diana and Gwyn. His back was very straight, the sun bright on his blue-black hair.

Kieran inclined his head to Diana and turned to Gwyn. Kieran had changed, Dru thought. She remembered the first time she'd seen him, bloody and furious and bitterly angry at the world. She had regarded him as an enemy of Mark, of all of them.

She had seen different sides of him since then. He had fought alongside them. He had watched bad movies with her. She thought of him complaining about his love life the night before, and laughing, and looked down at him now: Gwyn had laid a hand on his shoulder and was nodding, clear respect in his gestures.

People were made up of all sorts of different bits, Dru thought. Funny bits and romantic bits and selfish bits and brave bits. Sometimes you saw only a few of them. Maybe it was when you saw them all that you realized you knew someone really well.

She wondered if there would ever be anyone besides her family that she knew like that.

"We should go downstairs," Ty said, his gray eyes curious. "Find out what's going on."

He headed for the trapdoor that led to the stairs. Kit had just started to follow him when Drusilla tapped him on the shoulder.

Kit turned to look at her. "What is it?"

"Ty," she said in a low voice. Dru glanced over at her brother automatically as she said his name; he'd already disappeared down the steps. "I want to talk to you about him, but not with anyone else around, and you have to promise not to tell him. Can you promise?"

"Have a good watch," Jace said, ruffling Clary's hair. Diana and Gwyn had departed for Idris. Emma had watched them vanish until they were a speck on the horizon, disappearing into the haze of the Los Angeles air. Alec had gone to be with Magnus, and the rest of them had agreed to take turns at patrolling the perimeter of the Institute.

"We need to be alert," Julian had said. "This message from the Cohort is a loyalty test. They're going to be watching Institutes to see who races to Alicante to pledge themselves to the fight against Faerie. They know we'll delay as long as possible"—he gestured at Mark and Helen—"but I wouldn't put it past them to move on us first."

"That wouldn't be very clever," Mark had said, frowning. "All they have to do is wait, and they can declare us traitors soon enough."

"They're not that smart," Julian had agreed grimly. "Vicious, but not smart."

"Unfortunately, Manuel is pretty smart," said Emma, and though everyone had looked grimmer than ever, no one had disagreed.

Clary and Emma had the second watch after Jace and Helen; Helen had already gone inside to check on Aline, and Emma was trying to look off into the distance while Clary and Jace kissed and made cutesy noises at each other.

"I hope everything's all right in Alicante," she said eventually, more to determine if they were still kissing than anything else.

"It can't be," said Jace, breaking away from Clary. "They all think I'm dead. There had better be a mourning parade. We should find out who's sending flowers."

Clary rolled her eyes, not without affection. "Maybe Simon or Izzy can make a list. Then when we come back from the dead, we can send them flowers."

"Women will be in mourning to hear of my passing," Jace said, bounding up the steps. "Garments will be rent. Rent, I tell you."

"You're taken," Clary called up at him. "It's not like you're a single dead hero."

"Love knows no bounds," said Jace, and sobered. "I'm going to go check on Alec and Magnus. I'll see you two later."

He waved and vanished. Clary and Emma, both in gear, started to cut across the grass toward the path that led around the Institute.

Clary sighed. "Jace hates being away from Alec at times like this. There isn't anything he can do, but I understand wanting to be with your *parabatai* when they're suffering. I'd want to be with Simon."

"It's not like he's there just for himself," Emma said. The sky was dark blue and chased with fading clouds. "I'm sure it's better for Alec, having him there. I mean, I think part of what was so awful for the Alec in Thule was that he must have felt so alone when he lost Magnus. So many of his friends were already dead, and his *parabatai* was worse than dead."

Clary shuddered. "We should talk about something more cheerful."

Emma tried to think about cheerful things. Julian getting the spell taken off him? Not a topic she could discuss. Zara being squished by a boulder made her seem vengeful.

"We could discuss your visions," she said carefully. Clary looked at her in surprise. "The ones you told me about, where you said you saw yourself die. In the Unseelie Court, when you looked through the Portal—"

"I realized what I'd been seeing, yes," Clary said. "I was seeing me, and I was dead, and I was also seeing the dream I'd been having." She took a deep breath. "I haven't had it since we came back from Faerie.

I think the dreams were actually trying to tell me about Thule."

They had reached the place where grass turned into desert and scrub; the ocean was a thick line of blue paint in the distance. "Did you tell Jace?" Emma asked.

"No. I can't do it now. I feel so stupid, and like he might never forgive me—and besides, Jace needs to focus on Alec and Magnus. We all do." Clary kicked a small stone out of her path. "I've known Magnus since I was a little girl. The first time I met him, I pulled his cat's tail. I didn't know he could have turned me into a frog or a mailbox if he wanted."

"Magnus will be okay," Emma said, but she knew she didn't sound sure. She couldn't be.

Clary's voice shook. "I just feel like, if the warlocks are lost—if the Cohort succeeds in pitting Shadowhunters against Downworlders in war—then everything I ever did was useless. Everything I gave up during the Dark War. And it means I'm not a hero. I never was."

Clary stopped walking to lean against a massive boulder, one that Ty liked to climb. She was clearly struggling not to cry. Emma stared at her in horror.

"Clary," she said. "You're the one who taught me what being a hero means. You said heroes don't always win. That sometimes they lose, but they keep fighting."

"I thought I *had* kept fighting. I guess I thought I had won," Clary said.

"I've been to Thule," Emma said fiercely. "That world was the way it was because you weren't in it. You were the crisis point, you made all the difference. Without you, Sebastian would have won the Dark War. Without you, so many people would be dead, and so much goodness would be gone from the world forever."

Clary took a deep breath. "We're never done fighting, are we?"

"I don't think so," Emma said.

Clary pushed away from the rock. They rejoined the path, curving through the desert among the shrubs, deep green and chalky violet. The sun was low over the horizon, lighting the desert sand to gold.

"In Thule," Emma said as they rounded the corner of the Institute, "Jace was under Sebastian's mind control. But there was something I didn't say in the library. Sebastian was able to control Jace only because he lied about his involvement in your death. He was afraid that even under a spell, no matter how strong the spell was, Jace would never forgive him for letting you be hurt."

"And you're telling me this because?" Clary eyed Emma sideways.

"Because Jace would forgive you for anything," said Emma. "Go tell him you were being a butt for a good reason, and ask him to marry you."

Clary burst out laughing. "That's romantic."

Emma grinned. "That's just my suggestion about the sentiment. The actual proposal is up to you."

Helen had given Magnus and Alec one of the largest rooms. Jace suspected it had probably belonged to the Blackthorns' parents at one time.

It was odd, actually, even to think of Blackthorn parents and not to think of Julian—quiet, competent, secretive Julian—as the one who took care of the children. But people became what they had to be: Julian probably hadn't wanted to become a parent at age twelve, any more than Jace had wanted to leave Idris and lose his father at age nine. He would not have believed it if someone had told him he would gain a new and better family in New York, just as Julian would not have believed that he would love his siblings so fiercely it would all be worth it. Or so Jace suspected, at least.

Jace looked over at Alec, the brother he had gained. Alec sat propped on one side of the big wooden bed in the room's center:

Magnus lay beside him, curled on his side, his black hair stark against the white pillow.

Jace hadn't seen Alec this drained and exhausted-looking since Magnus had vanished into Edom five years ago. Alec had gone to get him back: He would have gone anywhere for Magnus.

But Jace was afraid—worse than afraid—that Magnus was going somewhere that Alec couldn't follow.

He didn't want to think about what would happen if Magnus went; the story of Thule had sent icy needles through his veins. He suspected he knew what would happen to him if he lost Clary. He couldn't bear to think of Alec in such insupportable pain.

Alec bent over and kissed Magnus's temple. Magnus stirred and murmured but didn't wake. Jace hadn't seen him awake since the night before.

Alec looked over at Jace, his eyes deeply shadowed. "What time is it?"

"Sunset," said Jace, who never carried a watch. "I can go find out if you need to know."

"No. It's probably already too late to call the kids." Alec rubbed the back of his hand across his eyes. "Besides, I keep hoping I can call them with good news."

Jace stood up and went to the window. He felt like he couldn't breathe. *Take this pain away from Alec*, he prayed to the Angel Raziel. *Come on, we've met. Do this for me.*

It was something of an unorthodox prayer, but it was heartfelt. Alec raised an eyebrow at him. "You're praying?"

"How did you know?" Out of the window, Jace could see the grass in front of the Institute, the highway and the ocean beyond. The whole world going on in its ordinary way, not caring about the problems of Shadowhunters and warlocks.

"Your lips were moving," said Alec. "You hardly ever pray, but I appreciate the thought."

"I don't usually have to pray," said Jace. "Usually when things go wrong, we come to Magnus and he fixes them."

"I know." Alec picked at a stray thread on his cuff. "Maybe we should have gotten married," he said. "Magnus and me. We've been unofficially engaged all this time, but we wanted to wait for the Cold Peace to be over. For Downworlders and Shadowhunters to be able to be properly married."

"In Shadowhunter gold and warlock blue," said Jace. He'd heard this before, the explanation for why Alec and Magnus hadn't married yet, but planned to someday. He'd even gone with Alec to pick out rings for the day Alec and Magnus would finally tie the knot—simple gold bands with the words *Aku Cinta Kamu* etched on them. He'd known the rings were a secret from Magnus, because Alec wanted to surprise his partner, but he hadn't known there were fears and worries behind something they seemed so sure would happen all in due time.

It was always hard to tell the truth of other people's relationships.

"Then Magnus would at least know how much I love him," Alec said, leaning forward to brush a stray hair from Magnus's forehead.

"He knows," Jace said. "You should never doubt he knows."

Alec nodded. Jace glanced back out the window. "They just switched over watch," he said. "Clary said she'd come see how Magnus was doing when she was done with this shift."

"Should I take a turn at watch?" Alec asked. "I don't want to let anyone down."

The lump in Jace's throat ached. He sat down next to his *parabatai*, who he had sworn to follow, to live beside, to die with. Surely that also encompassed the sharing of burdens and grief.

"This is your watch, brother," he said.

Alec exhaled softly. He put one hand on Magnus's shoulder, the lightest of touches. He reached out with his other hand and Jace took it, lacing their fingers together. They held fast to each other in silence as the sun went down over the ocean.

"So what happens?" Aline said. They stood at the edge of the bluffs, overlooking the highway and the sea. "If Magnus starts turning into a demon. What happens?"

Her eyes were red and swollen but her back was straight. She had talked to her father, who had told her only what he knew: That guards had come in the early morning to take Jia to the Gard. That Horace Dearborn had promised no harm would come to her, but that "a show of good faith" was necessary to reassure those who had "lost confidence."

If he thought it was all lies, he didn't say so, but Aline knew it was and had called Dearborn every name in the book to Helen the minute she had hung up the phone. Aline had always known an impressive number of curse words.

"We do have the Mortal Sword," said Helen. "The one from Thule. It's hidden, but Jace knows where, and what to do. He won't let Alec do it himself."

"Couldn't we—I don't know—try to capture the demon? Turn it back into Magnus?"

"Oh, honey, I don't know," Helen said wearily. "I don't think there's any coming back from being turned into a demon, and Magnus wouldn't want to live like that."

"It's not fair." Aline kicked a good-size rock. It sailed off the edge of the bluffs; Helen could hear it tumbling down the slope toward the highway. "Magnus deserves better than this garbage. We all do. How did everything get like this—so bad, so fast? Things were all right. We were happy."

"We were in exile, Aline," Helen said. She wrapped her arms around her wife and rested her chin on Aline's shoulder. "The cruelty of the Clave tore me from my family, because of my blood.

Because of what I cannot help. The seeds of this poison tree were planted long ago. We are only now watching it begin to flower."

The sun had set by the time Mark and Kieran began their watch. Mark had hoped to be paired up with Julian, but for some reason Emma had wanted to go with Clary and they'd ended up oddly matched.

They walked for a while in silence, letting the dusk settle into darkness around them. Mark hadn't talked to Kieran about anything significant since they'd come back from Faerie. He had wanted to, ached to, but he had been afraid of making a confusing situation even worse.

Mark had started to wonder if the problem was him: if his human half and his faerie half held contradictory ideas about love and romance. If half of him wanted Kieran and the freedom of the sky and the other half wanted Cristina and the grandeur and responsibility of earthbound angels.

It was enough to make someone go out into the statue garden and bang their head repeatedly against Virgil.

Not that he'd done that.

"We might as well talk, Mark," Kieran said. A bright moon was rising; it illuminated the dark ocean, turned it to a sheet of black-and-silver glass, the colors of Kieran's eyes. The night desert was alive with the sound of cicadas. Kieran was walking beside Mark with his hands looped behind him, deceptively human-looking in his jeans and T-shirt. He had drawn the line at donning any gear. "It does us no good to ignore each other."

"I have missed you," Mark said. There seemed no point in not being honest. "Nor did I intend to ignore you, or to hurt you. I apologize."

Kieran looked up with a surprised flash of silver and black. "There is no need to apologize, Mark." He hesitated. "I have had, as you say here in the mortal world, a lot on my mind."

Mark hid a smile in the dusk. It was irritatingly cute when Kieran used modern phrases.

"I know you have as well," Kieran went on. "You were fearful for Julian and for Emma. I understand. And yet I cannot keep myself from selfish thoughts."

"What kind of selfish thoughts?" Mark said. They were near the parking lot, among the statues Arthur Blackthorn had paid to have shipped here years ago. Once they had stood in the gardens of Blackthorn House in London. Now Sophocles and the others inhabited this desert space and looked out on a sea far from the Aegean.

"I believe in your cause," Kieran said slowly. "I believe the Cohort are evil people, or at least power-hungry people who seek evil solutions to the problems their fears and prejudices have created. Yet though I may believe, I cannot help but feel that no one is looking out for the welfare of my homeland. For Faerie. It was—it is—a place that possesses goodness and marvels among its dangers and trials."

Mark turned to Kieran in surprise. The stars were brilliant overhead, the way they only ever were in the desert, as if they were closer to the earth here.

The stars will go out before I forget you, Mark Blackthorn.

"I have not heard you talk about Faerie that way before," Mark said.

"I would not speak of it that way to most." Kieran touched the place at his throat where once his elf-bolt necklace had rested, then dropped his hand. "But you—you know Faerie in a way others do not. The way the water tumbles blue as ice over Branwen's Falls. The taste of music and the sound of wine. The honey hair of mermaids in the streams, the glittering of will-o'-the-wisps in the shadows of the deep forests."

Mark smiled despite himself. "The brilliance of the stars—the stars here are but pale shadows of those in Faerie."

"I know you were a captive there," Kieran said. "But I would like to think you came to see something good in it as you saw something good in me."

"There is much that is good in you, Kieran."

Kieran looked restlessly toward the ocean. "My father was a bad ruler and Oban will be an even worse one. Imagine what a good ruler could make of the Lands of Faerie. I fear for Adaon's life and I also fear for the fate of Faerie without him. If my brother cannot be King there, what hope is there for my land?"

"There could be another King, another prince of Faerie who is worthy," said Mark. "It could be you."

"You forget what I saw in the pool," Kieran said. "The way I hurt people. The way I hurt you. I should not be King."

"Kieran, you have become a different person, and so have I," Mark said. He could almost hear Cristina's voice in the back of his mind, the soft way she had always defended Kieran—never excusing, only understanding. Explaining. "We were desperate in the Hunt, and desperation can make people unkind. But you have changed—I have seen you change, even before you touched the waters of the pool. I have seen how kind you were when you lived in your father's Court, and how you were loved because of it, and while the Wild Hunt cloaked that kindness, it did not erase it. You have been only good to me, to my family, to Cristina, since you returned from the Scholomance."

"The pool—"

"It is not only the pool," said Mark. "The pool helped to uncover what was already there. You understand what it means for another to suffer and that their pain is no different from your own. Most kings never understand such a thing as true empathy. Think what it would be like, to have a ruler who did."

"I do not know if I have that faith in myself." Kieran spoke quietly, his voice as hushed as the wind across the desert.

"I have that faith in you," said Mark.

At that, Kieran turned fully to Mark. His expression was open, the way Mark had not seen it in a long time, an expression that hid nothing—not his fear, nor his uncertainty, nor the transparency of his love. "I didn't know—I feared I had broken your faith in me and with it the bond between us."

"Kier," Mark said, and he saw Kieran shiver at the use of that old nickname. "Today you stood up and offered all your powers as a prince and faerie to save my family. How can you not know how I feel?"

Kieran was staring at his own hand, where it hovered at the edge of Mark's shirt collar. He gazed as if hypnotized at the place where their skin touched, his fingers against Mark's collarbone, sliding up to brush his throat, the side of his jaw. "You mean you are grateful?"

Mark caught Kieran's hand, brought it to his chest, and pressed Kieran's open palm against his hammering heart. "Does that feel like *gratitude?*"

Kieran looked at him with wide eyes. And Mark was back in the Hunt again, he was on a green hill in the rain, with Kieran's arms around him. *Love me. Show me.*

"Kieran," Mark breathed, and kissed him, and Kieran gave a small harsh cry and caught Mark by the sleeves, pulling him close. Mark's arms hooked around Kieran's neck, drawing him down into the kiss: Their mouths slid together and Mark tasted their shared breath, an elixir of heat and yearning.

Kieran pulled back from the kiss at last. He was grinning, the wickedly joyous grin Mark suspected no one else ever saw but him. Holding Mark by the arms, he walked him back several paces until Mark fetched up against the side of a boulder. Kieran leaned into him, his mouth against Mark's throat, his lips finding the hammering pulse point and sucking gently at it until Mark gasped and buried his hands in Kieran's silky hair.

"You are killing me," Mark said, laughter bubbling up softly from the depths of his chest.

Kieran chuckled, his hands moving to slip under Mark's shirt, caress his back, skate over the scars on his shoulder blades. And Mark answered his touch. He stroked his fingers through Kieran's hair, caressed his face as if mapping the curves of it, let his fingers stray to touch the skin he remembered like the substance of a dream: Kieran's sensitive throat, collarbone, wrists, the beautiful and unforgotten terrain of what he had thought was lost. Kieran breathed in harsh low moans as Mark slid his hands under the prince's shirt, stroking his uncovered skin, the silk-hardness of his flat stomach, the curves of his rib cage.

"My Mark," Kieran whispered, touching Mark's hair, his cheek. "I adore you."

Te adoro, Mark.

Mark's skin went cold; it all seemed suddenly wrong. He dropped his hands abruptly and slid away from Kieran. He felt as if he couldn't quite catch his breath.

"Cristina," he said.

"Cristina is not what keeps us apart," said Kieran. "She is what brings us together. All that we have said, all the ways we have changed—"

"Cristina," Mark said again, clearing his throat, because she was standing just in front of them.

Cristina felt as if her face might actually catch on fire. She had come out to tell Mark and Kieran that she and Aline were prepared to take over on watch, without even once thinking that she might be interrupting them in a private moment.

When she had come around the boulder, she had frozen—it had reminded her so much of the first time she had seen them together. Kieran leaning against Mark, their bodies together, their hands in each other's hair, kissing as if they could never stop.

I am an awful idiot, she thought. They were both looking at her now: Mark seemed stricken, Kieran oddly calm.

"I'm so sorry," Cristina said. "I only came out to tell you that your watch was ending, but—I—I will go."

"Cristina," Mark said, starting toward her.

"Don't go," Kieran said. It was a demand, not a request: There was a rich darkness in his voice, a depth of yearning. And though Cristina had no reason to listen, she turned slowly to look at them both.

"I really think," she said, "that I probably ought to. Don't you?"

"I was recently given a piece of advice by a wise person not to remain silent about what I wished for," said Kieran. "I desire you and love you, Cristina, and so does Mark. Stay with us."

Cristina couldn't move. She thought again of the first time she'd seen Mark and Kieran together. The desire she'd felt. She'd thought at the time she wanted something like what they had: that she wanted that passion for herself and some unnamed boy whose face she didn't know.

But it had been a long time since any face in her dreams had not been either Mark's or Kieran's. Since she had imagined any eyes looking into hers that were both the same color. She had not wanted some vague approximation of what they had: She had wanted *them.*

She looked at Mark, who seemed pinned between hope and terror. "Kieran," he said. His voice shook. "How can you ask her that? She's not a faerie, she'll never talk to us again—"

"But you will leave me," she said, hearing her own voice as if it were a stranger's. "You love each other and belong together. You will leave me and go back to Faerie."

They looked at her with expressions of identical shock. "We will never leave you," said Mark.

"We will stay as close to you as the tide to the shore," said

Kieran. "Neither of us wishes for anything else." He reached out a hand. "Please believe us, Lady of Roses."

The few steps across the sand and scrub grass were the longest and shortest Cristina had ever taken. Kieran stretched out both arms: Cristina went into them and lifted up her face and kissed him.

Heat and sweetness and the curve of his lips under hers nearly lifted her off her feet. He was smiling against her mouth. Saying her name. His hand on her side, thumb gently caressing the inward dip of her waist.

She leaned into him and reached out with her free hand. Mark's warm fingers closed around her wrist. As if she were a princess, he kissed the back of her fingers, brushing his lips across her knuckles.

Her heart was beating triple time as she turned in Kieran's arms, her back to him. He drew her hair away from the nape of her neck and pressed a kiss there, making her shiver as she reached out to Mark. His eyes glittered blue and gold, alive with desire for her, for Kieran, for the three of them together.

He let her draw him in and they tangled together as one. Mark kissed her lips as she leaned back against Kieran's chest, Kieran's hand in Mark's hair, trailing down Mark's cheek to trace the line of his collarbone. She had never felt such love; she had never been held so very close.

A great clamor burst out in the sky above them—a clamor they all knew, though Kieran and Mark knew it best.

They drew apart quickly as the air rushed around them: The sky swirled with movement. Manes and tails whipped in the wind, eyes glowed a thousand colors, warriors roared and shouted, and at the center of it all was a great black brindle horse with a man and woman seated on its back, pausing to look down at the earth below as the sound of a hunting horn faded on the air.

Gwyn and Diana had returned, and they were not alone.

* * *

Julian had always thought his studio—which had been his mother's—was the most beautiful room in the Institute. You could see everything through the two glass walls: ocean and desert; the other walls were creamy and bright with his mother's abstract paintings.

He could see it now, but he couldn't feel it. Whatever feeling it was that looking at beauty had always raised in his artist's soul was gone.

Without feeling, he thought, *I am dissolving, like royal water dissolves gold.* He knew it, but he couldn't feel that, either.

To know you were despairing but not to be able to feel that despair was a strange experience. He looked at the paints he'd arranged around the plain white cloth stretched over the central island. Blue and gold, red and black. He knew what he ought to shape with them, but when he picked up the brush, he only hesitated.

Everything instinctual about drawing had left him, everything that told him what would make one curve of the paintbrush better than another, everything that matched shades of color to shades of meaning. Blue was just blue. Green was green, whether light or dark. Blood red and stoplight red were the same.

Emma is avoiding me, he thought. The thought didn't bring pain, because nothing did. It was just a fact. He remembered the desire he had felt in her room the night before and set his paintbrush down. It was strange to think of desire as divorced from feeling: He had never desired anyone he hadn't already loved. Never desired anyone but Emma.

But the night before, with her in his arms, he had felt almost as if he could break through the dullness that surrounded him, that choked him with its nothingness; as if the blaze of wanting her could burn it down and he would be free.

It was better that she did avoid him. Even in this state, his need for her was too strange, and too strong.

Something flashed past the glass of the studio window. He went to look out and saw that Gwyn and Diana were on the lawn and that several of the others surrounded them: Cristina, Mark, Kieran. Gwyn was handing a glass jar to Alec, who took it and went running back toward the Institute, flying across the grass like one of his own arrows. Dru was dancing up and down with Tavvy, spinning in circles. Emma hugged Cristina and then Mark. Gwyn had an arm around Diana, who was leaning her head on his shoulder.

Relief washed through Julian, brief and cool as a splash of water. He knew he should feel more, that he should feel joy. He saw Ty and Kit standing a little apart from the others; Ty had his head tipped back, as he often did, and was pointing at the stars.

Julian looked up as the sky darkened with a hundred airborne riders.

Mark could not help but be conscious of Kieran's tension as the Wild Hunt began to land all around them, alighting on the grass like dandelion seeds blown by the wind.

He could not blame him. Mark himself felt dizzy with shock and the aftereffects of desire—already those moments with Cristina and Kieran by the boulder seemed like a fever dream. Had it happened? It must have—Cristina was smoothing down her hair with quick, nervous movements, her lips still red from kissing. Mark checked his own clothes quickly. He no longer had faith that he had not ripped off his own shirt and cast it into the desert with the announcement that he would never need shirts again. Anything seemed possible.

Kieran, though, had drawn himself up, his face a mask Mark knew well—it was the look he had always worn when the rest of the Hunt mocked him and called him princeling. Later he had won their respect and been able to protect both himself and Mark, but he had had no friends in the Hunt besides Mark—and perhaps Gwyn, in his own odd way.

Mark, though, had never won their respect. Or so he had always thought. As he gazed around the group of silent Hunters on their steeds, some faces familiar and some new, he saw that they regarded him differently. There was no contempt in their eyes as they noted the fresh Marks on his arms, the gear he wore, and the weapons belt at his waist, bristling with seraph blades.

The riotous celebration that had followed the arrival of Gwyn and Diana had quieted down upon the arrival of the Hunt. Helen had taken Dru and Tavvy and marched them back to the house, over their protests. Diana slid from Orion's back and went to stand beside Kit and Ty as Emma headed back to the Institute with Aline to see if they could help Alec.

Gwyn dismounted, removing his helmet as he did so. To Mark's astonishment, he inclined his head to Kieran. He wasn't sure he'd ever seen Gwyn bow his head to anyone before.

"Gwyn," said Kieran. "Why have you brought all the Hunt here? I thought they were delivering the water."

"They wished to acknowledge you before they left upon their mission," said Gwyn.

One of the Hunt, a tall man with an impassive, scarred face, bowed from his saddle. "We have done your will," he said. "Liege lord."

Kieran blanched.

"Liege lord?" echoed Cristina, clearly stunned.

Diana touched Gwyn lightly on the shoulder and strode back toward the Institute. Mark's head was spinning: "Liege" was what the Hunt often called a monarch, a King or Queen of Faerie. Not a mere prince, and not one sworn to the Hunt.

Kieran inclined his head, at last. "My thanks," he said. "I will not forget this."

That seemed to satisfy the Hunt; they turned their horses and took to the air, bursting up into the sky like fireworks. Ty and Kit ran to the edge of the clearing to watch them as they hurtled across the sky, riders and steeds blurring into the same silhouettes. Their hooves churned the air, and a deep boom of thunder sounded across the beaches and coves.

Kieran turned to stare at Gwyn. "What was that?" he demanded. "What are you doing, Gwyn?"

"Your mad brother Oban sits upon the throne of Unseelie," said Gwyn. "He drinks, he whores, he makes no laws. He demands loyalty. He musters an army to bring to his parley with the Cohort, though his advisers warn against it."

"Where is my brother?" said Kieran. "Where is Adaon?"

Gwyn looked uneasy. "Adaon is weak," he said. "And he is not the one who slew the King. He has not earned the throne."

"You would put a Hunter on the throne," said Kieran. "A friend to your causes."

"Perhaps," said Gwyn. "But regardless of what I want, Adaon is a prisoner in Seelie. Kieran, there will be a battle. There is no avoiding it. You must take the mantle of leadership from Oban as all look on."

"Take the mantle of leadership?" said Mark. "Is that a euphemism?"

"Yes," said Gwyn.

"You can't honestly be telling him to kill his brother in the middle of a battle," said Cristina, looking furious.

"Kieran killed his father in the middle of a battle," said Gwyn. "I should think he could do this. There is hardly family feeling between Kieran and Oban."

"Stop!" Kieran said. "I can speak for myself. I will not do it, Gwyn. I am not fit to be King."

"Not *fit?*" Gwyn demanded. "The best of my Hunters? Kieran—"

"Leave him be, Gwyn," Mark said. "It is his choice alone."

Gwyn placed his helmet on his head and swung himself onto

Orion's back. "I am not asking you to do this because it is the best thing for you, Kieran," he said, looking down from the horse's back. "I am asking you because it is the best thing for Faerie."

Orion sprang into the air. In the distance, Ty and Kit gave a small cheer, waving at Gwyn from the ground.

"Gwyn has gone mad," said Kieran. "I am not the best thing for any place."

Before Mark could reply, Cristina's phone beeped. She picked it up and said, "It's Emma. Magnus is recovering." She smiled all over her face, bright as a star. "The lake water is working."

25
By Lifting Winds

Sunlight poured into the library through every available window: They had all been flung open. It lay in squares on the floor and painted the table in bright stripes. It turned Mark's and Helen's hair to white gold, made Jace into a tousled bronze statue, and lit Magnus's cat eyes to tourmaline as he sat curled on the couch, looking pale but energized and drinking Lake Lyn water out of a crystal vial with a brightly colored straw.

He was leaning against Alec, who was grinning ear to ear and scolding Magnus to drink more water. Emma wouldn't have thought it was possible to do both at once, but Alec was used to multitasking.

"This water is making me drunk," Magnus complained. "And it tastes awful."

"It contains no alcohol," said Diana. She looked tired—not surprising, after her journey to and from Idris—but composed as always, in a tailored black dress. "It might have a slight hallucinatory effect, though."

"That explains why I can see seven of you," Magnus said to Alec. "My ultimate fantasy."

Dru covered Tavvy's ears, though Tavvy was playing with a Slinky Alec had given him and appeared deaf to the world.

Magnus pointed. "That one of you over there is extremely attractive, Alexander."

"That's a vase," said Helen.

Magnus squinted at it. "I'd be willing to buy it from you."

"Maybe later," said Helen. "Right now we should all focus on what Diana has to tell us."

Diana took a sip of coffee. Emma had tea; everyone else was mainlining caffeine and sugar. Alec had gone out in a state of mad happiness and bought dozens of cinnamon rolls, doughnuts, and pies for breakfast. This had had the effect of getting everyone to rush at top speed to the library, including Kit and Ty. Even the most secretive fifteen-year-old boy wasn't immune to glazed apple fritters.

"I told some of you last night, but it's probably best I explain it again," she said. "We were able to get a great deal of water from Lake Lyn with the help of the Wild Hunt; they are currently distributing it to warlocks all over the world."

"The Clave and Council have noticed nothing," said Helen. "Aline spoke to her father this morning and he confirmed it." Aline was in the office now, tracking the progress of the deliveries of the lake water to warlocks in even the remotest places.

Emma raised her Styrofoam cup of tea. "Good job, Diana!"

A cheer went around the table; Diana smiled. "I could not have done it without Gwyn," she said. "Or without Kieran. It is faeries who have helped us."

"The Children of Lilith will indeed be in debt to the Children of the Courts after this day, Kieran Kingson," said Magnus, staring intently in what he clearly thought was Kieran's direction.

"That was a very nice speech, Bane," said Jace. "Unfortunately, you're talking to a doughnut."

"I appreciate the sentiment regardless," said Kieran. He had blushed at Diana's words and the tops of his cheekbones were still pink. It made a nice contrast with his blue hair.

Diana cleared her throat. "We brought the lake water to the blight," she said. "It seemed to stop it from spreading, but the land is still ruined. I don't know if it will heal."

"Tessa says it will stop affecting the warlocks," said Cristina. "That the land will always be scarred, but the sickness will no longer spread."

"Did you see anything else in Idris?" Julian asked. Emma looked at him sideways; it hurt to look at him too directly. "Anything else we should know?"

Diana turned the cup in her hands around thoughtfully. "Idris feels—empty and strange with no Downworlders there. Some of its magic has fled. A Brocelind without faeries is just a forest. It is as if a piece of the soul of Idris is gone."

"*Helen—*" It was Aline, slamming the door behind her; she looked disheveled and worried. In her hand was a piece of slightly charred paper—a fire-message. She stopped dead as she seemed to realize how many other people were in the library. "I just talked to Maia in New York. A mob of Shadowhunters descended on a group of harmless faeries and slaughtered them. Kaelie Whitewillow is dead." Aline's voice was tight with strain.

"How dare they?" Magnus sat up straight, his face alive with fury. He slammed the vial down on the table. "The Cold Peace wasn't enough? Banishing Downworlders who have lived in Idris for centuries wasn't enough? Now it's murder?"

"Magnus—" Alec began, clearly worried.

Blue flame shot from Magnus's hands. Everyone jerked backward; Dru grabbed Tavvy. Kieran flung an arm across Cristina to shield her; so did Mark, at the same time. No one looked more startled than Cristina.

Emma raised an eyebrow at Cristina across the table. Cristina blushed, and both Mark and Kieran quickly dropped their arms.

The blue flame was gone in a moment; there was a streak of

char on the table, but no other damage. Magnus looked down at his hands in surprise.

"Your magic's back!" said Clary.

Magnus winked at her. "Some say it was never gone, biscuit."

"This can't go on," Jace said. "This attack was in revenge for *our deaths.*"

Clary agreed. "We have to tell people we're alive. We can't let our names become instruments of vengeance."

A hubbub of voices broke out at the table. Jace was looking sick; Alec had a hand on his *parabatai*'s shoulder. Magnus was grimly studying his hands, still blue at the fingertips.

"Be realistic, Clary," Helen said. "How do you plan to reveal yourselves and still keep yourselves safe?"

"I don't care about being safe," Clary said.

"No, you never have," Magnus pointed out. "But you are a significant weapon against the Cohort. You *and* Jace. Don't take yourselves out of the equation."

"A message from Idris came while I was in the office," said Aline. "The parley with the Unseelie King and Horace Dearborn will take place on the Imperishable Fields in two days."

"Who's going to be there?" said Emma.

"Just the Cohort and the King," she said.

"So they could say anything at all to each other, and we wouldn't know?" said Mark.

Aline frowned. "No, that's the odd thing. The letter said the parley would be Projected throughout Alicante. Everyone in the city will be able to see it."

"Horace *wants* to be observed," Julian said, half to himself.

"What do you mean?" Emma asked him.

He frowned, clearly puzzled and frustrated. "I don't—I'm not entirely sure—"

"Manuel spoke of this in Faerie," said Mark, as if suddenly

remembering something. "Did he not, Kieran? He said to Oban: 'When every Shadowhunter sees you meet and achieve a mutually beneficial peace, all will realize that you and Horace Dearborn are the greatest of leaders, able to achieve the alliance your forefathers could not.'"

"Oban and Manuel knew this would happen?" said Emma. "How could they have known?"

"Somehow, this is the unfolding of the Cohort's plan," said Magnus. "And that can't be good." He frowned. "It only involves half of Faerie. The Unseelie half."

"But they are the half who are trying to destroy Nephilim. The half that opened the Portal to Thule and brought the blight," said Mark.

"And it is a fact that many Shadowhunters will simply think that it is another sign the Fair Folk are evil," said Cristina. "The Cold Peace made little distinction between Seelie and Unseelie, though it was only the Seelie Court who fought on Sebastian Morgenstern's side."

"It was also only the Seelie Court who accepted the terms of the Cold Peace," said Kieran. "In the King's mind, it has been war between Unseelie and Nephilim since then. Clearly, Oban and the Cohort are planning to make that war a reality. Oban does not care about his people, and neither does Horace Dearborn. They plan for the parley to fail before all, and Dearborn and Oban will tear power from the ruins."

Julian was still frowning, as if trying to solve a puzzle. "Power does come from wartime," he said. "But . . ."

"Now that the warlocks are cured, it's time for us to stop hiding," Jace said. "We need to intercede in Idris—before this sham parley."

"Intercede?" said Julian.

"A team of us will go in," said Jace. "The usual suspects—we'll bring Isabelle and Simon, Bat and Maia and Lily, the core group we trust. We'll have the advantage of surprise. We break into the Gard, free the Consul, and take the Inquisitor prisoner. We get him to confess what he's done."

"He won't confess," Julian said. "He's a true believer. And if he dies for his cause, so much the better for him."

Everyone looked at Julian in some surprise.

"Well, you can't be suggesting we let the Cohort go on as they are," Cristina said.

"No," said Julian. "I am suggesting we raise a resistance."

"There aren't enough of us," said Clary. "And those who oppose the Cohort are scattered all over. How are we to know who is loyal to Horace and who isn't?"

"I was in the Council room before Annabel killed my sister," Julian said. Emma felt her spine freeze; surely the others would notice how flatly he spoke about Livvy? "I saw how people reacted to Horace. And at the funeral, too, when he spoke. There *are* those who oppose him. I'm suggesting we reach out to Downworlders, to faeries, to warlocks, and to the Shadowhunters we know are against the Cohort, to form a bigger coalition."

He's thinking of Livvy in Thule, Emma realized. *Her rebels—Downworlders and Shadowhunters together. But he should say rebels, then. Freedom fighters. Livvy inspired people to fight—*

Out of the corner of her eye, she saw Kieran get up and quietly leave the room. Mark and Cristina watched him go.

"It's too dangerous," said Jace, sounding truly regretful. "We could bring a traitor into our midst. We can't just go off your guesses about what people believe—"

"Julian is the smartest person I know," said Mark firmly. "He isn't wrong about how people feel."

"We believe him," said Alec. "But we can't take the risk of bringing someone into our confidence who might spill our secrets to the Cohort."

Julian's face was still, only his eyes moving, roving up and down the table, studying the faces of his companions. "What the Cohort has going for them is that they're together. They're united. We're individually throwing ourselves into danger to spare others from danger. What if instead we all stood together? We would be far more powerful—"

Jace cut him off. "It's a good idea, Julian, but we just can't do it."

Julian went quiet, though Emma sensed he had more to say. He wasn't going to push it. Maybe if he were more himself he would—but not this Julian.

Alec rose to his feet. "Magnus and I had better head to New York for tonight. If we're all going to go to Idris, we should get the kids to my mom. We can bring Simon and Izzy back with us."

"We'll stay here," said Jace, indicating himself and Clary. "This place is still vulnerable to an attack by the Cohort. We'll be the first line of defense."

"We should all be ready," Clary said. "If it's okay, Helen, we'll go up to the weapons room, see if we need to requisition anything—" She paused. "I guess we can't reach out to the Iron Sisters, can we?"

"They oppose the government in Idris," said Aline. "But they've shut themselves up in the Adamant Citadel. They haven't yet responded to any messages."

"There are other ways to get weapons," said Ty. "There's the Shadow Market."

Emma tensed, wondering if anyone was going to point out that the Shadow Market was technically off-limits to Shadowhunters.

No one did.

"Good idea," said Jace. "Weapons are gettable if we need them—there are weapons caches in every church and holy building in Los Angeles, but—"

"But you're not fighting demons," said Kit. "Are you?"

Jace gave him a long look; it was hard to miss their resemblance when they were at close quarters. "Not the usual kind," he said, and he and Clary headed to the weapons room.

Mark was on his feet too; he headed out of the room with Cristina by his side, and Ty and Kit followed shortly after. Dru left with Tavvy and his Slinky. Amid the scattering, Magnus looked across the table at Julian, his cat's eyes sharp.

"You stay," he said. "I want to talk to you."

Helen and Aline looked curious. Alec raised an eyebrow. "All right," he said. "I'll go call Izzy and let her know we're on our way back." He glanced over at Aline and Helen. "I could use some help packing. Magnus isn't quite up to it yet."

He's lying to get them out of the room, Emma thought. The invisible communication between Alec and Magnus was easy to read: She wondered if people could see the same with her and Julian. Was it clear when they were silently conversing? Not that they'd been doing that since they'd gotten back from Thule.

Magnus started to turn to Emma, but Julian shook his head minutely. "Emma knows," he said. "She can stay."

Magnus sat back while the others filed out of the room. In a moment it was empty except for the three of them: Emma, Julian, and Magnus. Magnus was regarding the two Shadowhunters quietly, his steady eyes moving from Julian to Emma and back again.

"When did you tell Emma about the spell, Julian?" Magnus asked, his voice deceptively bland. Emma suspected there was more to the question than was immediately obvious.

Julian's dark eyebrows drew together. "As soon as I could. She knows I want you to take it off me."

"Ah," Magnus said. He leaned back against the sofa. "You begged for that spell," he said. "You were desperate, and in danger. Are you sure you want me to remove it?"

The bright sunlight turned Julian's eyes to the color of tropical oceans in magazines; he wore a long-sleeved shirt that matched his eyes, and he was so beautiful it made her heart stutter in her chest.

But it was a statue's beauty. His expression was nearly blank; she couldn't read him at all. They had barely spoken since that night in her room.

Maybe it had been enough time now that he had forgotten what it meant to feel; maybe he didn't want it anymore. Maybe he hated her. Maybe it was best if he did hate her, but Emma could never believe it would be best if he never felt anything again.

After an excruciating moment of silence, Julian reached down and drew up his left sleeve. His forearm was bare of bandages. He stretched his arm out to Magnus.

YOU ARE IN THE CAGE.

The color drained from Magnus's face. "My God," he said.

"I cut this into my arm in Thule," Julian said. "When I had my emotions back, I was able to realize how miserable I'd been without them."

"That is—brutal." Magnus was clearly shaken. His hair had gotten quite shaggy, Emma thought. It was rare to see Magnus less than perfectly coiffed. "But I suppose you've always been determined. I talked to Helen while you were missing—she confirmed for me that you'd been running the Institute for quite a while on your own. Covering up for Arthur, who never recovered from his experience in Faerie."

"What does that have to do with the spell?" said Julian.

"It sounds as if you've always had to make hard choices," said Magnus. "For yourself, and for the people you care about. This seems like another hard choice. I still know less than I wish I did about the outcome of the *parabatai* curse. A friend of mine has been looking into it, though, and from what he's told me, the threat is very real." He looked pained. "You may be better off as you are."

"I'm not," Julian said. "And you know this isn't emotionality talking." Despite the bitterness of the words, his tone was flat. "Without my emotions, without my feelings, I'm a worse Shadowhunter. I make poorer decisions. I wouldn't trust someone who felt nothing for anyone. I wouldn't want them to make decisions that affected other people. Would you?"

Magnus looked thoughtful. "Hard to say. You're very clever."

Julian didn't look as if the compliment affected him one way or the other. "I wasn't always clever in the way you mean. From the time I turned twelve, when my father died and the kids became my responsibility, I had to learn how to lie. To manipulate. So if that's cleverness, I had it. But I knew where to *stop*."

Magnus raised his eyebrows.

"Julian without feelings," said Emma, "doesn't know where to stop."

"I liked your idea earlier," Magnus said, looking at Julian curiously. "Raising a resistance. Why didn't you push it more?"

"Because Jace wasn't wrong," Julian said. "We could be betrayed. Normally I'd be able to think past that. Imagine a solution. But not like this." He touched his temple, frowning. "I thought I'd be able to think more clearly, without feelings. But the opposite is true. I can't think at all. Not properly."

Magnus hesitated.

"Please," Emma said.

"You'll need a plan," Magnus said. "I know your plan before was exile, but that was when Robert could help you. Horace Dearborn won't."

"Dearborn won't, but another Inquisitor might. We must overthrow the Cohort in any case. There's a chance the next Inquisitor might be reasonable," said Julian.

"They don't have a history of being reasonable," said Magnus. "And we don't really know the time frame here." He drummed his fingers on the table. "I have an idea," he said finally. "You won't like it."

"What about one we *would* like?" Emma suggested.

Magnus gave her a dark look. "There are a few things that will, in an emergent situation, break your bond. Death, which I don't recommend. Being bitten by a vampire—hard to arrange, and can also end in death. Having your Marks stripped off and being turned into a mundane. Probably the best option."

"But only the Silent Brothers can do that," said Emma. "And we can't get near them right now."

"There's Jem," Magnus said. "He and I have both seen Marks stripped. And he was a Silent Brother himself. Together, we could make it happen." He looked slightly ill. "It would be painful and unpleasant. But if there was no other choice—"

"I'll do it," Emma said quickly. "If the curse starts to happen, then strip my Marks. I can take it."

"I don't . . . ," Julian began. Emma held her breath; the real Julian would never let her offer this. She had to get him to agree before Magnus took off the spell. "I don't like the idea," Julian said at last, looking almost puzzled, as if his own thoughts surprised him. "But if there's no other choice, all right."

Magnus gave Emma a long look. "I'll take this as a binding promise," he said after a pause. He stretched out a ringed hand. "Julian. Come here."

Emma watched in an agony of anticipation—what if something went wrong? What if Magnus couldn't remove the spell?—as Julian went over to the warlock and sat down on a chair facing him.

"Brace yourself," said Magnus. "It'll be a shock."

He reached out and touched Julian's temple. Julian started as a spark of light flew from Magnus's fingers to brush against his skin; it vanished like a firefly winking out, and Julian flinched back, suddenly breathing hard.

"I know." Julian's hands were shaking. "I already went through it in Thule. I can—do it again."

"It made you sick in Thule," Emma said. "On the beach."

Julian looked at her. And Emma's heart leaped: In that look was everything, all of her Julian, her *parabatai* and best friend and first love. In it was the shining connection that had always bound them.

He smiled. A careful smile, thoughtful. In it she saw a thousand memories: of childhood and sunshine, playing in the water as it rushed up and down the beach, of Julian always saving the best and biggest seashells for her. Carefully holding her hand in his when she'd cut it on a piece of glass and was too young for an *iratze*. He'd cried when they stitched it up, because he knew she didn't want to even though the pain was awful. He'd asked her for a lock of her hair when they both turned twelve, because he wanted to learn to paint the color. She remembered sitting on the beach with him when they were sixteen; the strap of her swimsuit had fallen down and she recalled the sharp hitch of his breath, the way he'd looked away quickly.

How had she not known? she thought. How he felt. How she felt herself. The way they looked at each other wasn't the way Alec looked at Jace, or Clary at Simon.

"Emma," Julian whispered. "Your Marks . . ."

She shook her head, tears bitter in the back of her throat. *It's done.*

The look on his face broke her heart. He knew there was no point arguing that he should be the one to have his Marks stripped instead, Emma thought. He could read her again, just like she could read him.

"Julian," Magnus said. "Give me your arm. The left one."

Julian tore his gaze away from Emma's and offered his scarred arm to Magnus.

Magnus ran his blue-sparking fingers with surprising gentleness along Julian's forearm, and the incised letters, one by one, faded and disappeared. When he was done, he released Julian and looked between him and Emma. "I'll give you a small piece of good news," he said. "You weren't *parabatai* when you were in Thule. That was an injury to your bond that's healing. So you have a small cushion of time during which the bond will be weaker."

Thank the Angel. "How long?" Emma said.

"That depends on you. Love is powerful, and the more you're together, and let yourself feel what you do, the stronger it'll be. You need to stay away from each other. To not touch each other. Not speak to each other. Try not to even *think* about each other." He waved his arms like an octopus. "If you find yourselves thinking fondly of each other, for God's sake stop yourselves right away."

They both stared at him.

"We can't do that forever," Emma said.

"I know. But hopefully, when the Cohort is gone, we'll have a new Inquisitor who can gift you with exile. And hopefully it'll happen soon."

"Exile is a pretty bitter gift," Julian said.

Magnus's smile was full of sorrow. "Many gifts are."

It wasn't hard to find Kieran. He hadn't gone very far; he was standing in the hallway near one of the windows that looked out over the hills. He had his palm pressed flat against the glass, as if he could touch the sand and desert flowers through the barrier.

"Kieran," Mark said, stopping before he reached him. Cristina stopped too; there was something remote in Kieran's expression, something distant. The awkwardness that had been between all of them since the night before was still there too, forbidding simple gestures of comfort.

"I fear my people will be murdered and my country will be destroyed," Kieran said. "That all the beauty and magic of Faerie will be dissolved and forgotten."

"Faeries are strong and magical and wise," said Cristina. "They have lived through all the ages of mortals. These—these *culeros* cannot wipe them out."

"I will not forget the beauty of Faerie and neither will you," said Mark. "But it will not come to that."

Kieran turned to look at them with unseeing eyes. "We need a good King. We need to find Adaon. He must take the throne from Oban and end this madness."

"If you want to find Adaon, we will find him. Helen knows how to reach Nene. She can ask Nene to find him in the Seelie Court," said Cristina.

"I did not want to presume she would do that for me," Kieran said.

"She knows how dear you are to me," said Mark, and Cristina nodded in agreement. Helen, part-faerie herself, would surely understand.

But Kieran only half-closed his eyes, as if in pain. "I thank you. Both of you."

"There is no need to be so formal—" Cristina began.

"There is every need," Kieran said. "What we had last night—I was happy in those moments, and I know now we will not ever have it again. I will lose one of you and possibly I will lose both of you. In fact, it seems the most likely outcome."

He looked from Mark to Cristina. Neither of them moved or spoke. The moment stretched on and on; Cristina felt paralyzed. She longed to reach out to both of them, but perhaps they had already decided? Perhaps it truly was impossible, just as Kieran said. Surely he would know. And Mark looked agonized—surely he would not look like that if he did not have the same fears she did? And Kieran—

Kieran's mouth set in a hard line. "Forgive me. I must go."

Cristina watched him hurry away, vanishing into the shadows at the end of the corridor. Outside the window, she saw Alec and Magnus emerge from the back door of the Institute into the bright sunlight. Clary and Jace followed. It was clear they were bidding Magnus and Alec good-bye for now.

Mark leaned his back against the window. "I wish Kieran understood he would be a great King."

The light through the window edged his pale hair with gilt. His eyes burned amber and sapphire. Her golden boy. Though Kieran's silver darkness was just as beautiful, in its own way.

"We must talk in private, Mark," Cristina said. "Meet me outside the Institute tonight."

Emma and Julian left the library in silence, and made it back to her room in the same silence before Julian finally spoke.

"I should leave you here," he said, gesturing at her door. He sounded as if his throat hurt—gruff and husky. His sleeve was still rolled up to the elbow, showing the healed skin of his forearm. She wanted to touch it—to touch him, to reassure herself he was back to himself. Her Julian again. "Will you be all right?"

How could I be all right? She reached for the knob blindly, couldn't make herself turn it. The words Magnus had spoken whirled in her brain. *Curse, Marks stripped, stay away from each other.*

She turned around, pressing her back against the wood of the door. Looked at him for the first time since they'd been in the library. "Julian," she whispered. "What do we do? We can't live without talking to each other or even thinking about each other. It's not possible."

He didn't move. She drank in the sight of him like an alcoholic promising themselves this was the last bottle. She had kept it together for what felt like so long by telling herself that when the spell was over, she'd have him back. Not as a romantic partner, even, but as Jules: her best friend, her *parabatai*.

But perhaps they had just exchanged one kind of cage for another.

She wondered if he thought the same. His face was no longer blank: It was alive with color, emotion; he looked stunned, as if he'd come up too quickly from a deep sea dive and the pain of the bends had just struck him.

He took her face in his hands. His palms curved against her cheeks: He held her with a light, gentle wonder that she associated with the reverent handling of precious and breakable objects.

Her knees went weak. Amazing, she thought; Julian under the spell could kiss her bare skin and she felt hollow inside. This Julian—her real Julian—touched her face lightly and she was swamped by a yearning so strong it was almost pain.

"We have to," he said. "In Alicante, before I went to Magnus to ask him to put the spell on me, it was because I knew—" He swallowed hard. "After we almost—on the bed—I felt my rune starting to burn."

"That's why you ran out of the room?"

"I could feel the curse." He ducked his head. "My rune was burning. I could see flames under my skin."

"You didn't tell me that part." Emma's mind whirled; she remembered what Diana had said in Thule: *Their runes began to burn like fire. As if they had fire in their veins instead of blood.*

"This is the first time it mattered," he said. She could see everything that had seemed invisible to her before: the bruise-dark shadows under his eyes, the lines of tension beside his mouth. "Before this, I had the spell on me, or we were in Thule and nothing could happen. We weren't *parabatai* there."

She caught at his left wrist. He flinched; it wasn't pain, though. She knew that instinctively. It was the intensity of every touch; she felt it too, like the reverberation of a bell. "Are you sorry that Magnus took the spell off you?"

"No," he said immediately. "I need to be at my best right now. I need to be able to help with what's happening. The spell made me into a person I don't want to be. A person I don't like or even trust. And I can't have someone I don't trust around you—around the kids. You matter too much to me."

She shivered, still holding his wrist. His palms were rough against her cheeks; he smelled of turpentine and soap. She felt as if she were dying; she had lost him, gained him back, was losing him again.

"Magnus told us we had a cushion of time. We just have to—to do what he says. Stay away from each other. It's all we can do for now," Julian said.

"I don't want to stay away from you," she whispered.

His eyes were fixed on her, relentless sea-glass blue. Dark as the sky in Thule. His voice was restrained, quiet, but the raw hunger in his gaze was like a scream.

"Maybe if we kiss one last time," he said roughly. "Get it out of our systems."

Did someone dying of thirst refuse water? All Emma had to do was nod and they fell into each other with such force that her bedroom door rattled in its frame. Anyone could come along the hall and see them, she knew. She didn't care. She grabbed his hair, the back of his shirt; her head hit the door as their mouths crashed together.

She opened her lips under his, making him moan and swear and pull her up against him, harder and harder, as if he could smash their bones to pieces against each other, fuse them into a single skeleton. She clawed his shirt into fistfuls in her hands; his fingers raked her sides, tangled in her hair. Emma was aware of how close they were to something truly dangerous—she could feel the strain in his body, not from the effort of holding her, but of holding himself back.

She felt behind her for the knob of the door. Twisted it. It swung open behind her and they stumbled apart.

It felt like having her skin ripped away. Like agony. Her rune ached with a deep pain. Halfway into her room, she hung on to the door as if nothing else would keep her standing.

Julian was gasping, disheveled; she felt as if she could hear his heart beating. Maybe it was her own, a deafening drumbeat in her ears. "Emma—"

"Why?" she said, her voice shaking. "Why would something this horrible happen because of the *parabatai* bond? It's supposed to be something so good. Maybe the Queen was right and it's evil."

"You don't—trust the Queen," Julian said breathlessly. His eyes were all pupil: black with a rim of blue. Emma's heart beat like a supernova, a collapsing dark star of frustrated longing.

"I don't know *who* to trust. 'There is a corruption at the heart of the bond of *parabatai*. A poison. A darkness in it that mirrors its goodness.' That's what the Queen said."

The hand at Julian's side clenched into a fist. "But the Queen—"

It's more than the Queen. I should tell him. What Diana said in Thule about parabatai. But Emma held back: He was in no state to hear it, and besides, they both knew what they needed to do.

"You know what has to happen," she said finally, her voice barely more than a whisper. "What Magnus said. We have a little time. We need to not—not push it."

His eyes were bleak, haunted. He didn't move. "Tell me to go away," he said. "Tell me to leave you."

"Julian—"

"I will always do what you ask me to do, Emma," he said, his voice harsh. The bones of his face seemed suddenly too sharp and pronounced, as if they were cutting through his skin. "Please. *Ask me.*"

She remembered the time all those years ago when Julian had put Cortana in her arms and she had held it so tightly it had left a scar. She remembered the pain and the blood. And the gratitude.

He had given her what she needed then. She would give him what he needed now.

She raised her chin. It might hurt like death, but she could do this. *I am of the same steel and temper as Joyeuse and Durendal.*

"Go away, Julian," she said, putting every ounce of steel she could into the words. "I want you to go away and leave me alone."

Even though he had asked her to say it, even though he knew it wasn't her real wish, he still flinched as if the words were arrows piercing his skin.

He gave a short, jerky nod. Turned with sharp precision. Walked away.

She closed her eyes. As his footsteps receded down the hall, she felt the pain in her *parabatai* rune fade, and told herself that it didn't matter. It would never happen again.

Kit was lurking about in the shadows. Not because he wanted to, precisely; he liked to think he'd turned over a new leaf and was less prone to lurking and planning underhanded deeds than he used to be.

Which, he realized, might be an exaggeration. Necromancy was pretty underhanded, even half-hearted participation in necromancy. Maybe it was like the tree falling in the forest: If no one knew about your necromantic activities, were they still underhanded?

Pressing himself back against the wall of the Institute, he decided that they probably were.

He'd come outside to talk to Jace, not realizing when he saw Jace heading out the back door that he was on his way to join Clary, Alec, and Magnus. Kit realized he'd wandered into their good-byes, and scrunched himself awkwardly into the shadows, hoping not to be noticed.

Clary had hugged Alec and Magnus, and Jace had given Magnus a friendly high five. Then he'd grabbed hold of Alec and they'd hugged each other for what seemed like hours or possibly years.

They'd patted each other on the back and clung on while Clary and Magnus looked on indulgently.

Being *parabatai* did seem like intense stuff, Kit thought, rolling his shoulders to get rid of the crick in his neck. And oddly, it had been a long time since he'd thought about being Ty's *parabatai*. Maybe it was because Ty was in no shape to make that kind of decision.

Maybe it was something else, but he pushed away from the thought as Alec and Jace let go of each other. Jace stepped back, sliding his hand into Clary's. Magnus raised his hands, and the blue sparks flew from his fingers to create the whirling door of a Portal.

The wind that blew from it kicked up dust and sand; Kit squinted, barely able to see as Alec and Magnus stepped through. When the wind died down, he saw that Alec and Magnus were gone, and Jace and Clary were headed back to the Institute, hand in hand.

Kit closed his eyes and banged his head silently against the wall.

"Do you do that because you enjoy it, or because it feels good when you stop?" said a voice.

Kit's eyes popped open. Jace was standing in front of him, muscular arms crossed, an amused look on his face. Clary must have gone inside.

"Sorry," Kit muttered.

"Don't apologize. It doesn't make any difference to me if you want to scramble your brains like eggs."

Grumbling, Kit stepped out of the shadows and stood blinking in the sun, dusting off his shirt. "I wanted to talk to you, but I didn't want to interrupt all the good-bye hugging," he said.

"Alec and I are unafraid to express our manly love," said Jace. "Sometimes he carries me around like a swooning damsel."

"Really?" said Kit.

"No," said Jace. "I'm very heavy, especially when fully armed. What did you want to talk to me about?"

"Actually, that," said Kit.

"My weight?"

"Weapons."

Jace looked delighted. "I *knew* you were a Herondale. This is excellent news. What do you want to discuss? Types of swords? Two-handed versus one-handed? I have a *lot* of thoughts."

"Having my own weapon," said Kit. "Emma has Cortana. Livvy had her sabers. Ty likes throwing knives. Julian's got crossbows. Cristina has her balisong. If I'm going to be a Shadowhunter, I should have a weapon of choice."

"So you decided?" Jace said. "You're going to be a Shadowhunter?"

Kit hesitated. He didn't know when exactly it had happened, but it had. He'd realized it on the beach with Shade, when he'd feared for a moment that he wasn't Nephilim after all. "What else would I be?"

Jace's mouth curled up at the corners in a cheeky grin. "I never doubted you, kid." He ruffled Kit's hair. "You don't have any training, so I'd say archery and crossbows and throwing knives are out for you. I'll find you something. Something that says *Herondale*."

"I could slay with my deadly sense of humor and wicked charm," said Kit.

"Now *that* says Herondale." Jace looked pleased. "Christopher—can I call you Christopher?"

"No," said Kit.

"Christopher, family for me was never blood. It was always the family I chose. But it turns out it's nice to have someone I'm related to in this world. Someone I can tell boring family stories to. Do you know about Will Herondale? Or James Herondale?"

"I don't think so," said Kit.

"Excellent. Hours of your time will be ruined," said Jace. "Now I'm off to find you a weapon. Don't hesitate to come to me any time if you need advice about life or weaponry, preferably both." He saluted sharply and jogged off before Kit could ask him what you were supposed to do if someone you really cared about wanted to raise the dead in an ill-advised manner.

"Probably for the best," he muttered to himself.

"Kit! *Kit! Pssst*," someone hissed, and Kit jumped several feet in the air and spun around to see Drusilla leaning out of an upper window and gesturing at him. "You said we could talk."

Kit blinked. Unfolding events had blown his agreement with Dru cleanly out of his mind. "All right. I'll come up."

As he jogged up the steps toward Dru's floor, he wondered where Ty was. Kit had been used to going everywhere with him—to finding Ty in the hallway, reading, when he got up in the morning, and to going to bed only after they'd both worn themselves out researching or sneaking around the Shadow Market under the amused eye of Hypatia. Though Ty didn't care for the clamor of the Shadow Market, everyone at it seemed to love him, the extremely polite Shadowhunter boy who didn't display weapons, didn't threaten, just calmly asked if they had this or that that he was looking for.

Ty was remarkable, Kit thought. The fact that tensions were escalating among Downworlders and Shadowhunters didn't seem to touch him. He was entirely focused on one thing: the spell that would bring back Livvy. He was happy when the search was going well and frustrated when it wasn't, but he didn't take his frustrations out on others.

The only person he was unkind to, Kit thought, was himself.

In the past days, though, since Julian and Emma had woken up, Ty had been harder to find. If he was working on something, he hadn't included Kit in it—a thought that hurt with surprising intensity. Still, they did have plans for that night, so that was something.

It wasn't hard to find Dru's room: She was hovering in the doorway, dancing up and down with impatience. On catching sight of Kit, she ushered him inside and shut the door behind him, locking it for emphasis.

"You're not planning on murdering me, are you?" he asked, raising both eyebrows.

"Ha-ha," she said darkly, and plonked herself down on the bed. She was wearing a black T-shirt dress with a screaming face on it. Her hair had been done up in braids so tight they stuck out perpendicular to her head. It was hard to recall her dressed as the vampy businesswoman who'd tricked Barnabas Hale. "You know perfectly well what I want to talk to you about."

Kit leaned his back against the desk. "Ty."

"He isn't okay," Dru said. "Not like he seems. Did you know that?"

Kit expected himself to say something defensive, or to deny that anything unusual was going on. Instead he slumped back against the desk, as if he'd put down a heavy weight but his legs were still shaking from carrying it. "It's like—I don't know how—people just aren't *seeing* it," he said, so relieved to be able to say the words that it almost hurt. "He isn't doing well. How could he be?"

When Dru spoke again, her voice was gentler. "None of us are okay," she said. "Maybe that's part of it. When you're hurting, it's sometimes hard to see how other people might be hurting differently or worse."

"But Helen—"

"Helen doesn't know us that well." Dru tugged a lock of her hair. "She's *trying*," she admitted. "But how can she see how Ty's different now when she doesn't know how he was before? Mark's been caught up in faerie stuff, and Julian and Emma weren't here. If anyone will notice, now that things have settled down a little, Julian will."

Kit wasn't sure how you could describe "society probably on the edge of a war" as "settled down," but he sensed the Blackthorns had a different scale for these things than he did.

"I mean, in some ways, he *is* okay," said Kit. "I think that's what's confusing. It seems like he's functioning and doing normal, everyday stuff. He eats breakfast. He washes his clothes. It's just that the only thing getting him through all that is—"

He broke off, his palms suddenly sweaty. He'd almost said it. Jesus Christ, he'd almost broken his promise to Ty just because Dru was a friendly face to talk to.

"Sorry," he said into the silence. Dru was looking at him quizzically. "I didn't mean anything."

She narrowed her eyes at him suspiciously. "You promised him you wouldn't say," she said. "Okay, how about I guess what he's up to, and you tell me if I'm right or wrong?"

Kit shrugged wearily. There was no way she was going to guess it anyway.

"He's trying to communicate with Livvy's ghost," she said. "The Thule story made me think of it. People who die, they exist in other forms. Whether it's as ghosts or in other dimensions. We just can't . . . reach them." She blinked very quickly and looked down.

"Yeah," Kit heard himself say, as if at an enormous distance. "That's it. That's what he's doing."

"I don't know if it's a good idea." Dru looked unhappy. "If Livvy's passed on, if she's in a good place, her spirit won't be here on earth. I mean, they say ghosts can appear sometimes briefly for something important . . . or if they're called in the right way. . . ."

Kit thought of Robert Lightwood's *parabatai*, at the side of his burning pyre. *Something important.*

"I could try to talk to him," Dru said in a small voice. "Remind him that he still has a sister."

Kit thought of the night Dru had come with them to con Barnabas. Ty had seemed lighter, happy to have her there even if he wouldn't admit it. "We're going tonight to—" No. Better not to tell her about Shade. "To get the last piece of what we need for the spell," he lied rapidly. "We're meeting down at the highway at ten. If you turn up there, you can threaten to tell on us unless we let you come with us."

Dru wrinkled up her nose. "I have to be the bad guy?"

"Come on," said Kit. "You'll get to boss us around. Don't tell me you won't enjoy it a little bit."

She grinned. "Yeah, probably. Okay, deal. I'll see you there."

Kit turned to unlock the door and let himself out. Then paused. Without looking at Dru, he said, "I've spent my whole life lying and tricking people. So why is it so hard for me to lie to this one person? To Ty?"

"Because he's your friend," said Dru. "What other reason do you need?"

Opening the drawer that held his paints had meaning to Julian again. Each tube of paint carried its own promise, its own personality. Tyrian red, Prussian blue, cadmium orange, manganese violet.

He returned to the fabric canvas he'd left blank the night before. He dumped the paint tubes he'd selected onto the tabletop. Titanium white. Raw umber. Naples yellow.

They were colors he always used to paint Emma's hair. The memory of her went through him like a knife: the way she'd looked in the doorway of her bedroom, her face white, eyelashes starred with tears. There was a horror in not being able to touch the person you loved, to kiss them or hold them, but an even worse horror in not being able to comfort them.

Leaving Emma, even after she'd asked him to, had felt like wrenching himself apart: His emotions were all too new, too raw and intense. He had always sought comfort in the studio, though he had found none the night before, when trying to paint had felt like trying to speak a foreign language he'd never learned.

But everything was different now. When he picked up the paintbrush, it felt like an extension of his arm. When he began to paint in long, bold strokes, he knew exactly the effect he wanted. As the images took shape, his mind quieted. The pain was still there, but he could bear it.

He didn't know how long he'd been painting when the knock came on the door. It had been a long time since he'd been able to fall into the dizzy dream-state of creating; even in Thule, he'd had only a short time with the colored pencils.

He placed the brushes he'd been using in a glass of water and went to see who it was. He half-expected it to be Emma—half-*hoped* it was Emma—but it wasn't. It was Ty.

Ty had his hands in the front pockets of his white sweatshirt. His gaze flickered across Julian's face. "Can I come in?"

"Sure." Julian watched Ty as he ambled around the room, glancing at the paintings, before coming to study Julian's new canvas. Ty had long wanted this room as an office or darkroom, but Julian had always held on to it stubbornly.

Not that he'd kept Ty out of it. When Ty was younger, experimentation with paints and paper had kept him distracted for hours. He never drew anything concrete, but he had an excellent sense of color—not that Julian was biased. All his paintings turned out as intense swirls of interleaving pigments, so bright and bold they seemed to jump off the paper.

Ty was looking at Julian's canvas. "This is Livvy's sword," he said. He didn't sound annoyed—more questioning, as if he weren't quite sure why Julian would be painting it.

Julian's heart skipped a beat. "I was trying to think of what would best symbolize her."

Ty touched the gold pendant at his throat. "This always makes me think of Livvy."

"That's—that's a good idea." Julian leaned against the center island. "Ty," he said. "I know I haven't been here for you since Livvy died, but I'm here now."

Ty had picked up an unused brush. He ran his fingers over the bristles, touching them to each fingertip as if lost in the sensation. Julian said nothing: He knew Ty was thinking. "It's not your fault," Ty said. "The Inquisitor sent you away."

"Whether it was my fault or not, I was still gone," said Julian. "If you want to talk to me about anything now, I promise to listen."

Ty looked up, his brief gray gaze like a light touch. "You've always been there for us, Jules. You did everything for us. You used to run the whole Institute."

"I—"

"It's my turn to be there for the rest of you," said Ty, and set the brush down. "I should go. I have to meet Kit."

When he was gone, Julian sat down on a stool pulled up to a blank easel. He stared unseeingly ahead of him, hearing Ty's voice echo in his mind.

You used to run the whole Institute.

He thought of Horace, of Horace's determination to have the whole Shadowhunter world see him speak with the Unseelie King. He hadn't understood why before. Without his emotions, he hadn't been able to understand Horace's reasons. Now he did, and he knew it was even more imperative than he had believed to stop him.

He thought of Arthur's old office, of the hours he'd spent there at dawn, composing and answering letters. The weight of the Institute's seal in his hand. That seal was in Aline and Helen's office now. They'd taken what they could from Arthur's office to help them with their new job. But they hadn't known about the secret compartments in Arthur's desk, and Julian hadn't been there to tell them.

You used to run the whole Institute.

In those compartments were the careful lists he'd kept of names—every important Downworlder, every Council member, every Shadowhunter at every Institute.

He glanced at the window. He felt alive, energized—not precisely happy, but buzzing with purpose. He would finish the artwork now. Later, when everyone was asleep, his real work would begin.

26
A Stir in the Air

Thunk. Thunk. Thunk.

Emma spun and threw the balanced knives one after the other, fast: overhead, overhead, sideways. They sliced through the air and jammed point-first into the target painted on the wall, their handles trembling with kinetic force.

She bent down and grabbed two more from the pile at her feet. She hadn't changed into training clothes and she was sweating in her tank top and jeans, her loose hair plastered to the back of her neck.

She didn't care. It was almost as though she'd returned to the time before she'd realized she was in love with Julian. A time when she'd been full of a rage and despair she'd attributed entirely to her parents' deaths.

She flung the next two knives, blades sliding through her fingers, their flight smooth and tightly controlled. *Thunk. Thunk.* She remembered the days when she'd thrown so many *bo-shuriken* that she'd made her hands split and bleed. How much of that rage had been about her parents—because a lot of it had been, she knew—and how much had been about the fact that she'd kept the doors of her awareness tightly shut, never letting herself know what she wanted, what would make her truly happy?

She picked up two more knives and positioned herself facing away from the target, breathing hard. It was impossible not to think about Julian. Now that the spell was off him, she felt a desperate desire to be with him, mixed with the bitterness of regret—regret for past choices made, regret for wasted years. She and Julian had both been in denial, and look what it had cost them. If either of them had been able to acknowledge why they shouldn't be *parabatai*, they wouldn't be facing separation from each other. Or exile from everything they loved.

Love is powerful, and the more you're together, and let yourself feel what you do, the stronger it'll be. You need to not touch each other. Not speak to each other. Try not to even think about each other.

Thunk. A knife sailed over her shoulder. *Thunk*. Another. She turned to see the handles vibrating where they stuck out from the wall.

"Nice throw."

Emma spun around. Mark was leaning against the doorway, his body like a long, lean spoke in the shadows. He was wearing his gear and he looked tired. More than tired, he looked weary.

It had been a while since she'd spent time with Mark alone. It was neither of their faults—there had been the separation in Idris, then Faerie and Thule—but there was another piece to it too, perhaps. There was an apprehensive sadness in Mark these days, as if he were constantly waiting to be told he had lost something. It seemed deeper than what he had carried back with him from Faerie.

She picked up another knife. Held it out. "Do you want a turn?"

"Very much so."

He came and took the knife from her. She stepped back a little while he took aim, sighting down the line of his arm toward the target.

"Do you want to talk about what's going on with Cristina?" she said hesitantly. "And . . . Kieran?"

He let the knife go. It sank into the wall beside one of Emma's. "No," he said. "I am trying not to think about it, and I do not think discussing it will accomplish that goal."

"Okay," Emma said. "Do you want to just throw knives in a silent, angry bro way together?"

He cracked a slight smile. "There are other things we could discuss than my love life. Like *your* love life."

It was Emma's turn to grab a knife. She threw it hard, viciously, and it hit the wall hard enough to crack the wood. "That sounds like about as much fun as stabbing myself in the head."

"I think mundanes discuss the weather when they have nothing else to talk about," said Mark. He had gone to lift a bow and quiver down from the wall. The bow was a delicate piece of workmanship, carved with filigreed runes. "We are not mundanes."

"Sometimes I wonder what we are," Emma said. "Considering I don't think the current powers that be in Alicante would like us to be Nephilim at all."

Mark drew back the bow and let an arrow fly. It whipped through the air, plunging directly into the center of the target on the wall. Emma felt a twist of grim pride; people often underestimated how good a warrior Mark was.

"It doesn't matter what they think," Mark said. "Raziel made us Shadowhunters. Not the Clave."

Emma sighed. "What would you do if things were different? If you could do anything, be anything. If this was all over."

He looked at her thoughtfully. "You always wanted to be like Jace Herondale," he said. "The greatest of all fighters. But I would like to be more like Alec Lightwood. I would like to do something important for Shadowhunters and Downworlders. For I will always be part of each world."

"I can't believe you remember I always wanted to be like Jace. That's so embarrassing."

"It was cute that you wanted to be such a fighter, especially when you were very small." He smiled a real smile, one that lit up his face. "I remember you and Julian when you were ten—both of you with wooden swords, and me trying to teach you not to smack each other in the head with them."

Emma giggled. "I thought you were so old—fourteen!"

He sobered. "I have been thinking that not everything that is strange is bad," he said. "Since I came from Faerie the way I did—it closed the gap of years between me and Julian, and me and you. I have been able to be much better friends with both of you now, rather than an older sibling, and that has been a gift."

"Mark—" she began, and broke off, staring out the west-facing picture window. Something—someone—was walking up the road toward the Institute, a dark figure moving purposefully.

She caught a flash of gold.

"I have to go." Emma grabbed a longsword and bolted out of the training room, leaving Mark staring after her. Energy was ping-ponging through her body. She took the stairs three at a time, burst out the front doors, and crossed the grass just as the figure she'd seen reached the top of the road.

The moon was bright, flooding the world with bright spears of illumination. Emma blinked away stars and gazed at Zara Dearborn, stalking toward her across the grass.

Zara was fully decked out in her Centurion gear, *Primi Ordines* pin and all. Her hair was tightly braided around her head, her brown eyes narrowed. In her hand was a golden sword that shone like the light of dawn.

Cortana. *A flash of gold.*

Emma stiffened all over. She whipped the longsword from its scabbard, though it felt like dead weight in her hand now that she was looking at her own beloved blade. "Stop," she said. "You aren't welcome here, Zara."

Zara gave her a narrow little smile. She was gripping Cortana all wrong, which blinded Emma with rage. Wayland Smith had made that blade, and now Zara had it in her sticky, incompetent hand. "Aren't you going to ask about this?" she asked, twirling the sword as if it were a toy.

Emma swallowed bitter rage. "I'm not going to ask you anything except to get off our property. Now."

"Really?" Zara cooed. "*Your* property? This is an Institute, Emma. Clave property. I know you and the Blackthorns treat it like it's yours. But it isn't. And you won't be living here much longer."

Emma tightened her grip on her longsword. "What do you mean?"

"You were sent a message," Zara said. "Don't pretend you don't know about it. Most of the other Institutes have shown up in Idris to prove their support. Not you guys, though." She twirled Cortana inexpertly. "You haven't even *replied* to the summons. And the names in your registry were a joke. Did you think we were too stupid to get it?"

"Yes," Emma said. "Also, it seems like it took you a week to figure it out, at least. Who got it in the end? Manuel?"

Zara flushed angrily. "You think it's cute, not taking anything seriously? Not taking the Downworlder threat seriously? Samantha's *dead*. She hurled herself out the window of the Basilias. Because of your faerie friend—"

"I already know what really happened," Emma said, with a feeling of immense sadness for Samantha. "Kieran pulled Samantha out of the pool. He tried to help her. You can twist things and twist things, Zara, but you can't just make facts whatever you want them to be. You stood around and *laughed* when Samantha fell into that water. And the cruelty she saw—the terrible pain she'd caused—that was because of you and what you made her do. And that's the truth."

Zara stared at her, her chest rising and falling rapidly.

"You don't deserve Cortana," Emma said. "You don't deserve to have it in your hand."

"I don't deserve it?" Zara hissed. "You were given it because you're a Carstairs! That's all! I worked and worked to get respect, and people just gave it to you like you're special because your parents died in the Dark War. A lot of people died in the Dark War. You're not special at all." She took a step toward Emma, Cortana shaking in her grip. "Don't you get it? None of this is yours. Not the Institute. Not this sword. Not the Blackthorns, who aren't *your* family. Not the reputation for being a great warrior. You didn't earn any of it."

"How lucky for you that your reputation as a bigoted asshole is totally justified," said Emma.

Zara's flush had faded. Her eyes glittered angrily. "You have twenty-four hours to come to Idris and swear loyalty to the Cohort. If you are even five minutes late you will be considered deserters and I will strike down every deserter myself. Starting with you."

Emma raised her sword. "Then strike me down now."

Zara took a step backward. "I said you had twenty-four hours."

Rage sizzled through Emma's nerves. "And I said *strike me down now*." She jabbed the sword toward Zara; it caught the edge of Zara's cloak and sliced through it. "You came here. You challenged me. You threatened *my* family."

Zara gaped. Emma suspected Zara had rarely ever had to engage in a fight that wasn't on her terms.

"You're a liar, Zara," she said, advancing with her sword drawn. Zara stumbled back, almost tripping over the grass. "You've never accomplished anything. You've taken credit for what other people do and used it to prop yourself up, but people can see through you. You pick on those who have less power than you to make yourself look strong. You're a bully and a thief and a coward."

Zara snarled, raising Cortana. "I am not a coward!"

"So *fight me*!" Emma swung her sword; Zara barely got Cortana up in the air and it clanged hard against Emma's blade, the awkward angle turning Zara's wrist back on itself. She yelped in pain and Emma slammed Cortana again—it felt beyond wrong to be fighting *against* Cortana, as if the world had been turned inside out.

She ought to feel sympathy for Zara's pain, Emma thought. But she didn't. She felt only a savage anger as she drove the other girl panting and gasping back and back across the tufted grass until they were at the edge of the bluffs, until the sea was below them.

Zara dug her heels in then and fought back, but when she raised Cortana and wheeled it through the air at Emma, the blade turned aside at the last moment, seeming to bend like a live thing in her hand. Zara shrieked, almost overbalancing; Emma kicked out and swept Zara's legs out from under her. Zara thumped to the ground, her body half-dangling over the edge of the bluff.

Emma stalked toward her, longsword in hand. A surge of power went through her like electricity coursing through a wire. She felt almost dizzy with it, as if she were rising above Zara to an immense height—looking down at her with the indifference of an avenging angel, a being of light gifted with power so great it had rendered them nearly inhuman.

I could bring my blade down and cut her in half. I could take Cortana back.

She raised her longsword. She could see herself as if from the outside, a massive figure towering over Zara.

Their runes began to burn like fire, as if they had fire in their veins instead of blood. People said that the blades of those who fought them shattered in their hands. Black lines spread over their bodies and they became monstrous—physically monstrous.

Emma stumbled back, Diana's voice echoing in her head. She stood without moving as Zara, gasping, scrambled back from the edge of the cliff, rolling onto her knees.

Emma's vision of herself as an avenging angel was gone. In its place, a cool and reasonable voice whispered in the back of her head, unmistakably Julian's, telling her that Horace Dearborn surely knew where his daughter was, would know who to blame when she went missing, that either hurting Zara or taking Cortana would bring the Clave down on the Los Angeles Institute.

"Get up," Emma said, her voice edged with contempt. Zara scrabbled to her feet. "And get out of here."

Zara was panting, her face smeared with dirt. "You little *pervert*," she hissed, all pretense at smirking gone. "My father told me about you and your *parabatai*—you're disgusting—I guess you want to be like Clary and Jace, huh? Wanting what's forbidden? And *nasty*?"

Emma rolled her eyes. "Zara, Clary and Jace *weren't related*."

"Yeah, well, they thought they were, and that's the same!" Zara screamed, a tower of howling illogic. "And they're dead now! That's what'll happen to you and Julian! We'll leave your corpses on the battlefield and the crows will pick out your eyes, I'll make sure of it—"

"What battlefield?" Emma said quietly.

Zara blanched. Her mouth worked, spittle flecking her lips. At last she raised Cortana between herself and Emma, as if she were warding off a vampire with a crucifix. "Twenty-four hours," she breathed. "If you're not at the gates of Alicante then, there won't be a single one of you left alive."

She turned and stalked away. It took every ounce of Emma's self-control not to follow her. She forced herself to turn away from Zara. To turn back to the Institute.

She raced across the lawn and up the stairs. By the time she reached the front door, her anger was turning into anticipation: She would need to talk to Julian. She had to tell him about Zara.

She yanked the front door open, already picturing what Julian would say. He would tell her not to worry. He would have an idea about what they should do. He might even make her laugh—

There was a flare of sharp pain against her arm.

Her rune. She gasped and flinched; she was in the entryway of the Institute. It was deserted, thank the Angel. She pulled up the sleeve of her shirt.

The *parabatai* rune there glowed on her upper arm like a brand, red against her skin.

She sagged back against the wall. If even *thinking* of Julian did this, then how much time did they have left? How much time before she had to go to Magnus and have her runes stripped forever?

Slumped against the wall of the Gard cell, Diego held his brother in his arms.

Jaime had fallen asleep at some point during the night before, or at least Diego assumed it was night—it was hard to tell when there was no way to measure the passage of time except for meals, and those were served irregularly. There was only sleeping, eating, and trying to conserve Jaime's strength.

Jaime breathed against him, low irregular breaths; his eyes were closed. Some of Diego's earliest memories were of holding his brother. When he was five and Jaime was three, he had carried him everywhere. He'd been afraid that otherwise Jaime, toddling around on his short little legs, would miss out on all the things in the world Diego wanted him to see.

Sometimes at the end of a long day, his baby brother would fall asleep in his arms, and Diego would carry him to bed and tuck him in. Diego had always taken care of his brother, and the helplessness he felt now filled him with rage and despair.

For so long, he had thought of Jaime as a little boy, quick and mischievous. Even when he'd run off with the Eternidad, it seemed like another of his games, one where he was always slipping out of trouble and playing tricks. But in these past few days, as Jaime had grown weaker but refused to speak a word to Zara about the heirloom, Diego had seen the steel beneath his brother's playful attitude, his commitment to their family and their cause.

He kissed Jaime on the top of the head; his black hair was ragged, messy and dirty. Diego didn't care. He was filthy himself. *"Siempre estuve orgulloso de ti,"* he said.

"I've always been proud of you, too," Jaime murmured without opening his eyes.

Diego gave a rough chuckle of relief. "You're awake."

Jaime didn't move. His brown cheeks were red with fever, his lips chapped and bleeding. "Yes. I'm awake, and I'm going to hold this over you forever."

Forever. Most likely neither of them had forever. Diego thought of the heirloom, its optimistic infinity symbol looping over and over, promising a never-ending future. *Eternidad.*

There was nothing to say. He stroked Jaime's hair in silence and listened to his brother breathe. Every breath a struggle, in and out like rough water through a broken dam. Diego's desperation for a stele was like a silent scream, rising in the back of his throat.

They both looked up as a familiar clanking sound announced the arrival of what Diego guessed was breakfast. Surely it had to be morning. He blinked at the dim light coming from the open door of the prison. A figure came closer to their cell; it was Anush Joshi, carrying a tray.

Diego looked at Anush without speaking. He'd given up begging any of the guards for help. If they were monstrous enough to sit back and watch Jaime slowly die, then there was no point asking them for anything. It only made Jaime feel worse.

Anush knelt down with the tray. He wore the livery of the Council guard, his dark hair tangled, his eyes red-rimmed. He set the tray on the ground.

Diego cleared his throat. "Jaime's too sick to eat that," he said. "He needs fresh fruit. Juice. Anything with calories."

Anush hesitated. For a moment Diego felt a flicker of hope. But Anush only pushed the tray slowly through the gap in the bottom of the door.

"I think he'll want to eat this," he said.

He stood up and hurried away, closing the prison door behind him. Keeping Jaime cradled against him, Diego pulled the tray toward himself with one hand.

A jolt of surprise went through him. Lying beside the usual bowls of gruel was a stele, and a note. Diego seized them both up with a shaking hand. The note read: *You were the only one who was kind to me at the Scholomance. I'm leaving Idris and the guards. I know there's a resistance out there. I'm going to find it.*

Take care of your brother.

"What's that?" Kit called; he could see Ty coming down the dirt road toward the highway, a witchlight rune-stone in his hand. It cast him into shadow, but the small crouched creature on his shoulder was still visible.

"It's a wood rat," said Ty. The witchlight blinked off as he joined Kit by the side of the highway. He was all in black, with the glimmer of Livvy's pendant at the collar of his shirt.

Kit, who was not a fan of rats, eyed the animal on Ty's shoulder with some wariness. It didn't look like the usual sort of rat: It had rounded ears and a furry face and tail. It appeared to be nibbling on a shelled nut.

"They're harmless," Ty said. "They like to collect things for their nests—bottlecaps and leaves and acorns."

The wood rat finished its snack and looked at Ty expectantly.

"I don't have any more," he said, plucked the rat off his shoulder, and set it down gently. It scampered off into the bushes by the roadside. "So," Ty said, dusting off his hands. "Should we go over everything we have for the spell?"

Kit's stomach knotted. He was half-wondering where Dru was, half-anxious about what Shade was going to do. If the warlock planned to stop Ty, he was certainly waiting until the last minute.

"Sure," Kit said, pulling the list out of his pocket. "Incense from the heart of a volcano."

"Got it at the Shadow Market. Check."

"Chalk powdered from the bones of a murder victim."

"Same."

"Blood, hair, and bone of the person to be brought over," Kit said, a slight catch in his voice.

Ty's pale face was like a half-moon in the darkness. "I have a lock of Livvy's hair and one of her baby teeth."

"And the blood?" said Kit, gritting his teeth. It seemed beyond grim to be talking about pieces of Livvy, as if she'd been a doll and not a living, breathing person.

Ty touched the pendant at his throat, still stained with rust. "Blood."

Kit forced a noise of recognition through his tight throat. "And myrrh grown by faeries—"

A twig snapped. Both of them swung around, Ty's hand going to his waist. Kit, realizing, put a hand on Ty's arm a moment before Drusilla stepped out of the shadows.

She held up her hands. "Whoa. It's just me."

"What are you doing here?" Ty's voice crackled with anger.

"I was looking out my window. I saw you walking down toward the highway. I wanted to make sure everything was okay."

Kit was impressed. Dru really was a good liar. Face open and honest, voice steady. His dad would have given her a gold star.

"Why were you talking about faeries and myrrh and all that other stuff?" she went on. "Are you doing a spell?"

Ty looked a little sick. Guilt hit Kit with the force of a whip. Ty wasn't good at lying, and he didn't do well with surprise changes to plans he'd made. "Go back to the house, Dru," he said.

Dru glared at him. "I won't. You can't make me."

Kit wondered if any of this was still playacting.

"If you send me back, I'll tell everyone you're doing weird spell stuff with evil chalk," said Dru.

Ty flushed with annoyance. Kit pulled Ty toward him by his sleeve and whispered in his ear, "Better let her come with us. If we don't, and she tells, we could get caught or get Shade in trouble."

Ty started to shake his head. "But she can't—"

"We'll make her wait outside the cave," Kit said. He'd realized they would have to do that anyway; the first words Shade said would undermine the careful half-truths Kit had told Dru.

Ty exhaled. "Fine."

Dru clapped her hands together. "Woo-hoo!"

They crossed the highway together, and Dru took off her shoes when they reached the sand. It was a soft night, the air tickling their skin, the ocean breathing in low, soft exhalations, rushing the tide up the beach. Kit felt a sort of ache at the center of him at how beautiful it all was, mixed with bitterness at his father for never bringing him here. Another truth denied to him: His city was beautiful.

As were other things. Ty kicked his way along the edge of the sand, his hands in his pockets. The wind lifted his hair, and the strands clung to his cheekbones like streaks of dark paint. He was purposely ignoring Drusilla, who was playing tag with the tide, running up and down the beach with her hair askew, the cuffs of her jeans wet with salt water. She looked over at Kit and winked, a conspiratorial wink that said: *We're helping Ty together.*

Kit hoped that was true. His stomach was in painful knots by the time they made it to the cave entrance. Ty stopped at the dark hole in the stone bluff, shaking his head at his sister.

"You can't come with us," he said.

Dru opened her mouth to protest, but Kit gave her a meaningful look. "It's better if you wait outside," he said, enunciating each word clearly so she'd know he meant it.

Dru flopped down in the sand, looking woebegone. "Okay. *Fine.*"

Ty ducked into the cave. Kit, after an apologetic look at Dru, was about to follow when Ty emerged again, carrying an angry gray ball of fluff.

Dru's face broke into a smile. "Church!"

"He can keep you company," Ty said, and put the cat into his sister's lap. Dru looked at him with shining eyes, but Ty was already ducking back into the cave. Kit followed, though he couldn't help but wonder if Ty had ever noticed how much Dru looked up to him. He couldn't help but think that if he had a little sibling who admired him, he would have spent all his time showing off.

Ty was different, though.

The moment they entered the tunnel, Kit could hear scratchy music—something like the sound of a song that hadn't downloaded properly. When they entered the main cave, they found Shade twirling slowly around the room to the sound of a mournful tune playing on a gramophone.

"*Non, rien de rien,*" Shade sang along. "*Je ne regrette rien. Ni le bien qu'on m'a fait, ni le mal—*"

Kit cleared his throat.

Shade didn't seem the least embarrassed. He ceased his twirling, glared, and snapped his fingers. The music vanished.

"I don't recall inviting you to come tonight," the warlock said. "I might have been busy."

"We sent a note," said Kit. Shade beetled his white brows at him and glanced down at the scratched wooden table. An empty vial sat on it, the kind they'd used to distribute the Lake Lyn water. Kit was pleased to see Shade had drunk the cure, although a little worried he might be hallucinating.

Ty took an eager step forward. "We have everything. All the ingredients for the spell."

Shade's gaze flicked to Kit quickly and then away. He looked grim. "*All* of them?"

Ty nodded. "Incense, blood, and bone—"

"An object from another world?"

"We have that, too," said Kit as Ty drew the folded letter from his pocket. "It's from a place called Thule."

Shade stared at the letter, the color draining from his face, leaving it the sickly hue of lettuce. "*Thule?*"

"You know that world?" Ty said.

"Yes." Shade's voice was toneless. "I know many other worlds. It is one of the worst."

Kit could see that Ty was puzzled: He hadn't expected Shade to react this way. "But we have everything," he said again. "All the ingredients. You said you would give us a power source."

"Yes, I did say that." Shade sat down at the rickety wooden table. "But I won't."

Ty blinked disbelievingly. "But you said—"

"I know what I said," Shade snapped. "I never intended you to find all the ingredients, you foolish child. I thought you would give up. You didn't." He threw his arms into the air. "Don't you understand this would be the worst thing you could possibly do? That its effects would follow you all your life? Death is the end for a reason."

"But you're immortal." Ty's eyes were huge and pale gray, silver coins against his stark face.

"I have a long life, but I won't live forever," said Shade. "We all have the life that's been allotted to us. If you pull Livvy to you from where she belongs, you leave a hole in the universe to be filled by black sorrow and miserable grief. That's not something you can walk away from unscathed. Not now. Not ever."

"So you lied to us," Ty said.

Shade stood up. "I did. I would again. I will never help you to do this thing, do you understand me? And I will spread the word. No warlock will help you. They will face my wrath if they do."

Ty's hands were working themselves into fists, his fingers scrabbling at his palms. "But Livvy—"

"Your sister is dead," said Shade. "I understand your grief, Tiberius. But you cannot break the universe to get her back."

Ty turned and ran for the tunnel. Kit stared at Shade.

"That was too brutal," he said. "You didn't have to talk to him like that."

"I did," Shade said. He slumped back into his chair. "Go after your friend. He needs you now, and God knows I don't."

Kit backed up, then spun and ran, following Ty's witchlight. He spilled out onto the beach to find Ty already there, bent over and gasping for breath.

Dru leaped to her feet, spilling a meowing Church onto the ground. "What's happened? What's wrong?"

Kit put his hand on Ty's back, between his shoulder blades. He was a little startled to find Ty's back more solid and lightly muscled than he would have thought. He always thought of Ty as fragile, but he didn't feel fragile. He felt like iron hammered thin: flexible but unbreakable.

Kit remembered hearing somewhere that it was soothing to rub circles on someone's back, so he did that. Ty's breaths began to regulate.

"It isn't going to work," Kit said, looking firmly at Dru over Ty's back. "We aren't going to be able to see Livvy's ghost."

"I'm sorry," Dru whispered. "I would have liked to have seen her too."

Ty straightened up. His eyes were wet; he rubbed them fiercely. "No—I'm sorry, Dru."

Kit and Dru exchanged a startled look. It hadn't occurred to Kit before that Ty might feel not just disappointed but as if he had let others down.

"Don't be sorry," Dru said. "Some things aren't possible." She put her hand out, a little shyly. "If you feel bad, I'll watch movies all night with you in the TV room. I can make cookies, too. That always helps."

There was a long pause. Ty reached out to take Dru's hand. "That would be nice."

Kit felt a wash of relief so enormous he almost staggered. Ty had remembered he had a sister. Surely that was something. He had expected much worse: a disappointment he couldn't calculate, a hurt so deep nothing he could have said would touch it.

"Come on." Dru tugged on Ty's hand, and together they started back toward the Institute.

Kit followed, pausing as they began to scramble up the first of the rock walls that blocked the way across the beach. As Ty and Dru climbed, he looked back over his shoulder and saw Shade watching them from the darkness of his cave entrance. He shook his head at Kit once before vanishing back into the shadows.

The wind was blowing from the desert; Cristina and Mark sat near the statues Arthur Blackthorn had imported from England and placed among the cacti of the Santa Monica Mountains. The sand was still warm from the sunlight of the day, and soft under Mark, like the deep pile of a carpet. In the Wild Hunt, he and Kieran would have found this a very fine bed.

"I am worried," Cristina said, "that we hurt Kieran earlier today."

She was barefoot in the sand, wearing a short lace dress and gold earrings. Looking at her made Mark's heart hurt, so he glanced up at the statue of Virgil, his old friend of frustrated nights. Virgil stared back impassively, without advice.

"His worries are my worries too," said Mark. "It is difficult to ease his fears when I cannot ease my own."

"You don't have to ease other people's fears to share yours, Mark." Cristina was playing with her medallion, her long fingers caressing the etching of Raziel. Mark wanted badly to kiss her; instead, he dug his fingers into the sand.

"I could say the same to you," he said. "You have been tense as a bowstring all day. You are fearful too."

She sighed and poked his leg lightly with her bare foot. "Fine. You tell me, and I'll tell you."

"I have been worried about my sister," Mark said.

Cristina looked puzzled. "That isn't what I thought you would say."

"My sister was exiled because of her faerie blood," said Mark. "You know the story—all of it. You know it better than most." He couldn't help it; he put his hand over hers in the sand. "All of my family has suffered because we have faerie parentage. Our loyalty has always been questioned. How much worse would it be for her and for Aline if I were with Kieran and he were the King of the Unseelie Court? It sounds so strange to say, and so selfish—"

"It is not selfish."

They both looked up; Kieran stood in the space between two statues, pale as a statue himself. His hair was black raven wings in the darkness, which washed all the blue from its color.

"You are worried about your family," said Kieran. "That is not selfish. It is what I have learned from you and from Julian. To want to protect others more than you want your own happiness—" He glanced sideways. "Not that I wish to assume that being with me would bring you happiness."

Mark was speechless, but Cristina stretched out her arms. Gold bracelets shimmered against her brown skin as she beckoned to Kieran. "Come and sit with us."

Kieran was also barefoot; faeries often were. He prowled like a cat through the sand, his steps kicking up no dust, his movements silent as he sank to his knees opposite Cristina and Mark.

"It would make me happy," Mark said. "But as you said—" He took a handful of sand and let it sift through his fingers. "There are other considerations."

"I might not become King," said Kieran.

"But you might," said Cristina. "I, too, am afraid. I spoke to my mother today. Someone had said something nasty to her about me. That I was involved with faeries. That I was a—a dirty girl, besmirched by Downworlders. You know I don't care what anyone says about me," she added hastily. "And my mother could withstand it as well, but—it is a bad time to be a Rosales. Our history of friendship with faeries has already brought us trouble. Jaime and Diego are in jail. What if I bring further trouble on them?"

"Now I will tell you something selfish," Kieran said. "I was afraid you both regretted what happened last night. That you both regretted—me."

Mark and Cristina looked at each other. She shook her head, the wind lifting her dark hair.

"There is no regret," said Mark. "Only—"

"I know," Kieran said. "I knew it when Gwyn came and told me I should be King. I knew what it would mean. Even what it would mean for me to be involved in the Court at all, as it seems I must be. The Clave wants to control access to the Courts. They always have. For two Shadowhunters they do not control to have the ear of the King would be anathema to them."

"But, Kieran—" Cristina said.

"I am not a fool," Kieran said. "I know when something is impossible." His eyes were shields of metal: one tarnished, one new. "I have always been an unquiet soul. In my father's Court, and then in the Hunt, I raged and stormed inside my heart." He bent his head. "I knew when I met Mark that I had found the person who gave my soul peace. I did not think I would find that in anyone else again, but I have. If I could just sit here quietly with both of you before this gathering storm, it would mean a great deal to me."

"And to me," Cristina said. She held out her small hand and took one of Kieran's gently. He raised his head as Mark took the other, and Mark and Cristina joined hands as well, completing the circle. None of them spoke: There was no need. It was enough to be together.

Emma still felt jittery when she walked into the kitchen in the morning, as if she'd drunk too many cups of the coffee she despised.

The hammer beat of Diana's words in Thule echoed in her head. She hadn't gone to Julian last night to tell him about Zara but had reluctantly woken up Helen and Aline to warn them instead. Then she'd headed back to the training room, in the hopes that kicking and punching and falling onto the hard mats on the floor would make her forget about the burning of her rune. About the *parabatai* of Thule. About the words of the Queen.

Later, when she'd fallen asleep, she'd dreamed about the *parabatai* rune in the Silent City, and about blood on the hilt of Cortana, and a ruined city where monstrous giants stalked the horizon. She still felt uneasy, as if she were half-trapped in nightmares.

She was glad to see the kitchen full of people. In fact, there were far too many to fit into the small eating area. Someone had had the brilliant idea of supplementing the existing table with an overturned weapons crate from the training room, and folding chairs had been dragged in from all over the house.

She'd been worried the morning would be grim as everyone rushed around getting ready to invade Alicante. She couldn't help but feel resentful that she and Julian wouldn't be going. It was their fight too. Besides, she needed the distraction. The last thing she wanted was to be left in the Institute with Julian and minimal supervision.

But the assembled group seemed anything but grim. If not for the space where Livvy should have been, the scene was almost perfect—Helen and Aline smiling at the kids over their coffee mugs. Mark between Kieran and Cristina, as if Mark had never been torn away from his family in the first place. Jace and Clary visiting the way the family had never really been able to have casual visitors when Arthur was in charge. Kit being the missing piece they had never known Ty needed, stealing a potato from Ty's plate and making him smile. Diana radiating her steady calm, bringing a level head to a family prone to dramatics. Even Kieran, who seemed to make both Mark and Cristina happier when he was around, had folded into the group at last: He was showing Tavvy and Dru the joys of dunking strawberries in maple syrup.

And Julian, of course, standing over the kitchen range, flipping pancakes with the ease of an expert.

"One pancake at a time, Tavvy," Helen was saying. "Yes, I know you *can* get three in your mouth, but that doesn't mean you *should.*"

Emma's eyes met Julian's. She saw the tension in his shoulders, his mouth, as he looked at her. *Be normal*, she thought. *This is a happy, ordinary meal with family.*

"You made pancakes?" she said, keeping her tone cheerful. "What brought that on?"

"Sometimes when you start a war, you want to make pancakes," Julian said, slipping two pancakes onto a plate and holding it out to Emma.

Jace choked on his toast. "What did you say, Julian?"

Julian glanced up at the clock that hung over the kitchen range. He flicked off the gas burner and began to calmly untie his apron. "They should be getting here any moment," he said.

"They should *what?*" Diana put her fork down. "Julian, what are you talking about?"

Tavvy was standing up on a wobbly chair, his face pressed to the window. He made an excited squeaking noise. "Who are all the people coming up the road, Jules?"

Kit and Ty immediately jumped to their feet and scrambled for a window view. "I see faeries—" Ty said. "I think those are werewolves—those black cars have to be vampires—"

"And Shadowhunters," said Kit. "So many Shadowhunters—"

"The Sanctuary's almost ready," said Julian, throwing down a dish towel. "Unless someone else wants to do it, I'll go downstairs and greet our guests."

Jace stood up. Clary looked up at him in concern: His golden eyes were flat with anger. "I'm not going to ask you a second time, Julian Blackthorn," he said, and his usually amused voice had no amusement in it at all. "What did you do?"

Julian leaned his hip against the counter. Emma realized with a shock that though he did look much younger, he was just as tall as Jace. "Remember when you said my coalition idea was a bad one because we couldn't trust other Shadowhunters to be telling us the truth about their loyalties?"

"Vividly," said Jace. "But I gather you invited everyone to a war council anyway?"

"They're here right now?" Clary sputtered. "But—I'm wearing a T-shirt that says 'Unicorn Power'—"

"There are no such things as unicorns," Jace said.

"I *know*," Clary said. "That's why it's *funny*."

"To return to the issue of betrayal—" Jace began.

"What if I told you I expected betrayal?" said Julian. "In fact, that I was counting on it? That it was part of my *plan*?"

"What plan?" said Jace.

"I always have a plan," said Julian calmly.

Dru lifted her coffee cup. "It's great to have you back, Jules. I missed your lunatic schemes."

Helen was on her feet now. Aline appeared to be trying not to giggle. "How did you invite them all here?" Helen said. "How would you even have gotten in touch with so many Downworlders and Nephilim, and so quickly?"

"I corresponded with them all for years," Julian said. "I know how to send fire-messages to warlocks and Shadowhunters, and acorn messages to Faerie, and the telephone numbers of every important vamp and werewolf. I knew how to reach the Downworlder-Shadowhunter Alliance. I had to know those things. For five years, it was my job."

"But didn't you usually write to them as Arthur, before?" said Helen, clearly worried. "Who did you pretend to be this time?"

"I wrote as myself," said Julian. "I know these people. I know their personalities. I know which of them will be on our side. I've been the Head of the Institute here for years. I called on my allies, because it's been my job to know who my allies are." His voice was quiet, but firm. There was nothing disrespectful in what he'd said, but Emma knew what he meant: *I've been a diplomat for years now, unknown and unacknowledged. But that doesn't mean I wasn't skilled at it. I've put those skills to use—whether you like it or not.*

"We can't fight the Cohort alone," he added. "They're part of us. Part of our government. They're not an outside threat like Sebastian was. We need these allies. You'll see."

And then he looked at Emma, as if he couldn't help it. The message in his eyes was clear. Though she was reeling from the shock of what he'd done, he was hoping for her approval. As he always had.

She felt a burning pulse through her *parabatai* rune. She winced, glanced down at her left arm: Her skin felt hot and tight, but the rune looked normal. It had just been a look, she thought. That was all.

"I'll help finish setting up the Sanctuary for the meeting," she said. "We'll need chairs—"

Kieran got to his feet, pushing sea-blue hair behind his ears. "I will also help," he said. "I thank you on behalf of my people for calling Downworlders to the table as equals. You are right. None of us can do this alone."

Diana stood up. "I will send a message to Gwyn," she said. "I know he will be pleased to come, and you will have the Wild Hunt on your side."

It was Cristina's turn to rise. "Did you reach out to the Mexico City Institute?"

"Yes," said Julian. "Your mother said she'd be pleased to attend."

Cristina looked alarmed. "I have to go change my clothes," she said, and fled.

The younger Blackthorns watched with wide eyes as Jace held up his hand. Emma tensed. Jace was a powerful Shadowhunter—not just physically but politically. He and Clary could upset every facet of this plan if they wanted.

"Did you invite Magnus and Alec?" he said. "Do they know our plans have changed?"

Our plans. Emma began to relax.

"Of course," said Julian. "I invited everyone I thought would be on our side. And I told everyone I invited they could reach out to others they trusted."

"This is probably a bad idea," Jace said. "Like, a record-breakingly bad idea. Like a go-down-in-history bad idea. But—"

Clary bounced to her feet. "What he means is, we're in," she said. "We love bad ideas."

"That's true," Jace admitted, a smile breaking over his face. Suddenly he looked seventeen again.

Aline was the last to rise. "Technically, this is my Institute," she said. "We do what I say." She paused. "And I do what Helen wants. What do you want, baby?"

Helen smiled. "I want a war council," she said. "Let's get ready."

27
Far and Free

They streamed in through the open doors of the Sanctuary, one after another: Downworlders and Shadowhunters in a seemingly never-ending cascade.

First came the vampires with their paper-white faces and cold elegance, enchanted black umbrellas held aloft as they took the few steps from their tinted-window cars to the Sanctuary doors, eager to escape the sun. Emma recognized Lily Chen among them, on the arm of a tall vampire with dreadlocks. A gaggle of blond Swedish vampires came in chatting with the Lindquists, who ran the Stockholm Institute.

There were werewolves from all over the world: Luke Garroway, scruffy and bearded in his flannel jacket, Clary's mother, Jocelyn, at his side. Werewolves in kilts and hanboks and qipaos. Maia Roberts and Bat Velasquez—Emma felt a pang, thinking of the other version of them in Thule: still together, still hand in hand.

There were warlocks, too, more than Emma had ever seen in one place. Catarina Loss, blue-skinned and white-haired: She marched in with Tessa and Jem, wearing nurse's scrubs, and looked around her thoughtfully. Her eyes lit on Kit, and she gazed at him with a quiet recognition that he, absorbed in talking to Ty, didn't notice.

Hypatia Vex, with her bronze hair and dark skin, regal and curious. Warlocks with bat's wings, with hooves and gills and rainbow eyes, with delicate antennae and curving stag's horns. A bat-faced woman who went up to Cristina and began muttering in Spanish. A dark-skinned warlock with a white mark on his cheek in the shape of a spiderweb.

And there were Shadowhunters. Emma had seen many Shadowhunters gathered together before—she'd been to quite a few Council meetings—but it was gratifying to see how many had answered Julian's call. He stood at the front of the room, where the Blackthorns and their friends had hastily assembled a long table. A rolled-up banner hung on the wall behind it. Julian leaned calmly against the table, but Emma could sense the tension running through him like electrical lines as the Shadowhunters began to file into the Sanctuary.

Julie Beauvale and Beatriz Mendoza, their *parabatai* runes glimmering on their forearms. Marisol Garza, wearing white in memory of Jon Cartwright. Magnus and Alec had just arrived with Maryse and their kids, and were standing by the door opposite Aline and Helen, greeting the Downworlders while the two women greeted the Shadowhunters. Kadir Safar of the New York Conclave gave Diana a somber nod before going to speak with Maryse, who was dandling little blue Max on her lap while Rafe ran around them both in circles.

The Romeros had come from Argentina, the Pederosos from Brazil, the Keos from Cambodia, and the Rosewains from Northern England. A dark-haired, petite woman darted over to Cristina and hugged her tightly. *Cristina's mom!* Emma had an urge to bow in acknowledgment of the woman who had named Perfect Diego.

"It's cool to see the Alliance in action," said Mark, who had been helping the others set up rows of chairs. He had put on a somber dark suit jacket in an attempt to look more serious. Like the careful arrangement of the food at the meeting the other day, the small gesture made Emma's heart spark with tenderness. There were many ways to serve your family, she thought. Julian's way was in large and passionate gestures; Mark's were smaller and quieter, but meaningful just the same. "Alec seems to know every Downworlder in the place."

It was true—Alec was greeting a werewolf girl who spoke in excitable French and asked him something about Rafael; a tall, dark-haired vampire wearing a T-shirt with Chinese characters on it slapped him on the back, and Lily and Maia darted over to confer with him in low voices.

Mark suddenly straightened up. Emma followed his gaze and saw that several faeries had come into the room. She laid her hand on Mark's arm, wondering if he remembered the last time he had been in this Sanctuary, when the Wild Hunt had returned him to his family.

Kieran had turned around—he had been speaking with Julian in a low voice—and was staring as well: Gwyn had come in, of course, which everyone expected, but following him were several others. Among the dryads and pixies and nixies Emma recognized several piskies, the Fair Folk she and Julian had encountered in Cornwall. Behind them came a tall phouka in a JUSTICE FOR KAELIE T-shirt, and after him, a woman in a long green cloak, her face hidden but a bit of white-blond hair escaping nonetheless.

Emma turned to Mark. "It's Nene."

"I must speak with her." Mark gave Emma's shoulder a pat and vanished across the room to greet his aunt. Emma caught sight of both Kieran and Cristina watching him, though Cristina had been firmly captured by her mother and clearly wasn't going anywhere.

Emma glanced over at Julian again. He had moved behind the table and was standing with his arms at his sides. Helen and Aline had joined him behind the table as well. The rest of the family was clustered in a group of chairs at the left of the room, Kit and Ty together, Dru with her hand on Tavvy's shoulder, turning around to squint at a figure who'd just come into the Sanctuary.

It was Cameron. He was alone, slouching a little as if he hoped no one would see him, though his bright red hair was like a beacon. Emma couldn't help herself; she darted over to him.

He looked surprised as she bore down on him and caught his hands in hers. "Thank you for coming, Cameron," she said. "Thank you for everything."

"The rest of my family doesn't know," he said. "They're pretty much—"

"On the Cohort's side, I know," said Emma. "But you're different. You're a good guy. I know that for sure now, and I'm sorry if I ever hurt you in the past."

Cameron looked even more alarmed. "I don't think we should get back together," he said.

"Oh, definitely not," said Emma. "I'm just glad you're okay." She glanced over at Julian, who was waving and giving Cameron a thumbs-up from behind the table. Looking terrified, Cameron bolted for the safety of the seats.

Someday maybe she'd tell him about Thule.

Maybe.

She waved to Simon and Isabelle as they came in, holding hands. Isabelle made an immediate beeline for her mother and Max.

Simon regarded Kieran with a look of surprised recognition before crossing the room to talk to Vivianne Penhallow, the dean of Shadowhunter Academy. Sometimes Emma wondered if Simon had enjoyed his time at the Academy. She wondered if *she* would like it there. But there was no point thinking about the future now.

She glanced over at Julian. The wide doors were still open and a breeze was passing through, and for a moment Emma saw Livvy—

not as she had been in Thule, but the Livvy of this world—like a vision or a hallucination, standing behind Julian, her hand on his shoulder, her ethereal hair rising in the wind.

Emma closed her eyes, and when she opened them again, Julian was alone. As if he could feel her gaze, Julian glanced at Emma. He looked incredibly young to her for a moment, as if he were still the twelve-year-old boy who had hiked a mile back and forth every week from the highway, dragging heavy bags, to make sure his brothers and sisters had groceries.

If only you had told me, she thought. *If only I had known when you needed help.*

She couldn't be Julian's *parabatai*, or his partner, now. She couldn't smile at him as Clary smiled at Jace, or put a reassuring hand against his back the way Alec did to Magnus, or take his hand as Aline had taken Helen's.

But she could be his ally. She could stand with the others at the front of the room and face the crowd, at least. She began to cross the room toward the table.

Mark reached Nene at the same time that Helen did. Their aunt seemed agitated, her long pale fingers working at the emerald material of her cloak. Her eyes darted between them as they approached, and she gave a small, stiff nod. "Miach," she said. "Alessa. It is good to see you well."

"Aunt Nene," Helen said. "It is good of you to come, and—is everything all right?"

"I was ordered to remain at Court after the Queen returned from Unseelie," said Nene. "She has been furious and untrusting since that time. For me to be here, I disobeyed a direct order of my monarch's." She sighed. "It is possible I can never return to the Court."

"Nene." Helen looked horrified. "You didn't have to come."

"I wished to," Nene said. "I have lived in fear of the Queen all my life. I lived in fear of what I wished for—to depart the Court and live as one of the wild fey. But you, my niece and nephew—you live between worlds, and you are not afraid."

She smiled at them, and Mark wanted to point out that he was afraid half the time. He didn't.

"I will do what I can to help you here," she said. "Your cause is righteous. It is time for the Cold Peace to come to an end."

Mark, who hadn't realized Julian had been promising an end to the Cold Peace, made a slight choking noise.

"Adaon," he said. "I know Helen wrote to you of him. He saved our lives—"

"I wished to bring you the news myself. Adaon is well," said Nene. "He has become something of a favorite of the Seelie Queen and has risen quickly in the Court."

Mark blinked. He hadn't been expecting this. "A *favorite* of the Seelie Queen?"

"I think Mark wants to know if he's the Seelie Queen's lover," said Helen, with her usual bluntness.

"Oh, most likely. It's quite surprising," said Nene. "Fergus is much put out, as he was the favorite once."

"Greetings, Nene," said Kieran, striding up to them. He had changed out of his jeans and looked every bit the faerie prince, as Mark had first seen him, in creamy linen and fawn breeches. His hair was a dark, night-ocean blue. "It is good to see you well. How is Adaon my brother? Not too much under the thumb of the Queen?"

"Only if he wants to be," said Nene cheerfully.

Kieran looked puzzled. Mark put his face in his hands.

"Emma!"

Halfway to the table, Emma turned and found Jem approaching her, a shy smile on his face. She had seen him come in earlier, with Tessa, who was now seated beside Catarina Loss. She blinked at him as he reached her; it felt like centuries since she'd seen him, the awful day of Livvy's funeral.

"Emma." Jem took her hands in his. "Are you all right?"

He sees how tired I look, she thought. *My puffy eyes, rumpled clothes, who knows what else.* She tried to smile. "I'm really glad to see you, Jem."

The light from the chandelier illuminated the scars on his cheekbones. "That's not really an answer to my question," he said. "Tessa told me about Thule. You have been on quite a journey."

"I guess we all have," she said in a low voice. "It was awful—but we're back now."

He squeezed her hands and released them. "I wanted to thank you," he said. "For all the help you and your friends have rendered us in curing the warlock illness. You have been a better friend to me than I have been to you, *mèi mei.*"

"No—you've helped me so many times," Emma protested. She hesitated. "Actually, there is a question I want to ask you."

Jem put his hands in his pockets. "Of course, what is it?"

"Do you know how to strip a Shadowhunter's Marks?" Emma said.

Jem looked stunned. "What?" He glanced around the room as if to make sure no one was looking at them; most people had taken their seats and were thankfully looking toward the front of the room expectantly. "Emma, why would you ask me about something so awful?"

She thought quickly. "Well—the Cohort. Maybe the way to remove them from power is not—not to hurt them, but to make them not Shadowhunters anymore. And you were a Silent Brother, so you could do it, or . . ."

Her voice trailed off at the horrified look on his face.

"Emma, not every decision rests on your shoulders. The Clave will be restored, and *they* will deal with the Cohort." Jem's voice gentled. "I know you are worried. But as a Silent Brother, I have been part of the ceremony of stripping the Marks from a Shadowhunter before. It is something so horrible that I would never repeat it. I would *never* do it. Not under any circumstances."

Emma felt as if she were choking. "Of course. I'm sorry I brought it up."

"It's all right." There was so much understanding in his voice, it broke her heart. "I know you are afraid, Emma. We all are."

She looked after him as he walked away. Despair was making it hard for her to breathe. *I am afraid,* she thought. *But not of the Cohort.*

Of myself.

Emma took her place behind the table at the front of the room; Mark had also joined the small group, and she stood beside him, some distance from Julian. The doors had been closed and the torches lit, and row after row of faces stared back at them from the lines of chairs set up in the middle of the room. They had run out of chairs, in fact, and quite a few Downworlders and Shadowhunters were leaning against the walls, watching.

"Thank you all for responding to my summons," Julian said. Emma could feel his nerves, his tension, speeding the pace of her own blood through her veins. But he showed none of it. There was an easy command in his voice, the room falling silent as he spoke without him needing to shout. "I won't drag out any explanations or introductions. You know who I am. You know my sister and brother; you know Aline Penhallow and Emma Carstairs. You know that Aline's mother, our Consul, has been illegally taken into custody. You know that Horace Dearborn has seized power in Idris—"

"He was voted in," said Kwasi Bediako, the warlock Emma had noticed before with the white spider mark on his face; Cristina had whispered to her that Bediako was the High Warlock of Accra. "We cannot pretend otherwise."

"No one *voted* for him to throw my mother in jail," said Aline. "No one *voted* for him to remove the Consul from power so he could be in charge."

"There are others in jail, as well," said Cristina's mother. Cristina, sitting beside her, turned bright red. "Diego Rocio Rosales has been jailed! For nothing!"

Kieran glanced at her, a small smile at the corner of his mouth.

"As has my cousin Divya," said Anush Joshi, a young man with a jagged black haircut and an anxious face. "What do you plan to do about it? Intercede with the Council?"

Julian glanced briefly down at his hands, as if gathering himself. "Everyone—all of us here—have always accepted a certain amount of prejudice from the Clave as normal, through choice or necessity."

The room was quiet. No one disagreed, but there were many eyes cast down, as if in shame.

"Now the Cohort has changed what we thought of as normal," Julian said. "Never before have Downworlders been driven from Idris. Never before have Shadowhunters jailed other Shadowhunters without even the pretense of a trial."

"Why do we care what Shadowhunters do to each other?" demanded the phouka in the Kaelie T-shirt.

"Because that's step one, and what they do to Downworlders will be worse," Emma said, surprising herself; she hadn't meant to speak, only to stand by Julian. "They've already registered many of you."

"So you're saying we need to fight them?" said Gwyn in his rumbling voice. "This is a call to arms?"

Julie Beauvale rose to her feet. "They may not be a good Clave, but they are still Shadowhunters. There are a lot of people who follow the Cohort who are scared. I don't want to hurt those people, and their fear is real, especially now that Jace and Clary are dead. They were our heroes, and I knew them—"

"Julie," Beatriz hissed. "Sit down."

"Jace and I were personally very close," Julie went on. "I wouldn't hesitate to call him my best friend, and I—"

"Julie." Beatriz took Julie by the tail of her shirt and hauled her back into her seat. She cleared her throat. "I think that what Julie *meant* is that you're saying the Cohort wants to destroy the government, but I'm guessing, given all the secrecy, that you *also* want to destroy the government, and I . . . don't know how we do that without hurting innocent people."

There was a hum of conversation. In the shadows, Emma saw them—she didn't know when they'd come in, but a single Iron Sister and a single Silent Brother stood motionless against the far wall, their faces in shadow.

A slight chill went through her. She knew the Iron Sisters were against the Cohort. She didn't know about the Silent Brothers. They both seemed like emissaries of the Law, standing there in their silence.

"We're not suggesting destroying the government," Julian said. "We're saying it's being destroyed right now, already, from within. The Clave was built to give all Shadowhunters a voice. If we are all voiceless, then it is not our government. The Law was enacted to protect us and to allow us to protect others. When Laws are bent and broken to put the innocent in danger, then it is not our Law. Valentine wanted to rule the Clave. Sebastian wanted to burn it down. We only want to return our rightful Consul to power, and to allow the government of Shadowhunters to be what it should be—not a tyranny, but a representation of who we are and what we want."

"Those are some pretty words," said the French werewolf

who'd been talking to Alec earlier. "But Jace and Clary were beloved of your people. They will want a war against those who harmed them."

"Yes," said Julian. "I'm counting on that."

There was no gesture, no signal that Emma could see, but the doors of the Sanctuary opened and Jace and Clary walked in, as if on cue.

At first there was no reaction from the crowd. The light from the torches was bright, and neither of the two were in gear: Jace wore jeans and Clary a plain blue dress. As they passed through the crowd, people blinked at them until finally Lily Chen, looking annoyed, stood up and said, in a loud, bored voice, "I cannot believe my own eyes. Isn't that Jace Herondale and Clary Fairchild, back from THE DEAD?"

The reaction that ripped through the crowd was electric. Clary looked over with some alarm as the roar grew; Jace just smirked as the two of them joined Emma and the others behind the long table. Lily had resumed her seat and was examining her nails.

Julian was calling for people to be quiet, but his voice was drowned out by the noise. Feeling that this was an area in which she could excel, Emma jumped up onto the table and shouted. "EVERY-ONE," she yelled. "EVERYONE SHUT UP."

The decibel level fell immediately. Emma could see Cristina giggling, her hand over her mouth. Beside her, Jace shot finger guns at Julie Beauvale, who had turned bright pink.

"Good to see you, bestie," he said.

Simon's shoulders were shaking. Isabelle, who had been watching with a half smile, patted his back.

Clary scrunched her nose at Jace and then turned to the crowd. "Thank you," she said, her voice low but carrying. "We're glad to be here."

The room fell pin-drop silent.

Emma jumped down from the table. Julian was surveying the assembly, hands looped behind his back, as if wondering what he thought of the situation he'd architected. People were staring, rapt and silent, at Clary and Jace. *So this is what it's like to be heroes,* Emma thought, looking at the expressions on the faces of the crowd. *To be the ones with angel blood, the ones who've literally saved the world. People look at you as if . . . almost as if you're not real.*

"Inquisitor Lightwood sent us to Faerie," Clary said. "To seek a weapon in the possession of the Unseelie King, one that would be deadly to Shadowhunters. We discovered that the Unseelie King had opened a Portal to another world, one without angelic magic. He was using the earth from that other world to create the blight you have heard of—the one eating through Brocelind Forest."

"That blight was eradicated the night before last," said Jace. "By a team of Nephilim and Fair Folk, working together."

Now the silence broke: There was a buzz of confused voices.

"But we are not the only Nephilim working with faeries," said Clary. "The current King of Unseelie, Oban, and the Cohort have been working together. It was the Cohort who arranged for him to be put on the throne."

"How do we know that's true?" shouted Joaquín Acosta Romero, of the Buenos Aires Institute. He was sitting beside the French werewolf girl, his arm around her shoulders.

"Because they have done nothing but lie to you," said Mark. "They told you Jace and Clary were dead. They told you faeries slaughtered them. Here they stand, alive."

"Why would the Unseelie Court agree to be part of a scheme in which they were blamed for murder?" said Vivianne Penhallow.

Everyone looked expectantly at Julian.

"Because the Cohort and the Unseelie King have already agreed on exactly what both of them will get from this parley," he said.

"The parley is a performance. That is why Horace is Projecting it so every Shadowhunter can see it. Because the performance is more important than the outcome. If he is seen to get what he wants from the Fair Folk, then confidence in the Cohort will grow so strong that we will never have a chance to unseat them."

Emma tried to hide a smile. *You're really back, Julian,* she thought.

"This is a government that will murder its own to control its own," said Jace. The smirk was gone from his face, and any pretense at amusement: His expression was stony and cold. "This time, it was us. By luck, we survived and are standing here to tell you our story. The Inquisitor is meant to uphold the Law. Not to hide behind it as an alibi for murdering their own."

"What about murdering those who aren't Shadowhunters?" called a naga sitting near some of the Keo family.

"We're against that, too," said Jace.

"We've had bad members of our government before," said Julian. "But this is different. They've broken the system that might fix the situation. They're manipulating the Clave, manipulating us all. They are creating the illusion of threats to control us all through fear. They claim that faeries murdered Jace and Clary so they can declare an unjustified war—and under the cloak of that chaos, they put our Consul in prison. Who can speak against the war now?"

A blond Nephilim raised a hand. "Oskar Lindquist here," he said. "Stockholm Institute. Are you saying we shouldn't go to Alicante? The parley is scheduled for tomorrow. If we do not arrive there tonight, we will be considered deserters. Traitors."

"No," Julian said. "In fact, we need you to join the other Shadowhunters in Alicante as if everything is normal. Do nothing to alarm the Cohort. The parley is going to take place on the Imperishable Fields. We—the resistance—are going to interrupt it, with everyone watching. We will present our proof, and when that is done, we need you there to stand up for us and hold the Clave accountable for what they've done."

"We're the proof," Jace added, indicating himself and Clary.

"I think they knew that," Emma muttered. She saw Jem, in the audience, give her an amused look, and tensed. *It is something so horrible that I would never repeat it. I would* never *do it. Not under any circumstances.*

She determinedly put his words out of her mind. She couldn't think about that right now.

"Why do this during the parley?" called Morena Pedroso, the head of the Rio Institute. A bored-looking girl about Dru's age, with long brown hair, sat beside her. "Why not confront them sooner?"

"Horace wants—no, he *needs*—everyone to see him triumph over the Unseelie forces," said Julian. "Every Shadowhunter in Idris is going to be watching him via a massive Projection." There was a murmur of surprise among the Downworlders. "That means they'll be able to see and hear not just him but, if we join him—us. This is our chance. The Cohort is bringing everyone together in a way we don't have the power to do. This is our opportunity to show all Shadowhunters what the Cohort truly is."

"And what if it comes to a battle? We'll be fighting other Shadowhunters," said Oskar Lindquist. "I'm sure I'm not the only one who doesn't want that."

"Hopefully we can do this without a fight," said Julian. "But if it comes to one, we must be ready."

"So you have a plan for Shadowhunters," called Hypatia Vex. She looked over at Kit and Ty and winked; Emma wondered what that was about but didn't have time to dwell on it. "What about us? Why did you bring Downworlders here?"

"To witness," said Julian. "We're aligned here. We're on the same side against the Cohort. We know we're better, stronger, when Downworlders and Shadowhunters work together. And we wanted you to know that even if the Cohort are loud and hateful, they're a minority. You have allies." He glanced around the room. "A few of you will be with us. Kieran Kingson. Magnus Bane. But as for the rest of you—after the Shadowhunters pass through the Portals to Idris, you will need to return home to your people. Because if you don't hear from us after the parley, you can assume we were defeated. And if we are defeated, you're in danger."

"We can withstand the Cohort," said Nene, and Mark looked at her in surprise. "There are many fewer of them than there are Downworlders."

"If we lose, it won't be only the Cohort you need to fear," said Julian. "Once good Shadowhunters can no longer stand up to them, they will begin to destroy and control Downworlders. And while they do that, there will be nobody left to stand against the tide of evil from other worlds. They care so much about their prejudice, their imagined purity, and their Laws, that they have forgotten our mandate: *Protect this world from demons.*"

A whisper went around the room; a sound of horror. *I have seen the world overrun by demons,* Emma wanted to say. *There is no place there for Downworlders.*

"We're an army. A resistance," Emma said. "We are seeking justice. It won't be pretty, but it'll only get worse. The longer we wait, the more damage they'll do and the more blood will be spilled stopping them."

"Horace doesn't want a war," said Diana. "He wants glory. If it looks like he's facing danger, I believe he'll back off."

"If we're an army, what are we called?" said Simon.

Julian turned and unpinned the rolled-up canvas hanging on the wall behind him, which had been held in place with tacks. A gasp went up as it unfurled.

Julian had painted a banner, the kind an army would carry before it in wartime. The central item was a saber, point down, painted a shimmering pale gold. Behind the saber spread a pair of angel's wings, while all around it clustered symbols of Downworld—a star for vampires, a spell book for warlocks, a moon for werewolves, and a four-leaf clover for faeries.

Dangling from the hilt of the saber was a locket with a circle of thorns on the front.

"We are called Livia's Watch," Julian said, and Emma saw Ty sit up straighter in his chair. "We carry this banner in honor of my sister, so that all who have been hurt by the Cohort will not be forgotten."

Jace swept his gaze around the room. "If there is anyone who doesn't want to fight alongside us, they can depart now. No hard feelings."

The room was silent. Not a chair moved. Not a single person rose. Still leaning against the wall near the doors, the Iron Sister and Silent Brother who had come to observe the proceedings were motionless.

Only Emma heard Julian's low exhale of relief. "Now," he said. "Let's finalize the plan."

Dru, sitting on a hillock of grass, watched as a dozen warlocks created Portals on the Institute's front lawn.

It certainly wasn't something she'd ever thought she was going to see. The occasional warlock or Portal, sure, but not this many of them at one time.

Through the Portals, she could see the fields in front of the walls of Alicante: It was impossible to Portal directly into the Shadowhunter city without advance permission; the closest you could get was the front gates. Which was fine anyway, because the Shadowhunters needed to check in with the Cohort and make sure Dearborn knew they were there. Dru was a little disappointed—she'd been hoping they'd be rushing into the city, swords flashing, but that wasn't Julian's style. If he could get what he wanted without a fight, he would.

A few feet away, Tavvy was humming, running an old toy car up and down a smooth-sided rock.

She'd sat by herself during the meeting, though Kit had given her an encouraging smile at one point. And she had seen Julian look at her when he'd said "Livia's Watch." He'd looked at them all, scattered through the room: Mark and Helen, Dru and Tavvy, and last of all, Ty.

Dru had been worried since the night before, when Ty had come out of that weird cave by the beach. Kit had followed him and hadn't been there, as she had, to see the look on Ty's face when he'd first stepped outside. It was a hard look to explain. Half as if he might cry and half as if he might break down the way he sometimes did when things overwhelmed him. Livvy had always been able to calm him down, but Dru didn't know if she could do the same. She was no replacement for Livvy.

Then Kit had come outside, and Ty's expression had changed, as if he'd realized something. And Kit seemed relieved, and Dru wanted to be relieved too.

She'd worried about Ty when Julian had revealed the banner, and there had been Livvy's locket, the one Ty wore now, curled around a saber. And when Julian had said the words "Livia's Watch," hot tears had burned the back of Dru's eyes. She'd felt proud but also hollow where the piece inside her that had been Livvy had been lost to the darkness.

Julian stood by the Sanctuary doors, speaking to the dark-haired Iron Sister who had come to the meeting. The last of the Shadowhunters were passing through the Portals. Some of the Downworlders remained inside the Sanctuary, avoiding the sun; others stood and looked at the ocean and chatted among themselves. Maryse Lightwood stood by the Portal Magnus had created, smiling as she watched Max and Rafe run in circles around Alec.

Rocks and sand crunched: Dru looked up and saw Julian standing over her, silhouetted by the sun. "Hey, kiddo," he said.

"What's going on with the Iron Sisters and Silent Brothers?" said Dru. "Are they on our side?"

"The Iron Sisters have already rejected the Cohort," said Julian. "They're backing us up. Sister Emilia even had a good idea about the Mortal Sword. The Silent Brothers are—well, not neutral. They don't like the Cohort either. But any defection on their part will be more obvious and might tip our hand. They're going to station themselves in Alicante to keep an eye on things and prevent the Cohort from getting suspicious."

This was one of the things Dru loved about Julian. He didn't talk down to her, not even about strategy.

"Speaking of Alicante," she said. "It's time for us to go, huh?"

She'd known this was coming. Julian had told her about it before the meeting. She'd thought she'd be all right with it, considering that she *wanted* to get into Alicante, and this was pretty much the only way it was going to happen.

Not that Julian knew that. She screwed her face into a woeful expression. "I don't see why you have to leave us behind."

"I'm not leaving you behind," Julian said. "I'm sending you ahead. You are part of Livia's Watch. Don't forget it."

Dru continued to scowl. Tavvy was still playing with his car, but he was also watching them out of the corner of his eye. "Semantics are nobody's friend."

Julian knelt down in front of her. Dru was surprised; she wouldn't have thought he'd want to get his knees dirty when he was wearing nice clothes, but apparently he didn't care.

"Dru," he said. "I can't leave you here. It isn't safe. And I can't take you where we're going. There could be a battle. A big one."

"I can fight," Dru said.

Julian put his fingers under her chin and lifted her face so that she was looking directly at him. She wondered if this was what it was like for most kids to look at their parents. This was the face she associated with praise and scoldings, with late-night nightmare assistance and hot chocolate when it was needed and Band-Aids when those were called for. Julian had held her hand through the application of her first Marks. He was the one who stuck her terrible drawings to the fridge with magnets. He never forgot a birthday.

And he was still a kid himself. It was the first time she'd been able to look at him and see it. He was young, younger than Jace and Clary or Alec and Magnus. And yet he'd stood up in front of that Sanctuary full of people and told them what they were going to do, and they'd listened.

"I know you can fight," he said. "But if I think you're in danger, I don't know if *I* can."

"What about Kit and Ty?"

He grinned at her. "Don't tell them, but Magnus promised to make sure they don't get near the actual battle."

Dru gave a reluctant smile. "It's going to suck not knowing if you guys are okay."

"We'll all be wearing Familias runes," said Julian. "So that's something. If you need to know how one of us is, activate yours." His eyes darkened. "Dru, you know I'd protect you to my last breath, right? I'd give my last drop of blood for you. So would Emma."

"I know," Dru said. "I love you, too."

He pulled her into a quick hug, then stood up and offered his hand. She let him pull her to her feet and dusted herself off as he picked up Tavvy. She trailed along behind the two of them as they headed toward Maryse, Max, and Rafe. She didn't want to look as if she were in any way eager to go to Alicante. She felt a little bad about deceiving Julian, but if there was anything she'd learned from Kit and Ty in the past weeks, it was that sometimes you had to trick a trickster at his own game.

"But why are the small ones going?" said Gwyn as Diana stood watching Max, then Rafe, then Tavvy pass through the Portal to Alicante. "It was my understanding that Julian wished to keep them all together."

Diana sighed and slipped her hand into Gwyn's. "It's because he loves them that he's sending them away. Battle is no place for a child."

"We have children in the Wild Hunt. As young as eight years, sometimes," said Gwyn.

"Yes, but we've also covered how that's a bad thing, Gwyn."

"Sometimes I forget all the lessons you teach me," said Gwyn, but he sounded amused. Dru was just stepping through the Portal to Alicante: She turned at the last moment and looked back at Julian. Diana saw him nod encouragingly as Dru stepped into the whirlwind and was gone. "It is not certain there will be a battle, either."

"It is not certain there won't be," Diana said. Julian had turned away from the Portal; the encouraging look he'd worn for Dru and Tavvy was gone, and he looked hollow and sad. He headed toward the Institute doors.

The false faces we wear for the ones we love, Diana thought. *Julian would bleed out for these children and never ask for a bandage in fear that the question would upset them.* "The children will be safe with Maryse. And not being frightened for them will free up Julian and the rest of us to do what we need to do."

"And what is it you need to do?"

Diana tipped her head back to look up at Gwyn. "Be warriors."

Gwyn touched a curl of her hair. "You are a warrior every day."

Diana smiled. Julian had reached the Sanctuary doors and had turned there, looking out on the group in front of the Institute: a motley collection of warlocks, Shadowhunters, and a group of werewolves playing hacky sack. "Time to come in," he said, his voice carrying over the sound of the sea. "The real meeting's about to start."

From the window of the Gard, Manuel could see Shadowhunters streaming in through the Great Gate, the main entrance to the city of Alicante. All the exits were guarded now and warded against the imaginary threat of encroaching Unseelie faeries.

"It does not seem the Blackthorns' meeting was a success," said Horace. He could see out the window from the Inquisitor's big desk. It was odd, Manuel thought; he still didn't think of Horace as the Inquisitor. Perhaps because he had never really cared who the Inquisitor or the Consul was. They were positions of power and therefore desirable, but they held no inherent meaning. "The families he invited to his little insurrection are still arriving."

Zara entered without knocking, as was her usual style. She wore her Centurion gear, as she always did. Manuel found it pretentious. "The Rosewains are here, and the Keos, and the Rosaleses." She was fuming. "They all arrived at once, through Portals. It's like they're not even *trying* to hide it."

"Oh, I don't know," said Manuel. "If we hadn't been tipped off about the meeting, I don't think we'd have noticed. Too many people coming and going."

"Don't *compliment* Julian Blackthorn," said Zara, scowling. "He's a traitor."

"Oh, clearly," said Manuel. "But now we get to punish them, which I'm going to enjoy."

"I'm sure you are." Zara gave him a superior look, but Manuel knew she was going to enjoy the punishment of the Blackthorns just as much as he was. They both hated Emma. Of course, Manuel had good reason—she'd shown him disrespect at the last Council Hall meeting—while Zara was merely jealous.

"We will make an example of them," said Horace. "After the parley. Not the younger Blackthorns—no one likes to see a child die, even if the seeds of evil are in them. But Julian certainly, and that half-breed brother and sister of his. The Carstairs girl, of course. Aline Penhallow is a tricky question—"

The door opened. Manuel looked around curiously; there was only one other visitor to Horace's office who, like Zara, never bothered knocking.

A tall, blond Shadowhunter stepped into the room. Manuel had seen him earlier, coming through the Great Gates. Oskar Lindquist, having separated himself from the rest of his equally blond family.

Horace glanced up. His eyes glittered. "Shut the door behind you."

Oskar made a sound between a growl and a laugh, closing and locking the office door. There was a slight shimmer in the air as he turned and began to change. It was like watching water spill over a painting, distorting and altering the lines of it.

Zara made a low noise of disgust as Oskar's head fell back and his body spasmed, his hair turning a dark brownish-black and falling to spill over his shoulders, his spine compacting as he shrank down into a smaller frame, the lines of his jaw softening into a new, familiar outline.

Annabel Blackthorn looked at them out of steady blue-green eyes.

"So, how was the meeting?" Horace said. "We surmised it hadn't gone well, considering the number of Shadowhunters returning to Idris."

"I believe it went as intended." Horace wrinkled his brow as Annabel sat stiffly in a chair opposite his desk. Zara watched her warily; Horace kept referring to Annabel as the Unseelie King's gift to him, but perhaps Zara didn't consider it a gift. "Except for the fact that I was there."

"No one guessed you weren't Oskar?" said Zara.

"Obviously not." Annabel was studying her hands as if they were unfamiliar to her. "Their plan is simple to the point of rudimentary. Which could be seen as an advantage—less to go wrong."

Horace leaned forward, arms resting on his desk. "Are you saying we should be worried?"

"No," Annabel said, touching the etched glass vial at her throat thoughtfully. Red liquid swirled within it. "The element of surprise was their only advantage. Foolish of them to assume they would not be betrayed." She sat back in her chair. "Let us begin with the basics. Jace Herondale and Clary Fairchild are still alive. . . ."

* * *

Emma stood at the doorway of the Institute. The last of the Downworlders had gone, and they would all be leaving for Brocelind soon. Brother Shadrach had assured Julian and the others that all the guards in Idris had been recalled to the city for the parley. The forest would be deserted.

The afternoon sun glimmered on the sea, and distantly she wondered if, after today, she would ever see the Pacific Ocean again. Long ago her father had told her that the lights that danced on the surface of seawater came from glowing jewels beneath, and that if you reached under the surface, you could catch a jewel in your hand.

She held her hand out in front of her now, palm up, and thought of Jem's words, and then of Diana's.

Their runes began to burn like fire, as if they had fire in their veins instead of blood. Black lines spread over their bodies and they became monstrous—physically monstrous.

Across the inside of her forearm, where the skin had been pale and smooth, was a dark webbing of black lines, like cracks in marble, nearly the size of the palm of her hand.

PART THREE

Lady Vengeance

Her strong enchantments failing,
Her towers of fear in wreck,
Her limbecks dried of poisons
And the knife at her neck,

The Queen of air and darkness
Begins to shrill and cry,
"O young man, O my slayer,
Tomorrow you shall die."

O Queen of air and darkness,
I think 'tis truth you say,
And I shall die tomorrow;
But you will die today.

—A. E. Housman, "Her Strong Enchantments Failing"

28

And Shadows There

It was cool in Brocelind Forest; encroaching autumn added a cold metal bite to the air that Emma could taste on her tongue.

Quiet had come suddenly after the rush of Portal travel, the setting up of tents in a cleared space among the ancient trees and green earth. They were far from the blighted areas, Diana promised them—in the distance, over the tops of the trees, Emma could see the glimmer of the demon towers of Alicante.

She stood on a rise overlooking where they'd made camp. There were about a dozen tents, set up in rows, each with two torches burning in front of its flap door. They were cozy inside, with thick rugs on the floor and even blankets. Alec had given Magnus a sharp sideways look when they'd appeared out of nowhere.

"I did *not* steal them," Magnus had said, looking studiously at his fingernails. "I borrowed them."

"So you'll be returning them to the camping store?" said Alec, hands on his hips.

"I actually got them from a warehouse that provides props for movies," said Magnus. "It'll be ages before anyone notices they're gone. Not," he added hastily, "that I won't be returning them, of course. Everyone, try not to set your tents on fire! They're not our property!"

"Does one normally set them on fire?" said Kieran, who had his own tent—Mark and Julian were sharing one, and Emma was sharing another with Cristina. "Is that a tradition?"

Mark and Cristina both smiled at him. The oddness going on with the three of them was growing more intense, Emma thought, and resolved to ask Cristina about it.

The opportunity came sooner than she'd thought it would. She'd been restless inside the tent alone—Cristina was helping Aline and Julian, who'd put themselves in charge of cooking dinner. Everyone was muttering around maps and plans, except Jace, who'd fallen conspicuously asleep with his head in Clary's lap.

Emma couldn't concentrate. Her body and mind hummed with energy. All she wanted was to talk to Julian. She knew she couldn't, but the need to tell him everything was painful. She'd never made such a life-altering decision without telling him before.

She'd ended up throwing on a sweater and taking a walk around the perimeter of the camp. The air smelled so different here than it did at home—pine, green woods, campfire smoke. Inland, no scent of salt or sea. She climbed the small rocky rise over the camp and gazed down.

Tomorrow they would ride out to challenge Horace Dearborn and his Cohort. Very likely there would be a confrontation. And her *parabatai*, the one who always fought by her side, would be lost to her. One way or another.

The sun was setting, sparking off the distant shimmer of the demon towers. Emma could hear the night birds chirping in the woods nearby and tried not to think about what else was in the forest. She felt herself shivering—no, she was *shaking*. She felt disoriented, almost dizzy, and her cognitive process felt strangely diffuse, as if her mind were racing too fast for her to concentrate.

"Emma!" Cristina was walking up the rise toward her, her dark eyes full of concern. "I looked for you in the tent but you weren't there. Are you all right? Or are you on watch?"

Pull yourself together, Emma. "I just thought someone should try to keep an eye on things, you know, in case a party of Cohort members decides to take a closer look at Brocelind."

"So you're on watch," said Cristina.

"Maybe," Emma said. "What's going on with you and Kieran and Mark?"

"*Ay ay!*" Cristina sat down on a rock, knocking her forehead gently against her hand. "Really? Now?"

Emma sat down next to her friend. "We don't have to talk about it if you don't want to." She pointed her index finger at Cristina. "If we both die in battle tomorrow, though, we'll never get to talk about it ever, and you'll never get the benefit of my enormous wisdom."

"Look at this crazy girl," Cristina said, gesturing to an invisible audience. "All right, all right. What makes you think anything new is happening, anyway?"

"I see the way you all look at each other. I've never seen anything like it," Emma said.

Cristina sobered immediately, her hand going to the angel medallion at her throat as it often did when she was nervous. "I don't know what to do," she said. "I love both of them. I love Mark and I love Kieran. I love them both in different ways, but with no less intensity."

Emma spoke carefully. "Are they asking you to choose between them?"

Cristina looked off toward the sunset, stripes of gold and red above the trees. "No. No, they're not asking me to choose."

"I see," said Emma, who was not sure she did see. "Then . . ."

"We decided it was impossible," Cristina said. "Kieran, Mark, and I—we are all afraid. If we were together, the way we want to be, we would bring misery on those we love."

"Misery? Why?" Emma's hands were shaking again; she shoved them between her knees so Cristina wouldn't see.

"Kieran fears for Faerie," Cristina said. "After so many terrible Kings, after so much cruelty, he wishes to go back and take up a place in the Court and see to the welfare of his people. He cannot turn away from that, and neither Mark nor I would want him to. But for us—we cannot know the future. Even if the Cohort is gone, it does not mean the end of the Cold Peace. Mark is afraid for Helen, for all the Blackthorns, that if he were involved with a prince of Faerie and everyone knew it, his family would be punished. I fear the same for my family. So it would never work. Do you understand?"

Emma twirled a piece of grass between her fingers. "I would never judge you," she said. "First because it's you, and second because I hardly have the right to judge anyone. But I think you're letting your fear get in the way of what you really want because what you really want is what you're afraid of."

Cristina blinked. "What do you mean?"

"From the outside, here's what I see," said Emma. "When Mark and Kieran are alone together, they get pulled into their difficult past. It consumes them. When Mark and you are together, he worries that he isn't good enough for you, no matter what you say. And when Kieran and you are together, sometimes you can't bridge the gulf between Shadowhunter understanding and faerie understanding. Mark helps you bridge that gulf." The sun was nearly down, the sky a deep blue, Cristina's expression lost in shadow. "Does that seem wrong?"

"No," Cristina said after a long pause. "But it doesn't—"

"You're afraid of what everyone is afraid of," said Emma. "Having your hearts broken, being made miserable by love. But what you're saying, that's what the Cohort wants. They want to make people afraid, to make them stay apart because they have created an environment of fear and suspicion where you could be punished for being with someone you love. If they got their way, they'd punish Alec for being with Magnus, but that doesn't mean Magnus and Alec should split up. Am I making sense?"

"A little too much sense," Cristina said, pulling at a loose thread on her sleeve.

"I know one thing for sure," Emma said. "Cristina, of all the people I know, you're the most generous, and you spend the most time thinking about what makes other people happy. I think you should do whatever makes *you* happy. You deserve it."

"Thanks." Cristina gave her a shaky smile. "What about you and Julian? How are you doing?"

Emma's stomach lurched, surprising her. It was as if hearing the words "you and Julian" had set something off inside her. She pushed down on the feeling, trying to control it. "It's really hard," she whispered. "Julian and I can't even talk to each other. And the best we can hope for after all this is over is some kind of exile."

"I know." Cristina took Emma's hand in hers; Emma tried to still her own shaking. Cristina's reassuring touch helped. For the millionth time, Emma wished she'd met Cristina earlier—that Cristina could have been her *parabatai*. "After the exile, if it happens, come and stay with me, wherever I am. Mexico, anywhere. I'll take care of you."

Emma made a sound halfway between a laugh and a sniffle. "That's what I mean. You're always doing things for other people, Tina."

"Okay, well, then I'm going to ask you to do something for me."

"What? I'll do anything. Unless it makes your mom mad. Your mom scares me."

"You want to kill Zara in the battle, if there's a fight, don't you?" Cristina said.

"The thought had crossed my mind. Okay. Yes. If anyone else takes her out, I'm going to be really angry." Emma mock scowled.

Cristina sighed. "We don't even know if there's going to be a fight, Emma. If Zara is spared or imprisoned or escapes, or if someone else kills her, I don't want you to dwell on it. Focus on what you want your life to be *after* tomorrow."

After tomorrow I'll be exiled, Emma thought. *Will I see you again, Cristina? Will I always miss you?*

Cristina narrowed her eyes in concern. "Emma? Promise me?"

But before Emma could promise, before she could say anything at all, Aline's and Helen's voices cut through the evening air, calling them down to dinner.

"Has anyone ever tried ketchup on a s'more?" Isabelle said.

"*This* is why you're a bad cook," said Alec. Simon, bundled up in a sweater and leaning back against a log, slunk down as if he hoped to become invisible. "You actually like disgusting food. It's not, like, an accident."

"I like ketchup and s'mores," said Simon loyally, and mouthed to Clary, *I don't like them.*

"I know," Clary said. "I can feel through the *parabatai* bond how much you don't like them."

"Julian is an excellent cook," said Emma, spearing a marshmallow. Magnus had produced bags of them along with the requisite chocolate and graham crackers. He gave Emma a dark look that seemed to say, *Stay away from Julian, and also his cooking.*

"I am also an excellent cook," said Mark, putting an acorn onto his s'more. Everyone stared.

"He can't help it," said Cristina loyally. "He has lived with the Wild Hunt for so long."

"I don't do that," said Kieran, eating a s'more in the correct fashion. "Mark has no excuse."

"I never pictured Shadowhunters eating s'mores," said Kit, glancing around the fire. It was like a scene out of dreams of camping he'd had when he was a little kid—the fire, the trees, everyone bundled up in sweaters and sitting around on logs, smoke in their eyes and hair. "On the other hand, this is the first s'more I've ever had that didn't come out of a box."

"That's not a s'more, then," Ty said. "That's a cookie. Or some cereal."

Kit smiled, and Ty smiled back at him. He leaned against Julian, who was sitting beside him; Julian put an absent arm around his younger brother, his hand ruffling Ty's hair.

"Excited for your first battle?" Jace said to Kit. Jace was sitting cross-legged with his arms around Clary, who was creating a massive s'more out of several chocolate bars.

"He's not going!" Clary said. "He's too young, Jace." She looked at Kit. "Don't listen to him."

"He seems old enough," said Jace. "I was fighting battles when I was ten."

"Stay away from my children," said Magnus. "I'm watching you, Herondale."

Kit felt a brief jolt before realizing Magnus wasn't talking to him. Then another when he realized he'd reacted unconsciously to the name Herondale.

"This is great," said Helen, yawning. "I haven't been camping in so long. You can't go camping on Wrangel Island. Your fingers will turn to icicles and snap right off."

Emma frowned. "Where's Cristina?"

Kit glanced around: Emma was right. Cristina had slipped away from the group.

"She shouldn't be walking around the edge of the forest," Magnus said, frowning. "There are booby traps there. Quite well hidden, if I do say so myself." He started to rise. "I'll get her."

Mark and Kieran were already on their feet.

"We will find her," Mark said hastily. "In the Hunt, we learned much about traps."

"And few know more about the ways of the forest than the fey," said Kieran.

Magnus shrugged, but there was a knowing spark in his eye that Kit didn't quite understand. "All right. Go ahead."

As they vanished into the shadows, Emma smiled and placed another marshmallow on a stick.

"Let's make a toast." Aline raised a plastic cup of water. "To never being parted from our families again." She gazed at the fire. "Once tomorrow comes, we're never going to let the Clave do that to any of us again."

"Not to be parted from family *or* friends," said Helen, raising her glass.

"Or *parabatai*," said Simon, winking at Clary.

Alec and Jace cheered, but Julian and Emma were silent. Emma seemed bleakly sad, staring down into her cup of water. She did not seem to see Julian, who looked at her for a single long moment before wrenching his gaze away.

"To never being parted," Kit said, looking across the campfire at Ty.

Ty's thin face was limned in light from the red-gold flames. "To never being parted," he said, with a grave emphasis that made Kit shiver for reasons he did not understand.

Maryse could no longer return to the Inquisitor's house, as Horace and Zara had moved into it. Instead she took Dru and the others to the Graymark house, the one Clary said she had stayed in when she'd first come to Idris.

Dru had gone to bed as soon as she politely could. She lay with the covers tucked up to her chin, looking at the last bits of sunlight fading from the circular windows. This side of the house faced onto a garden full of roses the color of old lace. A trellis climbed to the windows and circled them: At the height of summer they probably looked like necklaces of roses. Houses of old stone fell away down the hill toward the walls of Alicante—walls that tomorrow would be lined with Shadowhunters facing the Imperishable Fields.

Dru burrowed farther under the covers. She could hear Maryse in the room next door, singing to Max and Rafe and Tavvy, a lilting song in French. It was strange to be too old for singing to comfort you but too young to take part in battle preparations. She started to say their names to herself, as a sort of good luck charm: *Jules and Emma. Mark and Helen. Ty and Li—*

No. Not Livvy.

The singing had stopped. Dru heard footsteps in the hall and her door open; Maryse stuck her head in. "Is everything all right, Drusilla? Do you need anything?"

Dru would have liked a glass of water, but she didn't know exactly how to talk to Max and Rafe's imposing, dark-haired grandmother. She'd heard Maryse playing with Tavvy earlier, and she appreciated how kind this woman who was basically a stranger was being to them. She just wished she knew how to say it.

"No, that's okay," Dru said. "I don't need anything."

Maryse leaned against the doorjamb. "I know it's hard," she said. "When I was young, my parents always used to take my brother, Max, with them to hunt demons and leave me alone at home. They said I'd be frightened if I went with them. I always tried to tell them I was more frightened worrying they'd never come back."

Dru tried to picture Maryse young, and couldn't quite. She seemed old to Dru to even be a mom, though she knew she wasn't. She was actually quite a young grandmother, but Dru had gotten used to people who looked like Julian and Helen being like mothers and fathers to her.

"They always did come back, though," Maryse said. "And so will your family. I know it feels like what Julian is doing is risky, but he's smart. Horace won't try anything dangerous in front of so many people."

"I should go to sleep," Dru said in a small voice, and Maryse sighed, gave her an understanding nod, and closed the door. If she were home, a small voice said in the back of Dru's mind, she wouldn't have had to ask for anything—Helen, who knew she loved tea but that the caffeine kept her up, would have come in with a mug of the special decaffeinated blend they'd bought in England, with milk and honey in the mug the way Dru liked it.

She missed Helen, Dru realized. It was a weird feeling—somewhere along the way her resentment toward Helen had vanished. Now she just wished she'd said a better good-bye to her older sister before she'd left the Institute.

Maybe it was better that she hadn't said the right kind of good-byes to her family. Maybe it meant she was definitely going to see them again.

Maybe it meant they'd be more forgiving when they found out what she was planning to do.

The light blinked out in the hall; Maryse must be going to sleep. Dru threw off her blanket; she was fully dressed underneath, down to her boots and gear jacket. She slid out of bed and went over to the circular window; it was stuck shut, but she'd been expecting that. Taking a small dagger with an *adamas* blade out of her pocket, she started to jimmy it open.

Kit lay awake in the darkness, counting the stars he could see through the open flap of the tent.

Emma and Julian had said the stars in Faerie were different, but here in Idris they were the same. The same constellations he had looked at all his life, peeking through the smog above Los Angeles, shone above Brocelind Forest. The air was clear here, clear as cut crystal, and the stars seemed almost alarmingly close, as if he could reach out and catch one in his hand.

Ty hadn't come back with him from the campfire. Kit didn't

know where he was. Had he gone to talk to Jules or Helen? Was he wandering in the forest? No, Simon and Isabelle would have stopped him. But maybe Ty had found an animal he liked in the campsite. Kit's mind started to race. *Where is he? Why didn't he take me with him? What if he can't tame these squirrels the way he can the ones at home? What if he's attacked by squirrels?*

With a groan, Kit kicked off his covers and reached for a jacket.

Ty stuck his head into the tent, momentarily blotting out the stars. "Oh good, you're already getting ready."

Kit lowered his voice. "What do you mean, I'm getting ready? Ready for *what*?"

Ty dropped into a crouch and peered into the tent. "To go to the lake."

"Ty," said Kit. "I need you to explain. Don't assume I know what you're talking about."

Ty exhaled with enough force to make his dark fringe of hair flutter above his forehead. "I brought the spell with me, and all the ingredients," he said. "The best place to raise the dead is by water. I thought we'd do it next to the ocean, but Lake Lyn's even better. It's already a magic place."

Kit blinked dizzily; he felt as if he'd woken up from a nightmare only to discover he was still dreaming. "But we don't have what we need to make the spell work. Shade never gave us the catalyst."

"I thought he might not do it," said Ty. "That's why I picked up an alternate energy source last time we were at the Shadow Market." He reached into his pocket and took out a clear glass ball the size of an apricot. Red-orange flame blazed inside it as if it were a small, fiery planet, though it was clearly cool to the touch.

Kit jerked back. "Where did *that* come from?"

"I told you—the Shadow Market."

Kit felt a wave of panic. "Who sold it to you? How do we even know it'll work?"

"It has to." Ty slipped the crystal back into his pocket. "Kit. This is something I have to do. If there's a battle tomorrow, you know we're not going to be part of it. They think we're too young to fight. This is the way that I can help that isn't fighting. If I bring Livvy back, our family will be whole for the battle. It will mean that everyone will be happy again."

But happiness isn't that simple, Kit wanted to cry; *you can't rip it apart and put it back together again without seeing the seams.*

Kit's voice was ragged. "It's dangerous, Ty. It's too dangerous. I don't think it's a good idea to mess around with this kind of magic, with an unknown power source."

Ty's expression closed down. It was like watching a door shut. "I've already scouted for traps. I know how we can get there. I thought you would come with me, but even if you don't, I'm going to go alone."

Kit's mind raced. *I could wake up the camp and get Ty in trouble,* he thought. *Julian would stop him. I know he would.*

But Kit's whole mind revolted at the idea; if there was one thing his father had brought him up to understand, it was that everybody hated a snitch.

And besides, he couldn't bear the look on Ty's face.

"All right," Kit said, feeling dread settle in his stomach like a rock. "I'll go with you."

Shapes danced in the heart of the fire. Emma sat on a log nearby, her hands thrust into the sleeves of her oversize sweater to keep them warm. The group had drifted away from the fire when the meal was done, retiring to their individual tents to sleep. Emma stayed where she was, watching the fire die down; she supposed she could have gone back to her own tent, but Cristina wasn't there, and Emma didn't feel much like lying alone in the dark.

She glanced up as a shadow approached. It was Julian. She recognized him by the way he walked, even before the firelight illuminated his face—hand in his pocket, his shoulders relaxed and his chin upturned. Deceptively casual. The damp in the cool air had curled his hair against his cheeks and temples.

Julian hid so many things, from so many people. Now for the first time she was hiding something from him. Was this how he had always felt? This weight in his chest, the pinching pain at his heart?

She half-expected him to pass by her without speaking, but he paused, his fingers toying with the sea-glass bracelet on his wrist.

"Are you all right?" he asked, his voice low.

Emma nodded.

Sparks from the fire reflected in Julian's blue eyes. "I know we shouldn't talk to each other," he said. "But we need to discuss something with someone. It's not about you or me."

I can't do it, Emma thought. *You don't understand. You still think we could get my Marks stripped if things went wrong.*

But then again—her rune hadn't burned since they'd left Los Angeles. The black webbing on her forearm hadn't grown. It was as if her misery were holding the curse back. Maybe it was.

"Who's it about?"

"It's about one of the things we learned in Thule," he said. "It's about Diana."

Diana woke from dreams of flying to the sound of scratching at the door of her tent. She rolled out of her blankets and caught up a knife, rising to a crouch.

She heard the sound of two voices, one rising over the other: "Octopus!"

She had a vague memory that this was the code word they had all chosen earlier. She put her knife away and went to unzip the flap of the tent. Emma and Julian stood on the other side, blinking in the dark, pale and wide-eyed like startled meerkats.

Diana raised her eyebrows at them. "Well, if you want to come in, come in. Don't just stand there letting all the cold air in."

The tents were just high enough to stand up in, unfurnished by anything but rugs and bedding. Diana sank back into the nest of her covers, while Julian leaned against her pack and Emma sat cross-legged on the floor.

"Sorry for waking you up," said Julian, ever the diplomat. "We didn't know when else we might get to talk to you."

She couldn't help yawning. Diana always slept surprisingly well the night before a battle. She knew Shadowhunters who couldn't get to sleep, who stayed awake with pounding hearts, but she wasn't one of them. "Talk to me about what?"

"I want to apologize," Julian said, as Emma worried at the frayed knee of her jeans. Emma didn't seem like herself—hadn't for a while now, Diana thought. Not since they'd come back from that other world, though an experience like that would change anyone. "For pushing you to be the head of the Institute."

Diana narrowed her eyes. "What brought this on?"

"The Thule version of you told us about your time in Bangkok," Emma said, biting her lip. "But you don't have to talk about anything to us that you don't want to."

Diana's first reaction was a reflex. *No. I don't want to talk about this. Not now.*

Not on the eve of battle, not with so much on her mind, not while she was worried about Gwyn and trying not to think about where he was or what he might do tomorrow.

And yet. She'd been on her way to tell Emma and Julian precisely what they were asking about now when she'd found out she couldn't reach them. She recalled her disappointment. She'd been determined then.

She didn't owe them the story, but she owed it to herself to tell it.

They both sat quietly, looking at her. The night before a battle and they had come to her for this—not for reassurance, but to let her know it was her choice to engage or not to.

She cleared her throat. "So you know that I'm transgender. Do you know what that means?"

Julian said, "We know that when you were born, you were assigned a gender that does not reflect who you actually are."

Something in Diana loosened; she laughed. "Someone's been on the Internet," she said. "Yeah, that's right, more or less."

"And when you were in Bangkok, you used mundane medicine," said Emma. "To become who you really are."

"Baby girl, I've always been who I really am," said Diana. "In Bangkok, Catarina Loss helped me find doctors who would change my body to represent who I am, and people who were like me, to help me understand I wasn't alone." She settled back against the rolled-up jacket she'd been using as a pillow. "Let me tell you the story."

And in a quiet voice, she did. She didn't vary the telling much from the story she'd told Gwyn, because that story had eased her heart. She watched their expressions as she spoke: Julian calm and silent, Emma reacting to every word with widened eyes or bitten lips. They had always been like this: Emma expressing what Julian couldn't or wouldn't. So alike and so different.

But it was Julian who spoke first when she was finished. "I'm sorry about your sister," he said. "I'm so sorry."

She looked at him in a little surprise, but then of course—that would be what would strike a chord with Jules, wouldn't it?

"In some ways, the hardest part of any of it was not being able to talk about Aria," she said.

"Gwyn knows, right?" Emma said. "And he was good about it? He's kind to you, right?" She sounded as fierce as Diana had ever heard her.

"He is, I promise," Diana said. "For someone who reaps the dead, he's surprisingly empathic."

"We won't tell anyone unless you want us to," Emma said. "It's your business."

"I worried that they'd find out about my medical treatment if I ever tried to become Institute head," said Diana. "That I'd be taken away from you children. Punished with exile." Her hands tightened in her lap. "But the Inquisitor found out anyway."

Emma sat up straight. "He did? When?"

"Before I fled Idris. He threatened to expose me to everyone as a traitor."

"He's such a bastard," Julian said. His face was tight.

"Are you angry with me?" Diana said. "For not telling you before?"

"No," Julian said, his voice quiet and firm. "You had no obligation to do that. Not ever. "

Emma scooted closer to Diana, her hair a pale halo in the moonlight streaming through the tent flap. "Diana, these past five years, you've been the closest thing I've had to an older sister. And since I met you, you've shown me the kind of woman I want to grow up to be." She reached out and took Diana's hand. "I feel so grateful and so privileged that you wanted to tell us your story."

"Agreed," Julian said. He bent his head, like a knight acknowledging a lady in an old painting. "I'm sorry I pushed you. I didn't understand. We—I—thought of you as an adult, someone who couldn't possibly have problems or be in any danger. I was so focused on the kids that I didn't realize you were also vulnerable."

Diana touched his hair lightly, the way she often had when he was younger. "That's growing up, isn't it? Figuring out that adults are people with their own issues and secrets."

She smiled wryly just as Helen stuck her head in through the still-unzipped flap. "Oh good, you're up," she said. "I wanted to go over who's staying behind tomorrow—"

"I've got a list," Julian said, sliding his hand into the pocket of his jacket.

Emma got to her feet, murmuring that she needed to go find Cristina. She slipped out the door of the tent, stopping only to glance back once at Julian as she went, but he was deep in conversation with Helen and didn't seem to notice.

Something was going on with that girl, Diana thought. Once they'd gotten through tomorrow, she'd have to find out what it was.

29
Tempt the Waters

"Cristina! *Cristina!*"

Voices rang through the woods below. Surprised, Cristina stood up, peering down into the darkness.

It had been too painful at the campfire, looking at Mark and at Kieran, knowing she was counting down hours until one or both of them left her life forever. She had slipped away to sit among the trees and grass and shadows of Brocelind. There were white flowers here, among the green, native to Idris. She had seen them before only in pictures, and to touch their petals gave her a feeling of peace, though her sorrow remained beneath it.

Then she had heard the voices. Mark and Kieran, calling for her. She had been sitting at the top of a green rise of grass between the trees; she rose, brushed herself off, and hurried down the hill toward the sound of her name.

"*Estoy aquí!*" she called, nearly tripping as she rushed down the hill. "I'm right here!"

They burst from the shadows, both white-faced. Mark found her first and swung her up off her feet, hugging her tightly. After a moment he released her to Kieran's arms as they tried to explain:

something about Magnus and traps and being afraid she'd fallen into a pit lined with knives.

"I would never do that," she protested as Kieran stroked her hair back from her face. "Mark—Kieran—I think we were wrong."

Kieran let her go immediately. "Wrong about what?"

Mark was standing next to Kieran, their shoulders just brushing. Her boys, Cristina thought. The ones she loved. She could not choose between them any more than she could choose between night and day. Nor did she wish to.

"Wrong that it's impossible," she said. "I should have said it before. I was afraid. I did not want to be hurt. Isn't that what we all fear? That we will be hurt? We keep our hearts in prison, in terror that if we let them go free in the world they would be injured. But I do not want to be in a prison. And I think you feel the same, but if you do not—"

In his soft, husky voice, Mark said, "I love both of you, and I could not say I love one of you the most. But I am afraid. The loss of both of you would kill me, and here it seems I am risking having my heart broken not once but twice."

"Not all love ends in heartbreak," said Cristina.

"You know what I want," Kieran said. "I was the one to say it first. I love and desire you both. Many are happy like this in Faerie. It is common, such marriages—"

"Are you proposing to us?" said Mark with a crooked grin, and Kieran turned bright red.

"There is one thing," he said. "The King of Faerie can have no human consort. You both know that."

"It doesn't matter right now," Cristina said fiercely. "You are not King yet. And if you ever are, we will find a way."

Mark inclined his head, a faerie gesture. "As Cristina says. My heart goes with her words, Kieran."

"I want to be with you both," said Cristina. "I want to be able to kiss you both and hold you both. I want to be able to touch you both, sometimes at the same time, sometimes when we are just two. I want you to be able to kiss and hold each other because it makes you happy and I want you to be happy. I want us to be together, all three."

"I think of each of you all the time. I long for you when you are not there." The words seemed to burst from Kieran like undammed water. He touched Mark's face with his long-boned fingers, light as the brush of wind on grass. He turned to Cristina next and, with his other hand, caressed her cheek. She could feel that he was shaking; she put her hand over his, pressing it to her face. "I have never wanted anything so desperately as this."

Mark placed his own hand over Kieran's. "I too. I believe in this, in us. Love wakens love, faith wakens faith." He smiled at Cristina. "All this time we were waiting for you. We loved each other, and it was a great thing, but with you, it is even greater."

"Kiss me, then," Cristina whispered, and Mark pulled her close and kissed her warmly, then hotly. Kieran's hands were on her back, in her hair; she leaned her head against him as he and Mark kissed over her shoulder, their bodies cradling hers, their hands linked in each other's.

Kieran was smiling like his face would break; they were all kissing each other and laughing with happiness and touching each other's faces with wondering fingers. "I love you," Cristina said to both of them, and they said it back to her at the same time, their voices mingling so she was not sure who spoke first or last:

"I love you."

"I love you."

"I love you."

Kit had seen Lake Lyn before in pictures, the endless images of the Angel rising out of it with the Mortal Instruments that were inside every Shadowhunter building, on every wall and tapestry.

It was a different thing entirely in real life. It moved like an oil slick under the moonlight: The surface was silver-black but shot through with bursts of chromatic splendor, streaks of violet blue and hot red, ice green and bruise violet. For the first time, when Kit imagined the Angel Raziel, massive and blank-faced, rising out of the water, he felt a shiver of awe and fear.

Ty had set up his ceremonial circle by the edge of the lake, where the water lapped at a shallow sandy beach. It was actually two circles, one smaller within another larger, and in the border between the two circles Ty had etched dozens of runes with a pointed stick.

Kit had seen ceremonial circles before, often in his own living room. But how had Ty become an expert at making them? His circles were neater than Johnny's had ever been, his etchings more careful. He wasn't using Shadowhunter runes but a runic language that looked far spikier and more unpleasant. Was this where Ty had been all those times Kit had turned around to find him gone? Learning how to be a dark magician?

Ty had also set up their ingredients in neat rows beside him: the myrrh, the chalk, Livvy's baby tooth, the letter from Thule.

Having placed the velvet bag containing a lock of Livvy's hair carefully among the other objects, Ty looked up at Kit, who was standing close to the water's edge. "Did I do it right?"

A wave of reluctance came over Kit; the last thing he wanted was to get close to the magic circle. "How would I know?"

"Well, your father was a magician; I thought he might have taught you some of this," Ty said.

Kit kicked at the edge of the water; luminous sparks flew up. "Actually, my dad kind of kept me away from learning real spells. But I know a little."

He scuffed across the beach toward Ty, who was sitting with his legs crossed on the sand. Kit had often thought night and darkness seemed like Ty's natural environment. He disliked direct sunlight and his pale skin looked as if it had never been burned. In moonlight, he shone like a star.

With a sigh, Kit pointed at the glowing red ball Ty had gotten from the Shadow Market. "The catalyst goes in the middle of the circle."

Ty was already picking it up. "Come sit next to me," he said. Kit knelt down as Ty started to place the objects into the ceremonial circle, murmuring in a low voice as he did so. He reached up, undid the chain of the locket, handed it to Kit. With a deep sense of dread, Kit placed the locket near the edge of the circle.

Ty began to chant more loudly. "*Abyssus abyssum invocat in voce cataractarum tuarum; omnia excelsa tua et fluctus tui super me transierunt*. Deep calls to deep in the voice of your waterfalls; all your whirlpools and waves have passed over me."

As he chanted, one by one the objects in the circle caught fire, like fireworks going off in a row. They burned with a clean white blaze, without being consumed.

A strong wind started to blow off the lake: It smelled of loam and grave dirt. Kit started to hear a clamor of voices and twisted around, staring—was someone there? Had they been followed? But he saw no one. The beach was deserted.

"Do you hear that?" he whispered.

Ty only shook his head, still chanting. The lake shimmered, the water moving. Pale white figures rose from the dark water. Many were in gear, some in more old-fashioned armor. Their hair flowed down and around them, translucent in the moonlight. They reached their arms out toward him, toward Ty, who could not see them. Their lips moved silently.

This is really happening, Kit thought, chilled to the bone. Whatever tiny hope he'd had that this wouldn't work had vanished. He turned to Ty, who was still chanting, spitting out the memorized words like machine-gun fire. *"Hic mortui vivunt, hic mortui vivunt—"*

"Ty, stop." His hands shot out, grabbed Ty's shoulders. He knew he shouldn't—Ty didn't like to be startled—but terror was fizzing in his blood like poison. "Ty, don't do this."

The Latin choked off midsentence: Ty stared at Kit, confused, his gray eyes darting from Kit's collarbone to his face and back down again. "What do you mean? I don't understand."

"Don't do this. Don't raise her from the dead."

"But I have to," Ty said. His voice sounded stretched, like a wire pulled taut. "I can't live without Livvy."

"Yes, you can," Kit whispered. "You can. You think this will make your family stronger, but it will *destroy* them if you bring her back. You think you can't survive without Livvy, but you can. We will go through it together." Kit's face was cold; he realized he was crying. "I love you, Ty. I love you."

Ty's face went blank with surprise. Kit plowed on, regardless, hardly knowing what he was saying.

"She's gone, Ty. She's gone forever. You have to get through this. Your family will help you. I will help you. But not if you do this. Not if you do this, Ty."

The blankness was gone from Ty's face. His mouth twisted, as if he were trying to hold in tears; Kit knew the feeling. He hated seeing it on Ty's face. He hated everything that was happening.

"I have to get her back, Kit," Ty whispered. "I *have to.*"

He pulled away from Kit's grasp, turning back toward the circle, where the various objects were still burning. The air was full of the scent of char. *"Ty!"* Kit said, but Ty was already chanting Latin again, his hands outstretched to the circle.

"Igni ferroque, ex silentio, ex animo—"

Kit threw himself at Ty, knocking him onto the sand. Ty tumbled backward without a struggle, too surprised to defend himself; they rolled down the slight incline toward the water. They splashed into the shallows and Ty seemed to come back to life; he shoved at Kit, elbowing him hard in the throat. Kit coughed and let go; he grabbed for Ty again and Ty kicked at him. He could see that Ty was crying, but even crying, he was a better fighter than Kit was. Though Ty looked fragile as moonbeams, he was a Shadowhunter born and trained. He struggled free and darted up the sand toward the circle, thrusting his hand out to the fire.

"*Ex silentio, ex animo!*" he shouted, panting. "*Livia Blackthorn! Resurget! Resurget! Resurget!*"

The flame in the center of the circle turned black. Kit sank back on his heels, tasting blood in his mouth.

It was over. The spell was done.

The dark flames rose toward the sky. Ty stepped back, staring, as they roared upward. Kit, who had seen dark magic before, staggered to his feet. Anything could have gone wrong, he thought grimly. If they had to run, he'd knock Ty out with a rock and drag him away.

The water of the lake began to ripple. Both boys turned to look, and Kit realized the shimmering dead were gone. There was only one transparent figure now, rising out of the water, her hair long and streaming silver. The outline of her face, her eyes, came clear: her floating hair, the locket around her throat, the drifting white dress that didn't seem like something Livvy would have chosen.

"Livvy," Kit whispered.

Ty ran to the edge of the lake. He stumbled, fell to his knees at the waterline as Livvy's ghost made its way toward them across the water, scattering luminous sparks.

She reached the banks of the lake. Her bare feet trailed in the glowing water. She looked down at Ty, her body transparent as a cloud, her expression unfathomably sad. "Why have you disquieted me?" she said in a voice as sorrowful as winter wind.

"Livvy," Ty said. He reached a hand out, as if he could touch her. His fingers passed through the skirt of her dress.

"It's not really her." Kit wiped blood from his face. "She's a ghost."

Relief battled with misery in his chest: She wasn't undead, but surely raising a ghost against its will wasn't a good idea either.

"Why aren't you here?" said Ty, his voice rising. "I did everything right. I did *everything* right."

"The catalyst you used was corrupted. It wasn't strong enough to fully bring me back," Livvy said. "It might have other consequences as well. Ty—"

"But you can stay with me, right? You can stay with me like this?" Ty interrupted.

The outlines of Livvy's body blurred as she swayed toward her brother. "Is that what you want?"

"Yes. That's why I did all this," Ty said. "I want you with me in any way you can be. You were there with me before I was born, Livvy. Without you, I just—there's *nothing* if you aren't there."

There's nothing if you aren't there. Pity and despair ripped through Kit. He couldn't hate Ty for this. But he would never mean anything to Ty and never had: That much was clear.

"I loved you, Ty, I loved you even when I was dead," said Livvy's ghost. "But you have upended the universe, and we will all pay for it. You've ripped a hole in the fabric of life and death. You don't know what you've done." Tears ran down Livvy's face and splashed into the water: individual, glowing drops like sparks of fire. "You cannot borrow from death. You can only pay for it."

She vanished.

"Livvy!" Ty didn't scream the word so much as it was ripped from him; he curled up, hugging himself, as if desperate to keep his body from shattering apart.

Kit could hear Ty crying, awful dark sobs that sounded pulled out of him; an hour ago he would have moved Heaven to make it stop. Now he was unable to take a step, his own pain a searing agony that held him frozen in place. He looked up at the ceremonial circle; the flames were burning white again, and the objects inside were beginning to be consumed. The velvet bag turned to ash, the tooth blackened, the chalk and myrrh destroyed. Only the necklace still gleamed whole and unharmed.

As Kit watched, the letter from Thule caught fire and the words on the page flared up to burn a glowing black before vanishing:

I love you. I love you. I love you.

At the door of the Gard prison, Dru paused, picks in hand. She was breathing hard from her climb up the hill. She hadn't taken the normal paths, but crept through the underbrush, staying out of sight. Her wrists and ankles were torn from the whiplash scratches of branches and thorns.

She barely felt the pain. Now was the moment of reckoning. On the other side of this action there was no turning back. No matter how young she was, if Horace and the others prevailed and learned what she'd done, she'd be punished.

Julian's voice echoed in her ears.

You are part of Livia's Watch. Don't forget it.

Livvy wouldn't have hesitated, Dru knew. She would have hurtled forward, desperate to right any injustice she saw. She would never have held back. She would never have hesitated.

Livvy, this is for you, my sister.

I love you. I love you. I love you.

She went to work on the lock.

The entrance to the Silent City was just as Emma remembered it. A barely marked trail cut through a corner of Brocelind Forest, surrounded by thick greenery. It was clear that few passed this way, and rarely—her witchlight revealed a path almost unmarked by footsteps.

She could hear the twitter of night birds and the movement of small animals among the trees. But something was missing from Brocelind. It had always been a place where one might have expected to see the glint of will-o'-the-wisps among the leaves or hear the crackle of a campfire around which werewolves were gathered. There was something very present about its current silence, something that made Emma walk with extra care.

The trees grew together more thickly as she reached the mountainside and found the door in among the rocks. It looked just as it had three years ago: pointed at the top and carved with a bas-relief of an angel. A heavy brass knocker hung from the wood.

Acting mostly on instinct, Emma reached behind her and drew the Mortal Sword from its scabbard. It had a weight in her hand that no other sword, not even Cortana, had, and it gleamed in the night as if it emitted its own light.

She had taken it from Julian's tent where it had been hidden beneath the bedroll, wrapped in a velvet cloth. She had replaced it with another sword. It wouldn't pass close examination, but he had no reason to be racing to the tent every five minutes to check on it. After all, the camp was guarded.

She placed her hand against the door. Brother Shadrach's message had said that the Silent City would be empty tonight, the Silent Brothers serving as guards on the city walls the night before the parley. And still the door seemed to pulse against her palm, as if it beat like a heart.

"I am Emma Carstairs, and I bear the Mortal Sword," she said. "Open in the name of Maellartach."

For an agonizingly long moment, nothing happened. Emma began to panic. Maybe the Mortal Sword of Thule was different, somehow, its atoms too altered, its magic alien.

The door opened all at once, soundlessly, like a mouth yawning open. Emma slipped inside, glancing once over her shoulder at the silent forest.

The door slid shut behind her with the same silence, and Emma found herself in a narrow, smooth-walled passage that led to a staircase going down. Her witchlight seemed to bounce off the marble walls as she descended, feeling as if she were passing through memory. The Silent City in Thule, empty and abandoned. Circles of fire in rooms of bones as she sealed her *parabatai* ritual with Julian. Her greatest mistake. The one that had ended with this journey.

She shivered as she came out into the main part of the City, where the walls were lined in skulls and femurs and delicate chandeliers of bones hung from the ceiling. At least in Thule, she hadn't been alone.

At last she entered the room of the Speaking Stars. It was just as it had been in her dream. The floor glimmered like the night sky turned upside down, the stars curving in a parabola before the basalt table where the Silent Brothers sat when in session. The table was bare, and no Sword hung behind it in its usual place.

Emma stepped onto the stars, her boots clanking softly against the marble. In her dream, the floor had simply opened. Now, nothing happened. She rubbed at her exhausted eyes with her knuckles, feeling inside herself for the instinct that had guided her in opening the door of the City.

I am a parabatai, she thought. *The magic that binds me to Julian is woven into this place, into the fabric of Nephilim.* Hesitantly, she touched a finger to the blade of the Mortal Sword. Ran her fingertip down it gently, letting her memory fall back to that moment she had stood in the fire with Julian—*thy people shall be my people, thy God my God—*

A bead of blood formed on her fingertip and splashed down onto the marble at her feet. There was a click, and the floor, which had appeared seamless, opened and slid back, revealing a black gap below it.

In that gap was a tablet. She could see it far more clearly than she had in her dream. It was made of white basalt, and on it was a *parabatai* rune painted in blood so ancient that the blood itself had long dissolved, leaving behind only a red-brown stain in the shape of the rune.

Emma's breath caught in her throat. Despite everything, being in the presence of something so old and so powerful caught at her heart. Feeling as if she were choking, she raised the Sword in her hands, the tip of the blade pointed downward.

She could see herself doing it, driving the Sword down, splitting the tablet apart. She imagined the sound of it breaking. It would be the sound of hearts breaking, all over the world, as *parabatai* were cut apart. She imagined them reaching for each other in uncomprehending horror—Jace and Alec, Clary and Simon.

The pain that Julian would feel.

She began to sob silently. She would be an exile, a pariah, cast out like Cain. She imagined Clary and the others turning from her with looks of loathing. You couldn't hurt people like that and be forgiven.

But she thought again of Diana in Thule. *Their runes began to burn like fire, as if they had fire in their veins instead of blood. People said that the blades of those who fought them shattered in their hands. Black lines spread over their bodies and they became monstrous—physically monstrous. I never saw it happen, mind you—I heard this all thirdhand. Stories about ruthless, massive shining creatures, tearing cities apart. Sebastian had to release thousands of demons to take them down. A lot of mundanes and Shadowhunters died.*

She and Julian could not become monsters. They could not destroy everyone they knew and loved. It was better to break the *parabatai* bonds than to be responsible for death and destruction. It felt like forever since Jem had explained the curse to her. They had tried everything to escape it.

Eventually the power would make them mad, until they became as monsters. They would destroy their families, the ones they loved. Death would surround them.

There was no escape but this. Her hands clamped tighter around the sword's hilt. She raised Maellartach.

Forgive me, Julian.

"Stop!" A voice rang through the Bone City. "Emma! What are you doing?"

She turned, without moving from the Speaking Stars or lowering the Sword. Julian stood at the entrance to the chamber. He was white-faced, staring at her in total shock. He had clearly been running: He was breathless, leaves in his hair and mud on his shoes.

"Don't try to stop me, Julian." Her voice was barely above a whisper.

He held his hands out as if to show they were empty of weapons and took a step forward, toward her. She shook her head and he stopped. "I always thought this would be me," he said. "I never thought it would be *you* doing this."

"Get out of here, Julian. I don't want you to be here for this. If they find me here, I want them to find me alone."

"I *know*," he said. "You're sacrificing yourself. You know they'll blame someone—someone with access to the Mortal Sword—and you want it to be you. I *know* you, Emma. I know exactly what you're doing." He took another step toward her. "I won't try to stop you. But you can't make me leave you either."

"But you have to!" Her voice rose. "They'll exile me, Julian, at best, even if Horace is overthrown; even Jia wouldn't overlook this, nobody would or could—they won't understand it—if it's the two of us, they'll think we did it so we could be together, you'll lose the kids. I won't let that happen, not after everything—"

"Emma!" Julian held his hands out to her. The sea-glass bracelet on his wrist glittered, bright color in this place of bones and

grayness. "I will not leave you. I will not ever leave you. Even if you shatter that rune, I won't leave you."

A sob tore through Emma. And then another. She slid to her knees, still holding the Sword. Despair ripped into her, as strong as relief. Maybe it was relief. She couldn't tell, but she could sense Julian come up quietly and kneel down across from her, his knees against the cold stone.

"What happened?" he said. "What about the cushion of time Magnus said we had—"

"My rune has been burning—and yours, too, I know it. And there's this." She tugged up the sleeve of her sweater, turning her hand over to show him the mark on her forearm—a dark spiderweb-like pattern, small but growing. "I don't think we have time left."

"Then we could get our Marks stripped," Julian said. His voice was soft, reassuring—a voice he saved for the people he loved the most. "Mine as well as yours. I thought that—"

"I talked to Jem at the meeting," Emma said. "He told me he would never do it, never, and Magnus can't do it alone—" She caught her breath. "In Thule, Diana told me that when Sebastian started to take over, the *parabatai* in that world turned into monsters. Their runes burned, and their skin was covered with black marks, and then they became monsters. That's what's happening to us, Julian. I know it is. All that stuff about the curse turning us into monsters. It's like that monstrosity is hidden in the heart of the bond. Like—like a cancer."

There was a long pause. "Why didn't you tell me about this?"

"I didn't believe it at first," she whispered. "At least, I thought it was something that could only happen in Thule. But our runes have burned. And the black marks on my skin—I *knew*—"

"But we don't know," he said softly. "I know how you feel. You feel shaky, right? Your mind's racing. Your heart's racing too."

She nodded. "How—"

"I feel the same way," he said. "I do think it's the curse. Jem said it would give us power. And I do feel like—like I've been lit up with electricity and I can't stop shaking."

"But you seem all right," Emma said.

"I think recovering from the spell, for me, is like climbing up out of a pit," he said. "I'm not quite at the top yet, where you are. I'm a little protected." He looped his arms around his knees. "I know why you're scared. Anyone would be. But I'm still going to ask you to do something for me. I'm going to ask you to have faith."

"Faith?" she said. "Faith in what?"

"In us," he said. "Even when you told me why it was forbidden for us to be in love—even when I knew we shouldn't ever have become *parabatai*—I still had all the memories of how wonderful it was to be your partner, to have our friendship made into something holy. I still believe in our bond, Emma. I still believe in the bonds of *parabatai*, in the importance of it, in the beauty of what Alec and Jace have, or what Jem had in the past."

"But what if it can be turned against us?" Emma said. "Our greatest strength made into our greatest weakness?"

"That's why I asked you to have faith," he said. "Believe in *us* if you can't believe in the idea of it. Tomorrow we might go into battle. Us against them. We need Jace and Alec, Clary and Simon—we need *ourselves*—to be whole and unbroken on the battlefield. We need to be at our strongest. One more day, Emma. We've made it this far. We can make it one more day."

"But I need the Mortal Sword," said Emma, hugging the blade to her. "I can't do this without it."

"If we win tomorrow, then we can get help from the Clave," Julian said. "If we don't win, Horace will be happy to strip our runes off. You know he will."

"I thought of that," Emma said. "But we can't be sure, can we?"

"Maybe, maybe not," he said. "But if you do this, if you cut the bonds, then I'm going to stand by you and take the blame along with you. You can't stop me."

"But the kids," she whispered. She couldn't bear the thought of Julian being separated from them, of more pain and suffering coming to the Blackthorns.

"Have Helen and Aline now," said Julian. "I'm not the only one who can keep our family together. When I was at my worst, you were at your best for me. I can only do the same for you."

"All right," she said. "All right, I'll wait one day."

As if it heard her voice, the floor closed up at her feet, hiding the *parabatai* tablet beneath the protecting marble. She wanted to reach out to Julian, to touch his hands, to tell him she was grateful. She wanted to say more, say the words they were forbidden to say, but she didn't—just looked at him silently and thought them, wondering if anyone had thought these words before in the Silent City. If they had thought them like this: with equal hope and despair.

I love you. I love you. I love you.

30

The Riches There That Lie

A scratching noise at the tent flap woke Emma. She had slept dreamlessly all night, waking only when Cristina crept into the tent late and rolled herself up in her blankets. She struggled awake now, feeling groggy; she could see through the gap in the tent fabric that it was gray outside, the sky heavy with impending rain.

Helen was outside their tent. "Thirty-minute warning," she said, and her footsteps receded as she continued with the wake-up call.

Cristina groaned and rolled out of her blankets. They had both slept in their clothes. "My stele," she said. "We should"—she yawned—"Mark each other. Also, there had better be coffee."

Emma stripped down to her tank top, shivering as Cristina did the same. They exchanged runes—Swiftness and Sure-Footedness for Emma, Blocking and Deflecting runes for Cristina, Sure-Strike and Farsight for both. Cristina didn't ask why Emma wasn't getting her runes from Julian. They both knew.

They zipped and laced their way into their gear and boots and clambered out of the tent, stretching their stiff muscles. The sky was heavy with dark clouds, the ground wet with dew. It seemed as if everyone else was already awake and hurrying around the camp—Simon was zipping his gear, Isabelle polishing a longsword. Magnus, dressed somberly in dark colors, was helping a geared-up Alec strap on his quiver of arrows. Aline was drawing a Fortitude rune on the back of Helen's neck. Mark, his weapons belt bristling with daggers, was stirring some porridge over the fire.

Cristina whimpered. "I don't see coffee. Only porridge."

"I always tell you coffee's evil, addict," said Emma. "Give me your hand—I'll draw you an Energy rune."

Cristina grumbled but held her hand out; a good Energy rune worked much like caffeine. Emma looked at Cristina affectionately as she ran the stele over her skin. She had a suspicion she knew where Cristina had been the night before, though now wasn't the time to ask.

"I can't believe this is actually happening," Cristina said as Emma returned her hand.

"I know," Emma said. She squeezed Cristina's hand before putting her stele away. "I'll have your back if anything happens. You know that."

Cristina touched her medallion and then Emma's cheek, her eyes grave. "May the Angel bless you and keep you safe, my sister."

Raised voices drew Emma's attention before she could say anything else. She turned to see Julian standing with Ty and Kit; Ty was speaking loudly, clearly angry, while Kit hung back with his hands in his pockets. As she headed over, she saw Kit's expression more clearly. It shocked her. He looked utterly drained and despairing.

"We want to be there with you," Ty was saying. Mark had started over, abandoning the porridge. Helen, Aline, and Kieran stood nearby, while the others were politely not paying attention. "We want to fight beside you."

"*Ty.*" New runes stood out black and gleaming on Julian's wrists and collarbones. Emma wondered who had done them—Mark?

Helen? It didn't matter. It should have been her. "This isn't a fight. It's a parley. A peace meeting. I can't bring my whole family."

"It's not like you're invited and we're not," said Ty. He was in gear; so was Kit. A shortsword hung at Ty's hip. "None of us are invited."

Emma hid a smile. It was always hard to argue with Ty when he made good points.

"If we all show up, it'll be chaos," Julian said. "I need you here, Ty. You know what your job is."

Ty spoke reluctantly. "Give a warning. Stay safe."

"That's right," Julian said. He took Ty's face in his hands; Ty was still a head shorter than him. "Stay safe, Tiberius."

Mark looked relieved. Kit still hadn't spoken a word. Over Ty's head, Julian nodded at Magnus, who stood beside Alec in the shelter of a nearby tree. Magnus nodded back. *Interesting*, Emma thought.

The others had begun to approach now that it seemed the argument was over: Cristina and Kieran, Diana, Isabelle and Simon, Clary and Jace. Jace went over to Kit and touched the boy on the shoulder with all the gentleness Emma knew he was capable of, but which he rarely showed. As Emma watched, Jace offered Kit a slim silver dagger with a design of herons in flight etched on the handle. Kit took it carefully, nodding his head. Emma couldn't hear them talking, but Kit at least looked a little less miserable.

Kieran and Cristina had been speaking to each other in low voices. Kieran moved away from her now, coming to face Julian and the rest of those who were going to the Fields—Emma and Cristina, Alec and Mark. Kieran's dark hair curled damply around his face. "It is my time to go as well, I think."

"I am sorry you can't remain with us for this part of the plan," said Julian. "You have been a great help, Kieran. It feels as if you belong with us."

Kieran gave Julian a measuring look. "I did not see you clearly enough in the past, Julian Atticus. You do have a ruthless heart. But you also have a good one."

Julian looked faintly surprised, and then even more surprised as Kieran went to kiss Mark good-bye—then turned to Cristina and kissed her as well. Both smiled at him as everyone stared. *Guess I was right*, Emma thought, and raised an eyebrow at Cristina, who blushed.

Kieran murmured something to the two of them that Emma couldn't hear, and melted into the woods, vanishing like mist.

"Those of us leaving camp must go," said Diana. "The parley is soon and it will take an hour at least to walk to the Fields."

Clary was talking to Simon; she patted his shoulders and turned worriedly to Isabelle, who hugged her. Alec had gone to speak with Jace. Everywhere were *parabatai*, preparing to be parted, even if briefly. Emma felt a sense of unreality. She had expected the bonds to be broken by now. It was strange to be standing where she was—not yet fleeing, not yet hated or exiled.

Alec clasped Jace's hand. "Take care."

Jace looked at him for a long moment, and let him go. Clary moved away from Simon and went to stand with Jace. They watched as Magnus crossed the wet grass to Alec, inclined his head, and kissed him gently.

"I wish you could come," Alec said, his eyes bright.

"You know the deal. No Downworlders scaring Horace," said Magnus. "Be good, my archer boy. Come back to me."

He went to stand with Jace and Clary. Helen and Aline joined them, and so did Kit and Ty. They made a small and silent group, watching as the others turned and walked into the woods of Brocelind.

"Are you ever going to talk to me again?" Ty said.

He and Kit were sitting in a green hollow in the forest, close to the campsite. A gray boulder covered in green-brown moss rose behind them; Ty was leaning his back against it, his eyes half-lidded with exhaustion.

Kit barely remembered coming back from Lake Lyn the night before. Ty had hardly been able to walk. He had leaned on Kit most of the way, but Kit hadn't spoken then, either. Not even when it started to rain and they splashed through miserable dampness together. Not when Ty had to stop to dry-heave by the side of the path. Not when he doubled over and gasped for Julian as if somehow Julian would appear out of thin air and make everything better.

It was as if Kit's emotions were trapped somewhere in an airless killing jar. Ty didn't want him—not as a friend, not as anything. Every breath hurt, but his mind shied away from why: from who he really blamed for what had happened.

"We're supposed to be keeping quiet," was all he said now.

Ty gave him a doubtful look. "That's not it," he said. "You're mad at me, I think."

Kit knew he should tell Ty what he was feeling; it was more than unfair to expect him to guess. The only problem was that he wasn't sure himself.

He remembered returning to camp, remembered crawling into their tent together, Ty curling up into himself. Kit had wanted to get Julian, but Ty had only shaken his head, pressing his face into his blankets, chanting under his breath until his muscles had relaxed and he'd fallen into an exhausted sleep.

Kit hadn't slept.

He reached into his pocket. "Look—last night, after—well, before we left the lake I went back up to the fire." It had been ash and char, save one shining remnant. Livvy's gold necklace, glimmering like pirate treasure among the ashes.

Kit held it out now and saw Ty's eyes crinkle at the corners the way they did when he was very surprised.

"You got it for me?" Ty said.

Kit kept holding the necklace out. It swung between them, a shimmering pendulum. Ty reached his hand out slowly to take it. The blood had been burned away from the surface. The locket shone clean as he fastened it around his neck.

"Kit," he began haltingly. "I thought that you—I thought that it would be—"

Leaves crunched; a branch snapped. Kit and Ty fell instantly silent. After a moment, hand on the pendant at his throat, Ty rose to a crouch and began to whistle.

Emma and the others made their way in near-total silence through the woods, which were damp and green and thick with leaves and water. Cold drops of rain broke through the canopy occasionally and slid down the back of Emma's collar, making her shiver.

They had reached a fork in the road some ways back. Diana, Isabelle, and Simon had gone to the right. The others had gone to the left. There had been no good-byes, though Alec had kissed his sister on the cheek without a word.

They walked on now as a group of five: Julian first, then Mark and Cristina—not holding hands but close together, shoulders touching—and Alec and Emma, bringing up the rear. Alec was watchful, his bow ever ready, his blue eyes raking the shadows on either side of the path.

"Have you ever wanted a really big tapestry of yourself?" Emma said to him.

Alec was not the sort who rattled easily. "Why?" he said. "Do you have one?"

"I do, actually," said Emma. "I rescued it from the Inquisitor's office and carried it through the streets of Alicante. I got some pretty weird looks."

Alec's mouth twitched. "I bet you did."

"I didn't want the Inquisitor to throw it away," Emma said. "He wants to pretend that the Battle of the Burren didn't matter. But I've been to Thule. I know what it would mean if there had never been a Clary. Or a Jace. Or a you."

Alec lowered his bow slightly. "And imagine where we'd be now," he said, "if there hadn't been a Julian or a you or a Cristina or a Mark. There are times, I think, where we're each called. Where we can choose to rise up or not to rise up. What you did in Faerie—" He broke off. "You know, you should give that tapestry to Magnus. If anyone would enjoy having it, he would."

Light broke through the trees suddenly. Emma looked up, thinking the clouds had parted, and realized they had reached the edge of the forest. The trees thinned out, the sky arching overhead in shades of pearlescent gray and smoky blue.

They had left the forest. In front of them stretched the green field, all the way to the far walls of Alicante. In the distance, she could see dark figures, small as beetles, approaching the center of the Imperishable Fields. The Cohort? The Unseelie? Even with Farsight runes, they were too distant to tell.

"Emma," Julian said. "Are you ready?"

She looked at him. For a moment it was as if no one was there but the two of them, as if they faced each other across the floor of the *parabatai* chamber in the Silent City, the connection between them shimmering with its force. Julian's face was pale above the black of his gear; his blue-green eyes burned as he looked at her. She knew what he was thinking. He had come this far, to the edge of where there was no turning back. He needed her to take the last step with him.

She lifted her chin. "We choose to rise up," she said, and, stepping onto the grass of the Fields, they began to march toward the walls of Alicante.

And the sky was full of angels.

Dru stood by the side of the canal in front of the Graymark

house, holding Tavvy's hand. All through Alicante, Shadowhunters old and young lined the streets, gazing up at the sky.

Dru had to admit that what Horace had done was impressive. It was like looking at a massive movie screen, an IMAX or something bigger. When they had first come out of the house, Maryse shooing Rafe and Max ahead of her, they'd stopped dead to gawk at the enormous square in the sky. All they'd been able to see then was the green of the Fields and a piece of gray-blue sky.

Then Horace and Zara had come into the frame, striding across the grass, and because of the size of the Projection and the angle, they had looked like angels striding across the sky. Horace looked as he always had, with one marked difference: the sleeve covering his left arm hung empty from the elbow down.

Zara had her hair loose, which was impractical for fighting but dramatic as a visual. She also had golden Cortana strapped to her side, which made Dru's stomach turn.

"That's Emma's sword," Tavvy said crossly. Dru didn't reprimand him. She felt no less annoyed.

Horace and Zara were followed by a small group of guards—Vanessa Ashdown and Martin Gladstone among them—and a contingent of Centurions. Dru recognized some from the time they'd stayed at the Institute, like Mallory Bridgestock, Jessica Beausejours, and Timothy Rockford. Manuel wasn't with them, though, which surprised her. He'd always struck her as someone who liked to be at the center of things.

As they took their places on the field, Maryse shook her head and muttered something about Gladstone. She had been trying to corral Max and Rafe, neither of whom were interested in the dull sky-pictures, but now she looked at Horace and frowned. "The Circle all over again," she said. "This is just how Valentine was—so sure of his own rightness. So sure it gave him the right to decide for others how they should believe."

An audible gasp ran through the watching Shadowhunters. Not a reaction to Maryse's words—they were all staring upward. Dru craned her neck back and saw with a shock that the Unseelie Court army was now marching across the Fields toward the Cohort.

They seemed vast, a countless array of faeries in the dusky livery of the King of Unseelie. Knights on horseback with spears of silver and bronze gleaming in the early light. Squat goblins with stern-looking axes; dryads with stout wooden staffs and kelpies gnashing their knife-sharp teeth. Marching at the front were redcaps in their blood-dyed uniforms, their iron boots ringing on the earth. They surrounded a crowned man on a horse—the new King of Unseelie. Not the one Dru was familiar with from pictures; this King was young. His crown was cocked insouciantly to the side.

As he came closer, Dru could see that he resembled Kieran slightly. The same straight mouth, the same inhumanly beautiful features, though the King's hair was coal-black and streaked with purple. He rode up to the Inquisitor and the rest of the Cohort and gazed down at them coldly.

Maryse made a noise of surprise. Other Shadowhunters were gasping, and a few standing on Cistern Bridge clapped. As much as Dru hated Horace, she could tell this was good theater: The small band of the Cohort facing down a great Faerie army.

She was just glad she had some theater of her own planned.

"Greetings, my lord Oban," said Horace, inclining his head. "We thank you for agreeing to take parley with us this morning."

"He's lying," Tavvy said. "Look at his face."

"I know," Dru said in a low voice. "But don't say it where people can hear you."

Oban slid gracefully from his horse. He bowed to Horace. There was another collective gasp that rocketed up the streets of Alicante. Faeries did not bow to Shadowhunters. "The pleasure is mine."

Horace smiled expansively. "You understand the gravity of our situation," he said. "The death of two of our own—especially such famed Shadowhunters as Jace Herondale and Clary Fairchild—leaves a hole in the heart of our community. Such a wound cannot be borne by a civilized society. It demands recompense."

He means retribution, thought Dru. She knew the two were different, though she doubted she could have explained exactly how.

"We of the Lands of Unseelie do not disagree," said Oban pompously. "It seems to us proved that Downworlders and Shadowhunters cannot occupy the same space in safety. Better for us to be separated and respect one another from a distance."

"Quite," said Horace. "Respecting one another from a distance seems very fine."

"Seriously," Maryse muttered. "No one can be buying this crap, can they?"

Dru glanced sideways at her. "You really sound like a New Yorker sometimes."

Maryse smiled crookedly. "I'll take that as a compliment."

There was a sudden stir. Dru looked up and saw that Horace, who had been nodding in agreement with King Oban, was staring into the distance, his mouth open in shock.

Oban turned, and a scowl—the first genuine expression he'd shown—spread across his face. "What is this intrusion?"

Unable to stop herself, Dru clapped her hands together. Coming into the Projection's focus, striding across the green fields toward the Cohort, were Julian, Emma, and the rest of their group. Against all odds, they had arrived.

The wind had risen and whipped across the Fields, its force unbroken by walls or trees. The grass bent in front of Emma and the others, and Horace's Inquisitor robes flapped around him. Zara pushed her hair out of her face and glared furiously at Julian before turning her look of loathing on Emma.

"*You,*" she hissed.

Emma grinned at Zara with all the hatred sparked by the sight of Cortana hanging at Zara's side. "I always wanted someone to hiss '*you*' at me," she said. "Makes me feel like I'm in a movie."

Horace sneered. "What are you brats doing here? How dare you interrupt this parley? This is a serious matter, not a game for children."

"No one said this was a game, Dearborn." Julian stopped in between Horace and a milling crowd of faerie knights and redcaps, flanked by Mark and Alec on one side, Emma and Cristina on the other. "Nor are we children."

"I'm certainly not," Alec pointed out mildly.

A man standing in the center of the milling redcaps pointed at Mark. He had a look of Kieran about him, with messy purple-black hair and a gold circlet tilted slightly on his head. "I know you."

Mark glared. "Unfortunately, that's true." He turned to the others. "That is Prince Oban."

"*King* Oban," Oban snapped. "Horace—Inquisitor, see that they show me respect."

"They shouldn't be here at all," said Horace. "My apologies for this intrusion." He flipped a smug hand in their direction. "Ashdown—Gladstone—get rid of this trash."

"You heard him." Vanessa stepped forward, her hand at the blade at her waist.

"It's really hard to imagine what Cameron did to deserve relatives like you," Emma said to her, and had the satisfaction of watching her turn a blotchy color.

Alec raised his bow. So did Mark.

"If you do not surrender your arms," said Horace, "we will be forced to—"

"Is this really what you want everyone to see?" Julian interrupted. "After everything you said about the deaths of young

Shadowhunters—you want to be the cause of more of them?" He turned away from Horace, toward the walls of Alicante, and spoke in a clear, hard voice. "This parley is false. It is entirely for show. Not only is the Inquisitor allied with the Unseelie Court, but he has placed Oban on the throne as his puppet."

Zara gasped audibly.

Where Horace had looked smug, he now looked stunned. "Lies. These are disgraceful lies!" he roared.

"I suppose that you're going to say that he killed Jace and Clary as well," said Zara.

Julian didn't bother to look at her. He kept staring toward Alicante. Emma imagined the Shadowhunters in the city. Could they see him, hear him? Did they understand?

"I wasn't going to say that," said Julian. "Because they're not dead."

They're not dead.

A roar went up around Dru. There was chaos in the streets: She could hear people calling out in happiness and others in surprise or anger; she could hear Jace's and Clary's names, spoken over and over. Tavvy raised his fists to the sky, where the image of Julian towered above them, flanked by Emma and their friends.

That's my brother, Dru thought proudly. *My brother Julian.*

"It's in very bad taste to make such jokes," Gladstone snapped. "The world of Nephilim still mourns Jace and Clary—"

"And we found their bloodstained clothes," said Zara. "We know they're dead."

"People drop jackets sometimes, Zara," said Alec. "Jace is my *parabatai*. If he were dead, I would know."

"Oh, *feelings*," Horace said nastily. "This is all about your feelings, is it, Lightwood? We at the Cohort deal in facts! *Our* facts!"

"No one owns facts," Cristina said quietly. "They are immutable."

Horace gave her a look of disgust and turned to Oban. "Jace Herondale and Clary Fairchild are dead, aren't they?"

Oban's expression was a mixture of anger and unease. "One of my redcaps told me it was so, and as you know, my people cannot lie."

"There you have it," said Horace. "I am out of patience with you, Blackthorn! Guards, come and take them to the Gard. Their punishment will be decided later."

"We'll take them." Zara stepped forward, Timothy Rockford at her side. She slid Cortana from its sheath and raised it to gesture at the intruders. "Emma Carstairs, I arrest you in the name of—"

Emma reached out her hand. She reached out as she had through all the years since Julian had placed Cortana in her arms at the start of the Dark War. She reached out as she had in the thorn hedge of Faerie, as if she were reaching down through the past to touch the hands of all the Carstairs women who had held Cortana through the years.

Zara's hand jerked. Cortana's grip tore free of her fingers and the blade sailed across the space between them.

The hilt smacked into Emma's hand. Reflexively, she grasped it, and raised the sword high. Cortana was hers again.

They had been sitting on one of the campfire logs, chatting, though Helen was too nervous to keep her mind firmly on the conversation. She couldn't keep her mind off Jules and Mark, and the danger they were now facing.

"They'll be all right," Magnus said after he'd asked her a question twice and she hadn't answered. She was staring off into the profusion of trees, her whole body tensed. "Horace wouldn't harm them in front of so many people. He's a politician."

"Everyone's got a breaking point," said Helen. "We've seen people do some pretty strange things."

Magnus's cat eyes flashed. "I suppose we have."

"It's nice to see you again," Aline said to him. "We haven't spent much time together since Rome."

She smiled at Helen; Rome was where they had met, years ago.

"I keep telling myself I'm going to avoid wars and battles in the future," said Magnus. "Somehow they keep coming to me. It must be something about my face."

The sound of the whistle brought Helen to her feet, along with Aline. It wasn't much of a warning. The trees around them shook; Helen had just drawn her sword when a group of fifty or sixty heavily armed Cohort members burst from them, led by Manuel Villalobos, and headed straight for the camp.

Magnus hadn't bothered to get up off his log. "Oh my," he said in a bored voice. "A terrifying and unexpected attack."

Aline hit him on the shoulder. The Cohort members pounded up the slight hill and burst into the camp, encircling Magnus, Helen, and Aline. Manuel wore his full Centurion gear; his red-and-gray cloak swirled impressively as he seized Aline and yanked her back against his chest, his dagger out.

"Which tent is Jace and Clary's?" he demanded. He gestured with his dagger. "You two! Milo, Amelia! Grab the warlock's hands. He can't do magic without them." He shot Magnus a look of loathing. "You ought to be dead."

"Ah, indeed, but the thing is, I'm *immortal*," Magnus said cheerfully, as a beefy Shadowhunter—Milo, apparently—yanked his hands together behind him. "Someone ought to have told you."

Helen wasn't having as easy a time being cheerful. Aline shot her a reassuring look, but the sight of her wife in Manuel's grip was still more than she could stand. "Let her *go*!" she demanded.

"As soon as you tell me where Jace and Clary are," said Manuel. "In fact, let me phrase it in words you might understand. Tell me where they are or I'll cut your wife's throat."

Helen and Aline exchanged a look. "It's that blue one over there," said Helen, and pointed in what she hoped seemed a reluctant manner.

Manuel shoved Aline away from him. Helen caught her and they embraced tightly. "I *hated* that," Helen muttered against Aline's neck as Cohort members shot by them, their unsheathed blades flashing.

"I didn't love it either," Aline replied. "He reeks of cologne. Like a pinecone. Come on."

They glanced back at Magnus, who was whistling cheerfully and ignoring his guards, who looked sweaty and worried. Magnus nodded at them and they hurried after Manuel and the others, who were just approaching the blue tent.

"Grab them," Manuel said, indicating the tent stakes. "Yank it out of the ground."

The tent was seized, lifted off the ground, and hurled aside, collapsing in a pile of fabric.

Revealed beneath were Jace and Clary, sitting cross-legged on the dirt, facing each other. They had been playing tic-tac-toe on the ground with sticks. Clary had her hair in a ponytail and looked about fifteen.

Manuel made a sputtering noise. "Kill them," he said, turning to his companions. "Go on. Kill them."

The Cohort looked nonplussed. Amelia took a step forward, raising her blade—then started visibly.

The trees around the campsite were rustling loudly. The Cohort members who had remained at the treeline, weapons drawn, were glancing around in puzzlement and dawning fear.

Jace drew the third in a line of *X*'s on the ground and tossed aside his stick. "Checkmate," he said.

"Checkmate is *chess*," Clary pointed out, entirely ignoring the Cohort surrounding them.

Jace grinned. It was a bright, beautiful grin, the sort of grin that made Helen understand why, all those years ago, Aline had kissed him just to see. "I wasn't talking about our game," he said.

"I said *kill them!*" Manuel shouted.

"But, Manu," said Amelia, pointing a shaking finger. "The trees—the trees are moving—"

Aline grasped Helen's hand as the forest exploded.

There was a moment of stillness. Genuine wonder showed on nearly every face, even Oban's. As a faerie, perhaps he understood the significance of Cortana's choice, whether he liked it or not.

Emma's gaze met Julian's. He smiled at her with his eyes. Julian understood what this meant to her. He always did.

Zara gave a screech. "Give that *back*!" She advanced on Emma, who raised Cortana in triumph. Her blood sang in her veins, a song of gold and battle. "You *cheaters*! *Thieves!* Coming here, trying to spoil everything, trying to ruin what we're building!"

"Cortana doesn't want you, Zara," Julian said quietly. "A sword of Wayland the Smith can choose its bearer, and Cortana does not choose liars."

"We are not liars—"

"Really? Where's Manuel?" Mark demanded. "He was in Faerie when I was there. I saw him plotting with Oban. He spoke of an alliance with the Cohort."

"Then he spoke of this parley!" Horace roared. "This is an alliance—it is no secret—"

"That was long before you told the Clave that Jace and Clary had died," said Cristina. "Can Manuel see the future?"

Horace actually stamped his foot. "Vanessa! Martin! *Get rid of these intruders!*"

"My redcaps can take them," said Oban. "Shadowhunter blood makes a fair dye."

The Cohort froze. Julian gave a small, cold smile.

"Really, Prince?" said Mark. "How would you know?"

Oban whirled on him. "You will address me as your King! I rule the Lands of Unseelie! I took the title from my father—"

"But you didn't kill him," said Cristina. "Kieran did that. Kieran Kingson."

The army of Unseelie had begun to mutter. The redcaps looked on stonily.

"End this farce, Dearborn," Julian said. "Send the Unseelie army home. Come and face your people in the Council Hall."

"Face them?" Horace said, his mouth working in disgust. "And how do you suggest I do that when I have not yet arranged for justice? Would you simply forget those brave Shadowhunters, the ones who you claim as friends, who have died at the hands of Downworlders? I will not abandon them! I will speak for them—"

"Or you could let them speak for themselves," Alec said mildly. "Since, you know, here they are."

"Oh, look, and there's Manuel," said Emma. "We were awfully sorry to miss him, but I see he was . . ."

"Don't say it," warned Julian.

". . . tied up." Emma grinned. "Sorry. Can't resist a bad pun."

And tied up he was: Manuel, along with a group of fifty or more Cohort members, was being marched firmly across the Fields from the edge of Brocelind Forest. Their hands were tied behind their backs. They were being propelled forward by a crowd of Shadowhunters—Aline and Helen, Isabelle and Diana and Simon.

Walking alongside them, as casually as if they were out for a morning stroll, were Jace and Clary. Above them fluttered the banner of Livia's Watch, Clary holding the stanchion from which the banner flew. Emma's eyes stung—Livvy's locket and saber, flying high above the Imperishable Fields.

And behind them—behind them came a wave of all the Downworlders who had waited in the woods through the night: warlocks and werewolves and fey of all sorts, leaping and striding and stalking out from between the trees. Brocelind Forest was full of Downworlders once more.

Horace had gone still. Zara shrank in against his bulk, glaring through her tangled hair.

"What is *happening*?" said Zara in a dazed voice. Emma almost felt sorry for her.

Julian reached up and unbuckled the clasp holding on his cloak. It slid from his shoulders, revealing the hilt of the Mortal Sword, blackly burnished silver with angel wings outspread.

Horace stared at him, wheezing slightly. Emma couldn't tell if he recognized the Mortal Sword or not yet; he seemed beyond that.

"What have you done, you stupid boy?" he hissed. "You have no idea—the careful planning—all we have done in the name of Nephilim—"

"Well, hello there, Dearborn." Horace jerked back, as if the sight of Jace and Clary so close burned him. Jace held Manuel in front of them by the back of his uniform, the Centurion's expression sulky and annoyed. "It seems the rumors of our death have been greatly exaggerated. By you."

Clary thrust the stanchion she was holding into the earth, so the banner fluttered upright. "You've always wanted to say that, haven't you?" she asked Jace.

Alec looked at them both and shook his head. The rest of the Shadowhunters and Downworlders had spread themselves out across the field between the parley area and the walls of Alicante. Familiar faces were mixed into the crowd: Simon and Isabelle stood close by, and near them Emma recognized Catarina, Diana, Maia, and Bat; she looked for Magnus and finally found him standing near the edge of Brocelind Forest. What was he doing so far away?

"Dearborn," Alec said. "This is your last chance. Call off this meeting and return with us to the Council Hall."

"No," Horace said. Some of the color had come back into his face.

"But everyone can see you lied," Emma said. "You lied to every Shadowhunter—tried to frighten us all into obedience—"

"That's not Jace and Clary." Horace pointed at them with shaking fingers. "These are some—some imposters—some warlock magic meant to trick and deceive—"

"The Iron Sisters predicted you would say that," Julian said. "That's why they gave me this." He reached behind him and drew the Mortal Sword from its scabbard. The metal seemed to sing as the blade arced across the sky, scattering sparks. An audible gasp went up from the Cohort and the Unseelie faeries; Emma could only imagine the commotion occurring in the city. "The Mortal Sword, reforged."

Silently, Julian thanked Sister Emilia and her willingness to deceive the Cohort.

Horace's mouth worked. "A fake—a falsity—"

"Then you won't mind if Manuel holds it," said Julian. "Order him to take it."

Horace froze. His eyes darted from the Sword to Manuel and back again; it was, startlingly, Oban who broke the silence.

"Well, if it is a falsity, let the boy take it," he said. "Let us suffer this farce only briefly." His silvery eyes flicked to Manuel. "Take the Sword, Centurion."

Tight-lipped, Manuel reached out his hands, and Julian placed the Mortal Sword in them, the blade across his palms. Emma saw Manuel jerk as if in pain, and felt a cold relief. So the Sword's power was working. It was painful to be forced to tell the truth. The Sword's power hurt, and not just those who lied but any who wished to protect their secrets.

Julian crossed his arms and looked at Manuel. It was a hard, cold look, a look that went back generations of Blackthorns, to those who had been Inquisitors themselves. "Did you and the Cohort try to kill Clary and Jace just now?"

Manuel's face was blotched white and red, his careful hair disarranged. "Yes," he hissed. "Yes. I did." He shot Horace a venomous look. "It was on the Inquisitor's orders. When he found out they were still alive and would be in Brocelind Forest last night, he ordered us to slay them at dawn."

"But that didn't happen," Julian said.

"No. They must have been warned. They were waiting for us, and the woods were full of Downworlders. They attacked. We had no chance."

"So you were willing to kill fellow Nephilim and pin the blame on Downworlders," said Julian. "Why? Why foment war?"

"I did what Horace ordered me to do."

"And in Faerie," said Julian. "When you helped Oban become King. When you brokered an alliance between the Cohort and the Unseelie Court. Was that because Horace asked you to do it?"

Manuel was biting his lip so hard blood was running down his chin. But the Sword was stronger than his will. "It was *my* idea," he gasped. "But Horace embraced it—he loved the idea of pulling off a trick under the Clave's noses—we put Oban on the throne because Oban was a fool who would do what we wanted—he would stage this parley with us, and we would pretend to reach a deal, a deal where both parties would get what they wanted. The Unseelie Court would get the Shadowhunters on their side against Seelie and other Downworlders—and the Cohort would be able to say that they had forced the Unseelie Court into a peace agreement, that they had agreed never to enter Idris again. Both sides would look strong to their people. . . ."

"Enough!" Oban shouted. He reached to seize the Mortal Sword from Manuel, but Mark moved in front of him, blocking his way. "Silence this brat!"

"Fine," Julian said unexpectedly, and plucked the Sword from Manuel's grasp. "Enough with the junior leagues. Dearborn, take the Sword."

He walked toward Horace, holding the Sword. All around Horace drooped the members of the Cohort, looking alternately shocked and furious. It wasn't too difficult to tell who had been surprised by Manuel's revelations, and who hadn't.

"It's time you spoke to your people, Dearborn," Julian said. "They can see you. They can hear you. You owe them an explanation." He held the Sword out to him, level and ready. "Let yourself be tested."

"We will be tested in battle!" Horace screamed. "I will prove myself! I am their leader! Their rightful Consul!"

"Consuls don't lie to their Council members," said Julian. He lowered the Mortal Sword so that the flat of the blade lay across his left palm, wincing slightly as the truth-telling compulsion took hold. "You blamed Dane Larkspear's death on faeries. *I* killed Dane Larkspear."

Emma felt her eyes widen. She hadn't expected Julian to say *that.*

"Maybe a little too much radical honesty," Simon muttered.

"I killed him because you sent him into Faerie to murder me and to murder my *parabatai*," said Julian. "I'm holding the Mortal Sword. I'm not lying. You can see that." He spoke as if he were addressing only Horace, but Emma knew he was addressing every Shadowhunter and Downworlder who could hear him. "Samantha Larkspear was hurt when she tried to torture Kieran Kingson at the Scholomance. Possibly also on your orders." He gave a little gasp; the Sword was clearly hurting him. "You've set Shadowhunters against Shadowhunters and against innocent Downworlders, all in service of tricking the Council into adopting your bigoted reforms—all in service of fear—"

"Yes, I did!" Horace screamed. Zara flew to her father's side

and yanked on his empty sleeve; he seemed barely to notice her. "Because the Nephilim are *fools*! Because of people like you, telling them Downworlders are our friends, that we can live in peace beside them! You would have us stretch out our necks willingly to the slaughtering blade! You would have us die lying down, not fighting!" He flung his right arm toward Oban. "I wouldn't have had to accept an alliance with this drunken fool if the Clave had not been so stupid and so stubborn! I needed to show them—show them how to protect ourselves honorably from Downworlders—"

"'Honorably'?" Julian echoed, raising the Mortal Sword so it no longer touched his palm. It was a weapon again now, not a test of the bearer's veracity. "You drove the Downworlders out of Brocelind. You knew the Unseelie Court was spreading the blight that was killing warlocks and you did nothing. How is that honorable?"

"As if all he did was nothing," Mark spat. "He encouraged the King to spread his poisoned earth here—to slay the Children of Lilith—"

"I think we're done here." Alec spoke coldly, in a ringing voice. "It is time for the Unseelie Court to go, Horace. Your loyalty is in question and you are no longer able to negotiate on the behalf of either Downworlders or Nephilim."

"You have no power to send us away, boy!" snapped Oban. "You are not the Consul, and our arrangement is with Horace Dearborn alone."

"I don't know what Horace promised you," said Jace, cool satisfaction in his tone. "But he can't help you, Prince."

"I am the *King*." Oban raised his bow.

From the knot of Downworlders, a faerie woman stepped forward. It was Nene, Mark and Helen's aunt. She faced Oban proudly. "You are not *our* King," she said.

"Because you are Seelie folk," sneered Oban.

"Some of us are Seelie, some Unseelie, and some of the wild peoples," said Nene. "We do not acknowledge you as the King of the

Unseelie Lands. We acknowledge Kieran Kingson, who slew Arawn the Elder-King with his own hands. He has the right of the throne by blood in his veins and by blood spilt."

She stepped aside, and Kieran emerged from the circle of the fey. He had dressed himself in his clothes from Faerie: unbleached linen tunic, soft deerskin breeches and boots. He carried himself upright, his back straight, his gaze level.

"Greetings, brother Oban," he said.

Oban's face twisted into a snarl. "The last time I saw you, *brother* Kieran, you were being dragged in chains behind my horses."

"That is true," said Kieran. "But it speaks more ill of you than it does of me." He looked out over the ranged masses of silent Unseelie warriors. "I have come to challenge my brother for the throne of Unseelie," he said. "The usual method is a duel to the death. The survivor shall take the throne."

Oban laughed in disbelief. "What? A duel *now?*"

"And why not now?" said Nene. Mark and Cristina were looking at each other in horror; it was clear neither of them had known this part of the plan. Emma doubted anyone had but Kieran himself and a few other faeries. "Or are you afraid, my lord Oban?"

In a smooth, sudden move, Oban raised his bow and shot at Kieran. The arrow flew free; Kieran jerked aside, the arrow just missing his arm. It flew across the field and slammed into Julie Beauvale; she went down like a struck sapling, her whip flying from her hand.

Emma gasped. Beatriz Mendoza cried out and fell to her knees at Julie's side; Alec whirled and shot a flurry of arrows at Oban, but the redcaps had already closed in around the King. Several went down with Alec's arrows in them as he nocked arrow after arrow to his bow and flew toward the Unseelie warriors.

"After him! Follow Alec!" shouted Maia. Werewolves dropped to the ground on all fours, sprouting fur and fangs. With a shout, the Cohort surrounding Horace seized up their weapons and charged;

Julian parried a blow from Timothy with the Mortal Sword, while Jessica Beausejours threw herself at Emma, her sword whipping around her head.

Nene dashed forward to arm Kieran with a silver sword; it flashed like lightning as he laid about him. Oban's Unseelie faeries, loyal to their King, surged to protect him, a tide of bristling spears and swords. Mark and Cristina hurtled toward Kieran, Cristina armed with a two-edged longsword, elf-shot flying from Mark's bow. Redcaps crumpled at their feet. Simon, Jace, and Clary had already drawn their swords and leaped into the fray.

Timothy yelled as his sword snapped in half against the blade of Maellartach. With a whimper, he vanished behind Horace, who was screaming wildly for everyone to stop, for the battle to stop, but no one was listening. The noise of the battle was incredible: swords slamming against swords, werewolves howling, screams of agony. The smell of blood and metal. Emma disarmed Jessica and kicked her legs out from under her; Jessica went down with a scream of pain and Emma whirled to find two goblin warriors with their broken-glass teeth and leathery faces approaching. She raised Cortana as one rushed at her. The other went down suddenly, its legs caught in a snare of electrum.

Emma dispatched the first goblin with a blade to the heart and turned to see Isabelle, her golden whip snared around the legs of the second.

The trapped goblin yelled and Simon took care of it with the stroke of a longsword, his expression grim. Julian called out and Emma turned to see a faerie knight rise up behind her; before she could even lift Cortana, he staggered back with one of Julian's throwing knives sunk deep in his throat.

Emma whirled; Julian was behind her, the gleaming Mortal Sword in his hand. There was blood on him, and a bruise on his cheek, but with Maellartach in his hand he looked like an avenging angel.

Emma's heart beat in great, powerful strokes; it was so good to have Cortana in her hand again, so good to fight with Julian by her side. She could *feel* the *parabatai* warrior magic working between them, could see it like a shimmering cord that tied them together, moving when they moved, binding but never ensnaring them.

He gestured to her to follow him, and together they plunged into the heart of the battle.

The Projection in the sky burst apart like fireworks, the images tumbling toward the city in shining shards. But Dru had seen enough. They all had.

She swung around to see Maryse behind her, staring at the sky as if blinded by an eclipse. "Poor Julie—did you see—?"

Dru looked at Max and Rafe, who were clinging together, clearly terrified. "You have to get the kids into the house. Please. Take Tavvy."

"No!" Tavvy wailed as Dru pushed him toward Maryse and the red front door of the Graymark house. "No, 'Silla, I want to go with you! *NO!*" he shrieked, the word tearing her heart as she let go of him and backed away.

Maryse was staring at her, still looking stunned. "Drusilla—stay in the house—"

Behind Maryse the streets were full of people. They'd caught up weapons, dressed themselves in gear. A battle had begun, and Alicante would not wait.

"I'm sorry," Dru whispered. "I can't."

She took off running, hearing Tavvy screaming for her long after she was likely out of earshot. She wove in and out of crowds of Shadowhunters in gear, bows and swords slung over their shoulders, their skin gleaming with fresh runes. It was the Dark War all over again, when they had flown hectically through the cobblestoned streets, chaos all around them. She caught her breath as she cut through Cistern Square, darted through a narrow alley, and came out in Hausos Square, opposite the Western Gate.

The great doors of the gate were closed. Dru had expected that. Lines of Cohort warriors blocked the crowds of Shadowhunters—many of whom Dru recognized from the war council meeting—from accessing them. The square was quickly filling with Nephilim, their angry voices raised.

"You cannot hold us in here!" shouted Kadir Safar, from the New York Conclave.

Lazlo Balogh scowled at him. "The Inquisitor has decreed that no Shadowhunters leave the city!" he called back. "For your own protection!"

Someone grabbed at Dru's sleeve. She jumped a foot and nearly screamed; it was Tavvy, grubby and disheveled. "The Silent Brothers—why don't they do something?" he demanded, distress printed all over his small face.

The Silent Brothers were still standing at the watch points they'd been assigned, motionless as statues. Dru had passed many of them the night before, though none had tried to stop her or asked her business. She couldn't think about the Silent Brothers now, though. She seized Tavvy and almost shook him.

"What are you doing here? It's dangerous, Tavvy!"

He stuck out his jaw. "I want to be with you! I won't be left behind anymore!"

The crowd burst into a fresh spate of shouting. The Cohort guarding the gate was starting to look rattled, but none of them had moved.

There was no time to send Tavvy back. This could turn into a bloodbath at any moment, and even more than that, Dru's family and friends were on the Imperishable Fields. They needed help.

She grabbed Tavvy's hand. "Then keep up," she snapped, and they started to run, shoving and pushing their way through the crowd to the other side of the square. They ran down Princewater

Canal and over the bridge, reaching Flintlock Street in a matter of minutes. It was deserted—some houses had been abandoned so quickly that their doors still swung open.

Halfway down the street was the shop with its small sign. DIANA'S ARROW. Dru flew to the door and rapped on it hard—three fast knocks, then three slow. *Open up*, she prayed. *Open, open, open*—

The door flew wide. Jaime Rocio Rosales stood on the other side, dressed in black battle gear. He carried a gleaming silver crossbow, pointed directly at her.

"It's *me*," Dru said indignantly. "You know—the one who got you out of jail?"

"You can never be too careful, princess," he said with a wink, and lowered the bow, calling over his shoulder for Diego and the others. They began to pour out into the street, all in gear, bristling with brand-new weapons: longswords and rapiers, crossbows and maces, axes and bolas. "Who taught you how to pick locks like that, anyway? I never got a chance to ask you last night."

Kit Herondale, Dru thought. The thought of Kit reminded her of something else, too. Tavvy was staring round-eyed at all the gleaming weaponry: Diego was sporting an ax, Divya a two-handed *bidenhänder*, Rayan a Spanish *bola*. Even Jia was decked out with her favorite sword, a curved *dao*. "Okay, everyone," Dru said. "These weapons are Diana's, and after today, they have to be returned to the store."

"No worries," said Jaime. "I have written out a receipt."

"He has not written out a receipt," said Diego.

"I considered it," said Jaime.

"Sometimes it is not the thought that counts, little brother," said Diego, and there was a deep warmth in his voice that Dru had never heard before. She sympathized—she knew what it was like to lose a brother and get him back.

"We have to go," Tavvy said. "Everyone at the gates is shouting and the Cohort won't let them out."

Jia stepped forward. "They cannot keep us trapped in the city," she said. "Follow me."

Jia seemed to have a mental map of the city in her head. She cut across several bigger streets, through narrow alleys, and behind houses. In what seemed like minutes they came out into Hausos Square.

"Someone let the prisoners out!" shouted a voice, and then other voices joined in, with many calling Jia's name.

"Move aside!" Rayan shouted. He had set himself on one side of Jia, beside Diego. Divya and Jaime were on the other. Dru hurried behind, still holding Tavvy's hand, along with the others who had escaped the Gard. "Make way for the Consul!"

That cut through the shouting. The crowd fell silent as Jia carved a path among the throng like a battleship cutting through heavy weather. She walked proudly, the dim sun gleaming on her gray-black hair. She reached the center of the locked gate, where Lazlo Balogh stood, a spear upright at his side.

"Open the gate, Lazlo," she said in a quiet voice that nevertheless carried. "These people have a right to join their friends and family in battle."

Lazlo's lip curled. "You are not the leader of the Clave," he said. "You are under investigation. I am acting on the orders of Horace Dearborn, Inquisitor and temporary Consul."

"That investigation is over," Jia said calmly. "Horace Dearborn came to power unlawfully. He has lied and betrayed us. Everyone here heard the words from his own mouth. He unfairly imprisoned me as he has now imprisoned us in our city while lives are at risk on the Fields. Open the gates."

"Open the gates!" shouted a boy with dark hair—Dru saw Divya smile. It was Anush, her cousin.

"Open the gates!" Divya cried, thrusting her sword into the air. "Open the gates in the name of Raziel!"

Jaime whistled, his grin infectious. "*Abre las puertas!*"

The cry rose into the air. More and more Nephilim joined in—Kadir Safar and Vivianne Penhallow, the cry of "Open the gates!" lifting into a chorus. Tavvy and Dru joined in, Dru losing herself for a moment in the shouting, the feeling of being part of something bigger and stronger than herself alone. She climbed onto a bench, pulling Tavvy up beside her, so she could see the whole scene: the obviously uncomfortable Cohort, the shouting Nephilim, the few Shadowhunters who stood quiet and uncertain.

"We will not disobey the true Consul!" shouted Lazlo, his face darkening. "We will die here before you force us to betray the Law!"

The cries faltered; no one had expected that. Tavvy's eyes widened. "What does he mean?"

The crowd had frozen. No Nephilim wanted to be forced to harm another Nephilim, especially after the nightmare of the Dark War. Jia seemed to hesitate.

A Silent Brother stepped forward. Then another, and another, their parchment robes rustling like leaves in the wind. The crowd shrank back to make way for them. Dru couldn't help but stare. The last time she had looked at a group of Silent Brothers, it had been the day of her sister's funeral.

A silent voice echoed across the square. Dru could see by the expressions on the faces of the others in the crowd that everyone could hear it, echoing inside their minds.

I am Brother Shadrach. We have conferred among ourselves as to what the Law instructs us to do. We have concluded that the true Consul is Jia Penhallow. Brother Shadrach paused. He and the others made a soundless tableau, ranged against the members of the Cohort. *Open the gates.*

There was a silence. Balogh's face worked.

"No!" It was Paige Ashdown. There was a high, angry note in her voice—the same sharp and mean tone she'd always used when she called Ty names, when she sneered at Dru's clothes and weight. "You can't tell us what to do—"

Brother Shadrach raised his right hand. So did each of the other Brothers. There was a sound like something enormous tearing in half, and the gates blew open, slamming into the Cohort members as if they had been smacked by a gigantic hand. The air was full of the sound of their yells as they were knocked aside; the gates yawned open, and beyond them, Dru could see the Imperishable Fields, green under a gray sky and overrun with fighting.

"Nephilim!" Jia had drawn her *dao*; she lowered it to point directly ahead at the raging battle. "Nephilim, *go forth*!"

Roaring with the desire to fight, Shadowhunters began to pour out of the open gates of the city. Most of them stepped over the fallen Cohort as they rolled on the ground, groaning in pain. Only Cameron Ashdown, visible thanks to his red hair, paused to help his sister Paige to her feet.

Diego and the others began to move toward the gates. Dru saw Jaime reach over and tap his brother on the shoulder; Diego nodded, and Jaime peeled off from the group and ran toward Dru. She stood frozen in surprise on her bench as he flew through the crowd toward her. He was graceful as a thrown knife, his smile as bright as the edge of its flashing blade.

He reached her; with her standing on the bench, they were the same height. "We could not have done this without you," he said. "You are the one who set us free." He kissed her on the forehead, his lips light and quick. "On the battlefield, I will think of you."

And he was gone, running toward his brother as Dru wished she were running toward hers.

She had dreamed that she might fight too, alongside the others. But she could not leave Tavvy. She sat down on the bench and pulled him into her lap, holding him as they watched Diego and Jaime, Rayan and Divya, even Cameron Ashdown, vanishing into the crowd surging through the gates onto the Fields.

31
A Redder Glow

"I can't believe Magnus did this to us," said Ty. He and Kit were sitting in the hollow below the oak tree, near the half-destroyed campsite. Kit was chilled from sitting on the ground for so long, but it wasn't as if he could go anywhere. Before heading out to the battlefield with the others, Magnus had fastened both Ty and Kit to the roots of the oak tree with flickering chains of light.

"Sorry, guys," he'd said, blue sparks dancing from his fingers. "But I promised Julian you'd stay safe, and the best way to make sure that happens is to make sure you stay right here."

"If he hadn't, you'd be following Julian and the others to the Imperishable Fields," said Kit. "You can see his reasoning." He kicked at the chain around his ankle. It was made of glimmer—there was no real substance to it, just shining loops of light, but it held him in place as tightly as if it had been made of *adamas*. When he touched the light itself, he got a faint shock, like the shock of static electricity.

"Stop fighting it," said Ty. "We haven't been able to break out yet; we're not going to be able to now. We'll have to find another solution."

"Or we could just accept that we have to wait for them to get back," said Kit, sinking back against the roots. He suddenly felt very tired—not physically, but deep down.

"I don't accept that," said Ty, poking at the glimmering chain around his ankle with a stick.

"Maybe you should learn to accept things that can't be changed."

Ty looked up, his gray eyes flashing in his thin face. "I know what you're really talking about," he said. "You *are* mad at me."

"Yeah," Kit said. "I'm mad at you."

Ty threw the stick aside; Kit jumped. "You knew I was going to raise Livvy," he said. "You knew it all along and you told me it was fine. You went along with it until the very last minute and then you told me not to do it. I thought you cared, but you lied to me. Just like everyone else."

Kit gasped with the unfairness of it. *I thought you cared?* He'd told Ty how much he cared and Ty had treated it like nothing. The humiliation of the night before flooded back over him in a hot wave, sparking a bitter rage. "You only care about what's best for you," he said between his teeth. "You raised Livvy for you, not for her or anyone else. You knew the damage it might do. You only thought of yourself. I wish— I wish I'd never known you—"

Ty's eyes filled with sudden tears. Shocked, Kit fell silent. Ty was Ty; he didn't weep easily, but he was wiping tears from his face with shaking hands. Kit's rage vanished; he wanted to crawl across the hollow toward Ty, who was shaking his head, saying something under his breath in a low voice—

"I'm here."

Ty's expression changed completely. There were still tears on his cheeks, but his lips had parted in amazement. In wonder.

She knelt at the edge of the hollow, half-transparent. The wind didn't lift the edges of her brown hair, nor did she shiver in her long white dress. The dress he had wondered about the night before, thinking she would never have chosen it.

Only now did Kit realize that she hadn't: The dress was what she had been burned in, a Shadowhunter funeral dress.

"Livvy," Ty said. He tried to stand, but the cord of light around his ankle jerked him back down. He tumbled onto some moss.

The ghost of Livvy Blackthorn smiled. She came down into the hollow—not climbing or falling, but drifting, like a feather on the wind.

"What are you doing?" asked Ty as she knelt down beside him.

"I shouldn't have been so angry with you last night," said Livvy. "You meant well."

"You came to *apologize*?" said Kit.

Livvy turned to look at him. The gold locket gleamed at her throat. It was strange to see two of it—the one Ty wore, real and shining, and the one that flickered on Livvy's neck. A whisper of her memories? Death's way of projecting an image of what people expected Livvy to look like?

"I forgot," Livvy said. "You can see ghosts, Herondale."

She sounded like Livvy. But not like Livvy. There was a cool distance in her tone, and real Livvy would have called him *Kit*.

Still, she bent to touch Ty's ankle gently, and at her touch, Magnus's chain of light flickered and vanished. Ty struggled to his knees. "Why did you do that? Because you're sorry?"

"No," said Livvy. "Ghosts don't really do things because they're sorry." She touched Ty's cheek, or at least she tried—her fingers passed through the outline of his body. Ty shivered but kept his gaze locked on her. "Julian and Mark and Helen and Emma are at the Imperishable Fields," said Livvy, her eyes unfocused, as if she were seeing what was happening elsewhere. "You must go to help them. You must fight in the battle. They need you on their side."

As if it were an afterthought, she turned and touched Kit's chain. It vanished—and so did Livvy. She bent her head and was gone, not even a wisp of mist to show she had ever been there.

Devastation passed across Ty's face and Kit felt a stab of pity. What would it be like for him, even if Livvy came and went as a ghost? She would never stay long, and there was no way to be sure that if she did go, she would return. It would be like losing her again and again and again.

Ty got to his feet. Kit knew he would say nothing about Livvy. "You don't have to come to the battle," Ty said. "You can stay here."

He began to scramble out of the hollow. Wordlessly, Kit followed.

Cristina knew her Shadowhunter history better than most. As she raced across the green grass, she thought of the past: that here on the Imperishable Fields was where Jonathan Shadowhunter had battled a legion of demons. As she ran, slashing out with her sword, she followed in his footsteps.

Mark was at her side. He was armed with a bow, lighter and smaller than Alec's, but capable of shooting with speed and precision. The Unseelie army surged toward them as they pushed their way toward Kieran, and Mark's hand went to his bow over and over, felling trolls and ogres with elf-bolts to the throat and chest. Cristina swung at the smaller, faster redcaps, hacking and slashing, noting with a distant horror that their own blood vanished against their already bloodstained uniforms.

A roar went up from behind them. "What's that?" Mark demanded, wiping blood and sweat from his eyes.

"Reinforcements coming to join Horace and the others," Cristina said grimly. "They were on guard around the city."

Mark swore under his breath. "We have to get to Kieran."

Cristina imagined Mark was having the same panic she was—there was only one of Kieran, and a mass of redcaps and Unseelie foot soldiers, from kelpies to goblins, who had sworn loyalty to Oban. In whatever direction she glanced, she saw Unseelie folk locked in battle with Downworlders and Shadowhunters: Simon and Isabelle were holding off imps with sword and whip, Alec felling ogres one after another with his bow, Maia and Bat tearing at trolls with claws and teeth. In the distance, she saw Emma and Julian fighting back-to-back, and Jace, locked in a fight with Timothy Rockford—but why was Jace using the *flat* of his blade . . . ?

"There he is," Mark said. They had crested a hill; down the slope was Kieran. He carried the sword Nene had given him and was facing off against a broad-shouldered redcap in massive iron boots. Mark swore. "They call him General Winter because he can wipe out a whole village faster than a deadly frost."

"I remember him." Cristina shivered—she recalled the fierce fighting of the redcaps in the throne room of the Unseelie Court. "But—he'll kill Kieran. I've read about redcaps. Mark, this is bad."

Mark didn't disagree. He was gazing at Kieran with worried eyes. "Come on."

They made their way down the slope, running past a number of Unseelie soldiers who were racing for the thick of the battle. Oban was still surrounded by a circle of goblins, protecting him: A few redcaps had formed a loose group around Winter and Kieran. They seemed to have congregated to enjoy the fight.

The redcaps cheered as Winter lunged with his swordstaff, landing a glancing blow against Kieran's shoulder. Kieran's white shirt was already striped with blood. His hair was white, the color of snow or ash, his cheekbones blazing with color. He parried the next blow of the swordstaff and lunged for Winter's torso; the redcap general barely slid aside in time to avoid the thrust.

Winter laughed. "What a pity! You fight like a King," he said. "In a hundred years you might have been good enough to face me."

"*Bastard*," Mark hissed. "Cristina—"

She was already shaking her head. "If we go for Winter now, the other guards will fall on us," she said. "Quick—signal Gwyn. He'll attack Oban. It might give us a chance."

Mark's eyes flashed with realization. He cupped a hand around his mouth and whistled, the low, humming, Wild Hunt whistle that seemed to vibrate inside Cristina's bones.

A shadow passed across the sky. It wheeled and returned: Gwyn on the back of Orion. He flew low over the field; Cristina saw Diana turn and reach up her arms. A moment later Gwyn had swung her up beside him on Orion. They soared back up into the air, Diana and the leader of the Wild Hunt.

Together, they flew low over the goblins surrounding Oban. Diana, her dark hair flying behind her, bent low from the horse's back, swinging her sword down, slicing across the chest of a goblin guard. The others yelled and began to scatter as Diana harried them from the sky, Gwyn grinning beneath his helmet.

But Kieran was still in desperate trouble. He was barely holding off Winter, whose swordstaff rang again and again against his blade. As Cristina watched in horror, one of Winter's blows knocked Kieran to the ground; he rolled aside and sprang to his feet, barely missing a second, deadly strike.

Mark and Cristina took off running toward him, but a redcap guard who had been watching the fight swung around to block their path. At this close range, Mark's bow was of less use; he drew a shortsword from his belt and flung himself at the guard, hacking fiercely at the redcap as he tried to reach Kieran. Another guard rose up in front of Cristina; she dispatched him with a slashing blow, rolling under the stabbing path of another spear. A metal boot crashed into her side and she cried out, feeling her ribs break. Agonizing pain seared through her as she crumpled to the ground.

Meanwhile, Oban's goblin guard had had enough. Dropping their weapons in their haste to escape, they fled away from Oban into the thick of the battle, Diana and Gwyn following. Oban, abruptly alone in the field, looked around in furious panic before seizing up a goblin's sword. "Come back, you bastards!" he shouted. "Come back here! I order you!"

Gasping in agony, Cristina tried to push herself to her feet. The sear of broken bones made her jackknife against the ground; she saw two redcaps above her and thought: *This is the end.*

They fell, one on either side of her, both dead. A blood-covered Mark leaned over her, his face white. "Cristina! *Cristina!*"

Cristina caught at Mark, gasping in pain. "*Iratze.*"

Mark fumbled for his stele as Winter shouted aloud. "King Oban!"

Cristina turned her head to the side. Winter stood over Kieran, who was crumpled on the ground, his sword lying shattered at his side. Cristina's heart sank even as Mark drew a swift *iratze* on her skin.

She barely noticed the pain depart. *Oh, Kieran.*

"General Winter!" Oban cried, waving his hands at the redcap standing over Kieran as if he were swatting at a fly. Stained lace flew from his sleeves and his velvet breeches were crushed beyond repair. "I command you to kill the traitor!"

Winter shook his head slowly. He was a massive figure, his shoulders almost splitting the seams of his blood-dyed uniform. "You must do this, sire," he said. "It is the only way to render your claim on the throne a true one."

With a petulant frown, Oban, sword at his side, stalked forward, crossing the swatch of grass between himself and Kieran. Mark looked down at Cristina. She nodded, *yes*, and he thrust out a hand, raising her to her feet.

They looked at each other once. Then Mark broke to the right, darting toward Winter and Kieran.

Cristina strode to the left and stepped directly in front of Oban. "You will not touch Kieran," she said. "You will not take another step."

She heard Winter cry out in surprise. Mark had thrown himself on the redcap general's back. Winter flung him off, but not before Kieran had staggered to his feet.

Oban looked at Cristina with exasperation. "Do you know who I am, Shadowhunter girl?" he demanded. "Do you dare to cross the path of the Unseelie King? You are no one and nothing important."

Cristina raised her sword between herself and Oban. "I am Cristina Mendoza Rosales, and if you hurt or kill Kieran, then you will have to deal with me." She saw the flicker in Oban's silvery eyes and wondered why she had thought he looked like Kieran. They were nothing alike. "You are not such stuff as Kings are made of," she said in a low voice. "Run, now. Leave this behind you and live."

Oban glanced at Winter, who was battling both Mark and Kieran; they were pressing him back, and back. Dead redcaps lay scattered around the field; the grass was slippery with blood. In the distance, Gwyn and Diana circled on Orion.

In Oban's eyes Cristina saw his horror, not at the death around him but at the vision of all of it slipping away—kingship, riches, power.

"No!" he cried, and lunged at her with his sword.

Cristina met Oban's blow with her own, swinging her sword in a savage arc. Surprise flickered in his eyes as their blades rang together. He fell back in surprise, but recovered quickly. He was a drunk and a wastrel, but still a prince of Faerie. When he lunged again, teeth bared, his sword clanged against hers hard enough to ring down through her bones. She stumbled, caught herself, and slashed at him again—and again. He met her blows, his own sword swift and furious. The tip of it nicked her shoulder and she felt the blood begin to flow.

Cristina began to pray.

Blessed be the Angel, my strength, who teaches my hands for war, and my fingers to fight.

All her life she had wanted to do something to ease the pain of the Cold Peace. Here was her chance. Raziel had brought it to her. She would do this for Emma, for the Blackthorns, for Diego and Jaime, for Mark and Kieran, for all the Rosaleses. For everyone harmed by the peace that was truly a war.

A calm stillness filled her heart. She raised her blade as if it were Glorious, as if it were a shining blade of heaven. She saw fear in Oban's eyes, even as he moved to strike out at her again, bringing his sword around in a sideways arc. She spun in a full circle, avoiding his blow, and as she turned she drove her blade between his ribs.

A sigh seemed to pass through the world. She felt the metal of her sword grind against bone, felt hot blood splash over her fist. She jerked the sword back; Oban staggered, gazing down in disbelief at the blood spreading across the front of his doublet.

"*You*," he breathed, still in disbelief. "Who are you?"

No one important.

But there was no point speaking. Oban had slumped to the ground, his hands falling loose at his sides, his eyes filming over. He was dead.

Mark and Kieran were battling desperately and heedlessly on. Cristina knew they were fighting not for their own lives but for each other.

"Prince Oban is dead!" she shouted. "Oban is *dead*!"

She stepped forward on the blood-wet grass, calling to Winter, to Mark and Kieran, to everyone who could hear.

It was General Winter who heard her cry. He stood, as tall and forbidding as a wall between Cristina and the boys she loved. His red-capped head turned. His red eyes took in Cristina, and then what lay behind her, a heap of blood and velvet.

His knuckles where he held his sword went white. For a moment Cristina pictured him taking his revenge for his King on Kieran and Mark. Her breath caught in her throat.

Ponderous and terrifying as an avalanche, Winter sank slowly to his knees. He bowed his blood-darkened head. His voice boomed like thunder as he said, "My liege lord, King Kieran."

Kieran and Mark stood side by side, blades still held high, breathing in hard jolting unison. Cristina walked across the blood-drenched earth to stand so she and Mark were flanking Kieran.

Kieran's face was deadly pale. There was a forlorn, lost look about him, but his eyes searched Cristina's face as if he might find himself there. She clasped his hand. Kieran's eyes traveled from Cristina to Mark, and his chin lifted. He stood with his back straight as a blade. Cristina watched him set his slender shoulders as if preparing to bear a heavy burden.

She swore an oath silently to herself: She and Mark would help him bear it.

"Prince Oban is dead," Mark said. His voice lifted to the skies, to Diana and Gwyn circling high above their heads. "Kieran Kingson is the new King of Unseelie! Long live the King!"

They had made it to the edge of the forest, half-running the whole way, tripping over tree roots in their haste to get to the Imperishable Fields. There was no defined border between the Fields and the forest: The trees thinned out and Ty stopped dead, his breath catching. Kit stopped beside him, staring.

It looked like a movie. He couldn't help the thought, though he felt vaguely ashamed of it—like a movie with incredible effects and attention to every detailed piece. He had thought of battles as organized, two lines of soldiers advancing on each other. Instead, this was chaos—less a chess game than a collapsed Jenga tower. Soldiers fought in clumps, rolled into ditches, spread in haphazard patterns across the Fields. The air stank of blood and roiled with noise—the clang of metal on metal, soldiers shouting, the howl of wolves, the screams of the wounded.

The noise. Kit turned to Ty, who had gone pale. "I can't—I didn't bring my headphones," Ty said.

Kit hadn't remembered them either, but then he hadn't really expected to be in the fight. He hadn't even imagined there would *be* a fight on this scale. It was massive. The gates of the city of Alicante were open, and more Shadowhunters were pouring out, adding to the noise and chaos.

Ty couldn't do this. He wouldn't survive being at the center of that with nothing to protect his ears, his eyes.

"Do you see Julian?" Kit asked. Maybe if Julian was nearby, if they could just get to him—

Ty's expression cleared slightly. "Hold on." He checked the inside of his jacket, where he'd stashed several knives and a slingshot. He had a pocketful of stones as well; Kit had seen them earlier.

Ty jogged to the nearest tree—a big, spread-branched oak—and began to shinny up it.

"Wait!" Kit ran to the base of the trunk and looked up. Ty was already vanishing among the leaves. "What are you *doing*?"

"I might be able to see the others from a higher vantage," Ty called down. A branch rattled. "There they are—I see Alec. And Jace; he's fighting some of the Cohort. Mark and Cristina are over by the redcaps. There's Helen—a troll is coming up on her from behind—" There was a whistling rattle and a rustle of leaves. "Not anymore," Ty added in a pleased voice, and Kit realized he must have used his slingshot. "Kit, come up here—you can see everything."

There was no answer.

Ty leaned down through the branches, searching the forest floor below the oak. It was bare. Kit was gone.

Alec had found himself a rock, one of the few on the Fields. This was a good thing, because he was at his best from a slight elevation—as Jace jogged toward him, weaving through Unseelie soldiers and friendly Downworlders alike, he watched with brotherly admiration as Alec let arrow after arrow fly with deadly speed and more deadly precision.

"Alec." Jace reached Alec. A troll was running toward them, its tusks stained with blood, its ax raised. Its eyes gleamed with hate. Jace tugged a knife from his belt and flung it and the troll went down, gurgling, the blade in its throat.

"What is it?" Alec didn't glance at him. He nocked his bow again, drew, and impaled a glass-toothed goblin that had been running toward Simon. Simon gave him an offhand salute and went back to fighting a mossy thing Jace suspected was a dryad gone wrong.

"The gates of the city are open—"

"I noticed." Alec shot the dryad. It ran off toward the trees.

"More Cohort members are coming onto the field."

"So are more of our allies. Jia's here," said Alec.

"True." An ogre came at Jace from the left. He cut it down with quick efficiency. "Where's Magnus?"

Alec watched Simon with narrow eyes; he'd joined Clary in cutting down a redcap. The redcaps were the deadliest faerie soldiers on the field, but Jace was pleased to see Clary handle hers with aplomb. She slashed at its knees, and when it fell, Simon lopped off its head. Good solid *parabatai* work.

"Why do you want to know where Magnus is?" Alec said.

"Because these Cohort members are all *Shadowhunters*," Jace said frankly. "I've been trying not to kill them. I've been using the flat of my blade, whacking them on the heads when they go down, or letting Clary use her knockout runes, but it's a lot harder not killing people than killing them." He sighed and threw a knife at an attacking pixie. "We could use Magnus's help."

"You know," Alec said, "vampires are really good at taking people down without killing them. Just grab a person, drink enough blood to make them pass out, and voilà."

"Not helpful," Jace said. Another troll rushed at them. Jace and Alec reached for their weapons at the same time. The troll eyed them, turned, and ran off.

Alec laughed. "You're in luck, *parabatai*," he said, and pointed toward the edge of Brocelind Forest.

Jace followed his gesture. The edge of the trees was deeply shaded, but Clary had put Farsight runes on him earlier. He could even see a small figure perched halfway up an oak tree, using a slingshot to take down Unseelie soldiers. Interesting. He also saw Magnus, who had just stepped out of the shadows beneath the trees.

He was in full warlock regalia—a cloak of black sewn with silver stars, silver chains at his throat and wrists, hair spiked to maximum height. Blue fire spread from his hands. It flowed up into the air, and the already thick clouds began to draw together.

Clary jogged over to them, picking her way among dead trolls and ogres. She was beaming. "I thought he was worried he couldn't do it!" she exclaimed. "He looks so cool."

"Just watch," Alec said, winking at her. "And he does look cool." He shot an approaching troll, just in case anyone was worried he was slacking off.

Jace hadn't been. The field was starting to roil in chaos, werewolves and warlocks, faeries and Shadowhunters, turning to look at Magnus as blue-black magic unfurled from his hands, spreading into the sky.

The sky itself began to darken. It was as if a sheet were being drawn across it: Light filtered down, but not all light—a dim bluish light like the illumination of stars or moonshine. Gwyn and Diana circled against the darkening sky.

Magnus began to sway. Jace sensed Alec tensing up. This was immense magic—the kind that could drain a warlock's power.

Another figure stepped from the woods. A man with green skin and curling horns, hair as white as Catarina's. He wore jeans and a black T-shirt with white lettering.

He placed his hand on Magnus's shoulder.

"Is that Ragnor Fell in a 'Ragnor Lives' T-shirt?" said Clary in amazement. Ragnor was one of Magnus's oldest friends and had spent several years pretending to be dead and then several more pretending to be a warlock called Shade. Jace and Clary had good cause to know him well.

"I wouldn't wear a 'Simon Lives' T-shirt to a battle," said Simon, who was standing within earshot. "Seems like asking for trouble."

Alec laughed. "I think he'll be okay," he said as Ragnor held fast to Magnus and Magnus raised his hands, releasing more blue-black light. "He's just giving Magnus some of his strength."

The sky had turned dark as sunset, without the gleam of the setting sun. Magnus lowered his hands as from the woods behind him, protected by the new darkness, exploded the vampires—Lily in the lead, racing across the field to join the battle.

"I know what you said," said Jace, watching as the vampires closed the gap between themselves and the Cohort, "but did the vampires get the memo about not killing Shadowhunters?"

Alec grinned.

"By the Angel!" Aline swore, her mouth dropping open.

Helen whipped around, raising her sword. Fighting alongside the people you loved was always terrifying. You weren't just battling to protect yourself; you were fighting for them as well. She would have battled a Greater Demon bare-handed to save Aline.

Aline caught at Helen's sword arm. "My mom!" She was almost incoherent. "They're coming out of the city—and my mom is with them!"

The gates of Alicante had been thrown wide and Shadowhunters were pouring through. At the head of the cavalcade she could see

Jia, dressed in battle gear with a massive curved *dao* in her hand and Centurions—Diego, Rayan, Divya, and others—on either side of her. *Scariest mother-in-law ever*, Helen thought.

Helen and Aline raced toward the new arrivals. As they got closer, Aline broke free and ran to throw her arms around her mother. Jia lowered her sword and hugged her daughter fiercely with her free arm, their dark heads bent together.

"Where's Dad?" Aline said, drawing back to study her mother's face.

"Still in the city. He's coordinating with Carmen Rosales Delgado and the Silent Brothers to make sure that people inside stay safe."

"But how did you get out of the Gard?" Aline asked.

Jia almost smiled. "Drusilla let us out last night. She's a very enterprising child! Speaking of Blackthorns, Helen, come here."

A little hesitant, Helen approached Jia. She'd always thought her mother-in-law was impressive, but she'd never been more intimidating than in this moment.

Jia put an arm around her and hugged her so tightly Helen remembered her own mother Eleanor and the strength of her embrace. "My darling, you've done such a wonderful job at the Institute," Jia said. "I am so proud."

Divya sniffled. "That is *so* sweet."

Jia ended the hug, all business again. "All right, everyone, enough gawking. We are entering a battle, one where we will be fighting other Shadowhunters. Ones we would prefer not to kill. We need to make a Malachi Configuration."

Helen dimly remembered what a Malachi Configuration was—a temporary magical prison created by *adamas* and runes. It was sometimes used by the Inquisitor or the Silent Brothers when they had no other way to hold a prisoner.

Diego responded first. "On it!" He grabbed a seraph blade and crossed over into the edge of the Fields before kneeling to stab it into the earth. "I'll take north; Divya, you go south; Rayan, go east. We need to mark the four cardinal directions."

"Bossy, bossy," said Divya, but she was smiling. Aline moved to help as well, going to the western point. The rest of the newcomers were drawing weapons. Jaime had his crossbow out and was clearly itching to jump into the fight.

Jia said, "Remember what Drusilla said about the Watch's plan. Try not to kill Cohort members if you have a choice. Herd them back here toward the configuration. They're still Shadowhunters, even if they are misguided."

With whoops and cries the Shadowhunters raced onto the field and plunged into the battle just as a sweet chiming noise sounded and the Malachi Configuration flared up.

Light poured from the four angel blades, forming a cage whose walls were made of shifting light. It looked delicate as butterfly wings, prismatic as glass. Helen gazed at the configuration and hoped that their plan to spare the lives of the Cohort would not be in vain. The luminous walls of the prison looked too fragile to hold so much hate.

"Let me go!" Kit yelled. He knew it wouldn't do much good. Emma had him firmly by the back of the shirt and was marching him along the edge of the forest, keeping to the shadows. She looked absolutely furious.

"What are you doing here?" she demanded. She held her golden sword in her free hand, her gaze darting around in mingled anger and watchfulness. "When I saw you I almost had a heart attack! You're supposed to be at camp!"

"What about Ty?" Kit said, twisting against Emma's iron grip. "He's back there! He's *up a tree.* We can't just leave him alone."

Something whistled over their heads, and an approaching ogre went down in a heap, a neat circle punched into the middle of its forehead.

"He seems to be doing fine," Emma said dryly. "Besides, I promised Tessa I wouldn't let you near battles *or* faeries and this is a battle full of faeries. She's going to *kill* me."

Kit was stung. "Why no battles or faeries? I'm not that bad of a fighter!"

Emma swung him around so he faced her, thankfully letting go of the back of his shirt as she did so. "It's not about that!" she said angrily. Her gear was dirty and bloodstained, her face scratched and cut. Kit wondered where Julian was—*parabatai* usually fought in battle together, didn't they?

"I don't see what's so important about me," Kit said.

"You're more important than you think," Emma said. Her eyes went suddenly wide. "Oh *no*."

"What?" Kit looked around wildly. At first he saw nothing unusual—or at least, nothing unusual for a huge ongoing brawl between faeries and Shadowhunters.

Then a shadow fell over them, and he realized.

The last time he had seen the Riders of Mannan had been in London. There were six of them now, gleaming in bronze and gold; their horses were shod with gold and silver, their eyes inky black. The Riders wore armor without joints or rivets to hold it together—a smooth, liquidy bronze that covered them from neck to foot like the gleaming carapaces of insects.

"Get behind me, Kit." Emma had gone pale. She stepped in front of Kit, lifting Cortana. "Stay down. They're probably coming for me, not you."

The Riders hurtled toward them, like a shower of falling stars. They were beautiful and awful. Kit had taken only the Herondale dagger Jace had given him. He realized now how unprepared he had been. How foolish.

One of the Riders jerked and yelled, clasping at his arm. Ty's slingshot, Kit realized, and felt a rush of reluctant warmth and a sudden stab of fear—what if he never saw Ty again?

The struck Rider spat a curse; they were almost overhead, and Kit saw their faces—their bronze hair, their sharp cold features.

"Six of you against one?" Emma shouted, the wind whipping her hair. "Are you that dishonorable? Come down one by one and fight me! I dare you!"

"It seems you cannot count, little Shadowhunting murderer," said Ethna, the only woman among the Riders. "There are two of you."

"Kit is a child," said Emma, which annoyed Kit even as he realized she was probably right to say it. Kieran's voice was in his head: *The children of Mannan have never been defeated.*

Across the field, Julian was running toward them. Helen ran alongside him, and Aline. But they would never reach Emma and Kit in time.

"Kit is *the* child," said Etarlam with a smirk. "The descendant of the First Heir."

"Give him to us," said Karn. "Give him to us and we might spare you."

Kit's throat had gone dry. "That's not right," he said. "I have no faerie blood. I'm a Shadowhunter."

"One can be both," said Ethna. "We guessed it when we saw you in that dirty city."

She meant London, Kit thought dizzily. He remembered Eochaid looking at him, saying: *I know you. I know your face.*

"You look just like her," said Eochaid now with a smirk. "Just like Auraline. And just like your mother."

"We slew her," said Ethna. "And now we will slay you, too, and wipe out any trace of your tainted bloodline from this world and ours."

"What?" Kit forgot his fear, forgot Emma's exhortation that he stay behind her. Forgot that anyone was coming to help them.

Forgot everything except Ethna's words. "You killed my mother? *My* mother?"

"What did you think happened to her, child?" Ethna said. "Yes, we spilled her blood at the King's orders. She died screaming for you, though even when we tortured her, she never spoke your name or revealed your whereabouts. Perhaps that will be a comfort for you, in these last moments!" She burst out laughing, and in a moment, the Riders were all laughing, their horses rearing back against the sky.

Cold fire spread through Kit's veins; he moved toward the Riders, as if he could reach up and pull them from the sky.

He felt the Talent rune Ty had given him begin to burn on his upper arm.

Emma swore, trying to grab at Kit and draw him behind her. "You can't," she was saying. "You can't, they're unbeatable, *Kit*—"

The Riders drew their swords. Metal flashed in the sky. They blocked out the sun as they hurtled down toward Emma and Kit. Emma raised her sword as Ethna, blaze-eyed astride her stallion, smashed into her, blade against blade. Emma was lifted off her feet and hurled backward. She hit the turf with an impact Kit could hear. She scrambled to her feet as Ethna wheeled her steed around, laughing, and started to race to Kit, but the others were coming—they were driving their horses toward Kit with such force that the grass below them flattened—he raised his hands as if he could ward them off with a gesture, and heard Eochaid laugh—

Something inside him cracked apart, flooding his body with power. It surged through him, electric, exploding from the palms of his hands with enough force to press him to his knees.

Emma looked at him incredulously as white light shot from his hands and surrounded the Riders like a net. Kit could hear them screaming in horror and surprise; they urged their horses higher, into the sky—

He closed his hands into fists, and the horses vanished. Winked out of existence between one breath and the next. The Riders, who had already plunged high into the sky to get away, fell screaming through the air to the ground; they crashed down among the surge of battle and disappeared from view.

Kit rolled onto his back on the grass. He was gasping for breath. *Dying*, he thought. *I'm dying. And I cannot be who they said I am. It's impossible.*

"Kit!" Emma was crouching over him, pulling the collar of his shirt aside to place an *iratze* there. "Kit, by the Angel, what did you do?"

"I don't—know." He felt like there was no breath in his body. His fingers scrabbled weakly against the dirt. *Help me, Emma. Help me.*

Tell Ty—

"It's all right." There was someone else bending over him, someone with a familiar face and calming voice. "Christopher. Christopher, breathe."

It was Jem. Closing his eyes, Kit let Jem's gentle arms lift him from the ground, and darkness came down like the curtain at the end of a play.

"*Emma!*"

Dazed, Emma stumbled a little as she straightened up. She had been bending over Kit, and then Jem had come—and Kit was gone. She was still dizzy from the shock of the Riders' attack and the strangeness that had followed.

Kit had made the Riders' steeds disappear and they'd fallen into the crowd of battle, wreaking havoc. And now Julian was here, looking at her with worry and concern.

"Emma," Julian said again, putting his hands on her shoulders and turning her to look at him. "Are you all right?"

"Aline and Helen," she said breathlessly. "They were with you—"

"They went back to help the others," he said. "The Riders are causing chaos on the field—"

"I'm sorry," Emma said, "I didn't know that Kit—"

"I'm not sorry," Julian said, and there was a savagery in his tone that made her look up, her head clearing. Julian's face was smudged with blood and dirt. His gear was ripped at the shoulder, his boots thick with churned mud and blood. He was beautiful. "Whatever happened, whatever Kit did, he saved your life. The Riders would have killed you."

She was breathless with fear, not for herself but for Julian. The Riders hated them both. Gwyn and Diana were circling over the Fields, calling out that Oban was dead, that Kieran was King. Perhaps Kieran could order the Riders around—perhaps not. At the moment, they had not sworn allegiance to him. They were masterless, here for blood and vengeance, and very dangerous.

"Do you need an *iratze*?" Julian was still holding her shoulders. She wanted to hug him, wanted to touch his face and make sure he was whole and unharmed. She knew she couldn't.

"No," Emma said. Runes between them were too dangerous. "I'm fine."

Slowly he bent his head and touched his forehead to hers. They stood for a moment, motionless. Emma could feel the *parabatai* energy in them both, vibrating beneath their skin like an electric current. There was no one around them; they were at the very edge of the battle, almost in the woods.

She felt herself smile a little. "Ty's up a tree with a slingshot," she said, almost in a whisper.

Julian drew back, a look of amusement ghosting across his face. "I know. Safest place for him, I guess, though when I find out how he got out of Magnus's enchantment, I'm not sure which of them I'm going to kill." There was a sudden commotion; Emma looked over at the field and saw flashes of bronze. The Riders had regrouped; they were laying about themselves with their blades, cutting a path through the Shadowhunters. Several bodies lay crumpled on the ground: with a pang, she recognized Vivianne Penhallow's strawberry-blond hair, now flecked with blood.

Emma grabbed Cortana. "Julian—where's the Mortal Sword?"

"Gave it to Jace," he said as they both hurried across the trampled grass. "I hated carrying that thing around. He'll enjoy it."

"Probably," Emma admitted. She looked around: The skies overhead roiled blue-black. The bodies of Downworlders and Shadowhunters were scattered across the field; as they pressed on, Emma nearly stepped on a corpse in a Centurion uniform, eyes rolled to the sky. It was Timothy Rockford. She fought down a wave of nausea and turned away. A redcap surged up behind her.

She raised Cortana, the blade slicing the air.

"Emma!" Julian caught at her shoulder. "It's all right," he said as the redcap turned and vanished back into the crowd. "The Unseelie soldiers don't know what to do. Some are still following Oban. Some are retreating at Kieran's orders. It's chaos."

"So it could be ending?" she said, breathless. "We could be winning?"

He drew the back of his hand across his face, smudging more dirt on his cheekbones. His eyes were brilliant blue-green in the odd light of the clouds; his gaze ran up and down her, and she recognized his look as the embrace he couldn't give, the words he couldn't say.

"The Cohort won't give up," he said instead. "They're still fighting. We're trying not to harm them, but they're not making it easy."

"Where's Horace?" Emma demanded, craning her head to see what was happening across the field.

"He's kept himself surrounded by his followers," Julian said. "Jace and the others are trying to get to him, but the Cohort are willing to die for him and we don't want to kill them. Like I said, they're not making it easy."

"We should get back and help." She started to head across the field, Julian beside her. Downworlders flashed past them, hurling themselves at Unseelie faeries and Cohort Nephilim. Jessica Beausejours was struggling to fend off a black-haired vampire with a seraph blade, while nearby a werewolf rolled on the ground with a massive troll, two sets of fangs snapping.

Emma heard someone yell. It was Mark—she could see Cristina, too, not far away, sword to sword with Vanessa Ashdown. Cristina was fighting carefully, trying not to hurt Vanessa; Vanessa was showing no such care—she held a swordstaff in her hand and was pushing Cristina back with slamming blows.

Mark, though—Mark was facing Eochaid. A Rider had found him.

Emma and Julian took off instantly, racing toward Mark. He was backing away, bow in hand, taking careful aim, but each arrow that hit Eochaid seemed only to slow him down, not to stop him.

No one's killed one of Mannan's Riders in all the history I know.

Emma had killed one of the Riders. But Emma had Cortana. Mark had only an ordinary bow, and Cristina and Kieran were both caught up in the vast crowd. They could never make it to Mark in time.

Emma heard Julian whisper his brother's name. *Mark.* They were racing flat-out over the uneven ground—Emma could feel the *parabatai* energy driving them forward—when something reared up and struck her. She went flying, hit the ground, rolled to her feet.

Standing in front of her was Zara.

She was cut and filthy, her long hair matted in clumps of blood and dirt. Her colorful Centurion gear had been cut to ribbons. There were tracks of dirty tears on her face, but her hands, gripping a longsword, were steady. As was her gaze, fixed on Cortana.

"Give me back my sword, you *bitch*," she snarled.

* * *

Arrested by Emma's fall, Julian spun around and saw his *parabatai* facing Zara Dearborn. Zara was whipping her sword back and forth while Emma watched her with a puzzled look: Zara wasn't a very good fighter, but she wasn't *this* bad.

Emma met Julian's eyes as she raised Cortana: *Go, go to Mark*, her expression said. Julian hesitated a moment—but Emma could more than handle Zara. He whirled around and ran for his brother.

Mark was still fighting, though he was pale, bleeding from a cut across his chest. Eochaid seemed to be playing with him, as a cat might play with a mouse, thrusting his sword and then turning it aside to slash rather than stab. It would mean a slow death of cuts and bloodletting. Julian felt the sourness of rage in the back of his throat. He saw Cristina slam the hilt of her sword against Vanessa's head; Cameron's cousin went down hard and Cristina turned, sprinting toward Mark.

Another Rider cut her off. Julian's heart sank; he was nearly there, but he recognized Ethna, with her long bronze braid and vicious scowl. She carried a sword in one hand, a staff in the other, and swung out at Cristina, knocking her hard to the ground.

"Stop!"

The word was a gravel-toned bellow. Cristina and Mark were both on the ground; their opponents turned, staring. Kieran stood before them, his shoulder knotted with white bandages. It was Winter who had spoken: The redcap stood upright, swordstaff in hand. He pointed the sharp end of it at Eochaid.

"Stop," he said again. "The King commands that you stand down."

Eochaid and Ethna exchanged a look. Their metallic eyes simmered with rage. They would not soon forget being cast down from the sky and humiliated.

"We will not," said Eochaid. "Our King was Arawn the Elder.

He commanded us to slay the Blackthorns and their allies. We shall enact that command and no word from you shall change it."

"We have not yet sworn allegiance to you," said Ethna. "You are not our King."

Julian wondered if Kieran would flinch. He didn't. "I am your King," he said. "Leave them be and return to Unseelie or be considered traitors."

"Then we will be traitors," said Ethna, and brought her longsword down.

It never struck its target. The air seemed to ripple, and suddenly Windspear was diving toward Ethna, rearing back: He struck Ethna full in the chest with his front hooves. There was a clang as she was flung backward. A moment later, Cristina was on her feet, her wrist bleeding but her grip on her sword steady.

"Go to Mark!" she shouted, and Kieran leaped onto Windspear's back and plunged toward Eochaid; the Rider was like a fall of sparks, graceful and inevitable. He flew into the air, whipping around with his sword in hand, the blade clashing against Kieran's.

Mark leaped into the air—a spinning, graceful leap—and caught hold of Eochaid, wrapping his arms around the Rider's throat from behind. They tumbled to the ground together; Eochaid leaped to his feet. Julian raced toward Mark, hurling himself between his brother and the Rider, bringing up his sword to parry a slashing blow.

Eochaid laughed. Julian barely had time to help Mark to his feet when something struck him from behind—it was Karn the Rider, a roaring tower of bronze. Julian whirled and hit back with all his force. Karn staggered back, looking surprised.

"Nice hit," Mark said.

It's because of Emma. I can feel the parabatai *bond burning inside me.*

"Thanks," he said, raising his blade to fend off another blow from Karn. Kieran and Cristina were harrying Eochaid; Ethna was battling Winter to his knees. Even the *parabatai* strength wasn't enough,

Julian knew. The Riders were too strong. It was a matter of time.

There was another flash of bronze. Mark muttered a curse: It was Delan, the one-handed Rider, drawn to his siblings. Now there were four of them: only Etarlam and Airmed were still missing, somewhere in the battle.

Delan wore a bronze half mask and swung a golden spiked flail; he was running toward Kieran, the flail swinging—

An ax crashed into him from behind, sending him sprawling. It was Eochaid's turn to swear. Ethna yelled, even as Delan staggered to his feet and spun to face his attacker.

It was Diego Rosales. He winked at Kieran just as the flail swung toward his head; he fended it off with the flat of his ax. Kieran, who had looked both astonished and pleased at Diego's appearance, leaped from Windspear's back and raced toward Delan. Winter darted after him as Cristina swung at Ethna—

There was a shattering crack as Cristina's sword broke. She gasped, leaped backward—Mark and Kieran turned, stricken—Ethna raised her blade—

And was blown off her feet. Lines of golden energy laced across the field, lifting each of the Riders into the air and sending them tumbling across the grass like scattered toys. Julian turned in astonishment to see Hypatia Vex standing nearby with her hands raised, light cascading from her fingertips.

"Magnus sent me over," she said as the battling Nephilim stared at her. Even Winter was staring, looking as if he might have fallen in love. Julian suspected his chances with Hypatia weren't good. "This'll buy us some time, but they'll be back. The Riders of Mannan . . ." She sighed dramatically. "Shadowhunters. Why do I always end up mixed up in their business?"

Zara was fighting like a wild thing. Emma had remembered Zara as a mediocre warrior, and she was, but from the moment their two blades had touched, Zara had been electrified. She swung her blade as if she meant to hack down a tree with it; she flung herself at Emma over and over, sloppily leaving her defenses completely open. As if she didn't care if she lived or if she died.

And perversely, it was making Emma hold back. She knew she had every right and reason to strike Zara down. But Zara seemed wild with what Emma could only identify as grief—she *had* lost friends, Emma knew, dead on the field like Timothy. But Emma suspected her grief was more for the bitterness of losing and the sting of shame. Whatever happened, the Cohort would never regain their glory. The lies they had told would never be forgotten.

Julian had seen to that.

"You couldn't just leave well enough *alone*," Zara hissed, lunging at Emma with her wrist held stiffly. Emma evaded the blow easily without needing to parry. "You had to be the moral busybodies. You had to stick your nose in *everywhere*."

"Zara, you took over the government," Emma pointed out, stepping aside as Zara lunged again. At this rate Zara would tire herself out. "Your father tried to murder us."

"Because you wanted to hurt us," Zara hissed. "Because there's an us and a them, Emma, there always is. There's the ones who want to protect you and the ones who want to hurt you."

"That's not true—"

"Really?" Zara tossed her filthy, bloody hair back. "Would you have been my friend? If I'd asked you?"

Emma thought of the things Zara had said about Downworlders. About Mark. About *half-breeds* and *perverts* and registries and cruelties large and small.

"That's what I thought," Zara sneered. "And you think you're so much better than me, Emma Carstairs. I *laughed* when Livvy died, we all did, just at the looks on your smug, stupid faces—"

Rage flooded through Emma, white-hot. She slashed out with

Cortana, turning the blade at the last second so that the flat hit Zara, knocking her off her feet. She hit the ground on her back, coughing blood, and spat at Emma as she leaned over her, laying the tip of Cortana against her throat.

"Go on," Zara hissed. "Go on, you bitch, do it, *do it*—"

Zara was the reason they were all here, Emma thought, the reason they were all in danger: The Cohort had been the reason they had needed to fight and struggle for their lives, had been the reason Livvy had died there on the dais in the Council Hall. The yearning for vengeance was hot in her veins, burning against her skin, begging for her to thrust the blade forward and cut Zara's throat.

And yet Emma hesitated. An odd voice had come into her head—a memory of Arthur Blackthorn, of all people. *Cortana. Made by Wayland the Smith, the legendary forger of Excalibur and Durendal. Said to choose its bearer. When Ogier raised it to slay the son of Charlemagne on the field, an angel came and broke the sword and said to him, "Mercy is better than revenge."*

She had taken down the pictures in her room because she was done with vengeance. Cristina was right. She needed to be done. In that moment she knew she would never cut the *parabatai* rune, no matter what happened now. She had seen too many *parabatai* on the battlefield today. Perhaps being *parabatai* was a weakness that could trap you. But so was any kind of love, and if love was a weakness, it was a strength, too.

She moved the sword aside. "I won't kill you."

Tears spilled from Zara's eyes and streaked down her dirty face as Emma stepped away from her. A second later Emma heard Julian call her name; he was there, hauling Zara to her feet by one arm, saying something about taking her where the prisoners were. Zara was looking from him to Emma, not trying to struggle; she stayed passive in Julian's grip, but her eyes—she was looking past Julian, and Emma didn't like the look on her face at all.

Zara made a little choking noise, almost a laugh. "Maybe I'm not the one you have to worry about," she said, and pointed with her free hand.

Julian went white as chalk.

In a cleared space on the field, under the blue-black sky, stood Annabel Blackthorn.

It was as if the sight of her formed itself into a fist that punched Emma directly in the guts. She gasped. Annabel wore a blue dress, incongruous on the battlefield. A vial of red fluid glimmered at her throat. Her dark brown hair lifted and blew around her. Her lips curved into a smile.

Something was wrong, Emma thought. Something was very, very wrong, and not just the fact that Annabel couldn't possibly be here. That Annabel was dead.

Something was more wrong than that.

"You didn't really think you could kill me, did you?" Annabel said, and Emma saw that her feet were bare, pale as white stones on the bloody ground. "You know I am made of other stuff. Better stuff than your sister. You cannot make *my* life run out with my blood as I squeal for mercy—"

Julian let go of Zara and ran at her. He tore across the ground and flung himself at Annabel, just as Emma screamed his name, screamed at him that something was wrong, screamed at him to stop. She started toward him, and a blow hit her hard in the back.

The pain came a second later, hot and red. Emma turned in surprise and saw Zara standing with a small knife in her hand. She must have taken it from her belt.

The hilt was red and dripping. She had stabbed Emma in the back.

Emma tried to lift Cortana, but her arm felt as if it wasn't working. Her mind, too, was racing, trying to catch up to her injury. As she tried to call out to Julian, choking on blood, Zara slammed the knife into Emma's chest.

Emma's legs went out from under her. She fell.

32
Heaven Come Down

It was all happening again.

Annabel was in front of him and she was looking at him with a sneering contempt. In her eyes he could see the reflection of himself on the dais in the Council Hall, soaked in Livvy's blood. He saw her in Thule, screaming for Ash. He remembered the swing of his sword, her blood spreading all around her body.

None of it mattered. She would kill Emma if she could. She would kill Mark and Helen; she would cut Ty's throat, and Dru's, and Tavvy's. She was the ghost of every fear he had ever had that his family would be taken from him. She was the nightmare he had wakened and not been able to destroy.

He reached her without slowing and plunged his longsword into her body. It slid in as if there was no resistance—no bones, no muscle. Like a knife through air or paper. It sank to the hilt and he found himself staring into her bloodshot scarlet eyes, barely an inch away.

Her lips drew back from her teeth in a hiss. *But her eyes aren't red. They're Blackthorn blue.*

He jerked back, dragging the sword with him. The hilt was dark with blackish ichor. The stench of demon was everywhere.

Somewhere in the back of his head he could hear Emma calling to him, shouting that something was wrong.

"You're not Annabel," he said. *You're a demon.*

Annabel began to change. Her features seemed to melt, to drip like candle wax. Beneath her pale skin and dark hair Julian could see the outlines of an unformed Eidolon demon—greasy and white, like a bar of dirty soap, pocked all over with gray craters. The glittering vial made of etched glass still dangled around its neck.

"You knew my brother," the demon hissed. *"Sabnock. Of Thule."*

Julian remembered blood. A church in Cornwall. Emma.

He reached for a seraph blade on his belt and named it quickly, *"Sariel."*

The demon was grinning. It lunged at Julian, and he plunged the seraph blade into it.

Nothing happened.

This can't be. Seraph blades slew demons. They always, always worked. The demon yanked the blade from its side as Julian stared in disbelief. It lunged for him, Sariel outstretched. Unprepared for the attack, Julian raised an arm to ward off the blow—

A dark shape slid between them. A kelpie, all razor-sharp, pawing hooves and fanged, glassy teeth. The faerie horse reared into the air between Julian and the Eidolon, and Julian recognized the kelpie: It was the one he had saved from Dane Larkspear.

It slammed a hoof into the Eidolon's chest, and the demon flew backward, the seraph blade skidding from its hand. The kelpie glanced over its shoulder at Julian and winked, then gave chase as the Eidolon got to its feet and began to run.

Julian began to follow. He had gone only a few steps when pain went through him, sudden, searing.

He doubled over. The pain was all through him. His back, his chest. There was no reason for it except—

Emma.

He turned around.

It was all happening again.

Emma was on the ground, somehow, the front of her gear wet with blood. Zara knelt over her—it seemed as if they were struggling. Julian was already running, pushing past the pain, every stride a mile, every breath an hour. All that mattered was getting to Emma.

As he got closer, he saw that Zara was crouched beside Emma, trying to wrest Cortana from her red-streaked hand, but Emma's grip was too fierce. Her throat, her hair, were wet with blood, but her fingers on Cortana's hilt were unyielding.

Zara glanced up and saw Julian. He must have looked like death in human form, because she scrambled to her feet and ran, vanishing into the crowd.

No one else seemed to have noticed what had happened yet. A howl was building in Julian's chest. He skidded to his knees beside Emma and lifted her into his arms.

She was limp in his grasp, heavy the way Livvy had been heavy. The way people felt weighted when they had stopped holding themselves up. He curled Emma in toward him and her head fell against his chest.

The grass all around them was wet. There was so much blood.

It was all happening again.

"Livvy, Livvy, my Livvy," he whispered, cradling her, feverishly stroking her blood-wet hair away from her face. There was so much *blood. He was covered in it in seconds; it had soaked through Livvy's clothes, even her shoes were drenched in it.* "Livia." *His hands shook; he fumbled out his stele, put it to her arm.*

His sword had fallen. His stele was in his hand; the *iratze* was a muscle memory, his body acting even without his mind's ability to comprehend what was happening.

Emma's eyes opened. Julian's heart lurched. Was it working?

Maybe it was working. Livvy had never even looked at him. She'd been dead when he lifted her from the dais.

Emma's gaze fixed on his. Her dark brown eyes held his gaze like a caress. "It's all right," she whispered.

He reached to draw another *iratze*. The first had vanished without a trace. "Help me," he rasped. "Emma, we need to use it. The *parabatai* bond. We can heal you—"

"No," she said. She reached up to touch his cheek. He felt her blood against his skin. She was still warm, still breathing in his arms. "I'd rather die like this than be separated from you forever."

"Please don't leave me, Emma," Julian said. His voice broke. "Please don't leave me in this world without you."

She managed to smile at him. "You were the best part of my life," she said.

Her hand fell slack into her lap, her eyes slipping closed.

Through the crowd now Julian could see people running toward them. They seemed to be moving slowly, as if in a dream. Helen, calling his name; Mark, running desperately; Cristina beside him, crying out to Emma—but none of them would reach him in time, and besides, there was nothing they could do.

He seized Emma's hand and clutched it tightly, so tightly he could feel the small bones grind under his grip. *Emma. Emma, come back. Emma, we can do this. We've melted stone. You saved my life. We can do anything.*

He reached deep into his memories: Emma on the beach, looking back over her shoulder at him, laughing. Emma clinging to the iron bar of the Ferris wheel at Pacific Park. Emma handing him a bunch of limp wildflowers she'd picked on the day of his mother's funeral. His arms around Emma as they rode a motorcycle through Thule. Emma in her pale dress at the Midnight Theater. Emma lying in front of the fire in Malcolm's cottage.

Emma.

Her eyes flew open. They were full of flame, golden and bronze and copper. Her lips moved. "I remember," she said.

Her voice sounded distant, almost inhuman, like the ringing of a bell. Something deep inside Julian went cold with fear and exultation.

"Should I stop?" he said.

"No." Emma had begun to smile. Her eyes were all fire now. "Let us burn."

He put his arms around her, the *parabatai* connection burning between them, shimmering gold and white. The ends of her hair had begun to burn, and the tips of his fingers. There was no heat and no pain. Only the fire. It rose up to consume them in a fiery cascade.

Diego flung Zara into the Malachi Configuration. There were quite a few other Cohort members in there and she staggered, nearly tripping in her effort to avoid bumping into them. Most of them were looking at her with deep dislike. Diego didn't imagine that Horace's daughter would be very popular right now.

She whipped around to glare at him. There was no need for him to slam a prison door—the Configuration held whoever was inside, door or no door—but he wished he could.

"I would regard this an announcement that our engagement is over," he said.

Her face screwed up in rage. Before she could reply, a pillar of white fire rose from the east, hurtling up toward the sky. Screams echoed across the battlefield.

Diego whirled to take off running. A redcap loomed up in front of him, steel-tipped pike a shining arc across the sky. Agonizing pain exploded in his head before he tumbled into darkness.

Mark caught Cristina's wrist and pulled her back just as white flame exploded like a tower from the place where Julian and Emma had been moments before.

She knew she screamed Emma's name. Mark was pulling her back against himself; she could feel him gasping for breath. *Julian*, she thought. *Oh God, no, not Julian.*

And then: *This must be the curse. To burn them alive . . . it's too cruel. . . .*

Mark breathed, "Look."

Shining figures were emerging from the fire. Not Julian and Emma, or at least, not Julian and Emma as they had been.

The flames had risen at least thirty feet in the air, and the figures that emerged from them were at least that tall. It was as if Julian and Emma had been carved from shining light. . . . The details of them were there, their features and expressions, even Cortana at Emma's side, a blade of heavenly fire the size of a tree.

"They're giants," Cristina heard someone say. It was Aline, staring upward, awestruck. Helen had her hand over her mouth.

"Not giants," said Cristina. "Nephilim." *There were giants on the earth in those days, and also afterward, when angels came in to the daughters of men and they bore children to them.* She took a shuddering breath. "They were—the first."

More people were crowding forward, from both sides of the battle. As the flames subsided around Emma and Julian, the sky above roiled and snapped—it was as if the heavenly fire had burned away the darkness Magnus had brought down. The shadowy clouds began to break apart and disintegrate.

Terrified, the vampires began to flee the field, racing toward the forest. They ran past Magnus, who was on his knees, Ragnor beside him, blue sparks ringing his hands as if they were torn electrical wires. Cristina saw Alec running across the field; he reached Magnus just as the warlock slumped back, exhausted, into his arms.

Emma—or what Emma had become, a great, shining creature—took a hesitant step forward. Cristina could hardly breathe. She had never seen an angel, but she imagined this was what it might be like to be near one. They were meant to be beautiful, terrible and awful as Heaven was awful: a light too bright for mortal eyes.

No one could survive this, she thought. Not even Emma.

Julian was alongside Emma; they seemed to be gaining confidence as they moved. They didn't stomp as giants might: They seemed to drift, their gestures trailed by sweeps of light.

Cristina could hear the Cohort screaming as Julian bent down and picked up Horace, like a giant child plucking up a doll. Horace, who had escaped the whole battle by hiding behind his followers, was kicking and struggling, his voice a thin wail. Cristina had only a second to feel almost sorry for him before Julian caught Horace in both hands and snapped his spine in half.

He tossed him aside like a broken plaything. The silence that had gripped the field was broken as people began to scream.

Horace Dearborn's body hit the ground with a sickening thud, only a few feet from Manuel.

This isn't happening. This can't be happening. Manuel, already on the ground, began to scramble backward. The Cohort who were trapped in the Malachi Configuration were screaming. He wished they would shut up. He desperately needed to think.

Religious training from his childhood, ruthlessly quashed before now, stirred inside him. What shone above him was the power of angels—not fluffy white-winged angels, but the blood-dark angels of vengeance who had given their power to make the Shadowhunters.

And it came to pass on a certain night that the angel of the Lord went out, and killed in the camp of the Assyrians one hundred and eighty-five thousand; and when people arose early in the morning, there were the corpses—all dead.

But it made no *sense*. What was happening was impossible. People did not turn into enormous shining giants and stride around battlefields dispatching their enemies. This could not possibly have been a plan that the Blackthorns and their allies had. No mortal human had access to power like that.

The great shining thing that had been Emma Carstairs reached down one of its hands. Manuel shrank against the ground, but she was not looking for him. She seized hold of the crouching Eidolon demon that had been Horace's great trick and clamped her fist around it.

The Eidolon demon cried out, a howl that seemed to come from the abyss between worlds. The touch of Emma's shining hand acted on it like acid. Its skin began to burn and melt; it shrieked and dissolved and slid away between her fingers like thin soup.

And when people arose early in the morning, there were the corpses—all dead.

Terrified, Manuel crawled toward Horace's body, still dripping with blood, and dragged it over himself. Horace had failed to protect anyone while he was alive. Perhaps things would be different now that he was dead.

But how can they possibly live through this?

Mark still held Cristina; neither of them seemed able to move. Aline and Helen were nearby; many other Shadowhunters were still on the field. Mark couldn't tear his eyes away from Julian and Emma.

He was terrified. Not of them. He was terrified for them. They were great and shining and magnificent, and they were blank-eyed as statues. Emma straightened up from destroying the Eidolon, and Mark could see a great fissure running along her arm, where once her scar from Cortana had been. Flames leaped inside it, as if she were full of fire.

Emma raised her head. Her hair flew around her like golden lightning. "RIDERS OF MANNAN!" she called, and her voice wasn't a human voice at all. It was the sound of trumpets, of thunderclaps echoing through empty valleys. "RIDERS OF MANNAN! COME AND FACE US!"

"They can talk," Cristina whispered.

Good. Maybe they can listen to reason.

Maybe.

"Emma!" Mark called. "Julian! We're here! Listen to us, we're here!"

Emma didn't seem to hear him. Julian glanced down, entirely without recognition. Like a mundane gazing at an anthill. Though there was nothing mundane about them.

Mark wondered if this was what raising an angel had been like for Clary, for Simon.

There was a stir in the crowd. The Riders, striding across the field. Their blaze of bronze shone around them, and Mark remembered Kieran whispering to him stories of the Riders who slept beneath a hill until the Unseelie King called them out to hunt.

The crowd parted to let them by. The battle had ended, in any real sense: The field was full of onlookers now, staring in silence as the Riders stopped to look up at Emma and Julian.

Ethna craned her head back, her bronze hair spilling over her shoulders. "We are the Riders of Mannan!" she cried. "We have slain the Firbolg! We have no fear of giants!"

She launched herself into the air, and Delan followed. They sailed like bronze birds through the sky, their swords outstretched.

Emma reached out almost lazily and plucked Ethna from the air. She tore her apart like tissue paper, shredding her bronze armor, snapping her sword. Julian caught Delan and hurled him back to earth with a force that tore a furrow into the dirt: Delan skidded across the ground and was still.

The other Riders did not run. It wasn't in them to run, Mark knew. They did not retreat. They were without the ability to do so.

Each tried to fight, and each was caught up and crushed or torn, hurled back to the ground in pieces. The earth was slick with their blood.

Julian turned away from them first. He put out a blazing hand toward the Malachi Configuration and scattered it, sending the bars of light flying.

The screams of the Cohort pierced the air. Cristina tore herself away from Mark and ran toward Emma and Julian. "Don't!" she cried. "Emma! Jules! They're prisoners! They can't hurt us!"

Helen ran forward, her hands outstretched. "The battle is over!" she cried. "We've won—you can stop now! You killed the Riders! You can stop!"

Neither Julian nor Emma seemed to hear. With a graceful hand, Emma lifted a Cohort member from the screaming throng and tossed him aside. He shrieked as he sailed through the air, his howls cut off suddenly when he hit the ground with a crushing thud.

Mark had stopped worrying only whether Emma and Julian would survive this. He had begun to worry whether any of them would.

Dru stood just inside the gates and gazed out onto the Imperishable Fields.

She'd never seen a battle like this before. She'd been in the Accords Hall during the Dark War and seen death and blood, but the scale of this fight—the chaos that was hard to follow, the blinding speed of the fighting—was almost impossible to look at. It didn't help that she was too far away to make out details: She saw the bronze Riders come and felt terror; she saw them tumble into the fighting crowd, but not what had happened to them afterward. Occasionally she would see the blurry figure of a man or woman fall on the field and wonder: Was it Mark? Was it Emma? The sickness of fear had taken up residence in her stomach and wouldn't budge.

For the past hour, the wounded had been coming through the gates, sometimes walking, sometimes carried. Silent Brothers moved forward in swirls of bone-colored robes to carry Cohort members and ordinary Shadowhunters alike to the Basilias for healing. At one point, Jem Carstairs had come in through the gates, carrying Kit's unconscious body.

She had started to run to them, and paused when she saw Tessa Gray racing through the crowd of Silent Brothers, Catarina Loss with her. Both already had blood on their clothes and had clearly been treating the wounded.

She wanted to go to Kit. He was her friend, and he mattered so much to Ty. But she hung back, afraid that adults like Jem and Tessa would want her to go back to Amatis's house and she would be taken away from the gates, her only window to her family. She hung back in the shadows as Tessa helped Catarina load Kit onto a stretcher.

Jem and Catarina took hold of the ends of the stretcher. Before they began to move up the hill toward the Basilias, Tessa bent and kissed Kit gently on the forehead. It eased the knot of tightness in Dru's chest—though Kit had been hurt, at least he'd be taken care of by those who cared about him.

More wounded came in then, the injuries worsening as the battle raged on. Beatriz Mendoza was carried through the gates, sobbing brokenly. She wasn't visibly injured, but Dru knew that her *parabatai*, Julie, had been the first Shadowhunter slain in the battle. Dru wanted to turn Tavvy's face away from all of it. It wasn't the Shadowhunter way to shield children from the results of battle, but she couldn't help thinking of his nightmares, the years of listening to him scream in the darkness.

"Tavs," she said finally. "Don't look."

He took her hand, but he didn't turn his face away. He was staring at the battlefield, his expression intent but not fearful.

He was the one who saw the giants first, and pointed.

Dru's first instinct was to wonder if this was a plan of Julian's. She saw white fire blaze up and then great shining figures striding across the field. They filled her with a feeling of amazement, a shock at their beauty, the way she'd felt when she was small, looking up at illustrations of Raziel.

She scanned the field anxiously—the white light of the fire was piercing the sky. The clouds were breaking up and shattering. She could hear cries, and the dark figures of vampires began to flee across the field toward Brocelind's shadows.

Most of them made it. But as the clouds rolled back and the gray sunlight pierced down like a knife, Dru saw one vampire, slower than the rest, just at the border of the woods, stumble into a patch of sunlight. There was a cry and a conflagration.

She pulled her gaze away from the flames. *This can't be Julian's plan.*

Tavvy tugged on her hand. "We have to go," he said. "We have to go to Emma and Jules."

She gripped him tightly. "It's a battle—we can't go out there."

"We have to." There was urgency in his tone. "It's Jules and Emma. They *need* us."

"Dru!" A cry made her look up. Two people were coming through the gates. One was Jaime. The sight of him made her heart leap: He was still alive. Dusty and scratched, his gear filthy, but alive and bright-eyed and flushed with effort. He was half-carrying Cameron Ashdown, who had an arm slung over his shoulder. Cameron appeared to be bleeding from a wound in his side.

"Cameron!" Dru hurried toward them, pulling Tavvy with her. "Are you okay?"

Cameron gave Dru a half wave. "Vanessa stabbed me. Some kind of demon stuff on the blade." He winced.

"Your *cousin* stabbed you?" Dru said. She'd known the Ashdowns were split politically, but family was family in her view.

"Holiday dinners will be very awkward from now on," said Jaime. He gave the other boy a pat on the back as a Silent Brother swooped down on Cameron and bore him away to the Basilias.

Jaime wiped a dirty hand across his forehead. "You two should get farther away from the battle," he said. "Has no one told you not to stand in the gates?"

"If we don't stand in the gates, we can't see anything," Dru pointed out. "Is that—on the field—is that really Jules and Emma?"

Jaime nodded. Dru's heart sank. Some part of her had been hoping it was a terrible illusion.

"I don't understand what's happening?" Her voice rose. "Is this a plan of Julian's? Do you know about it?"

"I do not think it is a plan," Jaime said. "They seem entirely out of control."

"Can they be *stopped*?"

Jaime spoke reluctantly. "They killed the Riders of Mannan. Now soldiers are trying to form a wall of bodies to protect the city from them. All the children are here." He indicated Alicante. Dru thought of Max and Rafe with Maryse. Her heart skipped a beat. "I don't know what will happen." Jaime looked from her to Tavvy. "Come with me," he said abruptly. "I can get you into the woods."

Dru hesitated.

"We can't go away from them. We have to go to Jules and Emma," Tavvy said firmly.

"It's dangerous—" Jaime began.

"Tavvy's right. We have to go." Dru looked down at the incomplete rune that sprawled across her forearm. She remembered Julian putting it there yesterday; it felt forever ago. "You don't have to help."

Jaime sighed and drew his crossbow from the holder on his back. "I'll cover you."

Dru was about to follow Jaime out of the gates when Tavvy poked her in the side. She turned to see he was holding out her stele. "Don't forget," he said.

She exhaled—she nearly had forgotten. Dru put the tip of the stele to her arm and began to complete the Familias rune.

Kieran was surrounded by the Unseelie army, thirty faeries deep. This was bad enough, because he could see neither Mark nor Cristina over the churning mass of his people, but he could barely control Windspear, who was rearing and whinnying beneath him. Windspear liked neither crowds nor giants, and at the moment both were far too close.

Winter was at Kieran's side. He had stuck to him like glue through the battle, which Kieran found both admirable and startling. He was not used to such loyalty.

"The people have come to you, liege lord," said Winter. "What are your orders for them?"

Orders for them? Kieran thought frantically. He had no idea what they should do. This was why he had wanted Adaon to be King, but Adaon was prisoner in the Seelie Court. What would Adaon say about an army of faeries trapped on a field with rampaging part-angel giants?

"Why aren't they all running for the forest?" Kieran demanded. The forest was a place Fair Folk felt at home, full of natural things, water and trees. There had long been faeries in Brocelind Forest.

"Sadly, the woods are full of vampires," said Winter glumly.

"The vampires are our allies!" shouted Kieran, grasping Windspear's mane as the horse reared.

"No one really believes that," said Winter.

By all the Gods of Dark and Light. Kieran wanted to yell and break something. Windspear reared again, and this time, Kieran caught sight of a familiar figure. Mark. He would know him anywhere—and Cristina beside him. He said a silent thanks. *What would they tell me to do?* He thought of Mark's generosity, Cristina's kindness. They would think of the Unseelie soldiers first.

"We need to get our people off this field," said Kieran. "They cannot battle angels. No one can. How did you all arrive here?"

"Oban made a door," said Winter. "You can do the same, liege. Open a door to Faerie. As King you can do it. Reach out to your Land and it will reach back to you."

If bloody drunk Oban did it, I can do it, Kieran thought. But that wasn't all that helpful. He had to reach out to his Land, a place he had long cursed, and hope it would reach back to him.

He slid from Windspear's back as the horse stilled beneath him. He remembered Mark saying: *I will not forget the beauty of Faerie and neither will you. But it will not come to that.*

And he thought of what he himself had said, had remembered, when he had thought Faerie was threatened.

The way the water tumbles blue as ice over Branwen's Falls. The taste of music and the sound of wine. The honey hair of mermaids in the streams, the glittering of will-o'-the-wisps in the shadows of the deep forests.

Kieran took a deep breath. *Let me through*, he thought. *Let me through, my Land, for I belong to you: I will give unto you as the Kings of Faerie long have, and you will flourish when I flourish. I will bring no blight to your shores, nor blood to wither your flowers in the fields, but only peace and a kind road that rises to green hills.*

"My liege," said Winter.

Kieran opened his eyes and saw that the low hillock before him had begun to split apart. Through the gap he could see the great tower of Unseelie rising in the distance and the peaceful fields before it.

Several of the closer fey sent up a cheer. They began to run through the gap even as it widened. Kieran could see them emerging on the other side, some even falling on their knees with gratitude and relief.

"Winter," he said in an unsteady voice. "Winter, get everyone through the door. Get them to safety."

"All the fey?" said Winter.

"Everyone," said Kieran, looking at his first in command sternly. "Shadowhunters. Warlocks. Everyone who seeks sanctuary."

"And you, my liege?" said Winter.

"I must go to Mark and Cristina."

For the first time, Winter looked mutinous. "You must leave your mortal friends, lord."

Winter was a redcap, sworn in blood to protect the King and the royal line. Kieran could not be angry with him, and yet he must make him understand. He searched for the right words. "You are my loyal guard, Winter. But as you guard me, so must you guard what I love best, and Mark Blackthorn and Cristina Rosales are what I love best in this world and all others."

"But your *life*," said Winter.

"Winter," Kieran said flatly. "I know they cannot be my consorts. But I die without them."

More and more faeries were flooding through the door to the Undying Lands. There were others with them now—a few warlocks, even a band of lycanthropes.

Winter set his jaw. "Then I will guard your back."

Helen felt as if she were caught in the middle of a river going two ways at once.

Faeries were running in one direction, toward a hilly rise at the eastern end of the field. Shadowhunters were racing in the other, toward the city of Alicante, presumably to hide behind its walls. Aline had darted off to investigate, promising to be back momentarily.

Some still milled around the center of the field—the Cohort seemed to be shrieking and running in circles, willing to join neither the exodus of faeries nor fellow Shadowhunters. Helen had stayed near to where the others she knew had gathered—Kadir and Jia were helping wounded from the field, Simon and Isabelle were in conference with Hypatia Vex and Kwasi Bediako, and Jace and Clary had gone with a group of others, including Rayan and Divya, to put themselves between Emma and Julian and the Cohort prisoners.

"Helen!" Aline was jogging toward her across the grass. "They're not running away."

"What do you mean?" Helen said.

"The Shadowhunters. They're going to protect the city, in case the giants—in case Emma and Julian make a move toward it. It's full of kids and old people. And besides," she added, "Shadowhunters protect Alicante. It's what we do."

Spoken like the daughter of the Consul. "But Emma and Julian would never—they wouldn't—" Helen protested.

"We don't know what they'd do," Aline said gently, just as Hypatia Vex and Kwasi Bediako rushed past them. They raced toward the trampled grass where Emma and Julian stood, and Kwasi flung out his hands as Hypatia placed her palms on his shoulders. A shimmering golden net burst into the air over Emma and Jules: It settled on them like a fine spiderweb, but Helen sensed it was made of something much stronger.

Emma put up a great, shining hand to push against the net. It held fast. Kwasi was breathing fast, but Hypatia steadied him.

A cry broke from Martin Gladstone. "Do it now! Round up the Blackthorns! Show those monsters what will happen to their families if they don't stop!"

The Cohort sent up a cheer. Helen could hear Zara screaming that they should do it, that they had a right to protect themselves.

Aline stepped in front of Helen. "That *bastard*!" She glowered.

Julian hooked his fingers into the material of the shining net and tore it apart. It fell away, and Julian reached down to seize Gladstone.

With a flick of his fingers, he snapped Gladstone's neck.

Julian and Emma moved toward the other Cohort members, who began to scatter. Emma reached for Zara—

And Jace slid between them, between Emma's shimmering hand and Zara's fleeing figure. The Mortal Sword was sheathed on his back; he was weaponless. He tossed back his golden head and called out, "Stop! Emma and Julian! The battle is over! *Stop!*"

Expressionless as a statue of an avenging angel, Emma reached down and swept Jace out of the way. He was thrown several yards and hit the ground with an ugly thud. Clary screamed and went flying across the grass, racing toward Jace with her red hair trailing behind her like fire.

Get up, get up, Helen thought. *Get up, Jace.*

But he didn't.

Dru had never used the Familias rune before, and the experience was a strange one.

She felt herself tugged toward her siblings in a way she couldn't define. It felt like something was tied around the inside of her spine—which was gross but interesting—and was pulling her toward a destination. She'd heard the way Tracking runes felt described to her, and she suspected this wasn't dissimilar.

She let the tugging pull her, running along after it with her hand clasped firmly around Tavvy's wrist. They kept to the edges of the battlefield, Jaime beside them with his crossbow trained on anyone who might approach.

They left the shelter of the city walls and struck out for the edge of the forest, still following the pull of the rune. She tried not to look over at the field, at Emma and Julian. It was like looking at pillars of fire one moment, at terrible monsters the next.

There was a rustling overhead, and Ty dropped down out of an oak tree. Dru gave a little gasp of surprise, and then another one as

Ty walked straight toward her and hugged her tightly.

He let her go and frowned. "Why are you on the field? You should be in the city. Tavvy, too." He turned to Jaime. "It's dangerous."

"Yes," said Jaime. "I am aware of that."

"*You're* out here," Dru pointed out.

"I was up a tree," Ty said, as if that made it better somehow. Before Dru could get into a really enjoyable sibling argument about it, Helen had come rushing up, her pale blond curls fluttering. Aline was just on her heels.

"Dru! *Tavvy!*" Helen darted tearfully toward the two of them, reaching to pick Tavvy up; Dru noticed that he held his arms out to her automatically, something he only really had ever done for Julian before. Helen lifted him up and squeezed him, hard. "What are you two *doing* here? Dru, did you use the Familias rune on purpose?"

"Of course I did!" Dru said. "We have to get out there on the field. We have to stop Emma and Jules. We have to get them back—back to themselves."

"We've been trying," Helen said as she set Tavvy down. "Don't you think we've been trying?"

Dru wanted to grind her teeth together. Why didn't Helen *listen?* She'd thought things were better, but she needed her sister to hear her so badly she could feel it like a lump in her throat.

She knew what they had to do. It seemed so clear. How could she make the rest of them see it?

She felt a twinge in her arm, where the rune was, and then Mark was there, racing up with Cristina at his side. "Dru! You called us—" He saw Ty and smiled delightedly. "I was watching you with your slingshot," he said. "Your aim is true, little brother."

"Don't encourage him, Mark," said Helen. "He was supposed to stay back at camp."

"Look," Dru said. "I know it doesn't make much sense. But if we all go up to Emma and Jules together, if we go right up to them and *talk* to them, we can get through. We have to try. If we can't do it, no one can, and then everyone is in danger."

Helen shook her head. "But why is this happening?"

Cristina and Mark exchanged a glance that Dru couldn't decipher. "I think it is because of the *parabatai* bond," Cristina said.

"Because Emma almost died?" Aline said, bewildered.

"I do not know," Cristina said. "I can only guess. But there is heavenly fire burning inside them. And no mortal being can survive that for very long."

"It's too dangerous for us to approach them," Mark said. "We have to trust Emma and Julian. Trust that they can end this on their own."

There was a long pause. Jaime watched impassively as the Blackthorns and their extended family stood in the stillness of an intense silence.

"No," Helen said finally, and Dru's heart sank. Helen raised her eyes, blazing Blackthorn blue in her grime-streaked face. "Dru is right. We have to go." She looked at Dru. "You're right, my love."

"I will walk with you to the field," Jaime said to Dru.

She was glad for his company as they all set out, Blackthorns together. But it wasn't Jaime she was thinking about as they turned to walk toward the heart of the battle. It was her sister. *Helen believed me. Helen understood.*

In the midst of the darkness of battle, her heart felt a tiny bit lighter.

Jaime suddenly jerked upright. "Diego," he said, and then a torrent of Spanish. Dru and Helen whipped around, and Dru sucked in her breath.

Not far away, a redcap was dragging Diego's limp body across the field. At least, Dru guessed it was Diego: His clothes were familiar, and his mop of dark hair. But his face was obscured entirely by blood.

Helen touched Jaime's shoulder. "Go to your brother," she said. "Quickly. We'll be fine."

Jaime took off running.

Jace was awake. He had been blinking and starting to sit up when Clary reached him, and she'd been torn between throwing herself into his arms and smacking him for terrifying her.

She was drawing an *iratze* on his arm. It seemed to be doing its work—the long bloody scratch along the side of his face had already healed. He was half-sitting up, leaning against her to catch his breath, when Alec came running up and knelt down beside them.

"Are you all right, *parabatai?*" Alec said, looking anxiously into Jace's face.

"Please promise you'll never do that again," Clary said.

"I promise that I will never stand between Zara Dearborn and a marauding giant again," said Jace. "Alec, what's happening? You've been out on the field—"

"Julian and Emma just tossed Vanessa Ashdown about twenty feet," said Alec. "I think they're angry that she stabbed Cameron, though why, I couldn't tell you."

Clary looked over at Emma and Julian. They stood very still, looking down at the Cohort, as if choosing what to do with them. Every once in a while a Cohort member would break free and run, and Emma or Julian would move to pen them back in again.

It was almost like a game, but angels did not play. Clary couldn't help but remember the sight of Raziel, rising from Lake Lyn. Not many people had looked at an angel. Not many people had stared into the cold eyes of Heaven, with its indifference to petty mortal concerns. Did Emma and Julian feel a fraction of that indifference, that unconcern that was not cruelty but something stranger and altogether bigger—something not human at all?

Emma suddenly lurched and went down on one knee. Clary stared in shock as the Cohort howled and fled, but Emma made no movement toward them.

Julian, beside her, reached down a shining hand to lift her back up.

"They're dying," Jace said quietly.

Alec looked puzzled. "What?"

"They are Nephilim—true Nephilim," said Jace. "The monsters of old who once strode the earth. They have heavenly fire inside them, powering everything they do. But it's too much. Their mortal bodies will burn away. They're probably in agony."

He got to his feet.

"We have to stop them. If they get too maddened with pain, who knows what they'll do."

Emma began to move toward the city. Clary could see Isabelle and Simon running toward the blockade of Shadowhunters standing between Emma and Julian and the city of Alicante.

"Stop them how?" Alec said.

Grimly, Jace unsheathed the Mortal Sword. Before he could move, Clary put a hand on his shoulder.

"Wait," she said. "Look."

Not far away now, a small group was walking steadily toward the shining, monstrous figures of Emma and Julian. Helen Blackthorn, with all her siblings beside her—Mark and Tiberius, Drusilla and Octavian. They moved together in a strong and steady line.

"What are they doing?" Alec asked.

"The only thing they can do," said Clary.

Slowly, Jace lowered the Mortal Sword. "By the Angel," he said, drawing in his breath. "Those kids . . ."

"Diego. Wake up, my brother. Please wake up."

There had been only darkness, interspersed with bright sparks of pain. Now there was Jaime's voice. Diego wanted to stay in the darkness and the quiet. To rest where the pain was held at arm's length, here in the silent world.

But his brother's voice was insistent, and from childhood Diego had been trained to respond to it. To rise from bed when his brother cried, to run to help him up when he fell down.

He peeled his eyes open. They felt sticky. His face burned. Above him was roiling dark sky and Jaime, his expression starkly distraught. He was on his knees, his bow at his side; a distance away, a redcap lay dead with an arrow protruding from its chest.

Jaime was clutching a stele in his hand. He reached out and pushed back Diego's hair; when he drew his hand back, it was red with blood. "Stay still," he said. "I have given you several *iratzes*."

"I must get up," Diego whispered. "I must fight."

Jaime's dark eyes flashed. "Your face is sliced open, Diego. You have lost blood. You cannot get up. I will not allow it."

"Jaime . . ."

"In the past, you have always healed me," said Jaime. "Let me be the one who heals you."

Diego coughed. His mouth and throat were thick with blood. "How bad—how bad will the scars be?"

Jaime took his hand, and that was when Diego knew it was bad indeed. He begged Jaime silently not to lie to him or to pity him.

Jaime's smile was slow and crooked. "I think I will be the pretty one in the family now," he said. "But at least you are still very muscular."

Diego choked on a laugh, on the taste of blood, on the strangeness of it all. He wound his fingers into his brother's, and held on tight.

The walk across the field was surreal.

As the siblings came closer to Emma and Julian, other Shadowhunters drew nearer to the Blackthorns, sometimes looking puzzled, sometimes almost ashamed. Dru knew they felt that the group was walking toward certain death. Some called out that they should leave Tavvy behind, but he only pressed closer to his brothers and sisters, shaking his head.

Emma and Julian were clearly making their way toward the city. They moved like shining shadows, closing the distance between themselves and the barricade of Shadowhunters who stood between them and Alicante.

"We need to get to them," she muttered, but the crowd in front of them was forming another sort of barricade. She saw Shadowhunters she recognized among them—Anush and Divya Joshi, Luana Carvalho, Kadir Safar, and even some Downworlders—Bat Velasquez and Kwasi Bediako among them—who were calling out to them not to approach Julian and Emma, that it wasn't safe.

She glanced at the others in panic. "What do we do?"

"I cannot shoot them with elf-bolts," Mark said. "They mean well."

"Of course not!" Helen looked horrified. "Please!" she called out. "Let us pass!"

But her voice was lost in the roar of the crowd, which was jostling them back, away from the city, away from Emma and Jules. Dru had begun to panic when they heard the thunder of hooves.

Shadowhunters moved reluctantly back as Windspear, Kieran on his back, parted the crowd. His flanks were lathered with sweat; he had clearly raced across the field. Kieran's panicked eyes flew across the group until he found Mark, and then Cristina.

The three of them exchanged a swift and speaking look. Mark flung his hand up, as if he were reaching out to the new Unseelie King. "Kieran!" he shouted. "Help us! We need to get to Emma and Julian!"

Dru waited for Kieran to say that it was dangerous. Impossible.

Instead he bent low over Windspear's neck; he seemed to be whispering to the horse.

A moment later, the sky darkened with flying shapes. The Wild Hunt had come. Shadowhunters and Downworlders alike scattered as the Hunt swooped low. Suddenly the Blackthorns could move forward again, and they did, moving as fast as they could toward Emma and Julian, who had nearly closed the gap between themselves and the line of Shadowhunters guarding the city.

As they passed, Dru reached up to wave at Diana and Gwyn, who had detached themselves from the Wild Hunt and were preparing to land alongside the Blackthorns. Diana smiled at her and pressed her hand over her heart.

Dru fixed her eyes on the goal ahead. They were nearly there. Kieran had joined them. The crown of Unseelie gleamed on his brow, but his attention was fixed on protecting the Blackthorns. With Windspear rearing, he was keeping the crowd at bay on one side, while Gwyn and Diana did the same on the other.

The field leveled out. They were close now, close enough that Emma and Julian were shining blurs. It was like looking at trees in the forest whose tops you couldn't see.

Dru took a deep breath. "Okay," she said. "Just us now. Just Blackthorns."

Everyone went still.

Mark pressed his forehead to Cristina's, his eyes shut, before helping her up onto Windspear, beside Kieran. Kieran squeezed Mark's hand tightly and wrapped his arms around Cristina as if to say to Mark that he would keep her safe. Aline kissed Helen softly and went to stand by her mother among the crowd. They watched, a small and worried group, as the Blackthorns set off to close the distance between themselves and Emma and Jules.

They stopped a few feet from the giant figures of Julian and

Emma. For a moment, the certainty that had carried Dru this far faltered. She had thought only of getting here. Not of what she would do or say when they arrived.

It was Tavvy who stepped forward first. "Jules!" he shouted. "Emma! We're here!"

And at last Emma and Julian reacted.

They turned away from the city and looked down at the Blackthorns. Dru craned her head back. She could see their expressions. They were completely blank. No recognition lived in their glowing eyes.

"We can't just tell them to stop," said Mark. "Everyone's already tried that."

Tavvy moved a little bit farther forward. The eyes of the giants followed him like massive lamps, glowing and inhuman.

Dru wanted to reach out and snatch him back.

"Jules?" he said, and his voice was small and low and stabbed into Drusilla's heart. She took a deep breath. If Tavvy could approach them, so could she. She moved to stand behind her younger brother and tilted her shoulders back until she was looking directly up at Emma and Julian. It was like gazing into the sun; her eyes prickled, but she held them open.

"Emma!" she called. "Julian! It's Dru—Drusilla. Look, everyone is telling you to stop because the battle is won, but I'm not here to say that. I'm here to tell you to stop because we love you. We need you. Come back to us."

Neither Emma nor Julian moved or changed expression. Dru plowed on, her cheeks burning.

"Don't leave us," she said. "Who will watch bad horror movies with me, Julian, if you're gone? Who will train with me, Emma, and show me everything I'm doing wrong, and how to be better?"

Something shifted behind Dru. Helen had come to stand beside her. She reached her hands out as if she could touch the shining figures before her. "Julian," she said. "You raised our brothers and sisters when I could not. You sacrificed your childhood to keep our family together. And Emma. You guarded this family when I could not. If you both leave me now, how will I ever get the chance to make it up to you?"

Julian and Emma were still expressionless, but Emma tilted her head slightly, almost as if she was listening.

Mark came forward, laying his slim hand on Dru's shoulder. He craned his head back. "Julian," he called. "You showed me how to be part of a family again. Emma, you showed me how to be a friend when I had forgotten friendship. You gave me hope when I was lost." He stood straight as an elf-bolt, gazing into the sky. "Come back to us."

Julian shifted. It was a minute movement, but Dru felt her heart leap. Maybe—maybe—

Ty stepped forward, his gear dusty and ripped where bark had torn it. His black hair fell in dark strands across his face. He pushed it away and said, "We lost Livvy. We—we lost her."

Tears stung the backs of Dru's eyes. There was something about the tone of Ty's voice that made it sound as if this were the first time he had realized the finality and irrevocability of Livvy's death.

Ty's eyelashes shimmered with tears as he raised his gaze. "We can't lose you, too. We will be—we will wind up broken. Julian, you taught me what every word I didn't understand meant—and Emma, you chased off anybody who was ever mean to me. Who will teach me and protect me if you don't go back to being yourselves?"

There was a great and thundering crash. Julian had fallen to his knees. Dru covered a gasp—he seemed smaller than he had, though still enormous. She could see the black fissures in his glowing skin where red sparks of fire leaked out like blood.

There is heavenly fire burning inside them. And no mortal being can survive that for very long.

"Emma," Dru whispered. "Julian."

They weren't expressionless anymore. Dru had seen statues of mourning angels, of angels thrust through with fiery swords, weeping tears of agony. It was not easy to wield a sword for God.

She could see those statues again in the looks on their faces.

"Emma!" The cry burst from Cristina; she had broken away from the others and come running toward the Blackthorns. "Emma! Who will be my best friend if you're not my best friend, Emma?" She was crying, tears mixing with the blood and dirt on her face. "Who will take care of my best friend when I cannot, Julian, if you are not there?"

Emma fell to her knees beside Julian. They were both weeping—tears of fire, red and gold. Dru hoped desperately that it meant that they felt something, and not that they were dying, coming apart in twin blazes of fire.

"Who will drive me crazy with questions in the classroom if not you?" called Diana. She was coming toward them as well, and so were Kieran and Aline, leaving Gwyn holding Windspear's bridle, his face reflecting awe and wonder.

Aline cleared her throat. "Emma and Julian," she said. "I don't know you that well, and this giant thing is admittedly a huge surprise. That wasn't a pun. I was being literal." She glanced sideways at Helen. "But being around you makes my wife really happy, and that's because she loves you both." She paused. "I also like you, and we're going to be a family, dammit, so come down here and *be* in this family!"

Helen patted Aline's shoulder. "That was good, honey."

"Julian," Kieran said. "I could speak of the way Mark loves you, and Emma, I could speak of the friendship Cristina bears you. But the truth is that I have to be King of the Unseelie Court, and without your brilliance, Julian, and your bravery, Emma, I fear my reign will be brief."

In the distance, Dru could see Isabelle and Simon approaching.

Alec was with them, his arm around Magnus, and Clary and Jace walked beside them, hand in hand.

Tavvy reached up his arms. "Jules," he said, his small voice clear and ringing. "Carry me. I'm tired. I want to go home."

Slowly—as slowly as the passing of eons—Julian reached out with his bright hands, fissured with darkness from which heavenly fire poured like blood. He reached out toward Tavvy.

There was a burst of light that seared Dru's eyes. When she had blinked it away, she saw that Julian and Emma were no longer there—no, they had slumped to the ground; they were dark figures within an aura of light, growing ever smaller, surrounded by a pool of illumination the color of bloody gold.

For a terrified moment Dru was sure they were dying. As the awful light faded, she saw Emma and Julian—human-size again—crumpled together on the ground. They lay with their hands clasped together, their eyes closed, like angels who had fallen from heaven and now slept peacefully upon the earth again.

33
Reverence

"Wake up, Emma. It's time to wake up."

There was a gentle hand on her forehead, a gentle voice calling her out of the long dark.

For some time there had been only shadows. Shadows and cold after a long period of burning. The world had tilted at a distance. She had seen a place too bright to remember and figures that shone like blades in the sun. She had heard voices calling her name. *Emma. Emma.*

Emma means universe, Julian had said.

But she had not woken up. She had heard Julian's voice again, this time mixed with Jem's.

"It was a clever touch," Jem said, "having not one meeting but two. You knew any of the Shadowhunters might be loyal to the Cohort, so you had them attend only the first meeting. That way when they reported to Horace what your plans were, he was prepared only for you to interrupt the parley. Not for the Downworlder attack."

"Jace and Clary agreed to be the bait," Julian said. He sounded tired, even in her dream.

"We knew Horace would do anything to get his hands on them. That way we could march them in front of everyone and prove that

Horace wasn't just wrong that they were dead—he was trying to kill them."

There was a long pause. Emma floated in more darkness, though she could see shapes in it now, shapes and shadows.

"I knew there would be spies at the meeting," Julian said. "I admit they surprised me by sending a demon. I didn't even figure it out until I saw the Eidolon on the battlefield. How do you think it got into the Sanctuary? Just posing as Oskar Lindquist shouldn't have protected it."

"Demons have been known to use Shadowhunter blood to enter Institutes. Oskar Lindquist was found dead yesterday. It is possible his blood was used."

"But would that grant the demon the power to be invulnerable to seraph blades?" Julian said.

There was a long pause. "I know of no magic strong enough for that." Jem sounded troubled. "The Silent Brothers will want to know—"

Emma dragged her eyes open reluctantly, not wanting to leave the softness of the dark. "Jem?" she whispered. Her throat and mouth were incredibly dry.

"Emma!" She was pulled into a hug. Jem's arms were strong. She pressed her head into his shoulder. It was like being hugged by her father—a memory she kept always in the back of her mind, precious and unforgotten.

She swallowed past the dryness in her throat. "Julian?" she whispered.

Jem drew back. She was able to see where she was—in a small room with two white beds, a window in the wall letting in sunshine. Julian sat on the bed opposite hers, wearing a clean T-shirt and loose pants like training garments. Someone had put her into the same clothes; her hair was tangled, and her whole body ached like a giant bruise.

Julian looked unharmed. Their eyes met and his expression softened; his back was straight and tense, his shoulders a hard line.

She wanted to go and hug him. At least to hold his hand. She forced herself not to move. She felt fragile inside, her heart thundering with love and fear. She didn't trust herself to control her emotions.

"You're in the Basilias," said Jem. "I woke you, Emma, after Julian had woken. I thought you would want to see each other."

Emma looked around. Through a window in the wall, she could see a bigger room of white-sheeted cots, about half of which were taken up with patients. Silent Brothers moved among the rows and the air smelled of healing—herbs and flowers, the medicines of the Silent City.

Their room had a low arched ceiling painted with healing runes in gold and red and black. More windows faced out onto the buildings of Alicante: the red-roofed houses, the slim needles of the demon towers.

"The children, are they all right?" Emma said. "Helen—?"

"I already asked," Julian said. It was hard for Emma to look away from him, and also painful to look at him—he seemed different somehow. Changed. She tore her gaze free and stared at Jem, who had risen to stand by the window. "Everyone's all right, Emma."

"Even Kit? He saved my life—"

"He was quite drained and ill," said Jem. "But he has recovered well. He is in the Silent City. We lost good warriors on the battlefield, but your friends are safe. You have been unconscious for three days, so you missed the funerals. But then, you've attended too many funerals lately as it is."

Emma frowned. "But why is Kit in the Silent City? The Basilias—"

"Emma," Jem said. "I did not come to you to talk about Kit. I came to talk about you and Julian." He pushed his hair back from his face; he looked tired, the white streak in his hair more pronounced. "You asked me a long time ago about the *parabatai* curse. What happens when two *parabatai* fell in love. I told you what I knew, but I didn't dream you were asking for yourself."

Emma felt herself go still. She looked at Julian, who nodded.

"He knows," Julian said in a flat sort of voice. Emma wondered what he was feeling. She couldn't quite read him as she usually could, but they were likely both in shock. "Everyone does now."

Emma hugged her arms around herself. "But how—"

"I wish I had known," Jem said, "though I can understand why you did not tell me. I have spoken with Magnus. I know all that you did to try to combat the curse. No one could have struggled more. But this is not a curse that can be undone, save by the destruction of every *parabatai* bond in all the world." He looked at Emma with sharp eyes, and she felt the sudden weight of how very old Jem was, and how much he knew about people. "Or at least, that's what was believed, and every attempt to investigate the curse turned up no records of what might happen if the curse were to be realized. We only knew symptoms: increased power with runes, ability to do things no other Nephilim could do. The fact that you broke the Mortal Sword, Emma—I am sure it was partly the strength of Cortana and partly the power of the curse. But these were all things we only guessed at for many years. Then the battle of three days ago happened. What of it do you remember?"

"Emma was dying in my arms," Julian said. His voice shook. It was strange, though—normally Emma would have felt a twinge inside her ribs, a flicker of his pain. Now she didn't. "There was a white light—and we were giants, looking down. I don't *feel* what we felt, but I remember people looking like ants running around our feet. And feeling like we were on a mission, like we were being directed. I don't know how to explain it. Like we were being told what to do and we had no choice except to do it."

"As if something were working through you," said Jem. "A will greater than yours?"

Emma put her hands to her chest. "I remember now—Zara stabbed me—I was bleeding—" She remembered again the feeling of burning, and the world spinning away and down. "We were *giants?*"

"I need to tell you a piece of Nephilim history," said Jem, though Emma wished he would stick more closely to the topic of Giants: Had Emma and Julian Turned into Them? "Long, long ago, in the early history of Shadowhunters, there were huge demons that threatened the earth. Much bigger than any demon we have now save what Greater Demons can sometimes become. In that time, it was possible for Shadowhunters to become true Nephilim. Giants on the earth. We have old woodcuts and drawings of them, and the writings of those who saw them battling demons." He took a piece of paper from his pocket and read aloud: "'*The land that we have gone through as spies is a land that devours its inhabitants; and all the people that we saw in it are of great size. There we saw the Nephilim; and to ourselves we seemed like grasshoppers, and so we seemed to them.*'"

"But this is history," said Julian. "People don't turn into giants *now*."

A land that devours its inhabitants. Emma could not help but think of Thule and the stories of giants there.

"Most did not survive their transformations," said Jem. "It was the ultimate sacrifice, to blaze up with heavenly fire and die destroying demons. But it was noticed that many who survived were *parabatai*. Shadowhunters were more likely to live through the transformation if they had a *parabatai* who did not transform, anchoring them to earth."

"But we both transformed," said Emma.

"You understand," Jem said, "that for years we have tried to understand the *parabatai* curse and what it might be, but we certainly never tied it in to the time of Nephilim. The end of the time of

Nephilim came when the giant demons ceased to come to earth. We don't know why they disappeared; they simply did. Perhaps they were all slain. Perhaps they lost interest in this world. Perhaps they feared the Nephilim. This was eight hundred years ago, and many records have been lost."

"So when we turned into giants," said Julian, looking as if the words made him ill, "you realized the *parabatai* curse was tied to Nephilim somehow?"

"After the battle, we raced to turn up every record of the true Nephilim. In doing so, I discovered one tale of a terrible event. A Shadowhunter became a true Nephilim to battle a demon. Their *parabatai* was meant to stay behind as an anchor, but instead, they too transformed, uncontrollably. Both went wild. They slaughtered the demon and then they murdered their families and all those who tried to stop them until they burned alive from the heavenly fire." He paused. "They were a married couple. In those days there was no Law against loving your *parabatai*. Some months later it happened again, this time with another pair of lovers."

"And people didn't know about this?" said Emma.

"Much was done to cover it up. The practice of *parabatai* is one of the most powerful tools the Shadowhunters possess. No one wanted to lose it. And since the great demons had vanished, it was not thought that there would be a need to employ true Nephilim again. Indeed, no one ever has, and the method by which true Nephilim were made has been lost. It could have ended there, and indeed there are no records in the Silent City of what happened, but Tessa was able to find an archive in the Spiral Labyrinth. It was the tale of two Shadowhunters who became like warlocks—powerful magicians, whose runes were unlike others'. They razed a peaceful town to the ground before they were burned to death. But I suspect they were not burned to death by the townspeople. I suspect that they died from the heavenly fire." He paused. "Not long after the date of this tale, the Law was passed that no *parabatai* could fall in love."

"That's suspicious," muttered Emma.

"So what you're saying," said Julian, "is that the Shadowhunters destroyed their own records of why they created the Law about *parabatai* love being forbidden? They were afraid that people would take advantage of the power—but they valued the benefits of *parabatai* too much to give up the ritual?"

"That is what I suspect," said Jem, "though I do not think we will be able to prove it."

"This can't keep happening," said Emma. "We need to tell everyone the truth."

"The truth won't stop it happening," said Julian. He looked at her steadily. "I would have fallen in love with you even if I'd known exactly what the danger was."

Emma's heart seemed to trip over itself. She tried to keep her voice steady. "But if the horrible punishments are taken away," she said, "if people don't think they'll lose their families, they'll come forward. Mercy is better than revenge—isn't it?"

"The Silent Brothers have conferred and agree with you," said Jem. "They will make a recommendation to the Consul and the new Inquisitor when he or she is appointed."

"But Jia—Jia is still the Consul?" said Emma.

"Yes, though she is very ill. She has been for some time. I hope she will now have the time and space to rest and get well."

"Oh." Emma was surprised—Jia had seemed invulnerable to her.

"The Cohort members who survived are being held in the Gard prison. You did win the battle for us, after all. Though I would not recommend trying that tactic again."

"What's going to happen to us?" Julian said. "Will we be punished?"

"For what happened on the field? I do not think so," said Jem.

"It was a war. You slew the Riders of Mannan, for which everyone is grateful, and you slew several Cohort members, which you might have done anyway. I think you will be curiosities now—true Nephilim have not been seen in centuries. Also, you may have to do community service."

"Really?" said Emma.

"Not really," said Jem, and winked at her.

"I meant about the *parabatai* thing," said Julian. "We're still breaking the Law by feeling like we do about each other. Even if they make the Laws gentler, we'll still have to be separated, exiled even, so this never happens again."

"Ah," said Jem, and he leaned back against the wall, his arms folded. "When your clothes were cut from you so you could be healed, here in the Basilias, it was noticed that your *parabatai* runes had disappeared."

Emma and Julian both stared at him.

"Now, a *parabatai* rune can be cut from your skin, and you will not lose your bond," said Jem. "The rune is the symbol, not the bond itself. But it was curious, because there were no marks or scars where your *parabatai* runes had been; it was as if they had never been drawn. The Silent Brothers looked into your minds and saw the bond had been severed." He paused. "In most cases, I would feel I was giving you bad news, but in this case, perhaps not. You are no longer *parabatai*."

Neither of them moved or even breathed. Inside Emma's chest, her heart seemed to be ringing like a bell in a vast space, the deep echo of a cavern whose roof was so high all sound vanished into silence and dreams. Julian's face was as white as the demon towers.

"Not *parabatai*?" he said at last, his voice like a stranger's.

"I'll give you two a moment to digest the news," Jem said, a smile curling the edge of his mouth. "I will go to speak with your family. They have been worried about you." He left the room, and even though he wore jeans and a sweater, the shadow of robes seemed to move about him as he went.

The door closed behind Jem, and still Emma couldn't move. The terror of letting herself believe that the horror was over, that it would be all right, kept her frozen in place. For so long she had lived with a weight on her shoulders. For so long it had been the first thing she'd thought of when she woke up and the last of her thoughts before she slept; the food of nightmares and the close of every secret fear: *I will lose Julian. I will lose my family. I will lose myself.*

Even in the brightest moments, she had thought she would lose one of those things. She had never dreamed she would keep them all.

"Emma," Julian said. He had gotten to his feet, limping slightly, and Emma's heart broke: She knew this could be no easier for him than it was for her. She rose to her feet, her legs shaking. They faced each other across the space between their two cots.

She didn't know who broke and moved first. It could have been her, or him; they could have moved in unison as they had done for so long, still connected even though the *parabatai* bond was gone. They collided in the middle of the room; she flung her arms around Julian, her bandaged fingers digging into the back of his shirt.

He was here, really here, solid in her arms. He kissed her face feverishly and ran his hands through her hair. She knew tears were running down her face; she held on to him as tightly as she could, feeling him shaking in her arms. "Emma," he was saying, over and over, his voice breaking, shattering on the word. "Emma, Emma, my Emma."

She couldn't speak. Instead, she traced her fingers clumsily across his back, writing out what she couldn't say aloud, as they had for so long. *A-T L-A-S-T*, she wrote. *A-T L-A-S-T*.

The door flew open. And for the first time ever, they didn't leap apart: They kept hold of each other's hands, even as their family and friends poured into the room, tearful and bright with happiness and relief.

* * *

"They are quite afraid of you in Faerie now, Cristina," said Kieran. "They call you a slayer of kings and princes. A terrifying Shadowhunter."

The three of them—Mark, Cristina, and Kieran—were sitting by a dry fountain in Angel Square, outside the Basilias. Cristina sat between Mark's legs, his arms around her. Kieran leaned against his side.

"I am not terrifying," Cristina protested.

"You terrify *me*," Mark said, and Cristina turned and made a face at him. Kieran smiled but did not laugh: there seemed too much tension in him. Perhaps because it was difficult for him to be in Alicante. It had been heavily faerie-proofed during the Dark War, iron and salt and rowan strategically deployed in nearly every street. The Basilias was covered in hammered iron nails, so Mark and Cristina waited for news of Jules and Emma in the square with Kieran, letting the bright sun warm them as they rested.

After the Dark War, Mark knew, this square had been full of bodies. Corpses laid out in rows, their eyes bound with white silk, ready for burning and burial. Now it was peacefully quiet. There had been deaths in the battle three days before, and the next day a great funeral at the Fields. Jia had spoken: of the sorrow endured, of the necessity of building again and the importance of not acting in revenge against the Cohort, fifty of whom were now in the Gard jail.

"My mother is the one who is terrifying," said Cristina, shaking her head. She was warm in Mark's arms, and Kieran was a comforting weight against his side. If it had not been for worry over Emma and Jules, he would have been perfectly happy. "I told her about us last night."

"You did?" Mark was agog. Cristina's mother *was* terrifying—he'd heard that after the gates of the City had been opened by the Silent Brothers, she'd climbed up on one of the walls and thrown dozens of spears at the Unseelie faeries with a deadly precision that had sent redcaps scurrying away from the city. There was also a rumor that she'd punched Lazlo Balogh in the nose, but he decided not to confirm it.

"What did she say?" Kieran's black and silver eyes were worried.

"She said that it was perhaps not the choice she would have made for me," said Cristina, "but that what mattered was that I was happy. She also said she wasn't surprised it took two men to fill Diego's shoes." She grinned.

"Because Diego saved my life, I will absorb that slight without retort," said Kieran.

"And I'll tie his shoelaces together the next time I see him," said Mark. "Can you believe they found Manuel hiding under Horace's dead body?"

"I am only surprised he did not cut Horace's body open and hide inside it," said Kieran dourly.

Mark punched him lightly in the shoulder.

"Why do you strike me?" Kieran protested. "It has been done before in Faerie. Once a cowardly warrior hid inside a kelpie for a week."

Something white fluttered down from the sky. A moth, who deposited an acorn in Kieran's lap and winged away.

"A message?" Mark said.

Kieran unscrewed the acorn's top. He looked darkly serious, probably because he was now clad in the raiment of an Unseelie King. It still gave Mark a jolt to see him, all in black—black boots, black breeches, and a black waistcoat sewed with embroidered waves of gold and green to symbolize Kieran's nixie heritage. "From Winter," Kieran said. "All the Shadowhunters and Downworlders are now returned from the Unseelie Lands to their homes."

Kieran had opened the hospitality of the Unseelie Court to those who had fled the battle on the Fields. Alec had said he thought the gesture would go a long way toward rolling back the laws of the Cold Peace. A meeting to discuss how the Clave would go forward was scheduled for the next day, and Mark was anxious for it.

Kieran had not stayed long in the Unseelie Court. He had returned to Mark and Cristina the day after the battle, and they had been glad to have him back.

"Look!" Cristina cried. She sat up, pointing: One of the windows of the Basilias had opened and Dru had poked her head out. She was waving down at them, gesturing for them to come inside. "Emma and Julian are awake!" she called. "Come up!"

Cristina scrambled to her feet and the others followed. *Julian and Emma.* And Dru had been smiling. Now, Mark thought, *now* he was perfectly happy.

He started toward the Basilias, Cristina beside him. They were nearly there when they realized Kieran hadn't followed.

Mark turned. "Kieran—" He frowned. "Is the iron too difficult?"

"It is not that," Kieran said. "I should return to Faerie."

"Now?" Cristina said.

"Now and forever," said Kieran. "I shall not come back from there."

"*What?*" Mark strode back toward Kieran. The white letter from Winter fluttered in Kieran's hand like the wing of a bird. "Speak sense, Kieran."

"I am speaking sense," Kieran said softly. "Now that we know Emma and Julian will live, I must go back to Faerie. It is the bargain I made with Winter." He glanced down at the letter. "My general summons me. Without a King the Land is at risk of falling into chaos."

"They have a King!" Cristina had run to Kieran's side. She wore a light blue shawl; she drew it around herself tightly in agitation, shaking her head. "You are their King, whether you are there or here."

"No." Kieran closed his eyes. "The King is linked to the Land.

Every moment that the King is in the mortal world, the Land weakens. I cannot stay here. I did not want to be King—I did not ask to be King—but I *am* King, and I cannot be a bad one. It would not be right."

"We could come with you, then," said Mark. "We could not stay in Faerie all the time, but we could visit—"

"I thought that as well. But after even a short time as King in the Court, I know otherwise now," Kieran said. His hair had gone entirely black under the slim gold circlet that now encircled his brow. "The King is not permitted to have a mortal consort—"

"We know that," said Cristina, remembering her words in Brocelind. Even then she had believed Kieran might not become King. That a way would be found. "But your father had mortal consorts, didn't he? Isn't there some way around the rules?"

"No. He had mortal *lovers*." The word sounded ugly. "A consort is an official position. Mortal companions are playthings to be toyed with and tossed aside. He cared not how they were treated, but I do care. If I brought you to the Court as such, you would be treated with contempt and cruelty, and I could not stand to see it."

"You're the King," Cristina said. "They're your people. Can't you order them not to be cruel?"

"They have had years of a cruel reign," said Kieran. "I cannot teach them overnight. I did not know it myself. I had to learn kindness from both of you." His eyes glittered. "My heart is breaking and I cannot see a way out. You are all I want, but I must do what is best for my people. I cannot weaken my Land by coming here, and I cannot hurt you by bringing you there. We would never have peace in either place."

"Please, Kieran," said Mark. He caught at Kieran's wrist: *I am holding the arm of the Unseelie King*, he thought. It was perhaps the first time he had thought of Kieran as the King and not simply his Kieran. "We can find a solution."

Kieran pulled Mark to him and kissed him, hard and suddenly, his fingers digging into Mark's wrist. When he let him go, he was pale, his cheeks burning with color. "I have not slept for three days. This is why I wanted Adaon to be King. Others want the throne. I do not. I only want you."

"And you will be a great King because of it," said Cristina, her brown eyes glimmering with unshed tears. "What if it was only you and Mark? Mark is half-faerie—surely that must mean something—"

"He is a Shadowhunter to them," said Kieran, releasing Mark's hand. He strode over to Cristina. His eyes were smudged with tiredness. "And I love you both, my brave Cristina. Nothing can change that. Nothing ever will."

The tears she had been holding back spilled down her cheeks as Kieran cupped her face gently. "You're truly leaving? There must be another way!"

"There is no other way." Kieran kissed her, swiftly and hard, as he had kissed Mark; Cristina closed her eyes. "Know that I will always love you no matter how far away I am."

He let her go. Mark wanted to protest, but more than Cristina, he understood the cruel realities of Faerie. The thorns among the roses. What it would mean to be a toy and plaything of the King of a faerie Court; he could stand it for himself but not for Cristina.

Kieran leaped onto Windspear's back. "Be happy with each other," he said, his eyes averted as if he could not bear to look at them. "It is my wish as King."

"Kieran—" Mark said.

But Kieran was already riding away with thunderous speed. The flagstones trembled with Windspear's retreating hoofbeats; within seconds, Kieran was out of sight.

Kit hated it in the Silent City, even though his room was fairly comfortable, at least compared to the rest of the Silent City, which was all sharp-edged objects made out of human skeletons. Once you'd picked up three or four skulls and muttered "Alas, poor Yorick," to them, the novelty wore off quickly.

He suspected his rooms were a Silent Brother's chambers. There were a lot of books on a wooden shelf, all of them about history and glorious battles. There was a comfortable bed and a bathroom down the hall. Not that he wanted to think about the bathroom conditions in the Silent City. He hoped to forget them as soon as possible.

He had been left with little to do but heal and think about what had happened on the battlefield. He remembered over and over the surge of power that had gone through him when he'd struck the Riders and made their horses disappear. Was it dark magic? Was that why he was locked up? And how was it possible he had faerie blood? He could touch iron and rowan wood. He'd lived his whole life surrounded by technology. He didn't look anything like a faerie and no one in the Shadow Market had ever whispered at the possibility.

It was more than enough to occupy his mind and keep him from thinking about Ty. At least, it should have been.

He was lying on the bed staring at the stone ceiling when he heard footsteps approaching in the hallway outside his room. His first thought was food—a Silent Brother brought him a tray of plain, nourishingly boring food three times a day.

But the footsteps *clicked* on the stone. Heels. He frowned. The Consul? Diana, even? He'd play it cool and explain that he hadn't done anything wrong. He sat up, running his fingers through his hair and wondering how the Silent Brothers ever got anything done without owning mirrors. How did they know their robes weren't on backward?

The door opened and Tessa Gray came in. She wore a green dress and a hairband like Alice in Wonderland. She smiled at him affectionately.

"Please break me out of here," said Kit. "I don't want to be trapped here forever. I didn't do anything wrong, especially not any necromancy."

Tessa's smile faded. She came over to sit down at the foot of the bed, her gray eyes worried. *So much for playing it cool,* Kit thought.

"Christopher," she said. "I'm sorry for having left you here for so long."

"It's all right," he said, though he wasn't sure it was. "But don't call me Christopher. No one does."

"Kit," she said. "I'm so sorry that we left you here. We were looking after Julian and Emma, so we couldn't leave the city. It was touch and go for a while, but they just woke up." She smiled. "I thought you'd want to know."

Kit was glad to hear it. And yet—"What about the others, are they okay? What about Ty?"

"Ty and the others are fine. And Emma is all right in part thanks to you. You saved her life."

Kit slumped back against the metal headboard of the bed, relief coursing through him. "So I'm not in trouble for what I did on the battlefield?"

"No," Tessa said slowly. "But you need to know what it means. There is a story. One shrouded in mystery and misdirection. One that very few people alive know."

"Something about faerie blood," Kit said. "The Rider . . . He said, 'Kit is the child. The descendant of the First Heir.' But I don't see how that would be possible."

Tessa smoothed her skirt out over her legs. "Long ago, the King of Unseelie and the Seelie Queen formed an alliance to unite the faerie Courts. They brought magicians from all over Faerie to cast spells ensuring that the child they had would be the perfect heir. Not all the magic was good magic. Some of it was dark. The King dreamed of a son who would unite the realms, inspire perfect loyalty and perfect love, who would be braver than any faerie knight that had gone before."

"Sure sounds like me," muttered Kit.

Tessa flashed him a sympathetic smile. "But when the child was born, she was a girl, Auraline."

"Plot twist," said Kit.

"The King had expected a male heir and was . . . upset. In his eyes, the child was flawed, and eventually he set a faerie knight the task of having her killed, though the King had the tale put around that she had been kidnapped, and that is the story most believe."

"The King planned to kill his own daughter?"

"Indeed, and he has had every daughter of his killed since, in bitterness over Auraline. For she defied him—she was still the Heir. She called upon the knight's loyalty to her and he let her go. That is what the King tried to hide. He pretended Auraline's death was the fault of another, even when Auraline fled to the mortal world. There she met a magician who became her husband—a magician who was descended from a line of Shadowhunters who had left the Clave."

"The Lost Herondales," Kit guessed.

"Correct. They were your ancestors; their line led to your mother. Through all the past decades, the Unseelie King has hunted those he thought were descended from his daughter, and so the Herondales have hidden, concealed by false names and powerful magic."

"Why would the King do that?" said Kit.

"Auraline inherited a great deal of magic. The spells done on her before and after she was born were powerful. She is called the First Heir because she was the first faerie born who was heir to the Seelie and Unseelie Court both. And so are all her descendants. Your blood gives you claim to the High Kingship of Faerie."

"*What?*" said Kit. "But—I don't want it. I don't want to be High King of Faerie!"

"It doesn't matter what you want, not to them," Tessa said sadly. "Even if you never went near the throne of Faerie, there are warring factions who would love to get hold of you and use you as a pawn. An army with you at the head of it could take down the King or Queen or both."

Goose bumps flooded along Kit's arms. "But doesn't everyone know who I am now? Because of what happened with the Riders? Are they hunting me?"

Tessa put her hand on his wrist. It was a gentle, motherly touch. Kit could not remember such a touch in all his life. Only the memory of light blond hair and the sound of a lilting voice singing to him. *The story that I love you, it has no end.*

"Part of the reason we kept you here these last few days was to reach out into Downworld to see if anyone has been talking about you," said Tessa. "We have many connections, many ways of following gossip in the Markets. But with the chaos of the battle, all the talk is of the death of the Riders, what happened with Emma and Julian, and Kieran's ascension. There have been words of a warlock who made the great horses of the Riders vanish, but we have spread the word that it was Ragnor Fell." She rolled her eyes.

"I thought his name was Ragnor Shade?"

"It is Ragnor Fell," she said, and smiled in a way that made her look nineteen. "He is a scamp, and has been in hiding for some years. He resurfaced in grand style during the battle, and now everyone knows Ragnor Fell is back—and that he defeated the Riders, to boot." She chuckled. "He will be insufferable."

"He didn't actually do it," said Kit.

"That will not make a difference to Ragnor," said Tessa gravely.

"So . . . I'm safe?" Kit said. "I could go back to the Institute in Los Angeles?"

"I don't know." A line of worry had appeared between Tessa's brows. "We felt nervous enough before, leaving you, even with you in the Institute and Ragnor nearby to protect you. He even followed you when you went to the Shadow Market."

"Did he say why we were going to the Shadow Market?" Kit said, forgetting, in his sudden fear for Ty, not to act suspicious.

"Of course not," said Tessa. "He wasn't there to tattle on you, just protect you." She patted his shoulder absently while Kit mused on the strange loyalty of people you barely knew. "The thing is—before, we didn't realize you'd manifest any of the powers of the Heir. Few of your ancestors have before, save Auraline. We thought if we kept you away from things that might trigger the powers . . ."

"No faeries," Kit recalled. "No battles."

"Exactly. If it happens again, word might spread. Besides, faeries have long memories, and we want to make you as safe as possible."

"Does that mean leaving me in the Silent City? Because I don't like it here," Kit said. "I'm not good at Silent. And I don't want to talk about the bathroom situation."

"No," Tessa said. She took a deep breath, and Kit realized she was actually nervous. "What I'm saying is that you should come and live with me and Jem and the child we're going to have. After all our wandering, we've decided to settle down and build a home. We want you to—to build it with us. To be part of our family."

Kit was almost too stunned to speak, not the least at the revelation that Tessa was pregnant. "But—why?"

Tessa looked at him forthrightly. "Because a long time ago the Herondales gave both Jem and me a home, and we want to do the same for you."

"But am I actually a Herondale?" he asked. "I thought my father was a Herondale and my mother was a mundane, but it looks like they were both Shadowhunters. So I don't even know what my name should be."

"Your father's real last name isn't known," Tessa said. "He did have a small amount of Shadowhunter blood. It allowed him to have the Sight."

"I thought Shadowhunter blood bred true?"

"It does, but over the course of many generations it can become diluted. Still, your father could have trained and Ascended had he wanted. He never did. It was your mother who bore runes. It was your mother who has made you the Lost Herondale we searched for for so long. It is your choice, of course. You can bear any name you wish. We would still welcome you in our family whether you were called Kit Herondale or not."

Kit thought of Jace and of the mother he had never known, who he remembered now only in the songs she had sung him once. The mother who had given up her own life for his.

"I'll be a Herondale," he said. "I like the family ring. It's classy."

Tessa smiled at him.

"Anyway," Kit said. "Where are you planning to live?"

"Jem owns a house in Devon. A big old pile. We'll be going there. We know you care about the Blackthorns, so we'll understand if you want to stay with them," she added quickly. "We would be sad, but we would do whatever we can to protect you. Ragnor would help, and Catarina—we'd have to tell the Blackthorns why you needed the protection, of course—"

She was still talking, but Kit had stopped hearing her. The words spilled around him in a meaningless rush as all the memories he'd been trying to push back flew at him like sharply pecking birds. The Institute, the beach, the Blackthorns, always kind to him; Emma saving his life, Julian driving him to the Market and listening to him talk about Ty—even then, he'd wanted to talk about Ty.

All his energy had gone into Ty, all his devotion and hopes for the future. He *liked* the other Blackthorns, but he hardly knew them well. He probably knew Dru the best, and he liked her as a friend, but that was a small thing compared to the burning hurt and humiliation he felt when he thought about Ty.

He didn't blame Ty for what had happened. He blamed himself: He'd been too fixated on not losing Ty to tell him what he needed to hear. Everyone needed to be stopped from making bad choices sometimes, but he hadn't stopped Ty. And he'd gotten what he deserved, really. Now that he knew he meant nothing much to Ty, how could he live in the Institute again? See him every day? Feel like an idiot constantly, feel the pity of his family, listen to them tell him he should try to make other friends, survive in the same house with Ty while Ty avoided him? There was no real question about it. *I can't face going back there and living with them. This is my chance to start again and learn what it means to be who I am.*

"I'll go with you. I'd like to live with you," Kit said.

"Oh." Tessa blinked. "Oh!" She grabbed his hand and squeezed it, smiling all over her kind face. "That's *lovely*, Kit, that's wonderful. Jem will be so happy too. And it will be wonderful for the baby to have company. I mean, hopefully you'll like the baby as well." She blushed. Kit thought it would actually be kind of nice to have a small sibling-type person in his life, but he said nothing. "I'm babbling," Tessa said. "I'm just so excited. We'll go tonight—get you safe and settled as fast as possible. We'll arrange for you to have a tutor—for all the necessary protection spells to be done by the Silent Brothers—"

"That sounds good," Kit said, a little exhausted already by the thought of everything that needed to be done. "I only have this bag—no other luggage." It was true, and there was nothing he cared about much in the bag either, besides the Herondale dagger and the witch-light Ty had given him.

"I imagine you'd like to say good-bye to the Blackthorns before we go—"

"No," Kit said. "I don't want to see them."

Tessa blinked.

"It's better if they don't know about all this First Heir stuff," Kit said. "It's safer for them. Jem can tell them I just decided L.A. wasn't for me. They're all so far ahead of me in training, and I should learn from the beginning if I want to be a Shadowhunter."

Tessa nodded. Kit knew she didn't entirely buy his excuse, but she also knew enough not to pry. It was very reassuring.

"I do have one question before we go," Kit said, and Tessa looked at him curiously. "Will I be growing pointy ears? Maybe a tail? I've seen some weird-looking faeries in the Shadow Market."

Tessa grinned. "I guess we'll find out."

Everyone wanted to come by the canal house and say hello to Emma and Julian now that they had left the Basilias. People Dru was familiar with as well as people she wasn't flooded into the ground floor, bringing flowers and small gifts: new gauntlets for Emma, a gear jacket for Julian.

Some were overly bright and cheery and greeted Emma and Julian as if nothing odd had happened to them at all. Some complimented them as if they thought the whole "becoming enormous and almost dying" was part of a predetermined plan that had paid off nicely. Others were awkward—those who had been a little too close to the Cohort, Dru suspected—as if they wondered if Emma and Julian might grow huge at any moment and squash them right there in the kitchen. One kindly older lady complimented Julian on being tall and a terrible silence fell; Tavvy said, "What's going on?" and Dru had to drag him into the sitting room.

A few others seemed to have had major life experiences. "It just came to me on the field that I should spend more time with my family," said Trini Castel. "Moments of peace are precious moments. We'll never get them back."

"So true," said Julian.

He looked as if he was trying not to laugh. Everyone else nodded thoughtfully. It was very strange—for days, Dru had been worried that Emma and Julian would be punished in some way when they woke up: either officially, by the Clave, or by the ignorant judgment of other Shadowhunters. But it didn't seem to be happening.

She edged close to Magnus, who was sitting by the fire eating the chocolates out of a box someone had brought for Emma. He'd come over with Maryse, Max, and Rafe so they could play with Tavvy. Alec, Jace, and Clary were coming later, apparently with some sort of surprise. Isabelle and Simon had already returned to the New York Institute to keep an eye on things.

"Why aren't people mad?" she whispered. "At Emma and Julian?"

Magnus wiggled his eyebrows at her. Magnus had very amusing eyebrows; Dru had always found him an amusing person generally, with his immense tallness and refusal to take anything seriously. "Well," Magnus said, "without Julian's war council and his strategy for dealing with Dearborn, it's likely that the Cohort would have prevailed. The road the Cohort was traveling led to civil war and bloodshed. Everyone is glad it was avoided."

"True," said Drusilla, "but that *was* before they became giant angel monsters."

"Angels are messengers." Magnus dusted cocoa powder off his hands, looking thoughtful. "They speak in strange ways, even to you, their children. Horace and his Cohort spoke as if they were doing the angels' will, and because of it, people feared them. On the battlefield, burning with heavenly fire, Julian and Emma proved that wasn't the case. The angels spoke through *them*."

"So basically everyone who didn't like Horace wanted a big angel to squash the Cohort?" Dru said.

Magnus grinned. "They don't want to say that, but believe me, it was immensely satisfying to them."

At that moment Jace and Clary arrived with Alec and an enormous cake they'd iced themselves. Most of the strangers had already departed, and Ty helped them put it on the sideboard, where the cake box was opened to reveal that the lettering said: CONGRATULATIONS ON NOT BEING GIANTS ANYMORE!

Everyone laughed and gathered around to cut pieces of the lemon-chocolate cake. Julian and Emma leaned against each other, their shoulders touching. Since they had returned from the Basilias, it had seemed that a massive weight was off Julian's shoulders. He seemed lighter and happier than he had since before the Dark War. Dru knew that he and Emma were no longer *parabatai*: the angel magic had burned it out of them somehow. It didn't take a genius to figure out that they were probably very pleased about that, considering all the smiling and hand touching they were doing.

Mark and Cristina, on the other hand, seemed sad. They were quiet among all the bright chatter in the room. At one point Dru saw Emma take Cristina into the kitchen and hug her as if something bad had happened.

Dru didn't know what it was, but she did notice that Kieran wasn't there.

Ty was also quiet. Every time he passed Julian, Jules would pull him in for a hug and ruffle his hair the way he'd liked when he was little. Ty would smile, but he seemed unusually listless, uninterested even in eavesdropping on the guests' conversations and making notes for his detective manuals the way he usually did.

Eventually he went up to Magnus, who was sitting in a deep blue chair by the fireplace holding his deep blue son on his lap and tickling him. Dru edged closer to the hearth, wondering what Ty wanted to say to the warlock.

"Where's Kit, really?" Ty said, and Dru thought: *I should have known.* Jem had told them that Kit was coming to live with him and Tessa in Devon, but not why, nor why they had to leave in such a hurry. Julian and the others seemed to think Kit would visit them soon, but Dru wasn't so sure. "I keep asking, but no one will tell me."

Magnus looked up, his cat's eyes hooded. "Kit's all right. He's with Tessa and Jem. He's going to be living with them."

"I know," Ty said. His voice shook. "I know, but—can I say good-bye to him? If I could just talk to him once—"

"He's already gone," Magnus said. "He didn't want to say good-bye to you. To anyone really, but I suspect it was mostly you."

Dru had to stifle a gasp. Why would Magnus say something so flatly unkind?

"I don't understand," Ty said, his left hand fluttering at his side. He caught at his wrist with his right hand as if he could stop it.

Julian had always called Ty's hands his butterflies and told him they were beautiful, graceful, and useful—why not let them fly? But Dru worried. She thought they fluttered like hearts, a sign that Ty was uneasy.

Magnus's expression was grave. "Come with me."

Magnus gave his son to Maryse to carry into the sitting room and headed upstairs, Ty at his heels. Dru didn't hesitate. If Magnus was angry with Ty she was going to find out why, and defend Ty if necessary. Even if Magnus turned her into a toad. She followed.

There was an empty bedroom at the top of the stairs. Magnus and Ty went into it, Magnus leaning his long body against the bare wall. Ty sat down on the edge of the bed while Dru stationed herself by the crack in the mostly open door.

"I don't understand," Ty said again. Dru knew he'd probably been working on the problem in his mind all the way up the steps: What did Magnus mean? Why did Kit not want to say good-bye to him?

"Ty," said Magnus. "I know what you did. Ragnor told me. I wish he'd told me earlier, but then I was dying, so I understand why he didn't. Also, he thought he'd headed you off. But he didn't, did he? You got an energy source from the Market and you did the spell anyway."

The spell? The one to raise Livvy's ghost?

Ty stared. "How do you know?"

"I have sources in the Markets," said Magnus. "I'm also a warlock, and the son of a Greater Demon. I can sense the dark magic on you, Ty. It's like a cloud around you I can see." He sat down on the window ledge. "I know you tried to raise your sister from the dead."

He did what? Realization exploded in Dru's mind, along with shock: You didn't just try to raise the dead. Look what had happened to Malcolm. Trying to communicate with a spirit was one thing, necromancy quite another.

Ty didn't protest, though. He sat on the bed, his fingers knotting and unknotting.

"You are so, so lucky your spell didn't work," Magnus said. "What you did was bad, but what you *could* have done would have been so much worse."

How could you, Ty? How could you, Kit?

"Clary brought Jace back from the dead," Ty said.

"Clary asked *Raziel* to bring Jace back from the dead. Think about it—Raziel himself. You are messing about in magic reserved for gods, Ty. There are reasons necromancy is something people hate. If you bring back a life, you must pay with something of equal consequence. What if it had been another life? Would you have wanted to kill someone to keep Livvy with you?"

Ty lifted his head. "What if it was Horace? What if it was someone bad? We kill people in battle. I don't see the difference."

Magnus looked at Ty for a long time; Dru was afraid he might say something harsh to him, but the lines of Magnus's face had softened. "Tiberius," he said at last. "When your sister died, she didn't deserve it. Life and death aren't doled out by a judge who decides what is fair, and if it were, would you want to be that judge? Every life at your fingertips, and also every death?"

Ty squeezed his eyes shut. "No," he whispered. "I just want my sister back. I miss her all the time. It feels like there's a hole in me that will never be filled up."

Oh, Dru thought. How odd that it would be Ty who would most accurately describe what it felt like to lose Livvy. She pressed her hand to her side. *A hole where my sister should be.*

"I know," Magnus said gently. "And I know that you've spent a lot of your life knowing you're different and that's true. You are. So am I."

Ty looked up at him.

"So you think this feeling you have, of missing half of yourself, must be fixed. That it can't be what everyone else is feeling when they lose someone. But it *is.* Grief can be so bad you can't breathe, but that's what it means to be human. We lose, we suffer, but we have to keep breathing."

"Are you going to tell everyone?" Ty said in a near whisper.

"No," Magnus said. "Provided you promise never to do anything like that again."

Ty looked nauseated. "I never would."

"I believe it. But, Ty, there's something else I'd like you to do. I can't order you to do it. I can only suggest it."

Ty had picked up a pillow; he was running his hand over the rough, textured side of it, over and over, his palm reading messages in the fabric.

"I know you always wanted to go to the Scholomance," said Magnus.

Ty started to protest. Magnus held up a hand.

"Just let me finish, and then you can say anything you want to," Magnus said. "At the L.A. Institute, Helen and Aline can keep you safe and love you, and I know you might not want to leave your family. But what you *need* is mysteries to solve to keep your mind busy and your soul filled. I've known people like you before—they don't rest until their minds are flying free and solving problems.

I knew Conan Doyle back in the day. He loved to travel. Spent his third year of medical school on a whaling boat."

Ty stared.

Magnus seemed to realize he'd veered off course. "All I'm saying is that you have a curious mind," he said. "You want to solve mysteries, to be a detective of life—that's why you always wanted to go to the Scholomance. But you didn't think you could. Because your twin wanted to be *parabatai* with you, and you couldn't do both."

"I would have given up the Scholomance for her," Ty said. "Besides, everyone I met who went there—Zara and the others—was awful."

"The Scholomance is going to be quite different now," said Magnus. "The Cohort poisoned it, but they'll be gone. I think it would be a wonderful place for you." His voice gentled. "Grief is hard. Change can be all that helps."

"Thanks," Ty said. "Can I think about it?"

"Of course." Magnus looked weary and a little regretful. As if he wished things could have been different; as if he wished there were something else to say than the things he'd said. He turned toward the door—Dru shrank back—and paused.

"You understand that from now on you're tied to the ghost of your sister," Magnus said.

Tied to the ghost of your sister?

Livvy's ghost?

"I do understand," Ty said.

Magnus stared at the door of the bedroom as if he were seeing through into the past. "You think you do," he said. "But you don't *really* see it. I know she set you free in the forest. Right now this feels better than nothing, better than being without her. You don't yet understand the price. And I hope you never have to pay it."

He touched Ty's shoulder lightly, without looking at him, and left. Dru ducked into the next bedroom until Magnus's footsteps had disappeared down the stairs.

Then she took a deep breath and went in to talk to Ty.

He hadn't moved from the end of the bed in the empty room. He stared into the gathering shadows, his face pale as he looked up at her. "Dru?" he said haltingly.

"You should have told me," Dru said.

He furrowed his arched eyebrows. "You were listening?"

She nodded.

"I know," he said. "I didn't want you to stop me. And I'm not good at lying. It's easier for me to just not say."

"Kit lied to me," she said. She was furious at Kit, though she tried not to show it. Maybe it was better that he wasn't coming back with them. Even if he had shown her how to pick locks. "Livvy's ghost—is she really around?"

"I saw her today. She was in the Basilias when Emma and Julian woke up. She was sitting on one of the bureaus. I never know when she's going to be there or not be there. Magnus said she's tied to me, so . . ."

"Maybe you can teach me to see her." Dru knelt down and put her arms around Ty. She could feel the slight vibrations going through his body; he was shaking. "Maybe we can see her together."

"We can't tell anyone," Ty said, but he had put his arms around Dru, too; he was hugging her, his hair against her cheek as soft and fine as Tavvy's. "No one can know."

"I won't say anything." She held on to her brother, held on hard, as if she could keep him tethered to the earth. "I'll never tell."

Emma lay atop the covers of her bed, the only light in the room the reflected radiance of the demon towers as it shone through the window.

She supposed it wasn't surprising that she couldn't sleep. She'd slept for three days and awakened to a series of shocks: realizing what had happened, Jem's explanation, the house full of people. The odd feeling that followed her constantly that she'd forgotten something, that she'd put something down in the other room and needed to remember to get it.

It was the *parabatai* bond, she knew. Her body and her brain hadn't caught up to the fact that it was gone. She was missing it the way people who lost limbs sometimes still felt them there.

She was missing Julian. They'd been together all day, but always surrounded by other people. When the house had finally emptied of strangers, Julian had taken Tavvy up to bed, bidding her an awkward good night in front of the others.

She'd gone up to bed herself not long after, and had been lying there worrying for hours. Would everything be awkward now that they weren't *parabatai*? Now that they floated in a new, foreign place between being friends and lovers? They had never declared themselves because words like "boyfriend" and "girlfriend" seemed banal in the face of curses and giant monsters. What if everything that had happened was so devastating that they could never reach a place of normalcy?

She couldn't stand it. She rolled out of bed, got to her feet, and smoothed down her nightgown. She flung open her bedroom door, ready to march across the hall to Julian's room and make him talk to her, no matter how awkward it might be.

Just outside her door stood Julian, his hand outstretched, looking as surprised to see her as she was to see him.

He lowered his hand slowly, the distant moonlight glinting off his sea-glass bracelet. The hallway was dark and quiet, casting Julian's face into shadow. "I didn't know if you'd want me to come in," he said.

Relief made Emma sag against the doorway. "I do want you to come in."

She moved back into the room while he shut the door behind him. They were both in darkness now, only the light of the glass towers providing illumination. Julian, in all black, was a shadow among shadows as he looked down at her; his hair looked black too, striking against his pale skin. "I didn't know if you'd want me to kiss you."

She didn't move. More than anything else she wanted him to come to her and put his hands on her. She wanted to feel him against her when the space between them was no longer a space of cursed and forbidden things.

"I do want you to kiss me," she whispered.

He closed the distance between them in one step. His hands cupped the back of her head, his mouth slanting down over hers, hot and sweet as tea with honey. She ran her teeth lightly across his bottom lip and he made a guttural sound that raised the hairs along her arms.

His warm lips moved to graze her cheek, her jawbone. "I didn't know if you'd want me to touch you," he murmured against her skin.

It was a pleasure just to look up at him slowly. To know that none of this needed to be rushed. She slipped her nightgown over her head and watched his face go tight with desire, his eyes dark as the bottom of the sea.

"I want you to touch me," she said. "There's nothing you could do to me that I wouldn't want, because it's you."

He caught her in his arms and it was strange for a moment, her bare skin against his clothes, cotton and denim and metal rivets as he lifted her up and carried her to the bed. They crashed onto it together, Julian struggling out of his shirt, his jeans; Emma crawled atop him, leaning down to kiss his throat, to lick and suck at the pulse point there where she could feel the beating of his heart.

"I want to go slowly," she whispered. "I want to feel everything."

He gripped her hips and flipped their position, rolling over so that he was above her. He grinned down at her wickedly.

"Slowly it is," he said.

He started with her fingers, kissing each one; he kissed the palms of her hands and her wrists, her shoulders and her collarbones. He traced a path of kisses over her stomach until she was writhing and gasping and threatening him, which only made him laugh softly and turn his attention to even more sensitive places.

When the world had gone white behind her eyes several times, he rose up over her and brushed her damp hair away from her face. "Now," he whispered, and covered her mouth with his own as he joined their bodies together.

It was slow as he had said it would be, as it had never been before; there was no desperation beyond their desire. They lay crosswise on the bed, sprawled and hungry, yearning and touching. She stroked his face lightly, reverently: the curve of his mouth, his eyelashes fluttering against his cheekbones, and with every touch and moment his breath grew more ragged, his grip on the sheets tighter. Her back arched to meet him, her head full of sparks: they rose and blended together until everything was fire. And when they caught alight at last, neither able to wait a moment longer, they were one person. They were incandescent as angels.

From Mark's room, he could see the moon, and it troubled him.

There had been so many nights on horseback, the moon riding with them as if it, too, hunted the sky. He could hear Kieran's laughter in his ears, even now, clear laughter untouched by sorrow.

He hoped Kieran would laugh again like that someday.

He could only picture him sitting in darkness, in the blackened throne room of the Unseelie King, a bleak and lonely place. A King of shattered hearts and broken souls, solitary on his granite throne, growing older slowly through the ages of the world.

It was more than he could stand. He was grateful beyond measure when Cristina slipped into his room and crawled onto the bed with him. She wore white pajamas, her hair loose and dark. She curled up against his side, pressing her face into his neck. Her cheeks were wet with tears.

"Is this really how it ends? The three of us, all miserable?" he said.

She placed her hand over his heart. "I love you, Mark," she said, her voice gentle. "I hate to think of your heart torn as mine is."

"I am happier when you are here," he said, placing his hand over hers. "And yet . . ."

"And yet," she said. "I have an idea, Mark. Perhaps a mad one. But it might work. It might mean we could see him again." Her dark eyes were straightforward. "I would need your help."

He drew her up his body and kissed her; she went soft against him, her body curving into his. She was rich and sweet as honey, silken as a bed of wildflowers. She was the only woman he would ever love.

He thumbed the tears away from her cheeks and whispered, "My hand, my heart, my blade are yours. Tell me what I need to do."

Emma lay with her head on Julian's chest, feeling the beat of her heart slowly return to normal. Somehow most of the covers had come off the bed and were on the floor; they were half-wrapped in sheets, Julian's free hand idly playing with her hair.

"So I guess you feel pretty good about yourself," she said.

He blinked at her sleepily. "Why would that be?"

She laughed, her breath stirring the soft dark curls of his hair. "If you don't know, I'm not going to tell you."

He smiled. "How do *you* feel?"

She folded her arms on his chest, looking up at him. "Happy. So happy but also like I don't deserve to be."

His hand stilled in her hair. "Why not? You deserve to be happy more than anyone I know."

"If it wasn't for you, I would have done a terrible thing," Emma said. "I would have broken all the *parabatai* bonds. It would have caused so much devastation."

"You were half-crazy from the curse," Julian said. "You weren't thinking straight."

"Still. I let myself be manipulated by the Queen. Even though I knew she only cares about herself. I knew it, and I let her get into my head. I should have had faith."

"But you did," he said. "Faith isn't never having any doubts; it's having what you need to overcome them." He lightly stroked her cheek. "We all have things we regret doing. I regret asking Magnus to do that spell. I regret that we couldn't help Ash. He was just a kid."

"I know," she said. "I hate that we left him behind. But if he was here—someone would always be looking for him. All it would take is some spells from the Black Volume to make him so powerful everyone would want to use him."

"Good thing there aren't any Black Volumes left," said Julian. "For a while it was like a whack-a-mole game. I guess I contributed to that." He smiled crookedly. "Oh, and I regret killing Dane Larkspear."

"He was going to kill us," Emma said. "You did what you had to do."

"Ah, there's the murderous girl I know and love," said Julian. "I don't know how I'll ever make up for Dane. But I have the faith you'll help me figure it out."

"I believe *you* deserve to be happy," Emma said. "You're the bravest and most loving person I know."

"And I believe you deserve to be happy," said Julian. "So how about I believe it for you, and you believe it for me? We can believe it for each other."

Emma glanced toward the window. She could see the first traces of sunlight in the sky. Morning was breaking.

She looked up at Julian. Dawn touched the edges of his hair and eyelashes with gold. "Do you have to go back to your room?" she whispered.

He smiled down at her. "No," he said. "We don't have to lie or pretend now. We don't have to lie or pretend ever again."

It was the first time Emma had been in the Council Hall since Livvy had died.

It wasn't the only reason she was desperate for the meeting to be over, but it was certainly part of it. The blood might have been scrubbed out of the dais, but she would always see it there. She knew it was the same for Julian; he tensed beside her as they went in through the doors with the rest of the Blackthorns. The whole family was quiet, even Tavvy.

The Hall was filled to bursting. Emma had never seen it so full: Shadowhunters were smashed together on the rows of seats, and the aisles were filled with those who were standing; some were Projecting in from distant Institutes, their half-transparent shimmering forms glowing along the back wall. Emma recognized Isabelle and Simon among them and waved.

Thankfully, seats had been kept for the Blackthorns by Jaime and Diego. Jaime had held an entire row by lying across it; he popped up when they approached and let them all slide in, winking at several glaring Shadowhunters who had been hoping to find a seat.

People stared at all the Blackthorns, but especially Emma and Julian, as they took their seats. It had been the same at the house the day before: strangers gawking, wide-eyed. Emma remembered what she had thought about Jace and Clary at the war council meeting: *So this is what it's like to be heroes. To be the ones with angel blood, the ones who've literally saved the world. People look at you as if . . . almost as if you're not real.*

As it turned out, it made you wonder yourself how real you were.

Emma wound up sitting between Cristina and Julian, her fingertips touching Julian's discreetly on the seat between them. Now that she and Julian were no longer *parabatai*, all she wanted was to get home and start their new life. They would discuss their travel year and plan all the places they would go. They would visit Cristina in Mexico, and Jace and Clary in New York, and Great-Aunt Marjorie in England. They would go to Paris and stand in front of the Eiffel Tower holding hands and there would be nothing wrong with it and nothing forbidden.

Maybe it would be a short meeting? She glanced around the room, noting the serious expressions on everyone's faces. Knots of those who had been friendly to the Cohort, but had not fought with them on the field, huddled together on benches, whispering. Dearborn sympathizers like Lazlo Balogh, who had remained in the city for the duration of the battle, hadn't been arrested—only those who had raised weapons against other Nephilim would stand trial.

"People look grim," she murmured to Julian.

"No one wants to sentence the Cohort," he said. "A lot of them are young. It feels brutal, I think."

"Zara deserves sentencing," Emma muttered. "She stabbed me and she totally upset Cristina with that whole fake engagement."

Julian looked over at Cristina, who had her head on Mark's shoulder. "I think Cristina has moved on," he said. "And Diego, too."

Emma darted a look at where Diego—his cheek bandaged—was sitting and chatting with a glowing Divya, who had been thrilled Anush had fought on their side on the field. *Interesting.*

There was a rustle and a flourish as the guards closed the side doors and Jia entered through the back of the Hall. The room hushed as she moved down to the dais, her robes sweeping the steps. Behind her, wearing the flame-colored tunics of prisoners, were the captured Cohort members. There were perhaps fifty or sixty of them, many of them young, just as Julian had said. So many had been recruited through the Scholomance and its outreach. Vanessa Ashdown, Manuel Villalobos, Amelia Overbeck, and Zara herself, her expression defiant.

They filed onto the dais behind Jia, the guards guiding them into rows. Some were still bandaged from the battle. All bore *iratzes*. Their tunics were printed with runes meant to keep them trapped in the city. They could not pass the gates of Alicante.

Flame to wash away our sins, Emma thought. It was odd to see prisoners with their hands unbound, but even if each of them had been freely bearing two longswords, they would hardly have been a match for the hundreds of other Shadowhunters in the Council Hall.

She saw Diego lean over to whisper something to Jaime, who shook his head, his face troubled.

"We come together in a time of grief and healing," announced Jia, her voice echoing off the walls. "Thanks to the bravery of so many Shadowhunters, we have fought nobly, we have found new allies, we have preserved our relationships with Downworlders, and we have opened a new way forward."

Zara made a horrible face at the phrase "preserved our relationships." Emma hoped she would be sentenced to cleaning toilets for the rest of eternity.

"However," said Jia. "I am not the leader who can take us on that path."

Murmurs ran through the room; was Jia really saying what they thought she was saying? Emma bolted upright in her seat and looked over at Aline, but she seemed as shocked as the rest of the room. Patrick Penhallow, though, seated in the front row, seemed unsurprised.

"I will preside over the sentencing of the Cohort," Jia continued, unfazed. "It will be my last act as Consul. After that there will be an open election for a new Consul and a new Inquisitor."

Helen whispered to Aline, who took her hand. Emma felt a chill go through her. This was a surprise and the last thing she wanted was a surprise. She knew it was selfish—she remembered Jem saying that Jia was ill—but still, Jia was a known quantity. The unknown loomed.

"And when I say an open election," Jia continued, "I mean *an open election*. Everyone in this Hall will have a vote. Everyone will have a voice. No matter their age; no matter if they are Projecting from their home Institute. No matter," she added, "if they are members of the Cohort."

A roar went through the room.

"But they are criminals!" shouted Joaquín Acosta Romero, head of the Buenos Aires Institute. "Criminals do not have a vote!"

Jia waited patiently for the roar to die down into quiet. Even the Cohort were staring at her in puzzlement. "Look how full this Council Hall is," she said. People twisted around in their seats to stare at the overflowing rows of seats, the hundreds of Projections in the back of the room. "You're all here because over the past week, and especially since the battle, you have realized how urgent this situation always was. The Clave was nearly taken over by extremists who would have driven us into isolation and self-destruction. And everyone who stood back and allowed this to happen—through inattention, through apathy and overconfidence—" Her voice shook. "Well. We are all guilty. And therefore we will all vote, as a reminder that every voice counts, and when you choose not to use your voice, you are letting yourself be silenced."

"But I still don't see why criminals should vote!" yelled Jaime, who had apparently taken the "no matter their age" portion of the speech to heart.

"Because if they don't," said Diana, rising to her feet and addressing the room, "they will always be able to say that whoever the new Consul is, they were elected because the majority had no voice. The Cohort has always flourished by telling the lie that they speak for all Shadowhunters—that they say the words that everyone would speak if they could. Now we will test that lie. All Shadowhunters *will* speak. Including them."

Jia assented gravely. "Miss Wrayburn is correct."

"So what will be done with the prisoners, then?" called Kadir. "Will they walk among us, free?"

"The Cohort must be punished! *They must be!*" The voice was a raw scream. Emma turned and flinched; she felt Julian's hand tighten on hers. It was Elena Larkspear. She was alone; her husband had not come to the meeting. She looked as haggard as if she had aged fifty years in the past week. "They *used* our children—as if they were trash—to do the things too filthy or dangerous for them to do! They murdered my daughter and my son! I demand reparations!"

She fell back into her seat with a dry sob, covering her face with her hands. Emma stared at the Cohort, her throat aching: even Zara was having a hard time wiping the look of horror off her face.

"They will not go unpunished," said Jia gently. "They have been tested by the Mortal Sword and confessed to their crimes. They sent Dane Larkspear to murder other Shadowhunters, and were thus directly responsible for his death." She inclined her head toward Elena. "They murdered Oskar Lindquist that a demon might take his place at a meeting held at the Los Angeles Institute. Led by Horace Dearborn, this group used lies and intimidation to try to lead the Clave into a false alliance with Faerie—"

"And now you people are trying to lead the Clave into an alliance with the new King—how is that different?" Zara shouted, rallying.

Emma whipped her head around to study the room. Many

Shadowhunters looked angry or annoyed, but there were those who clearly didn't disagree with Zara. *Ugh.*

A voice rang out clearly, stony and cold. Alec Lightwood's. "Because open political engagement is very different from disavowing any relationship to Downworlders in public while conspiring to commit murder with them behind the backs of the people you're meant to be governing."

"The Cohort imprisoned loyal Nephilim and sent others to their deaths," said Jia after a withering glance at Zara. "We were brought to the brink of civil war." She looked out at the Clave. "You might think I want to punish them severely, strip their Marks and send them into the mundane world they so despise. But we must consider *mercy*. So many of the Cohort are young, and they were influenced by misinformation and outright lies. Here we can give them a chance to again rejoin the Clave and redeem themselves. To turn from the path of deceit and hate and walk once again in the light of Raziel."

More murmurs. The members of the Cohort looked at each other in confusion. Some seemed relieved, some angrier than ever.

"After this meeting," Jia went on, "the Cohort will be split up and sent to different Institutes. Several of the Institutes who attended Julian Blackthorn's war council have offered to take in former Cohort members and show them a better way. They will have a chance to prove themselves before they return to the homeland."

Now there was an eruption of chatter. Some shouted the punishment was lenient. Some shouted that it was cruel to "exile them from Alicante." Jia stilled the shouting with a gesture.

"Any who are not in favor of this punishment, please raise your hand or voice. Manuel Villalobos, you are not allowed to vote on this issue."

Zara pinned Manuel, whose hand was half-raised, with a scowl.

A few more hands were raised. Emma almost wanted to raise

hers and to say that they deserved worse. But then, she had spared Zara's life on the field, and the gesture had led to all of this: had led to the end of the battle, and her and Julian's freedom.

Maybe Arthur had been right. Maybe mercy was better than revenge.

She kept her hand down, as did all the other Blackthorns. No one she knew well raised their hand, not even Diego or Jaime, who had good cause to hate Zara and her friends.

Jia looked relieved. "And now," she said, "to the election of a new Consul."

Jace was on his feet before she finished speaking. "I nominate Alec Lightwood."

The Blackthorns clapped fiercely. Alec looked stunned and touched. Clary cheered, and the cheer spread—many in the room waved their hands in support, and Emma's heart swelled. Jace could have reached out for the position of Consul had he wanted; he and Clary were beloved; either would win handily. But he had put Alec forward for it, because it was what Alec wanted—and because Jace knew Alec was the right choice.

Delaney Scarsbury rose to his feet, his face red. "I object. Alec Lightwood is much too young. He lacks experience and notoriously consorts with Downworlders."

"You mean by heading up the Downworlder-Shadowhunter Alliance where his *job* is to consort with Downworlders?" called Julian.

"He does it in his free time as well, Blackthorn," said Scarsbury with a nasty smile. Emma rather wished Magnus was there and could turn him into a toad, but Downworlders weren't at the meeting. They had refused to be in the same room as the Cohort members, and Emma couldn't blame them.

"You know what they mean," called Zara. "He's a filthy pervert. Jace should stand for Consul instead."

"I am *also* a filthy pervert," said Jace, "or at least I aspire to be. You have no idea what I get up to in my spare time. Just last week I asked Clary to buy me a—"

Clary pulled him down next to her and belabored him with her fists. He grinned.

"What about Patrick Penhallow?" someone shouted. "He knows what he's doing!"

Patrick, seated in the front row, rose to his feet with a stony expression. "I will not stand as Consul," he said. "My wife has given enough. My daughter has given enough. It is time for my family to be allowed some peace and rest."

He sat down in dead silence.

Delaney Scarsbury said, "I nominate Lazlo Balogh."

Real fear stabbed through Emma for the first time that day. She and Julian looked at each other, both remembering the same moment—Lazlo rising in the Hall of Accords to deliver the words that sent Helen into exile and abandoned Mark to the Hunt. *Both Mark and Helen Blackthorn have the blood of faeries in them. We know the boy's already joined up with the Wild Hunt, so he's beyond us, but the girl shouldn't be among Shadowhunters. It isn't decent.*

Those who hadn't cheered for Alec's nomination looked pleased, as did the Cohort. "He'd be an awful Consul," Emma said to Julian. "He'd set everything back."

"We don't really have a better system," said Julian. "All we can do is ask people what they want."

"And hope they choose the right thing," said Cristina.

"Alec would look much better on the money," said Mark.

"We don't put the Consul on the money," said Julian. "And we don't print money, anyway."

"We could start doing both," said Mark.

"Alec Lightwood has never even lived in Idris," said Lazlo, rising up. "What does he know about governing our homeland?"

Alec rose to his feet. "My parents were exiled," he said. "And most Shadowhunters don't live in Idris—how will you govern them if you think the only Shadowhunters that matter live in Alicante?"

"Your parents were exiled because they were in the Circle!" snapped Balogh.

"And he has learned from his parents' mistakes!" Maryse snapped. "My son knows better than anyone else the horror that bigotry and prejudice can bring."

Alec gave her a nod, and spoke coolly. "You voted for my father for Inquisitor, Balogh, so it didn't bother you then," he said. "My father gave his life in this room for the Clave. What have you done besides exile Shadowhunter children because you were afraid of their faerie blood?"

"Damn," said someone in the back. "He's good."

"Lightwood would end the Downworlder Registry," said Lazlo. "And the Cold Peace."

"You're right, I would," said Alec. "We can't live in fear of Downworlders. Downworlders gave us Portals. They gave us a victory over Valentine. They gave us a victory on the Fields just now. We cannot keep pretending we don't need them, any more than they can pretend they don't need us. Our future depends on our mandate—we are the hunters of demons, not the hunters of our own allies. If prejudice sidetracks us, we may all die."

Lazlo's expression darkened. Applause rang through the room, though not all were applauding. Many Shadowhunters sat with their hands clasped firmly in their laps.

"I think it has come time for the vote," said Jia. She took a tarnished glass vessel from a stand on the dais and handed it down to Patrick in the front row. He bent his head and whispered into the vial.

Emma watched with interest—she had heard of the process of voting for Consul but had never seen it. The vial went from hand to hand, each Shadowhunter whispering into it as if confessing a secret. Those Projecting had the vial held out to them by obliging hands since Projections could speak but not touch objects.

When the vial came to her, she lifted it to her mouth and said, "Alexander Lightwood," in a firm, loud voice. She heard Julian chuckle as she passed it along to Cristina.

At last the vial had been shared with every Shadowhunter save the Cohort. It was given to Jia, who passed it along to Zara.

"Vote wisely," she said. "The freedom to choose your own Consul is a great responsibility."

For a moment, Zara looked as if she might spit in the jar. She jerked it out of Jia's hand, spoke into it, and handed it to Manuel on her right. He smirked as he whispered into the jar, and Emma's shoulders tightened, knowing that every Cohort vote was a vote against Alec.

At last the final vote was cast, and the jar returned to Jia, who took out her stele and drew a rune on its side. The vial shook in her hand as pale smoke poured from its open neck, the expelled breath of hundreds of Nephilim. It formed into words across the air.

ALEXANDER GIDEON LIGHTWOOD

Clary and Jace flung themselves at Alec, laughing, as the air exploded with cheers. Aline and Helen gave Alec a mutual thumbs-up. The Projections of Isabelle and Simon waved from the back of the room. The Blackthorns whooped and applauded; Emma whistled. Maryse Lightwood wiped away tears of happiness as Kadir patted her shoulder gently.

"Alec Lightwood," cried Jia. "Please rise. You are the new Consul of the Clave."

Emma had expected an outburst from Lazlo, or at least a look of black rage. Instead he merely smirked coldly as Alec rose to his feet among cheers and applause.

"This vote doesn't count! It shouldn't count!" shouted Zara.

"If those who died on the field could have voted, Alec Lightwood would never have won!"

"I will work toward your rehabilitation, Zara," said Alec evenly.

Silver flashed. Zara had snatched a long dagger from the weapons belt of a guard standing near her; he made no move to stop her. There were gasps as the rest of the guards tossed weapons to the other Cohort members, steel sparking in the light from the great windows.

"We refuse to recognize Alec Lightwood as Consul!" shouted Manuel. "We stand for our old traditions, for the way things always have been and always should be!"

"Guards!" Jia shouted, but the twenty or so guards were making no effort to stop the Cohort—in fact, they had joined them in a flurry of unsheathed daggers. Emma glanced at Lazlo Balogh, who was watching with folded arms, clearly unsurprised. Somehow, Emma realized, the Cohort's allies had planted guards who were sympathetic to their cause. But what on earth were they planning? There were still only a fraction of them compared to the overwhelming number of Shadowhunters who had voted for Alec.

Jia leaped down from the dais, unsheathing her *dao.* All over the Hall, Shadowhunters were rising to their feet and drawing arms. Alec had reached for his bow, Jace his sword. Dru reached for Tavvy, her face pale, as the rest of the family took out their weapons.

Then Zara raised her dagger and put it to her own throat.

Movement in the room ceased. Emma still gripped Cortana, staring as Manuel followed Zara's gesture, placing the blade of his own dagger against his throat. Amelia Overbeck did the same—Vanessa Ashdown followed, with Milo Coldridge—until all the Cohort members stood with blades to their throats.

"You can put your weapons down," said Zara, holding the knife against her throat so tightly that blood dripped down her hand. "We are not here to harm our fellow Shadowhunters. You have harmed yourselves enough with your foolish and shortsighted vote. We are acting to save Alicante from corruption and the glass towers from ruin." Her eyes glittered madly. "You spoke before of the value of the lands outside Alicante as if Alicante were not the heart of our people. Very well then, go out and embrace the mundane world, away from the Angel's light."

"Are you demanding we leave Alicante?" said Diana in disbelief. "We who are Nephilim as you are?"

"No consort of a faerie is as Nephilim as I am," Zara spat. "Yes. We ask—we demand—that you go. Clary Fairchild can create Portals; let her make one now. Step through it and go where you wish. Anywhere that is not Alicante."

"You're only a few people," said Emma. "You can't kick the rest of us out of Alicante. It's not your tree house."

"I am sorry it came to this," said Lazlo, "but we are not a few people. We are many more. You may have intimidated people into voting for Lightwood, but their hearts are with us."

"You would propose a civil war? Here in the Council Hall?" demanded Diana.

"Not a civil war," said Zara. "We know we cannot win against you in battle. You have too many filthy tricks. You have warlocks on your side." She glared at Alec. "But we are willing to die for our beliefs and for Alicante. We will not leave. We will spill Shadowhunter blood, yes. Our own blood. We will cut our own throats and die here at your feet. Either you will go or we will wash this room clean in our blood."

Jaime rose to his feet. "Call their bluff," he said. "They cannot hold us hostage—"

Zara nodded to Amelia, who plunged the dagger she held into her stomach and twisted it viciously to the side. She fell to her knees spurting blood as the room exploded with gasps of horror.

"Can you build your new Clave on the blood of dead children?"

Zara screamed at Alec. "You said you would show mercy. If you let us die, every time you step into this room from this moment onward, you will be walking on our corpses."

Everyone looked at Jia, but Jia was looking at Alec. Alec, the new Consul.

He was studying not Zara's face but the faces of the others in the room—those who looked at Zara as if she were the promise of freedom. There was no mercy on the faces of the Cohort. Not a one of them reached for Amelia as her blood ran out across the floor.

"Very well," said Alec with a deadly calm. "We will go."

Zara's eyes widened. Emma suspected she had not expected her plan to work, but had hoped to die as a martyr and destroy Alec and the rest of them in the process.

"You understand," Lazlo said, "that once you go, Lightwood, you cannot return. We will lock the wards of Idris against you, tear the Portal from the walls of the Gard, brick up the entrances from the Silent City. You will never be able to come back."

"Brick up the entrances to the Silent City?" said Diego. "You would cut off your own access to the Silent Brothers? To the Cup and Sword?"

"Who holds Idris holds the Mortal Mirror," said Lazlo. "As for the Silent Brothers, they have been corrupted, as the Iron Sisters have. We will cut them off from Alicante until they see the error of their ways. Until they see who the true Shadowhunters are."

"The world is bigger than Idris," said Jace, standing tall and proud beside Alec. "You think you are taking our homeland, but you are making it your prison. Just as we can never return, you will never be able to leave."

"Outside the wards of Idris we will fight on to protect the world," Alec said. "In here, you will rot as you play at being soldiers with nothing to fight but each other."

Alec turned his back on Balogh, moving to face the Clave. "Let's open the Portal now," he said. "Those who do not live in Alicante, return through it to your homes. Those who live here will have a choice. Gather your families and come with us or remain here, trapped forever, with the Cohort as your rulers. It is the choice of each Shadowhunter whether they wish to be imprisoned or free."

Clary rose to her feet and walked to the doors at the back of the room, taking her stele from her pocket. The Clave watched in silence as her stele flashed in her hand and a silvery-gray whirlwind began to grow against the doors, opening outward, shimmering along the walls until it had become an enormous Portal.

She turned to look at the room. "I'll keep this open for as long as anyone needs to leave Idris," she said, her voice firm and clear. "I'll be the last who passes through. Who wants to be the first?"

Emma stood, and Julian moved with her, acting together as they always had. "We will follow our Consul," Emma said.

"The Blackthorns will go first," Julian said. "Keep your prison, Zara. We will be free without you."

The rest of their family rose with them. Aline went to Jia and looped her arm through her mother's. Emma would have thought the room would have been full of cries and chaos, of arguing and fighting. But it seemed as if a cloak of stunned acceptance had been drawn over the Shadowhunters, both those leaving and those staying. The Cohort and their allies watched in silence as the majority of Shadowhunters either headed toward the Portal or went to gather up their things from their Alicante houses.

Alicante would be a ghost town, a ghost city in a ghost land, Emma thought. She looked for Diana, found her nearby in the crowd. "Your father's shop," she said. "Your apartment—"

Diana just smiled. "I don't mind," she said. "I was always coming back with you to Los Angeles, love. I'm a teacher. Not a shop owner in Idris. And why would I want to live somewhere Gwyn couldn't go?"

Cristina hugged Diego and Jaime as they stood, ready to return to Mexico City. Divya and Rayan were preparing themselves. So were Cameron and Paige Ashdown, though Vanessa still stood on the dais, glaring at them with narrowed eyes. Amelia's body lay at her feet. Emma felt a twist of pity. To sacrifice so much for a cause that cared nothing for you, and then to die unmourned. It seemed too cruel.

Cameron turned his back on Vanessa, heading for the stairs, joining the Blackthorns and their friends as Clary directed the Portal to return them to Los Angeles. He didn't look back at his cousin. Emma hoped he saw her smile at him encouragingly.

The Ashdowns weren't the only family that would be torn apart by this. But with every step she took toward the Portal, she knew they were doing the right thing. No shining new world could be built on blood and bones.

The Portal rose up before Emma, lucent and shimmering. Through it she could see the ocean and the shore, the looming shape of the Institute. Finally the Blackthorns were going home. They had passed through blood, through disaster, and now through exile, but they were going home at last.

She took Julian's hand, and they stepped through.

34
The City in the Sea

Kieran had been waiting in the meadow for some time now. No one ever told you, he thought, that when you became a King of a Faerie Court, you would have to wear very itchy velvet and silk nearly all the time. The boots were nice—the King had his own cobbler, who molded the leather to his feet—but he could have done without wearing a jeweled belt, heavy rings, and a doublet with five pounds of embroidery on it on a bright summer day.

A rustle in the grass announced the arrival of General Winter, who bowed deeply before Kieran. Kieran had told him many times not to do that, but Winter persisted.

"Adaon Kingson, your brother," he announced, and stepped aside, allowing Adaon to pass him and come close to Kieran.

The two brothers regarded each other. Adaon wore the green livery of a page of the Seelie Court. It suited him. He seemed rested and calm, his dark eyes thoughtful as he gazed at Kieran. "You sought private word with me, my liege?" he said.

"Winter, turn your back," Kieran said. In truth, he did not mind what Winter heard: He had not bothered keeping secrets from the head of his guards. It was better for a King not to have secrets if he could avoid it, in his opinion. It simply gave the tools for blackmail into enemy hands.

Winter walked a few steps away and turned his back. There was a rustle as the handful of redcap guards who had come with him did the same. Adaon raised an eyebrow, but surely he could not be surprised: The guards were good at making themselves invisible, but Kings did not stand around in meadows alone and unprotected.

"You have come all the way to the doors of an enemy Court to see me," said Adaon. "I suppose I am complimented."

"You are the only brother I have ever trusted," Kieran said. "And I came to ask you if you wished—if you would consider becoming King in my place."

Adaon's eyebrows flickered like bird wings. "Do you not enjoy being King?"

"It is not to be enjoyed or not enjoyed. It does not matter. I have left Mark and Cristina, who I love, to stand as King, but I cannot bear it. I cannot live like this." Kieran fiddled with his heavy rings. "I cannot live without them."

"And they would not survive the Court." Adaon fingered his chin thoughtfully. "Kieran, I am not going to become King, for two reasons. One is that with you on the King's throne and me beside the Queen, we can work toward peace between Seelie and Unseelie. The Queen hated Arawn, but she does not hate you."

"Adaon—" Kieran's voice was raw.

"No," Adaon said firmly. "Already I have made the Queen see the wisdom of a peace between the Lands, but if I leave her to become the King of Unseelie, she will hate me and we will return to being enemies."

Kieran took a deep breath. The meadow smelled of wildflowers, but he felt nauseated, sick and hot and despairing. How could he live without hearing Cristina's voice again? Without seeing Mark's face? "What was your second reason, then?"

"You've been a good King," Adaon said. "Though you have only held the position these past weeks, Kieran, you have already done many fine things—released prisoners, enacted a fair redistribution of land, changed the laws for the better. Our people are loyal to you."

"So if I had been an incompetent King, like Oban, I might have the life I want?" Kieran said bitterly. "A strange reward for work well done."

"I am sorry, Kieran," Adaon said, and Kieran knew it must be true. "But there is no one else."

At first, Kieran could not speak. Before him he saw the long days stretching away without love in them or trust. He thought of Mark laughing, wheeling Windspear around, his strong body and golden hair. He thought of Cristina dancing, smoke and flame in the night, her softness and her boundless generosity of spirit. He would not find those things again; he would not find such hearts again.

"I understand," Kieran said remotely. This was the end, then. He would have a life of dutiful service—a life that would stretch on many years—and only the pleasure of doing good, which was not nothing, to sustain him. If only the Wild Hunt had known this would be the fate of their wildest Hunter. They would have laughed. "I must uphold my duty. I regret that I asked."

Adaon's face softened. "I do not hold duty above love, Kieran. I must tell you—I heard from Cristina."

Kieran's head jerked up. "What?"

"She made a suggestion that I give you my cottage. It exists in a place on the Borderlands that is in neither Faerie nor the mortal world. It would neither weaken you as the mortal world would nor would Mark and Cristina be under threat, as they would be in the Court." Adaon laid his hand on Kieran's silk-and-velvet shoulder. "You could be with them there."

The raw emotion he felt nearly rocked Kieran off his feet.

"You would do that, Adaon? You would give me your cottage?"

Adaon smiled. "Of course. What are brothers for?"

Emma was sitting on her suitcase in the hopes of trying to get it to close. She thought regretfully of all the stuff she'd already snuck into Julian's bag. He was an organized and minimalist packer, and had had a zipped suitcase ready to go in the hallway for a week now. It was starting to look a little bulgy with the extra items she'd snuck in while he wasn't looking—a hairbrush, a bag of ponytail holders, flip-flops, and a few extra sunglasses. And a neck pillow. You never knew when you were going to need a neck pillow, especially when you were taking your entire travel year to wander the globe.

"Are you ready to go to the party?" It was Cristina, in an airy blue dress, a daisy in her dark hair. She wrinkled up her nose. "What are you doing?"

"Jumping up and down on this suitcase." Emma stood up and kicked off her shoes. "Submit," she said to the suitcase, and climbed on top of it. "Okay. I'm jumping."

Cristina looked horrified. "Have you never heard of a packing cube?"

"What's a packing cube? Is it some sort of extra-dimensional space?" She started to jump up and down on the suitcase as if it were a trampoline.

Cristina leaned back against the door. "It's good to see you so happy."

The suitcase made a horrible sound. Emma stopped jumping. "Quick! Zip it!"

Clucking, Cristina got down on her knees and yanked the zipper closed. Emma jumped down to the floor and they both regarded the bulging suitcase, Cristina with apprehension and Emma with pride. "What are you going to do next time you have to close it?" Cristina said.

"I'm not thinking that far ahead." Emma wondered if she should have dressed up a bit more—the party was meant to be casual, just a group of them celebrating Aline and Helen's official ascension to heads of the Los Angeles Institute.

Or at least, that was the story.

She'd found a silk midi dress from the sixties with laces up and down the back and thought it was playful and retro, but Cristina looked so elegant and calm that Emma wondered if she should have gone more formal. She determined to find her big gold hair clip somewhere and put her hair up. She just hoped it wasn't in her suitcase, because that was a definite No-Go Area. "Do I really seem happy?"

Cristina tucked a stray lock of hair behind Emma's ear. "More happy than I have ever seen you before," she said, and because she was Cristina, every word she spoke shone with sincerity. "I'm so, so glad for you."

Emma flopped back onto her bed. Something poked her in the back. It was her hair clip. She seized it up with relief. "But what about you, Tina? I worry you're not happy."

Cristina shrugged her shoulders. "I am all right. I am surviving."

"Cristina, I love you, you're my best friend," Emma said. And it was easy to say now, "best friend," because while Julian was still her best friend too, he was more than that as well and finally everyone knew it. "Surviving isn't enough. What about being happy?"

Cristina sighed and sat down next to Emma. "We will get there, Mark and I. We *are* happy, yet we also know that there is a greater happiness we could have had. And we worry about Kieran every day."

"Did you contact Adaon?" Emma asked.

"I did, but I have not had a reply. Perhaps it is not something Kieran wants."

Emma frowned. She found the whole business confusing, but one thing she was certain of—there was nothing Kieran wanted more than to be with Mark and Cristina.

"Cristina!" A voice echoed faintly from outside the Institute; Emma scrambled across the bed to the window and threw it open. A second later Cristina was beside her. They both poked their heads outside to see Diego and Jaime standing on the front lawn, waving their arms energetically. "Cristina! Come down!"

Cristina started to laugh, and for a moment, under her quiet sadness, Emma saw the girl she must have been in Mexico City when she was a child, tearing around with the Rosales brothers and getting into trouble.

She couldn't help but smile. *I wish I'd known you then, Tina. I hope we'll be friends our whole lives.*

But Cristina was smiling and Emma didn't want to break her fragile good mood with wistfulness. "Come on," she said, grabbing a pair of sandals. "Let's go down to the beach."

With help from Ragnor and Catarina, the sandy strip of coast below the Institute had been blocked off for their private use, the area encircled by glamoured signs claiming the beach was closed due to a terrible sand crab infestation.

Magnus had also thrown up muffling spells that quieted the sounds of traffic from the highway. Emma knew he hadn't been involved in the weather, but it was almost as if he had: a perfect day, the sky blue and deep, the waves like blue satin threaded with gold.

Shadowhunters and Downworlders dotted the beach, all up and down the curve of golden sand encircled with rocks. Alec, tall and handsome in an ivory sweater and black pants, was helping Catarina and Ragnor set up tables of food. Emma noticed that his hands shook slightly as he set out plates and chopsticks. Magnus had summoned dumplings from all over the world—Chinese *jiaozi*, Japanese *gyoza*, Polish cheese pierogi, buttery Russian *pelmeni*, Korean *mandu*. Ragnor had provided bottles of ludicrously expensive wine from his favorite Argentinian vintner, as well as French sparkling water and apple juice for the kids. Catarina had created a fountain of Swiss chocolate, which had already attracted the attention of Max and Rafe. "Sandy fingers *out* of the chocolate," Magnus was telling them. "Or I'll turn you both into sea sponges."

Cristina headed off down the beach with the Rosales brothers to catch up with Mark, who had been sitting alone on a hillock of sand, his eyes fixed on the middle distance. Emma bent to lace her sandal. When she straightened up, Julian had appeared, his jeans rolled to his knees and his bare feet sandy from playing at the water's edge with Tavvy and Helen. He looked carefree in a way she had almost never seen him: His blue-green eyes sparkled like the sea glass at his wrist, and his smile was slow and easy as he came up to slide his arm around her waist. "You look gorgeous."

"So do you," she said, meaning it, and he laughed and kissed her. She marveled a little—Julian, who had always been so careful, was the one who didn't care who knew about their relationship. She knew their family understood everything, that Jem had explained it to them in Alicante. But she always worried—would others wonder how long they'd been in love, how much it overlapped with their time of being *parabatai*?

No one seemed to care, though, and Julian least of all. He smiled whenever he saw her, caught her up and kissed her, held her hand proudly. He even seemed to enjoy the good-natured wailing of his siblings when they happened on Julian and Emma kissing in the hallways.

It was amazing not to have to be secret, not to hide. Emma wasn't used to it yet, but she kissed Julian back anyway, not caring who saw.

He tasted like salt and ocean. Like home. He nuzzled his chin against her forehead.

"I'm glad everyone came," she said.

It was quite a crowd. Down at the end of the beach, Maia, Simon, and Bat were playing volleyball with Anush. The vampires hadn't shown up yet since the sun was still out, but Lily kept texting Alec to make sure they'd be providing O negative on ice for later. Isabelle was decorating the layer cake Aline had baked with icing frills, and Marisol and Beatriz were making a sandcastle. They both wore mourning white, and seemed to share a quiet, meditative sadness. Emma hoped they would be good for each other: both had lost someone they loved.

Jace and Clary had braved the water and were splashing each other as Ragnor drifted by on a massive pool float, drinking a lemonade. Jocelyn Fairchild and Luke Garroway sat with Jia, Patrick, and Maryse some distance down the beach, and Diana and Gwyn were cuddled together on a blanket near the shoreline.

"We have a lot of allies," Julian said.

Emma's gaze slid down the beach toward Magnus and Alec. "This is going to be an important night," she said. "And it's being shared with us. That's not about having allies. That's about having friends. We have a lot of *friends*."

She figured he'd make a teasing retort; instead, his face softened.

"You're right," he said. "I guess we do."

Keeping an eye on the kids had become habit. Even while playing at the tide line, digging up hermit crabs and letting them fuss up and down her hands, Dru kept a side-eye on Tavvy, Max, and Rafe. She knew they were all well looked after by a cadre of warlocks and anxious Shadowhunters, but she couldn't help it.

"Drusilla?"

Jaime was coming down the beach toward her, just as he had when he'd come in response to Cristina's summons. He looked healthier than he had then—less skinny, more color in his cheeks. Same wild black hair whipped by the wind, same sparkling brown eyes. He smiled down at her, and she wondered if she should have worn something more bright and pretty like the other girls. She'd been wearing black dresses everywhere for so long she barely thought about it, but maybe he'd think it was odd?

"So what's in store for you after all this?" Jaime asked. "Are you going to go to the new Academy?"

The Downworlder-Shadowhunter Alliance had come together to build a new school for Shadowhunters in an already safe and warded location—Luke Garroway's farm in upstate New York. According to reports, it was nearly done—and according to Simon, about a thousand times nicer than the old Academy, where he'd once found rats in his sock drawer.

"Not yet," Dru said, and she saw the quick recall and realization in his eyes: She was too young to attend the new Academy, which began at fifteen. "Maybe in a few years." She kicked at a seashell. "Will I see you again?"

He wore an expression she hadn't seen on his face before. A sort of pained seriousness. "I don't think that's very likely. Cristina is leaving, so I've got no reason to come here any longer." Dru's heart sank. "I have to go back home to make things right with my father and the rest of my family. You know how it is. Family is the most important thing."

She bit back the words she wanted to say.

"But maybe I'll see you at the Academy someday," he added. "Do you still have that knife I gave you?"

"Yes," Dru said, a little worried. He'd said it was a gift—surely he wasn't going to ask for it back?

"Good girl," Jaime said. He ruffled her hair and walked away.

She wanted to run after him and yank on his sleeve. Ask him to be her friend again. But not if he was going to treat her like a child, she reminded herself. She'd liked him because he acted as if she had a fully functioning brain. If he didn't think so anymore . . .

"Dru!" It was Ty, barefoot and sandy, with a hermit crab he wanted to show her. It had a delicately spotted shell. She bent her head over his cupped hands, grateful for the distraction.

She let his voice flow around her as he turned the crab over in his careful, delicate hands. Things were different with her and Ty now. She was the only one besides Kit and Magnus who knew what had happened with his attempt to raise Livvy.

It was clear to her that Ty trusted her in a new way. That they kept each other's secrets. She was the only one who knew that sometimes when he looked away and smiled he was smiling at Livvy's ghost, and he was the only one who knew that she could pick a lock in under thirty seconds.

"There's bioluminescence down at the other end of the beach," Ty said, depositing the crab back onto the sand. It scurried for its hole. "Do you want to come see?"

She could still see Jaime, who had joined Maia and Diego and was chatting animatedly. She supposed she could go over to them and try to join the conversation, try to seem more grown-up and worth talking to. *But I am thirteen*, she thought. *I'm thirteen and I'm worth talking to without pretending I'm something I'm not. And I'm not going to bother with anyone who doesn't see that.*

She picked up her long black skirt and raced after Ty down the beach, her footsteps scattering light.

"Okay, here," Helen said, sitting down just at the tide line. She reached up to pull Aline down beside her. "We can watch the tide go out."

Aline sat, and then scowled. "Now my butt is wet," she said. "Nobody warned me."

Helen thought of several saucy things to say but held back. Aline was looking especially gorgeous right now, she thought, in a skirt and flowered top, her brown shoulders bared to the sun. She wore small gold earrings in the shape of Love and Commitment runes. "You never sat on the beach on Wrangel?" she asked.

"No way. It was freezing." Aline wiggled her bare toes in the sand. "This is much better."

"It is much better, isn't it?" Helen smiled at her wife, and Aline turned pink, because even after all the time they'd been together, Helen's attention still made Aline blush and play with her hair. "We're going to run the Institute."

"Don't remind me. So much paperwork," Aline grumbled.

"I thought you *wanted* to run the Institute!" Helen laughed.

"I think steady employment is a good idea," said Aline. "Also we need to keep an eye on the kids so they don't become hooligans."

"Too late, I think." Helen gazed down the beach fondly in the direction of her siblings.

"And I think we should have a baby."

"*Really*?" Helen opened her mouth. Closed it again. Opened it. "But—darling—how? Without mundane medicine—"

"I don't know, but we should ask Magnus and Alec, because it seems to me that babies just fall from the sky when they're around. Like toddler rain."

"Aline," Helen said in her *be serious* voice.

Aline tugged at her skirt. "Do you—want a baby?"

Helen scooted close to Aline, pulling her wife's cold hands into her lap. "My love," she said. "I do! Of course! It's just—I still think of us in exile, a little bit. As if we're waiting for our real life to truly start up again. I know it's not logical. . . ."

Aline lifted their joined hands and kissed Helen's fingers. "Every single minute I've spent with you has been my real life," she said. "And even on Wrangel Island, a better life than I ever had without you."

Helen felt herself starting to get teary-eyed. "A baby would be like a new sister or brother for Ty and Dru and Tavvy," she said. "It would be so wonderful."

"If it was a girl, we could name her Eunice," Aline said. "It was my aunt's name."

"We will *not*."

Aline grinned impishly. "We'll see. . . ."

When Alec came up to talk to Mark, Mark was in the middle of making balloon animals for Tavvy, Rafe, and Max. Max seemed content, but Rafe and Tavvy had grown tired of Mark's repertoire.

"It is a manticore," said Mark, holding up a yellow balloon.

"It's a snake," said Tavvy. "They're all snakes."

"Nonsense," said Mark, producing a green balloon. "This is a wingless, headless dragon. And this is a crocodile sitting on its feet."

Rafe looked sad. "Why does the dragon have no head?"

"Excuse me," Alec said, tapping Mark on the shoulder. "Can I talk to you for a second?"

"Oh, thank the Angel," said Mark, dropping his balloons and scrambling to his feet. He followed Alec toward the bluffs as Magnus moved in to amuse the children. Mark overheard him telling Rafe the dragon had lost its head in a game of poker.

Mark and Alec stopped in the shadow of a bluff, not far from the tide line. Alec was wearing a lightweight sweater with a hole in the sleeve and looked calmly pleasant—surprisingly so for a Consul trying to piece together a shattered government.

"I hope this isn't about the balloons," said Mark. "I don't have much training."

"It's not about the balloons," said Alec. He reached around to rub the back of his neck. "I know we haven't really had much of a chance to talk, but I've heard a lot about you from Helen and Aline. And I remembered you for a long time after we met you in Faerie. When you joined the Hunt."

"You told me if I went to Edom with you, I'd die," Mark recalled.

Alec looked faintly embarrassed. "I was trying to protect you. But I thought about you a lot after that. How tough you were. And how wrong it was, the way the Clave treated you, just because you were different. I always wished you were around to join the Downworlder-Shadowhunter Alliance. Working with it has been something I'm really going to miss."

Mark was startled. "You're not going to work with the Alliance anymore?"

"I can't," Alec said. "I can't do that and be Consul—it's too much, for anyone. I don't know how much you've heard, but the government is setting itself up in New York City. Partly because of me—I can't be too far from Magnus and the kids. And it has to be somewhere."

"You don't need to apologize about it," said Mark, wondering where this was all going.

"There's so much we have to do," said Alec. "We have connections all over the world, with every religious organization, with secret societies that know about demons. They'll all have to decide who they tithe to—us, or the government in Alicante. We have to face that we're going to lose at least some of our allies. That we'll be struggling—for funds, for credibility. For so much."

Mark knew that Shadowhunters survived on the money they were given by organizations—religious, spiritual, mystic—who knew of demons and valued the guarding of the world. He'd never thought about what would happen without those funds. He didn't envy Alec.

"I wondered if you'd want to join the Alliance," said Alec. "Not just join it but help us head it up. You could be an ambassador to Faerie, now that the Cold Peace is being dissolved. It's not going to be a short process. We have a lot of reconnecting to do with the fey, and we need to help them understand that the government in Idris no longer represents the majority of Shadowhunters." He hesitated. "I know things have been crazy for your family, but you would truly be a valuable asset."

"Where would I need to live?" Mark asked. "I don't want to be too far from my family or Cristina."

"We were going to ask Cristina to join us as well," said Alec. "Her knowledge of faeries will be helpful, and her family's relationship with them as well. You can both have a place in the New York Institute, and you're welcome to Portal back to see your family whenever you want."

Mark tried to wrap his head around the idea. New York seemed far away, but then, he hadn't paused at all to consider what he might want to do now that the crisis seemed to be over. He had no interest in anything like the Scholomance. He could remain in Los Angeles, of course, but if he did, he'd be away from Cristina. He already missed Kieran, as did she; he couldn't bear to miss her, too. But what would his purpose be, if he followed her to Mexico? What did Mark Blackthorn want to do with his life?

"I need to think about it," Mark said, surprising himself.

"All right," said Alec. "Take all the time you need." He glanced at his watch. "I've got something important I have to do."

Cristina sat with her legs tucked up under her, gazing out to sea. She knew she should join the rest of the party—her mother had always scolded her for hanging back in her room during social occasions—but something about the sea was comforting. She would miss it when she went home: the steady drumbeat of the tide, the ever-changing surface of the waves. Always the same yet always new.

If she turned her head a bit she could see Emma with Julian, Mark talking to Alec. That was enough for now.

A shadow fell across her view. "Hello, friend."

It was Diego. He sat down beside her on the large, flat-topped rock she'd found. He looked more casual than she'd seen him in a long time, in a T-shirt and rolled-up cargo pants. The brutal, vicious scar across his face was healing quickly, as Shadowhunter scars did, but it would never fade to invisibility. He would never quite be Perfect Diego again on the outside. But he had changed so much for the better on the inside, she thought. And that was what truly mattered.

"En qué piensas?" It was the same question he'd always asked her, so common it was an inside joke between them. *What are you thinking about?*

"The world seems so strange to me now," she said, gazing at her toes in their sandals. "I can't quite fathom that Alicante is lost to us. The Shadowhunter homeland is our home no longer." She hesitated. "Mark and I are happy to be together but also sad; Kieran being gone feels like a wedge cut out of our relationship. It's like having Idris cut out of the world of the Shadowhunters. A piece that's missing. We can still be happy but we won't be whole."

It was the first time she had spoken to Diego about the odd nature of her relationship. She had wondered how he would react. He only nodded. "There is no perfect world," he said. "What we have now is a wound, but it's still better than the Cold Peace was, and better than the Cohort was. Very few people have the opportunity to reach out and change the injustices they see in the world, but you did, Cristina. You always wanted to end the Cold Peace, and now it's over."

Oddly touched, she smiled at him. "Do you think that we'll ever hear anything from Idris?"

"Ever is a long time." He folded his arms on his knees. There had been no communication so far. Alec—the Consul—had sent a fire-message to Idris the day the Cold Peace was officially dissolved, but there had been no response. They couldn't even be sure it had been received; the wards around Idris now were thicker and stronger than any wards seen before. The Shadowhunter homeland had become both prison and fortress. "Zara is very stubborn. It could be a long time." Diego paused. "Alec offered me the position of Inquisitor. Of course there has to be a vote, but—"

Cristina flung her arms around his wide shoulders. "Congratulations! That's wonderful!"

But Diego didn't look entirely happy. "I feel as if I do not deserve to be Inquisitor," he said. "I knew the Council guards, the ones who work in the Gard, were under the sway of the Cohort. I said as much to Jaime when they came in escorting Zara and the other prisoners. But I did not raise an objection. I believed it could not be possible that I alone saw a potential problem."

"No one could have foreseen what happened," said Cristina. "No one would have imagined that suicide gambit, and nothing else would have worked, even if they did have the guards on their side. Besides, being the Inquisitor isn't a favor or reward. It is a service you give. It's a way of paying back the world."

He started to smile. "I suppose so."

She winked. "Also, I'm happy to know that if I need someone to bend the Law in my favor, I will have a powerful friend."

"I see you have learned way too much from the Blackthorns," Diego said darkly.

A shadow passed over them—darker than a cloud, and too large to be a seagull. Drawing back from Diego, Cristina tipped her head back. A flying figure soared through the sky, shimmering white against the dark blue. It circled, and then began to descend, preparing to alight on the sand.

Cristina bolted to her feet and began to scramble down the rocks toward the beach.

* * *

The sun had dipped to touch the edge of the horizon. It was a massive glowing ball of orange and red now, illuminating the ocean with bands of metallic gold.

Julian stood at the high-water mark, a defined darker stripe on the sands. Emma was beside him, her pale gold hair escaping the clip she'd put in to hold it back; secretly, he was pleased. He loved her hair. He loved being able to stand next to her like this, to take her hand and have no one blink. In fact, nearly everyone they knew seemed so extremely fine with it that he wondered if many of them hadn't already had suspicions.

Maybe they had. He didn't mind.

He'd been painting again—Emma, when he could get her to sit still and be a model. He had painted her for so long in secret, the paintings his only outlet for his feelings, that painting her moving and laughing and smiling, a blur of golds and blues and ambers, was almost more than his heart could take.

He painted Ty, down by the water's edge, and Dru looking thoughtful or scowling, and Helen and Aline together, and Mark with his eyes raised to the sky as if he were always looking for the stars.

And he painted Livvy. He painted the Livvy he had always known and loved, and sometimes he painted the Livvy in Thule who had helped heal his heart from the wound of his sister's loss.

It would never be entirely healed. It would always hurt, as his mother's death did, as his father's death did. As Arthur's death did. He would be as everyone was, especially Shadowhunters: a patchwork of love and grief, of gains and losses. The love helped you accept the grief. You had to feel it all.

He knew that now.

"Can I talk to you, Jules?"

Julian turned, still holding Emma's hand; it was Mark. The gold light of the sun made his golden eye shine brighter; Julian knew he was still mourning Kieran's loss, but at least now, on the beach with his family, he was smiling.

"No worries," Emma said with a smile. She kissed Julian's cheek and headed down the beach to talk to Clary, who was standing with Jace.

Mark shoved his hands into the pockets of his jeans. "Jules," he said again. "Alec has offered me a job—helping run the Alliance—and I'm not sure whether I should take it. I feel like I should stay here and help Helen and Aline while you have your travel year so you don't have to worry. You took care of everything for so long. I should be taking care of things now."

Julian felt a rush of love for his brother—if there had ever been any jealousy, it was gone. He was only glad to have Mark back.

He put his hands on his brother's shoulders. "Take the job," he said.

Mark looked surprised. "Take it?"

"You don't need to worry. Things aren't the way they were anymore," Julian said, and for the first time, as he said the words aloud to his brother, he truly believed them. "In the past, I had to take care of things because there was no one else who could do it. But now Helen and Aline are home. They want to take care of the Institute, the kids—it's all they wanted for years." He dropped his voice. "You've always been part of two worlds. Faerie and Nephilim. This sounds like a way you can make having both a strength. So do it. I want you to be happy."

Mark pulled him into a fierce hug. Julian held his brother, with the tide crashing over both their feet, held him as tightly as he had imagined clinging to him during all the years he was away.

"Mark! *Mark!*"

The brothers drew away from each other; Julian turned in surprise to see Cristina racing toward them along the beach, zigzagging between the startled partygoers. Her cheeks were bright red with excitement.

She reached them and seized hold of Mark's hand.

"Mark, *mira*," she said, her voice rising with excitement. "Look!"

Julian craned his head back—everyone was, the whole party transfixed by the sight of a Faerie horse circling over them. A white horse with scarlet eyes, two gold hooves and two silver. It was Windspear, and Kieran was on his back.

The sun was setting in a final blaze as Windspear landed on the beach, sand puffing up around his hooves. Max yelled in delight at the sight of the pony, and Magnus grabbed him back hastily as Kieran leaped down from the horse's back. He was all in dark blue, the sort of elaborate costume Julian could only barely begin to understand—there was definitely velvet and silk involved, and some kind of dark blue leather, and rings on all his fingers, and his hair, too, was dark blue. He looked ethereal and startling and a little bit alien.

He looked like a King of Faerie.

His eyes roved restlessly around the group of partygoers and locked in on Mark and Cristina. Slowly, Kieran began to smile.

"Remember," Mark said, his hand in Cristina's, whispering in a voice so low Julian wondered if he was supposed to hear it at all. *"Remember that all of this is real."*

He and Cristina began to run. Windspear took off into the air, circling happily overhead. Julian saw Emma, standing near the chocolate fountain, clasp her hands together in delight as Mark, Kieran, and Cristina threw themselves into each other's arms.

"So," Alec said. He and Magnus had found shelter in the lee of a large rock, its surface worn to a granular texture by years of salt and wind. Magnus, leaning against it, looked young in a way that made Alec's heart break with a mixture of love and nostalgia. "Since I'm the Consul now, I guess I make the rules."

Magnus raised an eyebrow. In the distance, Alec could hear the sounds of the party: people laughing, music, Isabelle calling to Max and Rafe. She'd been put in charge of watching them while Alec and Magnus took a moment to themselves. Alec knew that by the time they got back, both kids would be covered in glittery eyeliner, but some sacrifices were worth the makeup remover.

"Was that flirting?" Magnus said. "Because I have to tell you I'm more in than I thought I would be."

"Yes," said Alec. He paused. "No. A little bit." He laid a hand over Magnus's heart, and Magnus looked at him with thoughtful green-gold eyes, as if sensing that Alec was serious. "I mean I make all the rules. I'm in charge now."

"I told you already I was in," Magnus said.

Alec slid his hand up to cup his boyfriend's jaw. There was light stubble on Magnus's skin, which Alec always loved. It made him think of the way Magnus looked when he first woke up, before the rest of the world saw him, before he put on his clothes like armor, when he was just Alec's.

"We could get married," he said. "In warlock blue and Shadow-hunter gold. The way we always wanted."

An incredulous smile spread over Magnus's face. "You're really asking me . . . ?"

Alec took a deep breath and knelt down in the sand. He looked up at Magnus, watching his face go from amused to something else. Something soft and serious and tremulously vulnerable.

"I almost lost you," Alec said. "I've gotten so used to thinking of you as immortal. But none of us are." He tried to keep his hands from shaking; he was more nervous than he thought he would be. "None of us are forever. But at least I can do everything I can to let you know how much I love you with every day that we do have." He took a deep breath. "I wish I could promise you a completely uneventful, peaceful life at my side. But I have a feeling we'll always be surrounded by adventure and chaos."

"I wouldn't have it any other way," said Magnus.

"When I found you, I didn't know what I was finding," Alec said. "Words about things that are beautiful and precious to me don't come easily. You know that. You know me better than anyone." He licked his dry lips. "And when one day people look back on me and what my life meant, I don't want them to say, 'Alec Lightwood fought in the Dark War' or even 'Alec Lightwood was Consul once.' I want them to think, 'Alec Lightwood loved one man so much he changed the world for him.'"

Magnus's eyes shone bright as stars. He gazed at Alec with eyes full of joy, of a feeling so profound Alec felt humbled to be a part of it. "You know you've already changed the world for me."

"Will you marry me?" Alec whispered. His heart was beating like a frantic bird's wings. "Right now? Tonight?"

Magnus nodded wordlessly and pulled Alec to his feet. They wrapped their arms around each other, and Alec leaned up just that little bit, since Magnus was just that little bit taller, which he had always loved.

And they kissed for a long time.

The beach was a hive of activity. The sun had gone down, but the sky still glowed an opaline blue. Simon and Jace were setting out a wooden platform on the sand, where the view of the coastline was best. Julian and Emma were lighting candles around the platform, Clary, who had changed into a blue dress, was scattering flowers, Ragnor and Catarina were arguing while plates of delicious-looking food were summoned up to weigh down the already creaking tables. Isabelle was stuffing Max and Rafe into adorable outfits trimmed in gold and blue while Max wailed and Rafe looked resigned.

Helen and Aline were helping the younger Blackthorns place their golden runes of commitment and love, faith and grace. Cristina, runed at her wrists and throat, had volunteered to help line the beach with torches. She hummed as she worked, surrounded by Shadowhunters and Downworlders laughing together. She knew there would be difficult times coming, that the Clave-in-exile would have no simple time of it. Alec would have difficult decisions in front of him; they all would. But this one moment, these preparations, felt like a moment of happiness enclosed in a bubble, safe from the harshness of reality.

"Take this." With a smile, Kieran pressed a torch into her hand; he had set himself to work alongside all the others as if he were not the King of the Unseelie Court. In the dusk, his hair looked as black as his clothes.

"And I have more." Mark, barefoot and starlight-haired, placed several more torches in the sand opposite Cristina's. As they settled, they began to burn with a dim light that would soon grow stronger: they were weaving a path of fire across the beach, to the sea.

"Kieran," Cristina said, and he glanced at her through the torches, his expression curious. She wasn't sure if she should ask him, but she couldn't help it. "I sent our message to Adaon ages ago and we didn't hear anything back. Did it take you a long time to decide what to do?"

"No," he said firmly. "Adaon did not tell me immediately that you had sent him a message. I was unaware you had contacted him. I was trying to forget the two of you—I was trying to be a good King, and to learn how to live a meaningful life without you." A stripe of his hair turned silver-blue. "It was awful. I hated every minute of it. Finally, when I could stand it no more, I went to Adaon and asked if he would be willing to trade places with me. He refused, but that was when he offered me the cottage."

Cristina was indignant. "I can't believe he did that! He should have gotten in touch with you right away!"

Kieran smiled at her. She wondered that she had ever found anything about him harsh or distant. They moved closer to each other, a quiet group of three among the fire and the laughter, their heads bent together.

"Will it really work?" Mark looked troubled. He reached over to brush sand from Kieran's velvet sleeve. "Is there really a place we can be together?"

Kieran produced a key from a chain around his throat—it looked ancient, blackened with age, a brassy silver. "The cottage is ours now. It will give us a place where there are no kings, no queens, no mortals or faeries. Just the three of us together. It won't be all the time, but it will be enough."

"For now I will take any time with the two of you that I can have," Cristina said, and Kieran leaned in to kiss her softly. When he drew back, Mark was smiling at them both.

"Cristina and I will be very busy, I think," he said. "Between our families in different Institutes and our work with the Alliance. And you too will be busy with your new kingdom. The time we spend together will be precious indeed."

Cristina patted her pocket. "Diego and Jaime both said they'd be grateful if I'd keep watch over the Eternidad. So all you need to do is send us a message, Kieran, and we will come to you."

Kieran looked thoughtful. "Will you bring me one of those cat calendars of which I have grown fond? I would like to decorate the cottage."

"There are actually other kinds of calendars. Ones with otters and rabbits and puppies," Mark said, grinning.

Looking beatific, Kieran tipped his head back to see the stars. "This is truly a land of marvels."

Cristina gazed at them both, her heart so full of love it hurt. "It truly is."

When Alec and Magnus returned to the beach, it had been transfigured.

"You *planned* this?" Magnus said, looking around in wonder. He'd had no idea—none at all, but it was unmistakeable. Magnus and Alec had lain awake so many nights in their apartment in Brooklyn, as the ceiling fan spun slowly overhead, and whispered their thoughts and plans for that far-off day when they would make their promises in gold and blue. They had both known what they wanted.

Their friends had worked quickly. The Shadowhunters had donned wedding runes, proclaiming their witness to a ceremony of love and commitment. The Downworlders had tied silk strips of cobalt blue around their left wrists, as guests at warlock weddings ceremonially did. It had been so long, Magnus thought, since he had attended a wedding for one of his own. He had never thought it would happen for him.

Glimmering torches, their flames untouched by the wind, described pathways on the beach, leading to a wooden platform that had been placed in view of the sea. Magnus had grown up able to see the ocean, and he had once—only once—mentioned to Alec that he would like to be married within the sound of its waves. His heart felt as if it were being crushed into a thousand joyous pieces now, since Alec had remembered.

"I'm just glad you said yes," said Alec. "I'd hate to have to explain to everyone that they have to put the decorations away. And I already told the kids I had a surprise for you."

Magnus couldn't help himself; he kissed Alec on the cheek. "You still surprise me every day, Alexander," he said. "You and your damn poker face."

Alec laughed. As their friends waved them forward eagerly, Magnus could hear their greetings and cheers, carried on the wind. Runes shimmered gold under the torchlight, and deep blue cobalt silk rustled in the wind.

Jace stepped forward first, in a gear jacket printed with golden runes, and held out a hand to Alec.

"I stand as *suggenes* to Alexander Lightwood," he said with pride.

Magnus felt about Jace the way he had felt about many Shadowhunters over the years, Fairchilds and Herondales and Carstairs and others: fondness and faint exasperation. But in moments like this, when Jace's love for Alec shone true and untrammeled, he felt only gratitude and affection.

Alec took Jace's hand and they began to walk the pathway of light. Magnus made to follow them, warlocks having no tradition of *suggenes*—a companion to the altar—but Catarina stepped forward, smiling, and took his arm. "I fought our mutual green frenemy for the privilege of escorting you," she said, indicating a fulminating Ragnor with a tilt of her head. "Come on, now—you don't think I'd let you approach the altar alone? What if you got cold feet and ran off?"

Magnus chuckled as they passed by familiar faces: Maia and Bat, Lily wearing a tipsy crown of flowers, Helen and Aline whistling and clapping. Helen had a blue band around her wrist as well as gold runes on her clothes; so did Mark. "My feet have never been warmer," Magnus said. "They're positively toasty."

She smiled at him. "No doubts?"

They had reached the end of the lighted path. Alec stood waiting, Jace beside him on the platform. Behind them was the ocean, stretching out silvery-blue as Magnus's magic, all the way to the horizon. Their closest friends ringed the platform—Clary with her arms full of blue and yellow flowers, Isabelle carrying Max and sniffling back tears, Simon alight and smiling, Maryse with Rafe by her side: he looked solemn, as if aware of the significance of the occasion. Jia Penhallow stood where a priest would stand in a mundane ceremony, the *Codex* in her hand. They had all donned shawls or light jackets of silk, runed in gold; silk banners hung suspended in the sky, printed with runes of love and faith, commitment and family.

Magnus glanced down at Catarina. "No doubts," he said.

She squeezed his hand and went to stand beside Jia. There was a second ring around the platform: The Blackthorns and their friends were all there, clustered in close. Julian smiled his slow quiet smile at Magnus; Emma glowed with happiness as Magnus crossed the wooden platform and took his place opposite Alec.

Alec held his hands out, and Magnus took them. He looked into Alec's blue eyes, the precise color of his own magic, and felt a great calm descend over him, a peace beyond all other peace he had ever known.

No doubts. Magnus didn't need to search his soul. He'd searched it a thousand times, ten thousand, in the years he'd known Alec. Not because he doubted, but because it shocked him so much that he didn't. In all his life, he had never known such surety. He had lived happily and had no regrets, he had made poetry out of wondering and wandering, had lived untethered and gloried in freedom.

Then Magnus had met Alec. He had felt drawn to him in a way he couldn't have explained or anticipated: He had wanted to see Alec smile, to see him be happy. He had watched Alec turn from a shy boy with secrets to a proud man who faced the world openly and unafraid. Alec had given him the gift of faith, a faith that Magnus was strong enough to make not just Alec happy, but a whole family happy. And in their happiness, Magnus had felt himself not just free, but surrounded by an unimaginable glory.

Some might have called it the presence of God.

Magnus just thought of it as Alexander Gideon Lightwood.

"Let us begin," Jia said.

Emma had risen to her tiptoes in excitement. They had all known that there was going to be a surprise wedding on the beach—a surprise to Magnus, at any rate. If Alec had been nervous, he'd done a good job of mostly hiding it. No one else had thought Magnus might say no, but Emma remembered the slight tremble of Alec's hands earlier, and her heart bubbled with happiness that it had all worked out.

Jace stepped forward to help Alec into a dark blue gear jacket printed with golden runes, while Catarina draped a cobalt-and-gilt silk jacket around Magnus's shoulders.

They both moved back, and a hush fell over the crowd as Jia spoke.

"Through the centuries," she said, "there have been few unions between Shadowhunters and Downworlders that have been recognized as such. But a new age has dawned, and with a new age come new traditions. Tonight, as Magnus Bane and Alec Lightwood blend their lives and hearts, we stand ready to recognize this union. To witness a true bond between two souls who have cleaved to each other." She cleared her throat. She looked a bit drawn, as she had in the Council Hall, but much less tired. There was delight and pride in her face as she gazed around the gathered group. "Alexander Gideon Lightwood. Hast thou found the one thy soul loves?"

It was a question asked at every wedding: part of the Shadowhunter ceremony for a thousand years. The crowd hushed, the hush of holiness, of sacred ritual observed and shared. Emma couldn't help but reach out to hold Julian's hand; he drew her against his side. There was something about the way Magnus and Alec looked at each other. Emma had thought they would be smiling, but they were both serious: They looked at each other as if the other person were as brilliant as a full moon that could blot out every star.

"I have found him," Alec said. "And I will not let him go."

"Magnus Bane," said Jia, and Emma could not help but wonder if this was only the second time in history that this question had been asked of a warlock. "Hast thou gone among the watchmen, and in the cities of the world? Hast thou found the one thy soul loves?"

"I have found him," Magnus said, gazing at Alec. "And I will not let him go."

Jia inclined her head. "Now it is time for the exchanging of runes."

This was the moment when, in a traditional ceremony, Shadowhunters would Mark each other with wedding runes and speak the words of the vows. But Magnus could not bear runes. They would burn his skin. Puzzled, Emma watched as Jia pressed something that flashed gold into Alec's hand.

Alec moved closer to Magnus and Emma saw that it was a golden brooch in the shape of the Wedded Union rune. As Alec moved toward Magnus, he spoke the words of the Nephilim vows: *"Love flashes out like fire, the brightest kind of flame. Many waters cannot quench love, nor can the floods drown it."* He pinned the brooch over Magnus's heart, his blue eyes never leaving Magnus's face. *"Now place me as a seal over thine heart, as a seal over thine arm: For love is strong as death. And so we are bound: stronger than flame, stronger than water, stronger than death itself."*

Magnus, his gaze fixed on Alec's, laid his hand over the brooch. It was his turn now: Alec drew aside his jacket and rolled up his sleeve, baring his upper arm. He placed a stele in Magnus's hand and clasped Magnus's fingers within his own. With their hands entwined, Alec traced the shape of the Wedded Union rune onto his own arm. Emma assumed the second rune, the one over his heart, would be added later, in private, as it usually was.

When they were done, the rune stood out stark and black on Alec's skin. It would never fade. It would never leave him, a sign of his love for Magnus for all time. Emma felt an ache deep down in her soul, where unspoken hopes and dreams lived. To have what Magnus and Alec had—anyone would be lucky.

Slowly Magnus lowered his hand, still clasped in Alec's. He gazed at the rune on Alec's arm in a sort of daze, and Alec looked back at him, as if neither of them could look away.

"The rings now," said Jia, and Alec seemed to start out of a dream. Jace stepped forward and put one ring into Alec's hand, and another into Magnus's, and said something quietly to both of them that made them laugh. Simon was rubbing Isabelle's back as she sniffled even more loudly, and Clary was smiling into her flowers.

Emma was glad of her Night Vision rune. With it, she could see that the rings were Lightwood family rings, etched with the traditional design of flames on the outside, and with words inscribed on the inside.

"*Aku cinta kamu,*" Magnus read out, gazing at the interior of the ring, and he smiled at Alec, a brilliant, world-spanning smile. "My love for yours, my heart for yours, my soul for yours, Alexander. Now and for all time."

Catarina smiled at what must have been familiar words. Magnus and Alec slid the rings onto each other's fingers, and Jia closed her book.

"Alexander Lightwood-Bane. Magnus Lightwood-Bane. You are now married," she said. "Let us rejoice."

The two men folded into each other's arms, and a great cheer went up: Everyone was shouting, and hugging, and dancing, and the sky overhead burst into golden light as Ragnor, finally over his temper tantrum, began to fill the air with fireworks that exploded in the shapes of wedding runes. In the center of it all, Magnus and Alec held each other tightly, rings gleaming on their fingers like the slivers of a new sun breaking over the horizon.

The wedding ceremony had broken up into a party, ebullient guests crowding up and down the beach. Ragnor had magicked up a piano from somewhere and Jace was playing, his jacket slung over his shoulder like an old-time blues musician. Clary sat on the piano's soundboard, tossing flowers into the air. Dancers spun barefoot in the sand, Shadowhunters and Downworlders lost in the music.

Magnus and Alec danced close together, their children between them, a happy family tangle.

Diana and Gwyn sat some distance away. Gwyn had put down his cloak for Diana to sit on. She was touched by the gesture: The cloak of the Wild Hunt's leader was a powerful item, but he didn't seem to think twice about using it as a beach blanket.

Diana felt ebullient, light with happiness. She touched Gwyn on the wrist and he smiled at her.

"It is good to see so many happy. They deserve it," he said. "Not just Magnus and Alec, but Mark and Kieran and Cristina as well."

"And Emma and Julian. I always wondered . . ." Diana trailed off. In hindsight, of course, their love seemed perfectly clear.

"I assumed it," said Gwyn. "They looked at each other as I look at you." He cocked his head to the side. "I am glad they are happy now. All true hearts deserve such."

"And what of the leader of the Hunt? What of his happiness?" said Diana.

He moved closer to her. The wind from the ocean was cool, and he drew her shawl closer about her throat to keep her warm. "Your happiness is my own," he said. "You seem pensive. Will you tell me your mind?"

She dug her fingers into the cool sand. "I was so worried for so long," she said. "I kept it all secret—being transgender, using mundane medicine—because I was afraid. But now I've told everyone. Everyone knows, and nothing terrible happened." She smiled a bittersweet smile. "Our whole world has been turned upside down, and my secret now seems like such a small thing."

Two days after they returned from Idris, Diana had gathered the inhabitants of the Los Angeles Institute and told her story to everyone who mattered to her. She had made it clear that it was no secret from the Consul. She had already talked to Alec, who had readily admitted he knew less than he thought he should about transgender Shadowhunters (or mundanes, for that matter) but was eager to learn.

She had done everything right, Alec had said; she had kept their secrets from the mundane doctors, she had brought no risk to Shadowhunters. He was only sorry she had ever lived in fear, as he once had himself. "But no longer," he had said, his conviction audible. "The Clave has always attended to the strength of Shadowhunters but not to their happiness. If we can change that . . ."

She had promised she would work with him. The Blackthorns had responded to her story with love and sympathy, and as for everyone else—they could find out or not. She owed nothing to anyone.

"You're smiling," Gwyn observed.

"I had two secrets. Now I have none. I am free as the wind," Diana said.

He took her face in his big hands. "My lady, my love," he said. "We will ride the wind together."

The music of the piano had been joined by the music of the flute, played—surprisingly enough—by Kieran. He wasn't half-bad, Julian thought, as Simon joined the two of them, carrying his guitar. Maybe all three of them could start the world's strangest band.

Emma and Cristina were dancing together, both laughing so hard they kept doubling over. Julian didn't want to interrupt them: He knew their time together was precious before he and Emma left. He let himself watch Emma for just a moment—she was lovely in the argent light of the torches, her hair and skin gleaming gold like wedding runes—before he made his way around the dancers, down to the wet sand where the incoming waves lapped the shoreline.

Ty and Dru stood close together there, Ty leaning in to explain to his younger sister what made the waves sparkle and glow. "Bioluminescence," he was saying. "Tiny living animals in the ocean. They glow, like underwater fireflies."

Dru peered doubtfully into the water. "I don't see any animals."

"They're microscopic," Ty said. He scooped up a handful of seawater; it shone in his hands, as if he were holding a spill of shimmering diamonds. "You can't see them. You can only see the light they make."

"I wanted to talk to you, Ty," Julian said.

Ty looked up, his gaze fixed on a point just to the left of Julian's face. Livvy's locket glittered around his throat. He was starting to look older, Julian thought with a pang. The last of the childish roundness was gone from his face, his hands.

Dru gave them both a salute. "You guys talk. I'm going to see if Lily will teach me the Charleston." She skipped off down the beach, scattering luminous sparks.

"Are you sure you're all right with me leaving?" Julian said. "Emma and I, we don't have to go."

Ty knew, of course, that Julian was going on his travel year. It was no secret. But Ty was the most change-averse member of the family, and Julian couldn't help worrying.

Ty glanced over toward Magnus and Alec, who were swinging Max between them while he gurgled with laughter. "I want to go to the Scholomance," Ty said abruptly.

Julian started. It was true they were starting the Scholomance back up, with new instructors and new classes. It wouldn't be like it was. But still. "The Scholomance? But wouldn't the Academy be better? You're only fifteen."

"I always wanted to be able to solve mysteries," said Ty. "But people who solve mysteries, they know a lot of things. The Academy won't teach me the things I want to know, but the Scholomance will let me pick what I learn. It's the best place for me. If I can't be Livvy's *parabatai*, this is what I should be."

Julian tried to think of what to say. Ty wasn't the child that Julian had been so desperate to protect. He had survived the death of his sister, he had survived an enormous battle. He had fought the Riders of Mannan. For all Ty's life, Julian had tried to help him master all the skills he would need to lead a happy life. He'd known that eventually he'd need to let him go so he could live it.

He just hadn't realized that that moment would come soon.

Julian put his hand flat on Ty's chest. "All the way down in your heart, this is what you want?"

"Yes. This is what I want. Ragnor Fell will be teaching there, and Catarina Loss. I'll come home all the time. You've made me strong enough that I can do this, Julian." He put his hand over his brother's. "After everything that's happened, it's what I deserve."

"As long as you know home is always waiting for you," said Julian.

Ty's eyes were gray as the ocean. "I know."

The sky was full of sparks—gold and blue and purple, glimmering like ardent fireflies as the wedding fireworks died away. They floated up from the beach to reach the level of the bluffs where Kit stood with Jem and Tessa on either side of him.

It was a scene both familiar and unfamiliar. He had begged for this: a quick stop via Portal to see the Los Angeles Institute one last time. He'd wondered how it would be; he was surprised to realize he felt as if he could have easily walked into the wedding party and taken his place with Julian and Emma and Cristina and the rest. Dru would have welcomed him. They all would.

But he didn't belong there. Not after what had happened. The thought of seeing Ty at all hurt much too much.

Not that he couldn't *see* him. He could see all of them: Dru in her black dress dancing with Simon, and Mark and Cristina chatting with Jaime, and Kieran teaching Diego some kind of awkward faerie dance, and Emma with her hair like a waterfall of amber light, and Julian starting to walk up the beach toward her. They were always going toward each other, those two, like magnets. He'd heard from Jem that they were dating now, and since he'd never really understood the hazy "*parabatai* can't date" thing anyway, he wished them well. He could see Aline and Helen too, Aline holding a bottle of champagne and laughing, Helen hugging Tavvy and swinging him around. He could see Diana with Gwyn, the Wild Hunt leader with a big arm thrown protectively around his lady. He could see Alec lying in the sand beside Jace, deep in conversation, and Clary talking to Isabelle, and Magnus dancing with his two sons in the moonlight.

He could see them all, and of course he could see Ty.

Ty stood at the water's edge. He wouldn't have wanted to be close to the noise and the lights and shouting, and Kit hated that even now he wanted to go down to the beach and draw Ty away, to protect him from anything and everything that might upset him. He didn't look upset, though. He was facing the glittering waves. Anybody else would have thought he was splashing around in the bioluminescence by himself, but Kit could see that he wasn't alone.

A girl in a long white dress, with Blackthorn-brown hair, floated barefoot above the water. She was dancing, invisible to anyone but Ty—and Kit, who saw even what he didn't want to see.

Ty threw something into the ocean—his phone, Kit thought. Getting rid of the Black Volume and its images forever. At least that was something. Kit watched as Ty waded out a little bit, tipping his head back, smiling up at the Livvy only he could see.

Remember him like this, Kit thought, *happy and smiling.* His hand crept up to touch the faded white scar on his left arm where Ty had drawn that Talent rune what felt like so long ago.

Jem put his hand on Kit's shoulder. Tessa was looking at him with deep sympathy, as if she understood more than he'd guessed.

"We should go," Jem said, his voice gentle as always. "It does no one any good to look backward for too long and forget that the future lies ahead."

Kit turned away to follow them both into his new life.

Dawn was starting to break.

The wedding party had lasted all night. Though many of the guests had staggered off to sleep in the Institute (or were carried off, protesting, by their parents and older siblings), a few still remained, huddled up on blankets, watching the sun rise behind the mountains.

Emma couldn't remember a better celebration. She was curled up on a striped blanket with Julian, in the shelter of a tumble of rocks. The sand under them was cool, silvered by the dawn light, and the water had just begun to dance with golden sparks. She leaned back against Julian's chest, his arms around her.

His hand moved gently up her arm, fingers dancing against her skin. *W-H-A-T A-R-E Y-O-U T-H-I-N-K-I-N-G A-B-O-U-T?*

"Just that I'm happy for Magnus and Alec," she said. "They're so happy, and I feel like one day—we could be happy like that too."

He dropped a kiss on the top of her head. "Of course we will be."

His complete confidence spread warmth through her, like a comforting blanket. She glanced up at him.

"Remember when you were under the spell?" she said. "And I asked you why I took down all that stuff in my closet, about my parents. And you said it was because I knew who'd killed them now, and he was dead. Because I got revenge."

"And I was wrong," he said.

She took one of his hands in hers. It was a hand as familiar to her as her own—she knew every scar, every callus; she rejoiced in every splash of paint. "Do you know now?"

"You did it to honor your parents," he said. "To show them you'd let go of it all, that you weren't going to let revenge control your life. Because they wouldn't have wanted that for you."

She kissed his fingers. He shivered, drew her closer. "That's right." She looked up at him. Dawn light turned his wind-tangled hair to a halo. "I do keep worrying," she said. "Maybe I shouldn't have let Zara go. Maybe Jia and the Council should have arrested every Cohort sympathizer, like Balogh, not just the ones who fought. People like him are the reason things turned out the way they did."

Julian was watching the ocean as it slowly lightened. "We can only arrest people for what they do, not what they think," he said. "Any other way of doing things makes us like the Dearborns. And we're better off with what we have now than we would be if we'd become like them. Besides," he added, "every choice has a long afterlife of consequences. No one can know the eventual outcome of any decision. All you can do is make the best choice you can make in the moment."

She let her head fall back against his shoulder. "Do you remember when we used to come down here when we were kids? And make sandcastles?"

He nodded.

"When you were gone earlier this summer, I came here all the time," she said. "I thought about you, how much I missed you."

"Did you think sexy thoughts?" Julian grinned at her, and she swatted his arm. "Never mind, I know you did."

"Why do I ever tell you anything?" she complained, but they were both smiling at each other in a goofy way she was sure any bystander would have found intolerable.

"Because you love me," he said.

"True," she agreed. "Even more now than I used to."

His arms tightened around her. She looked up at him; his face was tight, as if with pain.

"What is it?" she said, puzzled; she hadn't meant to say anything that would hurt him.

"Just the thought," he said, his voice low and rough, "of being able to talk about this, with you. It's a freedom I never imagined we would ever have, that *I* would ever have. I always thought what I wanted was impossible. That the best I could hope for was a life of silent despair as your friend, that at least I would be able to be somewhere near you while you lived your life and I became less and less a part of it—"

"Julian." There was pain in his eyes, and even if it was a remembered pain, she hated to see it. "That would never have happened. I always loved you. Even when I didn't know it, I loved you. Even when you didn't feel anything, even when you weren't you, I remembered the real you and I loved you." She managed to turn around, slide her arms around his neck. "And I love you so much more now."

She leaned up to kiss him, and his hands slid into her hair: She knew he loved to touch her hair, just as he had always loved to paint it. He drew her into his lap, stroking her back. His sea-glass bracelet was cool against her bare skin as their mouths met slowly; Julian's mouth was soft and tasted of salt and sunshine. She hovered in the kiss, in the timeless pleasure of it, in knowing it wasn't the last but was one of the first, sealing the promise of a love that would last down the years of their lives.

They came out of the embrace reluctantly, like divers unwilling to leave the beauty of the underwater world behind. The circle of each other's arms, their own private city in the sea. "Why did you say that?" he whispered breathlessly, nuzzling the hair at her temple. "That you love me more now?"

"You've always felt everything so intensely," she said after a moment's pause. "And that was something I did love about you. How much you loved your family, how you would do anything for them. But you kept your heart closed off. You didn't trust anyone, and I don't blame you—you took everything on yourself, and you kept so many secrets, because you thought you had to. But when you opened up the Institute for the war council, you made yourself trust other people to help you execute a plan. You didn't hide; you let yourself be open to being hurt or betrayed so you could lead them. And when you came to me in the Silent City and you stopped me breaking the rune—" Her voice shook. "You told me to trust not just you but in the intrinsic goodness of the world. That was my worst point, my darkest point, and you were there, despite everything, with your heart open. You were there to bring me home."

He laid his fingers against the bare skin of her arm, where her *parabatai* rune had once been. "You brought me back too," he said with a sort of awe. "I've loved you all my life, Emma. And when I felt nothing, I realized—without that love, I *was* nothing. You're the reason I wanted to break out of the cage. You made me understand that love creates far more joy than any pain it causes." He tipped his head back to look up at her, his blue-green eyes shining. "I've loved my family since the day I was born and I always will. But you're the love I chose, Emma. Out of everyone in the world, out of everyone I've ever known, I chose you. I've always had faith in that choice. At the edge of everything, love and faith have always brought me back, and back to you."

At the edge of everything, love and faith have always brought me back. Emma didn't have to ask; she knew what he was thinking about: their friends and family lined up before them on the Imperishable Fields, the love that had brought them back from a curse so strong the whole of the Shadowhunter world had feared it.

She placed her hand over his heart, and for a moment they sat in silence, their hands remembering where their *parabatai* runes had once been. They were bidding good-bye, Emma thought, to what they had been: Everything from this moment on would be new.

They would never forget what had gone before. The banner of Livia's Watch flew even now from the roof of the Institute. They would remember their parents, and Arthur and Livvy, and all they had lost, but they would step into the world the new Clave was building with hope and remembrance mixed together, because though the Seelie Queen was a liar, every liar was truthful sometimes. She had been right about one thing: *Without sorrow, there can be no joy.*

They lowered their hands, their gazes locked. The sun was rising over the mountains, painting the sky like one of Julian's canvases in royal purple and bloody gold. It was dawn in more than one sense: They would step into the world's day from this moment onward without being afraid. This would be the true beginning of a new life that they would face together, in all their human frailty and imperfections. And if ever one of them feared the bad in themselves, as all people did sometimes, they had the other to remind them of the good.

Epilogue

The Queen sat upon her throne as faerie workmen swept in and out of the room.

Everything had changed. The color of triumph was gold, and the Unseelie King was dead. His favored son had become the Queen's closest adviser and loyal friend. After so long immured in the ice of grief over the loss of Ash, the Queen had begun to feel alive again.

Workmen had polished the marble floors, removing the signs of burning. Gems had been placed in the walls where holes had been: They glimmered now like winking eyes, red and blue and green. Butterflies with shining wings circled the roof, casting shifting, prismatic patterns over the silk-draped throne and the low couches that had been carried in for her courtiers to lounge upon.

Soon the new Unseelie King, Kieran, would pay a visit and he would not find the throne room any less than dazzling. She was curious about the boy King. She had met him before, one of the Unseelie King's pack of feral children, wounded and leaning upon Shadowhunters for support. That he had risen so high surprised her. Perhaps he had hidden qualities.

The new closeness of the Shadowhunters and the Unseelie Court was disturbing, of course. She had lost several good courtiers to the wiles of the Shadowhunters, Nene among them. Perhaps she should have tried harder to get the Blackthorn boy and the Carstairs girl to destroy the *parabatai* rune and weaken their army. But you could only plant the seeds of discord; you could not be assured that each of them would grow. The game was a long one, and impatience served no one well.

She had been distraught, too, over the loss of her son. She had been searching for him since, but with little hope. Other worlds were not magic that faeries understood well.

The golden velvet curtain that hung at the throne room's entrance rustled, and Fergus entered. He wore a permanently sour expression these days since his place in her favor had become Adaon's. There was more than sourness in it now, though. There was more than a little alarm. "My lady," he said. "You have visitors."

She raised herself up in her chair to show her white silk gown, clinging and gossamer, to better advantage. "Is it the Unseelie King?"

"No," he said. "A Shadowhunter. Jace Herondale."

She slitted her eyes at Fergus. "Jace Herondale is forbidden to enter my throne room." The last time he had, he'd nearly stabbed her. It was irresponsible of Fergus to forget such a thing. "Are you unwell, Fergus? Why did you not send him away?"

"Because I think you will want to see him, my lady. He surrendered his blades to me willingly, and he is . . . not alone."

"This had better be worth my time, Fergus, or it will cost you your second bedroom." She waved an angry hand in his direction. "Let him in, but return as well to stand guard."

Fergus departed. The Queen idly considered having Jace pecked by pixies, but it seemed like trouble and would unnecessarily annoy the new Shadowhunter government. The word was that they had put Alec Lightwood in charge—unfortunate, as she had disliked him since he had killed Meliorn, her last champion—and he would be unlikely to forgive trouble visited on his best friend.

Perhaps this was why Jace was here? To forge an alliance? She had only just had the thought when the curtain rustled again and Fergus came in, escorting two companions, one robed and hooded.

The other was Jace Herondale, but it was not the Jace Herondale she knew. The Jace she knew had been beautiful as angels were beautiful: this Jace was older, haggard. Still handsome but in the manner of a granite cliff seared by lightning. There was no gentleness in his eyes, and he was muscled like an adult, with nothing childish left in him. There was a dark light about him—as if he carried a miasma of ill magic with him wherever he walked.

"I have his swords," said Fergus. "You might wish to see them."

He laid them at the Queen's feet. A larger sword with stars imprinted on its dark silver blade, its pommel and grip coated in gold. A smaller sword of black gold and *adamas*, a pattern of stars down its center ridge.

"Heosphorus and Phaesphorus," said the Queen. "But they were destroyed."

"Not in my world," said Jace. "In Thule, much lives that is dead here, and much is dead there that lives in your world, Queen."

"You speak in riddles," said the Queen, though her ancient heart had begun to beat with a rare swiftness. *The land of Thule is death and it will rain down death here.* "Are you from the world the Unseelie King called Thule?"

He swept a mocking bow. His clothes were filthy with dust, and they resembled no Shadowhunter gear she had ever seen. "I am not the Jace Herondale you know or have ever met. I am his dark mirror. I have indeed come from that world. But my friend here was born here, in your Courts."

"Your friend?" the Queen breathed.

Jace nodded. "Ash, take down your hood."

His companion raised his hands and drew back the hood of his cloak, though the Queen knew already what she would see.

White-silver curls tumbled over his brow. He was some years older than he had been when he had gone through the Portal in the Unseelie King's throne room. He looked a mortal in his teen years, his face already beginning to show signs of her own beauty. His eyes were green as grass as the true eyes of his father had been. He regarded her with a calm, straightforward gaze.

"Ash," she breathed, rising to her feet. She wanted to hurl her arms around her son, but she held back. No one gave something for nothing in the Courts. "You bring my son to me," she said. "And for that I thank you. But what do you wish in return?"

"A safe place for Ash to live. To remain with him as he grows up."

"Both those wishes can be easily granted," said the Queen. "Is there nothing else?"

"There is one more thing," said the Jace that was not Jace, his golden eyes hard. "I want you to bring me Clary Fairchild."

Meet the Shadowhunters
of Edwardian London in

Chain of Gold,

BOOK ONE OF THE LAST HOURS.

James Herondale was in the middle of fighting a demon when he was suddenly pulled into hell.

It wasn't the first time it had happened, and it wouldn't be the last. Moments earlier, he had been kneeling at the edge of a slanted roof in central London, a slim throwing knife in each hand, thinking about how disgusting the detritus that collected in the city was. In addition to dirt, empty gin bottles, and animal bones, there was definitely a dead bird wedged into the rain gutter just below his left knee.

How glamorous the life of a Shadowhunter was, indeed. It *sounded* good, he thought to himself, gazing down at the empty alley below him: a narrow space choked with rubbish, lit dimly by the half-moon overhead. A special race of warriors, descended from an angel, gifted with powers that allowed them to wield weapons of shining *adamas* and to bear the black marks of holy runes on their bodies—runes that made them stronger, faster, more deadly than any mundane human; runes that made them burn brightly in the dark. No one ever mentioned things like accidentally kneeling on a dead bird while waiting for a demon to turn up.

A yell echoed down the alley. A sound James knew well: Matthew Fairchild's voice. He launched himself off the roof without a moment's hesitation. Matthew Fairchild was his *parabatai*—his blood brother and warrior partner. James was sworn to protect him, not that it mattered; he would have given his life for Matthew's, vows or not.

Movement flashed at the end of the alley, where it curved around behind a narrow row of houses. James spun just as a demon emerged from the shadows, roaring. It had a ribbed, gray body, a curving, sharp beak lined with hooked teeth, and splayed paw-like feet from which ragged claws protruded. A Deumas demon, James thought grimly. He definitely remembered reading about Deumas demons in one of the old books his uncle Jem had given him. They were meant to be notable in some way. Extremely vicious, perhaps, or unusually dangerous? That would be typical, wouldn't it—all these months of not running across any infernal activity at all, and he and his friends happened on one of the most dangerous demons out there.

Speaking of which—where *were* his friends?

The Deumas roared again and lurched toward James, ichor spilling from its mouth in long strings of greenish slime.

James swung his arm back, ready to throw his first knife.

The demon's eyes fixed on him for a moment. They were coruscating, green and black, filled with a hate that turned suddenly into something else.

Something like recognition. But demons didn't recognize people. They were vicious spirits driven by pure greed and hatred. As James froze in surprise, the ground under him seemed to lurch. He stumbled back, the world going gray and silent. The buildings around him had turned to ragged shadow, the sky a black cave speared with white lightning.

He closed his hand around his knife—not the handle, but the blade. The jolt of pain was like a slap to the face, snapping him out of a stupor. The world came rushing back at him in all its noise and color. He barely had time to register that the Deumas demon was in midair, claws extended toward him, when a swirl of cords whipped through the sky, entangling the demon's leg and yanking it backward.

Thomas! James thought, and indeed, his massively tall friend had appeared behind the Deumas, bolas in his hand. Behind him was Christopher, armed with a bow, and Matthew, sword at his side.

The Deumas hit the ground with another roar, just as James let both his knives fly. One plunged into the demon's throat; the other sank into its forehead, just between its eyes. Its eyes rolled back, it spasmed, and James suddenly remembered what it was he'd read about Deumas demons.

"Matthew—" he began, just as the creature burst apart, showering Thomas, Christopher, and Matthew in ichor and burned bits of what could only be described as goo.

Messy, James recalled belatedly. Deumas demons were notably messy. Most demons vanished when they died. Not Deumas demons.

They exploded.

"How," Christopher sputtered, at a clear loss for words. Of all the three, he was the most coated in slime. It dripped off his pointed nose and delicate gold-rimmed spectacles. "But how . . . ?"

"Do you mean how is it possible that we finally tracked down the last demon in London and it was also the most disgusting?" James asked. He was surprised how normal his voice sounded to his own ears; he was already shaking off the shock of his glimpse into the shadow realm. At least his clothes were untouched: the demon seemed to have exploded entirely over the other end of the alley. "Ours is not to question why, Christopher."

James had a feeling his friends were gazing at him resentfully. Thomas rolled his eyes. He was scrubbing at himself with a handkerchief that was also half-burned and covered in ichor, so it was doing little good.

"This is an outrage," said Matthew. "Do you know how much I spent on this waistcoat?"

"No one told you to go out patrolling for demons dressed like an extra from *The Importance of Being Earnest*," said James, tossing him a clean handkerchief. As he did, he felt his hand sting. There was a cut across his palm from the blade of the knife. He closed his hand into a fist to prevent his companions from seeing it.

"I don't think he's dressed like an extra," said Thomas, who had turned his attention to cleaning off Christopher.

"Thank you," said Matthew, with a slight bow.

"I think he's dressed like a main character." Thomas grinned. He had one of the kindest faces James had ever known, and gentle hazel eyes. None of which meant he didn't enjoy mocking his friends.

Matthew mopped at his dull gold hair with James's handkerchief. "This is the first time in a year that we've patrolled and actually found a demon, so I'd supposed that my waistcoat would probably survive the evening. My mistake."

"Stop scrubbing at me, Thomas," said Christopher, windmilling his arms. "We should go back to the Devil and clean up there."

There was a murmur of assent among the group. As they picked their sticky way back to the main street, James considered the fact that Matthew was right. James's father, Will, had often told him about the patrols he used to do with his *parabatai*, Jem Carstairs—now James's uncle Jem—back when they had battled demons nearly every night.

James and other young Shadowhunters still faithfully patrolled the streets of London, seeking out demons that might harm the mundane population, but in the last few years demon appearances had been few and far between. It was a good thing—of course it was a good thing—but still. It was decidedly odd. Demon activity was still normal as far as the rest of the Shadowhunter world was concerned, so what made London special?

There were plenty of mundanes out and about on the streets of the City, though the hour was late. None glanced at the bedraggled group of Shadowhunters as they made their way down Fleet Street; their glamour runes made them invisible to all eyes not gifted with the Sight.

It was always strange to be surrounded by a humanity that did not see you, James thought. Fleet Street was home to the newspaper offices and law courts of London, and everywhere were brightly lit pubs, with print workers and barristers and law clerks who kept late hours, drinking into the dawn light. The Strand nearby had spilled the contents of its music halls and theaters, and well-dressed groups of young people, singing and boisterous, chased the last omnibuses of the night, laughing.

The bobbies were out working their beats too, and those denizens of London unfortunate enough to have no homes to go to crouched muttering around cellar vents that sent up drifts of warm air. As they passed a group of such huddled figures, one looked up, and James caught a glimpse of the pale skin and glittering eyes of a vampire.

James looked away. Downworlders weren't his business unless they were breaking the Law. And he was tired, despite his energy runes; it always drained him to be dragged into that other world of gray light and black ragged shadows. It was something that had been happening to him all his life: a remnant, he knew, of his mother's warlock blood.

Warlocks were the offspring of humans and demons, capable of using magic but not of bearing runes or using *adamas*. They were Downworlders, like werewolves and the fey. James's mother, Tessa Herondale, was such a warlock, but her mother had been not just human but a Shadowhunter. Tessa herself possessed the power to shape-shift and take on the appearance of anyone, living or dead, a power no other warlock had. They had all wondered what this would mean for James and his sister, Lucie, the first-ever known grandchildren of a demon and a human being.

For many years, it appeared to have meant nothing. Both James and Lucie could bear runes and seemed to have the abilities of any other Shadowhunter. They could both see ghosts, but that was not uncommon in the Herondale family. It seemed they might both be blessedly normal, or at least as normal as a Shadowhunter could be.

When James was thirteen he first traveled into the shadow realm. One moment he had been standing on green grass, the next, charred earth. A similarly scorched sky arced above him. Twisted trees emerged from the ground, ragged claws grasping at the air. He had seen such places in woodcuts in old books. He knew what he was looking at: a demon world. A hell dimension.

Moments later he had been jerked back to earth, but his life had never been the same again. For years the fear had been there that he might at any moment hurtle back into shadow. It was as if an invisible rope connected him to a world of demons, and at any moment the rope could be pulled taut, snatching him out of his familiar environment and into a place of fire and ash.

See where the adventures begin in

City of Bones,

BOOK ONE OF

THE MORTAL INSTRUMENTS.

"You've got to be kidding me," the bouncer said, folding his arms across his massive chest. He stared down at the boy in the red zip-up jacket and shook his shaved head. "You can't bring that thing in here."

The fifty or so teenagers in line outside the Pandemonium Club leaned forward to eavesdrop. It was a long wait to get into the all-ages club, especially on a Sunday, and not much generally happened in line. The bouncers were fierce and would come down instantly on anyone who looked like they were going to start trouble. Fifteen-year-old Clary Fray, standing in line with her best friend, Simon, leaned forward along with everyone else, hoping for some excitement.

"Aw, come on." The kid hoisted the thing up over his head.

It looked like a wooden beam, pointed at one end. "It's part of my costume."

The bouncer raised an eyebrow. "Which is what?"

The boy grinned. He was normal-enough-looking, Clary thought, for Pandemonium. He had electric blue dyed hair that stuck up around his head like the tentacles of a startled octopus, but no elaborate facial tattoos or big metal bars through his ears or lips. "I'm a vampire hunter." He pushed down on the wooden thing. It bent as easily as a blade of grass bending sideways. "It's fake. Foam rubber. See?"

The boy's wide eyes were way too bright a green, Clary noticed: the color of antifreeze, spring grass. Colored contact lenses, probably. The bouncer shrugged, abruptly bored. "Whatever. Go on in."

The boy slid past him, quick as an eel. Clary liked the lilt to his shoulders, the way he tossed his hair as he went. There was a word for him that her mother would have used—*insouciant*.

"You thought he was cute," said Simon, sounding resigned. "Didn't you?"

Clary dug her elbow into his ribs, but didn't answer.

Inside, the club was full of dry-ice smoke. Colored lights played over the dance floor, turning it into a multicolored fairyland of blues and acid greens, hot pinks and golds.

The boy in the red jacket stroked the long razor-sharp blade in his hands, an idle smile playing over his lips. It had been so easy—a little bit of a glamour on the blade, to make it look harmless. Another glamour on his eyes, and the moment the bouncer had looked straight at him, he was in. Of course, he could probably have gotten by without all that trouble, but it was part of the fun—fooling the mundies, doing it all out in the open right in front of them, getting off on the blank looks on their sheeplike faces.

Not that the humans didn't have their uses. The boy's green

eyes scanned the dance floor, where slender limbs clad in scraps of silk and black leather appeared and disappeared inside the revolving columns of smoke as the mundies danced. Girls tossed their long hair, boys swung their leather-clad hips, and bare skin glittered with sweat. Vitality just *poured* off them, waves of energy that filled him with a drunken dizziness. His lip curled. They didn't know how lucky they were. They didn't know what it was like to eke out life in a dead world, where the sun hung limp in the sky like a burned cinder. Their lives burned as brightly as candle flames—and were as easy to snuff out.

His hand tightened on the blade he carried, and he had begun to step out onto the dance floor when a girl broke away from the mass of dancers and began walking toward him. He stared at her. She was beautiful, for a human—long hair nearly the precise color of black ink, charcoaled eyes. Floor-length white gown, the kind women used to wear when this world was younger. Lace sleeves belled out around her slim arms. Around her neck was a thick silver chain, on which hung a dark red pendant the size of a baby's fist. He only had to narrow his eyes to know that it was real—real and precious. His mouth started to water as she neared him. Vital energy pulsed from her like blood from an open wound. She smiled, passing him, beckoning with her eyes. He turned to follow her, tasting the phantom sizzle of her death on his lips.

It was always easy. He could already feel the power of her evaporating life coursing through his veins like fire. Humans were so stupid. They had something so precious, and they barely safeguarded it at all. They threw away their lives for money, for packets of powder, for a stranger's charming smile. The girl was a pale ghost retreating through the colored smoke. She reached the wall and turned, bunching her skirt up in her hands, lifting it as she grinned at him. Under the skirt, she was wearing thigh-high boots.

He sauntered up to her, his skin prickling with her nearness.

Up close she wasn't so perfect: He could see the mascara smudged under her eyes, the sweat sticking her hair to her neck. He could smell her mortality, the sweet rot of corruption. *Got you*, he thought.

A cool smile curled her lips. She moved to the side, and he could see that she was leaning against a closed door. NO ADMITTANCE—STORAGE was scrawled across it in red paint. She reached behind her for the knob, turned it, slid inside. He caught a glimpse of stacked boxes, tangled wiring. A storage room. He glanced behind him—no one was looking. So much the better if she wanted privacy.

He slipped into the room after her, unaware that he was being followed.

"So," Simon said, "pretty good music, eh?"

Clary didn't reply. They were dancing, or what passed for it—a lot of swaying back and forth with occasional lunges toward the floor as if one of them had dropped a contact lens—in a space between a group of teenage boys in metallic corsets, and a young couple cooing affectionately to each other in Japanese, their colored hair extensions tangled together like vines. A boy with a lip piercing and a teddy bear backpack was handing out free tablets of herbal ecstasy, his parachute pants flapping in the breeze from the wind machine. Clary wasn't paying much attention to their immediate surroundings—her eyes were on the blue-haired boy who'd talked his way into the club. He was prowling through the crowd as if he were looking for something. There was something about the way he moved that reminded her of something . . .

"I, for one," Simon went on, "am enjoying myself immensely."

This seemed unlikely. Simon, as always, stuck out at the club like a sore thumb, in jeans and an old T-shirt that said MADE IN BROOKLYN across the front. His freshly scrubbed hair was dark brown instead of green or pink, and his glasses perched crookedly on the end of his nose. He looked less as if he were contemplating the powers of darkness and more as if he were on his way to chess club.

"Mmm-hmm." Clary knew perfectly well that he came to Pandemonium with her only because she liked it, that he thought it was boring. She wasn't even sure why it was that she liked it—the clothes, the music made it like a dream, someone else's life, not her boring real life at all. But she was always too shy to talk to anyone but Simon.

The blue-haired boy was making his way off the dance floor. He looked a little lost, as if he hadn't found whom he was looking for. Clary wondered what would happen if she went up and introduced herself, offered to show him around. Maybe he'd just stare at her. Or maybe he was shy too. Maybe he'd be grateful and pleased, and try not to show it, the way boys did—but she'd know. Maybe—

The blue-haired boy straightened up suddenly, snapping to attention, like a hunting dog on point. Clary followed the line of his gaze, and saw the girl in the white dress.

Oh, well, Clary thought, trying not to feel like a deflated party balloon. *I guess that's that.* The girl was gorgeous, the kind of girl Clary would have liked to draw—tall and ribbon-slim, with a long spill of black hair. Even at this distance Clary could see the red pendant around her throat. It pulsed under the lights of the dance floor like a separate, disembodied heart.

"I feel," Simon went on, "that this evening DJ Bat is doing a singularly exceptional job. Don't you agree?"

Clary rolled her eyes and didn't answer; Simon hated trance music. Her attention was on the girl in the white dress. Through the darkness, smoke, and artificial fog, her pale dress shone out like a beacon. No wonder the blue-haired boy was following her as if he were under a spell, too distracted to notice anything else around him—even the two dark shapes hard on his heels, weaving after him through the crowd.

Clary slowed her dancing and stared. She could just make out that the shapes were boys, tall and wearing black clothes. She couldn't have said how she knew that they were following the other boy, but she did. She could see it in the way they paced him, their careful watchfulness, the slinking grace of their movements. A small flower of apprehension began to open inside her chest.

"Meanwhile," Simon added, "I wanted to tell you that lately I've been cross-dressing. Also, I'm sleeping with your mom. I thought you should know."

The girl had reached the wall, and was opening a door marked NO ADMITTANCE. She beckoned the blue-haired boy after her, and they slipped through the door. It wasn't anything Clary hadn't seen before, a couple sneaking off to the dark corners of the club to make out—but that made it even weirder that they were being followed.

She raised herself up on tiptoe, trying to see over the crowd. The two guys had stopped at the door and seemed to be conferring with each other. One of them was blond, the other dark-haired. The blond one reached into his jacket and drew out something long and sharp that flashed under the strobing lights. A knife. "Simon!" Clary shouted, and seized his arm.

"What?" Simon looked alarmed. "I'm not really sleeping with your mom, you know. I was just trying to get your attention. Not that your mom isn't a very attractive woman, for her age."

"Do you see those guys?" She pointed wildly, almost hitting a curvy black girl who was dancing nearby. The girl shot her an evil look. "Sorry—sorry!" Clary turned back to Simon. "Do you see those two guys over there? By that door?"

Simon squinted, then shrugged. "I don't see anything."

"There are two of them. They were following the guy with the blue hair—"

"The one you thought was cute?"

"Yes, but that's not the point. The blond one pulled a knife."

"Are you *sure?*" Simon stared harder, shaking his head. "I still don't see anyone."

"I'm sure."

Suddenly all business, Simon squared his shoulders. "I'll get one of the security guards. You stay here." He strode away, pushing through the crowd.

Clary turned just in time to see the blond boy slip through the NO ADMITTANCE door, his friend right on his heels. She looked around; Simon was still trying to shove his way across the dance floor, but he wasn't making much progress. Even if she yelled now, no one would hear her, and by the time Simon got back, something terrible might *already* have happened. Biting hard on her lower lip, Clary started to wriggle through the crowd.

"What's your name?"

She turned and smiled. What faint light there was in the storage room spilled down through high barred windows smeared with dirt. Piles of electrical cables, along with broken bits of mirrored disco balls and discarded paint cans, littered the floor.

"Isabelle."

"That's a nice name." He walked toward her, stepping carefully among the wires in case any of them were live. In the faint light she looked half-transparent, bleached of color, wrapped in white like an angel. It would be a pleasure to make her fall. . . . "I haven't seen you here before."

"You're asking me if I come here often?" She giggled, covering her mouth with her hand. There was some sort of bracelet around her wrist, just under the cuff of her dress—then, as he neared her, he saw that it wasn't a bracelet at all but a pattern inked into her skin, a matrix of swirling lines.

He froze. "You—"

He didn't finish. She moved with lightning swiftness, striking out at him with her open hand, a blow to his chest that would have sent him down gasping if he'd been a human being. He staggered back, and now there was something in her hand, a coiling whip that glinted gold as she brought it down, curling around his ankles, jerking him off his feet. He hit the ground, writhing, the hated metal biting deep into his skin. She laughed, standing over him, and dizzily he thought that he should have *known*. No human girl would wear a dress like the one Isabelle wore. She'd worn it to cover her skin—all of her skin.

Discover the origins
of Jem and Tessa in

Clockwork Angel,

BOOK ONE OF

THE INFERNAL DEVICES.

The demon exploded in a shower of ichor and guts.

William Herondale jerked back the dagger he was holding, but it was too late. The viscous acid of the demon's blood had already begun to eat away at the shining blade. He swore and tossed the weapon aside; it landed in a filthy puddle and commenced smoldering like a doused match. The demon itself, of course, had vanished—dispatched back to whatever hellish world it had come from, though not without leaving a mess behind.

"Jem!" Will called, turning around. "Where are you? Did you see that? Killed it with one blow! Not bad, eh?"

But there was no answer to Will's shout; his hunting partner had been standing behind him in the damp and crooked street a few moments before, guarding his back, Will was positive, but now Will was alone in the shadows. He frowned in annoyance—it was much less fun showing off without Jem to show off *to*. He glanced behind him, to where the street narrowed into a passage that gave onto the black, heaving water of the Thames in the distance. Through the gap Will could see the dark outlines of docked ships, a forest of masts like a leafless orchard. No Jem there; perhaps he had gone back to Narrow Street in search of better illumination. With a shrug Will headed back the way he had come.

Narrow Street cut across Limehouse, between the docks beside the river and the cramped slums spreading west toward Whitechapel. It was as narrow as its name suggested, lined with warehouses and lopsided wooden buildings. At the moment it was deserted; even the drunks staggering home from the Grapes up the road had found somewhere to collapse for the night. Will liked Limehouse, liked the feeling of being on the edge of the world, where ships left each day for unimaginably far ports. That the area was a sailor's haunt, and consequently full of gambling hells, opium dens, and brothels, didn't hurt either. It was easy to lose yourself in a place like this. He didn't even mind the smell of it—smoke and rope and tar, foreign spices mixed with the dirty river-water smell of the Thames.

Looking up and down the empty street, he scrubbed the sleeve of his coat across his face, trying to rub away the ichor that stung and burned his skin. The cloth came away stained green and black. There was a cut on the back of his hand too, a nasty one. He could use a healing rune. One of Charlotte's, preferably. She was particularly good at drawing *iratzes*.

A shape detached itself from the shadows and moved toward Will. He started forward, then paused. It wasn't Jem, but rather a mundane policeman wearing a bell-shaped helmet, a heavy overcoat, and a puzzled expression. He stared at Will, or rather *through*

Will. However accustomed Will had become to glamour, it was always strange to be looked through as if he weren't there. Will was seized with the sudden urge to grab the policeman's truncheon and watch while the man flapped around, trying to figure out where it had gone; but Jem had scolded him the few times he'd done that before, and while Will never really could understand Jem's objections to the whole enterprise, it wasn't worth making him upset.

With a shrug and a blink, the policeman moved past Will, shaking his head and muttering something under his breath about swearing off the gin before he truly started seeing things. Will stepped aside to let the man pass, then raised his voice to a shout: "James Carstairs! Jem! Where *are* you, you disloyal bastard?"

This time a faint reply answered him. "Over here. Follow the witchlight."

Will moved toward the sound of Jem's voice. It seemed to be coming from a dark opening between two warehouses; a faint gleam was visible within the shadows, like the darting light of a will-o'-the-wisp. "Did you hear me before? That Shax demon thought it could get me with its bloody great pincers, but I cornered it in an alley—"

"Yes, I heard you." The young man who appeared at the mouth of the alley was pale in the lamplight—paler even than he usually was, which was quite pale indeed. He was bareheaded, which drew the eye immediately to his hair. It was an odd bright silver color, like an untarnished shilling. His eyes were the same silver, and his fine-boned face was angular, the slight curve of his eyes the only clue to his heritage.

There were dark stains across his white shirtfront, and his hands were thickly smeared with red.

Will tensed. "You're bleeding. What happened?"

Jem waved away Will's concern. "It's not my blood." He turned his head back toward the alley behind him. "It's hers."

Will glanced past his friend, into the thicker shadows of the alley. In the far corner of it was a crumpled shape—only a shadow in the darkness, but when Will looked closely, he could make out the shape of a pale hand, and a wisp of fair hair.

"A dead woman?" Will asked. "A mundane?"

"A girl, really. Not more than fourteen."

At that, Will cursed with great volume and expression. Jem waited patiently for him to be done.

"If we'd only happened along a little earlier," Will said finally. "That bloody demon —"

"That's the peculiar thing. I don't think this is the demon's work." Jem frowned. "Shax demons are parasites, brood parasites. It would have wanted to drag its victim back to its lair to lay eggs in her skin while she was still alive. But this girl—she was stabbed, repeatedly. And I don't think it was here, either. There simply isn't enough blood in the alley. I think she was attacked elsewhere, and she dragged herself here to die of her injuries."

"But the Shax demon—"

"I'm telling you, I don't think it *was* the Shax. I think the Shax was pursuing her—hunting her down for something, or someone, else."

"Shaxes have a keen sense of scent," Will allowed. "I've heard of warlocks using them to follow the tracks of the missing. And it did seem to be moving with an odd sort of purpose." He looked past Jem, at the pitiful smallness of the crumpled shape in the alley. "You didn't find the weapon, did you?"

"Here." Jem drew something from inside his jacket—a knife, wrapped in white cloth. "It's a sort of misericord, or hunting dagger. Look how thin the blade is."

Will took it. The blade was indeed thin, ending in a handle made of polished bone. The blade and hilt both were stained with dried blood. With a frown he wiped the flat of the knife across the rough fabric of his sleeve, scraping it clean until a symbol, burned into the blade, became visible. Two serpents, each biting the other's tail, forming a perfect circle.

"Ouroboros," Jem said, leaning in close to stare at the knife. "A double one. Now, what do you think that means?"

"The end of the world," said Will, still looking at the dagger, a small smile playing about his mouth, "and the beginning."

Jem frowned. "I understand the symbology, William. I meant, what do you think its presence on the dagger signifies?"

The wind off the river was ruffling Will's hair; he brushed it out of his eyes with an impatient gesture and went back to studying the knife. "It's an alchemical symbol, not a warlock or Downworlder one. That usually means humans—the foolish mundane sort who think trafficking in magic is the ticket for gaining wealth and fame."

"The sort who usually end up a pile of bloody rags inside some pentagram." Jem sounded grim.

"The sort who like to lurk about the Downworld parts of our fair city." After wrapping the handkerchief around the blade carefully, Will slipped it into his jacket pocket. "D'you think Charlotte will let me handle the investigation?"

"Do *you* think you can be trusted in Downworld? The gambling hells, the dens of magical vice, the women of loose morals . . ."

Will smiled the way Lucifer might have smiled, moments before he fell from Heaven. "Would tomorrow be too early to start looking, do you think?"

Jem sighed. "Do what you like, William. You always do."

Southampton, May.

Tessa could not remember a time when she had not loved the clockwork angel. It had belonged to her mother once, and her mother had been wearing it when she died. After that it had sat in her mother's jewelry box, until her brother, Nathaniel, took it out one day to see if it was still in working order.

The angel was no bigger than Tessa's pinky finger, a tiny statuette made of brass, with folded bronze wings no larger than a cricket's. It had a delicate metal face with shut crescent eyelids, and hands crossed over a sword in front. A thin chain that looped beneath the wings allowed the angel to be worn around the neck like a locket.

Tessa knew the angel was made out of clockwork because if she lifted it to her ear she could hear the sound of its machinery, like the sound of a watch. Nate had exclaimed in surprise that it was still working after so many years, and he had looked in vain for a knob or a screw, or some other method by which the angel might be wound. But there had been nothing to find. With a shrug he'd given the angel to Tessa. From that moment she had never taken it off; even at night the angel lay against her chest as she slept, its constant *ticktock, ticktock* like the beating of a second heart.

She held it now, clutched between her fingers, as the *Main* nosed its way between other massive steamships to find a spot at the Southampton dock. Nate had insisted that she come to Southampton instead of Liverpool, where most transatlantic steamers arrived. He had claimed it was because Southampton was a much pleasanter place to arrive at, so Tessa couldn't help being a little disappointed by this, her first sight of England. It was drearily gray. Rain drummed down onto the spires of a distant church, while black smoke rose from the chimneys of ships and stained the already dull-colored sky. A crowd of people in dark clothes, holding umbrellas, stood on the docks. Tessa strained to see if her brother was among them, but the mist and spray from the ship were too thick for her to make out any individual in great detail.

Tessa shivered. The wind off the sea was chilly. All of Nate's letters had claimed that London was beautiful, the sun shining every day. Well, Tessa thought, hopefully the weather there was better than it was here, because she had no warm clothes with her, nothing more substantial than a woolen shawl that had belonged to Aunt Harriet, and a pair of thin gloves. She had sold most of her clothes to pay for her aunt's funeral, secure in the knowledge that her brother would buy her more when she arrived in London to live with him.

A shout went up. The *Main*, its shining black-painted hull gleaming wet with rain, had anchored, and tugs were plowing their way through the heaving gray water, ready to carry baggage and passengers to the shore. Passengers streamed off the ship, clearly desperate to feel land under their feet. So different from their departure from New York. The sky had been blue then, and a brass band had been playing. Though, with no one there to wish her good-bye, it had not been a merry occasion.

Hunching her shoulders, Tessa joined the disembarking crowd. Drops of rain stung her unprotected head and neck like pinpricks from icy little needles, and her hands, inside their insubstantial gloves, were clammy and wet with rain. Reaching the quay, she looked around eagerly, searching for a sight of Nate. It had been nearly two weeks since she'd spoken to a soul, having kept almost entirely to herself on board the *Main*. It would be wonderful to have her brother to talk to again.

He wasn't there. The wharves were heaped with stacks of luggage and all sorts of boxes and cargo, even mounds of fruit and vegetables wilting and dissolving in the rain. A steamer was departing for Le Havre nearby, and damp-looking sailors swarmed close by Tessa, shouting in French. She tried to move aside, only to be almost trampled by a throng of disembarking passengers hurrying for the shelter of the railway station.

But Nate was nowhere to be seen.

"You are Miss Gray?" The voice was guttural, heavily accented. A man had moved to stand in front of Tessa. He was tall, and was wearing a sweeping black coat and a tall hat, its brim collecting rainwater like a cistern. His eyes were peculiarly bulging, almost protuberant, like a frog's, his skin as rough-looking as scar tissue. Tessa had to fight the urge to cringe away from him. But he knew her name. Who here would know her name except someone who knew Nate, too?

"Yes?"

"Your brother sent me. Come with me."

"Where is he?" Tessa demanded, but the man was already walking away. His stride was uneven, as if he had a limp from an old injury. After a moment Tessa gathered up her skirts and hurried after him.

He wound through the crowd, moving ahead with purposeful speed. People jumped aside, muttering about his rudeness as he shouldered past, with Tessa nearly running to keep up. He turned abruptly around a pile of boxes, and came to a halt in front of a large, gleaming black coach. Gold letters had been painted across its side, but the rain and mist were too thick for Tessa to read them clearly.

The door of the carriage opened and a woman leaned out. She wore an enormous plumed hat that hid her face. "Miss Theresa Gray?"